D0794089

SEASONS

SEASONS

Anna Dillon

St. Martin's Press
New York

SEASONS. Copyright © 1988 by Anna Dillon. All rights reserved. Printed in the United States of America. No part of this book may be used or reproduced in any manner whatsoever without written permission except in the case of brief quotations embodied in critical articles or reviews. For information, address St. Martin's Press, 175 Fifth Avenue, New York, N.Y. 10010.

Library of Congress Cataloging-in-Publication Data

Dillon, Anna.
      Seasons / Anna Dillon.
          p.   cm.
      ISBN 0-312-02978-0
        1. Ireland—History—Sinn Fein Rebellion, 1916—Fiction.
I. Title.
PR6054.I416S44   1989
823'.914—dc19   89-4100
                                      CIP

First published in Great Britain by Sphere Books Ltd.

First U.S. Edition

10 9 8 7 6 5 4 3 2 1

For A. . . . . .
C. . . . . .
P. . . . . .

ACKNOWLEDGMENTS

It would be impossible to acknowledge all of those who gave so freely of their time and were willing to share their experiences of the Easter Rising, 1916, but two deserve mention: P.O.T. (who planted the seed) and D.O.B. (who made it grow).

With the exception of the recognized historical personages, all the characters in this novel are fictitious. The events are all too real.

PART ONE

For Everything there is a Season,
and a Time for Every Affair under Heaven . . .
Ecclesiastes 3:1

CHAPTER ONE
May 2nd, 1898

'I think I'm going to hate this country.'

It was raining when Katherine Lundy stepped off the boat in Kingstown, a fine mist that clung to everything and quickly soaked through the thin material of her coat. She hesitated a moment on the quayside breathing in the damp salt air, while around her the crowd hurried past, meeting and being met by relatives and friends. Their accents were broad and flat, some harsh, others musical, but all sounding strange and a little intimidating to her ears.

And for the first time the realization that she was alone in a strange land struck home.

The young woman experienced a brief moment of panic and she clutched at the metal rail for support, desperately blinking back the tears. She tilted her burning face to the leaden skies, the rain cooling, and then, taking a deep breath and brushing her hand across her eyes, she hurried down the quayside, following the straggling crowd into a long shed-like building.

A hand touched her sleeve. 'Miss Lundy?'

Katherine started. Although she had known she would be met, it was still shocking to hear her name spoken aloud in the strange flat accent which she would later come to recognize as peculiarly Dublin. She stopped, turning towards the tall woman in black, taking in the long thin face beneath the round black bonnet but noting the warmth in the rather faded grey eyes.

'I am Katherine Lundy,' she said, her head bobbing nervously. She brushed back a rat's-tail of hair that had escaped from beneath her hat and now snaked across her face.

'I'm Mrs O'Neill, cook in the Lewis household. Mrs

11

Lewis asked me to come an' meet you, an' bring you back to the house.'

'That was thoughtful of Mrs Lewis.'

'Well, now, we wouldn't want you getting lost on us, an' it's a fair old trip back to town,' she smiled.

Katherine pulled a slip of paper from her pocket. 'Oh, I have the address, I think I would have found it eventually.'

Moire O'Neill liked what she saw. The girl had a mind of her own; it showed in her eyes and the determined set of her jaw. Mrs O'Neill knew the girl was only eighteen – Mrs Lewis had told her – and she thought her pretty in a rather plain, unassuming way. She was a little above middle height, but carried herself well which made her appear taller. Her face was long and oval, with a square chin and a straight nose. Her eyes were wide and deep brown, and Mrs O'Neill discovered almost immediately that she had the disconcerting habit of looking people straight in the face. Suddenly conscious that she herself was staring, she said briskly, 'We'd better hurry on, there's a train in a few minutes, and we don't want to miss it.'

The girl shifted her small bag from one hand to the other and fell into step beside the older woman.

Mrs O'Neill glanced sidelong at her. 'This is your first time in Ireland?'

'It is, although my father has told me a lot about it.'

'Did he live here?'

'Very briefly – he served under Captain Lewis,' Katherine added. Mrs O'Neill nodded; she had wondered how the girl had got the job.

Katherine didn't have much of a chance to see Kingstown, the gateway to Dublin, the second capital of the Empire. The weather had closed in and the skies were grey with low clouds. But, from what she did see of it, it looked like any other seaside town on a rainy day – miserable.

The fact that the train pulled out of Kingstown Station on time surprised her and she was equally surprised that

12

it was crowded. Somehow she had imagined that the Irish trains would be late and half-empty, especially early on a wet Monday morning. She looked down the length of the long carriage, the passengers sitting hunched and silent, bundled up against the weather, their sodden clothes steaming. Opposite her, Mrs O'Neill sat with her hands folded in her lap and her eyes closed. Praying or dozing, Katherine wondered.

She rubbed the back of her hand against the fogged-up glass, creating a little window of her own. Billows of white steam fled past her window, adding to the already impenetrable banks of mist and low cloud. With nothing to see, she sat back into the seat, rested her head against the red cloth and closed her eyes, allowing the clacking rhythm to soothe the bitterness that bubbled within her.

She had not wanted to come to Ireland in the first place, and she certainly hadn't wanted to come over as a skivvy. From the little she knew of Ireland, she guessed it to be a dirty, backward, rather dangerous country. However, she was also honest enough with herself to know that one of the reasons she disliked Ireland so much was because it had taken her father away from home for such a long time, and when he had finally come back to Lancashire it had been as a cripple, with a knee that would never bend and a meagre army pension.

And, of course, that was one of the reasons she had been sent away – her family needed the money. Her father's pension went nowhere towards feeding and supporting his family and, while James Lundy supplemented his pension by doing odd jobs around the nearby army camps, it wasn't enough to support a wife and six children. Katherine was the eldest of the six and the only girl amongst five boys. She was eighteen, but her brothers were twelve, ten, seven, six and three. She had been born while her father was serving with his regiment in South Africa, and all of her brothers had been conceived when he had been home on leave. And in three months' time there would be another mouth to feed.

13

Her father had spent his life in the service of his Queen and country, and while they had never been particularly wealthy they hadn't wanted for anything either. They had been comfortable, and unlike many other children of their generation they hadn't been forced out to work as soon as possible. Katherine had received a brief but thorough education in a local convent-run school, where she showed a surprising aptitude for figures, and the nuns who taught her had intimated that they would have been able to find her a job in an office locally.

But her father's accident had changed all that; suddenly, she was forced to work. Leaving school, she took the first job she could find – working in a tea-shop in Blackpool – but the wages were poor, and it also meant that she was still living at home and therefore a drain on the meagre resources.

And then James Lundy had met his former captain, John Lewis . . . and suddenly she was to be a maid in his house in Dublin. Of course, it was too good an opportunity to lose – the chance for her to earn ten pounds a year, including board and lodging. He had arranged with Captain Lewis that the major portion of her wages would be paid directly to him in Lancashire, while she would receive a small allowance.

Which made her little more than a slave, Katherine reflected bitterly, and ensured amongst other things that she would probably never be able to save enough for the fare to return home.

The train thundered into a tunnel, plunging the carriage into darkness, startling her. Katherine stared out into the darkness, images forming on the glass.

Everything had moved so quickly. It was less than a month since her father had first spoken with Captain Lewis. The captain had, it seemed, returned home a few days later and spoken to his wife. A week later a letter had arrived, confirming the position was still available if Katherine was interested.

There hadn't really been any discussion. Katherine didn't want to leave her mother – with the baby on the

14

way, she would be needed more than ever – but it wasn't her decision to make, nor was she consulted.

The train broke out of the tunnel, the sudden light blinding. 'You must be exhausted, my dear,' Mrs O'Neill said suddenly, startling her.

Katherine looked up to find the older woman's soft grey eyes staring concernedly at her. She shook her head, 'I'm sorry?'

'You look tired.'

'I am,' she confessed.

It was still raining heavily when Mrs O'Neill and Katherine walked down the steps under the arched portico of Amiens Street Station. The older woman shook open her umbrella, and then took Katherine's arm and tucked it into hers. 'If we hurry, we should catch the tram,' she said. 'We'll cross here.'

Katherine peered out beneath the fringed edge of the umbrella as they dashed across the cobblestones. 'Where are we?' she wondered.

Mrs O'Neill's head moved quickly, left and right, 'That's Amiens Street – that fancy building you can just about see on your right is the Customs House, but I'll give you the tour on a finer day. This is Talbot Street,' she added, as they stepped on to the pavement of the street facing the tall pillared frontage of the station.

The wind was now carrying the rain directly into their faces, and both women kept their heads down behind the umbrella. Katherine didn't have much chance to look at the shops – some of which were still in the process of opening for the day, and she glanced up only once and found herself looking down a squalid laneway. She had walked past the opening before she realized she had actually seen two children shivering in a rotten, mouldering doorway. She tilted her head to one side, and looked back, reading the nameplate high on the wall. 'Mabbot Lane'.

'What's down there?' she asked. 'Behind this street,'

she added, when Mrs O'Neill looked blank. 'Slums, my dear, an' praise God, but you'll never see them.'

The pillar and statue of Nelson took her breath away. She had known that it was big ... but the sudden unexpectedness of it, standing dead centre in one of the broadest streets she had ever seen, was shocking.

'Come on,' Mrs O'Neill said, 'there's our tram.' She gripped Katherine's fingers in her large, almost manlike hands and dragged her across the street, dodging around a covered cart with the legend, 'Johnson Mooney & O'Brien,' lettered in gold on the side. On the back of the cart, Katherine read the words, 'Machine Bread Bakeries,' and wondered what 'machine bread' tasted like. Awful probably.

Mrs O'Neill pushed Katherine on to a tram, closing her umbrella and giving it one final shake as she did so. The tram was crowded – but only because the top floor was uncovered and open to the elements, and therefore unused in this weather. Katherine didn't mind standing, she was still awe-struck by Nelson's pillar. The pillar was one Dublin monument she knew particularly well – it had been that which had crippled her father, but she thought she knew now what had tempted him to try and climb it. He – and a few others – had got drunk one night on leave and had attempted to climb up the base of the statue. He had apparently climbed the plinth and reached the column itself when he had slipped and fallen, and had narrowly missed being impaled on the spiked railings that surrounded the pillar, only to shatter his knee on the cobbles. It was impossible, of course; the column itself was smooth and sheer, and she was astonished that he had even managed to climb the massive plinth on which the column itself stood. The pillar was one hundred and thirty-four feet high, and that was topped by a thirteen-foot statue of the admiral – that much she had learned from her father.

As the tram's bell jangled and it clanged away, she

16

promised herself that she would climb it someday – but properly this time, by the stairway which she knew wound up inside the column.

As soon as the tram, which was drawn by two horses, jerked away, two young men – clerks or apprentices – stood up and courteously offered their seats to the two ladies. Mrs O'Neill nodded curtly, but Katherine smiled her thanks, catching the startled gaze of one of them. The young man touched the rim of his cap with his index finger. 'You're welcome, miss.'

'That was kind of them,' she said to Mrs O'Neill, as they settled back into the damp cloth seats.

'You'll find the Irish are not short of courtesy,' Moire said quietly. 'Well, the poorer folk certainly aren't,' she added. 'But I've found the gentry could do with a bit more.'

'This must be Sackville Street,' Katherine said.

'It is.' The older woman looked at the misted-up, rain-spattered windows. 'It's a pity you can't see it, but I'm sure you'll have plenty of opportunities later on.'

'I'm sure.'

'We'll be there shortly,' Mrs O'Neill said, 'then you can change out of those wet clothes.'

Katherine smiled shyly. 'Where exactly are we going?'

'We're going to Clonliffe Road. Captain and Mrs Lewis have a house right next to the college.'

'What college?'

'Holy Cross College; it's a seminary, where young men are trained to be priests . . .' She paused as a sudden thought struck her. 'You are a Catholic . . . ?'

Katherine nodded.

'The Captain and Mrs Lewis are Church of Ireland – and nothing wrong with that,' she said quickly, 'they're good, God-fearing people. Well, she is anyways,' she amended, 'I've little enough dealings with him, and I'm not sure I want any.'

'Why did the last maid leave?' Katherine wondered absently. 'They did have another maid . . ?'

'There have been a few,' Mrs O'Neill said slowly. 'None of them have lasted very long.'

'Why, is something wrong?'

'No, nothing wrong.'

Katherine turned to look at Moire, something in the older woman's voice catching her attention. 'Why did the other servants leave?' She continued staring at Mrs O'Neill's face, her dark eyes finally catching and holding the other woman's.

'There was a little difficulty about money with one girl,' Mrs O'Neill said finally. 'A small sum went missing, and it was eventually found hidden in the girl's room. She denied it of course, but the evidence was there for all to see. The captain was very generous, he didn't bring charges, but he wouldn't give her a reference.'

Katherine nodded sombrely. Good references were essential if one hoped to continue working; no reference usually meant the person had been fired for some reason.

'The last young girl we had, well, she found herself in a . . . certain condition.'

'What certain condition?' Katherine asked, intrigued.

Mrs O'Neill lowered her voice, until it was barely above a whisper. 'She found she was with child!'

'And she wasn't married?' she asked innocently.

'She was not!'

'What about the father of the child?'

Mrs O'Neill shrugged. 'There was none – or at least the silly girl wouldn't tell me his name, said her life wouldn't be worth living if she did.' She shook her head, tut-tutting softly to herself. 'It was such a surprise, and I thought she was such a nice, quiet girl. She wasn't even pretty, not like you anyway,' she smiled.

Katherine bowed her head, smiling shyly, unused to compliments. 'What happened to the girl?' she asked eventually.

'Mrs Lewis threw her out; I don't believe that the captain even knew about it until he came home that evening. As I said, Mrs Lewis is a very God-fearing,

18

righteous woman. She insists that the utmost propriety must be observed at all times.' She leaned forward, nodding with conviction. 'Of course, that may be one of the reasons behind their decision to employ an English maid.'

'Why?'

'Because you don't know anyone here, you won't have any gentleman callers.' The tram jerked and slowed and Mrs O'Neill looked up suddenly. 'Oh, we've arrived. Come on, it's only a short walk from here.'

As they stood in the gusting rain while the tram pulled away, Mrs O'Neill pointed across the cobbled road and down a long straight avenue, flanked by tall, elegant two- and three-storied houses of modern design. 'This is Clonliffe Road. Welcome to your new home.'

Katherine's room was at the top of the house. It had a low sloping ceiling on both sides, with two windows, one looking down on to Clonliffe Road, the other overlooking the rear garden. The only pieces of furniture were a bed, an old wooden dressing table with a spotted, dusty mirror, a rickety kitchen chair, and a wash-stand in the corner. Beneath the bed Katherine could see the chipped edge of a chamber pot.

'There's no fireplace,' Mrs O'Neill said, 'but the chimneys are just above your head and, if you feel this wall here . . .' she pressed her hand flat against the gable wall, '. . . you can feel the heat from the fires below.' Katherine touched the wall. The plaster was warm to her touch. 'When the fires below have built up,' Mrs O'Neill continued, 'this room will be like a furnace. You won't find it chilly.'

'But hot during the summer.'

Mrs O'Neill smiled. 'Just a wee bit,' she agreed. She looked around. 'Well, there's not much here, but I don't suppose you'll be needing much. Anyway, I don't think you'll be spending much time here – except for sleeping. You'll rise at half-past five, and I dare say it'll be after twelve before you're abed.' She pulled open the bottom

19

drawer of the dressing-table. Inside was a housemaid's uniform, neatly pressed and folded. 'I'm sure this'll fit you . . .'

'If it doesn't, I can always alter it . . .'

'Well, if you have any problems with it, you bring it down to me, and I'll help you sort it out.'

Katherine stifled a sudden yawn. 'Thank you.'

Mrs O'Neill smiled. 'Well, I'll let you settle in now. I've got the lunch to prepare. You'll want to unpack, and you should try and get some sleep, you look as if you need it.'

'I do,' Katherine said feelingly.

Mrs O'Neill nodded and stepped back, ducking her head at the low lintel, and pulled the door gently closed behind her.

Alone at last, Katherine unpacked slowly. There was little enough to do, but every girl going into service was required to bring her own caps, aprons and stockings, and indeed it was usual for them to bring their own uniforms. However, the hasty departure of Katherine's predecessor had ensured she had left her uniform behind. Katherine's only personal possessions included a print dress, a cotton nightdress, some calico underwear, a scarf, a pair of battered gloves and, beneath them all, a small much-thumbed bible. In the bottom of her bag was a small round hat-box which held a black bonnet with black velvet ribbons for Sunday and church wear. The rest of her possessions – her best dress, underwear, and a pair of black buttoned-boots – she was wearing.

She carefully folded her dress and laid it out on the bed, alongside her underwear. She pulled open the bottom drawer of the dressing-table and found the maid's uniform wrapped in tissue paper inside. She lifted it out and put it down on the bed, and then pulled the entire drawer out. There was a thin layer of dust in the bottom, and she crossed to the window that overlooked the rear garden, lifted the catch and pushed it open. A rich damp smell of raw earth touched with smoke drifted in. Katherine tilted the drawer and allowed the errant breeze to carry away the dust while she looked out over the garden.

The rear garden was long – not broad – and stretched back to a high stone wall and behind that was a second and higher wall. And Katherine guessed that there was a laneway running along behind the house. Beyond the wall – which, Katherine realized, was the wall of the college – she could see broad rolling fields dotted with clumps of trees and, in the distance, a sprawling many-windowed, much-chimneyed building. She looked at it for a few moments longer, and then the direction of the wind changed and stinging droplets of rain touched her face. With a shiver she closed the window and returned to her unpacking.

She ran her handkerchief around the edges of the drawer and then slid it back into the dressing table. She placed her dress in it, laid her slip and camiknickers on top and pushed it closed. She turned to her predecessor's uniform. The black alpaca dress, with its long sleeves and high, white, stock collar looked to be close enough to her own size and was still in very good condition – although she noticed that there was a tiny tear under the left armpit, and the right sleeve was frayed about the frilled cuff. She held it up against herself – it just about reached the floor – but when she examined the hem, she found there was enough to let down if the dress failed to cover her ankles when she tried it on.

Katherine yawned again. She would try it on later. She bundled the remainder of her clothes into the drawers, laid her bible on the dressing table, and then sat on the edge of the bed and bent over to unbutton her boots and pull them off. She wriggled her toes luxuriously; the boots were slightly too small and cramped her feet, but they were all she could afford.

Her eyes fell on the bible and she absently picked it up. It had been her mother's and her mother's before that, and from it Katherine had been taught to read and form her letters. When she had still been a young girl,

21

her grandmother had shown her what she called a 'small magic'. First she had told Katherine to concentrate on whatever problem was troubling her and then to take the bible and allow it to fall open. The old woman had always maintained that the first words that caught her eye when it fell open would have some bearing on whatever the problem was. For a while it had been something like a game, but she had soon tired of it, partly because she could rarely relate what she read to whatever her troubles were at that moment.

However, as she looked at the small battered book, she wondered, just what did the future hold for her in her new life in this strange land . . ? She picked it up, and then laid it down in her lap; of its own accord the book opened and the thin, close-printed pages fluttered, the noise sounding loud in the silence of the attic. Katherine found herself looking at the Book of Ecclesiastes, and reading . . .

'There is a season for all things, and a time for every affair under Heaven, a time to be born and a time to die . . .' She scanned down the verses, 'A time to plant . . . to kill . . . to weep . . . to mourn . . . to love.' She read the last lines again. 'A time to love and a time to hate, a time of war and a time of peace . . .'

She still wasn't sure how the verse answered her unasked questions. Was it telling her that there would be a time for all those things, and that she would experience all those different emotions? She hoped not, because she wasn't sure she could handle them, she didn't think she was strong enough. She closed the book softly and returned it to the dressing table. Katherine preferred not to think about it.

'I see you spell your name in the Irish fashion, with a "K" instead of a "C".' Anne Lewis looked up from the letter in her hand and smiled vaguely at Katherine.

'My grandfather was Irish, ma'am,· and my father served here briefly. He has a great fondness for things Irish.'

22

Anne Lewis nodded absently, looking down at the letter which James Lundy had given his daughter for the captain's wife. As she read through it Katherine looked down at the woman; she was, she decided, in her early thirties, a rather plain-looking woman with pale grey eyes and close-cropped mousy-brown hair that had far too many strands of silver in it to be called pretty.

Mrs Lewis folded the letter and looked up again. 'Your references are excellent, and my husband speaks very highly of your father . . .' her voice trailed away.

'Thank you, ma'am.'

She was about to speak again when something attracted her attention, and she stared out the window for a few moments before turning back to Katherine. She was sitting at a roll-top writing bureau, before a tall, broad window which looked out onto Clonliffe Road. Rain spattered the glass and ran in twisting rivulets down on to the window-ledge. These twisting streams seemed to mesmerize her.

The room was almost square but very tall and dark, and the fire in the grate sparkled and crackled, its light only serving to deepen the shadows that lingered in the corners, although it was now close to noon. The room was overcrowded with large ugly furniture, and the walls were covered with a grotesque floral wallpaper, much of which was mercifully hidden behind scores of framed prints and lithographs. It had taken a few moments for Katherine's eyes to adjust to the dimness, and to spot Mrs Lewis sitting absolutely still beside the writing desk.

'Yes, your references are excellent,' Mrs Lewis repeated. She looked at Katherine and smiled. 'I must admit I was a little apprehensive when my husband told me he had agreed to take on a new servant girl.' She paused. 'Has Mrs O'Neill told you what happened with our previous girl . . . ?'

'She did mention something about her leaving rather unexpectedly.' She was suddenly glad for the shadowed room so that the older woman couldn't see her expression.

'I'm sure she did,' Anne Lewis said shrewdly. 'I see you know how to be discreet – well that's one of the first lessons a servant must learn. Whatever happens within the walls of your master's house must never be repeated outside.'

'Oh, I wouldn't, ma'am.'

'No, I'm sure you wouldn't. Well,' she said, turning away from the window and glancing briefly at Katherine before looking into the fire, 'well, the captain and I have fairly simple needs, and I don't think you'll find your duties here arduous. As Mrs O'Neill may have already told you, you will be the only servant in the house; Mrs O'Neill comes in daily, and she has a woman who assists her whenever necessary.' Her eyes strayed back to Katherine. 'The captain and I are often away, and I think it would be possible for you to have a half day every Wednesday. However, if I need you, I would let you know on the Tuesday, or earlier if convenient.'

'Thank you, ma'am.'

'We also spend most Sunday afternoons with friends, and I feel sure that you could use that time for yourself.'

'Thank you.'

'However, we usually return by six on a Sunday, so I would expect to find you in the house at that time. Dinner is always at eight sharp.'

'Yes, ma'am.'

'There is one other thing . . .' Anne Lewis began, but her voice trailed away.

'Yes, ma'am?'

Mrs Lewis's eyes flickered momentarily to Katherine's. And like Mrs O'Neill, she found Katherine's habit of looking directly into her eyes disconcerting. 'My husband, the captain, is a very moral man, of high principles and strict morality. Under no circumstances will you be allowed to entertain young gentlemen while you are in our service.' She smiled briefly. 'I know this

24

may sound dramatic, but we have had some problems of a male nature with our last girl. You do understand?'

'Of course, ma'am.'

'Good. Now I think that's all. I know my husband has made all the monetary arrangements with your father.' She stood up and, crossing to the fireplace, tugged at the velvet rope that hung down by the huge ornately-framed glass mirror. 'I'll have Mrs O'Neill show you around the house after lunch. Afternoon tea is at four; I'm sure I will see you then.'

Katherine, realizing her interview was at an end, stood up. There was a single knock on the door and then Mrs O'Neill stuck her head around. 'You rang for me, ma'am?'

'Yes, Mrs O'Neill, when you have a few moments, perhaps you would be so kind as to show Katherine where everything is?'

'I'll do that.'

Mrs Lewis's gaze slipped off Katherine's face. 'Welcome to Ireland, Katherine, I hope you will be very happy here.'

'I'm sure I will be,' Katherine smiled tightly. I know I won't be, she thought.

CHAPTER TWO

By six-thirty Tuesday morning, Katherine had the fire in the dining room lit, and had cleaned out the coal-fired range in the kitchen and started a fire there.

Mrs O'Neill had insisted that the range in the kitchen was to be lit first every morning, as soon as the fire in the dining room was burning. She had explained that she came in at a quarter to eight and breakfast was served in the dining room at eight-thirty. She had insisted that, once the fire in the range was pulling strongly, the range had to be blackleaded and the fire-irons polished, and only when that was complete could she return to the dining room to open the shutters and dust the room, preparing it for the captain and Mrs Lewis who would be down promptly at half-eight for breakfast.

Mrs O'Neill had smiled. 'Well, when they say promptly at half-past eight, the captain means promptly at half-eight, Mrs Lewis might mean a quarter to nine. But the captain is always prompt.'

'So was my father,' Katherine put in.

'It's their military training; you can set your watch by him. Anyways,' she continued, 'Mrs Lewis usually lingers over her breakfast, so you can come on down here then, an' I'll put you up something to eat . . . '

Katherine threw back the dining room shutters and looked out on to Clonliffe Road. The sun was rising to her left further down the road, etching long sharp shadows on to the damp cobbles. The street was still deserted, although in the distance she could hear the rattle of a tram, and the street lights had been extinguished, so obviously someone was up and about. She looked down into the front garden and was surprised to find it was almost completely bare of flowers or shrubs of any kind, although the houses on the right and across the road were both bright with early spring flowers.

'Enjoying the view?'

Katherine spun around, her eyes darting first to the tall, rather handsome man standing in the doorway and then to the large round-faced clock standing on the mantelpiece. It was just after half-past seven.

'No, you are not late,' the man said with a thin, rather humourless smile, 'I am early this morning.' He stepped into the room and closed the door behind him. 'You must be Katherine Lundy, James Lundy's girl.'

Katherine bobbed a curtsey. 'Yes, sir.'

'I am Captain Lewis.'

'Yes, sir, pleased to meet you, sir.'

'Well, I hope your stay here will be a long and pleasant one . . .'

Katherine looked up to find the captain staring openly at her. He was a tall, broad-shouldered man, with a square face. His eyes were dark and deep-sunken, his nose sharp and his mouth was broad, but his lips were thin and lent his face a cruel cast. He was immaculately dressed in a dark business suit, and his black leather shoes shone with a mirror gloss.

'You are staring,' he remarked casually.

So are you, Katherine thought. 'I'm sorry, sir, but I expected to see you in uniform.'

'Well, not today,' he said, and then continued on a different subject. 'I have to go out early; will you tell Mrs Lewis that I shall be home for dinner at the usual time?'

'Yes, sir.'

He opened the door of the dining room and stepped out into the hall. 'And will you also tell her that I am afraid I will not be available this Saturday.' Something like a smile touched his lips. 'I think my wife wishes to make the final arrangements today for the dinner party.'

'Yes, sir, I will tell Mrs Lewis.'

27

Captain Lewis lifted his heavy overcoat off the stand in the hall and threw it over his arm. As he strode to the front door there was a sudden clatter of wheels in the street which stopped in front of the house. 'Ah, my cab is here.'

Katherine handed him his umbrella.

His eyes met hers briefly but Katherine, suddenly mindful of her position as a servant, dropped her gaze first, but not before the man had seen the determined expression in her eyes.

He turned the key in the lock and slid back the two bolts, one each at the top and bottom, and then pulled the front door open. A draught of fresh, cold air blew into the house as he stepped out. Katherine shivered and quickly closed the door without waiting to see if he looked back.

Mrs Lewis arrived down for breakfast a little after eight-thirty. She was pale and her eyes looked sunken and were shadowed. Katherine had already laid the table, and the smell of frying bacon seeped up from the kitchen.

'Good morning, Katherine.'

'Good morning, Mrs Lewis. Did you sleep well?'

'No, I'm afraid I had a restless night. It was rather hot and stuffy, didn't you think?'

'Yes, ma'am.'

'Did you see Captain Lewis this morning, Katherine?'

'Yes, ma'am. He asked me to tell you that he would be home for dinner at the usual time, but he was afraid that he would be unable to attend the dinner this Saturday. He wanted you to know so you could make the arrangements today.'

Katherine saw the other woman's mouth tighten into a thin line. She guessed that it had been more than the heat of the night that had kept her awake last night. She took a quick look at the table, checking to make sure that Mrs Lewis needed nothing, then silently left the room to snatch her own hurried breakfast in the kitchen below.

'Mrs Lewis looks tired,' Katherine said to Mrs O'Neill as she entered the warm, cosy kitchen.

'Ah, she probably had a barney with the captain. When you're married, lass, you'll find you have the best arguments at night, when you're lying beside him an' he can't get away, an' it's dark an' you can't see his face and see how the words hurt.'

'I didn't think you could have a "best argument",' Katherine said with a smile, sitting down on one of the high-backed wooden kitchen chairs and resting the palms of her hands flat on the smoothly polished wooden table.

Mrs O'Neill was standing by the range, stirring a round fat-bellied pot with a long wooden spoon. She glanced back over her shoulder, her grey eyes twinkling. 'Ah well, the best thing about having an argument is the making up afterwards!'

Katherine coloured and dropped her eyes, smiling shyly.

'You left no young beau behind you in England then?' the cook continued.

'Oh, I never had much time for a young man of my own; I was too busy looking after my mother, father and five brothers.' She paused, and then added, 'Well, maybe I'll meet a young man here.'

Mrs O'Neill turned from the range, shaking her head. 'Don't even think about it, lass. The mistress will not allow you to have any gentlemen suitors . . .'

Katherine nodded. 'She did say something about that . . .'

'An' she'll be keeping an extra eye on you, especially after what happened to Sheila.'

'Is she very strict?'

Moire O'Neill thought about it for a few moments. 'She's a harsh enough woman all right, severe, I'd say. There's not much humour in her . . . but then I don't suppose there's much humour in her life.' She saw

29

Katherine's sidelong look and laughed quickly, rubbing her hands in her apron. 'Ah, but I do go on, don't I?'

'I thought she looked sad,' Katherine said, looking at the cook for a reaction. Instinct told her that she was missing something. 'Does she get on well with Miste . . . Captain Lewis?'

'They could get on better,' Mrs O'Neill said, turning and busying herself at the range.

'What's he like?'

'You be careful of him,' the cook said quickly, and then, seeing the young woman's startled expression, corrected herself, 'I mean, mind what you say and how you treat him; remember your place.'

'Of course.' Katherine nodded. She watched the cook for a few moments, and then said, 'And have you anyone yourself, Mrs O'Neill?'

Moire O'Neill began spooning thick porridge into a bowl. She shook her head. 'No, not now. My Pat passed away eight, going on nine years ago now.' She put the bowl on the table in front of Katherine, and then set a spoon, some milk and salt beside it.

'I'm sorry . . .' Katherine began.

'Sure an' there's no reason to be. He was a docker, an' worked on the quays unloading the boats. It wasn't good money nor regular, but what with him working and me in service an' with no little ones to feed, we were never short of a few bob.'

Katherine tasted the porridge. It was hot and burned her lips; she added some milk.

'But he was fond of his drink,' Mrs O'Neill continued, turning back to the range, and moving the kettle closer to the heat. 'An' dockers, you see, are paid in pubs. One day he had one or two more than he should an', on the way home, he slipped and fell in the river. An' drowned.' Her voice cracked. 'He drowned,' she whispered. 'He had worked for over thirty years on the docks, an' he had never learned to swim . . .' She shook her head. 'Can you imagine the stupidity of it . . . ? Well, neither can I,' she continued, without waiting for

an answer. She poured water from the kettle into a plain squat teapot, and then almost immediately poured the tea into a cup. It was pale and weak. 'I know you English like your tea weak,' Mrs O'Neill said over her shoulder.

'Well, I prefer mine a little stronger,' Katherine confessed.

'Where I come from in the poorer part of the city, a pot of tea is made first thing in the morning, an' is then kept on the boil all day,' Mrs O'Neill said. 'The last cups are like tar – and taste just as bad.' She poured Katherine's cup back into the pot and then tried again; this time the tea was a rich bronze-gold colour.

Katherine lifted the cup and looked at Mrs O'Neill. 'What should I do first? This is the first time I've been in service. I suppose I should clean . . .'

Mrs O'Neill shook her head. 'Not yet.' She glanced up at the large, round-faced clock that hung above the kitchen door. 'Mrs Lewis should be finishing breakfast about now. She'll then go up and dress . . .'

'Should I help her?'

'No,' Mrs O'Neill frowned, 'she dresses herself – although she may ring if she needs help with buttons or fasteners. While she's dressing you can set a fire in the sitting room and then clear off the dining room. By the time you've done that, Mrs Lewis will probably be down and you can go up and do the beds, and clean the bedroom. Then you can wash and polish the bathroom floor – and don't forget to polish the taps. Oh, an' don't forget to trim the lamps and clean the globes.'

Katherine finished her tea and stood up, smoothing down the front of her dress. 'I'll get started then.'

Mrs O'Neill nodded. 'That's a good girl. Mrs Lewis goes out every Tuesday morning before lunch, so I'll give you a shout about twelve an' we'll have a nice cup of tea.'

Captain John Lewis stood on the top floor of the General Post Office, commonly known as the GPO,

and stared down into the street below. To his left and at the foot of the pillar a half-dozen flower-sellers were gossiping together, their blossoms, in sheafs, bundles, pots, basins, pans and bottles, scattered in a riot of colour on the drab cobble stones around them. There was a large woman selling fruit beside them, and the sharp reds and greens of her apples and the vivid oranges almost outdid the flowers.

He heard the door open behind him and turned, and then stiffened and saluted, although the older man standing in the doorway was not in uniform.

'Sir!'

'At ease.'

Captain Lewis relaxed, but only fractionally, as the older grey-haired man closed the door and crossed the room, finally sinking down into the captain's creaking leather-backed chair. He set his silver-topped cane down on the table, removed his hat and then pulled off his grey gloves. 'Sit, captain, sit, please.' He indicated a seat, a straight-backed wooden chair against the wall by the window. 'Your report, sir?' The older man, whom the captain knew only by the title 'brigadier', produced a slim, red, leather-bound notebook and a gold pen, which he laid down beside his hat and cane.

'There is little to report, sir,' John Lewis said, staring straight ahead at a point a little above and to the left of the other man's head.

'Begin with your work here. Does anyone suspect?'

'Not to my knowledge, sir. I have been officially appointed as staffing officer for the General Post Office and sub post offices. I have also allowed a rumour to circulate that I am looking into the possibility of trimming the staff numbers.'

'And?'

'Mr Creswell, the Secretary, reports that there has been an unprecedented increase in efficiency and timekeeping,' Captain Lewis said with a smile.

The older man nodded. 'Perhaps it would be as well

if you were to let a few staff go; I'm sure they can be easily replaced.'

'Easily.'

'It would help with your cover.'

'But it might also antagonize the workers,' Captain Lewis protested, 'and I do not want to draw unnecessary attention to myself at the moment. I intend to conduct a series of interviews with every member of staff here, and of course, in future, all further appointments will be conducted through me.' He paused and added, 'With your permission, of course . . ?'

'You may do what you wish, as long as you can remain here unsuspected.'

'I don't see any difficulty with that,' Captain Lewis said slowly. 'Officially, I have retired my commission for health reasons.'

'You are still using your military title,' the brigadier nodded towards the door, where 'Captain John Lewis' was inscribed in cursive script on the opposite side.

'Most people still refer to me by my military title,' John Lewis said stiffly.

'Your wife remains unaware of your real task here?'

'Yes, sir.' He turned to look at the older man and said slowly and carefully, 'I remain unconvinced of the usefulness of my being here . . . sir.'

'You consider it to be a waste of time, then?'

Captain Lewis hesitated. 'I would not have phrased it so bluntly, but yes, sir, I can only see it as a waste of time.'

The older man sat back in the creaking leather chair and brought both his hands together, flat against each other, with the thumbs touching his lips. His sharp grey eyes regarded the captain for a few moments. 'Captain Lewis,' he said finally, 'it is my belief – my firm belief – that Dublin is a city hovering on the brink of bloody revolution. It is only a matter of time . . .' He raised his hand as the other man began to speak. 'No, hear me out. You are aware, no doubt, that there have been three minor uprisings in Ireland in the last one hundred years,

33

that of Emmet in '03, the Young Irelanders in '48, and then there was the Fenian Insurrection as recently as '67, a little over thirty years ago.' He stood up and walked to the window to stand beside the captain who had remained seated. And, although he was seated, John Lewis was taller than the dapper little man.

The brigadier looked into his face, and then nodded to the street. 'Look beyond the grand façades, the hotels, the shops of O'Connell Street . . .'

'Sackville Street,' Captain Lewis automatically corrected him.

'What do the common people call it?' the older man snapped.

'O'Connell Street, sir,' John Lewis said stiffly.

'If you're going to spy on these people, Lewis, then I suggest you become a trifle more familiar with them!'

'Yes, sir!'

'Not one hundred yards behind O'Connell Street is a vast warren of streets and stinking tenements, each one inhabited by scores of families. They have nothing, and have therefore nothing to lose if there is a revolution here. And all they need is a focus – some firebrand or unscrupulous moneygrabber – who will weld them into a mass, and they will march out of their slums and hammer on all those fancy houses and shops down there demanding their share.'

'The police and army . . .'

'And what will they do – kill them all?'

Captain Lewis hedged. 'I'm sure it will never happen,' he said condescendingly.

The other man turned around and stood with his back to the window, his thin face in shadow. 'You're a fool, Lewis. A blind fool. It is happening now, even as we speak. In the slums behind this grand façade, there are people coughing their lungs out in damp foul-smelling rooms, there are children starving – yes, starving – to death, there are women and young girls selling themselves for the price of a meal; whole families are living

34

in buildings that have long been condemned, buildings where the rats have grown so big and so vicious that they contend with the dogs and cats. All the people down there need is a leader, and they'll get one,' the older man promised. 'Sooner or later, they will get one. And when they do, you can count on it, we English will be the most obvious target.'

'You seem sure,' Captain Lewis said.

'I am sure. And you're here because when it happens this will be the most likely place for us to spot it. This is the heart of Dublin. A revolutionary leader will need to have some men working here in this building where they would be able to monitor the post and telegraphs coming from the government and army, and where their men here can allow parcels of certain goods to pass through unrecorded and unsearched. For a revolution of any sort to succeed, they will need someone here.'

'And what do I do if I discover one or more of these people?'

'You take the relevant action.'

'And what form should that be? Should I allow them to operate and watch them, or should I take steps to neutralize them?' He paused. 'You must forgive me, sir, but I've never done anything like this before. I am only a soldier, I'm not sure of the politics in a case like this.'

'You are still a soldier, and I would expect you to act like one. This is a war, captain – or perhaps I should say the eve of a war. It is a war that may not happen for a year, or five years, or even ten years, but it will come, mark my words. Whatever action you take will, I hope, partially delay the outbreak of that war.'

'And my course of action?'

'One of the reasons I picked you,' the thin, hard-faced man said, crossing to the desk and picking up his cane and gloves, 'was because you have a certain reputation for ruthlessness.' He stepped over to the door, but stopped with his hand on the handle. 'You must deal with the situation as you see fit, captain. I will back whatever action you take as long as it does not implicate

35

the government, the army or the police in any way. Is
that understood, captain?'

Captain Lewis saluted. 'Yes, sir!'

Captain Lewis turned back to the window ledge and
stared down the length of Sackville Street – O'Connell
Street, he corrected himself with a wry smile – towards
the bridge. This side of the street was now in shadow
and the windows on the far side were burning with rich,
golden-brown light. It was going to be a fine evening,
just the sort of evening to go for a stroll along the leafy
lanes of Drumcondra near his new house with his wife
... But no, there was work to do – there was always
work to do.

He returned to his desk, opened one of the drawers
and pulled out a thick ledger. From another drawer he
produced a pile of brown envelopes. He opened the first
envelope and read, 'Stone, Charles M. Address: Room
3, No. 10, Gloucester Street Lr ...' He opened the
relevant page of the ledger and began to enter what
information he had on the man. He didn't know Charles
Stone, he had never met him, but his address in Goucester
ter Street, one of the roughest areas of the city, made
him suspect, and one of the first tasks the brigadier had
given him was to compile a list of all possible trouble-
makers. By troublemaker, the brigadier meant anyone
of notoriety from the poorer districts – and there were
a lot of these – or anyone who professed strong nation-
alistic tendencies or belonged to one of the many Gaelic
clubs or societies which were now springing up. John
Lewis was unsure how the brigadier would use the list,
the man had merely said that it was for his files, but it
did make him wonder if he himself was on a list or in a
file somewhere. He tapped his fingers on the desk,
frustration beginning to well up within him again. He
could do with a drink, but later, he promised himself,
when he was finished with these damned files. He was
certain he was in one of the brigadier's files ...

* * *

John Lewis had first met the man he knew only as the brigadier nearly eighteen months previously. It had been in early December, and he recalled that it had been a bitterly cold night, the cobble stones already sparkling with a hard frost although it was not yet six o'clock. He had gone to the bar in the Imperial Hotel directly across from the GPO, as he often did, for a tot to warm him up, when the small, thin man of late middle years had slid into the polished, buttoned, leather seat beside him. The bar had been almost empty, with plenty of vacant seats, and the captain had bridled, opening his mouth to insist that the man leave when the waiter came over, placed two hot whiskeys on the table and moved silently away. John looked from the man to the drinks and then back to the man.

'Captain John Lewis?'

Surprised, he nodded silently.

'You are familiar with Lord Roberts?'

Captain Lewis nodded again. Field Marshal, the Right Honourable Lord Roberts, V.C., was the general officer commanding the Crown forces in Ireland.

'And are you also familiar with the name of Sir Andrew Reed?'

Again the silent and by now puzzled nod. Sir Andrew Reed was the Inspector General of the Royal Irish Constabulary.

The thin man smiled, pulling back his lips from his yellowed teeth. 'Well suffice it to say that I am speaking with their full authority and, if not their blessing, then their cognisance.'

'I really don't see what this is all about . . .'

'Bear with me.'

'Look, mister . . .' the captain began, rising to his feet.

'Brigadier! You may call me brigadier. Sit down, captain, people are beginning to stare.'

Captain Lewis subsided into his seat. 'What do you want . . . brigadier?' he demanded. He finished his own drink in a swallow and then made to stand up again. 'I'm going . . .'

The thin man smiled and then, not looking at the captain, said very softly, 'Nine hundred pounds . . . captain!'

John Lewis sank back into the chair. He reached for the second drink in front of him and drained half of it in one swallow. 'How do you know about that?'

The man shrugged. 'We have been watching you for some little time now, and we are well acquainted with your . . .' he hesitated fractionally, and then said, 'interests.' He pulled out the small, red, leather-bound notebook which John Lewis would eventually come to hate. 'Let's see now, on the 12th of August of this year you lost one hundred pounds at the gaming tables; on the 16th August, you lost another hundred. In September, on the 5th to be precise, you lost two hundred pounds, on the following day another hundred.' He flipped over a page. 'There is a little gap until . . . the 28th September, and then you lost another hundred; on the 5th October two hundred lost, and the 30th October again a hundred.' He closed the book and took a sip from his drink. 'Nine hundred pounds lost – quite a sum of money for an army captain. Added to that, this money was lost in what are, I think, commonly called flash houses, in the Montgomery Street district.' He drank again. 'An area of some ill-repute. Does your lovely wife know that you're keeping company with prostitutes?' he asked casually.

'What do you want?' John demanded icily, 'Is this some attempt to extort money from me? If it is, you're wasting your time – I have none.'

'Oh, I am well aware of that, captain. No, all I want is a little of your time.'

'Well, that's cheap enough.'

'Ah, but I'm willing to pay for it.' The thin man pulled a bundle of papers from his pocket and pushed them across the table to John Lewis.

'What are they?'

'Of interest, I'm sure,' the brigadier said, lifting his head, catching the waiter's eye and pointing to the two glasses. Captain Lewis took the opportunity to open the papers – and found they were his notes and pledges made to the various banks and moneylenders.

'Where did you get these?' he whispered.

'I bought them.'

John stared at him incredulously. Here, spread out in tattered slips of paper on the table before him, were his ruin and disgrace.

'Listen to me for a while, and they're yours,' the brigadier added.

'What do you mean, they're mine?' the captain demanded.

'Well, I have no use for them, I'm sure.' The brigadier smiled, and John saw the malice behind his eyes.

'What do you want?' he asked, feeling his stomach churn.

The brigadier ran his thin fingers down the glass and for a moment seemed at a loss for words. Finally, he looked up at John and said simply, 'We want you to work for us.'

'I'm in the army . . .'

'Not if these papers come to light,' the small grey man said very quietly.

John Lewis turned the papers around on the table, an idea beginning to form at the back of his mind. These were the original papers, his signature on all of them . . . and there were no copies.

'You will resign your commission for whatever reasons you think fit to give,' the brigadier continued.

'I don't understand.'

'Resign honourably or be dismissed dishonourably – the choice is yours. If you choose the former, although officially a civilian, you will continue on the army payroll and we would place you in suitable employment.'

'What sort of employment?' John Lewis finished his drink with a single swallow, feeling the hot, spiced, malt whiskey sear its way down his throat and settle into his stomach. By now, he knew he should be feeling slightly drunk – but he was still stone-cold sober.

'A civil servant office . . .' he paused and shrugged, 'the title of the job has yet to be determined.'

'But why – for what purpose?' John asked impatiently, wondering if he was missing the point.

The brigadier smiled again, his thin lips curling back from his teeth, but the smile never touched his eyes. 'Why, you will be a spy, Captain Lewis, a spy! Your task will be to keep us informed of the movements and activities of the various underground organisations in this city.'

In the long silence that followed the ticking of the grandfather clock in the corner seemed suddenly louder. John Lewis ran his finger through the damp ring on the table, tracing a circle around again and again. Finally he looked up at the thin neat little man. 'Why me?'

'You have several desirable qualities, captain.'

'Such as?'

'You are discreet – when you have to be – ruthless when the need arises and . . .' the brigadier tapped the crinkled papers with the tip of his index finger, 'and you can be bought.'

CHAPTER THREE

'Well at least you've a good day for it,' Mrs O'Neill said, opening the kitchen door and staring up into the pale, blue, cloudless May sky. She shivered and pulled her shawl tighter around her shoulders; there was still a winter nip in the air. She turned back to the younger woman. 'Now, are you sure you have the address, in case you get lost?' she asked for the third time.

'Of course I have,' Katherine smiled. 'College House, Clonliffe Road,' she paused and then continued because the older woman was still looking expectantly at her, 'beside Holy Cross College.'

'And where will you get the tram?'

'At the pillar.'

'And what time do you have to be in by?' Mrs O'Neill asked, smiling now, realizing that she sounded just like every other mother she knew.

'Nine o'clock. But I'll be home long before that.'

Mrs O'Neill nodded. 'Aye. Fine then; be off with you.'

Katherine nodded and walked slowly down the path that led from the kitchen door to the laneway that ran along behind the house. She slipped the latch on the gate and stepped out into the lane, but just before she pulled the gate shut she turned and waved to Mrs O'Neill.

'Enjoy yourself,' the cook called.

'I will!'

Mrs O'Neill turned from the door and made her way over to the range where the kettle was just beginning to boil. She glanced up at the clock; it was just after half-past two, but the old woman was exhausted. When the new maid had turned and waved to her from the gate – just as if she had been her own daughter – Mrs O'Neill had felt the tears spring to her eyes and a knot settle into her throat. Usually her childlessness never affected her; the years had given her a thick skin, and she compensated for her own lack of a family by adopting other people's. She was 'Granny O'Neill' to a lot of children in and around Summerhill.

Katherine spotted the young man looking at her as she took her place in the tram queue on Drumcondra Road. She tried not to look at him, but she was only too aware of deep, intense eyes staring at her. Finally, she looked up and used the ploy one of the older girls she had worked with in Blackpool had taught her – she stared directly at him. The young man held her gaze for a single long moment, then he dropped his eyes and looked away. Katherine watched him openly for a score of pounding heartbeats and then she too turned away.

But when she turned back a few minutes later, she caught him looking at her again. She glared at him, and this time he coloured and rather self-consciously turned his back. He was a rather slight young man, about nineteen or so, she guessed, with a long sallow face that was dominated by a pair of deep-set, intense, black eyes and topped by a thick head of wiry, black hair. From his sober dress, Katherine guessed that he was a clerk of some kind.

The tram appeared drawn by a pair of high-stepping horses moving slowly down the slight hill on Drumcondra Road towards the stop. When it had rattled to a halt, the queue filed forward slowly, some, mostly the women and girls, stepping inside, while the rest climbed the outside stairs to the upper deck. Katherine saw the young man step inside and made a quick decision; she took the stairs to the top deck. It was uncovered and chill and, at this height, the breeze was cutting, but she was well wrapped up and was so excited at the prospect of exploring Dublin on her own that she barely noticed. She took a seat near the front of the tram and sat down, and looked down on to the street below. She felt someone sit down beside her and glanced around – and found it was the young man who had been staring at her earlier.

'I-I-I'm s-s-sorry I s-s-stared,' he immediately stammered before she could say anything.

Katherine continued looking at him, but said nothing.

'I-I-I know it's r-r-rude, but . . .' He had turned a bright pink colour and his stammering had become embarrassing.

Taking pity on him, she smiled and shook her head. 'There's no need to apologize; I think I stared too.'

'You are English!' he said in surprise, his stammer disappearing with the shock.

'From Lancashire.'

'You-you're in s-s-service here?'

'How did you know?'

'Just guessed,' he smiled, and then he added, 'My name's Dermot Corcoran.'

Katherine hesitated before answering, but finally decided that this young man was relatively harmless. 'Katherine Lundy,' she said.

'What an unusual name,' Dermot said.

'I don't think there's anything wrong with Katherine,' she smiled.

'I didn't mean that.'

'It doesn't sound half as strange as Corcoran.' She smiled, deliberately overpronouncing it as Kor-Korean.

'Is this your first visit to Dublin?' he asked, all trace of his stutter completely gone now.

'My first.'

'What do you think of it?' he asked eagerly.

Katherine shrugged. 'I don't know. I arrived on Monday, and it was raining so heavily I didn't get much of a chance to see anything. This is my afternoon off . . .' She smiled and shrugged again, 'And so here I am, off to see Dublin city.'

'One of the finest – if not the finest – capital cities in Europe,' Dermot said proudly.

'What about London?'

'Well, I've never seen London, and so I'll reserve judgement until I see what it looks like,' he added with a smile.

'I've never seen it myself,' Katherine confessed, 'although I did see Liverpool and I worked in Blackpool for a while, and they were grand big cities.'

'But dirty; I've heard they are dirty?' Dermot asked eagerly, his voice questioning.

'Liverpool is,' Katherine nodded, 'but Blackpool isn't too bad, and in the summer it can look really beautiful.'

The conductor arrived. 'Fares, please?'

While Katherine scrambled for her purse, Dermot slipped the man two copper pennies. 'Two to the pillar,' he said.

The conductor punched two tickets on the long roll he carried and passed them to Dermot. Dermot separated them and handed one to Katherine. She took it but handed him a penny. Dermot shook his head. 'No . . . no . . . allow me . . . please?'

She shook her head, 'I can't.'

'Why not?' he smiled, 'it's only a penny.'

'That's not the point; you might need it for the fare home,' Katherine snapped, and then saw him blush and knew she had struck the truth. 'You don't even know me, anyway.'

'It was only a penny,' Dermot mumbled, but sheepishly took the coin and slipped it into his pocket.

'What do you do?' Katherine asked, to cover his embarrassment.

'I'm a junior reporter for the *Freeman's Journal*,' Dermot said proudly.

'That's a newspaper?' Katherine asked.

Dermot nodded. 'The best in Dublin, with a circulation of upwards of thirty thousand people.'

Katherine dipped her head, hiding a smile. He made it sound as if he were personally responsible for the newspaper's circulation.

'And what do you do?' he asked.

'I'm in service,' she said softly.

'I know, but where?' he asked, wondering if she were living close to him.

'With Captain and Mrs Lewis, on Clonliffe Road.'

Dermot Corcoran's face lit up with a delighted smile. 'I know it well. You tell Granny O'Neill that I was asking after her.'

It took Katherine a moment or two to realize that he was talking about the cook, Mrs O'Neill. She was about to ask why he called her 'Granny', when the tram turned from Dorset Street into North Frederick Street which rolled down into Sackville Street, and the question died on her lips, unasked. The panorama that had opened out in front of her just took her breath away.

The main street of the second capital in the Empire was reputed to be one of the longest and broadest streets in Europe. And certainly, as the tram came down the gently sloping hill, Sackville Street seemed to stretch on forever, its broad straight line broken only by the tall column of Nelson's pillar in the centre of it. The afternoon had turned hazy and the far end of the street beyond the pillar was lost in the smoke.

Dermot leaned over the rail and stared down the length of the street; he was well-used to the sight, but it never failed to astound him.

'It's magnificent,' Katherine whispered. 'How long is it?'

'It's over a thousand feet long and about a hundred and fifty feet across, I believe,' he said.

'And this is Sackville Street?'

'Officially,' Dermot said with a grin.

'What do you mean?'

'Well, I think you'll find it more often called O'Connell Street,' Dermot said, 'on account of the statue of the Liberator, Daniel O'Connell, standing down at the far end near the bridge.'

'My father told me about Daniel O'Connell,' Katherine said.

'The greatest leader Ireland ever had.' He stood up. 'Come on, we get out here.'

Katherine stood up and followed him down the length of the tram, noticing that they were the last two left on board. As they stepped off the footboard onto the cobbles, she turned and pointed to an impressive-looking building with a pillared, arched doorway and curiously rounded roof. 'What's that?'

'That's the Rotunda, the Lying-In Hospital,' Dermot said, 'Dublin's first maternity hospital.'

Katherine looked again. The building looked nothing like a lying-in hospital. But then the city seemed to be full of surprises. Because of its width and length the main street seemed empty, the few people scattered, giving it a slightly deserted air. The buildings on either side were a curious mixture of the elegant and the austere, red and ivory stone alternating, a mixture of shops, hotels and offices.

'What are you going to do today?' Dermot asked suddenly.

Katherine turned, realizing Dermot was talking to her. She shrugged. 'I don't know. Wander around for a bit, I should imagine. I'd like to see the pillar close up.'

'I'll walk down with you if I may. The *Freeman*'s offices are in Princes Street, which runs down alongside the GPO . . .'

'The GPO . . ?' Katherine asked.

'The General Post Office,' Dermot explained, 'everyone knows that.'

'Every Dubliner,' Katherine corrected him.

He laughed, with genuine good humour, and Katherine joined in with him, while passers-by looked disapprovingly at them. 'Come on,' he said finally, 'I'll be late for work if we don't hurry – some of us don't have an afternoon off.'

Katherine stood looking up at the column of stone which had claimed her father's army career, and contemplated climbing it herself – by taking the stairs which ran up inside the pillar to the top. But she had promised Dermot she would wait until they next met, and then they would climb it together. He had rather sheepishly admitted that, although a Dubliner born and bred and although he worked not a hundred yards from the pillar, he had never climbed it. And it was only when he had run off, saying that he would see her next week, that she realized she had actually made a date with him.

She turned around and faced the GPO and thought about going inside. But there was nothing she wanted in there – she had brought a few stamps with her – and it would be a shame to go indoors now, just when the sun finally seemed about to burn through the afternoon haze. So, following Dermot's instructions, she slowly made her way down the length of Sackville Street – her father had always called it Sackville Street – towards O'Connell Bridge.

The first thing she noticed about the bridge was how peaceful it was. Everyone around it seemed so casual and relaxed, strolling easily, no-one in a rush anywhere. She found herself slipping easily into the same frame of mind and she idled for nearly twenty minutes on O'Connell Bridge, staring upriver at the humped back of the Metal Bridge, the Ha'penny Bridge, and down into the grey-green waters of the Liffey flowing beneath. Finally, conscious of the passing time, she turned away from the river and, mindful of Dermot's directions, headed for Trinity College, which she could just about see down the street, which in turn would lead her round into Grafton Street.

After the broad cobbled expanse of Sackville Street and then the wide open space of College Green, Grafton Street looked almost narrow, and the striped and col-oured awnings that hung over the windows of most of the shops only increased the feeling of claustrophobia. Also, because it was far narrower than Sackville Street, it looked crowded, with people thronging the footpaths and overflowing on to the road where the cabs, drays and bicycles had almost come to a halt.

The sudden crowd made Katherine nervous; although she had worked in Blackpool during the summer months, where there was a steady influx from the cities to savour the sea air and salt baths, she had never seen so many people gathered together in one place. She thought about turning around for a moment, but instead, remembering Dermot's instructions, decided to press on. She would walk up one side of Grafton Street – 'to St Stephen's Green,' Dermot had told her – and then cross over and walk down on the far side.

It was the people that took her attention first. She paused on the corner, standing beneath the huge pair of glasses that hung above the door of the optician's Yeats & Son and watched them for a moment. There were ladies in the finest of clothes, with rich stoles and mantles, rolled parasols and hats, walking arm in arm with men whose dress and air proclaimed them members of the upper classes. They strolled casually, with all the time in the world and no cares, stopping now and again to look into the richly-furnished, elegantly-dressed windows. Moving more quickly, no time to stop and stare, were younger men and women, clerks and shop girls on errands, mingling with older women of more impoverished means, perhaps servants shopping for their mistresses, and old men and boys selling newspapers on the street corners.

And wandering through them all were the beggars. It wasn't so much their wretchedness or filth which shocked the young woman – Lancashire was not short of beggars of its own, and Blackpool had its own seasonal quota – rather it was their age. The majority of them were children.

Katherine watched one small urchin – boy or girl, she was unable to tell – dogging a richly dressed couple, its filthy hand outstretched. Even from a distance, Katherine could make out its pleading eyes, until, either because its whining had touched him or more likely from frustration and to be rid of it, the man threw it a coin. The child deftly snatched the coin from the air and

48

darted off, snaking through legs and across the crowded street, running beneath a stalled dray, and popping up on the far side. Katherine watched the child dart into a side street across to the right and disappear. She felt in her purse for a coin – and then reconsidered. If she gave to one, she would have to give to all. And then she looked down at her own slightly shabby clothes and worn coat, and smiled inwardly. She didn't think she would be bothered by the beggars.

Katherine was crossing the bottom of Grafton Street and Suffolk Street on her way to the tram when the carriage passed, the iron-shod wheels rattling on the cobbles, the high-stepping horses' hooves striking sparks from the stones. She glanced up at it – and then stopped in amazement. The carriage was an open one, drawn by a matched pair of fine chestnut geldings and driven by a coachman in plum-coloured livery. There were six women in the carriage, quite lovely if you looked at them quickly, although a second glance revealed the excess of powder, the too-bright rouge, the tired eyes. They were dressed in the most magnificent gowns Katherine had ever seen, all of them in the latest styles, each one a different colour and cut to a slightly different but revealing design.

She saw the women nodding and acknowledging the stares of the men, although they ignored the women, and more than one passer-by doffed his hat. Katherine was amazed and surprised, and, as the carriage crossed Trinity College Gate and passed around into Westmorland Street, she wondered who the women were; she would ask Mrs O'Neill when she reached home . . .

'They're fallen women, ladies of easy virtue,' Mrs O'Neill scoffed angrily, surprising Katherine with her vehemence. 'They parade down Grafton Street as if they own it – but all they're doing is showing themselves off, flaunting themselves like a length of cloth for sale in Clery's shop window.' She placed a steaming cup of tea down in front of Katherine and then settled herself in the armchair before the fire. 'And what else did you do – beside gawk at tarts,' she asked curtly, and then immediately shook her head. 'I'm sorry, that was unkind, but I've little enough time for that sort of woman. It's just that it galls me to see them swanning around the streets in their fine carriages; even the police salute them. Mind you, I don't mean those who have to sell themselves just to live, that's different,' she amended. 'Tell me about your day . . .'

'Are there many . . . prostitutes in Dublin?' Katherine stumbled over the word.

'Too many.' Mrs O'Neill used a long poker to dig at the fire, prodding savagely at the glowing coals. 'Ach, but there's many a one you can't blame for it. A mother earning a few shillings to feed her childer; a girl bringing home money for her parents or brothers, or to pay the rent – they're not the ones I blame. It's those others – the fancy women in furs and gowns, and foreigners too – earning more in a single night than honest folk can earn in a month or a year. They're the ones I blame.'

Katherine wasn't sure what Mrs O'Neill blamed them for or why, but she wasn't prepared to ask. She sipped some more of the bitter-tasting tea, and wondered what had driven the old woman into such an unpleasant mood.

'They were more than likely from one of the flash houses – you don't find any from the stews parading themselves around Grafton Street.'

'What are the stews?'

'Tenement rooms, love, an' pray to God you never see the inside of one. Places where the poorer classes of girls can hire for the night to bring their "gentlemen" customers.'

'I heard one of the women call out to a tall, white-haired gentleman, and I thought I recognized an English accent.'

'A lot of those women came over from London, Liverpool and Manchester; this is a barracks town, love, and there's always a ready trade for that sort of person.

Why, when there's a troop ship in, well . . . it isn't safe for an honest woman to walk the streets.' She looked up at the clock and then stood up. 'And now look at the time, you've kept me late with your nattering. Mrs Lewis will be ringing for dinner any minute.' Even as she spoke the bell high on the wall jangled . . .

CHAPTER FOUR

Saturday started with an argument.

Captain and Mrs Lewis had argued over the breakfast table, obviously continuing with something that had begun the previous night. Katherine, who was serving, did her best to look uninterested and unconcerned.

'I have told you once and for all, I will not attend . . .' Captain Lewis snapped, looking over the top of his *Times* and glaring at his wife.

'It will only be for a few hours . . .'

'It will seem like years,' Captain Lewis growled. 'The last party of yours went on for what seemed like an eternity.'

'But there was even a mention of it in the *Freeman's Journal* . . .'

Captain Lewis ignored her.

'John, please, for my sake . . . ?'

'No. I will not be here tonight.'

Anne Lewis threw down her knife and fork, and then stood up so violently that the chair tilted and went crashing over backwards. 'And why? Where will you be?' Her rather plain face had grown hard and ugly, and her eyes were bitter. 'And who will you be with, then?' she almost spat, and turned and ran from the room.

Captain Lewis carefully folded the newspaper and placed it beside his plate. He looked up at Katherine, standing white-faced with embarrassment in the corner. 'Would you pick up Mrs Lewis's chair, please?'

'Of course, sir,' she whispered, stooping to pick up the chair and straighten it against the table. She was aware of the captain's eyes on her, watching her every movement and felt strangely self-conscious. When she

52

glanced up, his eyes caught and held hers. 'My wife has been unwell,' he said finally, by way of explanation.

'Yes, sir.'

'And how are you settling in?'

'Very well, sir, thank you, sir.'

Captain Lewis nodded. 'Good,' he mumbled. He slipped his watch from his vest pocket and glanced at it, then dabbed at his lips with a napkin and stood up. 'I must be off. You may tell my wife – if she asks – that I will not be in tonight,' he stressed.

'Yes, sir.'

'Pull again, Katherine.'

'Yes, ma'am.' Katherine took a firmer grip on the corset laces, grimaced and pulled. Anne Lewis winced and gasped, and then straightened up to look at herself in the full-length mirror on the back of the wardrobe door. The lace-and-ribbon-trimmed corset served to emphasize her slim waist and accentuate her rather small bosom. She took a deep breath, testing the movement of the steel-stayed corset.

'Can you breathe, ma'am?' Katherine asked, looking over her shoulder into the mirror and biting down hard on the soft flesh of the inside of her cheek, trying to keep the smile from her lips.

'Yes, quite freely,' Anne Lewis said, but she spoke slowly and there was a distinct gasp between words. 'I think I will sit . . . sit down for a moment to make sure it's adjusted properly,' she added, carefully lowering herself on to the edge of her bed. She gasped, she felt as if her ribs were breaking. 'Perhaps you might loosen it off a little, Katherine!'

Katherine bent her head behind Anne Lewis's back and fumbled with the laces.

'Hurry up, can't you, girl?'

'I'm sorry, ma'am, I've had little experience with laces . . .'

Anne Lewis glanced sharply at Katherine in the mirror. She wasn't sure if there was more than a touch

53

of insolence in the maid's tone. But Katherine kept her head bent, knowing Mrs Lewis was still looking at the mirror and that she would see even the sightest hint of a smile . . .

'Has Mrs O'Neill got everything ready?' Anne Lewis asked.

'Yes, ma'am, and I've just finished setting out the table.'

'When the guests arrive, you will take their hats and coats, the ladies' wraps and stoles, and place them in the cloakroom. Try and keep them together. That dress please.' She stood up carefully and pointed to a long, low-cut gown in heavy, royal-blue velvet in the wardrobe. 'You will remain throughout the meal,' she continued, her voice becoming muffled as she threw her head forward to allow Katherine to settle the gown over her head and to do up the tiny pearl buttons. 'But once the meal is obviously over, you will take the dishes – silently! – to the kitchen. Then I think you may retire for the night.'

'Thank you, ma'am. Will you not be requiring anything else for the guests, ma'am, before they go?'

Anne Lewis shook her head, while pointing to a pair of shoes complete with tiny bows. 'Those I think. No; following dinner there will be a series of readings by the guests from their latest works – I think the wine and port will be more conducive to a pleasant, well-modulated voice than tea or coffee.'

'Of course, ma'am.'

Anne Lewis turned around and faced Katherine. It was the first time Katherine had seen her close up, and she hadn't realized that the woman was actually smaller than herself. She noted that beneath the make-up there were deep dark shadows under her eyes, and there were grey hairs at her temples, but these had a reddish cast to them where they had obviously been treated with henna to colour them. 'This is your first dinner party with us, Katherine,' Mrs Lewis said slowly, turning her head slightly to look back over her shoulder at her reflection

54

in the mirror. She turned back to Katherine again. 'I expect you not to let us down.'

'I'll do my best, ma'am.' Katherine bobbed a curtsey.

The first guests began arriving just before eight. It was a surprisingly cold night for May and, every time she opened the hall door, the chill night air gusted through the house. Katherine was shivering in her black alpaca dress, but at least it was buttoned to the throat and had long sleeves; she wondered how Mrs Lewis was feeling with her low-cut – almost shamelessly so – short-sleeved gown.

Katherine took the guests' coats and capes in the hallway and then ushered them into the sitting room where they were received by Mrs Lewis. There were three couples, obviously husbands and wives, all of them older than Katherine but about Anne Lewis's age, and two rather prim ladies who arrived together who looked like mother and daughter. But the guests shared one characteristic: they were all very nondescript. Even as they were stepping past her into the sitting room, Katherine found she was already forgetting details of their faces.

She had just pulled the door closed behind the last of them when it opened again, and Anne Lewis stepped out into the hall.

'Is there no-one else, Katherine?' She looked up and down the hall.

Katherine stifled a smile. Did she think she was hiding one of the guests? 'No, ma'am.'

Mrs Lewis frowned and shook her head. 'There is one more . . .' she began, and then the doorknocker banged solidly, twice. Her face lightened. 'Aaah, that must be . . .'

Katherine opened the door, a tight smile fixing itself to her face.

'Good evening! Good God, but you're new!' The tall, rather gaunt figure of a man stepped into the hall, and then, catching sight of Mrs Lewis, boomed, 'Ah, Anne, but you're a sight to stir a stone!' He brushed past Katherine and strode down the hallway to snatch up Anne Lewis's hand and press it to his lips. 'William,' she murmured, colour rising to her cheeks.

Katherine remained standing with the door open for a moment and then hastily shut it.

'Katherine, will you take Mr Sherlock's cape?' Anne Lewis asked.

The man turned around and smiled at Katherine, his long craggy face breaking up into scores of tiny wrinkles. 'You're new?' he repeated.

'Yes, sir,' she said, looking with interest on what was certainly the evening's most flamboyant guest.

William Sherlock was tall and thin, probably in his mid-forties, Katherine guessed, with an erect bearing and short clipped moustache which immediately suggested a military background. His eyes were pale and colourless, but the light from the gas-lamps caught them and burnished them copper-yellow as he moved. He undid the clasp that held his crimson-lined opera cloak about his neck, removed it with a flourish, and handed it to Katherine. He turned back to Anne Lewis and patted his pockets, then removed a slim, leather-bound notebook. 'We shall have a good night, tonight, I think.'

'Yes, I hope so.'

'And has your husband honoured us with his presence?' he asked, as they moved towards the sitting room door.

'His work and his duty keep him away tonight, I'm afraid,' Anne Lewis said with a tight smile.

'Ah, a pity. Next time perhaps, next time ...' The sitting room door swung shut on the murmur of conversation.

Katherine sat in the large lonely kitchen, sewing in the light of an oil lamp while above her the sounds of conversation and laughter drifted down. Although dinner had finished and the guests moved back to the sitting room, Mrs O'Neill had advised her to hang on

56

until after the guests had departed, in spite of what Mrs Lewis had said.

It was a little after a quarter past nine by the round-faced kitchen clock when the noise from upstairs died down. A few minutes later Katherine heard a single voice, a strong male voice – Mr Sherlock's, no doubt – declaiming loudly. There was a pause and then some scattered applause. This was followed by another voice – female this time – and Katherine thought she recognized it as being Mrs Lewis, also reciting. She too was followed by polite applause. This went on for over an hour, with each of the guests obviously reciting their latest poem or collection of verses. Even though she couldn't make out the words Katherine found herself yawning, and she began to understand why the captain avoided these dinners.

Shortly before eleven the front door slammed for the first time, and then it closed again at regular intervals after that. Katherine stood up and went to the kitchen door to listen, and clearly heard Mrs Lewis call out good night. She yawned and stretched; it would be good to get to bed. After a full fifteen minutes of silence, she finally judged her mistress to be in bed. She raked the embers in the kitchen fire, gathered up her sewing, extinguished the oil lamp and climbed wearily to the attic; it had been a long day and, added to her usual chores, the preparations for the party had exhausted her.

She couldn't decide whether she liked the house or not. There was a lot of work to do, and while it was pleasant and relatively easy work, what bothered her was that she was doing the work of a score of maids: a chambermaid, a housemaid, and a scullery maid. She had worked far harder at home, looking after her crippled father, mother and five brothers, but at least she had company there – while here there was no-one to talk to. Mrs O'Neill was usually down in the kitchen, or out shopping, and she only saw her three or four times a day, and very briefly at that. The captain was out all day, and also long into the night – although he certainly wouldn't talk to her – and when Mrs Lewis was in, which was rarely, she was usually locked away in the parlour, writing poetry. It made the big house seem very lonely and empty.

She undressed quickly, tugging on her cotton nightdress, and pulled back the cold blankets. The room was freezing and the bed was icy, and she found she was shivering – and silently crying. Shocked, she touched her face and her fingers came away wet. She was suddenly furious with herself for this attack of tears! She missed her home, yes, and her mother, father and brothers, but she also bitterly resented the fact that she had been bundled off so that there would be one less mouth to feed. Katherine was homesick, and she knew it, but she wouldn't surrender to self-pity.

Angrily, she got up and padded around the room, a blanket draped around her shoulders for warmth. The sky was cloudless and the moon full, and the back garden was bright with silver and shadow. She stood by the chimney casing, feeling the last vestiges of heat through the stones, looking down the garden while memories of her past trickled to the surface, of the places she had known, people she had met . . . and Dermot . . .

Katherine shook her head, jerking awake. She was falling asleep on her feet, her thoughts becoming confused; what had made her think of Dermot? She smiled slightly, wondering if she would see him again – and was almost surprised to find that she wanted to.

She began to shiver as the cold crept up from her feet, her toes tingling painfully and her ankles beginning to throb. The wall was cooler now and she felt her nipples stiffen with the chill. Pulling her blanket tightly around her shoulders she leapt back into bed, squeaking with surprise as the sharp iciness of her own feet surprised her. She had to try and get some sleep; tomorrow was the Sabbath.

CHAPTER FIVE

Dermot Corcoran straightened when he saw the slim figure in the dark coat turn the corner and stride resolutely down the street towards the tram stop. He saw her look up and he half raised his hand in greeting, and then, feeling suddenly foolish, dropped it again.

'Hello.' He smiled nervously, finding his second encounter with the young English girl more nerve-wracking than the first for some reason. 'I thought you weren't coming.'

'I was held up,' Katherine said shortly. The truth was she had deliberately delayed, hoping he would have gone on.

'I've been looking forward to seeing you again,' Dermot said.

'Oh.' Katherine turned, her deep brown eyes widening as she stared him straight in the face. 'Why?' she asked, her uncertainty making her sound rude.

Her apparent ill-humour took him off balance and her direct question unnerved him even more. 'I don't know.' He shrugged, 'I'm not sure. I just wanted to meet you again.' He paused, and then added shyly, 'I had hoped you might be looking forward to it too.'

The tram appeared in the distance; it was one of the new electric models and it clanked and rattled along, sparking as it changed points.

'I was,' Katherine said suddenly, surprising herself that she even said it, 'and I wasn't.'

'Oh,' Dermot said quietly, confused now, a frown transforming his rather boyish face into that of a man. 'I'm not sure how to take that.'

Katherine continued looking at him, almost expecting him to continue, but he said nothing and then the tram clanked up, exuding a smell which Katherine would grow to love, a rich odour of ozone and oil, of leather and wood, sweat and hot air. They climbed the outside stairway and went down to the front of the tram, just as they had done the previous week.

As the tram clanged away, Dermot said suddenly, 'I kept thinking of you during the week; I was half tempted to stop by the house – I even changed my route home so as to walk past the door hoping to see you.'

Katherine was studying the buildings on either side of the road. Without looking at the young man, she said, almost absently, 'I have Sunday afternoon off.'

'Maybe we could walk out together next Sunday?' Dermot said immediately.

Katherine turned and nodded somewhat doubtfully. 'If the Lewises are out . . .'

'Oh, of course, I understand. I've taken the afternoon off,' he said abruptly, turning to face her.

'Why?'

'Because I'm going to show you around Dublin, introduce you to its streets. But only if you would like that,' he added hastily.

'I think I'd like that,' Katherine said with a smile, 'I think I'll probably be in Dublin for a long time.'

'You've no plans to return home then?'

Katherine shrugged. 'I'd go back tomorrow if I had the chance . . .' Another tram clanged by, blasting noise and heat up at them and she used the opportunity to fall silent. She deliberately turned to look at something on the street below, but not before Dermot had spotted the moisture sparkling in the corner of her eye.

'I'm sorry,' he said into the long silence that followed.

'It's not your fault.'

'I shouldn't have brought the subject up.'

'I'll get used to it, I suppose . . .'

'Do you want to talk about it?' Dermot asked, looking at her closely, watching how the pain in her eyes was expertly masked.

Katherine shook her head. 'Not now; let me get used

to the idea that my own family threw me out . . . sold me as a servant . . .'

'Surely not!'

'Well, that's how it seems. Look,' she said, deliberately lightening her tone, 'let's not ruin the day. Why don't you tell me about all these places . . . what about this church here?' she asked as the tram turned on to the gently sloping hill that led down into Sackville Street.

Katherine and Dermot crossed the top of Grafton Street, nimbly dodging a trio of lady cyclists, and entered St Stephen's Green. They had walked from the top of Sackville Street, down past Nelson's pillar and the GPO, around Trinity College, up Grafton Street, and Katherine was now beginning to flag although Dermot's enthusiasm remained unabated. Dermot had kept up a running commentary on every building, every street and laneway they had passed, until Katherine, at the point of screaming, had asked him not to spoil it by telling her everything on the first day. So they had come to an agreement that she would point out a particular feature and he would tell her about it.

'And where are we now?' she asked as they enterred through the iron gates of the huge park.

'This is St Stephen's Green,' Dermot said proudly.

Katherine looked around in amazement; as far as she could see, there were shaded gravel walkways and green lawns, and through the trees ahead and to her right she could see the brittle sparkle of water. It was like another world, far removed from Dublin's grimy streets. 'It's huge,' she whispered.

'Twenty-two acres,' Dermot said. 'It's only been open to the public for the past eighteen years, but already it's become part of every Dubliner's life. There's nothing more relaxing than a walk in the Green,' he added self-importantly.

He led her down to the lake where he produced a crumpled brown paper bag from his pocket. Inside there were a few stale and mouldy crusts of bread. Even

61

before he had begun to toss the bread on to the water, the ducks and drakes gathered round and began squabbling for the crumbs. Dermot squatted down and tossed the bread out, trying to place it near the younger and smaller birds, avoiding the larger, more aggressive ducks.

Katherine stood back and watched him, smiling wryly, watching his expression change, becoming rather pensive as he threw the scraps to the small birds. And for a moment she saw the boy, rather than the scholarly young man. 'Penny for your thoughts . . ?'

He looked up, startled, 'I'm sorry, I was miles away . . .'

Katherine smiled. 'I know.'

He nodded to the squabbling birds. 'I was thinking that people rather resemble birds – they are noisy, boisterous, always fighting, getting in each other's way, and the larger ones always seem to come out on top.'

'Sometimes the little ones win through, though.'

He tossed a piece of bread to a duckling, who snatched it from the air and then darted away before any of the larger birds noticed. 'Sometimes they need a little help,' he said.

'I think we all need help, at one time or another – only we don't realize it.'

'True.' He crumpled the empty bag and stuffed it into his pocket. 'Sometimes you live so close to something you don't see it – it has to be pointed out to you.'

Katherine frowned, puzzled.

'I'm talking about the injustices here,' Dermot explained. 'We've lived so long in England's shadow; suffered the injustices, the oppression for so long now, most people don't even recognize it as such.' The young woman was astonished at the depth of feeling in his voice. Smiling shyly, as if realizing that he had said too much, Dermot stood up and stretched, working his stiff shoulder muscles. 'Let's sit for awhile,' he said, indicating an empty seat.

They sat back on the hard wooden seat, a foot or so

separating them, but the silence between them was an easy one, as if they had known each other for a long time. The sun was beginning to dip in the sky, warm on their backs, sending their shadows darting out across the water. The ducks, sensing that there would be no more food, began to drift away, although some of the smaller ones lingered for a while until they too swam away, squawking disconsolately. Eventually, Katherine looked over at Dermot, 'I'm not sure I should be here; I know very little about you.' She smiled at his confused expression.

'There's little enough to know,' he said. 'My name is Dermot Corcoran, and I'm a junior reporter on the *Freeman's Journal*.' He shrugged in embarrassment. 'What else do you want to know?'

'What about all those questions you asked me, as we came down Sackville Str . . . O'Connell Street,' she corrected herself. 'Like, where I came from, where my mother and father came from, what my father did for a living, how many brothers and sisters I had, why I had come to Ireland, whether I liked it here or not and would I stay . . .' she finished breathlessly.

'I didn't ask all that, did I?' Dermot said colouring.

'You did,' Katherine corrected. 'Perhaps not directly, but you asked them nonetheless.'

'It's my training,' Dermot said apologetically, 'I'm trained to ask questions. And I suppose I'm just nosy,' he added with a boyish grin. He turned sideways and rested one elbow across the back of the seat, and crossed his legs, pulling one up under him. 'I was born in 1879, the last child and only son of Mr and Mrs Richard Corcoran. But I have three sisters, all older than me, to keep me in line. My mother and father run a small newspaper and tobacconist's shop at the end of Dorset Street just over the bridge. It's a thriving business and, while we're not rich by any means, we're not poor either. When I left school, I decided I wanted to be a journalist and so my father, who knows one of the chief editors there, found me a place as a junior.'

'Why didn't you follow your father into the shop?' Katherine wondered.

Dermot shrugged. 'No interest, I suppose. I've been helping out in that shop since . . . well, ever since I can remember, and besides, my sisters work there. They know far more about the business than I.'

'Why did you want to become a journalist?' Katherine asked, watching Dermot's face intently.

He shrugged. 'I don't know. No,' he shook his head immediately, 'I think I do. When I worked for my father, delivering messages around the city, I saw . . . things – tenement housing, people literally starving on the streets, children in rags – things which made me realize that something was wrong with this country. But we were not an established and wealthy family, we had no influence, and the only way I knew to set things right was to bring them to people's notice by writing. That's why I became a journalist.'

'And what do you do as an apprentice journalist?' Katherine asked with a smile.

'Everything,' Dermot said. 'I'm usually given the petty jobs to do. I do the research for their articles – which I don't really mind, since it allows me to wander around the libraries, reading up on all sorts of things.'

'Aren't you afraid you'll catch some dreadful disease?' Katherine asked. 'Mrs O'Neill was telling me that she had heard something about the libraries refusing to give books to families stricken with disease.'

Dermot nodded and tapped his chest proudly. 'There was an article in the *Freeman* recently; I was involved in it,' he said. 'And it's true; the medical authorities are afraid that disease may be transmitted on the pages of books, so they want the libraries to keep a stock of two copies of certain books – and one copy only should be lent out to the unfortunate household that has been struck down with disease.' The anger in his voice surprised her.

'And what's wrong with that?'

'Nothing. Except that if a well-to-do household is

struck with typhus, let's say, and it sends to the library for a book, you can be sure it'll get the better copy. But if an uninfected but poor family go to the library, even though they may not be diseased nor show any signs of disease, you can be sure they'll get the "sick" copy of the book.'

'But that's not fair,' Katherine said indignantly, 'that's two laws.'

Dermot nodded, suddenly angry. 'I'm not sure how it is in England, but in Dublin there's always been two laws – one for the rich and another for the poor, or,' he added with a savage grin, 'one for the English and another for the Irish.' He stood up suddenly, 'Come on, let's walk.'

Katherine stood up and followed the young man down along the path, surprised by the obvious intensity of his feelings, and wondering what he wasn't telling her.

Captain Lewis took the newly installed hydraulic lift to the first floor of the Junior Army and Navy Stores in D'Olier Street. The only other occupants of the lift were a matronly woman accompanied by a young woman who seemed to be her daughter, who giggled every time the lift lurched and clanged. At the first floor, the lift shuddered to a halt and the doors rolled back. The two women hurried out, obviously pleased to be free of the noisy contraption, and Captain Lewis, who followed them, saw them cross to the section of the floor selling perfumery.

The captain glanced up at the large four-faced clock hanging in the middle of the ceiling. It read a few minutes off four, and the captain's appointment with the brigadier was not until four. From previous experience, he knew the brigadier would be punctual to the minute.

To pass the time, the captain crossed the floor to the section dealing with guns and ammunition. He wandered down the long glass cases, looking at the rifles and shotguns and revolvers of various makes and calibres, all of which he was familiar with.

The young man on the counter, who knew the captain by sight, nodded courteously to him. 'Good day, sir.'

'Anything new?' Captain Lewis asked.

'We have one of the new Mauser automatic pistols, sir.' He moved down a case and produced a ring of keys and unlocked it, removing a long, rather square and ugly gun with a fat tube of a handle. 'It holds a clip of ten rounds, in 7.63 mm. There is also a detachable wooden stock, which enables the gun to be transformed into a carbine. This stock also doubles as a holster.' He demonstrated how the holster could be attached to the pistol and used as a stock, and then removed it and handed the pistol across to John Lewis. It felt awkward in his hand, and the long handle was distinctly uncomfortable. He shook his head, 'I don't think so.'

'Thank you, sir.' The assistant took back the gun and slid it back beneath the glass case. 'Good day, sir.'

'Good day.' He turned from the counter – and found the brigadier standing behind him. The small, sharp-faced man nodded at the pistol. 'What do you think?'

'It handles poorly,' Captain Lewis said immediately.

'But it has a ten-shot capacity,' the brigadier said, moving away, 'and they are developing new clips which will hold fifteen or twenty rounds.'

'I'm not sure it will ever replace my service revolver.'

'Don't be too sure,' the brigadier said. 'Imagine it, fifteen or twenty rounds without having to stop to reload. You must be prepared to accept change, captain. Come,' he nodded towards the lift, 'we'll go upstairs and get ourselves some tea.'

The Junior Army and Navy Stores was laid out on four floors, and its boast was that if an object could be purchased the establishment could supply it. It was a private society and its doors were open only to shareholders, members or ticket-holders. And it sold everything. Its telegraphic address was simply 'Supplies, Dublin', and it was no idle boast. Amongst the many attractions for its members were reading and writing rooms, containing a fine reference library, and paper and ink, where members could either write letters or receive mail. There were ladies' and gentlemen's cloak-rooms and, for the exhausted shopper, a small but select restaurant on the second floor. In many respects it was more than just a shop, it was a club.

A coal-eyed young maid, with at least a touch of Spanish blood in her veins, escorted them to a small side table, and then stood back deferentially while they glanced through the menu. The brigadier looked up and ordered tea, and Captain Lewis nodded, adding, 'And some buttered scones, please.'

She bobbed a curtsey and hurried away, Captain Lewis following her progress through the tables appreciatively. He looked back to find the brigadier regarding him cynically.

'Haven't you learned your lesson?'

'There's no harm in looking,' Lewis smiled.

'Not in looking,' the brigadier agreed. He fell silent then and the minutes dragged by until the waitress returned and set down the tray, placing fine bone china cups with their ornate floral decoration down in front of them, and the plate of hot buttered scones before Captain Lewis.

'Will that be all, sir?' she looked from the captain to the brigadier.

The brigadier nodded. 'It will, thank you.' He poured tea for them both, added milk to his own and passed the jug to Lewis. 'I understand you had a little difficulty with a servant recently,' he said softly, watching Lewis over the rim of his cup.

The captain raised his cup to his lips and then put it down again, untasted. 'What are my domestic concerns to you?'

'You are in my employ, captain, and I like to keep an eye on my employees.'

Lewis bridled; the word employee rankled. 'I have a commission in the army,' he said stiffly.

67

'Indeed you have – you are a captain,' the brigadier reminded him with a sly smile. He suddenly swallowed his tea and sat back. 'I really have no interest in your sordid affair with your servant – except perhaps deploring your taste. And, of course, the possibility that men in the throes of passion, or in the drowsy aftermath, often reveal things best left unsaid . . .' He leaned over and poured another cup of tea. 'You take my meaning,' he said, sharp eyes watching John Lewis closely.

'I can assure you . . .'

'Your assurances mean nothing to me.'

'I said nothing to her!' The captain bristled angrily.

'And how can you be sure?'

'I'm sure,' the captain said, lowering his voice when he realized he was attracting stares.

'But this young lady would have been aware of your rather odd hours, would have had access to whatever papers and documents you might have been carrying around in your pockets.'

'I'm sure . . .' Captain Lewis began.

'Do you know where she is now?' the brigadier interrupted him.

'No . . . yes . . . I mean, I don't know.'

'But you could find out?'

'Possibly.'

The brigadier drained his cup in another long swallow. 'Well then, I suggest you do so.'

'To what end?'

The brigadier looked surprised. 'Why, to talk to the young lady, to impress upon her the importance of saying nothing – nothing! – regarding your activities. I'm sure the Fenian brotherhood would be interested in whatever she had to say, and you wouldn't like to lose that nice house in Drumcondra that your wife is only now getting used to.'

'Leave my wife out of this.'

'Then find the girl.' The brigadier leaned across the table, his face turning ugly and malicious. 'You are too important a player to lose now.'

'And when – if – I find her?'

The brigadier smiled. 'Then talk to her, captain, talk to her.'

Captain Lewis leaned back in the chair and patted his lips with a linen napkin. 'That was a very fine meal, Katherine. Please convey my regards to Mrs O'Neill.'

The maid bobbed a curtsey. 'I will, sir. Would you like some tea or coffee?' she asked, watching him closely.

'Tea would be fine; but take your time. I'm in no hurry.' He glanced up at the ticking clock on the mantelpiece. 'What time did Mrs Lewis say she would be home?'

'I'm afraid she didn't say, sir. I could ask Mrs O'Neill if you wish. Perhaps she might know.'

He shook his head. 'It is of no consequence,' he said, slipping a heavy silver cigarette case from his pocket and snapping it open. He pulled out a short, fat, tube-like cigarette and struck a match, the light throwing his face into sharp relief, giving it a slightly sinister cast. Pungent smoke curled lazily about the stuffy room, catching Katherine off-guard and sending her into a spasm of coughing.

'I'm sorry . . .'

'No, my apologies,' the captain said hurriedly, waving his hand through the thick grey wreath. 'I should have been more considerate.'

'Really, sir, it's nothing, it just caught at the back of my throat . . .'

The captain tossed his cigarette into the fire. 'It's these wretched Turkish smokes, they are rather strong, but I've grown rather fond of them by now. Are you all right; you look rather red in the face.'

'I'm fine, sir.'

'Have something to drink; some water, no – some wine, that will ease your throat.'

'Really . . .'

'I insist.' The captain jumped to his feet and poured a

69

small amount of wine into his own glass and passed it to Katherine. 'Drink,' he urged her, smiling encouragement.

She smiled, tasting the réd wine carefully. It was rich and sweet, almost cloying, totally unlike the thin red wines she was used to, and it went down her throat like syrup. She drank more deeply, pressing her hand to her chest as it burned within her. 'Thank you, sir, I'm much better now.'

'Good.' He reached for the glass, and his fingers touched hers momentarily, leaving a burning impression in their wake. He filled the glass to the brim and then drank from it himself, and Katherine experienced a peculiar sensation seeing his lips touch the same spot where hers had rested a moment before. It was an almost intimate moment, and it disturbed her in a curious, frightening fashion.

The captain moved back to the fire and then stood with his back to it, one hand leaning on the tall marbled mantel, watching her as she moved around the table, loading the plates on to a tray to be carried down to the kitchen. Katherine was conscious of his eyes on her, watching her, and colour rose, burning to her cheeks; she was glad the room was dimly lit. When the table had been cleared she looked over in his direction, her eyes involuntarily catching his. They stared at each other for a moment, then Katherine, remembering her station, averted her gaze.

'How are you settling down?' he asked suddenly, something like amusement touching his voice.

'Very well, thank you, sir.'

'And your room?'

'It is very comfortable.'

He nodded, sipping carefully from the glass, his eyes never leaving Katherine. 'Good.' He placed the glass on the mantelpiece, looking up at the clock at the same time. 'I wonder what can be keeping my wife?'

Katherine hesitated, unsure whether the captain was

finished, or indeed if she was expected to answer the question.

Captain Lewis suddenly turned to her. 'Do you intend to remain with this household, Katherine?'

Caught unawares, she floundered for a moment. 'Why yes, I suppose,' then more firmly added, 'Of course, sir.'

'Good. I'm glad we've found someone trustworthy at last.' His eyes never left hers. 'You have been told what happened to the last maid?'

'Yes, sir.'

'It was such a betrayal of trust; we treated that girl like a daughter and my wife was particularly fond of her. It was a great shock to my wife, and she is a delicate woman.' His tone changed, becoming harder. 'I would not like her to be hurt again.'

'No, sir.'

'In fact, I will go so far as to insist that you have no gentlemen callers; if there is no temptation, there can be no sin.' He drank again, smiling easily to take the sting from his words. 'I know Mrs Lewis has already said this to you, and I'm sure it is unnecessary to mention this to you at all, but you are more than just another maid; you're the daughter of one of my men, and I have a duty to him as well as to myself.'

Katherine hesitated, unsure what to say, unsure what was expected of her, unsure why he had even brought up the subject. Finally she said simply, 'Thank you, sir.'

'Yes, well,' he smiled slightly, 'perhaps I'll have that tea now.'

CHAPTER SIX

'Can I buy you a drink?'

Tilly Cusack turned around, a smile automatically fixing itself on to her face, until she saw who was standing in the shadows and then the smile became genuine. 'Johnny!'

Tilly moved away from the door of the Hotel Metropole and into the shadows thrown by the awning of the Café Metropole that adjoined it. 'You were the last person I expected to see.'

Captain Lewis stepped out of the shadows, taking her hand and squeezing it briefly. He jerked his head behind him. 'I was posting a letter in the post office, and I thought I'd have a quick drink before I went on home.' He smiled, 'It was just luck meeting you here.' The truth was that John Lewis had spent the last two nights going from hotel to hotel looking for Tilly Cusack.

Tilly was a tall, rather willowy blonde, with a small heart-shaped face, bright blue eyes and a clear complexion – and only her clothes, the bright harsh colours, the cut of her dress, the tilt of her hat betrayed her profession. Tilly Cusack was a prostitute. It showed in her eyes – they were cold and weary and cynical – and in her over-ready, automatic smile. She was one of the hundreds who operated in Dublin at the turn of the century.

'Are you going to buy me that drink then?' Tilly asked, slipping into her natural English accent. Like many of the street women, she was a consummate actress, adjusting the image of herself to her customer. For John Lewis she assumed the role of an English lady, discreet whilst in company but brazen when they were alone together and during their lovemaking.

Captain Lewis nodded. 'But not in here,' he said nodding in the direction of the plush hotel behind him.

'Where then?'

He nodded across the road, towards North Earl Street, 'Kenny's.'

Tilly nodded. 'I know it. I'll meet you there in five minutes,' and then she turned away and walked straight across Sackville Street, darting nimbly between the trams, both horse-drawn and electric, that were beginning to queue up at Nelson's pillar, their first and last stop. Captain Lewis watched her stop and look into Clery's windows, admiring their new display of Irish linen and glassware, and then he turned and retraced his steps past the post office. He stopped for a moment, looking at what remained of the flower-seller's stock at the foot of the pillar, and then he continued across Sackville Street and slowly ambled down North Earl Street towards Kenny's Pub.

Tilly had found a corner booth in the dimly lit, smoky pub, and there were two drinks on the stained table before her when John Lewis slid on to the cracked and soiled leather seat beside her. He lifted the whiskey and silently toasted her.

'I haven't seen you for, oh . . .' she smiled wickedly, '. . . well, not since that night in the carriage.'

John Lewis grinned, recalling their last passionate encounter when they had made love in a carriage as it circled around St Stephen's Green making its way towards the Shelbourne Hotel. 'God alone only knows what the cabman must have thought was going on,' he murmured.

'Oh, I think he had a fair enough idea,' Tilly laughed.

John Lewis glanced nervously around, but this early in the evening the pub was half empty. 'Not so loudly,' he hissed, 'do you want everyone to know?'

She reached over suddenly, running the back of her hand down his cheek, the gesture both intimate and affectionate. 'Who cares, Johnny? It doesn't matter to anyone other than you or me – and no-one's interested.'

73

'My wife might be,' he muttered.

'I doubt it; why should she care that you have a mistress. I thought your marriage was a marriage only in name?'

'It is,' Lewis snapped. 'But what about my career; it would be ruined.'

'Blighted, Johnny, but hardly ruined.' She finished her porter and reached for her bag. 'Would you like another . . ?'

'I'll get it.'

Tilly watched the captain as he waited to be served at the bar. When she had embarked upon her trade, she had made a vow never – never! – to become involved with a client. It was a vow she had come close to breaking on three different occasions, but never so closely as with Captain Lewis. He had been one of her first customers, a bored young army officer, with a marriage that was solid but unexciting. She found him a fascinating mixture of man and boy, and his ruthlessness and icy, vicious temper both attracted and repelled her. She had once seen him kick a tramp down a flight of steps simply because he had clutched at the captain's trousers while begging for money, and then coolly walk past the shocked and bleeding wretch without a second glance. Over the past few years their relationship had changed; the captain still sought her out regularly, and they slept together, but more often they met just for a drink and a chat. She supposed, if things had been different, they might have fallen in love.

The captain returned with a half of porter and another whiskey and water for himself. 'I'm glad I met you, Tilly, there's something I want to ask you.'

'And what's that?' she asked archly.

'I'm looking for someone,' he continued, ignoring her implication.

Tilly smiled easily. 'A woman, no doubt.'

He nodded. 'A woman.'

'Are you growing bored with me too, Johnny?'

'Don't be silly, it's not that – although I think it's probably one of your street-sisters I'm looking for.'

Tilly picked up her glass of black porter and sat back into the shadows. 'And what do you want this woman for?'

'She was a servant in my house; you'll remember I told you about her. The young girl who discovered she was pregnant . . ?'

Tilly nodded and then, realizing the captain couldn't see her in the gloom, said, 'Yes.'

'Well, I'm looking for her.'

'Why?'

'My wife is worried about her,' Captain Lewis said, launching into his prepared story. 'She feels we may have acted hastily in throwing her out – but after all, what choice had we?'

'What choice?' Tilly asked, putting her drink down, untouched.

'But Anne wants to make sure the girl's in good health and has enough money.' Captain Lewis sipped from his drink, trying vainly to see Tilly's face. If he had been able to see her expression he would have been able to judge how well his story was going over. If she didn't believe him, then all his plans would have to be changed. 'I couldn't see her finding another position . . .'

'Did you give her a reference?' Tilly interrupted.

'Ahem, no.'

'Well, then, I can't see her getting another position,' she said coldly.

'That's why I imagine she may be trying to earn some money on the streets.'

'Would she have gone to one of the back street abortionists?'

Captain Lewis shook his head emphatically. 'She's a Catholic.'

Tilly laughed bitterly. 'That means nothing, I'm afraid. Most of the Irish girls working the streets are Catholics, but when they're desperate enough, they'll go to these quacks.'

'I need to find her, Tilly,' Captain Lewis said earnestly.

'There's a lot of working girls in Dublin, Johnny . . .' Tilly said doubtfully.

'But how many of them are pregnant and new to the job?'

She reached out and picked up her drink, swallowing half of it in one go. There was something awry here, but she couldn't quite put her finger on it. 'What do you want her for?'

John patted his pocket. 'I've the address here of one of Anne's cousins in the west of Ireland. She's an old woman, a kindly enough soul, and she's agreed to take Sheila on as a servant. We'll pay her wage,' he added.

'That's very generous . . .' Tilly said slowly. She sat forward, dusty light falling across her face. 'How long was Sheila with you?'

'A year and a half, two years, around that,' John said quickly.

Tilly's suspicions that something was wrong immediately deepened. 'You're being very generous to a girl who was with you only a short time,' she remarked.

Captain Lewis stared her straight in the eyes, without flinching. 'It's my wife's doing, more or less. I think she feels guilty that the girl fell into disrepute and became pregnant while she was employed in our household.'

'And you've still no idea who the father is?' Tilly asked, watching the captain intently.

'None whatsoever.'

Tilly nodded. However, she had always had her own suspicions about the father's identity, suspicions which, she imagined, she had just had confirmed in a round-about way.

'Will you help me find her?'

She sighed. 'I'll meet you here tomorrow – no, the day after tomorrow, at about this time. I'll know something – one way or the other – then.'

He stood up and his hand reached out and pressed her fingers gently. 'Thanks Tilly,' he said earnestly, 'you're doing me a great service.'

She nodded awkwardly, watching him make his way through the tables towards the door – and wondered what sort of service she was doing the young woman in question.

Tilly bought herself another drink, thinking about the young woman Captain and Mrs Lewis had more than likely forced to go on the streets, and recalled the time she had first walked Dublin's cobbled streets trying to make up the price of a meal . . .

Tilly Cusack had come to Dublin four years previously, fleeing charges of assault, attempted murder and robbery. At least, that's how the charges had read; the truth was very different.

The daughter of Irish emigrants, she had been a servant in the house of a Reverend Hodgson. The Reverend – who had been ordained by no recognized church – was a strange, eccentric man who worked as a missionary in the East End of London, mainly with prostitutes. He sallied forth every evening armed with his bible, a flask of whiskey or brandy, and a five-pound note. If he had any success – and five pounds ensured that his successes were many – he would invite the convert back to his home, where she would remain for a week or more while he instructed her in the Christian way. However, although Tilly never saw the slightest sign of impropriety between the Reverend Hodgson and his converts, she was wise enough in the ways of the world, and cynical enough, to accept without question that his interest in them was more than spiritual.

She had been there almost a year before the Reverend approached her. It had been late on a hot June evening – she remembered it clearly – and she had been washing herself in the ewer in the corner of the room she shared with one of the other servants. She had been standing up wearing only her long cotton drawers, splashing tepid water across her shoulders and well-developed breasts when she had heard the door open. She had turned, expecting to see the other girl, but instead it was

77

the Reverend Hodgson – naked except for a large black leather bible. His intentions had been obvious.

'Repent,' he had called, stretching out both arms, 'and lie with me in the love of the Lord!'

Tilly had struck him full in the groin with the ewer and, as he doubled over, had smashed it across his head. It was only as he had lain unconscious with blood pumping from a six inch gash across his scalp that the full enormity of what she had done had sunk in. She had also known that, even though he was lying naked and bleeding in her room, she was still only a servant, while he was a man of the cloth – and she had no illusions whom the law would believe.

And so she had rifled the money box he kept in his study, packed her few belongings in a bag and left for the mail boat. The following morning she had arrived in Dublin, with twenty-five pounds in her pocket.

She had stayed for a while with her father's elderly sister, who lived in a squalid flat off Mabbot Street. Although the old woman never spoke of her earlier life, Tilly guessed that she had once worked either the streets or the brothels; now she eked out a living supplying some of the fancier brothels – the flash houses – with costumes and dresses.

When Tilly's money ran out – and the old woman had ensured that it disappeared very quickly – it was almost inevitable that Tilly should turn to the streets for a living.

She had walked the streets for a week, been beaten up twice and robbed an equal number of times, before her aunt had taken her to see one of Dublin's most infamous madams – the notorious Bella Cohen. Mrs Cohen's flash houses, as the fancier brothels were called, catered for the better-off, wealthy merchants and so-called 'gentlemen'. They were not only brothels either; drink and gambling were also freely available. The huge woman ruled with a rod of iron and competition had a way of disappearing without trace. It was only later – much later – that Tilly discovered that the thugs who had beaten and robbed her during her first week on the streets were actually in the employ of Bella Cohen.

Tilly opened her tiny handbag and looked at her watch; a little after four. She would have to be getting back soon; although business didn't begin until nine at the earliest, there were always one or two early birds.

On her way back to the Hotel Metropole, Tilly watched a young woman strolling by on the arm of a prosperous-looking clerk, and she wondered how many men that woman would sleep with in her life; one, two perhaps, three at the outside – and you could nearly be sure that they would all be husbands. If tonight was busy, she would sleep with three or four men, or perhaps even more, know three or four or more different bodies.

Well, it was a living, the more practical side of her nature whispered. But for how much longer? She had been working for four years, and so far she hadn't become pregnant, nor had she caught any of the usual diseases that prostitutes succumbed to. That luck wouldn't – couldn't – last. Obviously the thing to do was to get out of the game and set herself up in her own house like Annie Mack, Peg Arnott, Mrs Meehan or Bella Cohen, who, between them, ran more than half the brothels in Monto, Dublin's red-light district.

But setting up a house called for money; and not only for the purchase or rent of the house itself. There was the decor, the upkeep of ten or more girls until they had started to pay for themselves, bills for food and liquor, light and heat, wages for the bullies and the payoffs to the police.

She had tried saving, hiding away a portion of her nightly earnings, but Bella Cohen had discovered it somehow, and one of the house bullies had given her such a beating that she had been unable to work for a week – and when she couldn't work, she fell further and further into debt with Mrs Cohen to whom she already owed money for her costumes, board and lodging. It was a vicious circle.

But all she needed was a rich client with a full wallet. She had heard stories of girls who had discovered clients with two hundred or more pounds in their wallets; such people rarely left Monto with their wallets intact – and the great beauty of it was that there was never any comeback. Monto, the red-light district, was a law unto itself, a place where the police rarely, if ever, ventured.

Tilly smiled at the thought . . . just one rich client.

CHAPTER SEVEN

The smells from the river were strong tonight, tainting the moist evening air with the stench of the city's waste, of offal and excrement, of rot and fish and decay. It was raining, a fine thin mist that had come down with sunset and looked set to continue long into the night. It sat above the surface of the water in a shifting smoke-like cloud, and tumbled out over the edge of the banks and drifted on to the quays, dulling sounds and insinuating damp fingers into every nook and cranny.

Although it was still relatively early – the bells upriver had only recently struck ten o'clock – the quayside was deserted. Even the traffic on O'Connell Bridge had lightened to a trickle, and the night had an unseasonal autumnal or even winter feel to it.

The young woman standing in the shadowed doorway shivered. She wore only a light coat and was soaked through, the thin cotton of her dress plastered to her body, plainly revealing her swollen belly. Sheila was six months pregnant.

There had been no business for her tonight; due to the damp weather and the fact that her twin attractions – her newness and pregnancy – were beginning to fade away. In the beginning, before the child was too obvious, the jaded sought her out because she was new, and when that passed, her obviously pregnant condition had made her an erotic novelty to some, but even they stopped coming as her belly became larger, hindering her performance.

Tonight would be her third night without working, and she was beginning to wonder if she would have to turn to theft when a tall figure came striding down from the bridge, a metal-tipped cane rapping the cobbles rhythmically. As the figure neared her she fixed a smile to her face and stepped into the light.

'Would the gentleman be prepared for some entertainment?' she asked, lowering her voice seductively.

'Ah, sure you were always able to entertain me, Sheila.'

Startled, her hands flew startled to her face. 'Captain Lewis!'

'The same.' He took a step towards her.

She pulled her sodden coat tight across her body. 'Stay away from me, you bastard. You're responsible for all this! You've ruined me!'

'I've come to help you . . .'

'I don't want your help.'

'You didn't think I'd abandon you, did you?' he asked, concern in his voice.

'You did abandon me,' Sheila said, puzzled.

'That was only for appearances' sake. I would have come sooner, but my wife had me watched, and when I went looking for you, you had disappeared. I've searched high and low for you, and I only learned last night where you were. This is the first chance I've had to slip away.'

'Who told you?'

'Another girl, an unfortunate like yourself.'

'Another whore, you mean?'

He nodded. 'Come on,' he said, 'let's walk for a bit, we've much to talk about.'

'We did all our talking a while ago,' Sheila said bitterly, staring up at his face.

'We'll shelter under the bridge and talk,' he said and, taking her arm, urged her down the quay towards the overhead railway bridge that crossed the Liffey at a point just above the Customs House.

It was dark under the railway bridge, with the nearest gas lamps throwing their sulphurous yellow pools of light over a hundred yards away. Behind them the black waters of the Liffey gurgled around the metal and stone supports of Butt Bridge, while above their heads the metal stays of the railway bridge whistled and moaned softly in an occasional breeze gusting up from the bay.

'I've thought about you . . . a lot,' John Lewis said softly, staring across the river towards the magnificent façade of the Customs House. He looked back over his shoulder at Sheila's dim shape, only the pale oval of her face barely visible. 'I've thought about our child.'

'You can't have it!' she said immediately. 'It's mine, and it's cost too dear already. I won't give it up.'

'That's not what . . .'

'I was thinking you might want it, seeing as how that cow of yours can't give you one,' she snapped.

Captain Lewis held his temper in check with difficulty. Whatever reaction he had been expecting from his ex-servant, it had certainly not been this one.

'I don't want your child . . . no,' he corrected himself, swinging around and looking at the woman. 'I do want the child, but I want you also. I want you, Sheila.'

Sheila was dumbstruck. 'You'll marry me?'

'Well, no . . . not yet.'

'More empty promises,' she spat. 'I'll give you this, an' I'll give you that,' she mimicked, 'an' all you wanted was a cheap whore.' She pronounced it Dublin fashion as 'hoor'. 'Well, I'm glad you came, because I've been thinking about you, Captain Lewis,' she continued, her voice rising, echoing slightly under the metal arches, 'I've been doing a lot of thinking about you. There's a lot of time for thinking when some old git's slobbering over your body . . .'

Captain Lewis took a step closer to the woman. 'And what were you thinking about . . ?' he wondered softly.

'Oh, this an' that, this an' that.'

He took another step closer to her. 'And what conclusions did you arrive at?'

Sheila put both hands on her hips and stared up at him. 'Oh, I'm thinking you're not all you seem. I'm sure someone would be interested in what I'd have to say . . .'

'Who, for example?'

83

She smiled maliciously. 'Oh, lots of people, for different reasons . . . including Mrs Lewis,' she added, her teeth flashing whitely in a grin.

'And what would Mrs Lewis like to know, do you think?'

'Maybe she'd like to know about her husband's gambling debts, an' maybe she'd like to know that Captain Lewis is well known in the flash houses of Monto . . ?'

He was now almost on top of the woman. 'And why should she believe you – she'd know it was only your vindictive spite talking.'

'Maybe I wouldn't be the one to tell her; but if it came from a good source, then I'm sure she'd look at it in a different light, eh?' Even in the dim light, he could see the contempt in her eyes, hear it in her voice. 'Let me tell you, Captain Lewis, I can make your life very difficult, very uncomfortable . . .' She let the sentence hang.

'Unless . . ?' he prompted.

'Unless we could come to some sort of an arrangement,' she smiled.

'You're talking about blackmail.'

'You call it what you like, Captain, but I need the money for me and the babe, an' I'm not too particular how I gets it.'

'And so you'd blackmail me to my wife,' Captain Lewis whispered very softly.

'I'm sure if I put my mind to it, there's a lot more I could do with what I know about you, Captain Lewis.' This time the threat was quite blatant.

'That's a pity,' John Lewis whispered, reaching out and touching her shoulder. She flinched, but continued to look defiantly into his face. 'Such a pity,' he murmured. His fingers tightened on the back of her neck and he struck her then, once, using the palm of his hand to strike hard at the point of her chin, snapping her head around sharply to the left. The bones at the base of her neck snapped, and the scream died in her throat. He caught her before she fell to the ground and dragged her over to the quayside. He stuck an empty gin bottle in the pocket of her coat and then he took his time positioning her, so that when he eventually pushed her over the side, her head smashed against the concrete support before the corpse splashed into the river.

Captain Lewis leaned over to look for the body, but in the darkness and the mist that clung to the water it was impossible to see anything. But there was nothing to worry about in any case; when it eventually came to the surface, the water and the rats would have done their work, and the corpse would be unrecognizable. And even if by any chance it was recognized and identified, no-one would associate him with the death; but the captain, being a cautious and meticulous man, had covered his tracks for the evening.

Captain Lewis walked across Butt Bridge and then turned left up towards the lights of Sackville Street, without a second thought for the murdered woman.

'You know, I really shouldn't be seeing you at all,' Katherine remarked casually as she sipped her tea and looked out on the crowds thronging Grafton Street.

'And why not?' Dermot asked in surprise.

Katherine smiled. 'Because the captain told me not to.'

Dermot almost choked on his tea, and his coughing and sputtering attracted disapproving stares from the other patrons of the XL Café and Restaurant. 'You t-t-told him about m-m-me?' he gasped, when he caught his breath.

Katherine took her time finishing off her tea before replying. 'No, it wasn't you in particular he was warning me about,' she said, 'but rather gentleman callers in general. He was concerned for my moral welfare,' she grinned.

Dermot made a face. 'Aye, an' he's a fine one to talk.'

'I think he's nice,' she protested. 'He even gave me some wine last week.'

Dermot had another choking fit. 'Wine?' he whispered hoarsely. 'And you took it from him . . . and drank it?' he asked incredulously.

'Of course – and it was lovely,' she added wickedly.

'I think you're pulling my leg,' Dermot said, although he didn't sound too sure.

Katherine shook her head vigorously. 'On my word of honour, he gave me a glass of wine . . .'

As they left the XL and turned left down Grafton Street, she told him what had happened, and was surprised to find his relief so obvious. They walked slowly down Grafton Street, taking their time in the brilliant sunshine around Trinity College, and continued down Westmorland Street towards O'Connell Bridge. But when they reached the bridge Dermot surprised her by turning right and following the quays towards Butt Bridge.

'Where are we going?' Katherine asked.

'You'll see,' Dermot said. 'Look, Katherine,' he said suddenly serious, 'you'll have to be careful of that Captain Lewis. He's a bad sort. I suppose you're sick and tired of people telling you what happened to the last maid . . ?'

Katherine nodded.

'But let me tell you anyway; she was fired because she became pregnant, and . . . and, well I've heard that Lewis was the father.'

Katherine managed to look shocked. 'But does Mrs Lewis know?'

'I'm sure she suspects – she must. And that's not all; I saw the captain a few months ago up in Monto . . .' He saw Katherine's blank expression and explained, 'Monto's where the . . . the . . . brothels are,' he finished in a rush.

'Oh, the stews and the flash houses,' Katherine said casually.

Dermot stopped suddenly while Katherine walked on. He reached out and grabbed hold of her arm. 'Hang

86

on; who told you about the stews and flash houses?' he exclaimed laughing in spite of himself.

She looked down at his hand which was still holding on to her arm, and he sobered immediately.

'I'm sorry . . .' he began.

'For what?' she asked.

He self-consciously released his grip on her arm. 'I'm sorry, I didn't mean to . . . that is . . . to touch you . . .'

She patted his hand. 'You've nothing to apologize for,' she said, and then added, 'Mrs O'Neill told me. And by the way, what were you doing around the brothels, eh?' she asked with a sly smile.

'Research . . .'

'Oh yes?'

He shook his head, smiling. 'The *Freeman* – the newspaper – was doing an article on the Metropolitan Police, and we were investigating rumours that no officer ever ventures into the Kips – that's what Monto is sometimes called – after nine in the evening.' He grinned ruefully. 'My job consisted of standing on the corner of Mabbot Street and counting the number of police who passed me.'

'And how many passed you?'

'None.'

'Why are we here?' she asked, nodding towards the bridge ahead of them.

'The police fished a girl out of the river here yesterday,' he said, looking quickly at her.

Katherine shuddered. 'Poor thing . . . was it an accident or . . .'

'Accident, suicide or murder,' he pulled a face. 'Well, who knows? You wouldn't believe the number of bodies that are fished out of the river every year. But this one was a little unusual. She was very pregnant and her neck had been broken.' He drew her in under the bridge, leading her around the pools on the cobbles which had formed from the constant dripping of moisture from the metal girders overhead. He pointed down into the

87

swirling, filthy water. 'She was found there, wedged between those two supports. She was a . . . a woman of the night,' he said delicately.

Katherine peered down into the murky water. 'How do you know?'

'By her clothing. Unfortunately,' he added, 'that's all that is known for certain about her – that, and the fact that she was pregnant. She carried no identification, or if she did the river took it, and there's no indication as to her age.'

The young woman drew her arms tightly about herself. 'What a terrible way to die.'

'She probably hit the stone support down there and broke her neck,' Dermot said absently.

'Dermot, don't!' Katherine pleaded.

He looked around, colour rising in his cheeks. 'Oh, I'm t-t-terribly s-s-sorry, I wasn't t-t-thinking . . .' he stuttered.

She smiled to ease his embarrassment. 'That's all right. But what have you come here for? Why are you interested in this poor woman?'

'I was wondering, did she jump or was she pushed?' he said quietly.

'You said yourself that a lot of bodies are fished up out of the river,' she said. 'The poor woman might have been drunk and fell in.'

'Probably; a gin bottle was found in the pocket of her coat.'

'Surely that's it then?' she asked.

He looked at her for a moment and then turned back to the filthy water. 'If I'm ever going to make it as a reporter,' he said quietly, 'I am going to have to specialize. But I've no interest in fashion or sport or court news; all I really know is Dublin and its people and places.' He glanced over his shoulder at her, seeing the puzzled look on her face. 'What I'm leading up to is that I want to try and discover the story behind this poor woman's death . . .'

'Why?'

'For several reasons. It will give me a chance to say something about the reasons why such women are forced to go on the streets, the housing problems, the absence of proper food and sanitation . . . the lack of jobs . . .' He shoved his hands into his pockets. 'Dublin is the second capital of the Empire. It is a beautiful city, wealthy and fashionable – and yet children are dying of hunger in its backstreets. I'm going to tell that story – and I'll start with this poor young woman, whoever she was.'

Katherine hugged her arms around her body. 'I don't know. It seems . . . well, wrong almost, to write something about the woman, intrusive, ghoulish.'

'Stories are being written about dead people all the time,' Dermot protested, 'What will make this one different is that it will be a true story.'

'Not a very nice one, though,' Katherine remarked.

'No,' he conceded, 'it will not be a particularly nice story. But it will tell the truth, with nothing covered up, nothing glossed over.'

'Dermot, even I know people don't want to know the truth.' She turned and walked a few steps away, and then glanced back over her shoulder at him. 'I think you're making a mistake.'

'You're late,' Mrs O'Neill said, turning round to look up at the kitchen clock as Katherine came rushing in through the kitchen door.

'I'm sorry,' she said, shrugging off her coat, and pulling on her apron, 'I hadn't realized it was so late.'

'Ach, no harm done,' the old cook said. She was clearing up the remains of baking, scraping the white dusting of flour back into the bag and gathering up the eggshells. The kitchen was rich with the smell of baking, and there were two trays of tarts cooling beside the fire. 'And where were you today?' she asked, brushing her hands together.

'Oh, Dermot and I . . .'

89

'Don't let either Mrs Lewis or the captain hear you say that,' Mrs O'Neill interrupted, glaring at Katherine.

'I'm sorry, I didn't mean . . .'

'Ach, I don't care. Dermot's a good lad, and a gentleman in every sense of the word. But remember what Captain and Mrs Lewis have told you . . ? We don't want you shipped home in disgrace, do we?' She stooped down and pulled the oven door open, looking in at two deeply golden loaves. She straightened slowly, pressing her hands to the small of her back. 'So tell me – what did you do?'

'We went for a walk around Trinity College, and Dermot told me all about its history. Did you know it was founded by Queen Elizabeth over three hundred years ago?'

'Imagine that!' Mrs O'Neill said, filling the kettle and moving it on to the range.

'And then he took me down Nassau Street and Kildare Street and showed me the gentlemen's clubs, and from there we went into St Stephen's Green . . .'

'It's usually just called the Green, love,' Mrs O'Neill said kindly.

Katherine smiled. 'The same way Sackville Street is called O'Connell Street?'

Mrs O'Neill laughed. 'Well, that's a little different.'

'Anyway,' she continued, 'we walked around the Green for a while, and listened to a band playing in the bandstand, and then we went down Grafton Street and he bought me tea in the XL Café. After that he brought me down to Butt Bridge and showed me where a young woman was pulled out of the river only yesterday.'

Mrs O'Neill crossed herself. 'God have mercy on her,' she said softly.

'She was also pregnant,' Katherine said, her voice barely above a whisper.

The cook crossed herself again. 'I'll pray for their souls. Did Dermot know anything about the woman . . '

Katherine shook her head. 'Even the police know

90

very little, but Dermot said that they suspect that she might be from the stews of Monto.'

Mrs O'Neill put her back to the range and folded her thin arms across her chest. 'But how pregnant was she – very pregnant, if she was noticeable,' she immediately answered her own question.

Katherine nodded. 'Very pregnant, about six months or so.'

'It's unlikely she'd be working in one of the houses. I can't imagine them wanting someone obviously pregnant around – it wouldn't be good for business, I'm sure.'

'So now Dermot is determined to write the poor woman's story. He feels it's his duty to publicize the plight of the poor in the city, and he's going to use the dead woman's story as an example.'

'I can't imagine her story being any different from the hundreds of stories I've heard from the young – and the not so young – women who've come to see me because I'm a midwife and because I live in Summerhill. They usually come to see me for the wrong reasons,' she added bitterly.

'What sort of reasons?' Katherine asked curiously.

Mrs O'Neill looked up in surprise. 'You really don't know?'

Katherine shook her head.

'They come to me thinking I do abortions – you know what abortions are?'

Katherine nodded dumbly. Finally, she asked, 'But why do they come to you?'

'Probably because of where I live,' Mrs O'Neill said, angrily. 'There are certainly two abortionists "working" – if that's the right word – quite close to me, an' I suppose that, while most people know a midwife can deliver a child, some of them think she can also bring it on early, too early for it to survive, that is.' The lid of the kettle started to rattle and Mrs O'Neill turned to lift it off the heat.

91

'Dermot did wonder if you might be able to help him at all,' Katherine said quietly.

Mrs O'Neill thought about it for a moment. 'I might, I might just do that.'

'He hopes to use the article to launch his career as a journalist . . .' Katherine said slowly, 'and once he has established his name, he intends to champion the cause of the lower classes.'

Mrs O'Neill shook her head slightly. 'I'm not sure Dermot is suited to the newspaper life. Perhaps he would be better joining his father in the shop.'

'He says all he needs is one big story to make his name,' Katherine said, 'and then think of all the good he will be able to do.'

Mrs O'Neill looked unconvinced. 'And is he going to change hundreds of years of history by himself?' She shook her head. 'I wish him all the best, but it cannot be done.' The cook spooned tea into the pot and added steaming water. 'No . . . and even if he does manage to write this woman's story, I don't think the death of one poor girl is going to make that much difference. God forgive us,' she added, crossing herself again, 'but what do people care about the death of a Dublin whore?'

'This one is a little different,' Katherine said slowly. 'You see, Dermot said that there is some doubt as to whether she was dead before she hit the water. It might be a murder, rather than an accident or suicide.'

'Maybe Jack the Ripper's come to Dublin,' the cook said with a shudder.

Katherine laughed, but just a little uneasily; Dermot had said the same thing, reminding her that the White-chapel Butcher had never been caught.

CHAPTER EIGHT

May drifted into a hot June, which rolled into a scorching windless July. Katherine had settled into College House and its simple routine. Every Sunday morning she went to church with Mrs O'Neill and every Wednesday afternoon she went into the city, sometimes with Dermot, if he was free, and he showed her Dublin both elegant and ugly. And she quickly learned to love and pity what Dermot called the city of contrasts.

But as the weeks passed Katherine began to be aware of the attentions Captain Lewis paid to her. She was conscious that he was watching her constantly; she could feel his eyes upon her as she waited at table when he dined alone, and sometimes she would turn around and find him staring at her. Strangely, she didn't feel disturbed by him, merely curious and, in an odd way, almost flattered that she should warrant his interest. Knowing – or at least suspecting – that he had disgraced her predecessor only added to the adventure – because that was what Katherine, in all her youthful innocence, took it to be. It was a game, played to unwritten rules. Unfortunately, Captain Lewis and Katherine Lundy were playing for different stakes.

When she thought of him, she had to concede that he was a handsome man, but it wasn't that which attracted her to him – rather it was his air of absolute authority and self-confidence. He spoke with the voice of a man used to being obeyed and yet rarely raised his voice above normal conversational level. Although she had never seen him in uniform, she could imagine him looking very dashing in the crimson and blue of the East Lancashire regiment.

Strangely, John Lewis's interest in Katherine was in

part stimulated by the poise and self-assurance with which she also conducted herself. Frankly he had had doubts when he had offered her father this position for his daughter. He knew then that she had never worked as a maid servant and, if the truth were known, had chosen her on the spur of the moment only to spite his wife.

Katherine Lundy had been more than a pleasant surprise. His promise to himself and to the brigadier to have nothing more to do with the maids was conveniently forgotten, and he began to toy with ideas of how to get the young woman into bed. On the evenings when Mrs Lewis would be out – and these seemed to be becoming more and more frequent – he took care to engage Katherine in conversation, chatting inconsequentially about her likes and dislikes, and, in a roundabout way, telling her a little about himself. Of course, by this time of night, Mrs O'Neill had always gone home. This made their conversations all the more private and personal and, for some reason which she didn't quite understand herself, Katherine never bothered to tell the cook about them. She told herself that she was merely chatting with her employer as she cleared up after dinner. Nothing more. He had a host of funny stories; amusing anecdotes about his early army life and stories about her father and their campaigns together. He made her laugh.

It was about this time that Katherine began to keep a diary of events in her life. Not a day-by-day account of everything that had occurred, but rather a brief note and a date when something which she considered relevant happened. She felt sure that, as the months and the years rolled by, all she would need to do was to look at her book and the memories would come flooding back.

At first she had collected the notes on small scraps of paper and stuck them inside the back cover of her bible, along with her other scraps of precious ephemera. Every time she looked at them, touched them, she recalled the memories they invoked, and felt the brief buzz of

94

homesickness. So then she had bought herself a note-book, and had re-written all her earlier recollections into it. The first diary events she had transferred had been taken from strips of paper, usually torn from old used envelopes, and Katherine had found she felt almost shy and embarrassed as she copied them.

'Sunday, 17th July. Met Dermot again. I think I'm falling in love with him.'

Katherine smiled as she re-read the last entry. She was sitting on the edge of her hard bed, writing in the events of the day – or rather the events of that evening.

'Thursday 21st July. Mrs Lewis returned home early tonight, and found Captain Lewis and myself laughing at a joke together. She didn't look too pleased.'

She chewed on the end of her pencil for awhile trying – vainly – to remember what the joke had been. She recalled the captain had been slightly drunk and in very good humour. He had complimented her on her looks and deportment as she cleared the table, and she had dropped him a curtsey. He had then launched into a series of jokes – nothing unsuitable of course – some of which had become almost unintelligible as he collapsed into laughter himself. His laughter had also proved infectious, and Katherine had soon found herself giggling uncontrollably as the captain struggled, red-faced and spluttering to finish one of his more uproarious stories.

She remembered she had been standing by the table, a laden tray in her hands, the plates and cutlery rattling together on it, when the door had swung open silently. Anne Lewis stood in the doorway, grim-faced and tight-lipped.

Her expression had wiped the smile from Katherine's lips, and Katherine's sudden silence had made the captain sit up and turn to face the door. Katherine had caught the look that passed between him and Mrs Lewis and seen nothing of love or compassion in it. It was like a look passed between two strangers. Mrs Lewis had stepped into the room, leaving the door deliberately open. 'That will be all, Katherine,' she had said frostily.

95

'Yes, ma'am.' Katherine bobbed a curtsey. 'Will you be requiring anything else, sir?' she asked, turning back to the captain.

He had opened his mouth to reply, when his wife said coldly, 'Captain Lewis will be requiring nothing else tonight. That will be all.'

Katherine curtseyed again. 'Yes, ma'am,' she whispered.

She tapped the paper of her notebook with her pencil, re-reading the single line again and again, and wondering if there would be trouble . . . 'Well what's done is done and cannot be undone,' she muttered, closing her book and returning it to the bottom drawer of the dressing table. It was a phrase of her mother's, but it seemed very appropriate right now.

The attic room was uncomfortably hot and stifling and, even with the one usable window wide open, there was no trace of a breeze. Although it was close to midnight, the July night was light and the few visible stars seemed wan and dull.

Katherine stripped down to her chemise and wandered listlessly around the room, too hot and still too keyed up to sleep. Her brief encounter with Mrs Lewis earlier that evening had left her disturbed; even though she knew that nothing untoward had occurred between her and the captain, she couldn't help wondering how Mrs Lewis would see it. And it was the look in the older woman's eyes – the look of contempt and something else, knowingness or certainty, which worried her more than anything else.

She hadn't seen either Mrs Lewis or the captain again that night – and, what was even more unusual, they hadn't rung for their night-time drinks. She had found occasion to pass by the sitting room door more than once, hoping to overhear something. There had been no conversation between them, and all she had heard had been the rustle of a newspaper – and that had disturbed Katherine even more.

She let down her hair and threw back her head,

shaking the long, thick tresses loose, working the stiff muscles at the base of her neck. She felt tense, like a coiled spring, and she was painfully aware of the dull pounding of a pulse in her temples and throat. The room was so hot and airless that she found it difficult to draw breath, and when she touched the wall that housed the chimney she found it uncomfortably hot – no wonder the room was scorching.

A bead of sweat formed at her hairline and trickled its way ticklingly down her face and dripped off her chin. She shook her head again, touching the tips of her fingers of both hands to her temples, pressing against the pounding. She could feel her chemise beginning to stick to her skin.

On an impulse she checked the door; there was no lock on it, but she had devised a triangle of wood which she could slide under the end of her door at night to guard her privacy. She slipped it from the niche above the door and then pushed it home, sliding the wood between the bottom of the door and the floor. The door was now wedged shut. Then, catching the hem of her chemise she pulled it over her head and stood, wearing only her calico drawers. She rolled her chemise into a ball and threw it on the bed followed, after a moment's indecision, by her drawers. Naked, she flopped down beside them, waiting for her headache to ease, trying to cool down.

The house settled down for the night, with creaks and sighs, and strange snappings and groanings. Noises which were inaudible during the day came into their own, and the slow, solemn clicking of the grandfather clock in the hall could be heard through the entire house, from the kitchens to the attic. The pipes clunked and banged, and hissed behind the walls and under the floorboards, then thumped and fell silent.

And Katherine, still sprawled across the top of her bed, her naked body covered in a fine sheet of sweat, heard the clipped murmur of voices from below.

The sounds made her sit up, her head tilted to one

side, listening. On tingling feet she got up and moved around the room, trying to gauge the spot where the voices were loudest. She discovered it was over by the wall which housed the chimneys. She put her head close to the bricks and found she could hear the voices quite clearly. Pulling her long hair away from her ear, she pressed herself against the flesh-warm stones, her face flat against the wall.

'. . . and I won't have it, John, do you hear me, I will not allow it . . .'

'You're imagining things.'

'I don't think so.'

The captain's voice sounded weary and cynical, Katherine thought, almost as if he were bored.

'Look, you will think what you want to think no matter what I say, but I've already told you, there is nothing going on betwen me and the maid.'

Katherine shivered, and became painfully conscious of the sudden pounding of her heart in her breast, the sound so loud and frightening that it blocked out the sounds of the voices.

'So, you found us laughing together – where's the sin in that?' Captain Lewis sounded exasperated, 'It's not as if you had caught us rolling naked in each other's arms.'

The very idea sent a quiver through Katherine.

'There's no call to be vulgar,' Mrs Lewis snapped.

'Well, if you refuse to be either serious or reasonable, then I'm afraid I can only answer in kind.'

'That's childish!'

'Very possibly. But if we're going to be difficult this evening, where were you? Oh, you needn't bother answering,' Captain Lewis hurried on, 'I can guess where – at one of your literary meetings no doubt.' Even though the sounds were muffled slightly, Katherine could clearly make out the amusement and disbelief in his voice.

'Yes, and we were addressed by George Russell!'

'And is that supposed to mean anything to me? All I

98

know is that my wife – whose duty is supposed to be here with me – spends more time away from home than is seemly.'

Katherine's face and body were becoming almost uncomfortably hot, and she turned her head and presented the other cheek to the hot brickwork, sucked in her belly, and pressed one hand across her breasts to keep from touching the wall.

'I don't think you can talk. What about you and your strange appointment in the post office. You cannot even tell me the truth about that . . . I've lived around the army long enough to know that there's something going on. Why did you take a civilian position in the GPO, that's what I want to know?' Katherine could hear the vindictiveness and derision in Mrs Lewis's voice.

Even through the muffling and distorting stone Katherine could make out the anger in Captain Lewis's reply. 'My new appointment enabled me to buy this house; enabled you to play the gracious hostess, with your own cook and servant; enabled you to mix with the literary and artistic classes; enabled you to attend and hold your precious "evenings". Even enabled you to attend this literary society. So don't you dare talk to me about my post. It is no concern of yours – except in as much that it brings in a respectable income, more than I could ever earn on a regular commission. Enough to pay for all this, remember!'

In the long silence that followed, Katherine wondered just what Captain Lewis's post was; something official, and secret too, by the sound of it. There was no possible way that a mere captain could afford a house like this, but obviously Captain Lewis's salary was more than that of an ordinary army captain. She was intrigued – just what was his civilian post?

Breakfast was a brief, silent affair with only Mrs Lewis in attendance, the captain having left the house before even Katherine had arisen. Mrs Lewis didn't bother acknowledging the maid's presence, nor did she speak

99

through the meal, and Katherine was very conscious that she was being reminded of her place and the tenuousness of her situation. Mrs Lewis was still wearing her long, heavy dressing-gown, with the lace collar turned up, but Katherine couldn't help noticing the red bruise mark just beneath her ear on her jawline.

As Katherine was clearing up, Mrs Lewis spoke directly to her for the first time that morning. 'You may tell Mrs O'Neill that Captain Lewis will not be joining us for dinner this evening, Katherine. He has some official business and will be out of town for the next week or ten days.'

Katherine curtseyed. 'Very good, ma'am.' As she turned to go, Mrs Lewis called her back.

'And Katherine . . .'

'Yes, ma'am?' She had been expecting Mrs Lewis to speak to her about last night at some stage, and now that it was coming, she felt very calm.

'I expect the servants in my employ to conduct themselves with a certain amount of modesty and reserve.'

'Yes, ma'am.'

Anne Lewis waited, almost as if she expected Katherine to try and defend herself. Finally, she spoke. 'Well, I am pleased to see that you didn't try to pass on the blame. That indicates a certain amount of self-control and common sense. I will expect you to exercise that same self-control and common sense in future.'

'Yes, ma'am.'

'Now,' she said, turning away to the window and staring out into the road, which was already pale and washed with sunshine, 'will you inform Mrs O'Neill that there will be a small, informal gathering here tonight; three guests, no more. I should like her to prepare a light supper, and I would like you to bring it in around ten or so.'

Katherine curtseyed. 'Yes, ma'am.'

* * *

'Well, sure this is the first I've heard of it,' Mrs O'Neill fumed, when Katherine passed on the message. 'An' where am I supposed to get meat for their suppers, this being a Friday an' a fast day. It'll mean a trip into town, an' no mistake . . .'

'Can I go in and get it for you?' Katherine asked.

'No love, thanks all the same for the offer, but I'll tell you what, you can come in with me an' help me to carry some of the food home.'

Katherine inclined her head upwards. 'What will she say?'

'Oh, don't worry about her; I'll tell her I need you. An' we won't be long in any case.'

'When do you want to go?'

'We'll go directly after lunch. There's a tram about two or so, an' sure we'll be home by four at the latest. Now leave that, it can wait,' she said as Katherine began piling the dishes into the large basin for washing, 'you get on with your work upstairs. She'll be wanting the place sparkling.'

Even as she spoke the dining room bell high on the kitchen wall jangled. Mrs O'Neill smiled broadly. 'What did I tell you . . . ?'

Although Katherine had travelled into Dublin regularly with Dermot she didn't think she had ever actually discovered the real heart of the city. True, he had shown her the grand mansions and the slums, the fine parks, churches and cathedrals, the galleries, the bridges, the statues. But he had never shown her the shops, had never taken her into one of the grand establishments on Grafton Street, or even into Clery's, the huge shop facing the GPO. One thing her father had told her, and which had remained with her, was that a nation's character was most clearly seen in its shops and markets. Of course, she was as much to blame; Dermot was always talking – about her, about himself, about his plans and schemes, and she would get caught up in them, and that would take up their time together. But

101

her visit to the city with Mrs O'Neill was different; Moire O'Neill took Katherine behind the bright façades of Sackville and Grafton Streets to the meaner streets, alleys and lanes; places that were teeming with life. In her diary she would record that it was her first introduction to the real Dublin.

Mrs O'Neill took her first to Moore Street, which was just off Sackville Street, and behind the GPO. The street itself was quite small, a few hundred yards in length, and it was thronged with people – and not the 'quality' that frequented Grafton, George and Wicklow Streets, but rather working-class Dubliners. Both sides of the street were lined with street-traders, mainly fruit- and meat-sellers, but with some flower-sellers at the top of the street. And most of the shops seemed to be victuallers, greengrocers and fishmongers.

It was a busy bustling street, the noise and the stench almost overpowering. Overlaying the usual Dublin street noises, there were shouts and cries as each seller attempted to attract potential customers – and also to outshout each other. Some moved through the crowd with their wares on trays around their necks, singing little ditties and bellowing imprecations and pleas at each passer-by; there were snarling, barking, howling dogs everywhere, and hordes of screaming and shouting children raced through the whole mêlée.

And the smell. On top of the permanent Dublin smell – a mixture of smoke, soot, animal droppings and the stench from the river, which was little better than an open drain – there was the sickly sweet stench of putrefaction as fruit rotted in the gutters, and the stink of offal black beneath a covering of flies in barrels outside the butchers' doors. Too many people – too poor to afford the luxury of washing and insensitive to their own odours – added to the pervasive miasma.

Katherine stopped as the atmosphere hit her, tears starting to her eyes. There was the smell of something long dead and she gagged. 'You're not going down there .. ?' she asked Mrs O'Neill, aghast.

'An' why not . . ?' Moire wondered, surprised.

'But the smell . . . it's disgusting,' Katherine exclaimed.

Mrs O'Neill smiled knowingly. 'Ah sure, but you'll get used to it; it's the smell of Dublin. Now,' she continued, becoming practical, 'we need some fruit and vegetables for tonight, and this is the best an' cheapest place to buy.' She took off down the street and, after a moment's hesitation, Katherine hurried along behind. She stopped by a fruit-seller leaning against the wall of The China and Glass Warehouse, which looked startlingly out of place amidst the squalor of the rest of the street. The slight, drawn, and painfully thin woman smiled at Mrs O'Neill.

'I'm not sure if you're late this week or early for next week,' she said with a gap-toothed grin.

'Ah sure neither. I did what shopping I had to do earlier on, but the missus is having a party tonight, and I'm short of a few bits and pieces.'

'Isn't that grand for her?' the fruit-seller commented, as Mrs O'Neill rooted through the selection of fruit and berries on the tray before her.

'I'm sure it is, but I won't be invited,' Mrs O'Neill said with a smile.

'True enough.' The fruit-seller nodded at Katherine. 'An' who's this? A relation.'

Moire shook her head. 'Katherine came into service with the missus a couple of months ago. She's from England,' she added, with a smile.

'Imagine!' The fruit-seller turned to Katherine. 'An' what do you think of Dublin, dearie?'

'Well, I haven't had much chance to look around yet – I only have half a day off each week – but what I've seen I've liked.'

The woman nodded, satisfied. 'You'll come to love it,' she said confidently.

'I'm sure I will.'

Mrs O'Neill turned to Katherine. 'I'll be awhile here; if you like I'll meet you here in an hour's time . . .'

103

'Really . . ?'

Moire nodded. 'I'm sure you've things to do.'

'I'd like to get some stamps in the post office.' She was about to turn away when she paused, 'if you're sure you don't need me . . ?'

'Not now I don't, but later, when I'm finished with the shopping I will.'

'Thanks, Mrs O'Neill. I'll be back here in an hour,' she promised.

'Make it an hour and a half,' Mrs O'Neill smiled.

Katherine made her way up Moore Street, through the throng and turned left into Henry Street, which let out into Sackville Street, directly facing the impressive height of Nelson's column. As Katherine passed the flower-sellers at the base of the pillar, she promised herself again that she would climb it 'someday'.

Katherine turned right into the GPO. It was bright inside, the large high windows allowing the afternoon sunlight to stream in, but nevertheless, it was cool and quiet and the air smelt faintly of polish. Katherine had the immediate urge to walk on her toes, and she noticed that everyone seemed to be talking in whispers. The long mirror-bright tables were shimmering with light and it looked as if the people standing by them, writing their letters or affixing their stamps, were doing so on beds of light.

She choose the shortest queue and, while she was waiting to be served, she examined the people around her. She watched with amusement as she noticed that class distinctions even crept into the selling of stamps; the queue to her right seemed to be composed of well-to-do businessmen and clergy, while the queue she had automatically chosen was composed mostly of ordinary Dublin labourers and serving girls, some of whom looked – and smelt – as if they had come in directly from the market.

Katherine bought six penny stamps and was moving away from the grill, carefully folding them into her purse, when a group of men stopped a few feet ahead of her, deep in conversation. She glanced up as she walked around them – and found she was staring directly at Captain Lewis.

He spotted her at the same time and his eyes flashed in warning as she opened her mouth. He gestured with his head in the direction of the square, four-faced clock in the centre of the room; puzzled, she nodded and moved towards it.

Captain Lewis joined her a moment later, stopping by the clock and slipping his pocket watch from his waistcoat. Without looking at her, he said, 'Well done; you're a smart girl. I'll meet you outside in a minute or two.' And with that he moved away. Intrigued now, Katherine was about to go after him, but then changed her mind and turned and walked out of the opposite door. She stepped out into the street just in time to spot Captain Lewis darting across Sackville Stret. He paused at the island in the middle, looking up and down the street as though watching out for someone. Katherine, taking advantage of a break in the traffic, hurried across the road after him.

'Good girl,' he said abruptly, as she reached him. 'I don't want any awkward questions being asked, you understand,' and then added more gently, 'Look, why don't we get some tea? Follow me.'

Remaining a few paces behind, Katherine followed him across Sackville Street, turned right past Clery's colourful window displays, crossed a small side street and then turned left into Lower Abbey Street. It was only as they left the main street that Captain Lewis stopped and allowed Katherine to catch up with him.

'I know a quiet place down here,' he said, striding along looking neither right nor left, almost as if he were ashamed to be seen with her – which was probably true, she realized. They passed the Salvation Gospel Hall and then the captain stopped outside Erskine's Temperance Hotel. He stood back and almost pushed Katherine up the steps before him. 'We'll get some tea in here; it's never very busy.'

The long hallway was quiet and dim, and the tea-rooms, which lay off to the right hand side were almost empty, only two old ladies there gossiping together near the window. A waitress in a stiffly starched uniform hurried over to them.

'We'll have a seat here,' Captain Lewis said, indicating a table in an alcove behind the fire.

'I could put you over beside the window . . ?' the waitress suggested.

'I think we would prefer this table,' the captain said firmly, moving towards it. 'Don't you think so?' he asked, turning to Katherine.

She nodded briefly. 'Yes, that should be fine.'

The waitess bobbed. 'Yes sir; this way, ma'am.'

As she seated them Katherine caught the girl's look of contempt – and possibly envy – as her eyes raked over Katherine's plain and worn clothing while taking in the captain's well-cut suit and military bearing. 'I'll just get you some menues . . .' the waitress began, but the captain raised his hand and she fell silent.

'We'll just have some tea . . . and scones,' he looked to Katherine for confirmation, but, receiving none, nodded to the girl. 'Tea and scones.'

As the girl hurried away, the captain leaned back in his chair, an amused smile playing on his lips. 'She can't quite make us out,' he said, 'although she obviously has a few ideas.'

'I was just thinking the same thing,' Katherine said softly, suddenly feeling embarrassed.

'Well, you know what she thinks you are, don't you?' Captain Lewis said, leaning forward, placing both hands flat on the table.

'No, what . . ?' Katherine began, and then suddenly coloured. 'Oh, I see what you mean.'

'Ah, not to worry, not to worry.' He folded his arms and stared silently at Katherine for a few moments. 'You acted with great presence of mind back there.'

'It was just so unexpected seeing you. Mrs Lewis told me only this morning that you would be away for the next week or ten days on official business.'

The captain frowned. 'Well, that's true . . .'

The maid returned balancing a tray with their tea in a large squat pot, and their scones hot and delicious from the oven. The captain remained silent while she placed the teapot, milk, butter and plate of scones down on the table. 'Will that be all, sir?' she asked, ignoring Katherine.

'That will be all – thank you!' Katherine broke in sharply startling the young woman.

'Yes, ma'am,' the maid said softly, looking from the captain to Katherine and back to the man, unsure of the situation. Initially she had had them pegged as whore and client, but now she wasn't so sure, in fact, on reflection, she realized it was highly unlikely that a prostitute would bring a client to a Temperance Hotel.

'You've a lot of fire, young woman,' John Lewis said with a grin, as the waitress disappeared.

'She annoyed me.'

Captain Lewis poured milk into the two cups and then added the pale weak tea. 'I hope you like it weak,' he said, returning the silver pot to its round base and pushing Katherine's cup across the table. 'Do you take sugar?'

She shook her head. 'No.'

'I'm afraid I rather over-indulge,' he said, pouring three heaped spoonfuls into his own cup.

'Syrup,' Katherine smiled.

'So, how is it you're in town today – your day off is Wednesday, isn't it?'

'It is, but Mrs O'Neill needed some help with the shopping. Mrs Lewis is having a small gathering this evening.'

'No doubt taking advantage of my absence.'

Katherine drank her tea and remained silent.

'How was my wife this morning?'

'To me, you mean?'

The captain smiled and nodded.

'A little cool,' Katherine said carefully, 'she told me

she expected me to conduct myself with a certain amount of modesty and reserve.'

'She was a little upset last night,' he said absently. He regarded her silently for a few moments, looking at her over the rim of his cup. Katherine was conscious of his eyes on her as she nibbled at a hot buttered scone. Finally, she looked up and stared directly into his eyes. 'Why have you brought me here?' she asked.

'So we could talk with some degree of privacy.'

'But we're not talking,' Katherine remarked pointedly.

'Not so much the servant now, eh?' the Captain observed, amused but with a hint of acid in his voice.

'I don't think I need to be now – do I?'

Captain Lewis looked at her appraisingly. The girl fascinated him; not only her looks but her intelligence, her humour and fire. His casual interest was beginning to blossom into an all-consuming lust – if he could, he'd have taken the girl upstairs right now. But he knew she wasn't ready and he had no idea how he should proceed. He sensed that she wouldn't respond to presents, that she couldn't be bought in that way. He ran his fingers around the lip of his cup, watching her. She was interested in him, he was sure – all he needed was to extend that interest a little further. Perhaps some secret shared between them? And at that moment an idea came into his mind. 'I'll tell you then,' he decided.

'Tell me what?'

'First I must swear you to secrecy – I'll need your oath that what I tell you will go no further.'

Katherine was intrigued. 'You have my word on it.'

'Swear!' John Lewis insisted.

'I swear,' Katherine said seriously, genuinely puzzled now.

He nodded, seemingly satisfied. 'First you must tell no-one – no-one mind! – that you've seen me today. Not Mrs O'Neill and especially not my wife! Is that understood?'

Katherine nodded. 'I swear.'

'Now, my wife thinks I'm out of town on official business so, if she's asked – and I'm sure she will be – then she can answer truthfully.'

'I'm not sure what your business is,' Katherine said. 'I understood you were army, but I've never seen you in uniform?'

'You're a smart girl, Katherine, I prophesy you'll go far.'

Katherine shivered, disturbed by the uncharacteristic warmth in the captain's voice.

'Officially, I am the staffing officer for the General Post Office and the various sub-post offices. As you can imagine it is a very responsible job, for the postal service – and the General Post Office in particular – lies at the heart of our culture and life.' He paused and added conspiratorially. 'Unofficially, my brief is to ferret out those people disloyal to the Empire and Her Majesty's Government.'

'Oh . . .' Katherine took a few moments to allow the information to sink in. 'Then . . . then you're still in the army . . . ?'

He nodded.

'You're a spy,' she said, leaning across the table, her voice dropping to a whisper.

The captain smiled. 'Exactly.'

'But why are you telling me this?' Katherine asked, darting a look around the room to find the waitress in the corner staring intently at them, 'Why are you telling me?'

'Because I think it better to have you on my side than against me,' Captain Lewis said, 'because you're English, so your sympathies aren't in doubt.'

'That doesn't answer my question,' Katherine persisted.

The captain leaned forward. 'No, I suppose it doesn't.'

He lifted his teacup and sat back in the creaking chair, his eyes never leaving the young woman's. His opinion of her, and her apparent uninterest in him, made her seem all the more desirable. 'What do you think of Mrs Lewis?' he asked suddenly, seemingly changing the subject.

'I don't think it's my place to talk about my mistress, sir,' Katherine said pointedly, wondering where the conversation was leading now.

'Forget for the moment that she's your mistress; forget that she's my wife, and tell me. I'll not be reporting to her,' he added with a smile.

'She seems like a good enough woman,' Katherine said slowly, 'a little distant perhaps, but then I am nothing more than a servant,' she said bitterly.

Captain Lewis sat forward, his voice falling to a whisper. 'She is a good woman; she does a lot of work for charity, the church and hospitals.' He paused. 'She has, though, two faults; she is Irish and she is . . . cool.'

Suddenly uncomfortable with these revelations, Katherine shook her head. 'I'm not sure I understand.'

Captain Lewis shook his head. 'My wife is not a very passionate woman, Katherine and – although this may be shocking to your ears, I feel I know you well enough to say it – she is loath to perform her wifely duties. Now, you may think that that is not all that important, but in time you will understand that a man and a woman often feel the closest in the aftermath of their joining. That is something I cannot share with my wife.'

'You said she had two faults . . .' Katherine said quickly, anxious to change the direction of their conversation.

'She is Irish, her father has some land in Kildare and Meath, and, along with many others of her so-called literary friends, she is devoted to the nationalist cause. And the nationalists have sworn to overthrow the British presence in Ireland, to make this land independent. Their followers are everywhere, plotting, planning, seeking to undermine the presence of the Crown forces, and part of my brief is to counter their measures.' He shook his head slightly. 'You see, I cannot talk freely to her about my duties to the Crown for fear she might inadvertently – or even deliberately – let them slip to the wrong people.' He dropped his eyes and turned his teacup around and around in his hands. 'There are times when I feel as if I could burst with the need for someone to talk to. Someone I could trust.'

In the long silence that followed, Katherine said very slowly, 'You could trust me . . .'

Lowering his eyes again, but this time to conceal the flash of triumph, he continued very gently, 'Thank you; it will be nice to have someone to share my triumphs and laugh at my failures.' He reached over and patted her hand once and then again. 'I know I can trust you.'

CHAPTER NINE

The evening was warm and heavy and, as Mrs O'Neill left College House shortly after nine, she could hear the sounds of laughter drifting out through the open windows from the dining room, where Mrs Lewis was entertaining. She looked back as she closed the rear gate behind her, and spotted Katherine in her maid's uniform, moving around the kitchen, putting the desserts, which Mrs O'Neill had prepared earlier that evening, on to the trays.

Mrs O'Neill automatically pulled her shawl tighter around her neck – and then self-consciously loosened it. It was a beautiful mild evening, still bright, and the night smelt soft and smokey, without the stench that sometimes came up from the city at this hour. She was tired; it had been a long busy day, what with shopping and preparing the food for this dinner of Mrs Lewis's, and there was every prospect of a long night ahead. There were two pregnant girls she had been looking after who were due any day now and, what with her luck, both would decide to give birth tonight. All she wanted was one good night's sleep, but the summer months were her busy time. Most children, she knew, were conceived in the long dark winter nights, when a couple had nought else to do, when money was short and the pubs closed.

Although she was tired, it was such a mild evening that she decided to walk home; Summerhill wasn't that far from Clonliffe Road. As she moved into town the buildings became grander – but, paradoxically, poorer – and the streets meaner. The fine Georgian-style houses, three and four floors over a basement, had once been the town houses for the upper and rich merchant classes, but times had changed and the gentry had moved away and their houses had been let, and let again and then sub-let, until it was not unusual to find ten or more families occupying sixteen rooms and paying anything from one shilling to three shillings per room. There were two distinct types of houses; most were simply family dwellings, but others were brothels, and these in turn could be divided into two types, the lodging houses, sometimes called the flash house, and the stews, with the former being the better class of establishment. However, it was not unusual for prostitutes to hire rooms in respectable houses for the night for somewhere to bring their clients.

Mrs O'Neill took the short cut down Emmet Street and then into Upper Charles Street and thence into Summerhill. The steps of the tenements were crowded, with the men sitting on the lower steps, chatting quietly together, passing a bottle back and forth, while the women occupied the higher steps or sat on rickety wooden chairs and boxes enjoying the mild evening air.

As she turned into Summerhill, partially in shadow now, the last remnants of the setting sun slanting dusty light down the cobbled street, she spotted two young girls climbing into a cab almost directly across the road from her. With a flick of his whip the cabby brought the horses away from the kerb. Mrs O'Neill didn't need to be told what had just happened; some 'gentlemen' had just purchased their 'entertainment' for the evening. She crossed the road and climbed the steps to her own house, not feeling anything, not even surprise. Thank God it wasn't so bad up here in Summerhill, but a few streets away, in Gloucester Street and Montgomery Street, nearly every second house was a brothel, and a decent woman couldn't walk down there without being accosted. But prostitution was a way of life – sometimes the only way of survival for many a young girl in Dublin. She stood on the steps and looked up and down the street. In all her years the street hadn't changed much, merely grown dirtier and dingier. She saw a young man hurrying down the street from the direction of Sackville Street, his head bent, his movements almost furtive. Well, there was little guessing what he was after. As she turned away, she realized that there were some things which never changed.

Dermot Corcoran stopped and glanced once again at the scrap of paper in his hand, re-reading the address, and then looking up to check the numbers of the doors. Odd numbers on one side; evens on the other. A few doors up.

He knew this part of Summerhill quite well; Granny O'Neill lived only across the road. When he was finished he decided he might call in on her, although, he smiled, he wouldn't tell her his real reason for being in Summerhill. Dermot Corcoran was looking for a whore.

He ran up the few steps and stepped into the dingy hallway, wrinkling his nose at the ever-present smell of cabbage. Every tenement he had visited – and in the last few months he had visited quite a few – always smelt of cabbage. He knew if he took a few steps forward, the stairway would smell of urine, and when he climbed upstairs there would be the sweeter stink of corruption as something rotted.

It was now almost two months since Dermot Corcoran had set out looking for a lead on the pregnant prostitute whose body had been dragged out of the river. He needed this story; the one good story that would make his name. He had become a regular visitor to Monto in the past two months, talking to the girls and their clients. Usually both groups proved extremely close-mouthed but a few drinks could sometimes loosen their tongues. However, he was no closer now to discovering the identity of the dead woman than he had been when he first started on his quest. But his time hadn't been entirely wasted, since he did now have enough information to write an informative general article on the red-light district of Monto.

Nevertheless, he wasn't about to give up yet. He had

the address of a woman called 'Madam' – she had no other name – whose knowledge of both the brothels and the street girls was apparently encyclopaedic. If a girl wished to find a place in one of the flash houses then she first came to Madam who evaluated her and, if she thought she was suitable material, passed her on to one of the other madams, the Misses Curley, Moore, Carn, Mack or Cohen. In return she would receive a flat fee from the brothel owner and a portion of the girl's first month's 'wage'.

Of course, a lot of the girls didn't go through Madam; only those looking for the relative safety and security, and the higher earnings, of the brothels. The rest of the street-walkers – the poor, those desperate for money to survive or bring up families, girls in service trying to put together an extra few shillings to send home to their families – usually just went straight on to the streets. And that could be a dangerous place; although injury and death were relatively uncommon, beatings and robbery were frequent, and the 'tart's trinity' – gonorrhoea, syphilis and pregnancy – almost assured.

Dermot climbed up to the first floor, moving quietly on the balls of his feet, the fingers of his right hand trailing along the slightly greasy wall. He stopped outside the first door at the top of the stairs and then paused for a moment, listening, before knocking. The house was almost silent, although upstairs a child was crying plaintively and the sounds from the street outside seemed very distant. Dermot was aware that his own heart was pounding painfully, and his shoulder muscles were knotted. Before rapping softly on the door, he touched the long double-edged hunting knife which he had strapped to his forearm under his jacket. In the past month he had drawn it on three separate occasions – and fortunately that had been enough to send his would-be attackers running. But one of these days, he was afraid he was going to have to use it – and he wasn't sure if he would be able to do it.

He tapped on the door and then pressed his ear to the

115

stained wood. He heard the sounds of scuffling inside and then cloth rustled. The footsteps approached the door, and he pulled away.

'Who is it?' The voice was a rasp and the question was followed almost immediately by a coughing fit.

The young man knocked on the door again.

'Who is it, I say? Who's there?'

Experience told him not to reply; once the woman heard a man's voice, she wouldn't open the door.

There was another fit of coughing from inside. 'Ger away with yez, yez dirty little bastards, disturbing an old woman like that.' The footsteps started to retreat.

Dermot rapped on the door again, harder this time.

The occupier returned to the door in a rush and Dermot barely had time to reach into his pocket before the door was wrenched open and a ruined face peered out. Their eyes met and for a moment they stared – shocked, surprised – at each other.

Madam was mad – it showed in her wild eyes, her slack lips and terrifying expression. Dermot almost made an excuse, bid her a good night and turned around, but the woman on seeing a stranger had already started to close the door. As a result, Dermot instinctively stuck his foot in the jamb and pulled the bottle of Power's whiskey from his pocket. Madam's eyes fastened greedily on to it.

'I apologize for disturbing you,' Dermot said slowly and clearly, 'but I would like to have a few words. Can I come in?'

The woman didn't seem to hear him, and he had to repeat the question, shaking the small bottle before her face to attract her attention. She reached for it, her fingers clawed, the knuckles swollen, but he pulled it away. 'Let me come in first, and it's yours.'

She shambled to one side and Dermot stepped in. The woman snatched the bottle from his hand and hobbled away towards the window, breaking the seal on it at the same time. Dermot closed the door quietly and watched as she leant against the window ledge and drank deeply,

116

holding the bottle by the neck. A thin stream of the pale honey-coloured liquid ran down her chin. When she paused for breath she began coughing and, at one stage, Dermot thought she was going to choke to death.

The room was large and surprisingly clean and looking at it Dermot had the impression that someone came in to 'do' for Madam. Against one wall was a bed, piled high with blankets, while above it was a religious picture of the Holy Family. Dermot wondered if, as in the brothels, the wall behind it was hollow, the recess containing a length of lead pipe or a knife? There were two easy chairs on either side of the fire. They were leather but had obviously seen better days, and in the centre of the room was a plain table surrounded with four chairs. The only other item of furniture in the room was a large and incredibly ugly wardrobe.

When the woman had stopped coughing, she turned to Dermot. 'What do you want?' she demanded suspiciously, her eyes glittering dangerously.

'I want to ask you a few questions . . .' Dermot began, but the old woman started to shake her head. 'Oh no, oh no. I don't answer any questions . . .'

He took a step nearer her. 'I'll have that bottle back then.'

The woman drew in on herself, clutching the bottle tight in both hands. Seen close up, Dermot had to revise his estimate of her age. Initially he had put her at around sixty or so, but now, in what remained of the light coming in through the window, he moved that figure down by about twenty years or so. He could tell by her hands and her figure, though her hair was ash-white and as brittle and fragile as straw, and powder and rouge were caked on her face. Her eyes were discoloured and quite mad and her eyelids and lips trembled. Syphilis.

Something must have shown in his face, for the woman suddenly cackled. 'What are you staring at, eh?'

'I'd like to ask you a few questions,' Dermot said quickly, drawing back from the woman.

'What sort of questions?' Madam asked, swigging from the bottle and then gasping for breath.

'I'm looking for someone, and I think you might be able to help me.'

'A woman no doubt?' Madam asked with a leer.

He nodded. 'A woman.'

The woman laughed again, her cackle sending shivers up and down his spine. It was the sort of laugh a witch in a child's fairytale would have. 'Well, you've come to the wrong place, lad. You've got the wrong Madam.' She drank again. 'You go down to Gloucester Street or Montgomery or Purdon Streets – you'll find tarts aplenty there.'

'It's not that sort of woman I'm looking for. It's a missing woman.'

Madam glanced at him curiously but, before she could ask any questions, Dermot launched into his prepared story. 'I'm looking for my cousin who went missing a little while ago, about six months or so. In the beginning she wrote home occasionally, but we could never reply because her address seemed to change a lot – although it was usually within Monto – and then in May the letters stopped, and we've heard nothing since.'

'I don't see how I can help you,' the woman said.

'In her last letter she said that she had recently found a few friends who had put her on to a job that would finally make her some real money. Now, I don't know about you, but there's not many ways in Dublin for a pretty young country girl to make herself any real money – except one that is.'

Madam nodded and grinned ghoulishly. 'Only one that I know of.'

'Now, her family's not prepared to admit it,' Dermot hurried on, 'but I think – I know! – that she went on the streets, and, because of what she said in her last letter, I'd hazard a guess that she was working the quays.' He paused, watching the woman intently. 'I also think she was pregnant.'

Madam stopped with the bottle touching her lips. Her

118

eyes met his briefly and then she continued drinking – in the silence of the room, the gurgling, slurping sounds sounded almost obscene. 'And what makes you think that she was pregnant?' she asked very softly, her voice hoarse and raw.

'She said that she felt the food was not agreeing with her, and that she often felt ill, especially first thing in the morning. Now, my cousin was an innocent girl – it's doubtful if she would even realize that she was pregnant.'

'So, you're looking for a missing pregnant hoor who worked the quays?' Madam asked quietly. 'Oh, and what was her name?'

Right then and there Dermot knew the game was up; she knew! But he was determined to play it out to the bitter end. 'Mary ... Mary Cunningham,' he said quickly.

'I've never heard of any Mary Cunningham,' Madam said reflectively. She put the bottle down on the window sill and then pulled the window up, allowing the tainted night air to waft into the room. 'Do you know what will happen if I stick my head out this window and just scream?' she asked, her voice low and conversational but her eyes glittering crazily. 'Within minutes, every-one in the street would be in here – and where would you be then? What are you?' she asked bitterly, 'police, or newspaper – although I fancy you're a little too fresh-faced to be either. What are you then?' she demanded fiercely.

'I'm with the *Freeman's*,' Dermot said quietly, realiz-ing that he had badly underestimated the woman.

'Reporter!' The woman turned and spat out the window.

'Look,' Dermot reached into his pocket and pulled out another bottle of whiskey, 'can we start again – with the truth this time,' he added.

Madam's eyes never left the amber-filled bottle.

'What I've told you is more or less true. I'm looking into the death of a young pregnant woman – possibly a

119

prostitute – whose body was found beneath Butt Bridge last May.'

'Why?'

Dermot shook his head. 'Why? What do you mean, why?'

'Why are you looking into it?' she reached for the bottle, and Dermot, reluctantly, handed it across.

'It's possible she was murdered.'

Madam didn't even react.

'Did you hear me? I said that it is possible that she was murdered. I'm trying to find the man who murdered a six-months-pregnant woman.'

'That's a police job.'

'She was a prostitute,' Dermot said simply, and the woman nodded in understanding.

They both knew that the Dublin Metropolitan Police were not going to dig too deeply into the unfortunate death of a young woman of no account. Indeed, the police were more or less inclined to leave Monto alone; Dublin, at the turn of the century had the dubious distinction of having a recognized – if not authorized – brothel district. The reasons for not inquiring too closely into the goings on in 'the Village' – as the area was somewhat affectionately known – were many, some political, others just practical. But primarily it was felt that, once the prostitutes were confined within a certain area, they could be watched and, to a certain extent, controlled. Dublin was also a barracks town, and it was preferable to have the off-duty soldiers and sailors on leave in one particular spot rather than wandering around the city, wreaking havoc. On the other hand, some of the flash houses were frequented by officials, not only the police and judiciary but also by local councillors and the landed gentry. Indeed, whenever the Prince of Wales visited Ireland, he was rumoured to be smuggled into Monto for a night of drinking and carousing. Monto's attractions were not only of the flesh – they also offered round-the-clock drinking and gambling.

And Monto, after dark, was not a place for the Dublin Metroploitan Police to venture alone or even in pairs.

Madam sat back against the window, a bottle in either hand, watching the young man intently. 'You still haven't told me why you're looking for this man,' she said.

'Because he killed a pregnant young woman – a girl really, and I think he may kill again. I think it's important that he is caught.'

'You think he might kill again?' Madam asked, taking a quick swig.

'I'm sure of it. Remember Jack the Ripper?'

'An' he was never caught,' Madam whispered, crossing herself quickly. 'You don't think it was him do you?'

'No, I don't. All we have at the moment is one dead body thrown in the river.'

'Two,' Madam said surprisingly, 'there was a girl found in the river up beyond Christchurch late last night.'

'I heard nothing,' Dermot said surprised, 'surely the police . . .'

'The police don't know – and they won't ever,' she suddenly snapped.

'What happened?'

She shrugged. 'I don't know; a fight with a man possibly. She was knifed,' she said simply.

'Was the man caught?'

'Not yet, but he will be.' She spoke assuredly.

'And when he is . . . ?' Dermot wondered.

'He'll be taken care of,' Madam said, almost casually.

'How?'

'Well Monto has its secrets and I think that'll have to be one of them.'

'What about the girl whose body was found in the river last May?' Dermot asked. 'Did you know her?'

A gleam came into the old woman's eyes. 'I may have; but I think that information's worth more than a bottle of booze.'

121

'Two,' Dermot reminded her.

'Two, then,' she smiled. 'I'll need a few more than that.'

'How many?'

'A dozen bottles,' she said drunkenly.

'You'll have them. Now who was she?'

'In advance . . . !'

'You have my word . . .'

Madam laughed. 'Your word is worthless here. Goods first – then information.'

Dermot stood up and jammed his pencil and notebook back into his pocket. 'Forget it, old woman. I don't believe you know. I don't believe you ever knew.' He turned towards the door when the woman called out for him to stop.

'If I tell you, will you swear to bring me the bottles?' she asked pathetically.

'I said I would.'

'You see I can't get out much . . .' she lifted the hem of her skirt and showed bulbous ankles and swollen feet.

'I'll bring you the bottles.'

'I'll tell you then.' She sat back into a chair. 'Not that I know much about her of course, except from what she told me, and the rest I guessed.' She drank deeply again. 'She was called Sheila, and she said she had been a servant in a house in the suburbs and that she had been seduced by the master of the house.'

'It's a plausible enough story.'

She nodded. 'Aye, it happens too. She was carrying his child and she had been thrown out of the house. That's all I know.'

'You don't know where she was in service, do you?'

'The suburbs . . . Drumcondra, Clontarf, Glasnevin . . . someplace like that . . .'

'And how do you know it's the same girl?' Dermot wondered.

Madam shrugged. 'She wanted to work in one of the houses, but I know no-one would have taken her in her

122

condition. And the only beat open at the time was that end of the quays. It's the same girl all right.'

Dermot stood up to go. 'Thank you for your help; I'll deliver the bottles tomorrow evening.'

'I'm trusting you,' the old woman called as he pulled the door closed behind him.

It was only as Dermot stepped out into the street that the full enormity of what he had just heard struck him. He began to shiver and he felt his stomach heave. He leaned against the door jamb, breathing in great gulps of the evening air, attempting to clear his head and settle his stomach.

He knew whom the old woman had been talking about. He knew the identity of the murdered girl!

CHAPTER TEN

The room in the Imperial Hotel overlooked O'Connell Street and was almost directly facing the GPO. Tilly Cusack, naked except for a pair of long white gloves, peered out through the net curtains and down into the street. Behind her, Captain Lewis lay on the bed, watching her drowsily.

'If they could only see what's going on in here,' Tilly said, turning away from the window and sauntering back to the bed, crossing her arms over her large swaying breasts.

'I'm glad they can't,' John Lewis said with a grin.

Tilly jumped on to the bed and curled up tight against him, both arms around his neck, her head close to his. 'Do you ever walk down a street at night, looking at all the lighted windows and wondering what's going on inside?'

Captain Lewis thought about it. 'Only if I'm coming home very late – or very early in the morning – and I see a light burning in a window, then I wonder what's happening in that house.'

'Did you ever creep up to the window and peep in?'

'No, never. Did you?'

Tilly shrugged, the movement sending ripples down her flesh. 'A few times.'

'And what did you see?'

Tilly drew up her legs and pulled the sheet out from under her, and then pulled it up over her body. She drew even closer to the captain, her head now resting on his chest, her toes curled around his. John tweaked her ear. 'What did you see, eh?'

'I remember once I saw a couple arguing. This was in London, and it was late in the evening. They were

124

shouting and swearing, and then I saw him strike her. She fell against a table and a bottle fell over. I saw her grab the bottle and break it across his head, and when he fell to the ground, with blood gushing from a score of cuts, she just stood there and screamed and screamed. Another time, and this was in Dublin now, I saw a wake. I was coming home very early, and there was a light burning in the window, and when I peeped in there was an old woman, all dressed up in her Sunday best, lying cold and grey on the bed with her family kneeling around. At the head of the bed, a priest was telling his beads, and all the people were murmuring softly together. It sounded like a beehive.' She giggled. 'And then once I saw a couple making love.'

'What's so funny?'

'Well he was at least sixty, red-faced, bald and stick-thin and the woman was a hugely fat creature. I saw her roll on to him and he absolutely disappeared. Drowned – smothered in flesh.'

'I can think of nastier ways to go,' John said.

'I wonder, will I still be making love when I'm sixty?'

Captain Lewis ran his hand down her body and cupped her breast. 'Of course you will: you're made for lovemaking.'

He felt her shudder. 'Who knows what lies ahead of us? Who would have thought that I'd have ended up as a tart in Dublin? If anyone had said that to me ten years ago, I'd have slapped their face – and look at me now. So how do we know what will happen in the next ten years?'

'They'll be good to you,' Captain Lewis promised.

'Oh, I wish I could be sure. I've been lucky so far, but one slip, just one, and I'm finished. Why . . .' she patted her flat belly, 'I could be pregnant right this minute and now wouldn't that put an end to my career in double-quick time?'

'You're not,' Captain Lewis said, forcing a smile and a hollow laugh.

'Oh, I know I'm not – but I could be. It happens so

125

easily. What about that servant girl of yours ... what was her name ... ?'

'Sheila.'

'Aye; look at her. A good job in service and then she gets herself pregnant, and now what has she got ... ?' She paused and then amended it slightly. 'Well she is a little luckier than the rest. At least you took care of her.' She twisted her head around to look up at him. 'You did find her – you did take care of her?'

Captain Lewis smiled thinly. 'Oh yes, I found her; I took care of her.' He stopped and then said, 'She's in the west with an aunt of Anne's. She can look after her and we'll pay the wages.'

'That's good of you.'

'Merely Christian.'

'Christian!' Tilly snorted. 'You've just spent the afternoon in bed with a whore and you talk to me about Christian.'

'Ah, but the sin isn't mine – it's my wife's,' Captain Lewis said seriously. 'If she would fulfil her wifely duties, I wouldn't be forced to have recourse to other women.'

Tilly wasn't sure if he was joking or not. 'You found a replacement for the servant girl?'

He nodded. 'Yes, in a strange and roundabout way. I had a chance meeting with an old soldier who had been invalided out of my regiment. When I enquired after his family, he told me that his daughter was presently looking for a position. So I hired her there and then ...'

'Sight unseen?'

'Sight unseen,' he agreed.

Tilly grinned. 'And what did your wife say?'

'She wasn't too pleased; she likes to employ the staff herself, but somehow she always ends up with girls who are a little ... slow.'

'And what's the new girl like?' Tilly asked, reaching across the captain's chest and flipping up the cover on his pocket watch. Half-past four. She squeaked with alarm and hopped out of bed, and then dashed around the hotel bedroom, gathering up her clothing.

'She's bright,' Captain Lewis said, answering her earlier question, 'intelligent and pretty in a rather simple way – discreet too,' he added.

'Well, you make sure she doesn't end up like the last girl,' Tilly said, struggling back into her dress, but watching the man carefully all the time.

John Lewis sat up in bed and tossed back the sheets. 'Oh, you needn't worry about that. She's not allowed to have any gentleman callers. I won't have any more little accidents of that sort in my house.'

Katherine sat on the edge of her bed and lit the stub of the candle on the dressing table. By candlelight the attic room seemed larger than it actually was, and the shadows dancing in the corners hid its drabness and lent it an air of mystery. Although it was close to midnight, the sliver of sky which Katherine could see through the back window was still pale purple, shot through with long lines of darker-coloured cloud. Three points of brilliant light burned above her head – stars, each one a wish, Katherine thought. Well, if she had three wishes, she would wish for . . . well, what would she wish for?

When she had played the game as a child, her first wish had always been for 'three wishes a day for the rest of her life', and her second wish had been for 'all the money in the world', and 'an island'. And now that she was older, she found that her wishes – while they had changed slightly – still held true to her original desires. She still wanted three wishes a day until the day she died, and she still wanted wealth but only a small amount. Large sums of money brought their own problems, unless of course, one was fabulously wealthy – like the Queen – and then you didn't have to worry about the worries. And she still wanted an island – well, not really an island, but a house of her own. Not too big, of course, something like the one she was in now.

127

But it must be hers, and not owned, or part-owned, by any man.

She opened a drawer and pulled out some sheets of white writing paper, and then took the stub of a pencil from her pocket. She positioned the paper under the candle's warm yellow glow, licked the end of the pencil, grimaced at the sharp taste and began to write.

'My Dearest Mama . . .'

She stopped and chewed the end of the pencil, staring at the dancing candle flame, searching for inspiration.

'My Dearest Mama, It seems such a long time since I last wrote to you, but I can assure you that you have never been far from my thoughts. Papa and the boys are well, I trust, and how is little David, well, I hope? It saddens me to think that he will be quite the young man before I see him, unless, of course, you and Papa managed to come over, although I realize how difficult that would be.

'Now that I have settled in, I can give you a better idea of my situation here . . .'

Katherine paused, and licked her pencil stub reflectively, wondering just how much to tell her mother, knowing the truth was impossible and a lie equally difficult to tell, even on paper. From experience she knew her mother would immediately spot a lie.

'As I said in my last letter, the house is rather lovely, set on a quiet road and backing on to a religious college for the training of Roman Catholic priests.

'I have made some friends here, especially with the cook, Mrs O'Neill. She is a lovely person, a fine cook as well as a midwife.

'Mrs Lewis is nice, if a little distant. She is a writer, and has had one book of poetry published. I do not see her that much as she spends a lot of time out of the house, doing her charity work, or attending her literary courses, and, when she is at home, she locks herself away to write. Mrs O'Neill told me that she is writing another book.

128

'Captain Lewis is a very nice man. He is kind and considerate . . .'

She stopped; she would have to be very careful what she said about the captain, otherwise her mother might put two and two together very quickly, and guess her feelings for the captain. And that, of course, raised the question – just what were her true feelings for Captain John Lewis? And, even more importantly, just what were his feelings towards her? True, he had told her he wanted her as a friend he could trust, but she felt there was more to it than that – and this was from the man who had seduced her predecessor. So, if he had any feelings towards her, it was unlikely they went very deep, or indeed much beyond mere physical attraction.

He was very charming though, not forward, just attentive. He always had a few words for her in the morning – although he seemed to be spending less and less time in the house now, and, on the few occasions he had remained overnight, Katherine had heard raised voices from the bedrooms below. He had met her once again in town, outside the GPO this time, while she had been waiting for Dermot to finish in the *Freeman's Journal* whose offices were just around the corner. He had stepped out of the GPO and was standing beside her before she had even noticed him. This time they had chatted together openly for a few terrifying moments, and then the captain had bid her a good day and strolled across the road towards the Imperial Hotel. He had just rounded the corner into North Earl Street when Dermot had appeared, red-faced and gasping, with what Katherine called the 'newspaper smell' about him, a mixture of inks and paper, of presses and sweat.

And of course there was Dermot Corcoran. She couldn't write to her mother about him, could she? A letter, either from her mother or father, would come by return post, informing the captain or Mrs Lewis what was happening. And that would be that. But just how did she feel about Dermot?

Katherine got up and paced around the room, her

129

shadow dancing and leaping up the wall. When she realized what was happening, she leaned over and blew the candle out – waste not, want not – and then breathed in the thick tallow fumes which always reminded her of those sharp winter nights when, as a child, she had huddled by her mother's skirts. A thin plume of grey-white smoke hung stock still on the air, until Katherine crossed to the window and pushed it open gently. Then, leaning on the window frame she stared out over the garden and beyond the college walls, breathing in the warm, sultry night air.

What were her feelings for Dermot? Well, it was difficult to say. He was a likeable chap, kind, thoughtful and considerate. He seemed to be genuinely interested in her for herself, always listened to what she had to say and treated her ... as a person. Yes, that was it – he treated her as a person.

The moon slipped behind a long streak of black and silver cloud, plunging the gardens below into darkness, highlighting the lights in the college windows in the distance. She noticed that most of the ground-floor windows were alight, and guessed that there was a function in progress.

She idly wondered how she would feel if she found out that Dermot was seeing another woman. Would she be angry, annoyed, jealous ... would she have any right to be? She thought she might be both angry and jealous, but was that an indication of her true feelings? Then she remembered her impetuousness, and the habit she had of making quick decisions and her sudden passions. However, she also knew that the same passions, quick to flare, were usually equally quick to subside, but, significantly, she thought, her feelings for Dermot remained with her.

She rested her chin in both cupped hands and stared out over the garden attempting to compose the rest of the letter in her head.

'Dublin is a very lovely city, but so small. I am allowed a half day every Wednesday, and I usually go into "town" – because that is what Dubliners call the city – and I am constantly surprised by the number of familiar faces I recognize.

'I have not done much exploring into the side streets yet, and there are some areas of the city which I have been warned to avoid, places where it is not safe for a woman to be out walking, even during the day.

'The city has many fine and beautiful buildings, but some of the lovely town houses of the gentry have been turned into slums. Dozens of families occupying the house, living one family – and sometimes more – to a room, and remember, in Ireland, the families tend to be large. It makes me a little sad and ashamed to think how small I thought our cottage was back home . . .'

She was going to mention that she had an entire room to herself, but, remembering that her whole family, mother, father and six children had lived in two rooms, each one smaller than her present attic, she decided not to.

'Dublin people are kind for the most part – especially the poor, but I think that is always the case. And Dublin is a city with a lot of poor. Sometimes, on my afternoon walks in town, I can be accosted up to a dozen times by beggars, and I am only sorry that I have nothing to give . . .'

She suddenly thought of Dermot; he was particularly vocal on the subject of Dublin's poor and diseased, and he swore that when he was a successful newspaper journalist he would champion their cause and work for better housing and medicine, better wages and conditions and generally improve their lot.

'. . . It is late now, Mama, and I will finish up, but I will write again soon. My love to you all, always . . .'

Katherine straightened up and stretched. She would try and wake up a little earlier in the morning and write the letter before she went down to start her day's duties. She knew she could ask Mrs O'Neill to post it for her.

As she undressed and prepared for bed, the contents of her letter still running around in her head, images of

131

Captain Lewis and Dermot Corcoran alternating with each other, she wondered what they were both doing right now . . .

In fact, at that moment Captain John Lewis and Dermot Corcoran were standing not three hundred yards apart, although naturally neither was aware of the other's presence.

Dermot Corcoran stood on O'Connell Bridge, looking down towards the pale outline of the Customs House on the left-hand side, breathing in the warm night air, ridding himself of the stink of the *Freeman's* presses. He often came here at night when his shift was done, to lean against the wall and compose his thoughts after the incredible noise and bustle of the *Freeman's* offices. At this time of night, the bridge was practically deserted, and he could stand above the blackness of the water, with the lights on either side, and pretend that he was somehow apart from the city. Usually he would walk away having regained his peace of mind – but he knew that tonight there would be no peace, and that not even the black waters could ease his troubled conscience.

He had discovered a murderer – or rather he had discovered the identity of the young woman who was murdered and thrown into the Liffey, not two minutes' walk from where he was standing. And there was only one man who would have had any reason for wanting her dead.

It was his duty to bring the information to the police – but unfortunately it wasn't so clear cut. The man involved was an officer in the army, now holding a highly placed civilian position, respectable, married, while his information had not exactly come from the most respectable of sources.

He knew what would happen if he accused a man like that; he knew whose word would be taken. He needed more proof, solid evidence, and not just the word of a drunken madam. The only problem would be finding that proof – but find it he would, that much he promised himself.

Captain Lewis stood in the middle of the Ha'Penny Bridge and stared down into the turgid foul-smelling water below. Red and yellow and gold reflections from the street lamps touched the black water, but instead of lending it an air of mystery, they merely picked out the filth that floated on its surface, the rotten fruit and vegetables, the drowned animals and birds, and accumulated offal, litter and excrement: the waste of the city dumped directly into the river that bisected it.

The captain drew heavily on his cigar, and then – almost delicately – dropped the butt into the water. It fell on something floating at the surface and remained lighted for a moment, a tiny red star, before it finally hissed out.

The wooden boards of the bridge echoed as someone began to cross from the far side and Captain Lewis glanced covertly to his left, while his right hand went to the pistol tucked into his belt. It was only when the second person stepped under one of the light bowls on the arches of the bridge, and he could clearly see the brigadier's rather slight figure, that he relaxed.

The brigadier joined him and then they stood silently for a few moments, both looking into the dark waters of the Liffey.

Finally, after what seemed like an age, the brigadier spoke, his voice no more than a whisper. 'There may be a problem.'

Captain Lewis nodded. 'I thought there might be something wrong after your rather cryptic summons this evening.'

'We have certain . . . associates and followers in most of the poorer parts of the city as you know; indeed most of them don't even know that they're working for us. However, that is beside the point. Over the past weeks a few snippets of information have trickled in from different sources concerning a young man – a newspaper

133

man – who is beginning to make something of an annoyance of himself up in Monto.'

'Newspaper men have a habit of doing that,' Captain Lewis remarked.

'It seems he is investigating the rather strange death of a pregnant prostitute who was dragged out of the river recently.'

The captain was aware of the brigadier's hard stare, but he managed to keep his face straight and seemingly unconcerned. 'Indeed.'

'Yes, indeed,' the brigadier snapped.

'And what is this newspaper man looking for?'

'As far as we can determine, some clues to her identity. It would seem that he intends to use her as a basis upon which to hang a series of stories about the Dublin poor. Now, while you do not seem too concerned, captain, I should point out that, once he has her identity, it should be easy enough for him to trace her background, eh captain? And we do not want any embarrassing questions raised either by him or the police.'

'He's unimportant,' John Lewis blustered. 'Who is he anyway?'

'We do not have a name for him yet. But we do know that he has attended several of the Gaelic League meetings – and I am sure you are aware of the aims of that organization?'

Captain Lewis nodded dumbly.

'It aims to restore the Irish nation through – what is the phrase they use? – de-anglicization. What do you think they would make of an English army captain on charges of murdering a prostitute who was carrying his child, eh?'

John Lewis bit his lips and kept his eyes firmly fixed on the waters below.

'This man will have to be taken care of, warned off but not killed. Is that understood – he is not to be killed; we don't need another death to spark off further inves-

134

tigations. Last reports indicated that he had visited a woman known as "Madam" . . .'

'I've heard of her.'

'Is it possible that this woman knew the dead girl, captain? And if she did, could this newspaper man wheedle or buy the information from her, eh? Think about that. Find out who he is and warn him off – decisively!' he snapped and then he walked off leaving Captain Lewis cold and shivering on the draughty wooden bridge.

CHAPTER ELEVEN

Katherine and Dermot sat on a bench in St Stephen's Green beside the lake and watched the ducks bobbing for the crusts of bread she had thrown into the water. Although it was high summer the park was almost empty, as the weather had turned unseasonally wet and there had been showers on and off throughout the afternoon.

Dermot had just told Katherine what he had discovered about the murdered woman, and added that he had an idea as to her identity and possibly the identity of the killer, but something had made him hold back from mentioning Captain Lewis's name.

'But I need proof,' Dermot said quietly, staring at the green, leafy water, 'solid proof.'

Katherine broke a crust of bread in half, and then in half again and nodded. 'You can do nothing without it.'

'But how do I go around finding proof?' Dermot asked, desperately, 'I've gone over this time and again, but I don't see any way out of it. All I have is this woman's word and no-one is going to take the word of someone like that against that of a . . . a gentleman.'

'But does this woman not keep some sort of records?' Katherine asked.

'I doubt it.'

'But if she's supplying girls to various houses, she must be owed money . . . Did you ask?' she persisted.

'No, I didn't ask,' Dermot said, 'I just assumed . . .' He sat back on the bench and tilted his head back, squinting up into the lowering sky. 'I think we'll have some more rain,' he remarked.

'Then she must be paid for her services,' Katherine said, continuing her train of thought.

'Twice; once by the brothel, and then she gets a portion of the unfortunate girl's first wage.'

'Then there have to be records of some sort, some sort of reckoning.'

Dermot shook his head savagely. 'Don't be stupid,' he snapped, 'what tart's going to keep accounts? I'm sorry,' he said, immediately contrite, 'I shouldn't have shouted at you.'

Katherine crumpled up her bag and placed it down on the seat beside her. She reached out one hand and rested it on Dermot's shoulder, and squeezed comfortingly. 'I know what you must be feeling. I'm sorry, and I wish there was something I could do.'

Dermot reached up and covered her hand with his. 'Thanks,' he smiled. 'Look,' he said, coming to a decision, 'I'll go back and speak to the old woman again; maybe she'll remember something else, something which might be of use.'

Katherine nodded, and then she shivered as a raindrop as big as a penny splashed off her cheek. She pulled Dermot to his feet and almost dragged him on to the path. 'Come on; we'll shelter in the XL Café.'

They cut out through the side gate and, although there was no reason for either of them to continue holding hands, neither of them felt like letting go.

The rain, Captain Lewis reflected, was an even better cover than darkness. Footsteps at night on a darkened street might attract attention, and the house would be that much quieter at night, so that sounds would carry. But in this downpour, everyone was hurrying for shelter, heads ducked, hats pulled down low, umbrellas straining against the wind, and the house would be filled with the usual daytime noises, cries, shouts, children playing, singing, banging and whistling.

The captain hurried up the steps, his slouch hat now sodden, his shabby coat hanging limp; to any casual watcher, he was merely another working man returning home. Once inside the door, however, he stopped and

137

allowed his eyes to accustom themselves to the dim light. The stench caught at the back of his throat and he coughed, and then he pulled a small hip flask from his pocket and drank deeply, allowing the rich whiskey fumes to dispel the odour of faeces, urine and cabbage, which was always strong in the summer weather and was now seemingly intensified by the rain. He drank again, more deeply this time, almost draining the flask before stuffing it back into his pocket. He shook water from his coat and slowly climbed the stairs, eyes and ears alert. Captain Lewis stopped at the first door, and tapped gently on it.

There was a long silence and then a voice finally cackled, 'Who is it?'

'It's me,' Captain Lewis said, pitching his voice low, making it into an obvious whisper.

'Who?' The voice was querulous.

'Newspaper,' the captain said, turning his brief answer into a cough. It was a ruse that would not work with anyone else, but he was counting on the fact that the woman was slightly deaf and his reports indicated she was more than a little mad.

'I've nothing more to say to you,' she snapped.

'Just one more question?' he wheedled.

'It'll cost you.'

The captain wondered what this newspaper man paid the old woman with – money or drink?

'I know; I brought something for you,' he said.

There was a moment's hesitation and then he heard the lock turning and the door opened slightly. He stood to one side and waited until the old woman peered out, and then he stepped out in front of her. There was a moment of shocked surprise and she scurried back and tried to slam the door again, but the captain hit it with his shoulder, forcing it open, knocking her back into the room. She staggered against the table, and the sudden bruising pain in her hip strangled her scream. The captain locked the door behind him and then advanced on the old woman; before she could cry out, his fingers

138

were on her throat, forcing her head up and back, stretching her neck, squeezing the flesh.

'One word, one word, woman,' he warned, 'and I'll snap your neck like a mangy chicken. Do you hear me – do you?'

Madam nodded her head tightly, her eyes wild and terrified, her heart thundering in her chest. There were colours, and black and white spots, swimming before her eyes, and she knew if she didn't breathe right now she was going to die. At that moment she would have promised the tall ill-kempt man anything just for a single breath of air. And then mercifully the pressure was gone and she could breathe again. She bent double, leaning up against the table, breathing in great lungfuls of tainted air. And then she began to cough, a harsh, racking sound that ended with her spitting blood. 'Drink,' she gasped, 'drink.' She waved her hand in the direction of the windowsill.

The captain found the bottle of cheap spirits on the windowsill and passed it to her. The old woman drank deeply, and began to cough again, but not so badly. 'I've no money,' she said when she could breathe easily.

The captain moved around the room, checking the wardrobe, under the seats of the chairs and behind the pictures. He finally came back to where Madam was standing by the table. 'I don't want your money,' he snapped.

'Then what do you want, for pity's sake?' she rasped.

The captain swung around to face her; his face was only inches from hers and he recoiled from the stench of her, mingled with the sweeter stink of the cheap whiskey. 'I want the name of the newspaper man you've been talking to.'

'I don't know any . . .'

He hit her – quite casually – an open-handed blow that rocked her head back and forth. For a moment she just stood there, holding her blazing cheek, not even feeling the pain, only the shock of having been struck registering. It had been many years since anyone had last laid a hand on her.

'Play games with me, old woman, and I'll cut your fingers off. Now, what was his name?'

'Really, I don't know. He never told me and I never asked.' She said it quickly, flinching in expectation of another blow.

'What newspaper did he work for?'

'The *Freeman*.'

Having established that the old woman was capable of telling the truth, Captain Lewis proceeded to extract a detailed description from the woman of the *Freeman*'s reporter. Armed with that description he felt confident he would be able to trace the name of the reporter in question.

'And what was he looking for?'

'A name.'

'What name?' The captain raised his fist. 'Don't make me drag this out of you a piece at a time,' he warned.

'He wanted to know the name of a young woman who was killed earlier this year. All I told him was that her name was Sheila and that she was walking the quayside beat, and that she was pregnant with her employer's child.'

'How do you know that?' Captain Lewis asked quickly, his face set and emotionless.

'Because she told me.'

'She told you?' he hissed. 'What else do you know about her?'

Madam shrugged. 'Nothing else, except that she was previously in service somewhere in the suburbs.'

'Names, I want names.'

The old woman shook her head, her eyes terrified. 'I don't know any names.'

'You must know something else. A bitch like you'll have dragged every scrap of information out of the girl, just in case you might be able to use it.' His eyes narrowed dangerously. 'So tell me, what else do you know?'

Madam recoiled from the look on his face. She had only seen such a look once before, and that was when one of the brothel bullies – Malley, his name – had beaten a man to death with a length of lead pipe. An unwanted client had made the mistake of attacking Malley with his swordstick, but had missed in his drunkenness. And the bully, enraged, had pulled the pipe from his pocket and hit the man, with the same look of mad satisfaction in his eyes as this terrifying stranger now had. Madam might be far gone on the road of disease and madness herself, but she was still conscious enough to recognize the look of a killer when she saw it.

'Tell me,' he urged menacingly.

'I don't know the name of the family,' she said quickly, gulping desperately from the bottle, 'but I know they were living somewhere near Clonliffe College, and that he was English and in the services. And also, I think, the woman of the house was Irish – landed gentry – and was a writer of some sorts. It should be easy enough to find them,' she added, wheedling now.

Captain Lewis nodded, his eyes vacant, his heart thundering. 'Easy enough,' he murmured. His eyes focused on the woman's face. 'And did you tell the reporter all this . . . ?'

She shook her head. 'No, no, I swear it.'

'Don't lie to me, woman!'

'I swear to you, I didn't tell him everything.'

'Why not?'

'I knew he'd be back. I needed something to sell to him.'

Captain Lewis nodded decisively. He had heard enough. He reached out and took the bottle from the woman's trembling fingers. He placed it carefully on the table, and then put both hands on the woman's shoulders, moving her a little away from the table.

'What . . . ?' she whispered.

In a swift, sudden movement, the captain thrust her forcefully back against the window. She staggered and fell, the back of her head smashing against the window-sill. The sound of her skull cracking was almost inaudible in the room with the rain smattering on the window.

The captain searched quickly through the room's meagre and shabby belongings, his innate caution driving him to ensure no hidden evidence remained to connect him with the woman now lying unconscious and dying on the filthy floor. But there was nothing, apart from the woman's supply of costumes, all slightly shabby and worn in the style of a previous generation, hidden in a long box beneath the bed. That was all she had to show for a lifetime spent on the streets and working the brothels. He picked up a chemise; it was yellow and brittle now with age and there was a series of moth holes down one side. He had seen Tilly Cusack wearing something similar, he thought suddenly. He smiled at the memory – Tilly pulling off the chemise to stand naked before the long glass mirror in the room in the Imperial Hotel. It had been a while since he had seen her . . .

Without a backward look at the dying woman, Captain John Lewis left the room, pulling the door shut behind him, locking it, and discarding the key in one of Monto's filthy sewers.

It was close to seven when Dermot rapped softly on the door to Madam's room. It had been a long day, he was tired and half of him believed this was going to be a waste of time, but he couldn't let go without one more try. There was no answer and he knocked again – louder this time. The old woman couldn't be out. She had said she never left the room, that anything she wanted was usually bought for her by one of the children living in the room above. Perhaps she was asleep, or drunk – or dead. He smiled at the thought, and then the smile faded. He knocked a third time, hammering on the stout panels of the door, and then pressing his ear to the wood, listening for sounds. But there was nothing, no sounds of movement, no snores. Nothing.

Dermot stood by the door, wondering what to do. He tried the handle, but the door was locked. On impulse, he knelt down and peered through the large keyhole – it was empty, and then he saw one twisted foot.

With a cold chill settling into the pit of his stomach, Dermot began hammering on the door, pounding on the panelling just above the lock. A heavy hand fell on to his shoulder, making him grunt with surprise. He turned and found a tall, powerfully-built man standing behind him. The man was coated in a layer of coal dust, and in the black mask of his face his eyes seemed unusually large and bright. 'What's wrong, lad?' he asked gently.

Dermot suddenly found he was panting and his heart was pounding. 'It's . . . it's Madam,' he said breathlessly. 'I've tried knocking, but there's no answer, and when I looked through the keyhole . . . I think there's been an accident . . .'

'You're the young man who was round here before, isn't that right?' the coalman said, stepping up to Madam's door and pounding on it with a massive fist. 'I'm Mick Donnelly, I live upstairs.'

'Have you got a key . . . ?' Dermot panted.

The large man shook his head. 'No key,' he said shortly. 'Madam, Madam, open up. Are you all right in there?' His roar brought the rest of the house's occupants out on to the landings above, where they hung over the bannisters, enjoying the excitement.

The large man stooped down and put his eye to the keyhole. He looked up at Dermot and nodded, 'I see it.' He stood up and pressed hard against the door, top, middle and bottom. It gave slightly at the top and bottom, but remained fast in the middle. 'There's only one lock on it,' he said – and then he stood back and kicked the door just above the handle, his thick-soled boot crushing the wood. The door flew open and slammed back against the wall, the force of the blow tearing it from its topmost hinge.

143

Dermot brushed past the man and knelt down beside the woman. The angle of her head and neck and the thick mat of dark blood on the floor beneath told their own story, as did the empty bottle beside her.

'Fell down drunk,' Mick Donnelly said, nudging the bottle with his foot.

Dermot bent his head, putting his ear close to her nose and mouth, but there was no sound. He went to lift her head, but his hands came away red and sticky and covered in coarse black and grey hairs. He felt the tea and scones he had had with Katherine in the XL Café rise to his throat and he had to swallow hard.

'Come on, lad, there's nothing you can do for her now.' The man put his hand on Dermot's shoulder. 'I'll have one of my lads run for the priest; you come on upstairs and have a cup of tea.'

'No . . . no thank you, . . .' The young man stood up shakily, suddenly feeling very sick, overcome by the realization that the scraps of gaudy cloth, the fleshy shell and the thin bones lying crumpled on the floor had been a living, breathing human being, someone he had talked to a few days ago.

In the long silence that followed, Dermot suddenly became aware that he was being watched. When he looked up Mike Donnelly said curiously, 'You don't look the sort that would know the likes of Madam now.'

'I'm a reporter with the *Freeman's Journal*,' Dermot said hoarsely, 'and I was doing an article on . . .' he glanced across at Donnelly, '. . . on this area.'

'There's no need to be shy, lad; we know where we're living, and what goes on around us.' He paused and then said slowly. 'I don't have much time for newspaper men . . . particularly those who interest themselves in . . .'

'I'm not doing a sensational article,' Dermot said quickly, 'I am following up on a murder that took place last May. I came to Madam, because I was told that she might have had some information on the girl who was killed then.'

Mick Donnelly nodded. 'Ah, well then . . . that's different, I suppose,' he added doubtfully. 'And was the old lady of any help to you?'

'A little; she told me something about the girl's background, but I'm afraid I'm still no nearer finding the murderer.'

'What's so important about finding him?' Mick asked.

'Because he could strike again – like Jack the Ripper in England,' he said slowly, playing his trump card, watching the look that came into the man's eyes. The Ripper's activities were legendary. 'Of course, now with Madam gone, I don't suppose the truth will ever come out . . .'

Mick Donnelly shook his head. 'It's terrible to think of a murderer running around free.'

'And there was another girl killed last week up beyond Christchurch – it could be the same man,' Dermot added.

'But what brought you to Madam in the first place?' Mick asked.

'Because of what she did – recommended girls to the . . . the houses.'

'Then why don't you see Bella Cohen? Madam used to work for her at one time.'

'*The* Bella Cohen?' Dermot asked.

Mick Donnelly smiled savagely. 'Aye, the Whoremistress.'

145

CHAPTER TWELVE

However, Dermot never got to see Madam Bella Cohen, the infamous Whore Mistress.

Two nights later, as he came out of the *Freeman's Journal* offices in the early hours of the morning following the long late shift, he was set upon and savagely beaten by three thugs who had been lying in wait for him. And, as he lay in a pool of his own blood, a fourth man came up to him, leaned over and spat venomously. 'Stay out of Monto – if you don't want to end up like the Madam.' The same man kicked him then, the point of his polished boot striking him in the temple.

When he regained consciousness he was in the Mater Hospital with a fractured skull, a broken arm, broken nose, and several cracked and broken ribs. It was ten days later.

Katherine let the first two trams go by, even though they had slowed and stopped for her; the drivers and conductors had come to recognize the tall dark-haired young woman who waited at the same stop every Wednesday afternoon. Finally, as the afternoon was drawing on and there was still no sign of Dermot, Katherine took the next tram into town. Perhaps something was wrong; perhaps he hadn't been able to get off work, or had caught an earlier tram and was even now waiting for her beside the pillar.

But there was no sign of the young man at the pillar. She stood, leaning against the tall pointed rail that ran around the monument and stared anxiously up and down the street, expecting at every moment to catch sight of his rather jerky, nervous stride as he rounded the corner of the GPO from the *Freeman's* offices, or came hurrying down the street.

She waited for over an hour before she finally admitted to herself that Dermot was not coming.

Katherine wandered around the town for the remainder of the afternoon, going to all the places she and Dermot usually visited. The only obvious place she didn't go – and that was because she couldn't – was the offices of the *Freeman's Journal* in Princes Street, beside the post office. She walked up and down the street, stopping to look at the billboards outside the Coliseum Variety Theatre until she knew them all by heart, and then crossed over and walked slowly past the newspaper offices, hoping to catch a glimpse of him inside.

Finally, she caught one of the new electric trams back to Drumcondra, and as it moved up and past the Rotunda and then out into Dorset Street and she could see the trees of the suburbs in the distance, she began to wonder seriously what had happened to Dermot. Was there something wrong, or had he just tired of her? She shook her head at that, the sudden savage movement surprising a young couple sitting across from her. Their stares caught her attention and she raised her eyes to look at them, catching and holding their gaze defiantly, embarrassing them into looking away. They bent their heads and began talking quietly together and then the girl glanced over at Katherine and suddenly laughed, but equally quickly sobered.

As the tram rolled noisily over Binn's Bridge and the stop loomed closer, she considered what possibilities were open to her. She could ask Mrs O'Neill; she was Dermot's godmother and would almost certainly know if anything had happened – but that in turn would reveal her interest in the young man, and she wasn't sure if she wanted to do that. She could contact the *Freeman's* offices – but that really was a last resort, as it would be embarrassing not only to Dermot but for her also. Or she could simply forget about him, she thought

147

suddenly, and then realized that she couldn't. Her feelings for Dermot went deeper than that.

Suddenly aware that the tram had almost reached the stop, she scrambled for her bulky bag and hurried clattering down the metal stairs. The young couple looked after her and shared a joke together, their laughter loud enough for Katherine's ears to burn red.

Once again Captain Lewis stood by the back gate and watched the light burning in the maid's attic room. That light had been a beacon – an almost fatal attraction – for him over the past few months, and he had paused here on many a night-time stroll, just watching the shadows leaping and twisting across the wall and ceiling and, occasionally, catching a glimpse of Katherine as she flitted past the window. He still was not sure just what attracted him to the maid. After all, he had his choice of women and, although his wife was unresponsive in bed, she was intelligent and uninquisitive and a credit to him at social functions; in fact she was everything a wife should be. And for his sexual gratification he had Tilly. Yet, here he was, standing outside the girl's window like any schoolboy hoping for a glimpse of the object of his lust. He shook his head chiding his own stupidity, and looking up saw that the light had died, and felt vaguely disappointed.

He walked slowly down the lane and then turned left on to the main road, towards his own house. There was a light showing in his bedroom window; Anne was still awake then – probably working on one of her damned stories. She had recently moved away from poetry to short stories, and was talking about writing a play for the new Irish theatre which would be opening soon. He found he didn't want to speak to her tonight – their last few encounters had been difficult and had ended in arguments, Anne threatening to return to her parent's country home, and he didn't really want that.

Ever since he had taken up this position with the brigadier, his relationship with his wife had changed, altered subtly so that they had drifted apart without either of them realizing it. Although if he was going to be truly honest, then he would have to say that his own gambling and womanizing would have driven them apart before long. Spying for the brigadier and, to some extent, the loss of face that Anne must have suffered when he had taken on this apparently undemanding job had only hastened the inevitable.

In the bedroom upstairs the light disappeared, and Captain Lewis breathed a sigh of relief; he hadn't really wanted to take another walk around the block.

Anne Lewis heard the front door close with a dull thump and knew her husband had returned. At least he wasn't drunk – and she was thankful for that. When he was drunk he slammed the door so hard that the entire house shook. Nevertheless, she pulled the quilt up so that it almost completely covered her head and closed her eyes, forcing herself to breathe softly and regularly.

It had been three days since she had last spoken with John; indeed it had been three days since they last had the opportunity to speak. Increasingly John arrived home late in the evenings – it was after twelve now – and he was always out early in the mornings. Twice or three times a week he failed to come home at all, and she had her own suspicions as to where he spent those nights.

Was it any wonder she had found other interests?

She had her writing, and of course there was William Sherlock and the literary society. She had met William through her writing, and he in turn had introduced her to a whole new world. She smiled in the dark, and then the smile faded as she heard her husband's step on the stairs. She was sure he had a mistress – she had no proof, but then there was a lot she didn't know for sure about her husband. She wasn't even certain what position he had taken up when he had left the army – she didn't believe the story he had peddled to her and from the little she had gleaned she thought he was somehow

149

involved in keeping an eye on prominent Irish personalities. She had noticed also that John, who had always had very little sympathy for the Irish, had become even more vehement in his condemnation of everything and everyone Irish.

Perhaps that was the reason she had accompanied William to a meeting of the Gaelic League. William had told her about the society many times. It had been set up about five years ago by two friends of his, Douglas Hyde and Eoin MacNeill, the aims being to propagate not only the dying Irish language but everything Irish – to make Ireland Irish again. Anne Lewis was Irish – and proud of it.

Sherlock had introduced her to Douglas Hyde, a small round-faced man with thick drooping moustaches, who had listened intently, his head thrust forward, when Sherlock told him of Anne's literary efforts. He had then looked at her, his eyes sharp and penetrating, and asked if he might see some of her work. She hadn't had anything with her then, but she had promised to send him some of her most recent work and a copy of her collection of poetry, *A Pot-Pourri of Verse*. Hyde's reply had come some days later, praising her work highly and making several suggestions. In particular, he had pointed out the possibility of using characters from the Celtic mythologies rather than drawing on Greek and Roman ones as she had done.

And that small comment had led her to discover the wonderful myths and legends of ancient Ireland. It had also brought her into contact with some remarkable people, such as the poet William Butler Yeats, and Lady Augusta Gregory, and many others involved in what was already becoming known as the Anglo-Irish literary revival.

Anne had visited Yeats and Lady Augusta on several occasions, and had occasionally attended Yeats's salons which were held on Monday afternoons and evenings. There she had been introduced to Maud Gonne; a tall stunningly beautiful woman with whom the poet was obviously besotted. After ten minutes in Maud Gonne's company, Anne Lewis had felt exhausted; the woman's energy and enthusiasm were boundless, and, while Yeats and Gregory treated Anne courteously if a little distantly, accepting her only because her introduction came through Sherlock, Maud Gonne had immediately taken to her as an old friend. When they talked together, she had a way of leaning forward and lowering her voice, as if imparting a vitally important secret, and Anne couldn't help but respond likewise.

These were her new friends, and the Irish literary revival her new interest. As footsteps sounded on the landing, Anne hugged herself closer, enjoying her secret. She had to admit she was doing this partly because she knew John wouldn't approve of it. She wanted to get back at him.

The bedroom door opened and she heard her husband walk softly across the carpeted floor, and then the wardrobe door creaked open. There was a rustle of cloth and the snap of studs as he undressed; she heard the wardrobe door creak again, and then the whispering of heavy cloth. But he didn't come over to the bed, as she had expected. Instead, she heard the chair in the corner of the room beside the window groan and settle, and then a match flared briefly, flooding the room with quick light, and moments later the sharp stench of sulphur drifted around the room. It caught Anne unprepared and she wasn't able to resist a short sneeze.

'I'm sorry, I thought you were asleep.'

Without turning over, she replied, 'I nearly was.'

'I won't disturb you,' Captain Lewis said quietly, his voice sounding weary. It was so unlike him that Anne turned around. 'Anything wrong?'

Silhouetted against the window, she saw the movement of his head. 'No, nothing; I'm just tired.'

'I would have had something for you to eat, if I had known what time you were coming home – indeed, if I had even known you were coming home tonight.'

He ignored the jibe. 'It's of no consequence; I wasn't

sure myself if I was going to make it.' He pulled hard on the cigarette, and his face was momentarily lit up from underneath by the sharp red glow and given an almost demonic cast.

Anne watched him in silence for a while.

'Something is wrong, isn't it?'

He pulled on the cigarette again, the smoke hanging still and grey just below the level of the ceiling. Anne was so used to it now that she didn't actually notice the pungent odour. Finally he nodded. 'I fell to wondering how long this could go on . . .' he said, very softly.

'How long what could go on?' she asked.

'Us . . . you and me.'

'I think you can best answer that,' she said defensively.

'You blame me?'

'Who else should I blame?'

The chair creaked as he turned toward her, although she knew he couldn't see her in the darkness. 'Are we not both equally responsible?'

Anne Lewis was honest enough with herself to pause before answering. 'Now, perhaps, but originally the blame was entirely yours.'

'Mine.' He said the word softly, neither an exclamation, nor a question. 'How?'

'When you resigned your commission . . .'

'A leave of absence . . .' He corrected her.

'Well whatever happened, when you changed position . . . or whatever.' She laughed bitterly. 'You see . . ? I don't know what position you hold now – or if you're even in the army any more.'

'I'm still a captain and . . .' he paused and added with a secret smile, 'I am associated with the army. My present position is now more administrative than anything else.'

'I've never heard of anything like it.' Anne sat up in bed, drew both her knees up to her chest and wrapped her arms around them. 'Maybe that's what's wrong with us, John, there is no honesty, no talking left between us.'

'And all because I accepted a new position – a better-paid position, I might add.'

'No, no, not entirely because of that, but yes, that was part of it. You changed then, you became harder, cruel even, and unapproachable. And you fell prey to other vices as well, your smoking, and drinking and . . .'

'And what?' he asked, in a gentle whisper.

'And . . .' But to say it would be to admit it, and she was not prepared to admit it, even to herself, not yet anyway. 'And . . . nothing.'

Captain Lewis leant back, exhaling smoke towards the ceiling, and then stubbed out his cigarette in the crystal ashtray on the window-ledge. 'And you're not to blame. Not even in part?'

'I don't think so,' she said surprised.

'And when did your literary adventures begin?' he asked accusingly.

'I don't know . . . about, about . . .'

'Two years ago?' Captain Lewis finished for her.

'About then.'

'And when did you begin holding your literary evenings and attending classes in the afternoons? When did I start coming home to an empty house, or arrive home after a hard day to find a house full of people I didn't know, who sometimes condescended to talk to me, but only sometimes because, after all, I was nothing more than an ignorant army captain? When did all of this start, eh? Well, let me tell you – about two years ago, that's when, about the same time I changed my post and about the same time you stopped being every-thing a wife should be.'

'And what's that? What is everything a wife should be?'

'You should be here.'

'I should be here . . . I should be here! And what about you? Should you not be here once in a while?'

153

'Perhaps I would if there was something to come home to.'

His reply shocked her speechless, and in the dimness she saw him rise to his feet and stand with his back to the window, looking towards the bed. 'So don't talk to me about my drinking and smoking and whatever else you may suspect me of, without examining your own conscience and recognizing exactly how much you helped drive me to them.' And then he turned and walked from the room.

Anne Lewis remained paralysed staring at the door for a full ten minutes after he had left, the enormity of what he had said and implied sinking in only gradually. It had its own crazy logic to it and her guilty conscience helped fuel the effect of his argument, but even so the whole idea was monstrous. And it was only then that Anne Lewis realized just how big the gulf that separated them had become.

CHAPTER THIRTEEN

The year turned and the long hot summer slipped almost unnoticed into a mild mellow autumn; the only real change was in the softening of the colours and the deepening of the night skies.

The Lewis household seemed to have entered a period of uneasy peace. John Lewis had taken to spending more and more time at home, while Anne Lewis became more involved in what she told her husband was the literary society but which was in fact the Gaelic League. Under Maud Gonne's tutelage and direction she also began working amongst Dublin's poor, and this helped to keep her away from Clonliffe Road four nights out of five.

Katherine had not seen Dermot in months.

Her initial concern had turned first to anger, and then to hurt and despair and then back to a slow glowing anger again. It was obvious what had happened. He had simply grown tired of her and no longer wished to spend his free time escorting her round Dublin. For weeks she continued to believe this until finally, after a lot of soul-searching, she asked Mrs O'Neill about the young man.

'Ah, why would you be wanting to know?' the old woman asked with a gap-toothed grin.

Katherine who was drying the dishes, didn't look around. 'No reason; I just haven't seen him for a while. I was wondering had anything happened to him?' The very casualness of her question betrayed her concern.

'I didn't know you had any feelings for him?' Granny O'Neill said, watching her carefully.

Katherine managed to avoid answering the question. 'I used to see him at the tram stop every Wednesday afternoon when I'd be on my way into town,' she said. 'Sometimes we'd ride into town together, but he hasn't been there for the past few weeks – months now, it must be.'

Mrs O'Neill shook her head. 'No, nor you won't see him there for a few more, I reckon.'

'Why?' Katherine turned around slowly, her dark eyes opening wide. She continued rubbing automatically at the plate in her hands. 'Is there anything wrong?'

'Ach, he's fine now – well more or less,' Mrs O'Neill amended, 'he's a good strong lad and a few broken bones heal soon enough in the young.'

'Broken bones?' Katherine whispered.

'Aye, but sure did you not hear?' She looked up and saw the tense frightened look on Katherine's face, and answered her own question. 'No, I reckon not. Well,' she continued, 'he was set upon and beaten some weeks ago by a group of thugs. He was hurt quite badly.'

'How badly? Who were they? Will he be all right?' The questions tumbled out rapidly and Granny O'Neill raised both hands.

'One at a time, one at a time. I thought you weren't really interested? You're asking a lot of questions for someone who's not interested.'

Katherine's eyes hardened. 'Is he badly hurt?' she asked evenly, her eyes holding the older woman's.

'He had a fractured skull, his left arm was broken, as was his nose, and he had a few cracked and broken ribs.'

'My God,' Katherine breathed.

Mrs O'Neill nodded and crossed herself. 'It was only by the mercy of God that he survived,' she said.

'But who did it – and why?' Katherine exclaimed.

'Well, Dermot says that there were three men, and when they were finished with him, he says he's sure one of them gave him a warning to stay out of Monto.'

'Monto?' Katherine squeaked in surprise.

'Aye, Monto, the red-light district,' Mrs O'Neill exclaimed. 'It seems Dermot was doing an article on the conditions in Monto . . .' She grimaced and shrugged.

'Sure, all he had to do was to come and ask me; I'd have told him. But anyway,' she returned to her story, 'one of them tells him to stay away from Monto, a warning like, so it looks as if they were flash-house bullies out to protect their employer's money. I suppose it's bad for business to have a reporter – even a junior reporter – snooping around.'

'And where is he now? At home? I don't suppose I could visit him there? His family wouldn't accept me.'

'Yes, he's back home now, and no, I don't think it would be proper for you to visit.'

Katherine sighed. 'No, I thought not,' she whispered. 'Can I get a message to him?'

The cook nodded. 'I'll be seeing him shortly . . .'

'Tell him . . . tell him to get well soon.'

Mrs O'Neill nodded, smiling kindly. 'I'll tell him that.'

It was only later, when Katherine sat down to record the day's events in her diary, that she realized that she did actually have feelings for Dermot, and only then did she care to acknowledge the true nature of those feelings.

As October moved towards November and the Indian summer faded, Captain Lewis once again met the man he knew only as the brigadier. He was sitting at his desk on the top floor of the GPO, indexing the files he had prepared on various suspect people and organizations, when the door suddenly opened and the slight dark man stepped in, closing it quickly behind him.

Captain Lewis went to stand up but the brigadier waved him back into his seat. The brigadier was dressed in his usual oatmeal-coloured tweeds and carrying his silver topped cane.

'I wasn't expecting you . . .' Captain Lewis began, 'I sent on a report earlier in the week.'

'I've read it,' the brigadier said brusquely. 'Your findings are excellent and your suggestions sound. Some of the names of possible agitators on your list we have

157

already gathered through other sources, and we can now confirm them as definite troublemakers; some of those are on the staff in this building. That list will be on your desk in a day or two.'

'Do you want me to act on it?' Captain Lewis automatically shuffled the papers on his desk to bring up the personnel sheets. Since taking on this job a little over two years ago, he had personally compiled a dossier on every employee working in the post office, from the Secretary to the humblest clerk.

'That is not my decision,' the brigadier said fussily, brushing lint from his tweeds, 'but I will be recommending that the men be allowed to remain here where they can be watched. If we allow them to go, then it will mean setting up another operation or multiple operations to keep them under surveillance.' He slipped his hand inside his coat and took out a small oblong case, from which he produced a pair of silver pince-nez. Captain Lewis was surprised; he hadn't known the brigadier wore spectacles – but then he knew very little about the man. When he had first been approached in the bar of the Imperial, he had attempted to check up on the man through the army and police intelligence services. After several fruitless weeks of inquiries, he had given it up. The brigadier was known, both in the army and police, but he took his orders and acted out of London, and seemed to be answerable only to London and at the very highest levels.

The sharp-faced man took out a sheet of paper and shook it open. 'It was surprising to discover how many of those employees with question marks over their allegiance and loyalties belonged to the Gaelic League,' he said slowly.

'It purports to be a non-political organization,' Captain Lewis said, pulling the folder he had compiled on the Gaelic League from his drawer, 'although naturally some of its members have certain political motivations.'

'Its principal aims are to revitalize the Irish culture,' the brigadier said, looking out over the edge of his spectacles at the captain, 'and its president – what's his name . . .' he glanced down at his paper.

'Hyde,' Lewis supplied.

'Hyde, that's the fellow; well he says he wants the de-anglicization of Ireland.'

'But he also insists that the movement is non-political; that it is merely a society promoting the Irish culture – language, dress, dance, history and music.'

'You're not defending this fellow are you?' the brigadier snapped.

'No, sir!'

The brigadier continued looking at him for a few moments and then folded the page and put it away. 'You have looked into this movement?'

'Yes, sir!'

'Well . . ?'

Captain Lewis pulled open the file. There were a score of sheets inside peppered with his neat precise handwriting. 'The society was founded in 1893, principally by Douglas Hyde, a Protestant of Ascendency background; Eoin MacNeill, a civil servant and a cleric, a Father Eugene O'Growney, a professor of Irish at Maynooth College. They have a newspaper called . . .' he paused and pronounced the Irish words carefully, 'called "*An Claidheamh Soluis*", which translates as the "Sword of Light" . . .'

'I know what it means!' the brigadier snapped.

'Its membership, which has been growing steadily since '93, is composed of Protestants and Catholics, nationalists and unionists, and there are English members also. There are Gaelic League branches all over the country, as well as in England and America.' He glanced down at the file again. 'Last year it held a . . . a *tOireachtas* . . . a sort of festival of Irish culture. It was well attended.' He closed the file. 'It has also been campaigning to have us – I mean the post office here – accept letters addressed in the Irish language.'

'You don't seem to be overly concerned about this organization?'

159

'Cranks, the lot of them. It's fashionable now to have a few words of Irish, to speak of the culture and quote from the legends. I've sat in the bar in the Imperial and heard two officers in the Lancers discussing the legend of Cucuhulain.'

The brigadier's icy stare finally quietened the captain. The small man continued to regard him for several minutes in silence, the fingers of his right hand absently brushing his knee. Eventually, he straightened and said, 'I find this attitude of yours very disturbing, Captain Lewis, very disturbing.'

'Sir?'

'You are no doubt aware of the GAA, the Gaelic Athletic Association.'

'Yes, sir.'

The brigadier leaned forward, placing both hands flat on the desk. 'And you are aware how this organization has developed?'

'I'm not sure . . .'

'Ostensibly an association for the promotion of Gaelic games, it is now a front for the Irish Republican Brotherhood! Surely you knew that, captain?'

'Yes, sir,' Captain Lewis said quietly.

The brigadier nodded his head and sat back. With his eyes half-closed and his lips pursed, he looked like a snake about to strike. 'And what do you know of the GAA, this Gaelic Athletic Association, captain?'

John Lewis pulled out another file, and suddenly the brigadier slammed his hand down flat on the desk. 'Dammit, man, do you have everything written down?'

'Yes, sir.'

'And what would happen if the material were to fall into the wrong hands?'

'It's locked up in my safe every evening, sir. If there is material of a particularly sensitive nature, I take it down to Dublin Castle myself, and then destroy any copies. I try not to keep dangerous or incriminating material in here.'

'Carry on, captain, carry on.'

'Yes, sir, thank you.' He glanced down at the file, and then looked over at the brigadier. 'The GAA was founded in November of 1884, with the principal aim of promoting and encouraging home-grown Irish games, and discouraging those of an English nature. Its members are bound by a set of rules which forbids them taking part in English games, and will not allow members of the army – even Irish-born soldiers – nor constables to become members. Anyone found even watching an "English" game is immediately expelled from the organization.' Captain Lewis glanced up at the brigadier, but the man was staring blankly at the ceiling.

'Continue,' he said.

'Presently, some of the GAA Clubs would seem to be run by the IRB, and it is more than likely that their members are being trained and disciplined by them.'

'Likely!' the brigadier snorted. 'I was at Parnell's funeral in '91, and I saw that GAA guard of honour with their hockey sticks . . .'

'Hurley sticks – camans, I believe they're called.'

'They were carrying them like rifles,' the brigadier continued, ignoring the interuption. 'What we now have, captain, is an organization of fit and dedicated young men who are loyal to the Irish cause. And you can be damned sure, captain, that those men are well versed in the use of arms. And now we have this Gaelic League; well, mark my words, captain, it's the same thing in another guise. If and when the revolution comes to this land, you'll find a lot of the prime movers and many other participants will have been involved either with the GAA or the League.'

Captain Lewis nodded, deciding to stay quiet.

'Now I want it watched. There is also a literary movement afoot, which is closely linked with this league. The leading lights of this are a fellow called Yeats, William Butler Yeats, a Lady Augusta Gregory and a Miss Maud Gonne. They may seem to be harmless, a poet, a pamphleteer and an agitato, but they can do more damage than an army if they try.' He lifted his pince-nez off his nose and slipped them into their case. 'But then I understand your wife is acquainted with these people, perhaps you should ask her about them, eh?' He stood up quickly and Captain Lewis rose with him. 'I've also come across some police reports on the recent death of a woman popularly known as the Madam,' he said smoothly. 'The police have connected it with the death of a pregnant prostitute some time ago since the women were known to have been acquainted. I think it would be unfortunate if there were any more deaths in Monto. Good day, Captain Lewis. I'll look forward to receiving your report in due course,' he said, and then closed the door behind him, leaving John Lewis staring at the polished wood, wondering at the reason for the man's visit in the first place. It was hardly to tell him about the GAA or the involvement of the IRB in the Gaelic League – was it?

His closing remarks then had been what he had come to say; he had wanted him to know that his wife was in a literary society. Or was it more than that? Was he telling him in a circuitous way that Anne was under observation? He wondered how much the brigadier knew about his personal life; did he also know how things stood between Anne and himself? He walked over to the window and stared down on to O'Connell Street, and realized that the little ferret of a man almost certainly knew everything about him.

And why the veiled warning about the deaths of two whores? Had it been a subtle warning or a threat?

He straightened up as he saw the dapper figure of the small man walk out between the pillars in front of the building and hurry across the street. The man stopped outside Clery & Co, and looked in the window; from across the street Captain Lewis saw the reflective sparkle of light, and knew the brigadier was looking at the display of Waterford Glass. The man turned to the left and strolled down O'Connell Street towards the Gresham Hotel. Lewis watched him curiously . . . and then he stiffened as an elegant lady hurried up beside the man and paused to talk with him.

Innocent enough perhaps, but as she joined the brigadier the captain had recognized her – Tilly Cusack – and suddenly a lot of things began to come clear.

CHAPTER FOURTEEN

Captain Lewis arrived home just after seven that evening. Katherine, who had recently finished setting the table, was surprised to hear him whistling in what seemed to be very good humour. She straightened up and smiled as he came into the room, his newspaper under his arm, his cigarette case in his hand.

'Good evening, sir. I didn't hear you ring.'

'I didn't ring,' he smiled. He looked down at the table and noticed that she had set only one place, and then looked over at Katherine for an explanation.

'Mrs Lewis is at a literary function . . .' Katherine began apologetically.

Captain Lewis nodded benevolently. 'No need to worry. You carry on there; I'll sit by the fire and read until dinner is served.'

'It will be another few minutes, sir,' Katherine said bending over to straighten the tablecloth. And then she stiffened suddenly, because as the captain had walked past her she could have sworn she felt his fingers caress her buttocks. She looked at him flushed and startled, but he was deep in the fireside chair, the paper spread before him as he struck a match to one of his foul cigarettes. He said nothing, and she wasn't sure, but she could almost have sworn he had touched her . . .

The captain ate a leisurely dinner and drank the best part of a bottle of wine. By the time Katherine came to serve the coffee, his humour, which had been good to begin with, had mellowed into an all-embracing geniality.

He was standing with his back to the fire when she entered the room, balancing the silver tray in one hand while she opened and closed the door behind her. There was a thick pall of smoke hanging just below the ceiling, which swirled and eddied as she entered, and Katherine immediately felt her throat dry and her eyes begin to water.

'I'll take coffee here, Katherine, if you please.' He indicated the side table beside the high-backed winged leather chair.

'Yes, sir.'

She began to transfer the cup and saucer from the tray to the table, but the Captain waved a hand. 'There's no need; leave them on the tray.' He watched as she bent to pour his coffee, and she was aware of his eyes on her, conscious that the material of her dress had tightened across her buttocks and that the swell of her breasts was prominent as she leaned forward.

'You're a very lovely girl, do you know that,' he said suddenly, softly, and Katherine felt her throat tighten and the muscles in her stomach began to flutter.

'So you've said, sir,' she whispered.

'Have I?' He sounded surprised.

'Often.' She knew if she looked up now she would see the hungry look in his eyes, that strange wanting she had glimpsed on several previous occasions. She added a single spoonful of sugar and then a tiny drop of hot milk to his coffee.

Captain Lewis drew on his cigarette. 'You know, I've been married to Anne for . . . for seven years – more! – and I don't think she knows how I like my coffee.'

'I'm serving your coffee most days, sir,' Katherine said quietly.

Captain Lewis sat down, his eyes on Katherine's face, trying to catch her eyes. He lifted his cup and held it to his lips. 'Are you happy here, Katherine?' he asked softly.

The question took her by surprise. 'I . . . I don't know . . . I suppose so. I've never really thought about it,' she said.

'But you're not homesick?'

'Not now. I was at first, but not any more.'

165

'Would you go back home?' he asked, turning away from her and staring into the fire.

She thought about it for a moment. 'I'm not sure; I don't think there's anything for me to go back home to.'

'But you have family, mother, brothers, sisters,' he persisted.

'I've no sisters,' she said automatically, wondering where his questions were leading, recognizing that he was well on the way to being drunk. 'I don't think there's anything there for me,' she said quietly, 'my father was quick enough to get rid of me when he had the opportunity.'

'So you'll stay here?'

'If I can.' She thought of something and a sudden note of alarm entered her voice. 'You're not thinking of letting me go, are you, sir? I mean, my work has been satisfactory?'

He waved a hand in the air. 'Yes, yes, more than satisfactory, I understand. No, you need not worry yourself on that account; it's merely my idle curiosity.' He finished his coffee and Katherine poured him a second cup, without his asking. He smiled his thanks and then indicated the chair opposite. 'Please . . . sit.'

Katherine smiled and perched on the edge of the opulent leather chair. It cracked, then groaned and sighed like a human person beneath her weight. Even though she and the captain had chatted like this on several previous occasions – and always when the house was empty – she didn't think she would ever get used to the idea of a mere maid conversing with the master of the house. But it lent their conversations a certain air of mystery; it was part of their secret.

'Coffee?' he asked, touching the pot with the back of his hand. 'It's still warm and there's another cup in it.'

She shook her head quickly. 'No. Thank you, really. I don't like coffee.'

Captain Lewis nodded and sat back into the chair. He watched her for a few moments, pulling hard on his

166

cigarette. Because he was so far back in the leather chair, the wings threw his face into shadow, and the red tip of the cigarette looked like an eye. 'Tell me, Katherine,' he said suddenly, 'what would you most like to do? In the future, I mean. Will you marry?'

Katherine shrugged. 'I don't know . . . I don't think so.'

'Is there no young man back in England waiting for you?'

She shook her head. 'I've never had a suitor.'

'And there's not much chance here, eh? Well, look,' he leaned forward, his elbows resting on his knees, looking straight into her face. 'I know Mrs Lewis and I insisted that you have no gentlemen callers when you first arrived, but since then . . . well, you and I have come to know one another in a very special way. I know you can be trusted. So if you do find a young man, come to me and I'll see what I can do to smooth things over.'

'But what would Mrs Lewis say?' Katherine breathed.

John Lewis smiled gently. 'Well, let it be our little secret for the moment. And if anything happens and she does find out, you can always say you had my permission.'

'Well . . . thank you . . . thank you very much.' She dropped her eyes and looked up at him again. 'You really are very kind to me, Captain Lewis.'

There was a long, almost embarrassed silence while Lewis continued to stare into Katherine's face. She met his gaze squarely and, although Katherine could usually outstare most people, she was the one to break contact this time. It seemed so . . . so intimate. The captain finally disturbed the silence by sitting back into the chair's shadow. 'If you weren't in service, what do you think you would like to do?' he asked.

'I think I would like to run a tea-room,' she said immediately.

He looked surprised. 'Why for heaven's sake?'

Katherine shrugged. 'No reason.'

167

'And how long do you think it will take you to achieve that goal?'

'I don't expect I ever will.'

'And why's that?'

'The wages in service aren't very high,' she said with a cheeky grin, 'I would never be able to afford it.'

Captain Lewis laughed, the sudden sound startling her. 'That's one of the things I like about you, young lady; you're not afraid to speak your mind. But what you need is backing,' he said seriously, 'someone prepared to put up the money. What do you know about running a tea-room for that matter?'

'Well, I worked in a tea-room in Blackpool, I know how they function, how to order, and set table.'

'Do you not think Dublin has more than enough tea-rooms?' Captain Lewis said slyly.

'Ah, but I'm talking about real English tea-rooms.'

Captain Lewis nodded, smiling. At last he had found the key to the girl, and all that he needed to do now was to reel her in. But she would have to be played gently. The slightest mistake and she would bolt. He knew that she was already sympathetic to him; he could see that in her face and eyes, and in her movements and the little things she did – like milking and sugaring his coffee, without asking. But to entice her to bed, she would have to be grateful to him, willing to repay him and his trust with the only coin she had available.

John Lewis leaned forward and tossed his cigarette into the fire. 'What would you say if I were to offer to finance it for you?' he said softly.

'I beg your pardon!' For a moment Katherine was stunned, but she recovered herself quickly. 'Why?' she asked bluntly. 'Why should you do that for me? What for?'

Her questions took him aback, and he stared open-mouthed at her for a few moments. 'Why?' he asked quietly.

The maid nodded decisively. 'Yes, why? And if you did, what would you want in return?'

Captain Lewis sat back in the chair and steepled the fingers of both hands before his face. 'Direct and to the point; I told you that's what I like about you, Katherine. You're direct, and you're honest too. What would I want in return? Well, my investment of course, plus a percentage of the profits also. I have – shall we say – certain monies which I would prefer not to bank in the normal fashion . . .' He saw the sudden hooding of her eyes and added quickly, 'legitimate monies, of course.'

'I'm not sure I understand,' Katherine said slowly.

'Well, there would be no need for you to understand. I would lodge money at regular intervals to your shop's account, which I would then draw upon at a later date.'

'But this would all be legal?' Katherine persisted.

He nodded sincerely. 'Completely.'

'Well then, sir, I hope you don't mind me asking you where the money will be coming from. Because I don't think I could do anything that might be illegal.'

'Smart girl,' Captain Lewis nodded. He had her, she was his; she was already thinking of the shop as hers. He had to be careful now. She was not stupid; she would recognize a lie. 'Shall we say that I am paid odd amounts by certain government departments for various services which I perform for them.'

'But why . . .' and then realization dawned. 'Ah, of course, your unofficial position . . .'

Captain Lewis raised his hands, silencing her. 'That's enough. Let us leave it at that, shall we?'

Katherine sat back into the chair and thought about it for a moment. She felt sure she was missing something – something important – and it wasn't anything he had said, but rather what he had left unsaid. She shook her head slightly; she would think about it later. 'But you still haven't answered my first question,' she said at last.

'And what was that?'

'I want to know why you would do this for me – for someone you barely know.'

'Because . . . because I like you,' he said cautiously. He pulled out his cigarette case and was about to light up, when he thought twice about it. He tapped the Turkish cigarette on the back of the silver box and stared into the fire. He looked up and found Katherine regarding him, her eyes intent. 'Look, you're a clever girl, Katherine, too clever to remain a maid for the rest of your life. You deserve better. I would like to give you that chance. It would also be the perfect investment for me.'

'I'm overwhelmed. You're a very kind man, Captain Lewis,' Katherine said softly, shyly, although somewhere at the back of her head she still felt uneasy.

'So, the offer stands – I will set you up in your own business as a proper English tea-room. The business will be yours, and yours alone, and my only connection with it will be the monies which I will pay into the shop account.'

'And what would you take in return?'

'Half of all the profits. If you agree, then I'll have my solicitor draw up the proper documents so that we'll know it's all legal and above board. So what do you say, eh?'

Katherine shook her head. 'I don't know what to say. What can I say – but yes, yes!'

Captain Lewis nodded, smiling. He had to admit that the idea sounded a very good one indeed, and he was almost tempted to do something along those lines. Like all good lies, there were enough elements of truth in it to make it plausible, and he only had to look at the girl's shining, trusting eyes to know that it had certainly served its purpose. 'Well now, before you get carried away, you should know that finding suitable premises for you may take a little time; location is very important of course.'

Katherine nodded happily. 'Of course.'

He stood up slowly and Katherine came to her feet before him. She was close enough to smell the wine on his breath. 'And, of course, you must say nothing of this to anyone, not Mrs O'Neill, and certainly not Mrs Lewis.'

170

'I'll tell no-one,' Katherine said very slowly. She suddenly felt very light-headed and was aware of a vague fluttering deep inside her.

'I know you won't,' Captain Lewis whispered, moving fractionally closer to the young woman. Her breasts brushed against his coat. He was about to continue when they both heard the front door close. Simultaneously, and without another word, they fell back into the roles of master and servant. When Anne Lewis entered the room a moment later, Katherine was busy clearing up the dishes, while Captain Lewis was deep in his newspaper, a thin cloud of smoke drifting over his chair.

CHAPTER FIFTEEEN

Katherine heard the argument clearly through the floor-boards. Although the words were dulled, the anger in both voices was clear. She quickly slipped out of bed and padded over to the chimney breast and pressed her head against the warm stones, listening.

'. . . too much time away from home . . .'

Anne Lewis murmured something and then she said quite clearly, 'What is there for me to come home to?'

'I am your husband.'

'You stopped being my husband some time ago,' Anne snapped, and Katherine found herself nodding; the captain had intimated that his wife was no longer interested in him. She wondered briefly if Mrs Lewis had a lover.

Her face was becoming warm and she moved her head, turning the left side of her face to the stone, but the rest of her body was beginning to shiver in the chill air. She made a quick dash to the bed to pull off the blanket, and wrapped it around herself and then hurried back to put her ear to the wall again. When she got back the captain was speaking.

'Look, we've had this conversation before . . . count-less times, and I'm sick of it. Just let it lie. You don't love me – you've made that perfectly clear . . .'

Anne Lewis murmured something which Katherine didn't catch, but the captain's reply was clearly audible.

'I'm afraid I can't believe that.'

There was silence for a while after that and then Katherine heard movement in the room below, and what sounded like a cupboard door slammed. She heard the captain speaking, but all she caught was the last word. '. . . going?' She heard the bedroom door slam shut and then there were footsteps – quick, angry steps – pounding down the stairs. And then the hall door slammed. Then silence.

Katherine darted to the window looking out on Clonliffe Road and, by standing up on her bed, she could just about peer down into the street below. She was in time to see a slim, dark figure hurrying up the road, a small hatbox swinging in her hand. She watched her until the woman turned to the left and disappeared out of sight.

She sat back down on the bed, feeling her head beginning to pound. Had Anne Lewis just left her husband? Just what had happened? Without really realizing what she was doing, she pulled her coat on over her nightdress and opened the door of her attic room. She stood in the doorway for a moment, hesitating, wondering what had happened downstairs, wondering whether she should go down and offer to help or whether to pretend not to have heard anything? Eventually curiosity got the better of her and she crept cautiously down the single flight of uncarpeted stairs.

The main landing was dimly lit with two gas globes at the far end, one at the top of the stairs and one between the Lewis's bedroom and the guest room. They had been turned low and gave off a faint cream-coloured glow. There was no other illumination except for a thin bar of light beneath the Lewises' door. Katherine padded along the landing and stood outside the door, her coat clutched in one hand, the other half-raised to knock. She pressed her ear against the smooth wood; there was no sound from within, and the ticking of the grandfather clock in the hallway below sounded almost ominously loud. She heard sheets rustling as if someone had turned over in the bed, and something clunked on to the floor. She stood with her ear pressed to the door for a few moments longer but heard nothing more and, gradually becoming aware of the night chill, she began to pad silently back towards the stairs.

A long rectangle of light sliced through the shadowed

landing, shocking her motionless. 'What are you doing here?' Captain Lewis's voice was cold and hard.

Katherine turned slowly. 'I'm sorry . . . I heard noises . . . I just wondered if everything was all right.'

He remained standing in the doorway for a few moments longer, the light behind him throwing his features into shadow. And then his shoulders slumped. 'Yes, yes . . .' He stepped away from the door and showed her the room. She noted the rumpled bed and the wardrobe door swinging open, and clothes lying scattered on the floor. 'Well, no,' he said quietly, 'everything is not all right.' He took a step into the room and Katherine followed him, looking around in wonder.

The room was a mess. As she had seen from the doorway one of the wardrobe doors – Mrs Lewis's – was open, clothes spilling out of it, and yet more clothes were scattered around the dressing table behind the door. There were shoes and boots lying on both chairs, and the window seat held two rather large suitcases, both of which were empty.

The captain meanwhile had crossed the room, and brushing off some odd shoes from one of the easy chairs sat down. He watched the maid closely, and, despite the outward expression of pain and hurt, his eyes were bright and sparkling and there was a twitch in his fingertips. 'My wife has left me,' he said quietly, with no inflection in his voice.

Katherine murmured sympathetically, looking around the room. 'Is there any reason?' She turned back to the captain, feeling her heart go out to him. What must he be feeling now? Even though his relationship with his wife was not a happy one, to have her suddenly walk out in the middle of the night must be devastating.

'It's been coming for quite a long time,' he said. 'My wife finds she has more time for her other pursuits than she has for her husband . . .'

Katherine wandered around the room, automatically

174

picking up the clothing and gathering up the shoes. The coat she had thrown on over her nightdress hung open, and the captain found he could clearly see the shape and swell of her breasts through the thin cotton as she bent over.

'Will Mrs Lewis be back?' she asked suddenly, straightening up and catching the captain's rather obvious stare. 'I mean where will she spend the night?'

He bent his head quickly, spreading his fingers and examining them. 'I'm not sure. She has plenty of friends.'

Katherine crossed to the dressing table and straightened the drawers, and then began to fold the articles of clothing and return them to their proper places. 'I'm sure she will come back, sir . . .' Katherine began. In the tinted mirror she saw the Captain rise from the chair and walk across the room towards her, his silk dressing-gown swishing gently but his bare feet making no sound on the carpeted floor. She forced herself to continue speaking normally. 'I mean in a day or two, I'm sure . . .' And then the captain was behind her, and his large hands were on her hips.

'Sir?' she whispered, her throat closing.

'I think this is why you came down here, isn't it?' he murmured, his breath warming her ear. One hand moved forward and up across the flat of her stomach towards her breasts, while the other continued down across her lower belly and on to her groin.

She twisted her head slightly to look up at the captain but she found she couldn't answer his question. Not truthfully, anyway.

John Lewis bent his head forward, and his lips touched hers briefly. He could feel the physical pounding of her heartbeat beneath her breasts, and he suddenly became aware that she was shivering slightly. 'You're cold,' he whispered.

She shook her head. 'No.'

'You're shaking,' he protested.

'But not with cold.'

The captain moved suddenly, stooping and sweeping her up into his arms, and she clung tightly to his neck. He carried her to the bed and gently – almost delicately – laid her down on the rumpled covers, and then he bent over her and kissed her deeply. He felt her stiffen in resistance, her body becoming as hard as a board, and then she relaxed and responded.

'Why did you come down here?' he asked again. He was still standing on the floor, leaning over the bed, supporting himself with both arms either side of the girl, his face inches away from hers, his breath warm on her face.

'Because . . .' she said.

'Because?'

'Because, I knew you would be here . . .'

'And alone?'

Katherine nodded. 'I knew,' she finally admitted. She pushed herself upright on the bed, allowing her coat to fall back off her shoulders, and then began to fumble awkwardly at her nightdress, but the captain shook his head fractionally.

'Let me.' He reached over and turned down the gas lamp, until the warm golden light diminished to nothing more than a deep red glow, giving the room a dusky mysterious air.

Katherine, meanwhile, slid quickly between the sheets and found they were still warm from the heat of Mrs Lewis's body. It sent a shiver through her entire frame, face to toes.

And then Captain Lewis lowered himself into the bed beside her. Katherine turned towards him, reaching out tentatively, and then gasped as her hands encountered his naked body.

'You still haven't told me why you came?' he persisted.

'Because I wanted to,' Katherine said fiercely, aware now of the desire building up inside her, 'Because I needed to.'

Captain Lewis reached out and caressed her breast

176

through the thin material of her nightdress. 'You're a strange girl, Katherine Lundy,' he said quietly. 'And I can tell you now that I wanted you from the first moment I set eyes on you.'

'Truthfully?'

'Truthfully.' His hands were on her body now, rolling up her nightdress and she eased herself upwards to help him. She raised her arms as he pulled it over her head and tossed it on to the floor. Captain Lewis reached out then and pulled her close to him, her face against his chest, her breasts against his stomach.

'Do you love me?' Katherine asked suddenly.

'I do,' Captain Lewis said soothingly, and at that moment he almost believed it himself. 'And do you love me, my dear?'

Katherine nodded. 'Oh yes.' And she meant it with all her heart.

He kissed her again, his hands busy exploring her body. He touched her pubic hair and felt her freeze against him. 'What's wrong?'

'I've never . . . I've never made love to a man before,' she whispered.

Captain Lewis breathed a sigh, and smiled in quiet satisfaction. She was a virgin. The idea excited him immensely.

Katherine awoke first with a feeling of indescribable panic. She lay rigid, unaware of where she was or what had happened, aware only of the ache in her loins and the stiffness of her back and leg muscles. She sat up in bed, and the blankets fell away, and the waft of cold air rippled across her skin, raising goose-flesh, but bringing memories of the night flooding back. She turned and looked at the captain lying beside her, one arm thrown across his face. She found she could look at him dispassionately, without longing, without curiosity. She was surprised – indeed, almost frightened – to find that she had no feelings for the captain; she didn't feel any of the love she had professed so ardently the night before. It was as if the night's lovemaking had burned the desire from her.

Katherine threw back the covers – and then stifled a scream. The was blood on the sheets, a reddish-brown stain, with tiny black specks in it. And there was more on her legs and between them; she looked at the captain and saw patches of blood on his leg and belly near to her, and she had a sudden desire to vomit. She began to shiver, and the trembling set her teeth chattering while her insides felt as if they were about to burst. The full enormity of what she had done – what had happened – struck home.

She scrambled from the bed and gathered up her nightdress and coat and slipped from the room. As she ran down the landing to the back stairs, she could hear the clock in the hallway below chime seven o'clock. She was going to be late starting today.

Mrs O'Neill remarked on how quiet and subdued Katherine seemed through the day, but Katherine passed it off, saying that she thought she was coming down with a cold. And even when the cook told her that Dermot would meet her at the tram stop next Wednesday, it did nothing to cheer her up, but only seemed to deepen her gloom.

Katherine served the captain his breakfast before he went out to work and then his main meal when he returned home that evening. On both occasions he made no mention of the previous night, and indeed, seemed to be almost cool and slightly distant from her.

But later that night, when the house was quiet and Katherine had gone off to her bed, he rapped softly on her door and entered her room. 'We'll have to be circumspect,' was all he said by way of explanation, but it was all Katherine needed. All her doubts and fears, her regrets and feelings of loathing, vanished, and she threw back the sheets. His hands touched her body and his fingers, warm and probing, drew a terrible, terrifying pleasure from her. They didn't speak much and,

178

although she was still sore and tender from the previous night, Katherine discovered her desire and capacity for physical love seemed to have increased, and this time it was the captain who fell asleep in her arms, exhausted, while she was still willing for more.

And when she awoke in the morning he was gone, and once again she was consumed by feelings of self-loathing. The doubts continued all through the day and she promised herself that if he came again that night she would say no.

But when Captain Lewis crept into her attic room around midnight, she merely threw back the covers and opened herself to him without a word.

CHAPTER SIXTEEN

Anne Lewis returned four days later, early Wednesday morning. Katherine was cleaning out the fire in the bedroom, setting it up in readiness for the evening when she heard the front door bell. Wondering who was calling so early in the day, she glanced quickly around the room; it was swept and tidied and the bed was neatly made with clean sheets. Katherine had quietly disposed of the blood-stained sheet two days previously, praying that its loss would never be noticed. The doorbell clanged again, insistently this time. Katherine brushed off her hands and dashed down the stairs, pausing only at the long ornamental mirror to straighten her cap and apron before opening the door.

'You took your time!'

Mrs Lewis swept roughly past her, leaving Katherine standing shocked and open-mouthed at the woman's return. She had tried to avoid thinking about Captain Lewis's wife over the past few days, and only in the mornings, when the pangs of guilt were strongest, did she pause to consider seriously what she was doing.

Mrs Lewis strode down the length of the hall to the foot of the stairs and then stopped, turned and looked back at Katherine, who was still holding the door open. 'Well, what's the matter with you, girl?' She looked up the stairs. 'Is my husband in?'

'No, ma'am, he left earlier at his accustomed time.'

'I'm surprised he bothered to come home at all during my absence,' she remarked acidly.

'He has arrived home regularly at six-thirty every evening, ma'am,' Katherine said, closing the hall door.

'That's most unlike him,' Mrs Lewis said, turning to stare at the maid.

Katherine turned and busied herself with the door, almost imagining that Mrs Lewis knew what had been happening for the past few days, imagining that she could see beneath her clothing to the bruises and scratches that now marked her body and the teeth marks on her thighs and breasts. 'I think he was rather expecting you to return sooner,' she said finally.

Mrs Lewis didn't react to that but began to climb the stairs, calling back over her shoulder. 'Have Mrs O'Neill prepare me a light breakfast, and I'd like you to run me a hot bath.'

'Which would you like first, ma'am?' Katherine asked.

'Food first, then a bath, and then I think I'll rest for a while. My little break over the past few days was rather exhausting.'

Not half as exhausting as mine, Katherine smiled secretly.

Shabbily dressed, in the rough clothes of a labourer, a short, stocky man stood before Captain Lewis's desk on the top floor of the GPO, twisting his cap around and around in his hand. 'The house is owned by a Mr William Sherlock, who is a well-known figure in literary circles. As far as I can find out, the woman has been there for the past three or four days.'

Captain Lewis nodded and made a note on the plain sheet of paper before him. 'Anything else?'

The man shook his head.

'Right.' The captain stood up and stretched out his hand and the man shook it. 'You've done a good job. Now, I want you to continue watching the house ...'

'Begging your pardon, sir, but I thought you might, so I took the liberty of applying for some part-time labour, and I've been taken on as a gardener. It's not much, but it does allow me to get into the kitchen where I can pick up all the gossip from the cook.'

'Excellent, that is excellent news indeed. Find out all

181

you can about this William Sherlock and his lady friend, and meanwhile, I'll do some research of my own.'

'Yes, sir!' The man took a step back and saluted smartly. Before he had been invalided out of the army, he had been a sergeant in the Royal Highland Fusiliers and his loyalty to the Crown was above question. As such he made an excellent spy for the captain's small and very select group of 'gentlemen'.

When the man had gone, Captain Lewis returned to his desk to mull over what he had learned about William Sherlock. It would seem that almost a week ago a strange woman had come to his house in the middle of the night; she had been admitted without fuss, but with apparent satisfaction and surprise on Sherlock's part; and she had remained there until earlier this morning, when she had left as suddenly as she had arrived, and wearing the same clothing.

Captain Lewis was not surprised by the fact that it looked as if his wife had a secret lover; indeed he had suspected it on more than one occasion. And he was not going to be at all surprised if, when he returned to Clonliffe Road that evening, he found that his wife had come home. A pity; his nights of lovemaking with Katherine had been exciting and exhilarating, and he had enjoyed her eagerness to learn. He was going to miss her – but there were always other women, and from experience he knew the best part was already over. For Captain John Lewis had always found that the excitement of the chase rarely survived the satisfaction of the capture.

Katherine didn't recognize him at first; the walk was no longer as bouncy, his head wasn't held so high and, although he had always been thin before, she was shocked by his now wasted appearance. His cheekbones were prominent and his eyes sunken, creating an almost skull-like effect.

Dermot came up to Katherine, his head nodding in recognition, a slight smile playing about his lips. 'It's

182

nice to see you again.' His voice too seemed less certain, and was barely above a whisper.

She smiled a little uncertainly herself, unable to recognize in this person the determined, self-assured Dermot she had known. 'It's been a long time.'

He nodded weakly. 'I know.'

'You're well again,' she said, suddenly becoming obscurely annoyed with herself and with Dermot also. They were behaving like strangers – and then looking at the young man she realized that this was not the Dermot she had known. Or was it that she was seeing him in a different light – comparing him now with the masterful John Lewis, contrasting the boy with the man.

'Yes, I'm recovered thank you.' He turned suddenly, his shoulders stiffening, and then relaxed. 'The tram's coming.'

The tram journey into town was uncomfortable and seemed unusually long. Katherine's few attempts to make conversation fell flat, her questions were answered in monosyllables, and Dermot himself made no effort to initiate conversation.

They walked side by side – but without communicating – down the length of O'Connell Street, past Nelson's pillar and the GPO. They crossed O'Connell Bridge and turned into Westmorland Street, and then continued on around Trinity College. Katherine knew where they were heading: into St Stephen's Green, to their usual seat beside the lake. It was as if Dermot knew something had changed in the weeks he had been away and was attempting to recapture a little of their former intimacy. However, instead of walking directly up Grafton Street, he touched her arm – a feather touch that she sensed rather than felt – and nodded down Nassau Street. 'We'll go this way, if you don't mind; there are fewer people.'

Katherine shrugged and followed him down Nassau Street, and then they turned to the right up Dawson Street. She noticed that Dermot seemed unusually nervous, avoiding large groups of people – especially men –

183

and deliberately moving out of the way whenever he saw a strange workingman approach.

It was an overcast October day, with every promise of rain and St Stephen's Green was almost deserted. They made their way along the gravelled paths, and allowed the peace of the place to wash over them. Here, amidst the trees and bushes, away from the bustle of the city, something of their old easiness together seemed to return. Still without speaking they turned off the path towards 'their seat'. It was empty and, like old times, Dermot spread out a copy of the *Freeman's Journal* on the wooden slats of the seat for Katherine to sit on.

Dermot seemed to relax a little and finally reached out and took Katherine's hand. 'I'm sorry,' he said simply.

'For what?' she asked, surprised, turning and noticing for the first time the strange look in his eyes. It took her a moment to realize that what she saw was distrust. 'What's wrong, Dermot?' she asked.

He shrugged briefly, and then suddenly there were tears in his eyes.

'Dermot . . ?'

He shook his head and pressed the heels of both hands into his eyes. 'Nothing . . . it's just that . . . it's good to see you again. I missed you, Katherine. You'll never know how much I missed you.'

Katherine leant over and gently eased his hands away from his face, and then kissed him lightly on the lips. For a moment, in shock, he resisted, and then he returned the kiss, clinging to her with a passion that amounted almost to desperation. Finally, he broke away and holding both of her hands in his, he whispered, very softly. 'Thank you.'

'For what?' she asked surprised, and then she smiled. 'That's two questions of mine you have to answer; what were you apologizing for and why are you thanking me now?'

Dermot smiled shyly. 'I was apologizing for my

strange behaviour, and I'm thanking you for your . . .'
he shrugged '. . . for your understanding, I suppose.'

'But I don't understand,' Katherine said, 'but I know,
if you want me to know, you'll tell me in your own
good time. I'm just concerned about you, about what
happened and about how you are now.'

'Did Granny O'Neill tell you what happened?'

Katherine nodded. 'I couldn't believe it. When I heard
nothing from you, I was angry . . . hurt . . . rejected.
And then when she told me what had happened to you
. . . I felt so angry, so guilty, so helpless. And of course
I couldn't even go and see you.'

'But why not?' Dermot asked surprised.

Katherine grinned. 'I am a servant girl, and you're the
son of a respectable middle-class family; I don't think
they would like the idea of their son being overly
familiar with a domestic servant.'

Dermot was about to protest, but he realized the
truth of what she was saying. He stared out over the
waters of the still lake, now clotted about the edges with
fallen leaves. With Katherine beside him once again he
felt the fear and anxiety of the last few months beginning
to diminish – the fear that he had lost her. While he lay
in hospital and later at home, recovering from his
injuries, he had discovered how much he had depended
on Katherine, on her silent strength and resolution, and
common sense. His experience had left him terrified and
when he first left his bed he had jumped at every shadow
and every knock on the door. But that fear was beginning to pass, although he knew it would never truly
leave him. His greatest fear however – the fear that had
lingered until the last few moments – had been that his
enforced absence might have cost him Katherine.

'I was unconscious for ten days,' he said quietly,
surprising her. 'And when I did regain consciousness, I
was blind, blind for another two weeks. Granny O'Neill
doesn't know that – no one outside my family knows –
but I was blind for thirteen days after the attack, and
I've never been more frightened in all my life.'

'Oh Dermot . . .' she squeezed his fingers, blinking at the sudden sting of tears at the back of her eyes.

'I told you about the Madam, didn't I?' he began quietly, his eyes fixed on the centre of the lake, watching a single bedraggled duck make its way across the lake. 'Well, she's dead. The police say it was an accident, but I think – I'm convinced – that she was murdered, probably by the same person who killed that poor pregnant girl.

'Anyway, the attack happened two days after the death of the old woman in Summerhill. I was coming off the night shift and had just walked into Princes Street when I was struck from behind by something. I was knocked to the ground, and then I was struck again and again by . . .' he shook his head, '. . . well, I didn't know at first what was happening; I was tired and the first blows left me dazed. But they were kicking me. Three or four men beat me, and I dimly remember seeing another who stood in the background and watched them. They were big men, workingmen, and I could hear their heavy steel-toed boots striking me again and again, even though after a while I felt nothing. And what was even more frightening was that they did it without anger; they didn't shout or swear, or even attempt to rob me. It was as if it was a job to them. After a while they stopped, and then that other man, the one who hadn't taken part in the attack, came up and bent over me . . .'

There was such a long pause that Katherine turned to look at him. 'Did he say anything . . ?'

Dermot nodded quickly. 'Aye, he did. He said, "Stay out of Monto, unless you want to end up like Madam," and then he kicked me, in the centre of the forehead.' He touched himself above the eyes, and Katherine could still see the last pale shades of the purple bruise. He shrugged then. 'And that's it. That's all. When I woke up I couldn't see.'

He sounded so scared, so lost, that Katherine pulled

186

him to her and held him close, his head on her breast. 'It's over now, it's done with.'

But Dermot shook his head and straightened up. 'Don't you see, Katherine, they were watching me, watching me all the time, and for all I know may still be watching me now. Someone knew I was visiting Monto, someone knew about Madam, and if he knew all that then he probably knows what I was looking for. And to be quite honest, Katherine, I think it's whoever killed that poor girl back in May, and who then probably killed Madam to stop her from talking.'

'But you don't know that,' Katherine protested.

'There's no other explanation. Is there?' he demanded fiercely.

She shook her head slowly. 'So, what are you going to do?'

'There's nothing I can do,' he said decisively, with the first sign of conviction he had shown so far. 'I can't go back into Monto – and the only leads I have are there.'

'But you can't just let it go now, you can't just forget about it!'

'Why not?' He turned to look at her. 'Katherine, if I go back into Nighttown, they'll kill me, I'm sure of it.'

'And you've no idea who they were, or at least who the speaker was?'

He hesitated a fraction too long before replying, or perhaps it was the way his eyes shifted and slid off hers that she knew he was lying. 'No.'

'And you've still no idea of the identity of the man who killed that poor girl, or the old woman?'

His answer came quicker this time, but again Katherine sensed he was lying.

'So, what are you going to do now?' she asked him again.

Dermot shook his head. 'I don't know. My parents want me to leave the *Freeman*.'

'But you can't – you've always wanted to be a journalist – you told me so yourself,' Katherine accused. 'You got into all this only because you wanted to expose

187

the terrible state the poor of this city live in. No-one else seems to be interested in doing it. I thought this was going to be your crusade. Are you just going to toss all this aside?' she demanded fiercely.

'I've been doing a lot of thinking over the past few weeks, and I've made a couple of decisions. When you can't see, some things become clearer.' He grinned humorlessly. 'And you know, my father is right; there's no money – only pain – to be had as a reporter. The shop would be mine; I could go and work there.'

'You would hate it,' Katherine stated flatly. 'And you'd end up hating yourself for what you had done.'

Dermot nodded. 'Probably.'

An icy wind ruffled the surface of the water and Katherine shivered. She snuggled closer to Dermot for warmth. 'What else did you decide?' she asked.

'I decided I should be wed.'

'Oh!'

'And I'd like you to be my wife!'

Tilly Cusack spotted the captain as he strode out of the GPO at six o'clock and headed across the street towards the Imperial Hotel. From beneath the awning in the front of Clery's shop windows, she wondered whether or not 'accidentally' to meet him. She shivered then; a cold wind, with every promise of rain, had sprung up and gusted down the broad length of O'Connell Street, and that more or less decided her. It was going to be a cold, wet night. If she dallied with the captain now, she would earn more from him than she would tramping the beat for the rest of the night and, even more importantly, he would be done with her in an hour or so. If she was extra nice to him, he might even let her have the room for the remainder of the night.

Putting on her smile, like another piece of cosmetic, she stepped out from beneath the awning . . .

The captain had, in fact, spotted Tilly Cusack from his office a few minutes before. This was the first time he

188

had seen her since he had spotted her following the brigadier. He quickly pulled on his coat, bundled the more important papers into the safe, and dashed down the stairs in an almost unseemly haste.

He pretended to be pleasantly surprised when the smiling young woman stepped out into his path. 'Well, it's been a while,' he said, taking her arm and leading her back under the awning where their faces were lost in shadow.

'I thought you'd found someone else, captain,' Tilly Cusack said with an engaging smile.

'Sure you know there's only you, Tilly,' Captain Lewis said with a grin. 'Are you in a rush?'

'You know I've always time for you, captain.'

Captain Lewis smiled. He could guess why. He raised his eyes slightly, indicating the rooms of the Imperial which looked out over the street. 'Shall we . . ?'

Tilly smiled: she didn't need to say anything.

The foyer of the Imperial Hotel was luxuriously appointed, with a crimson thick-pile carpet on the marbled floor. At this time of day it was filling up with guests either heading out for dinner and the theatre, or just coming in after a busy day's shopping.

The clerk behind the desk didn't even blink when the captain asked for a double room for a single night. His blank gaze settled on Tilly for a single moment, but she knew he had marked her face and would expect his cut either in cash or kind at some later date. It was the accepted practice in a lot of hotels around the city.

The captain had hired one of the cheaper rooms at the back of the hotel, overlooking Earl Place and looking directly down on to the stables of the Dublin United Tramways Company. The room itself, although clean, was dim and dark and smelt faintly of horse manure – although Tilly wasn't sure if she was only imagining that.

She looked out into the laneway. 'I think I prefer the room we had last time,' she said with a smile, reminding him of their last meeting when he had taken one of the more expensive rooms at the front of the hotel.

189

'It's all he had left,' Captain Lewis said, turning the key in the lock and then walking around the room, opening the single wardrobe and peering in. 'I think they're almost full,' he added.

But Tilly had heard him ask for one of the cheaper rooms, and she knew for a fact that the Imperial was nowhere near full; most of the street girls knew the guest quota of the large 'hotels by heart. It was their trade. She wondered why the captain had lied.

Tilly turned down the bedsheets and pressed both hands flat against them, and then put her face close to them, smelling them. It was one of the tricks the madam, Bella Cohen, had taught her, claiming that damp, unaired sheets had been 'the ruination of many a good girl'.

The captain sat down in one of the two, slightly shabby, easy chairs that came with the room, unlacing his boots and smiling at the girl. It was part of her ritual; first check the window, then the sheets, now she would look under the bed and then check the rest of the room. And only after that would she begin to undress.

But tonight was different. Instead of going through her usual routine, she went back and stood by the window again, looking down into the laneway, watching two boys sweeping out the stables. 'I don't think I like this room,' she said softly.

'Well, I didn't ask you here to look at the wallpaper, or the view,' Captain Lewis said shortly.

Tilly turned around quickly, an automatic smile fixing itself to her face and she begun to unbutton the front of her dress. 'I'm sorry, I was only thinking out loud.' She undressed quickly and efficiently, knowing the captain wasn't interested in the sensuous strip-tease she performed for some of her other clients. Finally she stood wearing only her transparent shift and drawers. 'Well . . ?' she asked, cocking an eyebrow.

The captain stood up and stepped over to her, and his arms slid around her, pulling her close. Tilly responded and turned her face up to his, expecting to be kissed –

190

but suddenly one of his large hands was at her throat, squeezing. 'Scream, or even try to struggle, and I'll crush this pretty throat of yours.' His voice was very low, almost casual, but Tilly never doubted that the man was deadly serious.

He pushed her back on to the bed and then reached inside his coat and pulled out a service revolver. In the silence of the room the double-click as he pulled back the hammer was unnaturally loud. He pointed the gun at her head, holding the heavy weapon easily, without a tremor. 'You see,' he said conversationally, 'One of the reasons I wanted a room at the back of the house was because it would be secluded. Why, I dare say I could pull this trigger and no one would hear a thing.'

'For God's sake, Johnny, what are you doing?' Tilly whispered in a small voice. 'Why?'

'Why? Well girl, it's because I don't like to be betrayed . . .'

'I don't know what you mean,' she interrupted, and then suddenly he shoved the gun into her face, the huge barrel resting lightly against her top lip. She could smell the bitter, oily scent, and a single bead of crimson blood trickled down her chin where she had bitten into her lip.

'I'm talking about a small, slim, grey-haired man, with the manners of a dandy and the eyes of a snake. I'm talking about a man who knows too much about me. That's who I'm talking about. I'm talking about the brigadier.'

She began to shake her head and then winced as the front sight on the barrel cut into the flesh of her nose. 'I know a man who fits that description, but he's not called the brigadier.'

'Tell me what you know about him,' Captain Lewis demanded.

'I don't . . .' she began.

'I'll kill you if you don't tell me,' the captain said, his voice again dangerously casual.

'And he'll kill me if I do!'

'Well then, you'll have to decide which one of us is holding the gun to your head.' He saw the look in her eyes and added with a grim smile. 'And don't try to lie to me either. You've no idea how much I know about the man, and so you'll never be able to tell if I know whether you're telling the truth or not.'

'I know only a little,' Tilly warned him.

'I want to know it.' The captain stepped back and dragged the wooden chair over to the side of the bed, and sat down. He eased down the hammer on the gun, but still kept it pointing at her face.

Tilly scrambled further up on the bed, until her back touched the bare wooden headboard. She suddenly felt naked – though she was still wearing her shift and knickers – and, although she had been alone before with many unpleasant men, this was one of the few times she had felt truly vulnerable. It wasn't the gun – she knew the man wouldn't fire it, not in this tiny room – but he was dangerous and she could tell just by looking at him, that he would take great enjoyment in hurting her.

'Well?' Captain Lewis demanded.

'His name is Richard – that's all I know him by – Richard. I think he's English, or maybe he's English-educated, but his accent's strange. I met him a couple of years ago; I thought he was just another client I had succeeded in winning but, as it turned out, it was actually he who had picked me up. Before we could get on with the business he sat down, and at first I thought he was either very nervous or else just a talker. There are some, you know, who are just talkers?' The captain grimaced and waved the gun. 'Anyway, he said he'd been recommended to me by a very good friend of his – a Captain John Lewis – and then he gave me a very accurate description of you. He said you had been friends in the army and that he had just been posted to Dublin. But it was only when I actually admitted knowing you that he changed; it was almost as if he hadn't been sure he had the right person, and was just questioning me to make certain.'

'What happened then?'

'Well, he pulled a knife – no, more than a knife, a sword of some kind – out of his walking stick, and he placed the tip of it against my throat . . .' her fingers touched the hollow of her throat as she remembered, '. . . and then he told me that, if I didn't do what he said, he would kill me. And I believed him!'

Captain Lewis nodded slightly. 'And I've no doubt that he would.'

'He said he wanted me to report on my every meeting with you, on everything you did and said, and how you were dressed and what you ate. He wanted to know if you ever carried papers, or had personal letters in your pockets, how much money you usually carried on you, and whether I had ever seen you carrying a gun.'

'And you agreed?'

'He would have killed me.' Tilly said simply, and then she added with a wry smile, 'But to ensure that I did as he wanted, he produced some documents relating to my past which I'd rather the Irish police didn't get hold of. He told me if I didn't co-operate, he would pass on the information to the authorities.'

The captain returned the gun to his inside pocket.

'I'm sorry,' she said quietly, but the captain waved his hand, his eyes distant. 'You had no choice in the matter, obviously.'

'What happens now?'

'You continue on as before,' Captain Lewis said quietly, standing up to remove his jacket, 'except now, you'll tell him what I want you to tell him.' He pulled off his cravat and extracted the stud from his collar. 'This man has brought me nothing but trouble,' he said slowly. 'Because of him my army career has come to a sudden halt, I've had to take up a post I don't care for, and all this has caused a rift between my wife and me. He has a lot to answer for.'

'What will you do?' Tilly asked, but the captain only smiled and pulled off his shirt.

CHAPTER SEVENTEEN

The attic room was cold, but that wasn't the reason Katherine was shivering. She was sitting up in bed, with the blankets pulled around her and another wrapped across her shoulders, and she had her diary in her hand. Her fingers had gone numb with the chill of the room and she found holding the pencil rather difficult, but nevertheless she decided to do the figures one more time.

The last time her monthlies arrived had been on Saturday, the 1st October, as she knew it would. For as long as she could remember, they had never varied by more than one day. Therefore, she should have been due again on Friday, the 28th, or Saturday the 29th, at the very latest. It was now Saturday, the 12th of November. And no matter how she did the figures, they still came out the same way. Katherine was terribly afraid that she was pregnant.

She had made excuses to herself over the past two weeks, the same excuses she had heard her mother making when she thought she was pregnant. It was the weather; her mother had firmly believed that when the weather changed dramatically, either for the better or worse, then her monthlies would go astray. And sure enough, November was cold, bitterly cold. And she had started eating different foods – another of her mother's excuses – and she had also been bending over, picking up vegetables in the garden. Then she had been reaching high over her head, and had been carrying heavy scuttles of coal upstairs, more so than usual now with the cold, and she had . . . of course, was it any wonder her body's cycles had been knocked awry?

She knew all her mother's excuses by heart, but deep

down she also knew they were worthless, that she was in fact pregnant.

And she was terrified.

Mrs O'Neill watched Katherine carefully the following morning. The old woman was shrewd enough to know when there was something wrong, and equally tactful enough to say nothing. But Granny O'Neill hadn't been a midwife for over forty years without developing what she called her 'pregnant nose' – her sense for knowing when a girl was pregnant. Often she had known someone was with child, even before the person themselves knew. Watching the young girl moving about the kitchen, looking at the dark rings under her eyes and the too-bright touch of colour in her cheeks, she hoped that her instincts were wrong. But somehow, she doubted it.

'I suppose you'll be seeing young Dermot today,' she said suddenly, startling Katherine.

The girl shook her head. 'No, not today; one of his sisters was coming down with a cold when I was speaking to him last week, and he promised her he would stay in over the weekend and read to her.'

'Ah, but he's a good lad, a kind lad,' Granny O'Neill agreed.

Katherine nodded. Dermot was a good lad, he was kind and considerate and would make someone a fine husband. But did she want him as a husband? For all her impetuousness and sudden whims, there was an eminently practical streak running through her, and she knew that, if she was pregnant, then marriage to Dermot would be a very convenient solution. But would it? His family would ostracize him, as would the neighbours; his inheritance would, in all probability, be cut off, and his job would surely become untenable when it became known that he had married a servant girl. She wasn't sure if she loved him – she wasn't sure that she really knew what love was – but she did like him, and she liked him too much to use him in this way.

When he had proposed to her, she had been so shocked that she had been unable to answer. He had asked her to think about it, but he obviously expected an answer – a positive answer – this week.

Katherine smiled wryly. It looked as if the decision had been taken out of her hands; there was little chance of anyone marrying her if she was carrying someone else's child. Indeed, there was now little chance of her marrying at all. But that brought up the question of the captain – how was she going to tell him? And how was he going to react?

What were his feelings for her, she wondered. Her feelings for him were confused, loving him and loathing him in turn. When tidying up his bedroom that morning, she had stood for a long time staring at the bed in which the captain had taken her virginity, and her future. She was as much to blame, she knew. She had gone into the room knowing what could – or would? – happen; she had put herself and the captain in a situation where what transpired had been almost inevitable.

Strangely, she couldn't really remember the episode; all she retained were fragments, images – sensations rather – of touch and taste and smell, and then the pain, or rather a discomfort, a burning discomfort . . . They were her memories of that night.

And she wondered, yet again, how he would react.

If he really loved her then there would be little problem. He would support her and the child – their child – and they would set up that tea-shop as he had promised. But if he didn't . . . She shied away from the thought, but then forced herself to return to it. If he refused her, then she would be out of work, without a penny and no prospects. But he wouldn't be so cruel, so heartless. However, she hadn't any doubts that Mrs Lewis would send her away as soon as it became obvious she was pregnant, and that couldn't be more then a few months away.

Her mother would have to be told of course – or

would she? And then she realized that either Mrs Lewis or the captain – if things didn't work out – would almost certainly inform her parents. She wondered if she should tell her mother first . . . but that was something else to be shelved for the time being.

Katherine looked over at Mrs O'Neill; she must tell someone, and if she were going to tell anyone then perhaps it should be Granny O'Neill. She had caught the old woman watching her over the last few days, and on more than one occasion she had inquired about Katherine's health. The woman knew something was amiss, and Katherine had a feeling that her news would be no surprise to her.

And what of Dermot, what would he think, how would he react when he discovered that she had been sleeping with someone else? She bent her head and bit the inside of her cheek to stop the sudden sting of tears. Her few nights of pleasure were going to cost her dearly.

Anne Lewis watched the servant girl clear away the dishes after breakfast. Ever since she had returned from Sherlock's house she had felt there was something different about the girl, but she couldn't quite put her finger on it. Perhaps it was the way in which the younger woman seemed to avoid looking directly into her face, or the way in which she seemed almost too eager to do her bidding.

She looked at Katherine closely. The girl was pale this morning, apart from two spots of colour in her cheeks which seemed unnaturally bright and harsh. There were bags under her eyes, and the end of her nose was slightly red, as if she had been weeping. Anne Lewis wondered what could have so upset the girl – but then, she thought, servants were easily upset.

Still deep in thought she turned her attention to the pile of letters which Katherine had placed by her side during breakfast. She glanced through the white and cream envelopes, dividing them neatly into two sections, those to be read immediately and those that could wait

197

until later. One letter she set aside on its own. When it came to be opened, she paused, admiring the broad, elegant, copper-plate hand on the rich, cream, parchment-paper envelope, the most expensive the Junior Army and Navy Stores could supply. She had recognized William Sherlock's writing at once.

She lifted the long ivory-handled paper knife and tapped it against the paper for a few moments, debating whether or not to open it right now. She could guess what it was about: it would be concerning the few days she had spent at William's house in Ballsbridge on the south side of Dublin, and very probably begging her to return. She shook her head in exasperation; she had explained that she had come to him – and his house – only as a temporary place of refuge, a place where her husband couldn't possibly find her. She tapped the letter a final time and then slit it open.

Anne Lewis read it through with growing disbelief. Almost immediately after she had left, a bizarre catalogue of events had befallen him. First, the police had arrived to search the house, looking for stolen goods; they said they were acting on a tip-off that Sherlock was involved in receiving and disposing of items of jewellery. He had then been visited by a member of the army High-Command, who claimed they had information that Sherlock had been openly attempting to solicit off-duty soldiers for immoral purposes. His two dogs had been poisoned, and all his rose bushes – his prize-winning bushes – had been doused with oil and set alight. And then finally, yesterday morning a card had arrived, which said simply, 'Stay away from Mrs Lewis'. That was all, nothing else, but the threat was explicit. His letter finished by explaining how frightened he was and that, for the moment, he felt it would be best if they didn't see one another for a while.

It was unbelievable, absolutely unbelievable. Someone was deliberately harrassing Sherlock, conducting some sort of sick campaign to terrify the man. But that would require someone with a certain amount of authority,

198

someone with connections in the police and army. And Anne Lewis knew only one person of her acquaintance who fitted that description.

'You initiated such action against this man Sherlock, as far as I can see, with no just reason at all.' The brigadier pulled gently on his cigarette and stared across the desk into Captain Lewis's unblinking eyes.

'No, not without reason, sir.' Captain Lewis had never liked the brigadier; he considered him a small-minded man with small-minded values and little vision. He was a civil servant in uniform. And now that he had discovered the brigadier had been spying on him through Tilly, his animosity had turned to something approaching hatred.

The brigadier leaned across the desk and rapped the curved and decorated silver handle of his walking stick on the desk, the sound echoing around the small office like a gun-shot. 'I would be interested in hearing your reasons – except those of a personal nature, of course,' he added maliciously.

'Of course.'

'And I should add that it would probably distress me to discover you had diverted men from legitimate posts to hound this man Sherlock.'

'Sherlock is associated with this Gaelic League which you told me to investigate,' Captain Lewis said slowly, deliberately looking down at the papers on his desk. 'He regularly holds classes in Irish folklore and creative writing. He is associated with Yeats, Miss Gonne and Lady Gregory, and is influential with several of the Irish publishers. As a matter of routine, I detailed a man to watch him.' He finished and looked up at the brigadier, with a slight smile. He didn't add that it was this man who had brought him the report on the strange woman who had arrived in the middle of the night. He didn't add that subsequent investigation had also revealed the woman's identity beyond doubt.

'And that is all?'

'Yes, sir.'

'But these activities constitute more than mere watching, and I have made it quite clear, captain, that I do not want these people disturbed. I would like you to ensure that this sort of thing does not happen again. It attracts attention from all quarters, it wastes manpower and it is childish. You will please see to it that Mr Sherlock isn't bothered again.'

'Yes, sir, I will take the proper steps.'

'Good. Now . . .' The brigadier flipped over a page of his notebook, 'I have it on very good authority that Her Majesty is considering a visit to Ireland in the next year or so. It will, as you can appreciate, fall to us to ensure her safety during the visit.'

'Well, we have plenty of time,' Captain Lewis remarked.

'Indeed. Time enough to identify those likely to cause trouble . . .'

When Katherine had cleared away the dinner dishes, Captain Lewis and Anne sat down in the two easy chairs on either side of the fire, he with a copy of the London *Times* and she with a book which, the captain was surprised to find, was entitled *The Celtic Twilight* by William Butler Yeats.

Katherine served the coffee, glancing at Captain Lewis now and again, willing him to look up and acknowledge her presence in some way, but he didn't even blink in her direction. She was about to pour, when Anne Lewis indicated for her to go.

The door clicked shut, and the captain looked up from his paper. 'Ah, coffee . . . excellent.'

'I think the maid is frightened of you,' Anne Lewis remarked, pouring from the fine bone china into the matching cups.

'Oh, and why is that?'

'She was staring at you, as she set down the tray, almost as if she thought you might bite.'

He nodded non-committally, and picked up his cup,

and then set it down again to add milk and sugar. 'This is pleasant,' he said finally.

'What is?'

'This; just you and me sitting quietly together on a Sunday evening. We haven't done it for a long time.'

Anne Lewis smiled. 'It reminds me of when we were first married, d'you remember? We spent most nights just sitting together, or you would read to me from the paper, and I'd read you a little from whatever I was reading.'

'I remember,' he said softly.

'Whatever happened to those days?' Anne Lewis asked almost wistfully.

'We grew up,' Captain Lewis said simply.

'Grew up or grew apart?' Anne sat back into the high-backed winged chair and stared at John. 'You're not the man I married, you know that?'

He shrugged.

'But what has changed us?' Anne asked.

'Circumstances,' he said.

'And can we not change those circumstances?'

'You can't turn back the clock, Anne. We've got to make the best of what we can.'

In the silence that followed, the hissing, sizzling of the fire seemed to fill the room. They both watched the flames dance over the sap-filled logs until, finally, Anne asked, 'Why are you persecuting William Sherlock?' She was watching him carefully and saw the change in his expression. She added hastily, 'And don't tell me you don't know who Sherlock is, or that you don't know what I'm talking about. I know you do.'

'I'm not persecuting Sherlock,' Captain Lewis said slowly, 'I'm merely giving him a warning . . .'

'To keep away from me?'

He nodded.

'Why?' she asked simply.

'Because I don't want him seeing you, nor you him.'

'But why should it bother you? Are you afraid some of your fellow officers might hear about your wife

201

spending time with another man – why, even staying overnight with him? What would they think? I don't suppose it would make any difference if I told you that it was totally innocent; William Sherlock is a perfect gentleman. But of course it's all right for you to fornicate with every little trollop you set your eye upon and get away with it, but I'm to remain pure and virginal for you. Is that it?' she snapped, her voice rising.

Surprisingly, he shook his head.

'Well then, why?' she demanded angrily.

'Because . . . because I love you,' he said very softly, stunning Anne Lewis.

'You love me?' she said, her voice heavy with sarcasm.

'I love you, no matter what I do, no matter whom I'm with, I still love you, I still come back to you. And it is only because I love you that I've held back from killing that man with my bare hands. But I love you,' he repeated earnestly, 'truly I love you, and I'll do all in my power to keep you to myself.'

'By Christ, I think you believe it yourself. You don't love me,' Anne spat. 'I don't think you've any feeling left for me now. You think of me only as a possession, something to be kept for your own private use.'

'That's not true . . .'

'What is the truth?'

'The truth is, I love you.'

Her face pressed against the warm wood of the door, Katherine clearly heard John Lewis say, 'The truth is, I love you.'

Katherine fled to the kitchen, trying to quell the sudden urge to throw up. She hadn't heard all the conversation, but she had heard enough. The fear that had grown inside her over the past few days welled up in a thick, cloying, suffocating wave. All the fragile plans she had made during the day – all the plans which had counted on a willing and helpful Captain Lewis – had been shattered into so much dust.

There was no future for her now.

CHAPTER EIGHTEEN

As a cold and wet November drifted into a chill and icy December, Katherine still hadn't told anyone about her condition, but she realized she couldn't delay much longer. On numerous occasions she had attempted to speak to Mrs O'Neill about her situation, but something always seemed to intervene and the moment was lost. In any case, Granny O'Neill hadn't been at all well herself over the last month; a dry rasping cough had turned deep and chesty and spasms of coughing left her doubled up and gasping for breath. On more than one occasion Katherine had had to help her to a chair until the coughing fit passed and she could stand up again. She felt she couldn't really burden Mrs O'Neill with her problem while the old lady had troubles of her own.

She daren't tell the captain – she knew now how deep his feelings for her ran. She couldn't go home – she hadn't the price of the fare in the first place, and even if she did somehow manage to raise the money what sort of welcome would await her there?

So, there was no-one else to turn to – no-one but Dermot, that was.

On the afternoon of the 20th of December they met in Dublin's City Centre at the foot of Nelson's pillar, which had become their usual meeting place on Katherine's afternoon off, instead of the tram stop in Drumcondra, which they had decided was too conspicuous.

The day was cold and overcast with a chill wind sweeping down the length of the broad street and, although it was not yet three in the afternoon the light was already fading and the street lamps were beginning to glow. Katherine stood with her back to the iron rails that surrounded the pillar and looked down O'Connell

Street towards the bridge, and then turned to look at the GPO. With the lights burning behind the windows and the gas bowls glowing outside, the entire building looked warm and homely and almost inviting. She wondered if the captain was in his office – more than likely, she thought.

She spotted Dermot as he wove his way through the crowd and she stepped out from the pillar to meet him. And then she spotted the captain. He was just coming through the door of the GPO, head bent and deep in conversation with a small, stocky man. He looked up and their eyes met – briefly, just briefly – and then Dermot stepped up to her, taking her hand familiarly, and when she looked back the captain had vanished into the crowd. But she knew he had seen Dermot . . .

'Let's get some tea,' Dermot suggested.

Katherine shook her head quickly. Although she was frozen through and through, she knew if they went into the crowded warmth of a café, she would have to face him, to look into his eyes, and she didn't think she would have the nerve to tell him then. 'Let's walk for a bit,' she said and, before he could protest she walked away.

Dermot hesitated a moment and then he followed her, catching up with her in a few long strides and linking his arm through hers. 'What's wrong?' he asked, with a shy smile, 'Are you annoyed with me? I'm sorry if I kept you waiting too long.'

Katherine shook her head. 'No, I had just arrived,' she lied, 'I just don't feel like sitting down in a cafe just yet. Later perhaps. But I want to talk to you.' She looked at him quickly and saw the sudden gleam of interest in his eyes, and could almost feel the increased tension in his fingers. 'Dermot,' she added quickly, 'I haven't made any decision yet. I told you before, I think we're too young to make a decision like that.'

'Well, I don't think so,' Dermot said, disgruntled, 'when am I going to get an answer out of you?'

'I gave you my answer last week,' Katherine said

quietly, 'I told you then that I'd give you my answer when we were older, but ... but now things have changed. I think I can give you some sort of an answer now.'

'What do you mean – a sort of an answer?'

Katherine squeezed his arm. 'Wait awhile, Dermot, just a little while. Let me tell you in my own way.'

They passed the tall statue of Daniel O'Connell, the Liberator, which gave O'Connell Street its name, and turned right on to Bachelor's Walk beside the river. The wind was icy, bitter and cutting, and Katherine felt the chill dig deep into her thin clothing and set her insides shivering. Her fingers, already numb, were now actually painful, and her ears and nose began to hurt so much she was afraid she was going to have a nose-bleed.

'Katherine, love, this is foolishness,' Dermot said, his teeth beginning to chatter.

But Katherine ignored him and merely dragged him across the road so that they were now walking along the riverside edge. Katherine's numb fingers trailed along the edge of the waist-high wall which grew progressively higher as they neared the metal bridge. Dermot shook his head in exasperation and trudged along beside her.

Finally, Katherine turned off the quayside and on to the metal Ha'penny Bridge. This was a hump-backed metal bridge that spanned the River Liffey midway between O'Connell Bridge and Essex Bridge. Dermot had once told Katherine that it was called the Ha'penny Bridge because a toll of one half-penny had once been charged for the privilege of the short cut. Half-way across the bridge Katherine stopped and looked out through the metal rails and down into the murky water below. It was slow and sluggish, and filthy with the city's waste.

'If you were looking for privacy we could have gone up to the Green,' Dermot said shrewdly.

'It would be closed by now,' Katherine remarked absently, 'you told me it closed at sunset. No, I wanted

205

it to be both private and public,' Katherine said looking quickly at him.

'What do you want to be both private and public? You're full of mysteries today.' Her unusual attitude was beginning to worry him. 'Is something wrong?'

She looked down into the dirty water; the oil lamps shining on the sludge lent it colour and the tall masts of the sailing ships down beyond O'Connell Bridge bestowed a superficial glamour which it certainly didn't deserve. She looked back at Dermot, but the grey dusk was beginning to claim his face – already it appeared as little more than an indistinct, grey smudge.

She had rehearsed what she was going to say so often now that she knew it by heart, but when the moment came all she said was, 'I'm pregnant, Dermot.' She spoke the words very softly, her voice cracking. She repeated it, realizing that she was also, in some obscure way, finally admitting it to herself. 'I'm going to have a baby.'

For a moment Dermot didn't react, and she thought that perhaps he hadn't heard her. 'I said . . .'

'I know what you said,' Dermot said, turning to look down the river, now wreathed in rising foul-smelling grey fog.

'Well . . ?' she whispered.

'Well, what?' he asked, sounding puzzled, 'Well, what do you want me to say? Congratulations?' She heard the hurt and anger in his voice, but her keen ear caught something else too, something that sounded like fear. 'Do you know who the father is?'

'Dermot!'

He shook his head. 'I'm sorry, I shouldn't have said that. But I thought you might have been raped . . . attacked and struck unconscious . . . or something like that,' he finished lamely.

'No, nothing like that,' she admitted with a smile, glad that, in the dusk, he wouldn't be able to see it.

'You sound very calm about it,' he remarked.

'I've known about it for some while now,' Katherine said, 'all my crying and panicking is done now.'

'What do you want me to do?' Dermot asked, and for a moment Katherine wasn't sure if he was being sarcastic or not, but then she realized that he was asking a genuine question.

'I don't think I want you to do anything,' she said finally. 'I'm just telling you because . . .' she realized she couldn't really think of a reason why she was telling Dermot, and finished lamely, '. . . because I have to tell someone and you're the only one I can trust.'

'I'm sorry, you know that, I'm truly sorry,' he said, his voice distant, his gaze fixed further down the river. 'What are you going to do?' he asked finally.

The question took her by surprise, and she was forced to shake her head. 'I don't know,' she admitted, 'what can I do?'

Dermot slipped his arm through hers and led her across the bridge, and they turned to the left to bring them down on to Aston Quay and back on to O'Connell Bridge. 'Do they know back at the house?' he asked.

Katherine took long enough about answering so that Dermot knew something was amiss. 'What is it?'

'No-one knows.'

'Not even Granny?' Dermot asked.

'No.'

'Perhaps you should tell her, she would know what to do,' he suggested.

'I really don't want to trouble her; she hasn't been well recently.'

'Well, you've got to tell someone, before your condition becomes obvious . . .' he paused, considering. 'When will that be?'

Katherine shrugged. 'I should start to show sometime early in the new year; February, I think, sometime around then, anyway.'

Dermot shook his head, more in exasperation than anything else. Katherine found herself disliking more and more his calmly clinical approach to her problem. Granted, it had nothing to do with him, but he had professed to love her. But she knew what the promises

207

of men were worth; that was a lesson she had already learned – and at what a cost. The captain had professed to love her, and there had been the promise of the shop, that he would support and take care of her, and yet ever since he had taken her virginity he had barely spoken to her, and seemed to be more than reconciled with his wife. Perhaps she was misjudging him, but somehow she didn't think so.

'What do you think will happen if – when – I tell?'

'You'll probably be sent home,' Dermot said simply, and Katherine found she didn't hear any trace of regret in his voice. He was simply stating a fact; like Captain Lewis, it looked as if he too had lost interest in her.

'I can't go back home.'

Dermot shrugged. At O'Connell Bridge, instead of turning right into Westmorland Street and then around by Trinity College, he continued down the quays, and Katherine found herself remembering the last time they had come down this way.

'Well then, they may just throw you out into the street,' he said continuing the conversation, his voice devoid of all emotion.

'But what will happen to me then?' Katherine said aghast, 'me and . . . and my child.'

Dermot shook his head, looking to the tall masts of the ships lying tied up on his left-hand side, unable or unwilling to face her.

'I'll end up as a thief or . . . or a whore, selling myself for a night's lodging and probably end up . . . up . . . like that girl you were investigating!'

That produced a reaction. Dermot halted suddenly and Katherine, who had continued on, had to stop and turn round. Dermot was staring at her, his face set, his eyes wide and horrified.

'Who's the father?' he whispered, his voice so soft it was almost lost in the thickening fog and the constant creaking of the ships' rigging.

'What?'

'Who is the father of the child you are carrying?' he

said, slowly and evenly, desperately trying to stop his teeth from chattering.

'I'm not sure what . . .'

'Who is it?' He gripped both her shoulders, his fingers biting deeply into the flesh, and Katherine suddenly realized that he was terrified.

'The captain!'

He looked as if he had been struck. He stepped back from her, shaking his head disbelievingly, his mouth working but no sound coming out.

'Dermot . . ?' She reached for him but he pushed her hand away and staggered to the quayside wall. 'Dermot, what's wrong?'

'You've got to get away,' he said suddenly, 'you mustn't tell anyone in the house, not Mrs Lewis, not Granny O'Neill and certainly not the captain. Especially not the captain.'

'I don't understand . . . why should I . . .'

'Listen to me,' he hissed, drawing her close to him, and even against the stench of the river at low tide she could smell the rank sweat of fear on him. 'If you don't get away, he'll kill you.'

'What!'

'He'll kill you,' he said fiercely, almost savagely.

'What are you talking about?' She tried to pull away from him, but his hold on her arms tightened, and she could feel her fingers beginning to tingle as the blood was cut off. 'You're hurting me!'

'Hey, iss everything a'righ up there?' a heavily accented voice suddenly shouted from the other side – the river side – of the wall.

Shocked, they both looked over to see the dark outline of a sailor staring up from the deck of the ship below. He repeated his question and raised a wickedly-curved boat-hook to emphasize the question.

'Yes . . . yes thank you,' Katherine said finally, when Dermot made no effort to reply.

'I thought maybe he hurt you,' the sailor said, moving away and fading back into the shadows.

209

Katherine turned round to find that Dermot had walked further down the quay and had almost reached Butt Bridge, the swinging metal bridge under which the body of the murdered girl, Sheila, had been found. When Katherine caught up with him, he was leaning over the low wall, staring down into the murky waters. As she came up he put his arm around her shoulders and drew her close. 'I'm sorry. I didn't mean to hurt you, it's just that I don't want you ending up down there . . . like Sheila.'

'Sheila?'

'The girl who was murdered,' he said simply.

'So you did find out something about her in your trips through Summerhill?'

He nodded, but didn't say anything.

'Do you want to tell me?' she asked quietly, feeling something of his fear beginning to settle into her bones.

'Do you want to know?'

'I want to know.'

Dermot sighed, and then he shivered. The fear which he had lived with ever since the attack, but which had gradually lessened over the past months, returned again, and he felt himself automatically looking over his shoulder. 'There's little enough to tell. But, simply put, it is this; the girl who was murdered and thrown into the river was a servant girl called Sheila Webb; she was in service in the Lewis household. She was made pregnant by the captain and then – for some unknown reason – attempted to blackmail him. In return he killed her.'

'But you don't know that!'

'It was the captain and his hired bullies who attacked me outside the *Freeman*'s offices; he told me if I didn't stay out of Monto I would end up like Madam.'

'The woman in Monto?' Katherine asked softly.

'She knew Sheila, she was able to tell me a little about her. The rest I pieced together myself.'

'And what happened to the madam?'

'She was killed – it was made to look like an accident,

210

of course, but she was murdered; murdered by your friend the captain,' he finished bitterly.

Katherine shook her head slowly, wishing she could disbelieve Dermot, wishing she could attribute his accusations to jealousy but knowing that, whatever else, he himself believed them to be true.

'I'm not lying to you, Katherine, I wouldn't do that to you. Why do you think I stopped the investigation . . . because he said he would kill me. And he meant it. Katherine, don't tell him about the baby. Just leave, I've some money, you can have it . . .'

'Dermot . . . Dermot . . .'

'There are people in Summerhill, doctors, medical men who look after the whores when they find themselves . . .'

Katherine struck him open-handed across the face. 'Don't even suggest it. Whatever decision I come to includes this child.' Both hands closed protectively across her stomach.

'I'm sorry, I just . . .' He bent his head, and Katherine was shocked to see his eyes glistening with water. 'I love you, you see,' he whispered, 'and I don't want anything to happen to you.'

'Well, you've got a strange way of showing it,' she said. She reached out and touched his cheek gently where she had hit it. 'Do you love me, truly?'

He nodded. 'What ever made you think otherwise?'

'I thought you didn't care. You didn't seem regretful when I said I might have to leave; you didn't even look upset.'

'Oh Katherine,' he sighed, 'you don't really know me at all. And I'm sorry we didn't get to know one another better . . . But know this, I do love you, more, much more than I can say.'

'I'm sorry too, sorry for a lot of things. Oh, I wish things were different,' she said suddenly, and was almost surprised to find tears in her own eyes.

'Marry me,' Dermot said softly. 'I asked you before I knew about this, and now I'm asking you again. It

211

would be a way out; we could say the child was mine. And I'd love it as my own.'

'Oh Dermot!' Katherine went to him, wrapping her arms around his neck, while he held her close. 'Dermot that would be so easy . . . but so unfair. I couldn't do that to you – you deserve better than a pregnant servant girl, Dermot Corcoran . . .'

He pressed his fingers across her lips, silencing her. 'Marry me,' he insisted. 'I want to marry you. I want us to be together.'

'No, Dermot, no, I cannot . . .'

Dermot ignored her protests. 'I might even be able to get us a special licence for Boxing Day . . .'

'No!' Katherine struggled free and began backing away from him. 'No, I won't.'

'What other choice have you?' Dermot demanded angrily.

Katherine turned and ran. 'I make my own choices from now on!'

CHAPTER NINETEEN

The morning of Christmas Eve dawned cold and sharp, with the faintest dusting of snow on the ground and an icy wind whispering in from the north and east. Katherine stood by the window of her attic room, dancing from foot to foot on the cold floor, looking out across the rooftops to where the first tendrils of colour were coming up from the east. Tomorrow was Christmas Day – and she felt nothing; no regret that she wouldn't be at home, no excitement at this, her first Christmas away from home, not even regret for what had happened. Tomorrow was just another Sunday.

After breaking the ice in the water jug, and splashing some water on herself, she dressed hastily, her fingers numb and fumbling with the buttons and hooks, and hurried downstairs to get the fires started.

She was surprised – indeed, shocked – to find a light burning under the kitchen door, and was even more surprised when she opened it to find the room rich and warm with the smells of cooking and Mrs O'Neill standing before the stove. 'Are you early or am I late?' she asked.

The cook smiled. 'You're early and so am I. I like to get things over early on Christmas Eve; it'll give me a little more time to spend with friends this evening.' She waved a flour-white hand in the direction of the range. 'Here, heat yourself for a few moments, you look half-frozen.'

'It is cold up there,' Katherine agreed. She went and stood with her back to the range, allowing the radiating heat to soak into her bones. She looked over the cook; the old woman had become thinner in the last few weeks and, although her persistent cough had disappeared, her voice was now harsher and she spoke slowly as if her throat hurt, and Katherine could hear her breath rasping in her chest.

'You're looking pale,' Mrs O'Neill observed quietly, 'are you feeling well?'

'Just cold and shivery,' Katherine said with a quick smile. Beyond a slight queasiness early in the morning, Katherine had not yet suffered from morning sickness, although this morning, for some reason, her stomach felt delicate.

'Perhaps you're coming down with a cold,' the cook said with a slight smile, her dark eyes concerned.

'Perhaps,' Katherine agreed. She reluctantly moved away from the heat. 'I suppose I had better set up the fires, I'm sure Captain and Mrs Lewis will be down shortly.'

'There's tea fresh made,' Mrs O'Neill said, nodding to the table, and the squat, floral teapot that stood beside two mismatched cups.

Katherine thought about the tea, and felt her stomach squirm. 'I'd best see to the fires first,' she said, and gathering up her shovel and bucket from behind the door, fled from the kitchen.

As the door clicked shut, Mrs O'Neill nodded. All her suspicions had just been confirmed. She wondered who the father was – and prayed it wasn't the captain.

Mrs Lewis breakfasted without the captain who had left before dawn on some business which he said he wished to complete early so as to be home with his wife on Christmas Eve. As she lingered over her coffee, she idly watched the maid, once again wondering had anything happened between the young woman and her husband while she had been away. Looking critically at Katherine she noted that, although the maid's uniform did nothing for her, there was the hint of a nicely-rounded figure beneath it and if the girl had a little colour in her cheeks and let her hair down, she could be pretty – never beautiful, but certainly pretty.

Anne Lewis had no real grounds for her suspicions of the maid and her husband – except that latterly her husband seemed to show no interest in the young woman at all, and that in itself was curious. Indeed, he had been more than attentive towards Anne over the past few weeks – ever since he had discovered that she had stayed with William Sherlock. He was home nearly every evening, was considerate and gentle – and never once mentioned Sherlock. He was very like the man she had married – and the change in him was so sudden and so dramatic that she distrusted it completely.

Anne looked at the girl again, wondering. She tapped the fine china cup against her slightly crooked teeth, and remembered how the girl had once seemed to be infatuated with the captain; why, every time Anne had looked at her, the girl was staring at him with her big brown eyes. Nowadays, she barely acknowledged his presence.

And looking closely at the girl, Anne Lewis saw that she was pale – very pale – and her brow was sheened with sweat. 'Katherine?' The girl looked up, her eyes wide, startled – and guilty! Anne Lewis knew that look; she had seen it often enough in her husband's eyes when he lied to her. 'Katherine, are you ill? You're looking pale.'

'I'm fine, thank you, ma'am. Mrs O'Neill thinks I might be coming down with a chill,' she added, looking at the curious – almost triumphant – expression on Mrs Lewis's face.

'I thought you might be ill,' Anne Lewis added, watching closely for any reaction.

'A little chilled, ma'am.'

'Ah,' she nodded, seemingly satisfied and reached for her cup again. The maid started to turn away when Mrs Lewis added, very casually and softly. 'By the way, Katherine, just what did happen between you and my husband while I was away?'

Katherine froze momentarily before she turned. She wasn't sure if she had heard correctly, but when she

215

looked at Mrs Lewis she found the woman was wearing an almost predatory expression. 'I'm sorry ma'am?'

'I was wondering what had happened between you and my husband, Katherine. Did he seduce you – or you him? The former I think, from the look of you.'

'I'm sorry, I don't know what you mean . . .' Katherine began, praying desperately that her face or eyes wouldn't betray her, although she could already feel the burning in her cheeks and her queasy stomach seemed to explode with butterflies. She was going to throw up.

'Oh come, come. I've been married to that man for over seven years now; I know him well enough to be sure he couldn't resist the temptation of a fresh young girl alone in the house with him without trying something. And, judging by your expression this morning, and indeed on previous mornings, he gave you more than you bargained for. You're carrying his child, aren't you?'

Katherine began to shake her head, but Anne Lewis suddenly slammed her hand palm down on the table, rattling the cups and upsetting a salt cellar. 'What's the point in lying to me?' she screamed. 'I know, girl, I know! Did he tell you he loved you – aye, he tells them all that, but only the most stupid believe it. Did he take you girl, did he have you, or did you give yourself to him . . ?' Her face had turned feral and her lips were bright with saliva. 'But no, I don't suppose he took you against your will – otherwise you wouldn't still be here, eh? And where did he have you? In my bed I suppose!' She slammed a fist down on to the table, and then suddenly swept the dishes and plates on to the floor. The coffee pot shattered against the marble fireplace and the room was suffused with the odour of rich, bitter coffee.

Katherine backed away from the woman and the stench of the bitter coffee grounds which made her already delicate stomach reel. She took a deep breath and made a conscious effort to keep herself from throwing up. She felt as if she had just slipped into some sort of nightmare. This was not the sort of conversation she should be having at ten o'clock on Christmas Eve morning.

'Mrs Lewis, I think . . .'

'I don't care what you think!' Anne Lewis spat. 'What were you thinking about when you took my husband, eh? What were you thinking about when he bedded you? Was it the house you wanted; the money, or just the respectability? Or did you think you might get it all, eh? Hah!' She laughed, the sound ugly and hysterical.

'No, that never actually crossed my mind,' Katherine said quietly, looking the woman in the face.

Anne Lewis moved around the table and stood before Katherine. They were almost the same size, but in her rage, Mrs Lewis looked enormous. 'You're nothing more than a slut,' she said contemptuously, 'a whore.'

'At least I am capable of loving a man, Mrs Lewis,' Katherine said softly. 'I can take pleasure from the act of love. I understand it has been a long time since you have been capable of such pleasure,' she added, slyly. All her bitterness, her anger and fear were welling up inside her now. 'You may call me a whore, madam, but at least I'm honest with myself – I knew what I was doing. I went into it with my eyes open. What about you – I think you've known about your husband's affairs for a long time, now, but have deliberately closed your eyes to them. And why, because you're frightened of losing him, and envious of the women he's with – they may be only servants or whores, but at least they're real women, with real women's feelings and desires.'

'Get out of this house,' Anne Lewis whispered, beginning to shiver.

But Katherine was already pulling off her lace-trimmed apron. 'I'm going,' she said simply. She turned and walked to the door. 'Have a happy Christmas, Mrs Lewis.'

Mrs O'Neill looked up in surprise when Katherine returned to the kitchen empty-handed, and then she saw the look on her face. 'What's wrong?' she demanded,

217

wiping the flour off her hands, taking the young woman by the hand and leading her to a chair. 'What happened?'

'Oh, Granny, I'm in such trouble,' she said in a whisper, and only then the tears came.

The old woman held her, gently stroking her back, while the girl shivered and sobbed. Granny O'Neill didn't press for details; they would come soon enough, she knew, and, in any case she could probably guess what had happened. Something had sparked an argument upstairs and Mrs Lewis had discovered the girl was carrying a child. More than likely she had ordered the girl from the house.

Eventually Katherine stopped crying and while she dried her eyes, Mrs O'Neill made them both some tea. She was just pouring it when the door slammed open and Mrs Lewis stepped into the kitchen.

'I want that girl out of this house now,' she shouted, and even from across the room Mrs O'Neill caught the stench of liquor.

'I'm going,' Katherine said, beginning to stand, but Granny O'Neill's hand pressed her firmly back into the chair again.

'You'll allow the lass a cup of tea first,' she suggested.

'I want her out of the house this minute!'

'Well, of course, an' if she goes, then I goes also,' Mrs O'Neill said with just a touch of a smile. 'An' I won't be back, either,' she added.

Anne Lewis stared at the cook for what seemed like an eternity, while the ticking of the kitchen clock grew louder and more oppressive. Finally she turned on her heel and left the room, slamming the door behind her so hard that one of its glass panes cracked.

'Without me, there's no Christmas dinner,' the old woman said with a grin. She pushed a cup of tea in front of Katherine. 'Drink it; it's hot and strong and sweet; it'll do you good.'

'You shouldn't have said anything to her, I don't want to get you into any trouble.'

'Don't you worry your head about it, luv, there's naught she can do about it.'

Katherine sipped the tea cautiously, and then grimaced. It was foul. She put the cup down and found Granny O'Neill staring intently at her. 'I suppose you know what's happened?' the girl asked.

'I've a good enough idea.'

'I'm carrying the captain's child,' Katherine said quietly, watching Granny O'Neill closely, looking for any sign of disapproval, but all she found in her face was a deep and genuine sorrow. 'Mrs Lewis has just found out. We had words and she's just ordered me out of the house.' Her fingers tightened around the cup in her hand. 'What am I going to do?' she suddenly cried.

Granny O'Neill patted her hand again, and then said, 'Pack what you need into one small bag, and you can come and stay with me for the next few days. After Christmas we can see about fixing you up with something . . .'

'But I can't just . . .'

'Of course you can; I'll be alone this year – I'd welcome the company.'

Katherine sensed she was lying, but she was feeling too low and dispirited to argue with her.

'I'll pick up the rest of your things later. I think the first priority now is to get you home and into bed, where you can rest for a bit.'

'Thank you,' Katherine said simply.

'Now you finish your tea and then pack what you need, and then you can go on. I'll finish up here – we don't want to give her ladyship any excuses, do we – and when I'm done I'll follow you home. Off with you now.'

Katherine stood up and carried both cups to the sink. She was about to wash them when Mrs O'Neill waved a hand at her. 'Leave them now, they're not important. I want you out of the house before the captain returns.' She looked over at Katherine. 'I take it he doesn't know.'

She shook her head.

'Well, there's no telling how he might take it. So I think it best if you were already gone. If things work out somehow, an' he has an ounce of sympathy for you, you can always get in touch with him after Christmas.' However, Mrs O'Neill's tone made it clear that she thought the likelihood of that happening was very small.

Katherine paused at the door, her fingers just touching the handle and looked back at the cook. 'Thank you,' she said simply.

'For what?' Moire O'Neill asked with an almost shy smile.

'For not accusing me,' Katherine said, and then she pulled the door shut behind her.

The attic room already felt empty, as if she had left it in spirit a long time ago. She gathered up her few things and, after a few moments trying to decide what to take with her, decided that she could easily take everything now, and therefore there would be no need for her to return.

She quickly pulled off her maid's uniform, and dressed in the same long print dress – a summer dress and entirely unsuitable for icy weather – which she had been wearing when she arrived in Ireland . . . and was it only last May? She pulled out the battered army kitbag and dropped it on to the bed. She emptied the drawers of the dressing table on to the bed beside it and bundled all her underclothes into the bag. Finally, she dropped her bible in on top of it all.

And she suddenly realized that she was ready; she had arrived in this house with her entire belongings in this same bag, and she was leaving the same way. She touched her flat stomach briefly, and realized that she was going away with just a little more than she had arrived with.

On her way downstairs, she paused briefly on the landing and looked into the captain's and Mrs Lewis's room thinking she might feel something – regret perhaps, or excitement, or even love. But she felt nothing; it was just another room, and it held no particular memories for her.

Mrs O'Neill was waiting for her when she got back to the kitchen, filled with all the rich seasonal smells of Christmas. 'I'm sorry this had to happen today – I know you could do with a little help.'

'Sure an' it's not your fault at all,' Granny O'Neill said. 'Now look, here's the address; it's at the top of Summerhill, near Portland Row. But if you get lost, you just ask anyone for Granny O'Neill's place, and they'll show you. You won't need a key, it's not locked. Now I'll be home as quick as I can; them upstairs are dining out tonight, they're going to a party, so I'll be leaving early. Off with you now. We'll talk later.'

Katherine took the slip of paper from the old woman's flour-covered hands and Granny O'Neill squeezed her fingers. 'Don't worry yourself overmuch; we'll sort out something.'

Katherine kissed her quickly on the cheek. 'Thank you . . . Granny.'

It took Katherine the best part of an hour to find the address, and when she did she was shocked; it was a tall, dingy tenement-building with rows of dirty windows identical to the rest of those on the long street. The hall door was open – as were all the others on the street – and she slowly walked up the stone steps and looked inside. The floor was nothing more than bare wooden boards, worn smooth with the passage of countless feet in the centre, dark and fouled around the edges. The stairs were similarly marked, the walls filthy with hand prints and finger marks, and the whole building seemed to stink of cabbage and urine.

Granny O'Neill's room was on the second floor, and from the outside seemed identical to all the others on the landing. She placed her hand flat against the wood – there was no handle on the outside – and pushed. The

221

warped door resisted and then reluctantly swung open on groaning hinges.

Katherine was shocked when she saw the interior of the room. It was clean – she had expected that – but it was so stark. There was a bed in one corner, piled high with blankets and clothing, a table with a single wooden chair beside it, an old dresser with a score of mismatched plates on it, and set into the opposite wall, an open fire on which, Katherine guessed, Granny O'Neill did most of her cooking. The room's single window overlooked a tiny boxed-in backyard, and in every direction there were scores of similar tenements.

It was so depressing – not only the grinding poverty, but the very atmosphere of the stark room and the dingy building seemed to sap her energy. Was this her future now – was this all she had to look forward to? Dropping her bag on the floor, keeping only her purse, she almost ran from the room, pulling the door shut behind her. She knew she couldn't stay in that terrible room on her own any longer. She would walk around for a while until Granny O'Neill came home; with someone to talk to and a cheery fire in the grate, the room might seem more welcoming. But somehow she doubted it.

Katherine walked down Summerhill and then on into Great Britain Street, where she turned left before the Rotunda Lying-In Hospital and out into O'Connell Street. Although it was now just past noon, the street was crowded – this being both a Saturday and Christmas Eve, she supposed. She made her way, as best she could, down along the left-hand side of the street, past Findlaters', the wine, tea and spirit merchants, and the Sackville Drug Hall, the chemists, and then Mackey's the seed merchants, and then the hotels, The Gresham, The Crown, The Granville, The Hammam Hotel and the Turkish Baths. The hotels seemed to be doing a good business and revellers – celebrating Christmas early – had spilled out on to the street in front of them. She looked at the people as if they were animals, another

222

species; their laughter was bright and loud, the voices shrill and harsh and their movements quick and spasmodic. Theirs would be a happy Christmas.

Unlike hers.

The thought slipped into her head unbidden and an almost immediate depression spilled over her, like a cloak. Up to then she had managed to distance herself from what had happened, but now, the realization that she was without a home, without a position, pregnant and with no money on Christmas Eve, sank in.

Katherine walked past the pillar, unconscious of her surroundings, conscious only of her despair.

Revellers laden with parcels jostled against the young-looking woman, but she didn't feel them, didn't notice them. She was trying to balance out the ills, trying to look on the bright side – and found she couldn't find one. She wondered where she would be this time next year, with a child and . . . and . . . She shook her head angrily; she wasn't going to cry now, even though she could feel the burning in her throat and at the back of her eyes; she wasn't going to give in. There must be something she could do . . . there had to be, not only for her sake – but for her baby's also!

Katherine found herself on O'Connell Bridge, shivering in the chill breeze whipping up the Liffey from Dublin Bay. Icy water – either rain or spray, she wasn't sure which – stung her face, but she was glad of it in a strange self-pitying way. She stared down into the oily water, looking past the head of one of the river gods carved into the archway of the bridge, and watched the flotsam and jetsam of the city drift past. And she wondered what it would be like to die in that water.

The thought was insidious, and absolutely chilling. It was so easy, an answer and an ending to all the problems; and it was so simple. So simple.

Katherine walked slowly across the bridge and then turned to her left down the quays, heading towards Butt Bridge. This short length of the quays seemed to have some form of fatal attraction for her. This was where

223

Dermot had told her about the pregnant young girl who had been found dead in the water; this was where she had told him the name of the father of her child. And, if Dermot was to be believed, the father of her child and the father of the child of the dead girl were one and the same. The coincidence was eerie.

She walked out on to the metal part of the bridge, her footsteps ringing hollowly. Dermot had once told her that it had been built in 1879, and was designed to swing to allow masted ships to moor upriver. She looked over the edge. The water here was deep, deeper than at O'Connell Bridge and seemed somehow cleaner – although she was sure that was only her imagination. It would be easy . . . too easy. And if she gave in to it, then Captain and Mrs Lewis would have won; to them she was obviously nothing, a thing to be used. Mrs Lewis considered her nothing more than a servant and a whore, and the captain had obviously seen her as something to be won and enjoyed and then discarded. Well, she was going to prove them wrong – she owed it to herself . . . and her child.

Granny O'Neill arrived home a little after three, a few bits of food and half a bottle of cheap cooking wine hidden in her skirts. She didn't know what was going to happen with Katherine, but that could wait for the moment. Tomorrow was Christmas Day, and she was determined that they would celebrate it as best they could. Life could begin again on Monday, the twenty-sixth.

The room was dim and dark and completely silent and for a few moments Granny O'Neill thought that Katherine might be sleeping, but when she lit the oil lamp she saw that the bed was empty and the only sign that Katherine had been there was the battered kit bag in the corner beneath the window. Perhaps Katherine had slipped out for something – although Granny O'Neill knew she had very little money, and where could she possibly go?

224

The old woman checked with her neighbours on either side and with the people on the floor below; but they had seen no-one strange going upstairs.

Not really worried, but a little concerned, Granny O'Neill went back upstairs to her room, wondering what had happened to the girl, wondering when she would come in. She spent the rest of the afternoon sitting by the window, staring down into the wretched backyard, watching the lights come on one by one in the tenements all round her, little pools of yellow light in the smoky night. Gradually the house quietened down and frost began to sparkle on the cobbles.

It was only when the church bells tolled the Angelus at six o'clock that Mrs O'Neill began to grow frightened.

Katherine started awake with the sound of the bells. She realized she had fallen asleep leaning on the cold stone of the bridge. She was frozen through and every joint in her body ached. Her fingers had turned blue and there was no feeling in them, and her lips had cracked.

She looked around. Traffic had died away to almost nothing, everyone heading home early to enjoy the festive season. Wrapping her arms around herself, Katherine turned and headed back towards Summerhill.

She had walked a hundred yards before she realized she was lost.

Katherine stopped and tried to orientate herself. She could go back to the metal bridge and walk up to O'Connell Bridge, and then take a right and head back down O'Connell Street to Summerhill. Was there not a quicker way, though? If she continued on straight, surely that would place her in Talbot Street, with Amiens Street Station on her right? She knew her way back to Granny O'Neill's then.

Moving hurriedly through the unusually deserted streets, Katherine cut out into Talbot Street and found herself facing Mabbot Lane. She darted across the

225

cobbled street; if she cut through the lane, that would lead her out into . . .

'Well, what 'ave we got here?'

'Where's the rush, love . . ?'

The figures had materialized out of the shadows, half-way down the narrow lane, and now stood before her, blocking her path. In the vague light she saw that they were male and in uniform, although she couldn't identify the regiment.

Katherine moved to one side, and the men moved with her, cutting off her exit.

'We've been looking for you,' one of the men said, startling her. Were these the captain's men, sent to bring her back?

'Yea, where've you been hiding – none of the girls are on the street tonight.'

'You got a friend – we could 'ave a party?'

Katherine breathed a sign of relief; their accents were English, and she guessed that they were army privates on leave for the holiday season, and now looking for a woman to spend the night with. 'I'm not what you think,' she said quietly.

'Oh, she's not what we think – an' what do we think she is, eh?' They had now moved close enough for her to smell the cheap drink on their breaths.

'I'm a respectable woman,' Katherine said loudly.

One of the men laughed. 'Respectable women don't come down 'ere, do they?' he asked his companion, and both men laughed raucously.

'I'm taking a short cut,' Katherine said tightly, beginning to move backwards.

'A short cut!' The man darted forward and wrapped his hand into the young woman's coat, hauling her forward, 'We'll show ye a short cut . . .'

Katherine lashed out, the pointed toe of her buttoned boot catching him low on the shin. The man swore and his grip momentarily loosened on her coat. Katherine wrenched away and turned – only to run full tilt into

226

the second man, who caught her by the shoulders and held her at arm's length. 'Ah, you're a wild one. I like a bit of spirit . . .'

The first drunk wrapped his hands into Katherine's hair and pulled her head so far back that she heard her neck creak. 'Kick me, ye bitch . . .'

Katherine kicked him again, lashing out backwards with her foot, catching him just below the knee. He howled in pain and staggered backwards, falling against a pile of refuse, his feet slipping on the muck, toppling him into it.

The man holding Katherine was laughing so hard that it took a moment for the pain to register; it started low in his groin and then ripped up into his stomach, doubling him over. Katherine turned to run, and his flailing arm caught her across the legs, sending her crashing forwards against the slimy tenement wall. Her head exploded with bright red pain and she collapsed on the ground; the last thing she was aware of was two shapes standing over her. . .

'Christ . . . I think she's done for . . .'

CHAPTER TWENTY

There were faces, pale, painted faced with wide eyes and open mouths surrounding her. The mouths were working, but she could hear only a vague buzzing. She was aware of movement – sudden, stomach-churning movement – and then the faces were no longer looking down at her, but rather on a level with her. Something moved before her eyes – a bottle – and then there was fire in her mouth, scorching its way down her throat and into her stomach. But it cleared her head, and she could see and hear again – and it also brought the pain.

The right side of her head was pounding, and she could feel where the flesh of her face had been scraped raw; there was no feeling in her right arm and her hip was stiff.

There were half a dozen women standing around her, their faces and clothing betraying their occupations. 'You all right, love?'

'. . . Bastards did that to you . . .'

'. . . We'll see they get theirs tonight . . .'

'Poor thing.'

'Leave her be, let her get a little air.' One of the group around her, a tall, blond-haired young woman, pushed the others aside and stepped up to Katherine, looking into her eyes. 'Given yourself a good solid bang, you have.' She was smiling slightly, but her expression seemed to be one of genuine concern.

'There were two men . . . they thought . . . they thought . . .'

'We know, we saw them running off.' The blonde grinned. 'The girls will pass on their descriptions – they'll be in for a nasty surprise sometime tonight.' She reached out and touched Katherine's grazed face, brush-

228

ing strands of hair from her forehead. 'That's a nasty scrape you have there, you'll need it washed. Are you hurt anywhere else?'

'My arm ... fingers ...' She lifted her right arm gingerly, opening and closing her fist. 'I hurt my hip.'

'Bastards,' one of the women muttered.

'What were you doing up here anyway?' the blonde asked. 'You don't work the streets.'

'I was trying to find my way back to Granny O'Neill's.' The women muttered together when they heard the name. 'You know her?' Katherine asked, surprised.

'We all know Granny O'Neill,' one of the women said, 'all Summerhill knows the Granny.'

'I worked with her ... and ... and now I'm spending a few days with her ...' Katherine fell silent, realizing that she had been babbling.

'What you need is a cup of tea,' the blond-haired woman said quickly, 'it'll settle you, an' then I'll take you to Granny O'Neill.' She turned to the other women, 'I'll take her across to the cabmen's shelter on the quays.'

'There's no need ...' Katherine began, but the women were already beginning to drift away, leaving her alone with the blonde woman. Katherine looked up at her, squinting painfully as the throb in her head threatened to close one eye. 'Thank you ...'

The woman shrugged. 'I owe it to Granny O'Neill ... I think a lot of us owe Granny.' She paused and added. 'You said you worked with her.'

'Until today. I was fired.'

'You must have done something spectacular to get yourself fired on Christmas Eve,' the woman said shrewdly.

Katherine nodded tiredly. 'It was spectacular. You're English,' she said suddenly, realizing the accent was one which she hadn't encountered for a while.

'London, born and bred. Where are you from yourself, love? Further north, I reckon.'

'Lancashire,' Katherine said, almost shyly.

'Thought I recognized the accent,' the woman said. 'My name is Tilly, Tilly Cusack,' she added.

'Katherine Lundy.'

'Come on then.' Tilly linked her arm through Katherine's and led her back across Talbot Street towards the metal bridge and turned right when they reached the quays. They walked a few yards to a small wooden building with red and white striped woodwork. 'It's the cabmen's shelter,' Tilly said, and Katherine nodded; she had seen a similar building at the top of O'Connell Street. 'If you stay here, I'll see if I can get us some tea or coffee.'

Katherine leaned against the quayside wall, watching the woman as she crossed to the shelter. She was still dizzy and sickened by her encounter with the drunks, and for the moment was quite content to allow this woman to take charge. She saw a tall thin man in an ill-fitting hat stand up as the woman – what was her name, Tilly? – approached him, then he stepped to one side and held the door open for her. Tilly said something to him and the man looked in Katherine's direction, and nodded once. When the door closed behind Tilly, he ambled across to Katherine.

'Evening, miss,' he tipped his hat.

'Did she tell you to keep an eye on me?' Katherine demanded, suddenly frightened by the stranger.

'Ah, sure, an' I wouldn't have to be told to keep an eye on a pretty lass like yourself.'

For a moment his impertinence shocked her speechless and, while she was trying to think of a suitable reply, the door of the shelter opened and Tilly returned, holding two steaming mugs. She handed one to Katherine and then nodded to the tall man, 'Thanks, Joe.'

'Anytime, Tilly, love, ' he said, touching the brim of his hat and sauntering away towards O'Connell Bridge.

Tilly walked over and leaned against the Liffey wall, both hands wrapped around the cup, but not drinking from it. Katherine joined her, holding the cup close to

230

her chest for warmth, shivering now, but whether from reaction or from the chill she wasn't sure. She breathed in the rich coffee aroma, but wasn't too sure she liked the look of the thick black liquid in the cup. She leaned against the wall, feeling the rough stone chill and hard through her thin skirt and sipped the scalding liquid. It tasted as bad as it looked. She looked at Tilly. 'Thank you,' she said simply.

The other woman glanced sidelong at her. 'You said you worked with Granny O'Neill . . .' she remarked, and then asked, 'where?'

'In Drumcondra.'

Tilly looked at her again, and then reached out and turned one of Katherine's hands over. 'You're in service.'

'How do you know?'

'Well, you're not a tart, your manners are good, and your hands are rough enough for service work.'

'I was in service, I was let go today,' Katherine said grimly. 'What do you do?' she asked.

Tilly stared her straight in the face, and said evenly, 'I'm a tart.' She sipped her coffee, not even tasting the foul liquid. 'Why were you let go?' she asked.

Katherine shrugged. 'Oh . . . I'd a disagreement with the mistress.'

'Pregnant?'

Katherine almost dropped her cup with shock; one hand automatically went to her stomach, and then Tilly laughed and shook her head. 'Ah, it's not noticeable, don't worry about it. It was only a wild guess; but it was either that or they had caught you lifting the household silver. I've found that one thing the wealthy do not do is inconvenience themselves – and believe you me, firing the maid on Christmas Eve is a major inconvenience. How pregnant are you?'

'About two months,' Katherine said miserably.

'I'm sorry, I'm so sorry.' She sounded so genuine that Katherine looked at her properly for the first time. She wasn't what she had expected a tart to be; the woman

231

was young and pretty, and the hands wrapped around the chipped cup were slim and elegant, with long and brightly-painted nails. She looked again and saw that only the eyes betrayed her; even in the dim light reflected from the cabman's shelter she could see their bright blueness was stone hard. There was a world of experience in those eyes, she decided.

'Do you want to tell me about it?' Tilly asked finally, when Katherine said nothing.

'There is little enough to tell. The man of the house made me pregnant, and his wife, who had her suspicions, discovered today. We had words, and I'm afraid I mentioned some of her own failings,' she added wryly.

Tilly leaned over the low wall and looked down-river and then asked casually, 'The master of the house, he wouldn't be a military man, would he?'

Katherine shook her head. 'He does hold some military post, I know that, because my father was in his regiment. But ... but how did you know?' she demanded.

Tilly waved her hand dismissively. 'Granny O'Neill only works for one family in Drumcondra,' she said softly, almost to herself, 'the Lewises.' She shivered then, although she was well used to the chill of Dublin's streets in December. 'Does this man know you are carrying his child?' she asked quietly.

Katherine shook her head. 'I didn't tell him, but I'm sure his wife will tonight.' She grinned mirthlessly. 'It'll make a nice Christmas present for them both.'

'What do you think he'll do if he finds out?'

Again Katherine shook her head. 'I'm not sure ... I'm really not sure. He said he loved me ...' she added uncertainly.

'They always do,' Tilly said, kindly. 'Will he come looking for you?'

'I don't know – but why would he want to come looking for me?'

'If he really loved you, he might,' Tilly said, but added silently, or if he feared you and what you knew.

232

She remembered the young girl she had known briefly, the pregnant servant girl who had walked the far side of the quay. And now here was another girl from the same house: it was a strange, alarming coincidence. Tilly was not a religious woman; experience had taught her that the only altar which all men truly worshipped was a woman's warm and willing body, but she felt something cold and sinister slide down her spine. She looked at the frightened face of the young woman and felt – somewhere deep inside – that she was partly responsible for her herself. In a way she owed it to her conscience, for she knew with an absolute certainty that she had betrayed Sheila – unknowingly, it was true – but she had betrayed her. And she had no doubt now that the captain had killed her. She could not allow it to happen again. 'Have you any place to stay?' she asked.

'Granny O'Neill has asked me to stay with her in Summerhill, but I don't want to . . . to impose on her. She may already have lost her job because of me – I don't want to cause her any more trouble.' Katherine shook her head, and Tilly saw the moisture sparkle in her eyes. 'I don't know anywhere else to go.'

Tilly finished the last of her coffee and grimaced; it tasted exceptionally foul and bitter tonight. She rested the battered cup on the curved stone while she considered what to do. She neeeded someplace to hide – yes, hide – this young girl, someplace where the captain would never find her, someplace where his network of spies and informants had no contacts. And that meant somewhere in the Village, the huge brothel area around Montgomery Street, Purdon Street, Gloucester Street and Summerhill tenements. It would have to be somewhere very safe – somewhere protected . . .

The idea came slowly, and at first she dismissed it, but when she considered the alternatives it was the only one which remained viable. There was one woman who might take the girl in, if the price and circumstances were right. She would need paying, of course, but Tilly could arrange to have money taken out of her own earnings. However, the madam in question would also need something more convincing than mere money . . .

'What can you do?' she asked Katherine suddenly. 'I mean can you read or write or anything like that . . ?' She saw the young woman's puzzled stare and continued quickly, 'There's a place I know where I might be able to . . . to put you up. But the woman who runs the house will need a good reason to take you, and if you can do something useful then it will make it easier to get you in.'

'Well, I can both read and write, and I know a little of the French language, and also some of the classics, Latin and Greek. I can keep accounts and do figures.' She paused considering, and added finally. 'I can cook and sew . . . and generally do all the work of a lady's maid and a housemaid.'

Tilly smiled, and squeezed Katherine's arm. 'I think that may be enough,' she said. 'Come on.' She linked her arm through Katherine's and helped her across the road.

'Where are we going?' Katherine called, conscious now of the stiffness in her arm and hip.

'We're going to see the Whoremistress!'

Tilly led Katherine down some of the meanest side-streets that Katherine had ever imagined possible, the cobbles broken and puddles of foul liquid scattered everywhere, stinking rubbish piled high in the corners. There were rats as big as cats and quite fearless, who stared at her with tiny evil eyes from the open sewers. There were no streetlights; the only illumination came from within tenement buildings which loomed tall and many-windowed on either side. Light streamed out through the doors which were all open, although the night was bitter, and she heard Tilly acknowledge the greetings – Christmas good wishes! – from some of the people standing in the shadows. The buildings exuded an almost physical miasma of decay and . . . despair, and she found herself gagging on occasions when the stench grew too strong.

Finally the lanes widened out and Tilly led her out into a broad street. 'Tyrone Street, once called Mecklenburgh Street, after the Princess Charlotte Sophia of Mecklenburgh-Strelitz who married George III,' she said proudly. 'I don't think she'd want to be associated with it now,' she added with a wry smile.

She led Katherine down the street which, Katherine noted, was busy, indeed almost bustling, even at this hour and despite it being Christmas Eve. There was a constant stream of carriages arriving and departing, and nearly every window on the street was ablaze with light. There were women on the street also – and they conformed more with Katherine's idea of a tart, with their garish make-up and over-bright too-revealing dresses. Some of the men recognized Tilly and called out to her, but she merely shook her head, pointed down the road, and called out, 'Number eighty-two.' They all seemed to understand her cryptic message.

It became clear a few moments later when she stopped at the foot of the steps to No 82, Tyrone Street Lower. Unlike some of the other houses its door was firmly closed and there were no girls standing on the steps, calling out their lewd invitations to the male passers-by.

Before she mounted the steps, Tilly turned to Katherine and laid her hand on her arm, her fingers squeezing slightly to emphasize her point. 'Now, you must trust me, Katherine; I'm doing what I'm doing for your sake. You must let me do the talking, but if you're asked a question, then answer truthfully.' She put her foot on the first step and then stopped and turned back to Katherine. 'We're going to see Bella Cohen,' she said, and then added, 'Always address her as ma'am or Mrs Cohen.'

Tilly rapped once on the solid wooden door, and it was opened almost immediately by a huge hulking man. 'Mickey,' Tilly said, nodding to him and walking into the lighted hallway as he held the door open.

He nodded briefly and then grunted something which might have been an acknowledgement or her name. He

235

had turned back to close the door when he spotted Katherine. He stared at her for a few seconds and then looked back over his shoulder at Tilly.

'It's all right, Mickey, Katherine is with me,' Tilly said quickly.

The man looked unconvinced, and almost reluctantly opened the door fully again and allowed Katherine to step around him and into the hallway.

'He keeps the peace,' Tilly whispered, 'keeps the undesirables out and the girls in,' she hurried on, and then continued in a normal voice. 'You wait in here, Katherine, while I go and speak to Mrs Cohen,' she nodded towards a parlour. Katherine stepped inside and Tilly pulled the door shut behind her. Katherine's immediate reaction was to turn and try the handle, but she guessed she would see the glowering Mickey standing outside.

There was no one in the parlour room, though there was evidence enough to suggest that it had only recently been vacated. Long curls of grey smoke still drifted up from the ashtrays, and there were half-finished glasses of red and white wine scattered around the room on the tables and mantelpiece.

Katherine suddenly realized that she was terrified. She almost felt as if she was being kidnapped. She sat on the soft, sagging sofa and looked nervously around the over-dressed room, her mind turning endless circles, wondering what she had let herself in for when she had agreed to accompany Tilly – what was her second name? – to see this woman, this mistress of whores?

She also realized that she didn't really know where she was. Oh, she knew she was in a house – number eighty-two – in Tyrone Street, and she knew that Tyrone Street was behind O'Connell Street, behind the Gresham Hotel, in fact, and she knew she was in Nighttown, The Village, Monto, the largest and most notorious brothel district in Europe. But that was all she knew, and what was even more important no-one knew she was there. And she doubted if anyone cared.

236

The door suddenly opened and a huge woman swept into the room, trailing an aura of smoke and sweat, wine, cheap perfume and something else, a raw musky smell that was vaguely familiar. Tilly stepped into the room behind the woman and closed the door quietly. Katherine scrambled to her feet as the woman crossed the room and eased herself into one of the sagging armchairs.

'Katherine,' Tilly said quietly, 'this is Mrs Cohen.'

The woman was huge, with a broad heavy face, and a large slightly flattened nose. Her eyes were black, and the thick make-up made them look even darker, giving her an intense expression. Her hair might once have been coloured red, but it was now bleached to a pale. gaudy orange, and the roots were black and grey. She was dressed in a full-length royal-blue gown, with a deep plunging neckline that left all of her chest and most of her enormous breasts exposed, and she carried a large white ivory fan which she waved constantly. Her dark eyes bored into Katherine's face for several long minutes. Suddenly she snapped the fan shut and pointed it at the young woman.

'Tilly here tells me you're in a bit of trouble.' The woman's voice was harsh and flat, her Dublin accent pronounced.

'Yes, ma'am,' Katherine whispered.

'Lost your position.'

'Yes, ma'am.'

'She says you've got a child coming.'

Katherine nodded.

'So have lots of others! Now tell me why I should take you in?' she demanded abruptly, the fan opening again and wafting the woman's fetid odour towards Katherine.

'I don't know why you should,' Katherine said simply. Her reply seemed to take the madam aback somewhat, and Katherine used the opportunity to continue quickly. 'But if you were to afford me lodgings, then I could make myself useful in a number of ways. I

237

can read and write, do accounts, read and speak some French, and I am familiar with household management.'

Mrs Cohen sat back into the chair which creaked and groaned aloud with her bulk. Her small eyes regarded Katherine keenly. 'Tilly tells me you could be useful in a house like this,' she said slowly, 'and Tilly, I know, don't make mistakes,' she added, glancing up over her shoulder at the pale-faced young woman standing behind her. Tilly smiled, but the warning in the other woman's voice was plain. Bella Cohen looked at Katherine again. 'Do you think you would be useful here?'

'I'm sure I would be,' Katherine said slowly, 'but whatever else I do, I won't act the whore,' she added defiantly.

Tilly closed her eyes and held her breath.

The enormity of what she had just heard took a few moments to sink into the older woman. She glared at Katherine, her fan tap-tap-tapping insistently against the many rings she wore on her fingers. And then she laughed! It was a guffaw, a bellow of mirth that set her enormous body quivering and shaking. Beads of sweat, which had formed at her hairline, trickled down her face, cutting through the heavy make-up, and the odour of sweat and stale perfume which she exuded as she moved became almost overpowering.

Katherine looked to Tilly, but the other woman just shrugged helplessly.

When Mrs Cohen finally regained control, she wiped her hands across her face, smearing her charcoaled eyes. 'I think you and me might get along just fine, you know, just fine.' She stood up and Katherine scrambled to her feet, and then the huge woman draped an arm across her shoulders. Close to, both physically and otherwise, she was overpowering, but beneath the thick make-up and layers of fat Katherine caught a glimpse of what Bella Cohen must have been like as a girl: a pretty and attractive woman.

'As it happens, you're a bit of a godsend. I've been looking around for someone to keep the accounts, but

238

you can't trust most people; they're only out for themselves, or what they can thieve off you. But you'll be different, you won't steal from me.' Again the voice hardened almost imperceptibly into a warning. 'I'll take you in,' she said, 'you can say you're my . . . my niece. No-one will believe it, of course, but . . .' she shrugged, unconcerned, 'I'll take care of you, and when the babe comes along, well, we take care of that too . . .'

'I'm keeping the baby,' Katherine said warily.

Bella Cohen didn't even blink. 'Of course you are – otherwise all of this wouldn't be necessary, now would it?' She smiled broadly. 'You'll be safe here in the Village, no-one has power here – no-one but the madams,' she added with a smile. She reached out and brushed Katherine's grazed face with a surprisingly delicate touch. 'You get that seen to – and Tilly, you tell Mickey to take care of the two boyos who did this.' Bella Cohen then pulled Katherine to her and kissed her forehead quickly. 'Welcome to my home, child,' she said and swept from the room, leaving Katherine and Tilly alone.

Katherine flopped back down on to the chair. 'And that's it? It's as simple as that?'

'Not quite so simple as you might think,' Tilly said wearily, sitting in the chair Mrs Cohen had recently vacated. 'She is the most powerful madam in Monto, and she's quite capable of having your legs broken as easily as smiling at you. If she's taking you on, she's doing it for a reason, and only because it suits her at the moment. But if you play fair with her, she should be good enough to you . . .' she stopped and yawned, and then added, 'Well, at least you'll be safe here, safe until the child is born, and then you can make whatever decisions you have to make.'

'I've a lot to thank you for,' Katherine said shyly.

'No, you haven't, not yet anyway. Tell me again in a couple of months when you're settled here.' She stood up suddenly, yawned again and stretched. 'Well, I'll be off then.'

239

'Where are you going?' Katherine asked, standing also.

'Work,' Tilly said with a grin. 'I'll leave you to Mrs Cohen's tender mercies . . .'

Six months later, on the 7th June, 1899, Katherine Lundy gave birth to an eight-pound-eight-ounce baby boy. She called him Patrick Montgomery Lundy; Patrick after her grandfather, and Montgomery after the area.

In that short time, Katherine had become very much a resident of the infamous Monto.

PART TWO

. . . a Time to Love and a Time to Hate . . .
Ecclesiastes 3:8

CHAPTER TWENTY-ONE·
Dublin, July 1907

The tall, regal woman, dressed almost entirely in black, read quietly through the day's papers while the maid set the table for tea. There was a sheaf of blank paper by her side on which she made occasional notes in a small precise hand. When she had read the various accounts of the event she was interested in, she folded the newspapers into a neat bundle and dropped them on to the floor by her chair. She then picked up the pages and scanned quickly through the notes she had made.

The day's headlines had been dramatic, overshadowing the visit of King Edward and his queen two days hence on Wednesday the 10th July. The Irish Crown Jewels – the insignia of the Order of Saint Patrick – had been stolen!

Katherine sat back into the winged leather chair, tapping her pen gently against her fine teeth, wondering what could be done – if anything! She smiled wryly: every situation could be used for profit and gain, that was one of the rules she had learned over the past few years. Every situation!

The years had been kind to Katherine Lundy, and although the lines on her face were firmer there was little evidence of the passage of time on her slim body. Only her hair, now touched with silver and grey, betrayed the passage of time and bore witness to her struggle to survive.

There was a single tap on the door, and before she could call out it opened and another woman entered. Time had not lain so lightly on Tilly Cusack; her face had hardened, the lines deepened – although she was still pretty – and her breasts, which had always been large, were now even heavier. But the gaudy tart's clothing was a thing of the past; it had been replaced by an elegant demure gown in the latest fashion, and what little make-up she wore was expertly applied. Tilly Cusack was no longer a tart, she was a lady.

'I've got the last 'pink' edition of the *Telegraph*,' she said, sitting gracefully into one of the chairs at the table. She looked over at the woman in black, offering her the neatly folded newspaper.

Katherine Lundy sat forward and removed the pince-nez from her nose and then massaged her tired eyes. 'Read it to me, Tilly; though it's probably nothing more than we already know.'

Tilly nodded and spread out the paper on the table before her, draping it casually over cups and saucers and moving carefully-placed cutlery to one side so that she could rest her elbows on the table. The maid returned with some side plates, and stopped in surprise when she saw the mess of her settings. She turned to Katherine in silent appeal.

'Perhaps if you were to leave it for a few moments, Nuala. I'll ring for you.'

The maid bobbed a curtsey. 'Of course, ma'am.'

Katherine nodded to Tilly to begin and then rested her head against the polished leather and closed her eyes.

' "Sensation of the hour," ' Tilly read slowly, tracing the words with her finger, ' "Burglary in Dublin Castle . . . consternation in official circles – the big function postponed – regalia and jewels gone . . . fifty thousand pounds' worth stolen . . ." '

Katherine suddenly opened her eyes and sat up. 'How much?'

'Fifty thousand pounds, it says here.'

'Nonsense; they were recently valued at between sixteen and seventeen thousand pounds. Twenty thousand pounds at the outside, I would estimate.'

'And have you any idea where they are now?' Tilly asked with a grin.

Katherine simply smiled and indicated that Tilly

should continue reading. 'I'll skip down to the official statement,' she said, and Katherine nodded. ' "About 2.30 P.M. on the 6th inst, an official connected with the Office of Arms, Dublin Castle, had occasion to put some articles into a safe in which the state jewels belonging to the Order of St Patrick had been kept. On trying to unlock the door he discovered that it had been previously unlocked, and on testing the lever the door readily opened.

"The last time on which this safe is known to have been opened was on 11th June last, when the jewels were inspected and found to be correct, and there appears to be no doubt that the door was locked when the inspection was over.

"There is no mark on the safe to indicate that any violence was used to open it, nor is there any indication to show that access to the building was obtained otherwise than by regular means . . . " ' Tilly finished a little breathlessly.

Katherine sat forward again, and rang the small silver bell which stood beside her plate. The door immediately opened and the maid entered. 'We'll have tea now, Nuala. Will you call Master Patrick?'

'Yes, ma'am.' She bobbed a curtsey again and backed from the room.

Katherine turned back to Tilly. She nodded to the paper, 'And what does all that suggest to you . . ?'

'Someone inside?'

Katherine nodded, pleased, 'Someone inside; there were no marks on the door of the safe, remember.'

'But when were they taken?' Tilly wondered. She looked down at the table and read the relevant section again, 'The last time on which this safe is known to have been opened was on 11th June last, when the jewels were inspected and found to be correct . . .' That's almost a month, Katherine, plenty of time for them to be smuggled out of the country.'

But Katherine shook her head. 'I would have heard if

245

they had left the country,' and Tilly nodded, realizing it was no idle boast.

Katherine Lundy, or Madam Kitten as she was more usually called, ran one of the most exclusive brothels in Dublin, catering to the tastes of some of the most highly placed men in government and society, so her information always came from impeccable sources. She also ran what was somewhat affectionately known as the 'Monto Intelligence' whereby she paid for any information that might possibly be of interest to her, or which might have some re-sale value. Here, her informants came from all classes – principally the lower and working classes of course – but again, her information was nearly always reliable. It was said that nothing happened in Dublin that Madame Kitten didn't know of.

'Could the jewels have been broken up?' Tilly asked. She looked down at the paper again, ' "A diamond star ... composed of brilliants consisting of points issuing from a centre enclosing a cross of rubies and a trefoil of emeralds and sky-blue enamel with ..." ' she paused, and then hurried on, 'with some Latin words in rose diamonds. There's a diamond badge set in silver, containing a trefoil of emeralds on a ruby cross, surrounded by a sky-blue enamelled circle with some more Latin words, cut out in rose diamonds in a circle of large Brazilian stones, surmounted by a harp in diamonds and a loop.' She glanced up at Katherine and continued on quickly. 'There were five collars of the Knights Companions of the Order of St Patrick, composed of gold, with roses and harps alternately tied together with knots of gold; leaves enamelled and an Imperial jewelled crown surmounting a harp of gold. There was also a badge of the Order composed of Brazilian stones and the Cross of St Patrick in rubies, in a blue enamel circle with a Latin motto in rose diamonds, the whole enclosed by a wreath of trefoil in emeralds on a gold ground enamelled in colours ...' She finished breathlessly. 'Whatever way you look at it, it's a lot of gold and

246

diamonds, rubies and emeralds, and it's easily broken up.'

Katherine shook her head. 'I've already checked with the jewellers, both legitimate and otherwise, here and in Cork and Belfast, and no-one has handled them.'

'What about London?'

'I'm looking into it.' Katherine shuffled her notes together and patted them into a pile. 'Is there anything else we should know about?'

Tilly shook her head. 'I don't think so. Everything is in readiness for the coming festivities. All the girls are confined to their rooms and have been checked by the doctor and certified fit and well. The wines arrived late last night – but I'm sure you know about that – and there was a special case of fine brandy and another of ten-year-old whiskey. I presume that is in case we have a special guest?' she asked with a sly smile.

Katherine smiled mischieviously, but didn't answer the question. 'And the champagne?'

'Arrived also.'

'The musicians?'

'All arranged,' Tilly said with a grin. 'What now . . .' she asked.

Suddenly a small boy, about eight years old and instantly identifiable by his mother's square chin and determined eyes, came charging into the room, 'Mother . . . Aunt Tilly!' he shouted, deafening them both, and then scrambled on to a chair.

'And now tea, I think,' Katherine said with a smile.

Katherine tucked her son into bed later that evening, running her fingers through his mousy-brown hair, a legacy from his father. When he was older, she decided, she would advise him to dye it: a deeper colour would give his face greater strength of character.

She rarely thought about his father, Captain – no, Major now – John Lewis, except when his name popped up on one of her reports. She hadn't seen him in over eight years, although she knew that he was still living in

Clonliffe Road, and still working in the GPO, where his somewhat shadowy position remained unchanged. She had a very good idea of what he was up to now, and she knew that some of the nationalist political groups also had their eye on him. She fully expected one day to receive a report saying that he had been found in some alley or floating face down in the river.

She bent over and kissed Patrick's forehead lightly, and moved quietly from the room. She had almost reached the door when he spoke from beneath the blankets, startling her a little, because she thought he was asleep. 'Will we see the King, mother?'

Katherine's eyes sparkled with amusement. 'Possibly,' she said, closing the door behind her; very probably, she decided, knowing Edward's inclinations and her house's reputation.

Her girls were waiting for her in the large drawing room; behind them stood four 'waiters' whose duties involved more than just waiting on customers. It had become Katherine's custom to speak to all her staff before the doors opened – although they never really opened, as admittance was by sight or recommendation only.

As she entered they chorused, 'Good evening, ma'am.'

Katherine crossed the room and sat down in the easy chair beside the fire, and looked each of them over in turn. The women were dressed in evening gowns of different colours and in the latest fashion. They weren't all young and slender, although they were pretty, but Katherine had spent some time in the brothels of Montmartre – learning the craft, as Madam Bella Cohen had jokingly called it – and she had realized then that men's tastes in women ran to different shapes and sizes. The European brothels catered to all tastes – and that was what had made them so successful and enduring. She was also quick to learn that, with proper care and treatment, a whore's brothel 'life' of five years could be almost doubled. What she had learned in Paris, and later

248

in London and Berlin, she had brought back to Dublin and applied to the running of the house in Lower Tyrone Street, turning it into something very special.

'Now ladies and gentlemen,' she said looking into each of their faces, catching and holding their eyes briefly, 'I think you all know how important the next few days are going to be. On Wednesday the King and his entourage arrive on the royal yacht for the start of their tour. Indeed, many of his company have already arrived and several more companies of military are on their way and should arrive over the next day or two. In addition to that there are various dignitaries, both local and otherwise, in town for the show, and just about every lord and lady in Ireland has come to Dublin for the event.

'Now this house has a certain reputation,' she smiled slightly, 'a reputation which should ensure that some of these wealthy people will venture our way. Every attempt should be made to welcome them, and to ensure that when they leave they will spread the word about this house. I want those words to be good ones. I want this house placed on the visiting list of just about everyone of importance in the British Isles.' Her hard eyes travelled over them again. 'We have the opportunity to make quite a lot of money over the next few days – and we must not lose sight of that – but it will be as nothing compared to what could be made over the next few months as our fame spreads.' She watched their eyes light up, and the heads begin to nod as the truth of what she was saying sank in.

'Now,' she turned to the four men standing quietly in the background, 'a special word to the boys.' The women giggled at the word 'boys'. They were all large and well-built and, with one exception, young men, all looking more than a little incongruous in their waiters' tails. The fourth man was Mickey, who had been the original doorman when Katherine had first arrived at Bella Cohen's. Although bullies (as they were commonly known) generally came and went, Mickey had remained with the one house down through the years. Now he acted the part of head waiter with a certain rude charm and great gusto.

Mickey had once been a constable with the Dublin Metropolitan Police, but a misdemeanour, which he never spoke about, had caused his rather hasty exit from that proud body of men. He was a handsome man, his iron-grey hair slicked well back from his broad forehead, his eyes grey and piercing, his nose straight and unbroken, and his jaw square and rather jutting.

'I think Mickey has told you that a certain amount of discretion is to be used should there be a disturbance of any kind. We cannot afford to injure anyone, but by the same token we must preserve the reputation of the house as a quiet, well-ordered, well-run and dignified establishment. Which means that, if any young buck or old rake takes it into his head to show off, then he is to be quietly – but firmly – removed from the room until he cools down. If he persists, then you will call a cab and ensure that he is returned to his house or hotel.'

'What if he threatens to return again, or bring the police?' one of the waiters asked.

'Make a point of taking his name and address – both here in Dublin and wherever he comes from – and promise that it will be published with a suitably lurid story. That should scare him off. If he persists, then promise to break both his legs.'

A ripple of laughter ran round the room, and Katherine took the opportunity to stand up, whereupon they all fell silent. 'Anyway, it's unlikely they would go to the police – what are they going to tell them, eh? That they were thrown out of a brothel?' She looked around the room. 'Any questions?'

'Do you think *he'll* be coming?' May, one of the younger girls, asked.

'Well, we know that as a young man during the time he was doing his military service in the Curragh, he did frequent the older fancy houses.' Katherine looked over at Mickey. 'What do you think?'

250

The older man smirked. 'Well, I personally saw him twice in this very room, once in '71 and again in '85, and I did hear tell that he visited Mrs Arnott's house next door in '68.'

'I also know that when he was in Dublin in 1903 and '04, he received the attentions of certain young women,' Katherine added, 'but, because he was King then, for reasons of security the girls were brought to him, instead of the monarch having to come down into this disreputable area,' she added with a smile. 'And I know because I arranged the visits. Oh,' she looked around the room again, 'if he does come here, he will not pay, nor will you ask for payment. However, the following day, something will arrive by messenger – usually two presents, one for the girl, and the other to the house. The last girl I know who received a present from Bertie sold it and retired on the money she made. Bear that in mind,' she said and swept from the room.

Mornings were Katherine's favourite time. The house was generally quiet, the girls sleeping off the previous night's exertions, and it allowed her to spend time with her son. If the weather was fine, she usually took him for a walk down O'Connell Street and up to St Stephen's Green where he would feed stale crusts of bread to the ducks. But not this morning; she couldn't afford to leave the house, even for a little while, not with so much happening.

She sat by the window of the large old house and watched her son walk hand-in-hand with Mickey down Tyrone Street. The pair looked just like any other grandfather and grandson taking a walk – Patrick even called Mickey 'Granddad', in the same way as he called Tilly Cusack 'Aunt'.

The idea of bringing her boy up in a brothel used to bother her at one time, but no longer. His education to date had been by private tutor, and when he was old enough she would have him entered in Trinity College, Dublin or perhaps send him abroad to Oxford.

However, there was time enough for that. At the moment he was a fine, healthy, handsome boy, advanced for his years, and lacking for nothing. She didn't think she had done too badly for her son.

Katherine crossed to her desk and leafed through her note-books, wondering what her plans for today were. Over the years, she had become an inveterate note-taker and diarist; the need to record everything in her small neat script was almost compulsive. First, she checked her appointments, but her diary for today, Tuesday 9th July, 1907, was blank, and there were no callers due. So, she returned to the notes she had made on the theft of the Irish Crown Jewels – that would certainly bear looking into; there was sure to be a profit in it somewhere . . .

Katherine wondered if there was a political connection to the theft, but she almost immediately dismissed it – the various political organizations were mainly rhetoric and promises and, in any case, they were so riddled with informants, both governmental and her own, that there was no possible way the robbery could have been planned or executed without some whisper of it leaking out.

She had been working steadily for an hour or so, when she became aware that the front door bell was jangling insistently. She jumped to her feet and crossed to the window, peering out through the dusty panes and down the flaking front of the building to the feet-worn steps below. But she could see no-one; the caller was obviously standing right up against the chipped wood. The exterior of the house had been deliberately allowed to run down; from the outside, it looked like just another of the decaying tenements on Tyrone Street; inside, it was a palace.

She heard the front door open and the ringing stopped, then Billy – one of the waiters – spoke, his soft Belfast accent buzzing up from below. Katherine crossed to the door and opened it a fraction.

'. . . no, I'm afraid not.'

252

'It will only take a minute.' The second voice was persistent, a Dublin accent but the rough edges rounded off with education. It sounded vaguely familiar.

'We are closed, sir.' She heard the door scrape as Billy pushed it over, and then he added quietly, 'If you don't take your foot away, sir, I think I'll just crush it.'

'I need to speak to Madam.'

'Impossible,' Billy said, and then Katherine clearly heard what sounded like a blow, followed by a yelp, and then the door slammed closed.

'Who was it, Billy?' Katherine called down, looking over the bannister.

Startled, the young man looked up. 'Someone who wanted to talk to you. I said no.'

'Did he give a name?'

'He wouldn't,' Billy said.

'Wait a moment,' Katherine said, and then dashed back to the window to stare down into the street. She was startled to see a young man standing on the street staring up at her window. He was leaning against the low wall in front of the building, holding one foot slightly off the ground. Katherine looked at him for several long minutes, feeling her heart beginning to pound. She took a deep breath and then sighed, her teeth chewing on her bottom lip. Finally, she ran back to the door and called down to Billy. 'I'll see him. But give me a few minutes before showing him in.'

'Yes, ma'am.'

As Katherine stepped back into the room she heard the front door scrape open and then Billy call out, 'Hey, you!' When he spoke again, his voice was softer, but she could guess that he was telling the man Madam would see him now.

When Billy rapped deferentially on the door a few moments later and ushered the visitor in, Katherine was standing in front of the window, gazing out at the houses opposite. She did not turn round, and all the young man could see was the tall, black figure silhoetted against the sunshine outside.

253

'You wanted to see me?' The voice was low and slightly muffled, almost as if the speaker was covering her mouth with a piece of cloth.

The young man nodded and then realizing that the woman couldn't see him, cleared his throat and said, rather loudly, 'Yes.' He coughed and repeated himself, pitching his voice lower this time.

'Please sit.'

He stepped over to the hard-backed chair that had been placed in the centre of the room and slowly sat down in it, his eyes darting around the high-ceilinged, elegant room, trying to reconcile the luxurious interior with the shabby exterior of the building. He found himself looking for something which would give him a clue to the speaker's personality. He knew of her only by reputation – indeed, all Dublin knew of her by reputation. But all that was really known about her was her name, Madam Kitten, though generally she was just called Madam.

'How I can I be of assistance to you?' the woman asked, her voice softer, and she turned her head slightly to look at something in the street below.

'But I should first caution you, that should you turn out to be from the police, either directly or indirectly, or should you be in the employ of one of the other madams, then I will have both your legs broken and your kneecaps shattered so that you will never walk properly again. So, with that in mind, if you still wish to continue, you may do so.'

'Yes ... well, no. I'm not from the police, nor am I from one of your competitors, although,' he added, with a brave grin, 'judging from some of the stories I've heard, you've no real competition in your trade in Dublin.'

'Yes ... I'm sure. Well, get on with it!' Katherine responded sharply, resisting the temptation to smile.

'Of course.' He was sweating freely, and his hands were damp. This had seemed a good idea to begin with – but now he wasn't quite so sure; he hadn't been so

254

frightened in a long time. There was a knife strapped to his left forearm under his coat in case of an emergency, but he found he could draw little comfort from it. 'I am interested in the Crown Jewels,' he said suddenly.

'So are a lot of people,' she remarked dryly.

'I'm willing to pay – handsomely too – for any information which might lead to their return.'

'And why have you come to me?'

'For two reasons. There is a little evidence that some of the gentlemen involved in this scandal have . . . shall we say . . . certain inclinations . . .'

'They are sodomites . . . homosexuals,' she said forthrightly.

'Yes, so I've heard.'

'And how does that bring you to Monto in general, and me in particular?'

'Well, because of Monto's reputation in catering to all tastes, and secondly because your sources are universally acknowledged to be excellent. I thought you might know,' he finished lamely.

'And what is your interest in all this?' Katherine asked.

'Professional,' he said.

'But you're not police?'

'No.'

'Then just what are you?' she demanded.

There was a few moments silence, and eventually he said, 'I would rather not say.'

'I don't believe you have any choice,' she said quickly. 'Don't play games with me, just answer my question. Who are you, what are you?'

'My name . . . my name is Corcoran . . . Dermot Corcoran, and I'm a reporter with the *Freeman*!'

CHAPTER TWENTY-TWO

'I know!' the woman whispered and turned around to face him.

The morning sunshine streaming through the grimy window haloed her dark hair around her head but still left her face partially in shadow. She placed both hands on her hips, and tilted her head slightly, quizzically.

And Dermot found the simple movement vaguely familiar, tantalizingly, almost frighteningly, so.

In the long silence that followed, Dermot touched the knife strapped along the inside of his forearm almost unconsciously, a nervous gesture. It had always lent him a certain amount of reassurance, a certain confidence – until now that was.

'Are you still carrying that knife strapped to your arm, then? And if you were attacked, do you really think it would do you any good? You would be dead before you had a chance to pull it.' The woman smiled, taking the sting out of her words.

'I . . . I really don't k-k-kknow what you mean,' Dermot said, his heart beginning to thump painfully in his chest and his old stutter returning. For some reason this dark mysterious woman made him feel like a boy, a mischievous schoolboy.

'You still stutter,' the woman said, sounding almost pleased. 'You always stuttered when you became nervous or excited,' she said quietly. 'Of course, that was a long time ago, but I suppose one never loses the nervous traits of childhood.'

'You know me . . .?' Dermot asked slowly, straining to make out her features.

'I know you.'

256

'I'm afraid you have the advantage of me, then,' Dermot said uncertainly.

'Do you not know me, Dermot Corcoran?' she asked clearly and distinctly – and her voice was familiar . . . so familiar.

Shaking his head, he stood up cautiously, and then paused, unsure if she was going to call out to the guard he was sure waited beyond the door, but she made no movement, no sound, and he took a step towards her. 'We have met . . ?' he asked, coming closer.

'You can be forgiven for not recognizing me, it was a long time ago.'

'You . . . you really must forgive me, but I'm afraid I do not count many women amongst my acquaintances and certainly no-one of . . .' he hesitated.

'Of my profession?' she asked gently.

'I was going to say of your obvious breeding.'

The woman bowed slightly. 'You are very kind,' she said, and then moved away from the window, out of the blinding light.

Dermot Corcoran stared at her for a full two minutes, while all around him he felt his world shift and jar, and then settle again. The face hadn't changed; it had matured certainly, the bones had become more prominent, the eyes were harder and the mouth slightly creased, but it was still the same face, the same clear-eyed challenging gaze. It was a face out of his past, a face that had haunted him down the last nine years.

'Katherine Lundy!' he gasped.

'At your service, sir,' she said, her voice mocking, but her eyes were cautious and suddenly terribly afraid.

'B-B-B-But I-I-I t-t-t-thought . . .'

Katherine reached out with both hands and he automatically clasped them in his. 'Oh Dermot, I'm sorry, I shouldn't have done it this way. It was cruel, I know, but . . . well, I didn't know how you'd react to seeing me again after all these years. I'm sorry . . .'

'Katherine?' Dermot whispered aghast.

Katherine led him to the sofa and pushed him gently

into it. He was sheet-pale, his eyes were sparkling far too brightly, and she was afraid he was about to faint. 'Billy?' she called, looking across the room.

The door opened immediately and Billy rushed in, a short length of lead pipe in his hand. He stopped and looked around in confusion, expecting ... well, he wasn't sure what he had been expecting, but certainly not to find the stranger sitting on Madam's sofa, looking as if he'd seen a ghost. Billy turned to Madam.

'Would you bring some tea for our guest, Billy – oh, and be sure to bring some sugar. I think the young gentleman has had something of a shock.'

'Of course, ma'am,' Billy said quietly. He had turned to go, when Katherine spoke to him again.

'Billy?'

'Yes, ma'am?'

'What have I told you about using lead pipe?'

He looked at the eighteen-inch length of quarter-inch thick pipe in his hand, and absently slapped it into the palm of his left hand. 'I'm sorry, ma'am,' he mumbled, 'old habits die hard ...'

'A lot more than old habits will die if you hit someone with that,' she said, and then waved her hand, dismissing him. She sank down gracefully into the sofa beside Dermot. 'In the old days lengths of lead pipe were often hidden behind the religious pictures in the bedrooms in some of the houses along here. If a client became difficult, then it was always ready to hand. I have told my staff about using such crude methods, but they sometimes fall back on the old reliables.'

Dermot was still staring at her, trying to reconcile the wild-eyed young servant girl he had last seen in the winter of 1898 with this hard-eyed, self-confident woman who, if his information was correct, ran one of the most exclusive and successful brothels in Dublin.

'You're staring,' she reminded him gently.

'I'm s-s-sorry,' he whispered, 'but you are Katherine ... Katherine Lundy, the same girl who worked in the house of Captain and Mrs Lewis as a servant girl ...'

'. . . And who left suddenly on Christmas Eve of '98,' she finished, 'Yes, I am the same.'

'But how . . ?' He looked around the room in wonder, the light streaming in through the window, picking out the luxurious furnishings, the gleaming table, the well-stocked bookshelves and the thick-piled marvellously-worked carpet on the floor, and then he turned back to the woman. 'How?' he repeated in a whisper.

There was a tap on the door and Billy entered again, this time carrying a silver tray complete with a tall, silver teapot and two china cups and saucers. There was milk and sugar in a matching jug and bowl of cut-crystal, and a pair of Irish linen napkins. The waiter placed the tray on a small side-table and then moved the table over beside the sofa. 'Will that be all . . ?' He looked at Katherine, and she silently nodded her head. He bowed briefly, and left the room.

'We will have some tea first, I think,' Katherine said, lifting the pot and beginning to pour. 'There will be time enough for talk later.'

The sense of unreality that had settled over Dermot from the first moments he had entered this room intensified. He tried to convince himself thst this wasn't really happening, that he wasn't having tea with a woman he had assumed to be dead, a woman he hadn't consciously thought about in far too many years. He imagined he would wake up quite soon; he would wake up cold and sweating, the sheets and his nightshirt soaked through, and it would be time to get up for work, and within minutes the dream would have faded.

They drank their tea in silence, Katherine seemingly absorbed in an examination of a dark Gustav Doré print on the wall, while Dermot was unable to take his eyes off her. Finally, he followed the direction of her gaze, and looked at the print in the heavy gilt frame which seemed far too opulent for such a dreary subject.

'It's Hell,' Katherine said softly, not looking at him, 'one of Doré's illustrations from *Dante's Inferno*.'

259

'Yes, I know,' Dermot replied softly, 'It's what I've always imagined Hell would be like.'

Katherine shook her head. 'No, Hell is a terrified pregnant girl living in a brothel while a man hunts for her – that's Hell.'

'The captain went looking for you?' Dermot asked in wonder.

'Yes,' she turned to him and smiled, 'you know, I didn't really believe it when you said he would, but you were right. St Stephen's Day, the 26th of December, he began making inquiries. He took this town apart looking for me – he threatened, cajoled and bribed – and he didn't stop looking until the middle of the year, although by then he was looking for a woman and a new-born child. But do you know how many there are in Dublin at any one given time? Perhaps that might make a suitable subject for your next article,' she added, her voice unintentionally acid. She saw his look of surprise and continued, watching him over the rim of her cup, 'Oh, I've been following your career carefully over the past few years; you've become very much the champion of the poor.'

'It's something I feel very strongly about,' Dermot said quietly. 'I've always felt strongly about it – you know that.'

Katherine nodded. 'I've heard you speak at the public meetings.'

'You don't approve?'

'It doesn't really matter if I approve or not, does it?' she asked.

'I would like to know.'

'I think there are ways to bring about change . . . but I don't think yours is the right way. The authorities will not listen to shouts and threats, but I think they might listen to the voice of reason.'

Dermot shook his head quickly, glad to be back on familiar ground. 'Words will only take our cause so far, Katherine. There comes a time – sooner or later – for action.'

260

'What sort of action? I can't say I like your idea of making slum-crawling fashionable, of inviting the upper classes to tour their "hidden city".'

'But if it opens their eyes . . ?'

'It will take more than a twenty-minute tour through the slums to open their eyes,' Katherine said coldly. Suddenly she smiled, and shook her head slightly. 'I'm sorry; I didn't mean to sound so harsh. I've no wish to argue with you.' She put down her cup and reached out to touch his sleeve. 'If you are going to stay, perhaps you should take off your coat,' she suggested, and Dermot realized with a start that he was still wearing his overcoat. He stood up and pulled it off, draping it over the back of a nearby chair, and when he sat down again he turned to face Katherine, his head tilted slightly to one side, one leg crossed over at the knee, one arm resting on the back of the chair, and the fingers of both hands interlocked. All at once he looked older and more responsible, and Katherine had the impression that it was a pose he had studied and practised many times.

'We've a lot to talk about,' he said quietly, watching her face, searching her eyes.

Katherine nodded. 'Aye, but first you must give me your word of honour that you will never reveal my wherabouts, or ever mention my real name again. I am Madam Kitten – that is how I am known now.'

Dermot smiled. 'Where did you get it?'

'The previous madam, Bella Cohen, found 'Katherine' to be rather a mouthful, and she always gave her girls what she called 'working names'. And so she called me Kit, short for Katherine, and then that gradually changed into Kitten.'

'It must have been terrible for you – living in such a place, I mean,' Dermot said. He reached into his inside pocket and produced a flat silver cigarette case. But before he could open it, Katherine waved her hand and nodded at the box. 'I'd rather you didn't. These are my private apartments, and I try to keep the stench of smoke from them. Outside, in the rest of the house, you

261

may of course do as you wish, but I tolerate neither drinking to excess nor smoking nor swearing in these few rooms, and proper dress must be worn at all times.' She saw his surprised – almost shocked – look, and grinned, and suddenly all the years fell away from her, and she was a young, wide-eyed girl again. 'It sounds terrible, doesn't it; makes me out to be a real tartar.'

'Well . . .' Dermot fumbled with the case before slipping it back into his pocket. 'I suppose you must have your rules.' He sounded surprised that rules would exist in such a place.

'It was something I learned in the brothels in Montmartre. The madams have very strict rules. When the girls are working, they may smoke, drink and wear their 'working clothes', but when they are off-duty, so to speak, then they must behave with all the due decorum of ladies.'

'But why?' Dermot asked, surprised.

'There may be certain men who prefer sluts,' Katherine said slowly, 'but this is a reputable house. My girls may sell themselves, but they remain, above all, ladies, and to remain ladies they must think of themselves as such. The rules enforce such a view.'

'And does it work?'

She nodded. 'It works. Most of my girls manage to find themselves good husbands after four or five years here. If they were on the street, they would be either diseased or dead in that time.'

A door slammed somewhere in the house, and they both clearly heard a child's voice raised in laughter. Katherine smiled at Dermot's startled look. 'My son,' she said softly.

'Your son?'

'I was pregnant when I left Clonliffe Road, remember?'

He nodded. 'I remember.'

'He's a fine young lad – and he knows nothing of his father. I want it kept that way,' she said quietly, and Dermot clearly heard the warning in her voice.

'I wouldn't dream of saying . . .'

'I know you wouldn't,' she said. She reached out and took his hand in hers. 'Dear Dermot, it's been a long time – too long.'

'Why did you never contact me?' he asked.

'I don't know. I've asked myself the same question – often, and especially when I read one of your articles. But I had started a new life . . . and I had left you free to get on with your life unencumbered with a pregnant servant girl. I didn't see the point in opening old wounds.' She paused and added, almost shyly. 'But I always knew we would meet again. I was waiting for you to come to Monto.'

'You might have been waiting a long time,' Dermot smiled.

'Oh, I don't think so. You've written articles on housing and sanitation, on the poor, the unemployed, the plight of the homeless children, the sweatshops, the crime. It was only a matter of time before you turned to the working girls, and the flash houses and kips. In fact, I'm surprised it took you so long. Is that what brings you here now?'

'My last experience with one of the working girls of Monto earned me a beating at the hands of your captain, remember?'

Katherine sighed and nodded. 'I remember.'

'And I'm not here to do an article on working girls,' Dermot said quietly, 'I told you, I am looking into the disappearance of the Crown Jewels. I thought the infamous Madam Kitten might be able to help me.'

'Oh,' Katherine shook her head and grinned. 'I'm afraid your trip to Monto has been wasted then, the Madam is as much at a loss as you,' she said, 'but I also know that she has had certain inquiries made which – who knows – might yield some results.'

'You don't sound very hopeful.'

'I'm not.'

'Can I ask you a question?' Dermot asked very quietly, watching her closely.

'You can ask – but I might not answer it.'

'Is it true what they say about you . . . about Madam Kitten?'

Katherine looked away, her gaze drifting back to the print of Hell on the wall. 'It is true that Madam Kitten runs one of the most exclusive brothels in Monto, and has an interest in a string of flash houses. It is also true that she deals in stolen goods and has financed several . . . well, shall we say, shady deals. It is also true that little happens in Dublin without her coming to hear of it.' She looked back to Dermot. 'But it is also true that Madam Kitten has survived – against all the odds.'

There was a brief knock on the door, and then a young boy came shyly into the room. He stopped a few paces from the chair, looking from Dermot to Katherine and then back to Dermot.

Katherine reached out her hand and the boy came eagerly to it, holding the outstretched fingers tightly, possessively, but his eyes never leaving Dermot's face. 'This is Patrick,' Katherine said proudly, 'Patrick, say hello to Mr Corcoran . . .'

The boy immediately extended his right hand, surprising Dermot, who then tentatively reached out with his own hand and shook it. 'I am pleased to make your acquaintance, Mr Corcoran,' the boy said gravely.

'I am honoured,' Dermot replied equally seriously, bowing his head.

'You had an enjoyable walk?' Katherine asked, automatically straightening the boy's jacket.

The boy, conscious of the attention focused on him, nodded seriously. 'Yes, thank you, mother. It was very enjoyable.'

Katherine smiled, and then felt a sudden pang of . . . regret? If things had turned out differently, this could have been Dermot's boy standing before her. She looked over at Dermot and, from the way he was looking at Patrick and the expression in his eyes, she imagined the same thoughts were running through his head. 'Patrick,' she said., 'will you tell Nuala that Mr Corcoran will be staying for lunch – and probably for dinner too.'

'Yes, mother.'

'And Patrick,' she added, 'will you ask Billy to have some more tea sent in. Mr Corcoran and I have a lot of talking to do.' When the door closed, she turned back to Dermot. 'Perhaps you should begin ...' she suggested.

'My story is short enough ...' Dermot protested.

'Exactly,' Katherine said with a smile, 'Mine, I'm afraid, is not.'

CHAPTER TWENTY-THREE

Although the two men were dressed as civilians, their walk betrayed them. They carried themselves tall and erect and had automatically fallen into step with each other, and it was immediately obvious that they were – or had been – military men.

'His Majesty is not pleased with the course of events, I take it?' the taller of the two men asked.

'He is inconvenienced,' the smaller man said with a thin smile. 'We had something of a struggle to prevent him from coming ashore.'

Major John Lewis grinned. The years had been kind to him; he was now a distinguished-looking man – tall, ruggedly handsome, with dark piercing eyes ringed with tiny wrinkles. There was grey at his temples. And he had affected a moustache which served to disguise his thin, somewhat cruel lips.

The brigadier, however, remained almost completely unchanged, and Major Lewis found the small man reminded him rather unnervingly of the character in that book by Wilde – Dorian Gray – which his wife had insisted on reading to him.

John Lewis looked out across Kingston Harbour to where the majestic lines of the royal yacht *Victoria and Albert* would soon be rocking gently on the swell, and nodded. 'No doubt, but I am happier having him out there than in the Castle, or even in the Lodge.'

The brigadier stopped and leaned on the metal railings that lined the pier, and stared out across the waves. 'Perhaps, but he makes the point that, if he is to be attacked, then the attackers will have every opportunity of doing so while he wanders around the town performing one of his dreary duties – his words,' he added, 'not mine. He claims he is coming to Ireland to visit his subjects, and he resents this interference.'

The major shook his head. 'Aye, that may well be so, but I'll still be happier with him sleeping out there in the evenings. However, having said that, I must admit that my spies, although aware of a growing feeling of ill-will in certain quarters towards British rule here, can find little or no signs of ill-will towards the royal couple, even amongst the nationalists. I don't think there will be any attempt on his life.'

'He believes the same. But then, the King always did have a soft spot for Ireland.'

'He did his military training here in the Curragh in '68, and has found time to visit the country on numerous occasions.' Major Lewis smiled thinly. 'You don't think he would try to come ashore illicitly, do you?'

The brigadier looked shocked; the idea hadn't occurred to him. 'I hope not! We couldn't guarantee his safety under such circumstances!'

'We cannot guarantee his safety under any circumstances,' Major Lewis remarked cynically.

Because of the uncertain political situation in the country, the King had been persuaded that the Viceregal Lodge and Dublin Castle might not be the most suitable places for the royal couple to stay, and so it had been suggested by Lord Aberdeen, the Viceroy, that they might stay on the royal yacht overnight and travel to and from their duties during the day. The King was dismayed, and said so in no uncertain terms. He claimed he had always been treated with courtesy and kindness by his Irish subjects, and he was sure nothing untoward would happen. His advisers had agreed, but it was not the Irish activists they were worried about. The situation in Europe had been deteriorating over the past few years, and they were afraid that one of the European political groups might attempt an assasination in an effort to gain publicity and recognition.

Officially, the royal couple were under the protection of the Dublin Metropolitan Police as well as certain units of the army, but unofficially the task of protecting them during their stay in the capital had fallen to the brigadier's office, and he had charged his most competent officer, Major John Lewis, with the assignment.

The major mobilized his spies, but surprisingly they could find very little anti-royalist feeling. Anti-English feelings were beginning to grow and there was certainly a considerable amount of ill-will felt towards the English government for its recent policies. But generally the royal couple were held in high regard, and looked upon with a certain amount of affection, especially by the poorer classes.

'When will the yacht arrive?' Major Lewis asked.

'Around four in the morning.'

'And he knows about the loss of the jewels?'

'He knows.' The brigadier turned to John Lewis. 'Have your people found anything yet?'

'Nothing. We've investigated every suspect, but perhaps the most interesting statement we received was from a Mrs Farrell.'

'And she is . . .?'

'Mrs Farrell is the cleaning woman in Dublin Castle; she is a woman of excellent character and reputation.' He pulled out his notebook and, leaning both arms on the metal rails, consulted it. 'Yes, here it is . . .' He glanced over at the slim, grey-haired man. 'This was in response to a question asking whether she had noticed anything unusual in the past few months . . . She says that about five or six months ago, when she was cleaning the rooms on the first floor, she heard someone moving about downstairs. She went out on to the landing and looked over the bannister, and says she saw someone – a man – pass on the landing below and cross to the library door. She says that she may have made some noise, or exclaimed in fright, because the man looked up and said something reassuring, like "That's all right" or "It's all right".

'The man in question then moved to the bottom of the long library table, but because the early morning sun was blinding her, Mrs Farrell was unable to see what he was doing. She thought he might be writing a note, but when she checked a few moments later after he had left, there was no note on the table.'

'Did she recognize the man?' the brigadier asked.

The major folded the notebook and slipped it into his pocket. 'She was able to positively identify the man.'

'We have our thief, then!'

'Not quite, sir; Mrs Farrell claims the man was the Lord-Lieutenant's son, Lord Haddo!'

'Impossible!'

'She is quite positive,' Major Lewis said slowly, staring out to sea. 'She is an independent witness, her testimony is lucid and not exaggerated, and interestingly she is not making an accusation but simply reporting what she saw.'

'What she thought she saw.'

Major Lewis hesistated before answering. 'Yes, sir.'

'This must go no further and the woman must not repeat the story.'

'I've already taken steps to ensure that nothing more will be said.'

The brigadier nodded. 'Good. What other steps have you taken?' He gestured suddenly and walked away, the major falling into step beside him.

'I have investigated the political angle thoroughly,' Major Lewis began. 'I was working on the theory that the jewels were stolen expressly to embarrass the government or the King. However, no-one connected even vaguely with the nationalists has any access to the keys of the safe. I was forced to conclude that this robbery was conducted from the inside.'

The brigadier grimaced. 'Messy . . . very messy.'

'It gets even messier,' Lewis said. 'Some of the men involved are . . . shall we say of a certain inclination with regard to women – or should I say, men.' He glanced quickly at the brigadier, and noticed with amusement that colour had come into the man's cheeks. 'I intend to pursue some inquiries in the establishments

269

in Monto which cater to such men. Perhaps we might hear of someone spending large amounts of money or boasting of coming into wealth.'

'It's doubtful.'

'I know, but I am following up every lead.'

'Anything else?'

'There is a woman in Monto, the madam of one of the flash houses who deals in information and news. She also has a reputation for handling stolen goods, and I was thinking that if the jewels were offered up for sale, she would be one of the first to hear of it.'

'Have you had any dealings with her before?'

'Some – but always through intermediaries. However, because of the sensitive nature of this case, this time I think I might pay her a visit myself.' He saw the brigadier's lip curl in disgust, and smiled inwardly.

'And what is the name of this woman?'

'I believe she is called Madam Kitten.'

'I learned you had gone the following day – Christmas Day,' Dermot said, turning the glass in his hand slowly, allowing the slanting light to catch the refractions and reflect ruby-coloured light on to Katherine's face. 'Granny O'Neill told me about you when she came to visit my family on Christmas morning.' He paused and glanced up at her, 'Do you have any contact with Granny O'Neill now?'

Katherine smiled fondly. 'She delivered Patrick, and we've kept in touch over the years. I make sure she wants for nothing.' She said this almost accusingly.

Dermot heard the new note in her voice, and shrugged. 'She's a proud woman – you know that – and she'll accept nothing from my family. We've tried, God knows we've tried, but she won't take charity.'

'Then don't give her charity – give her what she's due! Don't ask her what she wants – just give! She won't insult you by returning a gift.' Dermot opened his mouth to reply, but Katherine shook her head quickly. 'I'm sorry, I didn't mean to snap. It's just it angers me

270

to see the old lady left alone and friendless now.' She shook her head again. 'I'm sorry, I'm doing it again. Continue – please.'

Dermot sipped at the glass of wine Katherine had poured from the cut-glass decanter on the table. 'There is little enough to tell. I have remained in the *Freeman's Journal* – as you know – and over the years I've written several articles on the conditions of the working class in Dublin. I've tried to point out that those conditions will only improve when the authorities stop regarding the Irish as second-class citizens, a source of cheap labour and domestics.' He stopped, grinned and then shrugged. 'You shouldn't get me started . . . Anyway, my articles have gained me a certain notoriety, some admiration and more than a little enmity.'

'Why do you do it then?' Katherine asked, staring him straight in the face.

'I do it because it is the only way I know to highlight the problems in this country at the moment. I do it in the hope that something will be done . . . before it is too late, before words are no longer enough.' He paused and added softly. 'And I used to do it to honour the memory of a woman who told me that I had a duty, not only to myself but to the people of Dublin, to show up the injustices.'

'Used to – past tense?'

'That was before today – before I knew you were alive.'

Katherine smiled and bent her head to her glass to hide the sudden colour in her cheeks. 'And now, or rather in the future, whom will you write them for?'

Her direct question caught him unawares, and he stumbled and began to stutter as he attempted to answer. 'Well, I-I-I would of course like to c-c-continue dedicating them to you – as my wife!'

It was Katherine's turn to be startled. She shook her head slightly, and Dermot saw the lines in her face harden into resolution. 'I cannot,' she said simply.

'But why – why?'

Katherine got to her feet and went to walk past him, but Dermot reached out and gripped her hand, holding it tightly. She looked down into his pale – and still boyish – face and gently eased her hand free. 'I cannot, Dermot.' She crossed to the window, and stood, framed in the tall rectangle of light staring down into the cobbled street. 'Perhaps I should have said yes to you when you asked me to marry you all those years ago,' she said, without turning around, her voice wistful. 'In fact, I know I should have said yes. I realized it a few weeks after I left the Lewis house. Things would have been hard for us at first, but I would have been a good wife to you and I know you would have made a good father for Patrick.'

'It's not too late . . .'

'Oh Dermot, don't be so foolish.' She spun around, the early afternoon light behind her, lending her an ethereal unworldly quality. 'There are too many years, too many experiences between us. You have achieved your ambition, you are a fine reporter, a respected member of the community, championing the causes of the poor in this city. I am a madam in a brothel; I arrange the sale of women's bodies to sex-hungry men. My predecessor was called the Whoremistress – and I've inherited that title. How can there be any common ground between us now?'

'Not even love . . ?'

The simple question stopped her cold. She took a few steps forward and placed her hand against Dermot's cheek. His flesh was smooth and slightly flushed. He reached up and held her fingers against his skin, and kissed the ball of her hand.

'Not even love?' he whispered again.

'Affection perhaps, friendship and gratitude certainly, but I don't know about love,' she answered truthfully.

'You loved me once,' he said, almost accusingly.

Katherine shook her head. 'Perhaps. I don't know. I was fond of you, yes, certainly, and perhaps I even loved you a little. But now, I'm not so sure, I don't think I even know what love is any more. In my business love is something we sell nightly. Look!' she said suddenly, pulling away from him and crossing to the fireplace. 'Go now, but come back to me tonight . . .' She saw the look of surprise mingled with horror on his face and smiled at his reaction. 'We'll talk,' she said firmly, 'I take no part in my girls' activities. I've only ever slept with one man, Dermot, and you know who that was. And you also know what it cost me.' She crossed to the door and opened it slightly. 'Come back after nine or so; everyone should be busy then; we'll talk.'

Dermot stood up and pulled on his coat in silence and then walked to the door. He stood for a moment, staring into Katherine's eyes, trying to remember them as they had once been, clear and innocent, but he couldn't. This woman's eyes were worldly and wise, an older woman's eyes . . . a stranger's eyes. 'Tonight then?'

'Tonight,' she nodded.

As Dermot padded down the heavily carpeted stairs, Patrick came out of his room, which adjoined Katherine's, and peered over the bannister rail. 'I thought the man was joining us for lunch,' he said, looking back over his shoulder at his mother.

'He recalled a previous engagement,' Katherine said absently.

'Will he be back?' the boy asked.

'Oh, he'll be back.'

Number Eighty-Two officially opened for business around eight or eight-thirty, although naturally there was admittance at an earlier time by appointment for certain gentlemen who sometimes called in on their way home from their offices. But on a normal working day, all the girls were ready in the large sitting-room a little after eight. The gentlemen callers – who were admitted by sight or by personal recommendation only – were shown into the brightly lit room to find the young ladies engaged in the type of activities they were likely to find their own wives, fiancées or mothers engaged in: sewing, crocheting, reading, drawing or playing the recently restored antique harpsichord that took up one corner of the room. The mysterious black-clad and veiled madam would introduce the girls one-by-one to any newcomer, although most of the clientèle of the house were regulars who had regular girls. Wines would be brought from the madam's small but interesting cellar and, after a 'respectable' interval, the gentleman, with the lady of his choice on his arm, retired to one of the luxuriously appointed bedrooms on the floor above.

The girls had been chosen by Katherine herself, and she had tutored them in some of the erotic arts she had learned about during her travels. In addition, they were given speech lessons and a dancing instructor attended the house twice a week. He was a small dapper Italian who took his payment in kind rather than cash, and was currently working his way through every girl in the house. Katherine read to the girls from the daily newspapers each evening, bringing them up to date on world and home events, ensuring that they could at least converse with their clients.

Katherine insisted on strict cleanliness, and this applied to the clients also; any gentleman who refused to bathe before lying with one of the girls was asked to leave. If the girls thought a man to be diseased – which occasionally happened – then he was asked to leave, and instructed not to return! If some of these gentlemen were inclined to threaten to blacken the house's name, Katherine in turn threatened to reveal the reason the man had been thrown out in the first place.

Each of the girls also had a speciality, or took care of men with certain tastes, and there was one girl who catered for the needs of other women, but she more often than not attended her clients' homes rather than have a lady come down to Monto.

In a city with more than its share of brothels, Number Eighty-Two, Tyrone Street Lower was something very special, and certainly the most successful.

* * *

'How is business tonight?' Katherine asked as Tilly came into the room.

'Good; there are some guards and dragoons in. They're a bit rowdy, but generally good-humoured. I don't think they'll stay though, I think they find the atmosphere intimidating and not as free as they're accustomed to in a house of this kind.'

She sank down into a chair opposite Katherine and turned to face the fire's glowing coals. In the darkened room, it was the only light. 'I'll go back down again in a minute, when I catch my breath,' she said. 'You know, I think I'm getting too old for these long, late nights. I'm quite exhausted. I remember when I worked the streets, I'd be out from late afternoon until eight or nine doing the hotels and theatres, and then back here, where I'd certainly be awake most of the night.' She shook her head, remembering. 'God, but I remember those days . . . and I'm glad they're over,' she added feelingly.

Katherine laughed quietly, 'You're getting old – we're all getting old.'

Tilly grinned in satisfaction. 'That's better. You've been looking very glum today; do you want to talk about it?'

'Talk about what?' Katherine asked, looking deep into the fire, watching shimmering pictures form and reform within the flames.

'You had a visitor today,' Tilly suggested. 'Did he upset you? If he did, I'll get Mickey and one of the boys to have a few words with him.'

'No, no, it's nothing like that – and you really must stop worrying about me, you're like a mother hen sometimes. I can take care of myself.'

Tilly nodded, but without much conviction.

'It was someone out of my past, a young man called Dermot Corcoran. He's a journalist now, and was investigating the disappearance of the Crown Jewels. He thought Madam Kitten might have heard something.'

'And has she?'

'Nothing, but I hope to have some more information

on the people involved in the morning. Anyway, Dermot's visit brought back memories, some pleasant, some not so nice.'

'Does he know your identity?' Tilly asked.

'I told him.'

Tilly shook her head slightly. 'That might not have been such a good idea . . .'

'He won't say anything,' Katherine said confidently.

'Will he be back?'

'I've asked him to see me again tonight; we've some talking to do.'

'Don't tell him too much,' Tilly advised. The brass carriage clock on the mantelpiece chimed once – half-past nine – and she stood up slowly. 'I had better go down. That old army colonel is back again – you know the one who smokes those wretched cigars. All he wants to do is to talk to someone about his amorous conquests.' She sighed and smoothed down the front of her gown. 'I suppose I'll have to talk to him – at least it will leave one of the girls free to attend to someone else. But I'll stink of cigar smoke for days.' She paused by the door. 'Do you want anything?'

Katherine began to shake her head, but then changed her mind. 'If you'll just look in on Patrick for me. Oh, and when Dermot Corcoran calls, will you make sure we're not disturbed.'

'Of course.' One of the waiters came hurrying up the stairs and stood back, waiting for Tilly to finish. 'What is it, Pat?' she asked.

'There's a gentleman asking to see Madam.'

Tilly glanced back and smiled wickedly at Katherine. She turned back to the waiter. 'And does this gentleman have a name?' she said, smiling.

'He says his name is Major John Lewis!'

CHAPTER TWENTY-FOUR

'Don't panic!' Tilly snapped, seeing the look on Katherine's face. She rounded on the startled waiter. 'How did he ask for Madam?'

'He . . . he asked would it be possible to see Madam Kitten.'

'And those were his words? Now this is important Pat – were those his words?'

'His words exactly,' he said nodding.

'And how did you reply?'

'I told him that the Madam saw no-one, but he insisted, and said that he understood that Madam had access to certain information which he might be interested in purchasing.'

'Stay here,' Tilly commanded, and stepped back into the room, closing the door behind her. In the gloom, she could see Katherine's pale face and wide startled eyes. She felt her own heart pounding painfully, and there was a tight knot of apprehension in her stomach. It had been many years since she had last seen the Captain – now, Major – John Lewis. 'I think it's nothing more than coincidence,' she said slowly, trying to keep her voice as calm as possible. 'In fact, it's probably surprising that we haven't received a visit from him before this. After all, you are dealing in news and gossip and we know that he is a collector of information, and what with the theft of the Jewels, he's probably under a lot of pressure to discover as much as possible.'

Katherine was nodding her head before Tilly finished. With every word the explanation became more and more plausible, indeed, even probable.

'You're right, of course, and it only shows just how desperate he is that he's come to me . . .' She stood up and began pacing the floor. 'Tilly, Dermot will be here shortly; you see to him, keep him out of the way while Lewis is here. I'll speak to the major . . .'

'Is that wise? Why not allow me to speak to him?'

Katherine, who had crossed to the chest of drawers and was pulling out a long, black, lace veil, shook her head. 'No. He was acquainted with you for a long time; there is a possibility that he might just recognize you. But he only knew me for a few months and was intimate with me on only four occasions, and all of those were within the course of a single week. He knew you rather better,' she added with a sly grin.

Tilly laughed. 'Yes, he knew me slightly better,' and then sobered immediately. What Katherine was saying made sense. 'Be careful,' she advised. 'He's a wily one – and dangerous too, remember that,' she warned.

'I can't ever forget that. Have Mickey show him up, and then make sure some of the boys stay close at hand. But I hope I won't be needing them.'

Major John Lewis was still finding it difficult to equate the shabbiness of the exterior of the building with the plush interior. Stepping through the battered wooden door, with its stained and chipped paint, and into the hallway was like stepping into another world; the transition was so abrupt as to be shocking. He sat back in a tall, winged leather chair in the corner of the sitting room, sipping a very passable brandy, watching the elegant women make polite conversation to some of the best-known names in the city. It was unlike any other whorehouse he knew in Dublin and, although he had heard stories about some of the Paris and Berlin brothels, he wasn't widely travelled enough to make the comparison, but he imagined it would compare favourably.

A waiter refilled his glass and offered him a choice of fine cigars from a humidor, which he regretfully declined. He wondered what it must cost to run a house like this, with its servants – though, looking at the

278

waiters again, he guessed that they were more than just servants – its fine wines, cigars and food. On a tray in the corner there were salmon and fresh Dublin Bay prawns, along with lamb, turkey and at least a score of chickens. The women were dressed in the height of fashion, and he wasn't prepared to say that all their jewellery was paste. Looking around the room, he tried to arrive at an estimate of the value of the paintings, etchings and photographs on the walls; the carpet was thick-piled and ornately colourful – Turkish, he guessed – and the wallpaper seemed to be of the latest flocked French design. Running a brothel obviously paid, but then, this Madame Kitten was catering for a very exclusive clientèle.

He watched one of the waiters make his way across the floor, heading determinedly in his direction, and he was already on his feet by the time the man reached his chair.

'Madam will see you now, sir. If you will follow me.'

Major Lewis buttoned his dress coat and followed the waiter from the room. The man paused by the door and allowed the major to precede him, and once he had stepped into the hall, he closed the door to the dining room behind them.

There were two men in the hallway waiting for the major. They were both dressed as waiters, although their stance was too arrogant and self-assured for waiters, and the major noticed that the knuckles of both their hands were scarred and swollen. There was a sharp metallic click and then Major Lewis felt the ice-cold barrel of a gun placed against the base of his skull.

'You'll excuse us of course, major,' the older of the two men said. 'But a lot of folks want to see the Madam, and not all of them wish her the best of health – you understand?' He stepped forward and Major Lewis flinched, his hands tightening into fists. He simultaneously felt the gun barrel press even harder against his neck, and saw the second waiter produce a short, thick, wooden stick with a swollen, rounded end – lead-filled, no doubt.

The older man smiled. 'Now, no need to fret yourself. We have to take precautions and no disrespect meant.'

'None taken,' Major Lewis said slowly, unbuttoning his dress coat and pulling it open with both hands. The lanyard ring and checkered grip of his Webley-Fosbery was clearly visible in the special pocket cut into the coat under his left armpit.

The older man gently hooked out the heavy pistol between his forefinger and thumb, and then stepped back from the major.

'I am an army officer,' the major said slowly, unsure how these three men would take the presence of the pistol.

The senior of the three men nodded. 'We know that sir, an' we were told you might be carrying something like this. You'll understand, I'm sure, but we'll be holding on to this until you're leaving. Billy and Pat here will take you up to see Madam now.' He nodded to the major and then walked down the long corridor towards the back of the house, the pistol still held loosely in his hand. The heavy weight of the gun was removed from the major's neck, and he heard the double click as the hammer was let down. He glanced around in time to see the waiter return the gun under his arm. When he turned back to the other man, the ugly wooden stick was no longer visible. The man stepped away from the bottom of the stairs and gestured. 'This way, sir,' he said, his accent immediately betraying that he was from the north, most probably Belfast. He took the first few steps, then waited for the major to follow him, and the second waiter – the one with the gun – followed on behind.

While they climbed the stairs – and Major Lewis guessed that they were heading for the top floor, the only floor that had not been showing any lights from the street – he quickly reviewed what he knew of Madam Kitten. And that was precious little.

She had first come to his notice a few years ago, when the house was still being run by the notorious Madam Bella Cohen. Kitten, which was apparently Bella Cohen's pet name for the girl, was the old woman's assistant – although there were rumours which said that she was her daughter or niece. The day-to-day running of the house was left to her, and she was supposed to be well-educated and well-travelled. Even during Bella Cohen's time, she had begun making changes, turning Number Eighty-Two from just another brothel into something very special.

She had also begun to deal in information around this time, since her unique situation allowed her access to the most delicate and interesting secrets and snippets of gossip. One of the major's street spies had learned of the fees the woman was paying for verifiable news and had passed on the information to the major. He had dismissed it at first, assuming that this Kitten was only interested in gossip relating to her trade.

However, when, following a spectacular jewel robbery in Dublin's fashionable Grafton Street, it became apparent that the thieves had been aware of the gemstones' arrival date, and when he subsequently learned that Kitten had sold the information to the gang for a sizeable amount of money and a percentage of the profits, only then did he realize the seriousness of her interest. He had kept a check on her activities over the years – which was no easy task, as she remained a very secretive person, and both her staff and her girls were devoted to her, and could not be bought or intimidated into revealing any information about her.

Early the previous year, the Major had had one of the girls snatched on her way back from Sunday Mass and two of his men had attempted to extract information about her employer from her, at first by threats and then by a beating. For two days following the kidnapping the major received reports from his men, and then they suddenly ceased. When the major sent some of his people down to check up on them, they found that the

281

two men and the girl were missing. The men turned up three days later in the Mater Hospital with just about every bone in their bodies broken. Both subsequently died from their injuries and the doctor said that it looked as if someone had systematically worked them over with a hammer or a length of pipe.

The major had filed a report with the proper authorities, detailing his suspicions and requesting permission to bring in Madam Kitten and all her people for questioning. His request had been shuffled from department to department and was finally denied: Madam Kitten, it seemed, had friends in high places. Unofficially, he had received a warning to leave her alone. And, since then, he had maintained a respectful distance from the Madam.

Here, at the top of the house, the sounds of gentle revelry coming from the floors below were almost entirely muffled by the thick carpet and even thicker walls. The first waiter stopped and knocked twice on a smoothly polished wooden door and, without waiting for an answer, turned the handle and eased the door open slightly.

'You're expected,' he said.

The major nodded to him, and, taking a deep breath, he pushed the door open and stepped inside. One of the men immediately pulled the door shut, leaving him standing in a darkness relieved only by one oil lamp at the far end of the room, which had been turned down low. In the grate he could just make out the red glow of coals under the ashes.

'If you walk forward a few steps, you will find a chair.' The voice was low and harsh, slightly hissing, and not immediately identifiable as belonging to a woman.

He took a few tentative steps and felt the back of the hard wooden chair. Manoeuvring round it in the darkness, he sat down.

'You wished to speak to me, Major Lewis.' It was a statement, rather than a question.

'I'll come directly to the point . . .' he began.

282

'I would be very much obliged if you did!'

Major Lewis heard cloth rustle in front and a little to his left, where he judged the woman to be sitting. Now that his eyes had become accustomed to the gloom, he began to make out shapes in the room, a table to his left, another chair off to his right, and an oblong that might have been the woman. 'You deal in information, I understand?'

'Let us not toy with one another, Major Lewis, I am sure you know full well what I deal in.'

'Flesh and gossip,' he smiled, hoping for a reaction, but there was none. 'Very well. You are, no doubt aware of the theft of the Jewels of the Order of Saint Patrick?' When the woman still remained silent, he hurried on. 'I am looking for the Jewels, and am willing to pay quite generously for information that would lead to their recovery.'

'So are a lot of people.'

'You've had other offers?' He sat up straight in the chair, almost tempted to leave it and step forward to the shadowy figure, but guessing that the two armed waiters would be on top of him before he could reach her.

'Several parties are interested in the Jewels, it is true.'

'Do you know where the Jewels are now?' he snapped. 'Have you any idea who stole them?'

'How much are you prepared to pay, major . . ?' she paused and then said, 'You are acting on behalf of the authorities, I take it. But I am curious why they should pick you to undertake such a delicate task.'

Katherine took advantage of the long silence that followed to regain control of herself. She had been shaking with fear when the man had first stepped into the room, but the fear had left her as she began to realize he was just another 'buyer'.

'I liaise between the police and army,' Major Lewis said suddenly, startling her, 'and as such, I undertake tasks which are a little outside the ken of either force.'

'I am sure your brief does not include dealing with a brothel-keeper in Monto.'

Major Lewis amiled. 'My brief is a broad one.'
'Indeed,' Katherine said quietly.
'Are you prepared to deal with me?'
'I'll deal with the highest bidder.'
'No thoughts of patriotism or of what is right enters into your dealings?' he demanded, suddenly growing angry with this – this whore! – who presumed to treat him in this fashion.

'No, Major Lewis, no thoughts of patriotism, or of what is right or wrong, enters into my dealings. Do they really enter into yours, I wonder?'

Somewhere in the building a clock boomed, the reverberations long and slow and both the major and Katherine silently counted ten. 'If you are finished major . . ?' Katherine suggested.

'You haven't answered my question,' Major Lewis said quickly.

'What was your original question?'

He gritted his teeth and took a deep breath before answering. 'Do you know where the Jewels are, and do you know who stole them?'

'To be perfectly truthful, major, I cannot answer either question at the moment. I do not know where the Jewels are – they may well be out of the country by now, though if they are I have not heard of it – nor do I know who stole them – though again, I am sure you have your own ideas. Should any information come to hand I will contact you; we may be able to do business then.'

'Fine.' He stood up and backed away to the door, suddenly eager to leave the darkened room. He stopped with his hand on the handle. And looked back. 'Let me impress upon you the seriousness of this matter. And let me remind you that there would be a substantial reward – with no questions asked – for the return of the Jewels.'

'I will bear that in mind.'

John Lewis nodded, realizing that he would get no

further with the woman. 'I'll leave an address with one of your people.'

'Oh I know where to find you, Major John Lewis. Good night to you.'

Major Lewis opened the door and was unsurprised to find the two waiters waiting for him. In silence they marched him down the numerous flights of stairs to the ground floor, where they were met by Mickey who handed the major back his gun, holding it by the barrel, presenting it butt-first. He then held out his hand with five copper cartridges nestling in his palm.

'Perhaps you might load it later,' he suggested, and then one of the waiters opened the door, while another presented the major with his coat, hat, gloves and cane. 'Good night, sir.'

Without a word, the major slipped his gun into the pocket-holster of his coat, and dropped the bullets into another pocket. He then pulled on his coat and patted his hat on to his head. Stuffing his gloves into his overcoat pocket, he marched out into the night, feeling the anger inside him threatening to explode and over-whelm him. At the foot of the steps, he brushed brusquely past a young man, who was about to start up the steps. 'Why don't you watch where you're going, dammit,' he demanded.

The young man swung around to reply, and his eyes met with the major's. There was a moment of vague recognition, and then the two men turned away, both realizing that they had met before, both puzzling as to when and where.

Major Lewis lingered long enough to hear the young man speaking to the doorman. '. . . an appointment to see Madam Kitten . . .'

The doorman muttered something, and the major assumed that he was asking the young man's name, but the man bent his head forward and the major didn't hear the words. But he was curious; he had seen that man before, although for the life of him he didn't know where. But there could only be one reason for someone

285

inquiring to see the Madam this night, and that was surely in connection with the missing Jewels. He quickened his pace; by the time that young man left the house, he wanted to have someone in position to watch him. He would find out who he was – and by doing so he might identify the mysterious Madam Kitten in the process!

By the time Dermot was shown upstairs, all the lamps in the room had been lit and the fire coaxed to a flame of sorts. Katherine was adding a log to the fire when Dermot was shown in. She stood up and brushed her hands briskly together, smiling openly at him. 'Thank you for coming,' she said warmly.

'I'm sorry I wasn't here earlier, but I was held up in the *Freeman*'s offices. This Crown Jewel affair is causing all sorts of problems.'

'Not to worry,' Katherine said. 'In any case, I wouldn't have been able to see you. I had an unexpected visitor. He's just gone.'

'I passed someone on the way in,' Dermot said, pulling off his coat and draping it over the back of the chair Major Lewis had so recently vacated.

'Did you recognize him?' Katherine asked with a smile.

'His face looked terribly familiar, but I can't say I know his name. What is he, a lawyer, barrister, a politician . . ?'

Katherine shook her head, laughing, and then a sudden thought struck her and she sobered immediately. 'He didn't recognize you, did he?'

'I doubt it; he was moving far too fast, and seemed a little preoccupied. Who was it?' he asked.

'That was Captain John Lewis,' she said simply. 'He's a major now,' she added.

Even from the distance, she could see the colour drain from his face, and she poured him a whiskey and added a dash of water. 'Drink this,' she commanded.

Dermot tossed off the drink in one swallow, and then

proceeded to cough and choke for the next five minut
while tears streamed down his face. 'Sorry, I hardly ev
drink . . . I didn't know it was whiskey . . .'

'Suddenly my past seems to be catching up with m
Katherine said, pounding his back. 'First you, and no
the major. I suppose we'll have Mrs Lewis appeari
next.'

Surprisingly, Dermot shook his head. 'I doubt it.
used to see her regularly; she used to attend meetings
one of the literary organizations I belong to. She w
also a member of the Gaelic League a little while ag
But I haven't seen her for some time now – I heard s
was very ill.'

'Was she? Well, I find it difficult in my heart
forgive what she did to me.' Katherine went to sit in h
armchair by the fire. 'Although I'm surprised she w
accepted into the League.'

'Why?' Dermot asked, sitting down in the ch
opposite, his eyes never leaving her face. 'Why shou
she be excluded?'

'Because of her husband's activities,' Katheri
suggested.

'Mrs Lewis worked hard for the League; she was ke
and well respected.'

'Why did she stay in the League?' Katherine asked.

'She – like the rest of us – realized that the Gae
League will be a major force for change in this countr
Dermot said proudly, 'every right-minded Irishman ai
woman has a duty to join.'

'Nonsense!'

'We are endeavouring to make Ireland Irish agaii
Dermot said a little stiffly.

'That is impossible now,' Katherine said, sipping h
mulled wine. 'The two communities, the two culture
are inseparably intertwined.'

'I can't expect you to understand, I suppose,' Derm
said, a touch of anger creeping into his voice. 'After a
you aren't Irish.'

287

'And I'll thank you not to be so damned condescending,' Katherine snapped.

Dermot raised both hands, palm outwards. 'I'm sorry, I didn't mean to discuss politics; in fact, I've been promising myself over the past few months that I would refrain from mentioning politics at all. I'm getting a reputation at work which I don't really want, and ending up in far too many arguments.'

'And what sort of reputation is that?' Katherine asked, allowing her anger to die down.

'Ah,' he shrugged, 'a bit of a hothead, I suppose.'

'I've heard you called a revolutionary,' Katherine said quietly, watching him.

Dermot nodded reluctantly. 'Yes . . . well, I've been called that. And my articles are seen as proof that I'm out to undermine the very fabric of society.' He shook his head abruptly. 'Look, there I go again. Please forgive me. We've got so much to discuss, and I don't want to waste our time together on trivialities.'

'It's not trivial to me,' Katherine said with a smile. 'It helps me build up a picture of you and how you've changed over the past few years.'

Dermot shook his head. 'Don't remind me; tell me all about you.' He looked around the room, and waved an arm to encompass it. 'Tell me how you came to get all this,' he said. .

Major Lewis had walked past the GPO and was just crossing Princes Street, when he suddenly remembered the identity of that young man. He was . . . he was Corcoran, Dermot Corcoran, a prominent crusading journalist and a vocal and active supporter of the nationalists. He had a file on him – if his memory served him correctly – he had even tagged him as being one of those people to watch. He stopped in the middle of the street and looked down to the *Freeman's Journal* offices on the left-hand side of the street, remembering. Yes, Corcoran had been the reporter investigating the death of the young girl who had once been a servant in his

288

house. Looking into the darkened street, he could vividly recall the night he, with his hired bullies, had dragged the young man over into the shadows there on the right and beaten him as a warning to stay out of Monto.

And now here he was again, obviously looking for some leads on the Crown Jewel affair. Unless, of course, he was one of the people the Madam had mentioned who had already made inquiries. Or perhaps he was even one of her sources.

Major Lewis touched the pistol under his arm, and smiled. It was time he renewed his acquaintance with Dermot Corcoran.

CHAPTER TWENTY-FIVE

'It was a woman called Tilly Cusack who actually brought me here in the first place.' Katherine began, staring into the fire, watching the flames dance across the coals. 'I had been making my way back to Granny O'Neill's when I was accosted by two drunken soldiers and, in the scuffle, I'd fallen and struck my head on a wall. Tilly was one of the group of street-women who found me.' Katherine settled into the winged leather chair and looked back to the glowing coals. 'It was she who suggested that the safest place for me in Dublin would be Monto in one of the brothels; it was she who brought me to the Whoremistress, Madam Bella Cohen . . .

'Bella Cohen you will have heard about. She was notorious; one of the most powerful women in Dublin and virtual ruler of Monto. She ran a string of houses, with nearly a hundred girls and more than two-score of bullies to protect her work. She had a heart of stone, and was extremely bitter at the loss of her beauty over the years, and was often jealous of some of the prettier women working for her.

'But she was very good to me, and I grew to be very fond of her. When you saw what a lonely and sad old woman she was, it was easy to forgive her tempers, her petty jealousies, her drunkenness. She was religious too, with that sort of fervent religiosity only whores and fanatics have, and every room in this and all her other houses had at least one holy picture on the wall. Of course, there was often a hollow behind the picture which concealed a length of pipe or a stick for dealing with difficult customers.

'Anyway, she took me and insisted I move in with

her in her own private apartments on the ground floor. She lived in two connecting rooms, a dining room and a bedroom; they were both incredibly crowded, and Bella had a magpie-like tendency for collecting useless, shining things and never throwing them out. The bottom drawer of one of her dressers was completely filled with old scent bottles. Her bed was a double bed, although she never slept with any of the men – no, that's not true, there was one, an old man who visited twice a year. He was the captain of a freighter, I think, and an old sweetheart of hers, and I imagine they slept together for company or out of habit rather than anything else. There was a picture of the Sacred Heart above her bed, and another of the Holy Family across from it. There was a crucifix nailed above the sitting room door, and in a niche in the bedroom she kept a penny candle burning before an alabaster statue of the Blessed Virgin.

'For the first few weeks I was a curiosity, both for her and the girls, but they treated me well, very well, and the girls particularly seemed to take a great delight in bringing me presents of fruit and chocolate sweets. Although the girls were carrying on the most worldly of professions, they were very innocent and almost child-like in many ways.

'Tilly had warned the madam that I was being sought by the father of my child and, although I didn't understand then what was happening, it appears that a lot of people suddenly grew very interested in the whereabouts of a displaced pregnant servant girl. The captain probably thought I might go on the streets – like the poor girl before me – and a lot of the street-girls were picked up and questioned by the police. I think it was only then that I began to understand just how much authority Captain John Lewis actually wielded.

'And then things quietened down, although there was a sudden burst of interest later, around the time the child was due, and a lot of the midwives and doctors in the district were questioned then, including Granny O'Neill. In a strange way, all this interest by the police

291

only served to ensure my place with the Whoremistress, and dispel any doubts she might have had about the stranger living with her.

'Anyway, I started to work for Madam. I did the accounts, working out the takings, and then deducting the various expenses and bribes – which were numerous. I noticed that she was buying her alcohol from three different suppliers, and so I suggested buying it all from the one supplier and negotiating a larger discount. I knew that was how the restaurant I had worked in back in Blackpool had operated, but I'd no idea about how to put it into practice. Madam, however, was enthralled by the idea and insisted that I go around to her main supplier and work out a cheaper price. I was a bit wary about doing this on my own, and afraid I should be recognized, so she dressed me up in the black gown with the veil and sent one of her bullies – Mickey it was, the older of the waiters downstairs – with me. The wine and spirit merchant was more than a little loath to deal with a woman, but I think the presence of the huge thug encouraged him. I suggested a twenty-five per cent discount; the dealer laughed and said ten; I insisted, he compromised and went up to fifteen, but he wouldn't budge from that. And then Mickey put his huge hand on my shoulder and asked me, in one of the softest whispers I've ever heard from a large man, how much I'd settle for. I told him twenty per cent. So he grabbed the dealer by the throat, and growled, "We'll be taking twenty per cent." The dealer squeaked and nodded, and that was that. From that day on I could do no wrong in Madam's eyes. I bargained with all the tradesmen, hammering out discounts for Madam's houses, and even cut down on the number of bribes being paid to people who had no real power to harm or interfere with the day-to-day running of the house. Bella Cohen was delighted; she told me I was a natural madam and from then on she actually went out of her way to teach me all she knew about the workings of a bawdy house.

'In June of 1899, my son was born, and it was then I

met Granny O'Neill once again. Bella was fussing around like an old mother hen, complaining all the time that she could get no work from the girls as they waited for news. She offered to move me to one of the lying-in hospitals, but I didn't want to do that; I was terrified in case Captain Lewis had put a watch on them. He knew when I had become pregnant and it would have been a simple matter for him to work out roughly when the child was due, and so I insisted on having the child "at home". Bella became insistent. I went to hospital, but I worked myself up into such a state that in the end she merely nodded and said she would find the best midwife in Monto. Less than half an hour later, she returned with Granny O'Neill.

'I'm not sure who was the more shocked, but Granny O'Neill later said that she lost about ten years of her life when she was picked up by two bullies and escorted to one of the most notorious brothels in Dublin. And that when she saw just who it was lying in the Whore-mistress's bed, she lost another ten. But all her questions had to be saved for later, because the moment she walked into the room – almost as if he had been waiting for Granny O'Neill to arrive – my labour pains began in earnest.

'My labour was neither long nor difficult, I'm told, but it was one of the most frightening things I've ever experienced, and I was truly grateful that Granny O'Neill was there. I made myself a promise that, if ever I was going to undergo the ordeal of pregnancy again, I would make sure that the father of the child would be by my side.

'In the first few months following Patrick's birth Granny O'Neill came to visit me daily, and the friendship which we had begun in the Lewis household was renewed and strengthened, and has lasted to this day. I still see her now and again, and while she doesn't agree with what I'm doing we remain friends for all that.

'In 1900, I suggested to Bella that she allow me to travel to some of Europe's capital cities to visit their various red-light districts, to see how they ran their brothels. There was too much competition in Dublin, both on the streets and in the houses, and I thought we should turn the house into something different, something special. And the house as you see it today is the result of those travels. Anyway, we had the money, so over the next two years I travelled to London, Paris, Berlin, Rome, Madrid and Vienna, with very brief visits to Cairo and Algiers. Each time I returned to Dublin I had a list of suggestions for Bella as to what the Europeans were doing, and which of those we might emulate. Some of my suggestions she adopted, others she felt were just not suitable. We had our disagreements of course, but we were close enough at this stage not to allow an argument to hurt our friendship. She treated me like a daughter and my son Patrick called her "Nana" which pleased her no end.

'The most important thing I learned on the Continent was that the brothels were used for more than just selling flesh. They sold drink, yes, and gambling schools were arranged for interested parties; some of them dealt in opium and exotic potions. A few passed stolen goods, or harboured criminals on the run for a fee, but the one thing they all had in common was that they dealt in information and news, selling to the highest bidder or passing it over to another group to be acted upon in some way.

'I immediately realized that this house was in a unique situation as far as that was concerned, especially with the clientèle which we attracted from all walks and professions. Bella had instructed the girls that my word was to be obeyed as hers, so I told them to pass on to me any titbit of information, news or gossip – anything, no matter how inconsequential – that might be of interest to me. Initially, I paid them a straight fee for this, and then attempted to pass on the information myself for a profit. Of course, this was difficult, as what I was selling was often scrappy and disorganized. So I changed my rates and began to pay the girls according to the importance of what they discovered, adding a bonus if what they had passed on turned out to be really significant.

'You know, it is extraordinary the amount of information men tell to their bed partners; small things usually, which they think are of little or no account, small talk to pass the time away. But often when two or three pieces of this trivial information and chat are put together, they provide clues to something of importance: a shipment of gold or coin; someone going away for a spell and leaving a house unoccupied; a scandal; a shop opening; a shop closing . . . everything can be sold to the right bidder. As that field grew both in importance and lucrativeness, I began to buy news and gossip from the street people, the traders, the coachmen, the boot-blacks, the paper boys, the servants, the lower classes, the poor – the unnoticed, the type of people you never think are listening.

'And that's brought me to where I am today. And now – and I can say this without being accused of boasting – nothing happens in Dublin without me knowing about it. Well, almost nothing. The theft of the Crown Jewels was as much a shock to me as to anyone else.

'Bella finally "retired" a couple of years ago. And, although she came to regard me like a daughter and trusted me implicitly, I think she never really understood nor agreed with the selling of information to the highest bidder. She claimed it made me more of a prostitute than the girls working in the bedrooms. She left the house to me, and it's all signed and sealed, in a proper legal fashion.

'And the house . . . well, you can see how I've changed it. Outside it remains just another shabby Dublin tenement, but inside, ah, inside, it can rival any bordello in Paris, Berlin or Vienna.' Katherine finished with a rather breathless smile. 'And that, I'm afraid, is the rather sordid tale of the young maid you once knew.'

Dermot, who had sat through Katherine's story in complete silence, shook his head in astonishment. 'It's difficult to believe . . .'

'But it's true,' she assured him.

'I can't help feeling you've left out a few bits,' he said slowly.

'What; you mean like the time I was attacked by two knife-wielding apaches in the backstreets of Marseilles; or the time a German prince defended my honour solely because I claimed to be Irish; or the time I contracted cholera in Madrid, or when I was kidnapped in Algiers? And what about the occasion when one of the other madams in town sent her gang of bullies around to burn the house down?' she asked with a sly smile.

'You're joking!'

Katherine shook her head and lifted the almost empty bottle of wine. He held out his glass, his eyes never leaving her, trying to gauge whether she was indeed joking. She filled his glass and then added a small amount to her own. Katherine never allowed herself to fall under the influence of drink.

'If even half of what you tell me is true – and I'm certainly not doubting you,' he added hastily, 'then it would make a fabulous story.'

Katherine smiled. 'Why, do you want to write it?'

'Yes!'

'But surely it wouldn't do to write about the trials and tribulations of a madam, making her into a heroine of sorts, when your articles on the evils of Dublin are appearing, condemning the influence the madams have over this whole area? Surely there would be a conflict?'

'I'd write it as a book,' Dermot said quickly, 'a huge novel of contemporary society.'

'No publisher in Dublin would handle it,' Katherine said, suddenly standing up and crossing the room to the bell rope that hung down alongside the fireplace.

'We could have it published in France, yes, in Paris, the publishers there are much more adventurous.'

Katherine shook her head. 'Before you let your

296

literary ambitions run away with you, perhaps we should eat first.' She pulled the bell rope twice, and, although it could only have been his imagination, Dermot thought he heard a bell jangling somewhere deep in the house. 'And I don't think I want you to write my story yet,' she added reflectively. She saw his look of almost childish hurt and disappointment and reached out to stroke his cheek. 'But only because it's not finished yet. When the time comes, you will know when to write it.'

There was a rattle of cutlery outside the door, followed by a single knock, and then the door opened and two waiters appeared, pushing a trolley laden with two large silver tureens, and a score of smaller covered dishes.

'Dinner,' Katherine anounced.

They ate in silence, enjoying the meal which had been prepared in the kitchens of the nearby Gresham Hotel, and disposing of two more bottles of excellent wine from Katherine's cellar. Or rather, Dermot drank nearly all of it; Katherine succeeded in making two glasses last throughout the meal. The oil lamps had been doused and two candles lit, which made the meal into something special. The candlelight served to soften Katherine's features which had hardened over the years, and disguise the few threads of silver which streaked her hair.

'You're very lovely,' Dermot said suddenly, breaking a long silence.

'Thank you.'

Too much wine had dulled his senses and loosened his tongue, but Katherine was prepared to sit back and allow him to ramble on; she realized she would probably learn more about the present Dermot Corcoran this way than any other.

'Have you given any thought to what you're going to do in the future?' he asked her blearily. 'I mean, you know there are changes abroad, and that there is talk of clearing out the brothels.'

'There's been talk like that from the moment I arrived in Monto,' Katherine said with a smile.

'But this time it's different; this time there is a whole lot of social issues involved. We're talking about change, Katherine, major changes, not only here but all across Europe, across the world. And when that change comes, places like Monto will vanish . . .'

Katherine threw back her head and laughed. 'Dermot, listen to me. There have always been brothels, every country in every age has had its brothels and its working girls, and no movement, no change, no matter how wide-reaching will alter that.'

'But what about you?' he demanded beginning to slur his words. 'What will you be doing in five years, ten years, twenty years from now?'

'I haven't thought that far ahead.'

'Why not?' He sat forward and leaned both elbows on the table, staring earnestly into her face. Katherine returned his gaze and noticed how red and flushed his cheeks were, and that his eyes were now slightly glazed.

'Look Dermot, I don't really see where this conversation is leading . . .'

'I'm asking about your future,' he interrupted.

'I don't see any future for myself outside of this brothel,' Katherine snapped. 'I'll probably run this house until the day I die or retire.'

He nodded, seemingly satisfied. 'But I'm offering you a future,' he said, sounding pleased, as if this was where he had wanted the conversation to go to. 'I asked you before, nearly nine years ago, and I asked you earlier today, and now I'm asking you again to become my wife.'

'Well, you're nothing if not persistent,' Katherine said with a smile.

'I'm serious!'

'I gave you my answer today. My reply hasn't changed in a few hours.'

'Look, just think about it,' he said desperately, 'I am offering you the opportunity to leave this life, to live

298

respectably.' He realized he had said the wrong thing when he saw the expression change on her face. 'I'll adopt your son as my own,' he hurried on, 'we can say you're a widow, and . . .'

'No more!' Her voice was ice-cold, matching her eyes. 'What you're offering me is slavery. Yes, I could become your respectable wife, in your respectable home, with you in respectable employment. And what would I have? Nothing! What would I be? Nothing! Here, I have everything I want. Here, I am someone! Now go,' she said suddenly, standing up and walking away from the table.

Dermot stumbled to his feet and the room suddenly swayed around him. He held on to the table for support and then collapsed back into his seat.

Katherine walked back to the table and leaned over him. 'I've worked far too hard and too long to achieve all this; I'm not going to throw it away.' She stared at him for a few moments. 'Now, let's just say it was the drink talking then, and forget about it. But I still think I would like you to go now.' She walked over to the bell rope. 'I'll have someone walk you out of Monto; it's not safe for a well-dressed drunk to be wandering the streets.'

Dermot, realizing that he'd been dismissed, stood up slowly. He was aware that he had offended Katherine, although, in his befuddled state, he wasn't entirely sure just how he'd managed to do it. 'Can I see you again?' he asked.

'I am a busy woman – especially during the day, but most nights I'm free; you can come and see me then. Although,' she added as a sudden thought struck her, 'perhaps it would be better if you left it until the end of the week, or early next week, before you called again. With the royal party in town, business is apt to be hectic.' There was a knock on the door, and then one of the waiters appeared. 'Will you see Mr Corcoran home, or at least to a cab, whichever is the more convenient?' Katherine asked.

'Of course, ma'am.'

'I'm quite capable . . .' Dermot began, but Katherine had passed his coat to the waiter, and he was now holding it open for Dermot to put on.

'If you'll wait a moment, sir, I'll get my coat,' the waiter said in a soft, northern accent.

'There's no need,' Dermot protested, both to Katherine and the waiter. But they ignored him. Katherine and Dermot stood facing each other, waiting for the young man to return. As she stared at him, Katherine realized that he was at least a year – or possibly more, she wasn't sure – older than herself, and yet she felt infinitely older than him. But if one were to count experiences, then she supposed that she was.

The waiter reappeared and stood respectfully by the door. Katherine came over and Dermot took her hand and pressed the backs of her fingers to his lips. 'I'm sorry,' he said in a hoarse whisper.

'There's no need to be,' she smiled.

'I've so much to say to you, and I wanted this evening to have been so special, and now . . .' he shrugged.

'There will be other evenings,' Katherine said, and then looking over at the waiter said, 'Take care of Mr Corcoran for me, Billy, he's an old friend.'

'Yes, ma'am.'

The ragged tramp sitting on the steps of the house opposite Number Eighty-Two looked up as the door of the brothel opened, shafting light down the worn steps. Two men stepped out. One of them, the taller of the two, he recognized as Billy McMahon, one of Madam Kitten's waiters and a native of Belfast, who had accumulated a string of convictions for assault and malicious wounding in the north before he had disappeared a few years ago. The second man though . . .

The tramp squinted in the wan light from the street lights, and then grunted in affirmation. The second man certainly fitted the description the major had given him. He followed the two men down towards Marlborough

Street, where they turned to the right and crossed the road. They then made a left into Findlater's Place, went past the church and headed out into O'Connell Street. He hurried to the far end of Findlater's Place and watched the two men cross to the lines of cabbies in the middle of the street.

Satisfied, the tramp leaned back against the wall and pulled out a tiny notebook, and began making notes with the stub of a pencil . . .

A short length of lead pipe was rammed across his throat, pushing him up and back against the wall!

'Do you want to tell me what you were doing?' Even though he couldn't see his attacker, the northern accent was unmistakable.

'Don't know what you mean, guv'nor.'

The pipe was removed from his throat and, as he was gasping for breath, it came down hard on his wrist, shattering the bone. Before he could cry out, it was back across his throat, cutting off his air.

'Don't be lying to me. You were following me, and I want to know why, and I want to know who put you up to it.'

'You can go to hell!' the tramp spat.

Billy raised the pipe again . . .

CHAPTER TWENTY-SIX

Katherine knew something was badly wrong when she saw Mickey's pale face, and the sheen of sweat on his upper lip. Usually the old man was completely imperturbable, having once said to her that he had seen it all and done most of it anyway.

'What's wrong?' she demanded, sitting up in bed and reaching for her robe.

'We have a problem, ma'am; I think it would be better if you come down to the kitchen. I'll wait for you there.'

'Mickey?' Katherine called, but the old man was gone. As she pulled on her robe, she couldn't imagine what had so upset the man. But something serious, certainly. She glanced up at the ornate carriage clock ticking solemnly on her mantel-piece: half-past one – still early in Monto. She hurried down the stairs, pausing on the second-floor landing to listen to the various sounds of lovemaking, the moans and sighs, the laughter and coarse jests that seeped from beneath the different doors. Everything seemed to be fine here. Downstairs, however, she noticed that both Pat and Jimmy, two of her waiters, were hanging around outside the kitchen door, which was firmly shut. Both men looked anxious and troubled.

'What's wrong?' Katherine demanded.

Pat shrugged. 'We don't know, ma'am, except that it's something to do with Billy.'

'Well, don't hang around here, you'll find out soon enough what has happened, if indeed anything has happened. Now, return to your duties.'

'Yes, ma'am.' They both nodded and backed away rather reluctantly from the kitchen door.

Katherine waited until both men had disappeared into the sitting room before she opened the door to the long kitchen. There were three people waiting for her, Mickey, Tilly and Billy. Mickey was standing by the back door, his arms folded across his chest, staring straight ahead, his face set, Tilly was sitting by the plain wooden table, methodically cutting up a coat, while Billy stood by the large sink, stripped to the waist, washing himself.

The first thing Katherine noticed was the blood. The water in the sink was red with it, and there was blood splashed on Billy's face and caked in his hands. There was blood on the table, long streaks already turning brown on the scarred wood, blood on the coat Tilly was slicing into ribbons, and blood on the length of lead pipe that lay partially wrapped in a once-white cloth – a red-stained shirt – that was thrown on the floor.

'My God, what has happened?' Katherine gasped, and then she looked over at Billy, her eyes widening in horror. 'Dermot?'

But it was Mickey who replied. 'He's fine, ma'am, safe and home by now, I should think. You'd best sit down.'

Katherine shook her head defiantly, her fear crystallizing into anger. 'Just what the hell has happened?' she demanded.

'Billy's killed a police spy.' Tilly said very softly, still shredding the coat, 'beat him to death with the pipe.'

'My God in heaven,' Katherine whispered, crossing herself. She reached out for one of the hard wooden chairs, pulled it over and sat down, her eyes drawn again to the blood-stained water, and then to the ragged coat with its red-black stains. She opened her mouth to speak, but no sound came out.

'He was following us,' Billy said suddenly, his northern accent now harsh and raw with emotion. 'When I came out with your friend, he was sitting on the steps opposite, and then he got up to follow us.'

'Coincidence,' Katherine breathed.

303

'No, no, no,' Billy said, his teeth beginning to chatter. 'I took the long way around to the cab stop, and he followed us every bit of the way. And when I hurried back I found him writing in a little black notebook. I asked him what he was doing, and then there were words and then blows struck, and then I started hitting him . . . and then he was dead,' he sobbed.

'I believe I've spoken to you before about that bar you carry,' Katherine said absently. 'Who saw you?' she suddenly demanded.

'No-one,' Billy said, beginning to shake.

'What did you do when you discovered the man was dead? Think now. Did you come straight back here?'

'No, ma'am,' he whispered hoarsely, 'I went down Marlborough Street, and turned into Abbey street, then went around by Beresford Place and into Gardiner Street.' He had made an huge loop before finally coming back in at the top of the street.

'Were you followed?'

'No, ma'am. I'll stake my life on it.'

'You have,' she snapped, 'yours and ours. Now get dressed, and go to your room. Say nothing to any of the lads. We'll speak later.'

'Yes, ma'am,' he nodded, and then reached into his back pocket and pulled out a small, black-bound note-book. 'I took this from him. I thought it might be useful.' He reached over and placed it on the table beside Katherine. She looked at it as if it were a venomous spider which might suddenly scuttle across and bite her. Billy waited a moment, as if he expected her to say or do something, but when she made no move he wished her and the others a subdued good-night and hurried from the room.

With his departure, the atmosphere in the room seemed to ease a little. Katherine turned to Tilly who had by now almost completely destroyed the blood-stained coat. 'What are you doing?'

'I thought we'd burn these and then throw the ashes

in the river. You know this is going to bring down trouble.'

'I know it,' Katherine sighed. She nodded to the bloody pipe on the floor and looked at Mickey.

'It'll be in the river before the night is out.' He left his place by the door and crossed to the kettle, lifting and shaking it, listening to the water slosh around inside. He transferred the kettle to the stove. 'I'll make some tea.'

'He's a stupid bastard,' Tilly suddenly spat, 'even in Monto you can't kill a policeman and get away with it. We should never have hired him.'

'Well, it's too late for recriminations now,' Katherine said softly. 'We have to decide the best course of action.'

'We'd better get rid of Billy, ship him back to Belfast or even across to Liverpool.'

'No,' Mickey said quickly, 'we must be very careful to do nothing – or at least be seen to do nothing. When the police come looking, they'll want to know where he's gone and why. We've got to keep him for a while, in fact we'll have to make sure everything goes on as before.'

'Mickey's right,' Katherine said, 'we operate as before. Now the royal visit tomorrow – later today,' she corrected herself ' – should help us. The police will be more than busy keeping the crowds under control, and this, coming on top of the jewel robbery, will mean that their resources are going to be stretched to the limit. So it will probably take them a day or two before they get around to investigating . . .'

Mickey shook his head. 'No, I have to disagree with you there, ma'am. We're talking about the murder of a police officer, an' I think you'll find the police are very particular about investigating crimes against their own people. There will be a crew down here with the crack of dawn – if not before, you mark my words.' The kettle began to whistle and he stood up to make some tea.

'I don't suppose there's any way of disposing of the body?' Katherine asked softly, almost to herself.

305

Mickey spoke from beside the range. 'Not now. If Billy had come straight back to the house, I might have considered going out and dumping the body somewhere, but by going around the long way, he's left enough time for it to be discovered.'

'But if what Billy says is true, then the man was watching this house, and probably only this house. As soon as that body is discovered, they will come crawling all over us,' Tilly said, cutting up the last strip of material. She bundled it all up and crossed to the stove, pulling open the small grill and beginning to feed the material in, a piece at a time. Those that were still damp with blood hissed and spat, and the room began to stink with a thick acrid odour.

'There's something in what she says,' Mickey agreed.

'I know,' Katherine said. She reached out and touched the small notebook with the tips of her fingers, nudging it slightly. It was a cheap piece of leather, a skiver leather, and black, the shape and size of the regulation Dublin Military Police notebook. She lifted it and folded back the cover. The pages were covered with a small, fine, precise script, and Katherine immediately received the impression of a rather fussy man. She quickly flipped through the entries, noting the dates, until she reached the last page. There were only two entries, and the last of these was cut abruptly short. She read both entries aloud.

'9.10 Received instruction from maj. to take up position outside No. 82, and watch for small, thin, pale-faced, dark haired young man, wearing plaid overcoat, no hat, no cane, no gloves. Instructions to follow man to destination and report.

'11.35 Suspect left house in company of second man, identified as Billy McMahon, a Belfast criminal now in the employ of Madam Kitten. Suspect seemed to be drunk. McMahon led him to cab stand in Sackville St . . .'

Katherine looked up. 'It finishes there.' She shook her head, more confused than ever now. 'It looks as if he

306

was watching Dermot Corcoran,' she said slowly, 'but why would he be doing that?'

'Read the opening again,' Mickey advised.

'Received instructions from maj. to . . .'

'That's the place,' he said. 'Now who or what is a "maj."? "Received orders from maj." What maj.? What is a maj.?'

'It could be in cypher,' Tilly suggested.

'But the rest of his notes are plain enough,' Katherine said. 'No, it must mean something else.' She looked at Mickey. 'You're familiar with police slang, have you ever heard them use a phrase like that?'

He shook his head. 'Never. The only thing I can think of maj. standing for is major,' he said slowly. And then he looked at Katherine in horror. 'The major!'

'Could the major have seen Dermot when he was here tonight?' Tilly asked quickly.

'No, he left before Dermot arrived.'

'But one was only leaving as the other arrived,' Mickey put in. 'I know, because I had barely closed the door to the army officer when your friend knocked.'

'So they passed on the steps, or met on the street,' Katherine said slowly.

'Almost certainly,' Mickey agreed.

'And the major must have recognized Dermot,' Tilly said, 'and had a watch put on him.'

'We'll get a visit from the major then,' Katherine said slowly.

'But he can't prove anything,' Mickey said, pouring three cups of strong, black tea. 'There will be no evidence, nothing at all. I suggest we brazen it out; admit the young man was here, but deny knowledge of anything else.'

Tilly nodded. 'I agree.'

'I'll speak to Billy then,' Katherine said, sipping the scalding tea and suddenly remembered the last time she had drunk such a foul concoction. She looked over at Tilly, raising her cup in a silent salute, remembering the Christmas Eve standing by the Liffey walls drinking the coffee from the cabmen's shelter. Everything had seemed grim then, but it had all worked out for the best in the end. 'All we can do is to hold on, and say and do nothing out of the ordinary. Given time, it might just blow over.'

'Things like this don't blow over quite so easily,' Mickey said, shaking his grey head. 'Speaking from experience that is,' he added.

It was cold in the bedroom and John Lewis was dressing swiftly and silently when the bell went. He turned to look up in surprise at the clock on the wall over the fireplace. It was a little after half-two in the morning, and hardly the time for visitors. In the bed behind him, his wife mumbled and turned over in her sleep, and in the closeness of the room Major Lewis could smell the reek of stale wine from her. The bell rang again, and this time it was accompanied by an insistent knocking. He stooped down and reached under the bed, pulling out his service revolver and then crept downstairs in his stockinged feet. He stopped at the foot of the stairs. Through the ornately worked glass of the doorway, he could see two shapes, one wearing the distinctive helmet of the Dublin Military Police. He saw a hand raised and then the bell began to ring again, and this time it was obvious that they weren't going to stop until the door was answered.

Major Lewis crept to the door, his stockinged feet sliding on the polished wooden floor. 'Who is it?' he demanded.

The bell-ringer stopped, surprised at hearing a voice so close at hand. 'It's Moore, sir.' Martin Moore had been a decorated lieutenant in the Royal Irish Fusiliers until Major Lewis had asked for his services. Within two days he had been promoted to the rank of captain and had been posted to join Major Lewis in the GPO as his assistant.

John Lewis snapped the bolts back and flung the door

open, startling the young constable who was standing beside Martin Moore. 'What's wrong?' he demanded.

'Can we come inside, sir?' Martin Moore asked. John Lewis stood aside with ill grace, and then ushered both men into the sitting room. It stank of stale smoke and sour wine, and he could see Moore looking around with interest; this was the first time he had ever been inside his senior officer's residence – indeed, it was the first time he had had occasion to call on Major Lewis at home.

'What's wrong?' the major demanded again, placing his gun on the mantelpiece and crossing to the cabinet to pour himself a brandy. 'I'll not offer you one, constable, since you're on duty.' He didn't bother to offer one to Moore whom he knew to be a non-drinker.

'Harris is dead, sir,' Martin said quietly.

'What!' He drained the glass in one swallow and then immediately poured another. 'What happened?'

'Perhaps this constable could tell you; he found the body.'

'I'm Finegan, sir, and attached to the Great Brunswick Street station . . .'

Major Lewis waved his hand. 'Get on with it, constable.'

'Yes, sir. I was patrolling down Sackville Street, sir, and just coming up to Findlater's place when I thought I heard a cry or a shout. Well, it's not unusual to hear noises of that sort, particularly around that place. Some of the street-walkers use it for . . .'

'Constable . . .' Major Lewis said, the warning plain in his voice.

'Anyways, I investigates, sir, and at first I thought I had stumbled across a bundle of rags thrown up against the wall, but when I kicked it, it felt solid, so I flashed my bull's-eye on down over it and found it was a man, a tramp. Well, I was about to move on when I saw the blood. I bent down to have a closer look and . . . well, I'll tell you, sir, you being an army man an' all, he was a fair bloody mess. Someone had worked him over proper with a club, or a bar, or a brick, something solid like that. His head was fair beaten to a pulp.' His voice, which had fallen to a whisper, grew even hoarser as he continued, 'But the most terrifying thing about it, sir, was that he was still alive. I didn't know until he reached out and grabbed my trouser leg. Well, I fair shouted myself, sir; I'm not a coward, but this fair terrified me, sir.' He coughed and continued in a more normal tone. 'Well, I knew he hadn't got long – and I think he knew it too – so I bends down to ask him had he any idea who had done it. And he nodded.' The constable seemed to pause for breath, nodding his own head in affirmation. 'He actually nodded.'

'What did he say?' Major Lewis demanded.

'He said – or at least I think he said – "the lad in eighty-two" or "the lad at eighty-two, he's murdered me".'

'And that's it?'

'He then said the word "pocket", "pocket, pocket, the pocket". I wasn't sure what he wanted then, but I had a look through his pockets in any case. And I found the letter there, sir.'

Major Lewis nodded. The letter the constable was referring to was a single sheet of authorization signed by the Chief Commissioner and the army Commander-in-Chief, confirming that the bearer was acting on their authority. 'And then?'

'Well, when I reads the letter, I started blowing my whistle for assistance. We then got the lad to the hospital; we took him into the lying-in hospital, it being the closest, but he was already dead. Next, I contacted the Castle, and then Captain Moore here arrives.'

Lewis nodded, suddenly weary. This was not the first time he had lost an operative in the field, nor would it be the last, but it always annoyed him intensely. A good man wasted – although obviously not good enough, otherwise he wouldn't be dead – and now he would have to go to the trouble of finding and training a replacement! The clock in the hallway belled the hour,

310

and he suddenly remembered that he was supposed to be in Kingstown by sunrise. He was about to dismiss the constable when a sudden thought struck him. 'Had the man anything else in his pockets? A notebook, for example.'

'No sir. I was with him when they examined him in the lying-in hospital. There was no notebook.'

'Go back to the scene,' Lewis ordered, 'and search the area for a small, black notebook. You go with him, Moore, you know what to look for. Now, I must go, I'll speak to you later on today.'

Both men saluted, 'Yes, sir,' and hurried from the room.

'Find that notebook!'

In the chill dawn light, the royal yacht *Victoria and Albert* sailed into Kingstown harbour, graceful and elegant against the grey and pink skyline, and dropped anchor. The harbour walls were almost completely empty at this early hour, with barely half a dozen people watching the arrival of the vessel.

Muffled against the chill of the dawn, Major John Lewis and the brigadier stood against the newly painted rails and watched the vessel arrive. The brigadier glanced down at the full hunter in his hand. 'Four o'clock,' he said and snapped the face closed. 'It's on time,' he added, looking at Lewis, the rebuke plain in his voice.

'One of my men was murdered tonight,' John Lewis said, almost by way of apology. He had only just arrived, although he had arranged to meet the brigadier a quarter of an hour ago.

'Murdered?'

'Beaten to death with a blunt instrument in the street, within spitting distance of Sackville Street.'

'Has it any connection with the jewels?'

'Possibly; very possibly. My man Harris was watching a reporter named Corcoran with marked nationalist leanings, who you may remember was involved in a murder investigation some years ago, when an old

311

whore he had visited died in mysterious circumstances. Of course, there was no evidence, and he was never charged with anything. But now we have a similar death – and Mr Corcoran appears once again.'

'Almost too good to be true,' the brigadier mused, watching the various flags being run up on the royal yacht and answered on-shore. 'What are the details?'

'I was following up a certain line of inquiry on the jewels which led me to a brothel in Monto, the place run by Madam Kitten – I mentioned it before.'

'I remember,' the brigadier said softly.

I'm sure you do, the major thought, but aloud he said, 'She denied all knowledge of the whereabouts of the jewels, although she did admit that if she found out, she would be prepared to sell to the highest bidder, and led me to understand that she would consider any offer we had to make. When I was leaving, I passed a young man on the steps whose face was familiar. It took me a few moments to realize where I had seen him before. We had met on only one previous occasion and then in ... rather strained circumstances, so it's unlikely he would remember me. But I recognized him.'

'What newspaper?'

'The *Freeman*.' The brigadier nodded for the major to continue. 'I contacted Harris and gave him a full description of this person and instructions to follow him. I know it's a long shot, but I thought the only reason a reporter would be calling on Madam Kitten would be in connection with the missing jewels. I wanted to find out if he was buying or selling information.'

'Understandable.'

Major Lewis shook his head. 'And that's it; the next thing I know is that Harris turns up dead. But, before he died, he said that he had been attacked by, and I quote, "the lad at eighty-two, he's murdered me". I take that to be the man he was watching.'

The brigadier nodded. 'What do you want to do?' he asked, looking across at Lewis.

312

'Bring him in for questioning,' the major said, ducking his head into his muffler to hide his smile. He didn't for a single moment even consider that the reporter Corcoran was responsible for Harris's death, but the idea had come to him during the wild cab ride across town. The reporter was nothing – a nuisance – but Major Lewis wanted something else, something much bigger.

'Right, bring him in. Anything else?'

'I want to search Madam Kitten's brothel!'

CHAPTER TWENTY-SEVEN

Dermot Corcoran came slowly and painfully awake, dimly aware of shouts somewhere in the distance. He lay unmoving in his bed, aware of the pounding in his head, the foul taste in his mouth and the knowledge that if he moved he was going to vomit. His memories of last night were rather dim, and the events of the previous day had become twisted and distorted in a long terrifying nightmare which had kept him from any real rest, although never fully allowing him to come completely awake. A cold rational part of his mind knew that it was merely a combination of the shock of discovering Katherine again and of consuming far too much wine last night. Dermot wasn't a drinker; he couldn't hold it, and usually limited himself to a single glass of wine on social occasions.

He opened his eyes slightly, wincing at the sunlight that shafted through his window – and that, in some vague way, disturbed him. He closed his eyes again and allowed his mind to wander, wondering why sunlight on his bedroom floor should set alarm bells jangling deep inside his skull. And then he suddenly realized why. The sun didn't hit his bedroom until nearly ten o'clock ... but he should have been in work by eight. He sat up suddenly in bed – and felt the room explode around him, and he barely had time to roll over and pull out the chamber pot under the bed before he vomited the undigested food, wine and bile from the previous night. When the wracking spasms had passed, however, he felt better, although he was now cold and shivering, and his head was still pounding abominably. He found he could think reasonably clearly again, and he realized now that he was not due in until the afternoon shift. He

314

flopped back on to the pillow, which, like the sheets, was sodden with his sweat, and mentally reviewed the previous day and night . . .

He became aware once again of the shouting. It seemed to be coming from the sitting room below. Voices raised in anger, demanding, and then heavy footsteps on the stairs. He sat up in bed, holding both hands to his throbbing skull . . . and his bedroom door crashed open. He had a momentary glimpse of a huge constable in the dark uniform of the Dublin Military Police, and then the man was on top of him, wrenching his arm around and high up behind his back. Disorientated, he attempted to struggle, striking out at his attacker with his free arm, and then something solid cracked across the side of his skull. Before he blacked out his last conscious image was of the room filling with police and his mother's pale and terrified face behind them . . .

Mickey tapped on the door, and then turned the handle, opening it. 'It's Mrs O'Neill, ma'am,' he said respectfully, ushering the old woman into the sun-bright room.

Katherine came to her feet and crossed to her old friend, both hands outstretched, smiling warmly. 'Ah, it's such a pleasant surprise. We don't get to see you often enough these days.' She kissed the woman on both cheeks and helped her to a chair.

'I don't often come up this way,' Mrs O'Neill said, her voice soft and whispering, her flat Dublin accent blurred now by the disease which was attacking her throat. The years had not been kind to the old midwife. She had always been thin, but now she was incredibly gaunt, her hands and feet seeming too big and bony for her body. Her head, perched on a scrawny neck, was large and skull-like and her eyes had sunk back into her head.

'You know you're always welcome,' Katherine said, tugging on the bell rope and ordering tea when Nuala poked her head around the door.

315

The two women sat in silence for a while, neither speaking, measuring one another with their eyes; Katherine seeing in the old woman all that she could have become had things been different, Mrs O'Neill seeing in Katherine all that she despised.

'How is Patrick?' she croaked eventually.

'He's well, getting bigger every day,' Katherine said, watching her carefully, wondering what had brought her here. The last time she had stood inside this house had been nearly three years ago, when one of the girls had become pregnant and Katherine had asked her to assist with the birth. Katherine often visited Granny in her rooms in Summerhill, but these occasions had become less frequent over the past few years, although she still sent up food and clothes regularly.

Nuala brought in tea and set it out on the small side table, and then brought it over to them. 'Will that be all, ma'am?' she asked.

'Yes, thank you, Nuala.' The maid bowed slightly and slipped quietly from the room.

'You've done well for yourself,' Mrs O'Neill said suddenly.

'I have been fortunate,' Katherine said pouring the tea.

'You've come a long way from the days you were a maid yourself.'

Katherine smiled, realizing that this was the old woman's way of leading up to something. 'Oh, I've worked hard for it – and I've been very lucky,' she added with a smile.

'Do you ever see any of the people you knew then?' Mrs O'Neill asked casually, too casually, lifting her cup and carefully sipping the tea.

Katherine felt something cold settle into the pit of her stomach. The question disguised something, but coming as it did the day after both Dermot and Major Lewis had visited her, it was startling. 'I . . . I don't think they move in my social circles,' she said finally. 'Why do you ask?'

'For no particular reason,' Mrs O'Neill said, her eyes never leaving hers. 'But do you remember a young lad you were fond of once, a Dermot Corcoran?'

'I remember him,' Katherine said in a whisper.

'I saw him yesterday,' Mrs O'Neill said very slowly, 'he came to me, wondering if I would be able to get him the address of a Madam Kitten. He was doing an article on the theft of the Crown Jewels and he thought she might be able to help.'

Katherine watched her, saying nothing.

'He was arrested this morning an' charged with murder!'

Katherine dropped the cup, the fine china shattering against the edge of the table.

'I thought you might be interested,' the old woman added.

'But what happened, for goodness sake, tell me?'

'First tell me, was he here last night?'

'He was here; he came to ask if I had any information on the missing jewels.'

'Would you be prepared to swear to that in a court of law?' Mrs O'Neill demanded fiercely, her voice rasping painfully.

Katherine paused for a moment, considering, and then she finally shook her head. 'I don't know . . . I'm not sure . . . Yes, yes, I suppose so.'

The old woman relaxed, seeming to sag in the chair. 'I knew you would, Katherine, I know you've gone your way, an' I know we don't agree on that, but deep down you're a good girl, an' I knew you wouldn't see any harm come to Dermot.'

'For goodness' sake, tell me what has happened!' Katherine demanded.

'I don't really know,' Granny O'Neill confessed. 'Richard Corcoran, Dermot's father, sent a cab for me this morning, begging me to call round. When I arrived, I found the house in an uproar. The police had arrived just before ten, an' demanded to see Dermot. Richard, that's Dermot's father, was in the shop, an' Brigid, his

317

mother, was in the house at the time with two of Dermot's younger sisters, an' naturally she was confused an' upset. She sent one of the girls to fetch Richard an' tried to keep the police downstairs, but by the time Richard had returned the police had gone upstairs an' had dragged Dermot from his bed an' hauled him away, still in his nightclothes. Brigid also said that he was bleeding from some cuts to his head. When Richard arrived, they were gone an' so was his son. So he went around to the Castle, where they said they were taking him. After a bit of a wait, he got in to see the lad. Poor Dermot was terribly confused, an' shaken after the bit of a battering he had got, and he didn't really know what was happening. He told his father that they were questioning him about the death of a policeman just off O'Connell Street last night, an' had also brought up the death of an old woman in Summerhill back in '98. He swore he was innocent an' told his father that he'd been with the Kitten last night, an' insisted that his father tell me this, sayin' I'd know what to do. Naturally Richard didn't know what he meant an' apparently, before he could question him any further, he was ordered to leave.' The old woman put down her cup and looked into Katherine's eyes. 'Was he here last night?' she asked, her whispering voice becoming ragged.

'Yes . . . and no,' Katherine said slowly.

'Well, it's one or the other,' she snapped.

'He was here until about one in the morning; when he left, he was much the worse for drink, I should add.'

'They say he beat a policeman to death,' Mrs O'Neill croaked.

'He didn't do that.'

'I know . . . I know, but what will happen if the police charge him? They'll hang him for it . . . It'll kill his mother and father with shame.'

Katherine stood up and paced around the room, finally stopping before one of the tall windows over-looking the street. She stared across the cobbled road to the steps on which the policeman disguised as a tramp had sat last night. She closed her eyes and imagined she saw the ragged figure rise slowly to his feet and shamble down the road towards Marlborough Street, following the two men.

She turned back to Granny O'Neill. 'Look, go back to Dermot's parents, and tell them he's innocent. Tell them he spent the night with me until . . . until just before four o'clock . . .' She saw Moire's disapproving expression, and shook her head angrily, 'I know what they'll think, but better that than having their son charged with murder and hanged. Tell them I'll provide an alibi for him.'

Mrs O'Neill regarded Katherine shrewdly. 'I think you know a little more about this than you're telling.'

'News travels fast in Monto,' Katherine said. 'Now, go on, and I'll be around to your place a little later today, but I'm not sure when. I dare say I'll be having a visit from the police sooner or later.'

When Mrs O'Neill left, Katherine called for Mickey and Tilly, and told them briefly what had occurred and what she proposed to do.

'That's madness,' Mickey protested, 'they won't just accept your word that he spent the night with you. You and everyone else in this house will be taken in for questioning, we'll have police all over the place for days, and it will ruin business.'

'I think I know why you're doing it, and I understand it,' Tilly said, 'but Mickey is right; something like this could close us down. Think of what we stand to lose, both in earnings and in credibility.' She saw the look in Katherine's eyes and asked hopefully, 'Could you not wait until after the royal family have left before speaking up for Dermot, at least let us take in that business?'

'I think this is something best done soon, before the Dublin Military Police manage to extract a confession from him.' She turned to Mickey. 'Do we have anyone in the Castle?'

'There are two or three who owe us some favours,' Mickey said slowly, unsure where this was leading.

319

'I want a message got to Dermot. He's to say he spent the night with me until around four, and he's to stick to that story; I'll back him up.'

'I'll see that it gets to him.'

'And Billy's lead pipe . . . ?' she asked.

'In the river.'

'The clothing?' She looked at Tilly.

'Burned, and the ashes disposed of.'

'I burned the notebook this morning,' Katherine said, 'and scattered the ashes myself. Now, they may be suspicious, but they can prove nothing, and provided we keep our heads we can weather this storm. And that goes for Billy – and Dermot too,' she added reflectively. 'Now, I think it's time to call in a few favours, and at least try and tone down, if not completely call off, the police investigation of this house.' She looked back at Mickey. 'Make sure that message gets to Dermot.'

Mickey nodded and moved towards the door, but he stopped with his fingers on the handle. 'You realize, if any part of this goes wrong, we'll all be implicated, and probably charged with accessory to murder.'

Katherine nodded solemnly. 'I realize that, Mickey,' she said.

The cell was beneath ground level, cold, damp and foul-smelling. The ancient, large-blocked stone walls dripped with moisture and there was a green fungus growing in the mortar between the stones.

Dermot was dazed and in a state of shock. He still didn't know what had happened to him, although the realization that he had been accused of murder had sunk in. But it was all some ghastly mistake and they would soon release him – wouldn't they?

He was still dressed in his nightshirt, now torn and soiled from the filth on the floor and by the blood which had come from his head wound and cut lip both of which he had received while 'resisting arrest'. His right arm ached abominably, he couldn't move it prop-

320

erly, and there was a sharp stinging pain when he breathed deeply.

At every moment he expected to hear footsteps come down the long, echoing corridor, and then the heavy metal door would clang open and someone would step into the room and tell him that he was free to go . . .

But it hadn't happened yet. There had been a lot of movement in the corridor earlier, and he had heard the iron grill in the door clack open and shut half a dozen times, but it was a while now since the door had been opened. He had been questioned twice. Once when he had been brought in by a senior police officer, but he had been completely disorientated, cut and bleeding, and the officer had been unable to get any sense out of him. A doctor had been called and had cleaned out the gash in his skull, swabbing it none too gently with an acrid, stinging solution, and then he was marched down into the cell. The second time, the inquisitor had come down to the cell, and Dermot, who had been drifting in and out of a semi-conscious daze, opened his eyes when he heard the door clang open – and stared at his worst nightmare come to life. It was Major John Lewis.

The two men regarded each other for a few long minutes, and the major spoke. 'I see you remember me,' he said softly, pushing the door closed behind him.

'I don't think I've ever seen you before . . .' Dermot began, his teeth chattering, but the major suddenly kicked him, quite casually and without breaking stride, the point of his boot striking him high on the thigh, catching the muscle and completely numbing his leg.

'Don't lie to me, Mr Corcoran.' He slowly walked around the crouching man. 'Now this can be very easy for you – or . . .' he smiled, 'well, it can be difficult.'

'You can't keep me here . . .'

'Of course I can – and don't interrupt me again!' To emphasize his point he kicked Dermot again, this time catching him at the base of the spine. 'Now, I will ask you certain questions, which you will answer. I know

321

enough to know when you're telling me the truth, so don't lie to me,' he warned. 'Now, where were you last night?'

'Working!'

There was a hiss of air, and then the major's metal-tipped swagger stick struck the young man across the side of the head, re-opening the wound in his skull.

'I asked you a question.'

'I was in Monto,' Dermot sobbed, cringing, expecting another blow.

'And what were you doing there?'

'I was working on a story,' he said, closing his eyes, expecting another blow. When nothing happened he opened his eyes and looked up to find the major had retreated to the far side of the cell, and was almost lost in the shadows.

'What story?'

'I was looking into the disappearance of the Crown Jewels; it's an assignment from the *Freeman's Journal* — you can check it!' he added hastily as the major moved away from the wall.

'I will. But how did that bring you to Monto?' Major Lewis asked, coming to a halt directly in front of Dermot who was still squatting on the floor. The major slipped his swagger stick under Dermot's chin and tilted his head back. 'Well?' he asked softly.

'I went to Number Eighty-Two, Madam Kitten's place. She sells information,' he said quickly.

The major nodded. 'And then? What time did you leave?'

'I . . . I'm not sure . . . I had more than a little to drink,' he confessed. 'In the early hours of the morning . . . I think. Yes . . . it must have been then . . .'

'And you went straight home?'

'I did.'

The major stared at him for a few moments longer, his face implacable, and then he turned on his heel and marched out without another word. That had been over two hours ago.

The key rasped in the lock and then the bolt was thrown back and a small man, dressed in civilian clothes, stepped into the room. Dermot immediately took him for a clerk. He had a clipboard in his hands, and he sat down on the edge of the hard bed and took out a pencil. 'I have to ask you some questions for our records . . .' he began.

'What sort of questions?' Dermot said wearily.

'Name, address, occupation . . . that sort of thing. Oh,' the little man looked up, his dark eyes sparkling, 'when you're questioned again, you're to say you spent the night with Madam Kitten, and left there around four o'clock. She'll back you up on that. But you're to stick to the story, understand?'

Dermot nodded dumbly, too numbed and dazed to be even surprised.

'And now, name, and address please . . .'

Dermot was questioned about an hour later. Two police officers brought him up countless flights of stairs and left him in a long rectangular room that was devoid of furniture, except for a long table set in the centre of the floor, with three chairs on one side, and a single chair on the other, facing it. There was one window in the room, but that was set high up on the wall and covered with a thick grill.

The door behind him opened and three men entered. The only one Dermot recognized was Major Lewis; the second was a small, thin man with a sharp rat-like face and dark eyes, dapper in a morning suit with crimson cummerbund and top hat. The third man was a high-ranking officer of the Dublin Military Police resplendent in full-dress uniform and still wearing his ceremonial sword. When he saw them, for a brief terrifying moment Dermot imagined he was about to be sentenced, but it passed, leaving him covered in an icy sweat, and he remembered that King Edward and his Queen arrived in Ireland today.

The men took up positions behind the table and,

when they were seated, Dermot sat down on the hard chair facing them. Major Lewis produced a sheaf of papers and handed them to the senior officer. But the man didn't even look at them and seemed content to stare at Dermot as if he were some species of rare animal.

'You're accused of a very serious crime,' he said abruptly.

'I didn't do it,' Dermot said quickly, and then, seeing the expression on the man's face harden, immediately shut up.

'Major Lewis saw you entering a known brothel in Tyrone Street last night at or around ten o'clock. Because of your connections with the somewhat suspicious circumstances surrounding the death of an old prostitute known as "the Madam" in Summerhill some years ago, he set one of his officers to watch you. This officer is subsequently discovered beaten to death a few hundred yards from this brothel. It is perhaps coincidental that the woman known as "the Madam" was killed by a blow to the back of the head – which occurred, it was assumed then, by her falling against the windowsill.' The officer drummed his fingers on the file of papers. 'Perhaps an account of your movements last night might be in order.'

'I've already told this man here . . .'

'Tell me!' the officer roared, blood rushing to his face, turning it a livid purple.

Dermot swallowed hard. 'I was instructed by my newspaper to do a story on the disappearance of the Crown Jewels, and so I went to the house of a woman known as Madam Kitten, because I had heard that she bought and sold information, and I thought she might know something about the missing jewels. But she didn't, although she said she was already in the process of making inquiries. I then . . . then passed the night in the house.'

Major Lewis sat up straight.

The senior officer glanced across at him, and then

turned back to Dermot. 'And you left the house at what time?'

'Just before dawn, around four I think.'

'So you entered the house around nine and left some seven hours later, at four?'

'Yes, sir.'

'You told this officer that you had drunk too much and were unsure what time you had left the house,' he accused.

'He . . . he had struck me,' he said very quickly, 'I was unsure . . . confused. But I've had a little time to get my thoughts in order.'

The officer ignored his outburst. 'But you said you went to the house looking for information . . .'

'Initially, yes, sir.' Dermot felt his confidence growing. His claim hadn't been dismissed out of hand, and he had seen the look of dismay that crossed the major's face.

'I see. And when no information was forthcoming, you remained. Why?'

Dermot managed to look both abashed and shy. 'Well, sir, it is a . . . a house of a certain type.'

'Are you saying you spent the night with one of the women in the house?' the officer demanded.

'Yes, sir.'

'Her name?'

'Madam Kitten, sir.'

When the police arrived at Number Eighty-Two around five that afternoon, they were expected. Katherine had been forewarned and had also been supplied with a copy of the instructions from the officer in charge; there would be no search of the house, and only she would be questioned. Dermot Corcoran was costing Madam Kitten a lot of favours.

There was only one cab, but it was enough to draw the attention of just about everyone on the street. Two officers remained on the steps, while another two went inside. They remained there for about twenty minutes, and then the four men were driven away to the shouts and jeers of the crowd.

Katherine was standing by the window, watching the horse-drawn cab turn and rattle back towards Marlborough Street. In a long black gown, wig, and wearing too much make-up, she had told the two police constables that she had entertained Dermot Corcoran until dawn that day and that he hadn't left the house in all that time. It would be enough to have him set free, but she knew it wouldn't satisfy the major.

She shivered. Everything was changing, shifting; she felt as if things were beginning to run out of control. Her simple, ordered world had been disturbed by the theft of the jewels, which had been responsible for both Dermot's reappearance and the major's visit, and that in turn had led to the murder. The jewels were probably cursed, she decided with a smile, and were now exerting their evil influence over anyone even remotely interested in them. She shook her head, dismissing the facile idea, and turned away from the window, wondering how it was all going to end.

CHAPTER TWENTY-EIGHT

The alcohol helped ease the pain.

Usually by ten o'clock in the morning, Anne Lewis was well on the way to becoming drunk. But not this morning. Although the bells in the seminary behind the house were tolling the hour, she was still in her night-gown, with her hair uncombed and without her usual make-up, looking old and haggard. Her breakfast – mostly untouched – was on the tray which she had left on the chair by the side of her bed. She usually took the cup which was meant for her tea and filled it with wine from the cache she had secreted at the bottom of her wardrobe.

The pain was always at its worst in the mornings, and so – by drinking steadily – she usually managed to get completely drunk by eleven, and then remain in a state of intoxication through the rest of the day. Sometimes, in the dead of afternoon, the alcohol in her bloodstream seemed to dissolve and she became briefly, coldly sober, and in those lucid moments she knew what she had become, and she despised herself. At times like that she thought of suicide. But she always needed that extra drink to give her the courage to take the long final step, and somehow that extra drink always changed her mind.

Anne Lewis had syphilis. She knew – in her few lucid moments – just what she was suffering from. And she knew where she had contracted the disease: it was a gift from Monto.

And it gave her a strange consolation to know that her husband must also be suffering from the disease.

When she saw her husband – which was not often – they didn't speak, and indeed hadn't spoken for a long time now. Indeed, their contact with one another was minimal, and she could go for weeks without even seeing him once. She hadn't attended an official function in nearly two years now, and hadn't left the house in over half that time, but that wasn't entirely her own fault. Anne Lewis was virtually a prisoner in her own home.

When she was sober and she had the energy and the will to think back on it, she realized that she could trace the beginnings of her present situation back more than eight years ago, to the Christmas Eve when she had dismissed that servant girl. It was ironical; the girl had gone and probably had never given her another thought, and yet she had set in motion a train of events that had shattered Mrs Lewis's ordered life. And Anne Lewis couldn't even remember her name. If she was feeling really maudlin, she sometimes wondered what had happened to the girl and her child – if indeed she had kept it – but those times were few and far between.

The departure of the girl had forced her into the position of finally having to face up to the facts; not only was her husband the father of this maid's child, but he was almost certainly the father of the previous servant's child. Of course, she knew he would deny it, but for two girls in the one house to become pregnant was more than coincidental. So she had waited until Major Lewis had come home more than a little drunk that Christmas Eve, and she had questioned him about it . . .

And the Christmas of 1898 was not one she would easily forget.

When she had told him that she had dismissed the girl because she was pregnant and had been insolent, the major had flown into a rage, demanding to know where the girl had gone. Her accusations had only served to incense him even further, and he in turn had accused her of sleeping with William Sherlock . . .

Their argument had raged long into the night, and it had ended with him striking her across the face, two quick backhanded blows that had sent her reeling against a chair, cutting a three-inch gash in her scalp. She had spent the Christmas holiday in bed, her face bruised and swollen, her head bleeding on and off over the next few days. She knew it needed to be stitched, but her husband had refused to call a doctor. Alcohol had helped to ease the pain.

Then the major had begun his search for the girl, frequenting Dublin's mean and sordid streets, the wretched pubs, the brothels, the reeking tenements and the dives. But there was no sign of her. When he returned home, he was usually in a filthy rage, and he had taken out his frustrations on her many times. He had raped her on two separate occasions; they were bloody, humiliating affairs which had left her feeling befouled and sickened for weeks afterwards, but again the drink had helped ease her pain.

Mrs O'Neill had been her only comfort and help during those bitter days of 1899 – and then the major had dismissed her; without notice or warning, he simply told her that her services would no longer be required.

At first her friends called; the few neighbours, the members of her literary society, those she knew in the Gaelic League, but they were all rudely turned away by her husband who had informed them his wife was ill and unavailable to visitors. Soon he no longer even bothered to open the door to casual callers.

She sometimes wondered why he didn't just kill her and be done with it, but she realized that the monthly allowances which came from her father's estate – which, though it wasn't much, did supplement their budget, would immediately be cut off if she were to die in any but natural circumstances. And, even more importantly, her inheritance – which would be substantial – might not be forthcoming. There was no love lost between her aged Irish father and the arrogant British soldier.

Time lost its meaning, and even the grandfather clock in the hallway was allowed to run down. The front of the house was never used now, with only the kitchen, the dining room and the bedroom in regular use. Unable to get out to a doctor, Anne Lewis resorted to the bottle

329

to ease the pain of the disease that was eating its way through her body. When the pain became too much, she drank herself into a stupor.

Soon the drink and her writing became her only solace. She wrote in secret, terrified that her husband might destroy it, and that very secrecy lent it excitement. She still had her books, though, and if disease and alcohol were conspiring to destroy her mind, then the books somehow managed to correct the balance and keep her sane. Her friends, assuming her to be desperately ill, sent her copies of the latest publications from those writers whom she had known in the early days of the Irish literary movement. The works of William Butler Yeats and Lady Gregory fascinated her, and she found herself attempting to emulate their rather rich and colourful style.

She had good days and bad days; days when she wished for death, when she wished she had the strength of mind and will to throw herself from the window or to slice her wrists open and finish this life of degradation. But on the good days, before the drink took hold, or in the afternoons when it lessened its grip on her, she wondered why she allowed her bondage to continue, and knew that if she really put her mind to it she would be able to walk out of the house . . . to escape.

And today was a good day.

Anne Lewis looked longingly at the wardrobe as she dressed, where the bottles of wine appeared overnight, but then resolutely turned away again. One glass would settle her nerves, but too many good days had been destroyed by just a single glass to settle her nerves. She glanced up at the clock on the fireplace. Just after ten. If her husband followed his usual pattern, he would begin work a little after lunch. In the past few years he had taken to bringing his work home with him, and working on it in the sitting room below – at the same desk she had used for her writing.

She stepped out on to the landing and leaned over the bannister, listening for sounds from below. She was shaking slightly and desperately needed a drink, but she had resisted so far this morning and was determined to remain sober for as long as possible. She could hear nothing from downstairs; indeed, she hadn't heard anything all morning, but she still didn't know for certain whether her husband was in the house or not. And she couldn't afford to run the risk of being caught.

Anne darted back into the bedroom and lifted the small bag she had spent the morning packing and re-packing, and then stepped back out on to the landing again, easing the bedroom door closed silently. As quietly as possible she crept down the stairs, keeping well in close to the wall, stepping over the third step from the end – which squeaked – and down into the hall. She could see that the front door was locked and she knew if she attempted to lift the bolts she would make far too much noise. In any case, the sitting room overlooked the front garden, and if her husband was anywhere in the house he would be there. So, she would have to go out through the kitchen door, but that meant passing the sitting room door – which was slightly ajar.

She took off her shoes and stuffed them in the pocket of her coat and moved over to the wall. Turning her head slightly, she peered through the crack in the door into the room, but from this angle she couldn't see the writing desk. Interestingly, though, the fire was unlit. But, just to be on the safe side . . . with a quick smile, she slowly and silently eased the door shut, turning the handle gently so there would be no sound. Then she turned the key in the lock. Her husband might not be within, but she was taking no chances.

A few moments later, Anne Lewis walked out of the house on Clonliffe Road, determined never to return. She glanced in at the window as she passed, but the sitting room was empty, and she wondered idly where her husband was. And decided she didn't care. She had no idea where she was going, no idea what she was going to do. All she did know was that she was never

331

going back, and that she would be revenged on Major John Lewis.

Major Lewis had seen the inside of many brothels in his time, but never one like Number Eighty-Two. It looked even more astonishing in the daylight, its slightly shabby, run-down exterior blending in perfectly with the surroundings but giving no hint at all of the opulent interior concealed within.

He stood on the steps of the brothel, his right hand wrapped around the butt of the gun in his pocket, and knocked on the door. He looked up and down the street, noting how quiet and desolate it seemed at this hour of the morning, the only movement caused by two old tramps on the far side of the road, gossiping together. Major Lewis smiled; they were both men from his unit in disguise. He turned back and rapped on the door again, louder this time, and he saw faces beginning to appear at windows up and down the street. Few people, he realized, called on a brothel at noon.

He heard footsteps and then latches were lifted and a chain rattled behind the door. It opened smoothly and the large, grey-haired man he had seen previously looked out. 'Ah, Major Lewis,' he said expressionlessly, 'Madam is expecting you.'

The major hesitated a moment, and then, resisting the temptation to look behind him at the two men across the road, stepped quickly into the darkened hallway, flattening himself against the wall and pulling out his revolver at the same moment. But the hall was empty except for the large man who had let him in, who nodded at the pistol. 'I think that will be unnecessary,' he said, 'but if you want to see Madam, I'm afraid you will have to leave it with me.'

The major pulled back the hammer and extended his arm, until the dark barrel was almost touching Mickey's throat. He jerked his head in the direction of the stairs. 'Lead the way.'

Mickey smiled and folded his arms, leaning back

against the door. 'Put the gun away.' His voice hadn't altered its pitch, but the threat was implicit.

The major laughed. 'What you seem to forget, old man, is that I am holding the gun. I could shoot you.'

Mickey nodded. 'Yes, you could. But then I'm afraid my boys would have to shoot you.'

The major smiled indulgently . . . and the smile froze on his lips as he heard the ominous double-click of the hammers on a shotgun being pulled back behind him, and then someone else stepped out from the shadows under the stairs holding a revolver.

Mickey reached out and took the pistol from the major's hand. 'You can see Madam now.'

Mickey led the major up the stairs to the top of the house to Madam's private apartments. The two men with the guns followed behind him, and the major had no illusions that they would shoot him without hesitation if necessary and he was more than thankful that he had men waiting across the street – although by the time they got over here, he could be well dead.

The room he was ushered into was the same one he had been in on the previous occasion. The room was bright with light, and for a single moment Major Lewis thought he was actually going to see the mysterious Madam Kitten. He blinked, squinting towards the figure sitting in front of the window, but the light streaming in behind her effectively blinded him, rendering her a vague blur, and her features were completely invisible behind a veil. Mickey led the major to a soft chair and then nodded for him to sit down; then he crossed to the Madam and placed the major's gun down on the table before her. He gave the major a final look and walked quickly from the room, shutting the door quietly behind him. Major Lewis listened, but he couldn't hear steps moving away from the door and guessed that the three men were still outside, waiting for the woman to cry or call out.

'What brings you back to us, Major Lewis?' the woman asked, her voice whispering, hissing through her

333

silk veil. 'I told you I would contact you if I discovered anything about the missing jewels.'

'I've come on different business,' Major Lewis said quietly, wondering why this woman frightened him so. He had been in tighter situations, situations in which his life had actually been threatened, but he had never felt so . . . so diminished, as he did in her presence.

He saw her head nod against the light. 'Ah, the killing,' she said.

'You know about it? Curious that, because it hasn't been reported in the newspapers.'

'My dear major, all Monto knows about the killing of the policeman who was disguised as a tramp. Although why he should be disguised as a tramp is beyond me . . .' he felt her smile behind the veil, '. . . and I still cannot work out what those two men pretending to be tramps are doing across the road.'

'I'm not sure what you mean . . .'

'Come, come now major. Surely they are your men; no real tramp looks or behaves like them? Now, perhaps if you were to state your business,' she said brusquely.

'I want to know,' the major began, automatically coming to his feet, and then freezing. The woman had picked up his gun and was pointing it at him, holding it rock steady in both her long-fingered hands.

'Sit,' she commanded.

Major Lewis smiled uncertainly. Without being able to see her face, he was unable to judge just how serious she was, but her voice was cool and calm, and then she professionally thumbed back the hammer on the heavy gun in one smooth movement. The major made up his mind and sat down.

It was only when Lewis had stood up so suddenly and she had reached for the gun that Katherine realized that he still had the power to frighten her, even though she had him at a disadvantage here in her own territory. He was on-guard and edgy, not knowing her, not knowing what to expect, and while she maintained this aura of mystery his imagination would do the rest. She

334

despised herself for using the gun to threaten him, for she felt her authority had somehow been diminished by doing so, but it had been an automatic reaction. When he sat down, she lowered the weapon again, but kept it close to hand. 'State your business, Major Lewis.'

'I am investigating the murder of one of my men,' he said slowly.

'Your men?' she asked, 'I didn't think you had any men under your command. My understanding of your position was that you were merely a post office administrator, a . . . clerk of some sort.'

Major Lewis held his temper in check with difficulty. 'I have some men who serve under me.'

'And are these army or police officers?' Katherine wondered aloud.

'I really don't see what interest that can be to you.'

'It is of no interest really,' Katherine said slowly, 'it was just idle curiosity. However, would it be true to say that you and I are in a very similar business, eh . . . ?' Behind the veil, Katherine smiled at the man's embarrassment.

'And what business is that?' he asked, attempting to sound casual.

'We run spies, Major Lewis, you and I, we run spies.' She laughed at his expression. 'Oh, don't look so surprised, Major Lewis, you've never made any real secret of it, and you've been doing it for too long now not to have escaped notice. Your visit here to investigate the death of a police officer in disguise – one of your men, by your own admission, is conclusive, I think. But what brings you here specifically?'

'The man who was murdered was watching this house – your house,' Major Lewis stated bluntly.

'Why?'

'When I was leaving here last night, I saw someone I knew . . .'

'And do you have a name for this person?'

The major leaned forward, squinting against the sun-

335

light. 'Dermot Corcoran,' he said slowly, 'do you know him?'

'Vaguely.' Katherine smiled again.

'He said he came here looking for a lead to the jewels.'

'As did you,' Katherine smiled.

'And then he spent the night with you. Why?'

'I beg your pardon?' she asked, sounding surprised.

'Why did he spend the night with you, if all he wanted was information?' he demanded, half-rising to his feet but allowing himself to sink back into the chair when he saw the woman's hand move towards the gun.

'I am not at liberty to discuss any of my clients.'

'But this client stood accused of murder – and only your word saved him. You're involved in this one, Madam Kitten,' he warned.

Katherine nodded slowly, as if she were considering what he was saying. 'When he discovered that I could sell him nothing about the theft of the jewellery, he decided to take advantage of some of the services of the house. Perhaps he found it easier to stay here than to go home,' she added.

'And one of those services included you ... ?' the major said reflectively. He sat back into the chair, and a smile touched his cruel lips. 'And how much would it cost to spend a night with you?' he asked, 'you will of course excuse my forthrightness ... ?'

'I'm afraid that is impossible,' Katherine said quickly.

'Why?' Major Lewis demanded.

'One of the advantages of running my own house is that I can choose my partners,' Katherine said with a tight smile, feeling her heart beginning to pound. 'And I am very selective indeed.'

'You are presumptuous – for a whore,' the major said slowly. 'You seem to forget that I can have your house closed at any moment.'

Katherine laughed, the sound hissing behind her veil. 'I think you will find great difficulty in closing this house,' she said, glad to be back on safer ground now.

'You have friends in high places,' Major Lewis said, a

336

statement more than a question, 'but I think you will find your friends a little unwilling to defend a brothel.'

'Perhaps not openly – no. But I think you will find yourself blocked by an excess of red tape.' She sounded almost gleeful at the idea.

Major Lewis sat back into the chair and regarded the woman carefully. There was something anomalous about her, something which didn't quite add up. At times she seemed an old woman, self-confident, assured, almost arrogant, but then there were flashes of a young woman, a frightened woman almost. Someone with more self-confidence would not have used the gun; she would have simply called out to the guards outside the door. And then why did she hide her features behind the veil, and only give interviews in darkened rooms or with the light behind her?

'Who are you?' he asked suddenly, watching her closely, squinting against the light, trying to gauge her reaction. She was surprised, taken aback, that was obvious, and he counted the seconds it took her to formulate an answer.

'I am Madam Kitten,' she said finally and, Major Lewis thought, a little breathlessly.

'But what is your real name? Just who are you?' He stood up, but didn't move from his position beside the chair. 'I wonder what face lies behind the mask? And why won't you show it to me . . . ?' A sudden thought struck him and he asked, slowly, 'Is it because it's a face I would recognize?'

He still hadn't moved from his position by the chair, but Katherine lifted the heavy pistol again and held it steady in both hands, pointing it at him. She was sure he could hear the pounding of her heart, and her mouth was so dry she wasn't sure she would be able to speak properly. 'This interview is at an end. Leave now!'

'You fear me, don't you?' Major Lewis said savagely, almost triumphantly.

'I have no reason to fear you, Major Lewis. Mickey,' she called, raising her voice only slightly, but suddenly

337

the door opened and the three men burst in, the two younger men pointing their weapons at the major, while Mickey crossed over to the table and took the pistol from Katherine's hand. 'The major is leaving now,' she said quietly.

'You know me, don't you?' Major Lewis demanded. 'We've met somewhere before, I'm sure of it.'

Mickey stepped up to his side and nodded in the direction of the door. 'Let's go.'

The major turned on his heel and walked across the room without looking back, but paused at the door and glanced over his shoulder. 'I'll find out just who you are.'

When the door shut and the footsteps sounded on the stairs, Katherine stood up and went to the window which overlooked the street. She heard the front door slam and then she saw the major walk down the steps. He stopped on the bottom step and looked up, and she instinctively moved back, although she knew he couldn't see her behind the grimy glass. She was frightened, and she knew the major hadn't been making an idle threat. She guessed that he would start looking into her background – and that was something she couldn't afford. She wondered if she ought to consider providing Major Lewis with an accident.

The visitor came late to the house which, strangely, was dark and unlit, although the rest of the brothels in the street were ablaze with light as the houses made the most of the many visitors in town for the royal visit.

Around eleven, a closed carriage arrived before Number Eighty-Two and a slim young man, well-dressed but not so much as to attract attention, jumped out and ran up the steps. Before he had time to knock on the door, however, it was opened and he slipped inside. A moment later, he came out again and darted down to the still-waiting carriage. He stuck his head inside and spoke briefly, and then the door opened again, and another man stepped out. He was a tall and

338

broad man, swathed in a high fur-collared coat, with a broad-brimmed tweed hat pulled down low over his eyes, and he kept his head tucked down into his chest as he slowly climbed the steps, leaning on a silver-topped cane. When he stepped inside, the door closed immediately behind him, leaving the younger man standing outside, leaning up against the carriage, both hands dug deeply into his pockets.

Major Lewis, standing in the shadows across the street, shook his head in amazement. He had heard the stories, of course, but he had never truly believed them. But he realized then that his chances of having the house closed down were next to impossible. Madam Kitten hadn't been joking when she said that she knew some important people.

CHAPTER TWENTY-NINE

William Sherlock, very much a creature of habit, closed his book just as the antique German clock on the mantelpiece pinged half-past ten with a whirring of gears. He yawned and checked the leather bookmark in the pages once again. He had just stood up when the front door bell clanged.

He stopped, the sudden harsh sound bringing him up short, and looked up at the clock again. Although it was still early by some standards, no-one ever called at this hour, not on him in any case. Experiencing a vague feeling of unease he moved over to the window and lifted the heavy chintz drapes and peered out. But, as usual he had forgotten to light the brass lamp that hung outside his door and, in the almost total darkness, he could see nothing.

The bell clanged again, louder, more insistently this time, urging him to do something – although he was damned if he knew what to do. Finally, he picked up the long heavy poker from the grate and went out into the hall. Here, the lights were out and he was able to make out a vague shape through the smoked and coloured glass of the front door. The shape suggested one person, someone small.

He padded down the hall in slippered feet and stood peering out through the coloured side panels of the door which were of plain glass, unlike the centrepiece which was heavily decorated with a thick floral pattern. The night was heavy and overcast, with neither moon nor stars showing, and all he could distinguish was a single person standing on the steps – a woman by the general shape and size. He saw her hand reach for the bell again, but before she could pull it he called out, 'Who's there?'

She started and took two paces backwards to the edge of the first step, then she spotted the pale face peering out through the glass at the side of the door. She stepped up to the door again and peered in, and Sherlock drew back with a start; her face was pale and blotchy, discoloured by the glass and distorted slightly, and given an almost unhuman cast.

'Who is it?' he called again.

'I want to see William Sherlock,' the woman said, mouthing the words through the glass.

'Who are you?' he demanded.

'Open the door – please!'

'Not until you tell me who you are,' he said firmly.

'For Christ's sake, William, it's me, Anne Lewis!' she suddenly shouted.

William Sherlock started in horror at the distorted face in the glass, and began to make out in it the features of the woman he once knew. He fumbled with the bolts and locks and threw open the door, and Anne Lewis picked up a single small case and calmly walked inside. 'Hello, William; it's been a long time.' She walked past him and down the hall into the sitting room.

Sherlock looked after her in absolute astonishment for a few moments and then he slammed the door shut and raced down the hall after her.

Walking into the warm, book-lined, overcrowded sitting room was like walking back into her past. Anne Lewis stood before the glowing fire, warming her hands and looking around in wonder. In over eight years nothing seemed to have been touched, everything was just as she remembered it. She lifted her head as William Sherlock came running into the room, the look of stunned amazement frozen onto his face, a long black poker in his hand.

The look in his eyes was enough; he might be surprised, amazed and astonished, but his eyes were glad and welcoming. She smiled, tentatively, shyly, and suddenly all her new-found resolve and strength left her, and she sank down into a chair, ashen-faced.

341

William Sherlock came and knelt by the side of the chair and gently lifted her face in his hand. 'It really is you . . . it really is. My God, I never thought . . .' It was a face that had haunted his dreams, his nightmares too for a long time after their last meeting all those years ago. He had learned that she was desperately ill, and he could well believe it, looking at her now. She had never been beautiful, but she could once have been called pretty, though no longer. Her face was gaunt, her eyes sunken, and her hair was streaked through with grey and silver and had obviously seen neither water nor comb in a long time. She had lost a lot of weight, and her bones were prominent over tight flesh. Her skin was pasty and had an oily sheen to it, and there was a faintly rancid odour clinging to her or her clothes. 'What happened to you?' he whispered aghast.

'It's a long story,' she said wearily, 'and I'm afraid I can't stay.'

'I don't understand.'

'My husband may soon be here . . . I've run away, you see,' she said, looking up at him, and the sparkle in her eyes was far too bright to be natural.

'You've run away,' William Sherlock repeated slowly.

'He was keeping me a prisoner!' she suddenly screamed, shocking him with the sound. 'But he'll come here,' she said desperately, 'he'll know I've nowhere else to go!'

'Hush now, hush,' William said, attempting to wrap his arms around her, but she pushed him away savagely.

'Don't touch me . . . don't touch me!' she shuddered. 'He'll kill us!' she spat. 'He's not a man, he's a monster. All I need is some money, just a little, enough to get away. I'll pay it back when I can. Please, William . . . you're my only hope . . .'

'Look,' he said, reaching a decision. 'I can hide you here . . .'

'He'll find me, he'll find me . . .'

'He'll never find you,' Sherlock said confidently. 'Come on.' He reached out his hand and she slowly

342

took it, and he squeezed it comfortingly. Then, picking up her bag he led her from the room and up the stairs.

William Sherlock used the smallest bedroom of the four-bedroomed house as a library. It was covered wall to wall with books, and there was a tall double-sided bookcase in the centre of the floor. Even with the light on, the room was dim and smelt faintly of must and dust and something else, something which Anne Lewis always associated with old books. She looked at Sherlock, puzzled, but he merely shook his head and led her to the furthest, darkest corner of the room.

'I could put in better lighting,' he said quietly, 'but you'll see why I don't want to.' And then, grasping the bookshelves in both hands, he pulled – and the whole section moved out silently and smoothly, revealing a cupboard behind them. 'You'll be safe here,' he said, opening the door.

Anne Lewis craned her neck and peered into the dark cupboard; it was piled high with long rectangular boxes, each one covered in a thick, blocky script which she couldn't read in the dim light.

'I won't be able to give you a light, but I'll bring you up some food and something to drink,' he said. 'Do you think he'll come tonight?' he asked.

She nodded wearily and stepped into the darkened cupboard and perched on one of the wooden boxes. As he moved to close over the door she suddenly reached out and touched his cheek. 'Thank you,' she said softly.

William Sherlock nodded, curiously embarrassed by the simple gesture, and closed the door on the hidden cupboard, then pushed the bookcase back in front of it. He straightened some of the books on the shelves, and then piled some papers on the floor in front of it, before stepping back to inspect his handiwork, examining it critically. 'I'll be back in a few moments,' he said loudly, and without waiting for a reply, he stepped from the room and closed the door behind him.

He had barely reached the bottom of the stairs when he heard movement outside, booted feet crunching on the gravel in his driveway, the rattle of harnesses and the clink of metal on metal. He stopped, his heart pounding in his chest, memories of the last time the military had paid him a visit coming back painfully, and with terrifying clarity. Anne Lewis had been involved then, too, albeit indirectly.

He was already moving down the hall when the bell clanged. He stopped to turn up the gas, bathing the long hall in a soft yellow-white light, and then, taking a deep breath and attempting to ease his pounding heart, he went and opened the door. He was surprised – indeed, almost shocked – to find the officer on the step wasn't Major Lewis.

'What's wrong?' he asked immediately, idly wondering how an innocent person would react to finding the police and military at his door.

'Nothing wrong, sir.' A hard-eyed young police officer lifted a single sheet of paper and waved it in Sherlock's face. 'I am required to search your house, sir. I have the necessary papers.'

'For what purpose?' William Sherlock demanded, looking past him to the army captain.

'I am not at liberty to discuss that,' the police officer said and went to step into the hall.

William folded his arms and placed himself directly in the man's way. 'I demand to know by what authority you can just walk into my home, and I certainly demand to know for what reason.'

The officer regarded him steadily for a moment, and behind him the army captain's gloved hand came to rest almost casually on his holstered pistol. 'By the authority of His Majesty's Government, and this properly authorized and noted document.' He lifted the paper again, but when William reached for it he twitched it out of the way. 'But I am not at liberty to discuss why your house is being searched.'

'Is any other house in Ballsbridge being searched?'

'I cannot say.'

'I must protest . . .'

'Your protest is noted, sir, and now if you don't mind
. . .' He placed his hand in the centre of Sherlock's chest
and pushed him back out of the way.

The kitchen door opened and a burly police sergeant
poked his head out. 'There's nothing here, sir.'

'You've broken in!' Sherlock said, outraged.

'I'm sure if you submit a claim for any damages
incurred, you will be recompensed in the fullness of
time,' the army captain said, unholstering his pistol and
walking to the foot of the stairs. More men – police and
army – came out from the kitchen and others filed in
past Sherlock. The army captain looked for his sergeant
and then nodded upstairs. 'Sergeant . . . ?'

The short, stout man nodded and clumped up the
stairs in his heavy boots, a half dozen men following.
The captain, meanwhile, wandered into the sitting room
and looked around, noting the shelves of fine bindings
and the framed autographs of authors. He nodded
slowly. 'You are a literary man, I see.'

'I have some connections with the Irish Literary
Society.'

'Indeed. And you live here alone?'

'There is a housekeeper who comes in . . .' he said
slowly, realizing that, in an easy subtle way, he was
being interrogated.

'And you have had no visitors tonight?' The officer
rounded on him quickly.

'No-one,' William Sherlock lied, desperately praying
that Anne wouldn't do anything stupid or make a noise
that would betray him now.

Anne Lewis crouched in the darkened cupboard,
listening to the faint thumps from the room behind her
– William's bedroom, she guessed. She was beginning to
wonder why he was making so much noise when she
heard a crash, followed by a coarse laugh.

She knew then it wasn't William. They must be her
husband's men. They must have been right behind her,
she thought desperately . . . and what would happen if
someone had seen her come in here . . . or spotted her

345

talking to William on the doorstep . . . She was going to be sick.

And then the light went on in the book-lined room, thinly visible round the edges of her cupboard door, and she could hear men moving around.

'. . . Nothing in 'ere but books . . .'

'You're sure?'

'Positive.'

The light went out and the door slammed, and then she heard the booted feet descending the stairs. There were further distant thumps and thuds from below, vibrating up through the woodwork, and then she heard the front door slam. The silence that followed was almost frightening, and she immediately had a terrifying thought: what if they had taken William with them? What would happen to her? A sudden bout of claustrophobia struck her and she slid off the box she was sitting on and pushed on the cupboard door. Nothing happened. She pushed again, harder this time, throwing her full weight against it. It still didn't move. Panic seized her then and she flung herself against the door, pounding on it with both fists, already imagining she could feel the air in the tiny cupboard grow hot and stale, and she began gasping for breath. She could smell her own fear and terror, and that only served to frighten her further. They had taken William away for questioning and she was alone now in this tiny box where she was going to suffocate and die, and when they released him he would come home to find the house stinking with her decaying corpse, and when he opened the cupboard he would find . . .

Anne Lewis threw back her head and . . .

'Don't scream!'

She was aware of light and cool air and William pulling the door open. He reached in for her, and she tumbled into his arms, sobbing uncontrollably. 'I thought they'd taken you, and I was left, and, and, and . . .'

He held her close and rubbed her sticky hair, one part

346

of him enjoying her trust and obvious affection, while another, more abstract part was slightly revolted by the smell and dirt of the woman. He was a fussy and proper man, loving beauty in all things and finding dirt disgusting. It was hard to equate this slovenly creature with the cleanly beautiful woman he had once known.

'They've gone now; they found nothing; they won't be back,' he added hopefully.

'Was my ... was Major Lewis with them?' she wondered.

'No. They were a mixture of police and army, but I think the young army captain was in charge. I didn't recognize him.'

'John doesn't do his own dirty work much any more,' she said, sniffing back her tears.

'Come on,' William Sherlock said, 'we'll get you something to eat and then I think I'll draw a bath for you. What do you say?'

But she only burst into tears again.

Major Lewis stood by the window of his office in the GPO and looked down on to O'Connell Street. He was pale and irritable, having spent most of the day and night wandering around Dublin, trying to find his missing wife. He had been sure – in fact, he would have put money on it – that she would have gone to Sherlock's. She had run there before, and he didn't think that there was anyone else she knew well enough to shelter her in Dublin. But a search of Sherlock's home had revealed nothing. He pulled hard on a cigarette, the tip glowing in the darkened room, reflecting back from the glass like a single eye. He wasn't sure whether he should be worried or not; over the years he had put out the story of her 'nervous disorder' which made her 'imagine things', so that, even if she did reach one of her friends, they would be inclined to distrust what she said about him.

And he wondered where she was now ...

He turned away from the window and crossed to his

347

desk, turning up the gas on the wall behind it. There were three files sitting on it, along with three leather-bound ledgers, each one referring to a case. He picked up one, a slim, maroon-coloured file, but decided against opening it yet. He would dispose of the official business first.

The largest of the three by far was the file on the Crown Jewel affair. He had requested outside help in the investigation of the matter, and Chief Inspector John Kane of Scotland Yard would be coming over shortly from London to conduct his own investigation into the theft.

Major Lewis sat down at his desk and flipped open the file, and pulled out a two-page, closely written report made by Detective Officer Owen Kerr, whose duties included the checking and securing of the Office of Arms in the Bedford Tower of Dublin Castle every night, following the departure of the staff. The man's report was concise and to the point. There were two details of interest, both of them relating to Mrs Farrell, the cleaning woman. He read through the report quickly, and then pulled out Mrs Farrell's own statement. It stated that on the 3rd July, she had found the door to the Bedford Tower unlocked when she arrived at about eight o'clock that morning – the implication being that it had been unlocked all night. And then, some three days later, she had actually found the door to the Strong Room unlocked and, while the inner grill did seem to be locked, the key was still in the lock! And this was from the same woman who had actually seen the Lord Lieutenant's son, Lord Haddo, in the room.

Major Lewis was rapidly developing his own theory as to how the jewels had disappeared – and that was through sheer stupidity on someone's part. He turned back to Kerr's report. According to the detective, the jewels had actually been 'stolen' twice before, as a practical joke by someone on the staff, when Sir Arthur Vicars, the Chief Herald, had been overcome by drink.

He shook his head in amazement; it was absolutely

348

incredible, the jewels had almost begged to be stolen. But it was an inside job, of that he was almost certain. And the only place those jewels could be disposed of without any questions being asked was in Monto. And that brought him to the maroon-coloured file, and Madam Kitten.

The Dublin Metropolitan Police kept a file on just about every madam working in Dublin. Most of the material was pretty thin; just a real name, if it was known, the working name, the address of the house, and the number of girls working therein, if known. Also appended was a list of known clients – although, from experience, Major Lewis knew that these lists were never accurate, as influence was often brought to bear to ensure that certain names never reached the list. But strangely no file for Madam Kitten existed – well, that wasn't really true, her name was mentioned, but only as a footnote in Madam Bella Cohen's file, which was thick enough.

In an addition to the sheet dated '1901', it listed a 'Kit or Kitten', who was considered to be a niece of Madam Cohen. The note was brief enough, 'She does not appear to be a prostitute and would seem to assist the old woman in the day-to-day running of the house. However,' it continued in a tiny, crabbed hand, 'this Kit does travel to the continental brothels, and certainly bears watching, as it seems likely that she will be Cohen's successor.' Major Lewis grimaced. How bloody prophetic!

Well, that much he knew, but what he needed was detail on the woman. His own investigation into the lady was hampered by a curious lack of information. What little there was on the lady went back to the turn of the century, but it was almost as if she hadn't existed before that. No one had ever seen her face, although there were numerous rumours and wild stories about her origins and present identity, with two being particularly popular. One story said that she had once been a beautiful young courtesan who had been hideously scarred by one of her men and who was now forced to live in darkened rooms, always wearing a veil, while the second story said that she was a rich society lady, moving in the highest circles, who ran the brothel to finance her taste for fine living and expensive jewellery.

Major Lewis turned back to the file on Bella Cohen. Obviously that was the place to start. He thumbed through the numerous pages on this extraordinary woman, whose checkered past, he decided, would certainly keep novelists writing for generations. He finally reached a list of the girls working for her. He idly ran his finger down the list of names, not really sure what he was . . . looking . . . for . . . Tilly Cusack!

Now there was a name from his past, a name which brought memories flooding back, memories of numerous hotel rooms, of long afternoons and evenings spent in lovemaking. The good old days. What had ever happened to Tilly Cusack, he wondered. Why, he hadn't seen her in . . . must be over seven or eight years . . . not since the turn of the century, in fact . . . Not since the turn of the century – and Madam Kitten had only appeared then. He felt something cold settle into the pit of his stomach.

It was only coincidence – wasn't it?

He got up from the table and walked around it, pacing up and down his small office, not really thinking, simply allowing the various facts he had gathered and the different impressions he had gained on his two visits to the veiled woman to settle into position. Finally he stopped and, leaning both hands on the window-ledge, stared down across O'Connell Street, now bustling with the theatre crowd. He looked over at Clery's Shop where he had last met Tilly Cusack. That had been in . . . 1898, late '98, when he had discovered the brigadier's identity and found out that Tilly had been spying on him and reporting back to the brigadier. He had taken her into the Imperial and there threatened her, he remembered that, and he had never met her again. He had searched and asked questions, leaving messages at her haunts, but she had never turned up. Eventually, he had given up and, whores being so common in Dublin, he hadn't really missed her.

But about the same time, a little later in fact, this strange young woman appears with Bella Cohen, and travels abroad to the continental brothels. Well, it must have taken a lot of experience to travel to the continent, and Tilly certainly had that experience, and, of course, it would have kept her out of his way.

And now there was the veiled woman's reaction to him. She knew him – he was sure of that.

All the evidence pointed to the fact that Tilly Cusack was Madam Kitten!

Although she had never been naked before any man other than her husband, Anne Lewis felt no shame or embarrassment in standing naked before William Sherlock. But standing shamelessly, comfortably, before him, she suddenly realized that she had never felt completely at ease when her husband was looking at her. She stepped into the huge copper bath, easing her tired body into the steaming hot water.

'You've lost weight,' William Sherlock said suddenly. He was sitting on a hard chair at the foot of the bath, sipping a sherry, content to watch the woman bathe. He had been shocked by her thinness. She had never been fat, but now she was positively skeletal, and he could count her every rib. Her skin was pale and tinged with a faintly yellowish, unhealthy cast, and the same yellow tinge was echoed in her eyes. He had, however, expected to find her skin scarred or bruised, and was almost surprised to find she was unblemished.

'What are you staring at?' Anne asked suddenly, startling him.

'Oh. Nothing. You. I thought he might have hit you,' he explained.

She rested her head back against the tub and closed her eyes. She shook her head sleepily. 'No, he hasn't touched me in . . . well, in a long time. Not since he

351

raped me,' she added, opening her eyes and staring at him.

He looked at her for a few moments and then nodded. 'Where have you been over the past eight years?' he asked.

'I've never left the house,' she said, watching his expression change to one of startled disbelief. 'He kept me a prisoner in the house.'

'But how . . .'

Anne laughed bitterly. 'Simple; he passed on to me a filthy whore's disease – and then he wouldn't get me a doctor. When the pain got too bad, the only relief I could get was from a bottle. It not only eased the pain, it helped pass the time. I drank my way through the days.' She lifted the drink Sherlock had left on the stool beside the bath and downed it quickly, almost as if to emphasize the point. 'I didn't feel the years run on, I didn't feel the time passing. But do you know what I missed most; I missed my friends not calling. They all have short memories.'

'We couldn't get in,' he protested.

'But you simply stopped trying,' she almost accused him.

'The major put out a story that you were desperately ill, and were so bad that you didn't even recognize him, let alone your old friends. He said that during your lucid moments you had given him strict instructions that none of your friends were to be allowed to see you. They were to remember you as you had been and not as you were now.'

Anne began to laugh, but stopped when the sound grew too hysterical. 'And you believed him?'

'I even felt sorry for him,' Sherlock admitted.

'He's a grand liar, what you might call a professional liar. He has fooled you all; you and me, and everyone else who knows him. But do you know what he is? Do you know what my husband does?' She suddenly stood up in the bath, water cascading from her emaciated body. 'I'll tell you what he does,' she said, her voice becoming higher and higher. William Sherlock stood up and took a step closer to the bath. 'My husband is a spy. My husband is a British spy!'

Katherine was standing by the window of the dining room, looking down on the cobbled street below, watching the three men sitting on the steps opposite playing cards. Although they were dressed as tramps, they were all wearing socks. Tramps never wore socks!

She turned as the door opened, and Tilly came in with a sheaf of letters which she had picked up from the post office. No post was ever delivered directly to the house.

'There's one addressed directly to you,' Tilly said, running through them, handing it over.

Katherine looked at the thick white envelope and the small crabbed script centred on it. The writing looked vaguely familiar, although she couldn't place it for the moment. 'It's from Dermot,' she said in surprise when she had opened it. 'He wants to meet me in the Green!' She sounded almost pleased.

'But you can't!' Tilly protested, 'it's not safe, not now when the house is being watched.' She saw the expression on Katherine's face and continued on quickly, 'Katherine, you cannot be thinking . . .'

But Katherine only shook her head. 'And why not?'

CHAPTER THIRTY

Walking through the gates of St Stephen's Green was like walking back into her past. Suddenly, Katherine was eight years younger and a lot more innocent, and the days of running through the gates to meet with Dermot at their appointed seat facing the lake came back with poignant clarity.

The church bells began to toll noon and she automatically quickened her step, not wanting to be late. She smiled wryly, realizing that she was behaving like a girl on her first date. She found her feelings towards Dermot were a little confused at the moment; she wasn't sure what still attracted her to him. Perhaps it was his innocence or his boyishness which brought out the mothering instinct in her. And yet she had read all his articles; and they were virulent, impassioned attacks on the society and system that bred the worst slums in Europe, on a city that had one of the highest incidences of child mortality and one of the largest concentrations of prostitutes. These were not articles written by a shy, blushing boy, but rather by an angry, forceful, young man, strong-willed and dedicated to a cause. And she found it hard to reconcile the two.

But when he said or did something stupid or came out with what she considered to be nothing more than empty phrases, she forced herself to remember that he had been willing to marry her, even though it would have brought him nothing but trouble and disgrace.

Deliberately slowing her pace – in keeping with her appearance – Katherine realized that he would wait if she were a few moments late. She was dressed in what she called her 'widow's weeds', a fashionable dress of black velvet, with matching black gloves and a small hat

354

with a lace veil. It was a simple outfit, but it lent her an air of dignity and, coupled with some clever make-up, added about ten years to her age – which was what she wanted.

Getting out of the house presented no problem. Number Eighty-Two was linked by a tunnel to a building two houses down the street, and the three card-playing tramps had paid no attention to the hunched woman in black who had left there earlier that morning. Legend had it that many of the houses in Monto were linked by tunnels, or had secret rooms and hideaways, some concealing stills for brewing poteen, illegal whiskey, but in actual fact the truth was very different. Some of the houses were connected, it was true, but only by the simple procedure of knocking a hole through the connecting walls while the secret rooms tended to be basements or unused attics. And although alcohol, both legitimate and otherwise, was sold in Monto, none of it was ever made there. So, once she had left the building, Katherine had simply walked around the corner and hailed a cab, which had brought her to the top of Grafton Street.

Since the death of the policeman, Katherine had not dared to leave the house, except under the cover of darkness, and so this occasion was a treat, and she found the streets fascinating. They were bright with flags for the royal visit and seemed to be exceptionally busy for a weekday. The shop windows were filled with patriotic displays of linens or silver or glasswork, and nearly every window sported a flag or at least a picture of the royal family. She noticed too the unusually large number of army officers in town, and a lot of these were walking out with ladies on their arms – whose virtue, Katherine knew, was quite suspect, and who like herself were equally unused to being abroad during the daylight hours.

It was a beautiful day also, bright but cold, with a sharp breeze gusting through the streets and raising whitecaps on the lake, sending high clouds scudding

355

across the sky. Possibly because of the weather, St Stephen's Green was almost deserted, and the few people wandering around seemed to be mainly nannies pushing babies in hideous perambulators or soldiers walking arm-in-arm with their girls. Katherine smiled to herself as she walked past one couple and almost called out in greeting to the girl; she wondered what the girl would think if the rather staid, matronly woman suddenly shouted out her name, and she wondered if the soldier knew that his girlfriend was capable of performing the most extraordinary feats with two men at the same time.

She crossed the low, humped-back bridge and turned to her left, and there he was sitting, as she knew he would be – as he had always sat when he was waiting for her – with a mixture of studied casualness and impatience. She caught him stealing a look at the small watch he wore on his waistcoat.

'I hope I'm not too late.'

Dermot scrambled to his feet, simultaneously shaking his head and stuffing the watch back into his pocket. 'No, I mean . . . of course not . . . I was just . . .' He suddenly took control of himself, and then smiled and shrugged. 'Why do you always make me feel like a schoolboy? I'm actually older than you, if I remember correctly.'

Katherine sat down on the hard bench and arranged her dress in graceful folds. 'Yes, I believe you are. But I fancy I've experienced a little more, eh?'

Dermot shrugged, embarrassed, and sat down. Katherine glanced sidelong at him and noticed there was a slight flush to his cheeks. 'Have I said something to embarrass you?' she asked curiously.

'No, no, it's not you,' he said quickly, 'it's me. I think I've a long way to go . . .'

'A long way to go for what?'

He turned to look at her. 'Why, to become as sophisticated as you.'

Katherine suddenly burst out laughing. 'What;

356

sophisticated? Oh, Dermot, don't you realize that this is all an act, just an act. Unfortunately, I've lived with it for so long now that it's become part of me; it's not an act I can shake off. You don't think I like what I've become, do you? Dermot, I am nearly twenty-seven years of age but I dress and look like a woman nearly twice my years. I should be like you; I should still be young.'

Unsure what to say, Dermot sat back into the bench and then pulled a crumpled paper bag from his coat. He looked at Katherine. 'You know what this is?'

He saw her smile beneath the veil. 'Bread.' And then she produced a bag of her own.

They sat in silence for a while, tossing the bread to the ducks which had quickly gathered and now swarmed around their feet, pecking at the crumbs of bread. Dermot noticed that Katherine still deliberately tossed her bread to the smallest and weakest birds, as they had always done ever since they first met. When the last of the bread was gone, they remained silent, content to sit quietly in each other's company and enjoy the afternoon.

Finally, Dermot spoke, breaking the silence which he felt was becoming uncomfortable.

'I asked you to come here so that I could thank you . . .'

'Thank me? For what?' Katherine asked with a smile.

'You know full well,' he smiled in return.

'I hope it didn't place you in a difficult position at home?' she asked with a grin.

Dermot coughed in embarrassment. 'Well, it did a little, but in a curious way I think my father is rather pleased — no, not pleased, that's the wrong word, but proud perhaps.'

'I often have fathers bringing their sons to the house for instruction by the father's mistress,' Katherine said with a smile, taking a certain delight in the way the colour burned in Dermot's pale cheeks.

'Yes, well, ah . . . you know you saved my life –
literally,' he finished quickly.

Katherine shook her head. 'They could never have
made the charge stick. The evidence was circumstantial
at best.'

'But they were tying me in with the death of the old
woman called Madam whom I met in Summerhill back
in '98, when I was investigating that young girl's death.
They were saying the old woman's death might not have
been an accident.'

'No proof,' she said gently, and patted his hand
absently. 'Did Major Lewis question you himself . . . ?'

'He did. But I didn't say anything about you,' he
added quickly.

'I know that.'

'You do?' he asked, surprised.

She turned on the bench to look at him, and out of
the corner of her eye caught sight of a figure ducking
behind a tree. 'We had a visit from the major,' she said
slowly, and then continued on in the one breath. 'Keep
looking at me, Dermot, and don't look around. But did
you know you were being watched? Don't look!' she
warned.

'But why would anyone be watching me?' he said, his
voice falling to a strained and horrified whisper.

'It's probably one of the major's men. My advice to
you is to carry on with your usual routine, and I think
it would be best if we didn't see one another – for a
little while, at least.'

He started to nod and then stopped. 'But he's seen
me – with you,' he said suddenly. 'Surely that will link
us?'

'We are linked already, remember,' Katherine said
with a twinkle in her eye. 'But don't worry. The major
doesn't know who I am, although he suspects that he
and I have met before,' she continued on slowly, 'but I
dare say I'm the last person he expects to find.' She
stood up suddenly. 'Come on; let's try and lose the
man, and see if we can find somewhere to talk.' She

358

linked her arm through his and, like any other couple, they began to walk slowly around the lake.

The temptation to look over his shoulder was almost irresistible, but Dermot forced himself to look ahead and, at Katherine's insistance, to keep smiling. They swung around by the ornamental fountain and continued on down the flower-lined path, and then turned sharp right, but, instead of continuing to stroll on down the path, Katherine dragged Dermot into the bushes that lined the path. Moments later a dark-eyed, deeply-tanned, young man came hurrying around the corner and stopped almost beside the clump of bushes they were hiding in. He looked left and right in confusion and then, making a decision, took off down the left-hand path. Katherine and Dermot were just about to step out of the bushes when a second figure came puffing down the path; a tall, grizzled, grey-haired man. He peered around the corner of the bushes, following the progress of the first man. He was about to move off in pursuit when Katherine suddenly recognized him.

'Mickey!'

The man spun around, his hand falling to his pocket, and then he smiled rather sheepishly as Katherine stepped from the concealment of the bushes. 'Just what are you doing here?' she demanded.

'Well, now, Tilly and I were a little worried about you, and I decided to come along and keep an eye on things.' He jerked his head in the direction the man had gone. 'I thought I might be saving you a bit of bother, but I can see you had everything well in hand.'

Katherine shook her head, half angry, half amused. 'I'm not a child, you know, I can take care of myself.'

'Never said you couldn't, ma'am. But it doesn't hurt to have someone at your back.'

'No, I don't suppose it does,' she said, smiling. 'Well, we've lost him now, so you can get on with yourself.'

'I'll tally on behind – if you don't mind,' he added.

'I do mind!'

Dermot touched the sleeve of her dress. 'Perhaps it would be as well . . .'

Katherine turned, about to argue, but when she saw the fear lurking behind his eyes, she changed her mind. 'If you wish . . . I suppose so.' She turned back to Mickey. 'Police or major's man?'

'Army,' he said decisively. 'He didn't get that colour here in Ireland.'

'But who was he watching?' Katherine wondered, 'me or Dermot?'

Mickey shook his head. 'I'm not sure; he was here when I arrived, and both of you were sitting on the bench. If I had to guess, I'd say Dermot, but you know I never guess. I'd give it a little while to let things settle down, but perhaps you should go away for awhile . . . you too,' he added, turning to Dermot.

Both spoke at once. 'I can't!'

But Mickey only laughed, shaking his head. 'Oh, I know, you're both indispensable. The house'll fall down without you, ma'am, and the *Freeman* will cease publication.'

'Come on, Dermot,' Katherine said with a sigh, 'let's get some tea.'

They walked around the Green and crossed the top of Grafton Street into the DBC Restaurant. The restaurant was almost empty at this time of day, although it would shortly begin to fill with its regular lunchtime customers. Katherine chose a seat by the window, which afforded them a fine view across to the Green and down to the College of Surgeons.

While they were waiting for their tea and hot buttered scones, they watched four lady cyclists pedal furiously around the corner, narrowly missing a crowd of chatting sandwich-board men, who were about to set off down Grafton Street advertising their wares. The colourfully descriptive language they directed at the retreating ladies brought a grin to Katherine's face, but made Dermot blush again. She caught his expression and smiled.

'Surely you've heard worse?'

He nodded. 'But never when I've been in the presence of a lady.'

Katherine reached out and squeezed his hand. 'Oh Dermot, I'm no lady.'

'You are to me,' Dermot said shyly, but Katherine just smiled and squeezed his hand again.

They drank their tea and ate their hot buttered scones in silence, looking out through the large plate-glass windows. It was Dermot who finally broke the silence. 'If you sat here long enough you could see all Dublin pass by.'

'Not all of it,' Katherine said softly. 'There are many I know who never venture to this side of the city at all.'

The River Liffey divided Dublin into two halves, the north and south sides, with the south being the more fashionable, and including the exclusive Grafton and Dawson Streets and St Stephen's Green, as well as the colleges and the museums.

Dermot nodded. 'That's a good point. I could do a feature based around that, "The Dublin No-one Sees". People will be expecting something about the slums, but instead I'll be writing about the fashionable streets and shops which are never visited by the poor.'

Katherine smiled. 'That's a good idea.' She sipped some tea and then asked, 'You've given up the idea of a story on the jewels, then?'

'What else can I do? It's a dead end; there are just no leads to go on.'

Surprisingly, Katherine shook her head. 'I wouldn't give it up so soon. I don't think we'll ever find the jewels again; they've probably been broken up. But I think we may discover the thief – although I have a feeling the police already know the identity of the thief.'

'Well then, why won't they prosecute?' Dermot demanded. Katherine stared at him, a slight smile playing around her lips, and then he nodded, answering his own question. 'Oh, I see. Someone with friends, you mean?'

She nodded. 'Either that or it would be too embarrassing to bring a prosecution.'

'I'll leave the story for the moment, then.'

Katherine nodded again. 'Leave it be for a while – we'll see what happens . . .' She paused and then added, 'You know you'll have to be careful for a while, don't you, watch where you're going, whom you're seen with? You are being watched.'

'Nonsense!' he tried to laugh.

'You think the major is going to let you go so easily?' she asked. 'You evaded him, tricked him. He's not going to forgive that.'

'But I'm just a journalist . . .' Dermot began.

'Don't be so naïve,' Katherine said impatiently. 'Your political views are well known, and now here you are, suddenly "involved" in the death of a British spy. Now the major might not be able to prove anything at the moment – but do you think he's just going to walk away and leave you be?'

'Should I leave . . . go away for a holiday?' he asked.

Katherine shook her head emphatically. 'No, not now. It's too soon after the killing. I'm sure the police will want to ask you a few more questions – me too, in all likelihood – but in a few weeks' time it might be an idea. Let me know and I'll arrange for you to lose whoever's watching you.'

'Would . . . would you come too?' he asked shyly.

His question surprised her. 'Well, I don't know. I might, if you asked me.'

'I'm asking you.'

'Ask me again in a few weeks' time!'

'I lost him!' the young army officer said simply.

'What do you mean you lost him?' Major Lewis demanded, coming to his feet and moving around his desk to stand directly in front of the officer.

The man winced slightly at the smell of drink from the major, but his deeply tanned, impassive face betrayed nothing. 'He went to the park and was met there by a woman. They spoke for a while and got up and went for a stroll. They rounded a curve in the path and . . . well, they seemed to disappear. They were only out of my sight for a few moments, I don't know how they did it.'

'Perhaps they caught sight of you?' the major suggested.

'No, sir,' the young man said confidently.

'But you still lost them – or did they lose you?' Major Lewis crossed over to the window, leaving the officer still standing to attention, facing the desk. 'Describe the woman!' he snapped.

'Unfortunately, she was wearing black – rather like a widow – with a veil, and I was therefore unable to get a look at her.'

Major Lewis leaned both hands on the windowsill, his arms stiff. He smiled in triumph. So, Madam Kitten was meeting with the Corcoran lad away from the house. 'Did they seem close?' he asked, without turning around.

'They chatted together like old friends, they laughed, and when they got up she linked her arm through his.'

Lewis nodded. 'Double the watch on the lad's house. I want him followed everywhere he goes. I want to know where and when he meets the woman. Understand – everything about them.'

'Yes, sir!'

'Dismiss!' the major snapped.

The officer straightened and saluted and then hurried from the room, leaving the major still standing by the window, planning his strategy. Once he had some sort of pattern for them, he would take them both. Corcoran knew something about the death of his man – of that he was sure. His association with the various nationalist societies alone made him worth watching and his articles – which had won him a considerable following in the slums, where he was regarded as their champion – had been taking a more and more overtly political stance. And the last thing they wanted or needed now was some

363

troublemaker stirring things up in the slums. The major smiled; he could see a time when this crusading journalist might encounter a serious accident.

And then, of course, there was the mysterious Madam Kitten – well, not so mysterious now. He still found it difficult to believe that the whore he had known was now one of the most powerful figures in the Dublin underworld. Well, they would certainly have a lot to talk about.

He turned away from the window, rubbing his hands briskly together; everything was coming together very neatly. If he played his cards right, he might solve the Crown Jewel theft and the murder of his operative, and also close down Madam Kitten's brothel, and put her journalist boyfriend out of business. It would be quite a coup. The only fly in the ointment was that his wife was still missing.

'There's a man watching the house,' Anne said suddenly, turning to William Sherlock who sat close to the fire reading the morning newspaper.

He looked up. 'I know, Anne, he's been there since early morning. I think he's probably watching out for you.'

Anne crossed the room and sank down on to the floor by William's feet. She rested her head on his leg and stared into the glowing embers of the fire. 'You don't think my husband knows I'm here, do you?'

'If he did, his men would have torn the house apart last night looking for you. No; I think you're safe for the moment.'

'But what's going to happen to me?' she whispered. She looked up at him, her eyes sparkling with tears. 'I can't see any future for me.'

'What about a future for us?' he asked with a smile.

'You know that's impossible. My husband will never divorce me . . . and you're a Catholic. You couldn't marry a divorcee.'

'I could, in a civil ceremony.'

'But you would be cut off from your religion.'

'Jesus Christ said love is the greatest of His commandments. There would be no sin in loving you – not in His eyes in any case.'

Anne Lewis shook her head. 'I won't allow you to do such a thing for me.'

'Not even if I want it that way?'

'No,' she said firmly, shaking her head, quelling the feelings of panic welling up inside her. She had just escaped from one prison; she wasn't about to walk into another quite so easily. 'No, William; there's no point in even discussing it. John will never divorce me.'

William Sherlock nodded resignedly. 'You're right, of course. But if you were a widow . . . well, that would be a different matter, of course.'

Anne nodded. 'But there's not much chance of that happening, is there?'

'Come the revolution . . .' William said with a smile.

'We'll be old and grey before that happens.'

'Perhaps not,' William said slowly. 'There's a lot of talk at the moment, and it's a short step from talk to action.'

'I always thought it was the longest step one could take,' Anne said quietly.

'No, no, we'll have a revolution in this country soon. You mark my words. And then we'll be revenged on those who have betrayed us.' His voice, which had risen higher and higher as he spoke, now fell to a whisper. 'And preparations are already being made for that day.'

'What sort of arrangements?' Anne asked, curious and just a little frightened by the fanaticism she had heard in Sherlock's voice.

He bent and kissed her on the forehead, and then, taking her hands in his, stood up. She opened her mouth to speak, but he pressed his finger to her lips and, still holding her hand, led her from the room. He brought her upstairs to the same book-filled room in which he had hidden her the previous night, and once again pulled out the section of bookshelves concealing the little cupboard. Opening the door, he reached in and pulled out one of the oblong boxes Anne had sat on. In the light she could see that the dark blocky script she had noticed last night was actually German, and she immediately guessed what was inside. She had often heard John Lewis talk about the army's suspicions that the various organizations, both associated with or on the fringe of the Gaelic League, were being supplied with arms by the Germans. William pulled off the lid and reached inside . . .

In the box, each individually wrapped in heavy oiled paper, were a dozen rifles.

She looked at William as he almost reverently unwrapped one of the long, heavy-looking weapons and saw the strange glitter in his eyes. Anne shuddered; she had seen that look before – on the occasions her husband had raped her. It was a look of power, of rage, of lust. And yet, William Sherlock, for all his military bearing and rhetoric, was one of the gentlest of men, compassionate even, who was unable to pass a beggar in the street without dropping a coin.

'Why, William?' she asked.

He looked at her, uncomprehending, working the bolt on the rifle with monotonous insistence.

'Why have you become involved in this . . . this . . . foolishness?'

'Anne, we're going to liberate Ireland!'

'With a dozen rifles?'

'There'll be more when the time comes,' he said confidently.

'And will you be there, firing on the enemy?'

'Oh, I'll be there,' he promised, although Anne thought she saw something like doubt pass behind his eyes.

'And just who are the enemy?' she demanded.

Sherlock slammed the bolt home and then began wrapping the rifle in its oiled covering once again. 'All those who stand against us,' he snapped.

366

'You keep speaking in the plural. Just who are "we"?' she wondered.

A look of suspicion crossed his face. 'You're asking a lot of questions . . . for someone who doesn't support the cause,' he added.

'Who said I didn't support the cause? I'm Irish, and surely I've more reason than anyone else to loathe the British – well, one of them in particular. And don't forget,' she added, 'I did join the Gaelic Literary Society.'

'I hadn't forgotten.' William said slowly. 'Look, I shouldn't really have shown you all this . . .'

'Why not? Because you're afraid I am going to tell someone? Who can I tell – you're all I have now. I don't think guns are the way, I don't think you can win that way. But I don't suppose what I say will make the slightest bit of difference; your mind is made up.'

He nodded quickly. 'I made my decision a long time ago.'

'Whatever happens, William, I want to be part of it! If you're going to fight, I want to fight alongside you.'

William Sherlock pushed the box back into the cupboard. 'We'll win,' he promised.

'I don't think so. Not unless things have changed in the years I have been kept locked up.' She pressed her head against his chest. 'You'll not win, but I hope it'll be a close-run thing.'

William suddenly laughed.

'What's so funny?' she demanded.

'I was wondering why the women seemed to be the strongest amongst us. You remind me of Maud Gonne, or the Countess Markievicz.'

'Who?'

'Maud Gonne you've met, I think.'

'Briefly; wasn't she the one the poet Yeats was deeply in love with?'

'He still is,' Sherlock smiled.

'Constance Markievicz – the name is Polish, by the way, she married a Polish Count – is . . . well . . .' he shrugged. 'I don't know how to describe her. But when there is a revolution in Ireland, she will be in the thick of it.'

'I think I'd like to meet her,' Anne said slowly, an idea beginning to form at the back of her mind.

'You will,' Sherlock promised, 'you will.'

CHAPTER THIRTY-ONE

Major Lewis found that there was no pattern to Madam Kitten's or Dermot Corcoran's movements. Over the next few weeks, they didn't seem to meet at all, or more particularly Corcoran had made no attempt to visit the brothel. His spies reported that Madam Kitten rarely, if ever, left the house. He had their mail intercepted – that was one of the reasons his rooms were in the post office – but there was no communication between them. Yet, if they were lovers – and he suspected that they were – then surely they would be sending messages to one another.

Unless . . .

Unless, they were deliberately staying apart for a few weeks . . . perhaps allowing some time for things to quieten down. The more he thought about it, the more convinced he became that this was closer to the truth . . . and that indicated a guilty conscience . . . which meant that Kitten or Corcoran, probably both, were involved in either the Jewel Robbery or the death of his officer or both . . .

Meanwhile, the investigation into the death of his officer was carried out and a verdict of 'death by a person or persons unknown' was handed down, and, while the police doubled up on their patrols in the district for a while, and generally made life difficult for working girls operating around those streets, things soon returned to normal.

The investigation also continued into the theft of the Crown Jewels. Chief Inspector John Kane of Scotland Yard had arrived in Dublin on the 12th of July to carry out an independent investigation. His inquiries had led him to a homosexual vice ring that went all the way back to London and was connected with the highest offices of power both there and in Dublin Castle.

On the day before he returned to London, he submitted a full report of the theft of the jewels and named the person responsible. That report was read by both the brigadier and Major Lewis; both indicated that it would be better if it were destroyed.

Two days later a copy of the report ended up in Katherine's hands. When she read it, she spent the rest of the evening debating whether to release it to Dermot or not. It was a story that would make his career – but could very possibly destroy him in the process. Too many important people with too much power and money were involved, both in the theft and in the subsequent cover-up – Dermot would never be able to stand against them. Also, the practical business-side of her nature warned that the resultant scandal would be bad for business, and so, rather reluctantly, she consigned the thick folder to the fire, and watched the heavy pages darken and smoulder and then burst into flame. When it was completely consumed, she raked out the ashes herself, ensuring that no particle of text remained. But at least she was now content; she knew now that the jewels were gone – indeed had been taken some time before the theft had been discovered – and had very likely been broken up and sold off individually.

She stood up, dusting off her hands, staring into the ashes. From what she had read, no-one would ever know the secret of the Irish Crown Jewel Affair; too many lies had been told, too many names to protect. She smiled wistfully; she wondered if, in years to come, would anyone even remember it? She would; it was that event which had brought Dermot back to her -- but it had also brought the captain – the major – back into her life again.

Katherine crossed to the window and sat down on the high-backed, hard, wooden chair, and looked down into the street, watching the children playing. Knowing she would never see her own son playing there, principally because it would lead to too many questions, but also because she didn't want him to, she didn't want him mixing with the urchins and barefooted waifs. She smiled, leaning her forehead against the cool glass: she was becoming a snob. Whatever would Dermot think? Over the past few weeks he had been creeping more and more into her thoughts, and occasionally when she did or said something she would stop and wonder what his reaction would have been. But she also found that when she thought of him, almost naturally it seemed, her thoughts would also turn to the major – and with him always came the old fear . . . and the thrill, too, she had to admit, if she was to be totally honest.

As Dermot walked out of the *Freeman*'s offices in Princes Street, a small ragged street urchin came running up to him and pulled on his trouser leg. Dermot automatically waved his freshly printed copy of the *Freeman's Journal* at him, thinking him another beggar, but the boy handed him a slip of paper. He then turned and ran off without a backward glance.

The paper was thick, heavy parchment of the highest quality and very expensive, and it contained a six-word message written in a slightly sloping, elegant hand that set his blood pounding: '*I have thought about that holiday.*'

There was no signature.

'I can't stay here forever,' Anne Lewis protested, pulling aside the curtains and staring across the street at the shadowy figure of the man still watching the house.

'And why not?' William Sherlock looked up from the sheaf of papers he was sorting through. 'Your husband thinks you are definitely not here; surely this is the safest place for you to be at the moment, eh? Here,' he patted the seat beside him, 'come and help me sort through these.'

Anne crossed the room and sat down by his side. He was sorting through bundles of crudely printed posters,

371

inviting people to a public lecture featuring the Countess Constance Markievicz as the main speaker. The poster ended with the words IRELAND WILL BE FREE in large blood-red letters.

'Sort them into bundles of fifty or so,' William suggested, 'and they can then be passed on for distribution.'

'What do the authorities say about this sort of thing?' Anne wondered.

'They more or less turn a blind eye to it at the moment; I think they consider us nothing more than a harmless bunch of cranks. But they'll have cause to regret their laxity in the future,' he warned.

'How did you become involved ... ?' Anne wondered.

William thought about it for a moment, and then shrugged. 'I'm not sure. I think it was just a natural continuation of my activities in the Gaelic Literary Society. It brought me into contact with people like the countess, and Maud Gonne, Yeats and Stephens, and Pearse.'

'I'm not sure I know them all ...' Anne Lewis said slowly.

'The one to remember is Pearse, Padraic Pearse,' Sherlock said with a rather proud grin.

'Have I ever met him?'

William shook his head. 'If you had, you would undoubtedly remember him. All fire and energy, and force of will. He drains me. But he has the vision – they all have of course, but his is the clearest, I think – of a free Ireland, an Ireland ruled by the Irish people, making their own laws, running their own country without outside interference. And, when I'm with him, when I hear him speak, I can share that vision too! Anyway,' he continued, slightly embarrassed by his outburst, 'I started penning verses on heroic subjects, using as my models the Irish heroes and heroines, personifying Ireland in them. Oh, it's nothing new of course, Yeats did it years ago with the play *Cathleen ni Houlihan* . . .'

Anne shook her head again. 'You forget I've been locked in since the turn of the century. I spent the New Year's Eve of 1899 and 1900 sitting at the window of my room, drinking steadily through my third or fourth bottle of wine of the day, and watching the merrymakers wend their way homewards from their parties . . . and looking at all the candles burning in the windows . . . and listening to the bells and the ships sirens' sound in the century . . . and crying . . .'

William reached out and squeezed her hand. 'I'm sorry,' he said softly.

Anne shook her head. 'No, don't be sorry,' she said, sounding almost angry, 'just remember it. Remember I don't know what's been happening in the world since the turn of the century; I've had no contact with it, I've had no newspapers, I had no-one to talk to . . .'

'I'm sorry,' William said again. 'I'll take care to explain everything in the future.'

'Dear William,' Anne said softly, 'you're so patient with me . . .' She squeezed his fingers tightly.

'You know I love you, don't you?' he said suddenly. He cupped her chin in his hands and forced her to look into his eyes. 'You know I mean it,' he demanded, 'I love you.'

She could only nod dumbly; but she couldn't in all honesty say that she loved him. Respected him, yes, felt a certain affection for him, yes certainly, but love . . . she wasn't sure if she knew what love was any more.

William kissed her cheek, a fleeting feather touch and then turned back to the pile of posters on the table. 'What was I saying . . . ?' he asked vaguely.

'Oh . . . you mentioned *Cathleen ni Houlihan*,' she said, 'who or what is *Cathleen ni Houlihan*?'

William smiled at the memory. 'Oh, it was a play which Willy Yeats wrote for Maud Gonne. She plays the part of an old woman, bowed down by sorrows, but of course she is in reality the personification of the sufferings of Ireland. Maud Gonne is Ireland.'

Anne Lewis nodded. She remembered the tall, statu-esque, very beautiful woman, whom Yeats obviously adored, and she could very easily see how she could personify Ireland.

'The play was first performed in 1902 in Clarendon Street. I was there, and it was one of the most extraor-dinary productions I've ever seen ... Anyway,' he shook his head, annoyed at himself for rambling, 'to come back to me. I took the idea of using characters from Ireland's heroic age and wrote them into a series of political plays. It's all terribly allegorical and preten-tious, but the audiences seem to love it. Those plays brought me to the notice of some of those I mentioned earlier, especially Pearse and ... well, things have just gone on from that.'

'And now you've reached the stage of storing arms in your own home?'

'It's for the cause,' he said simply. 'And everyone needs a cause, either personal or public, something which they can throw themselves into, something which they believe in.'

Anne Lewis nodded vaguely. 'I know.' She turned to look at him. 'Do you think this cause has room for another volunteer?'

William pulled her into his arms. 'There's always room for one more,' he said happily.

As the evening rolled into dusk and the sun sank into the ocean, the chill of evening replacing the heat of the day, the beach gradually became deserted. Sounds which had been inaudible during the day regained their hold again, and the hiss of the surf against the sands, the rattle of the stones as the water washed over them, and the curious, mysterious, popping sounds of water over seaweed made the night a magical, mysterious place. The air seemed to change too. During the day it had been heavy and dry, leaden almost, but the night made it moist again; it was cold, but the chill made it refreshing.

Katherine stood by the water's edge and breathed in deep lungfuls of the salty sea air. It felt . . . extraordinary and, after the smogs and fogs and stenches of Dublin, it smelt like nectar. This was her first real holiday since she had come to Ireland and, although she had travelled abroad for Bella Cohen, this was the first time she had ever ventured to any part of Ireland outside the city of Dublin.

Katherine and Dermot were in Galway, on the western seaboard of Ireland, and the seas which hissed and rattled the sand and stones at her feet were the same seas that washed on the shores of America – and that thought excited her, it almost made the Land of Promise seem closer, and she could understand why so many of the people on the west coast had sailed to the Americas in the last decades. It was almost as if it lay just out of sight beyond the horizon.

Katherine felt like a young girl again. She had made a promise to herself not to think of the house, or Major Lewis, or any of the problems that were waiting for her in Dublin. This holiday was for her benefit as much as Dermot's.

Mickey had suggested Galway and at first Katherine had been reluctant to travel across Ireland just for a holiday. She argued that if anything happened, she would be that much further away. But Mickey and Tilly had pointed out that that was the idea. If she went to Galway, she would be several hours away and that, they pointed out, would help to remove the temptation both for them to call on her for help and for her to return early just to make sure everything was running smoothly. And so she had gone, half reluctantly, half eagerly, with Dermot who was like an excited boy starting out on his school holidays. And as the train chugged its way across the flat Irish countryside, Katherine noticed a curious change coming over them both, almost as if the proximity to the capital changed or altered their characters. Away from Dublin, she had no worries, no cares, and there was no longer any need to wear her 'widow's weeds' and play that role, and suddenly she was just another young woman starting out on a holiday, and she found herself relaxing, allowing Dermot to take over. Similarly, Dermot, with no deadlines to meet, no worries about the major, and no-one to order him about, gradually grew more assertive.

Katherine had written ahead some days earlier, and had reserved two single rooms in a small hotel on the waterfront, and, once they had deposited their luggage and freshened up, they set out to wander around the ancient city.

Dermot had visited the town before and was able to show Katherine some of its sights. Her first impression was of size; she thought it was tiny and, after Dublin, she supposed it was. But it was compact and snug and, although it was called a city, she found it hard to think of it as anything other than a town.

The buildings too had character and showed a strong Spanish influence as did many of the inhabitants, being dark-haired and dark-eyed, and the women especially were imbued with a distinctly exotic beauty. Dermot explained that it was because of the trade which Galway had traditionally carried on with Spain and also because some of the survivors of the ill-fated Spanish Armada had managed to come ashore along the west coast of Ireland. Here, too, she heard the Irish language spoken for the first time; a rich, flowing, musical language that took her so completely by surprise the first time she heard it that she stopped and stared.

'What are they saying?' she whispered in astonishment to Dermot, looking at the two women in their voluminous skirts and black shawls.

'They're discussing the recent catch of fish,' Dermot explained.

'But the language .. ?'

'That's Irish they're speaking,' he explained.

'And you understand it?' she asked, astonished, 'I never knew you spoke Irish.'

Dermot shook his head. 'I'm afraid I don't understand

all of it, they're using a West of Ireland dialect, but I can get most of it.'

She listened again to the rich, flowing, almost liquid sounds. 'It's beautiful,' she said at last. 'You must teach me.'

Dermot grinned and shook his head. 'Oh, I can't; I don't know enough. But there are places you can go in Dublin to learn . . .'

Katherine nodded eagerly, something of her old girlish impetuousness returning, and there and then she made up her mind to set about learning Irish as soon as she returned to Dublin.

Katherine fell in love with the city on the Atlantic coast, but a great part of its attraction was the sea. Even when she had been crossing over from England, she hadn't felt in awe of the sea as she did now, and when she worked in Blackpool on the seafront she had somehow been insulated from the raw power of the ocean, and hadn't appreciated it fully. She loved to walk along the beach each evening with Dermot. Dusk shaded the meeting of the sea and shore, and in the twilight all she could hear was the distant roar of the sea coupled with the hiss of the surf on the sands. As they walked down the beach, it sounded like some huge creature breathing gently by their sides. The beach became a quiet magical place, a place for lovers. It seemed almost natural that they should reach for each other's hands, and then Dermot's arm went around her shoulder, pulling her close. And suddenly the previous eight years, with all that had happened, all the fears, the successes, the failures, seemed to slip away and they were just another young couple, falling in love.

The days drifted by quietly. The weather was glorious, one of the hottest summers on record, and the single week they had planned gradually extended into two. They toured the city and its surroundings, venturing as far out as the tiny village of Spiddal and the surrounding Galway and Mayo countryside, which was one of the most rugged and beautiful in Ireland. They

377

talked together – constantly – and on every subject imaginable, speaking of their wishes and desires, their pasts and their futures, and somehow their futures always seemed to become entwined. They found they had become comfortable in each other's presence, and when there was silence between them it was no longer strained. But they never talked of their feelings for each other – not until the last day of their holiday.

They were sitting in a small restaurant that looked out over Galway Bay. They had booked early and had managed to secure a window seat, and they had a fine view of the fishing fleet moving sedately across the bay out towards the open sea. The restaurant was decorated with all the articles of the fishing trade, with nets and shells and even an upturned coracle on the wall above the fire which, because of the heat of the day, had been allowed to die down to a dull cherry-coloured glow. The light in the room had been turned down, and the main illumination came from the candles set into wax-encrusted bottles on the tables, which shed a soft yellow light over the diners. Katherine had found the idea of candles in bottles a little startling at first, especially in what was obviously an expensive restaurant – indeed the whole place was something of a novel surprise – but on the whole she decided she liked it. It was obviously popular because, even by eight o'clock, the twenty or so tables scattered around the room were all fully occupied, and Katherine saw several couples being turned away.

'How did you ever find this place?' she asked Dermot.

'I've never been here before,' he admitted, 'but I heard one of the reporters in the *Freeman's* talking about it. It's a strange place,' he added, looking around, 'it doesn't advertise and yet it's nearly always booked up. It's reputation is solely dependent on word of mouth.'

'It's very nice,' Katherine said, 'and a perfect ending to our holiday.'

Dermot nodded in understanding, reaching for her hand across the table and squeezing it. 'I'm sorry it has to end,' he said, looking directly into her eyes.

'So am I.'

'Will we see each other when we get back to Dublin?' he asked directly. The holiday had relaxed him greatly and Katherine's obvious delight and interest in everything he had to say had done much to restore his confidence. Although the nervous youth hadn't vanished entirely, something of the real, spirited Dermot had returned.

'I hope so,' Katherine said, toying with the heavy silver tableware.

'The last two weeks have been . . . well, something I'll treasure. They've let me see what might have been between us,' he said with a sad smile.

'I realize that. Perhaps I should have said "yes" to you when you asked me to marry you. I don't know. Things would have been different certainly. But I'm not sure whether we would still be in love.' She smiled quickly. 'And if I had said yes, we wouldn't have been able to enjoy this holiday.'

Dermot smiled. He stared down at his hand which was still resting on hers, realizing that it was something he would never have dreamed of doing barely fourteen days previously. He looked across at Katherine. The candlelight had softened the hard lines of her face and dipped her eyes into shadow, wiping years and hard experience from her age. 'I . . . I think I love you,' he whispered.

'You only think you love me?' Katherine asked with a slight smile.

He grinned and shook his head. 'No, I don't think it. I know I love you.'

She turned her hand in his and gripped his fingers tightly. 'I'm glad, because I think I love you too.'

'Think?' he mocked.

'It's not as easy for me to make a decision like that,' she said. 'I sell love daily, and I find it difficult to draw the line between love and lust.' She stared him straight in the face. 'And what is it you feel for me, Dermot, love or lust?'

His face flushed with the sudden, direct question, but he was saved from answering by the arrival of the food. The meal was magnificent, although afterwards he could never be sure precisely what he had eaten; he was only conscious of Katherine's slightly mocking gaze on his face, and he experienced a vague feeling of regret, knowing that with the ending of their holiday they were already slipping back into their respective city roles.

'Well,' Katherine asked finally, when the tea arrived, 'you never answered my question.' She saw the colour touch his cheeks again, and he started to shake his head. 'And don't ask me what question,' she warned.

'You know me too well,' he smiled. 'I think – I know! – I love you, and yes, I also want to hold you in my arms, and if that is lust, well then yes, I feel lust for you.'

'I think lust may be something stronger than just holding me in your arms,' she said softly.

They walked back to their hotel in silence, realizing that in the morning they would board the train to Dublin, the holiday would end, and they would return to normal, although they both realized that things would never be the same between them again. They had come to know each other too well during the fourteen days, had shared too much together for them not to make a commitment to one another, or break off all communication between them completely. They had shared nearly everything.

They stopped outside the door to Katherine's room and stood awkwardly together, unsure what to do, how to act. Finally Dermot dipped his head as if to touch his lips to Katherine's cheek, but she turned her head and her lips met his. He drew back in shock, but her arms went up around him and pressed his head against hers. Her lips opened under his and he felt the tip of her tongue against his mouth.

'Katherine . . . ?'

Her eyes were dark and moist, and when she spoke

380

her voice was so soft that he had to bend his head to make out the words. 'I want you to love me, Dermot.'

'I do love you,' he said, but she shook her head and touched her fingertips to his lips.

'No, no, you don't understand. I want you to love me – now!'

His eyes opened wide in astonishment and he wondered if he had heard her correctly.

Katherine kissed him passionately again, her lips and tongue exploring his, and when she pulled her head away, she said, 'I mean it. I want you to love me.'

She turned and opened the door to her room, leading him inside. The room was in darkness; she didn't bother with a light but crossed to the window and pulled back the heavy curtains, suffusing the room with the purple night light. Dermot crossed to the window and stood behind her, his hands encircling her waist. Her own hands covered his and they stood in silence for several pounding heartbeats, staring out across the sparkling bay. Finally, Katherine turned and moved her arms up around his neck. 'I meant it, I want you to love me – but only if you want to,' she added with a sly smile.

'I've wanted to for a long time,' Dermot confessed. 'I've often dreamt of it – and then woke up ashamed of my thoughts.'.

Katherine's hand moved to his throat and loosened his cravat, before pulling out the stud and allowing the hard collar to curl free.

'But Katherine,' his voice fell to an embarrassed whisper, 'Katherine, I've never made love to a woman before.'

She undid the buttons of his coat and slipped it off his shoulders, tossing it on to the floor, and then her hands went to the buttons of his waistcoat. 'I've only ever made love to one man,' she said slowly, 'and that was a long time ago. No-one has touched me since. I imagine I'll be just as unsure as you . . .'

Katherine undressed him slowly, while he stood unmoving, her nimble fingers working on the buttons and hooks and belts, until he stood completely naked before her. His body was pale and almost completely hairless, like a boy's, but he was well muscled and his reaction was certainly not that of a boy.

She then stood back and, with her eyes on his, began to undress herself, quickly stripping down to her shift and French silk knickers. And then Dermot, without any urging on her part, gently lifted the shift and bundled it up over her head and dropped it on the floor. His hands, the fingertips calloused from the typewriters, moved slowly down her shoulders and rested flatly on her breasts, his thumbs just touching her nipples. He kissed her then, deeply, passionately, and Katherine could feel him trembling, like an animal about to spring, and she knew that he was holding himself in check only with the greatest of difficulty.

His hands moved down her body, and he slowly sank to his knees, pressing his lips to the soft flesh under her breasts and down her belly. With a feather-light touch his fingers found the ribbons on her knickers and undid them, allowing the cloth to rustle down her legs. His hands moved around her body, warm and flat against her rounded flesh, and he looked up at her, palely outlined against the purple star-studded night.

'Make love to me – please.' Her voice was tight and strained, sounding almost forced.

Dermot pressed himself to her body, her groin against his chest, his hands on her buttocks, her hands on the back of his head. He could hear her heart thudding through her entire body, echoing his own, and he was painfully aware of the pulse throbbing in his groin. He suddenly stood up and pressed him against her, the touch of her breasts shocking, and he kissed her again, but this time with a hunger that was terrifying.

'I want you,' he hissed.

'I know,' she said, and pushed him backwards, urging him towards the bed. The back of his knees touched the mattress and he fell backwards, still clutching Katherine. She straddled him, her arms on either side of his head, while his hands worked at her breasts, fascinated by the hardening nipples. She moved herself against him, aware of the need growing inside her, a need she hadn't felt in a long time. She felt Dermot's hands, touching, pressing, caressing, and then moving down her body to touch her intimately and then draw back, almost in surprise, as they encountered moisture. She felt him touch again, his fingers exploring, spreading her flesh and then entering her. The shock was almost unbearable and they both stopped and remained still, experiencing the sensations of flesh against flesh, of warmth and moistness, of the closest intimate bonding that can exist between a couple. And then Katherine began to move slowly, rocking herself on Dermot's body. He became caught up in the rhythm and joined her, pushing upwards, his hands rigid against the small of her back as if to force himself deeper into her body.

'I . . . I . . . love . . . you,' he gasped.

She crouched lower against his body, wrapping her arms around his head. 'I love you so much,' she gasped.

But as they reached the shuddering culmination of the act, it wasn't Dermot's face Katherine saw beneath her. Time dissolved and she found she was looking into John Lewis's hard eyes.

CHAPTER THIRTY-TWO

Mickey was waiting for them with a carriage at the station, and Katherine immediately knew that something was wrong. It was etched into the hard lines on his face and the obvious signs of relief at her appearance.

'You're looking well; relaxed and refreshed,' he said, forcing a smile, taking the cases from Dermot and swinging them up behind the carriage. He held the door open and helped Katherine in, but touched Dermot on the sleeve before he could climb in also. 'I've taken the liberty of arranging for a separate cab for you, sir. I'm sure you won't mind, but I've some urgent business to discuss with Madam.'

Dermot looked from Mickey to Katherine in surprise, but smiled easily and shrugged. 'Of course; I'm sure you'll need to bring Madam up to date on all that's been happening over the past two weeks. I suppose it's partly my fault. I didn't mean to keep her away for so long.'

'Ah sure she deserved it,' Mickey said, raising his hand, and immediately another cab detached itself from the line and moved forward.

'I'll see you tonight?' Dermot asked, looking in at Katherine.

She glanced quickly at Mickey and then regretfully shook her head. 'Not tonight, if you don't mind, Dermot . . . but tomorrow night, certainly.'

Dermot had caught the look that had passed between the two and knew something had happened, and then nodded slightly. 'Of course; tomorrow then.' He was about to turn away when he popped his head back into the window and winked at Katherine. 'And thank you,' he whispered.

'For what?' she smiled.

But Dermot just shook his head and trotted over to the second waiting cab.

Mickey climbed in beside Katherine and tapped on the roof for the driver to move off. 'What's wrong?' she asked immediately.

'It's Tilly,' Mickey said softly. 'She's disappeared.'

She looked at him uncomprehendingly. 'What do you mean, disappeared? That's impossible.'

But he shook his head. 'I wish it was. She went out three days ago to get some fresh flowers from the market and she never came back. I've looked everywhere for her.'

'But why didn't you contact me?' Katherine demanded.

'I thought she might be back at any moment.'

'And you've no idea where she is?'

'Well . . . not exactly.'

'What do you mean?' The carriage lurched as it crossed the bridge and began the long drive down the quays into the heart of the city.

'This morning I noticed that the major's men are no longer watching the house,' he said slowly.

'You don't think . . .' she began, but then she nodded to herself, 'yes, he would.'

On the drive back to the house, Mickey told her that he had put out the word to his street spies and to all the prostitutes working in Dublin's Monto, but none of them had seen Tilly. He had then set about calling in various favours with higher-ranking police and army officers but, to the best of their knowledge, there were no special category prisoners being held at the moment. But when he enquired after Major Lewis at the post office, he found the man was on a week's leave of duty.

'I've had the house on Clonliffe Road watched since about noon today, when I finally discovered the major was on leave.'

'And was there anything to report?' Katherine wondered. Already her holiday, with its bittersweet echoes

385

of the past and what might have been, had faded to be replaced with the coldly terrifying present.

'There may be some news when we reach home,' he said.

The cab rattled on to Bachelor's Walk and then turned left into O'Connell Street, slowing only to allow scores of sandwich-board men to cross in front of it. Katherine idly read the advertisements for various hotels, and salves, and meats and breads, but the words were meaningless. If anything had happened to Tilly she would hold herself responsible – and her vengeance on the major would be terrible.

'Do you think he's taken her?' she asked suddenly.

Mickey nodded silently.

'And do you think he's holding her in the house in Clonliffe Road?'

Again the silent nod.

'How many men can you raise before nightfall?' she asked softly.

Mickey looked across at her, not sure if she were joking or not, but in the dimness of the cab her face was set in hard lines. 'You can't be thinking . . .'

'How many men?'

'As many as you need,' he said quietly.

'Find a dozen – and make sure they're trustworthy,' Katherine said, still staring through the small window. 'Hire them through intermediaries; there must be no connection with the house at all.'

'But surely you can't be thinking of . . .' he began, but looking at the expression on her face, he nodded and answered his own question, 'By God, I think you are . . .'

When Tilly awoke, she lay still and unmoving hoping – against hope – that the dusty wooden boards beneath her naked body would dissolve into the sheets of her bed and then she could wake up knowing it had been nothing more than a nightmare. But she knew it was no nightmare; it was real, all too real.

She sat up slowly, feeling the bare attic room swim around her, and hugged her arms around her breasts, shivering. She was naked. She had been stripped when she had been first brought to his house – two, three? – days ago, sickened from the pad which had been pressed over her face, her lips and nostrils blistered from the chloroform.

Later, when she had felt well enough to stand up, she found she was in a small attic room which had for its furniture a bed, a chair and a bedpan. There were two windows; one overlooking the grounds to a college of some sort, the other looking down on to a fairly prosperous road. Still dazed and sickened, it took her befogged brain a long time before she realized that the college behind her was Holy Cross College, and therefore she was in Major Lewis's house.

He had come for her later that evening, just as dusk was falling and the room was slipping into shadow. She had dragged the single blanket off the bed and was huddled in it, crouched in a corner, when the door suddenly opened and he stepped into the room.

'Good evening, Tilly,' he said quietly, his voice low and conversational, crossing to sit on the only chair in the room, 'or should I say, good evening, Madam Kitten?'

She was about to burst out and say she wasn't Kitten, when she realized his mistake, and something like humour sparked behind her eyes.

The major saw the look, but misinterpreted it. 'Ah, I see I've struck home.' He settled back into the chair, tilting it backwards on its two rear legs, and straightened the crease in his twill trousers. 'I told you I would discover your identity,' he said smugly, 'and for someone with my connections, it really wasn't too difficult. A little cross-referencing of dates and it all became very clear.'

'You have kidnapped me,' she said hoarsely, her mouth and throat still raw from the chloroform.

'Kidnapped is such a strong word,' he said, 'and I

don't think it applies here, especially as no ransom will
be demanded for your release, as is usual in a kidnap.
Your body is just as I remember it,' he continued on in
the same conversational tone, 'and I have very fond
memories of your body.'

'Why are you holding me?'

'Oh, for questioning,' he said. 'Yes, many's the night
I've awoken with your body in my dreams, inflamed
with lust for you. You were always my favourite. Why
did you leave?'

Tilly found it difficult to follow him. His eyes were
bright and glittering and his fingers were drumming
nervously – or excitedly – on the knee on his trousers,
but his face was expressionless and his voice a flat
monotone.

'Why did you leave?' he asked again.

'It was becoming unsafe on the streets,' Tilly impro-
vised, realizing that her only chance lay in playing along
with the major.

'But you could have told me where you were,' he
suggested.

'Madam Cohen wouldn't let me contact any of my
old customers. She . . . she sent me abroad to train in
some of the European houses.'

'Oh, I know that, I know a lot about you, Madam
Kitten,' Major Lewis gloated. 'But why didn't you
reveal yourself when I visited your house the first time?'

'I don't know . . . I didn't recognize you at first,' she
said, 'and when I finally realized just who you were,
well, I didn't know how you would react . . .'

'Don't lie to me, Tilly,' Major Lewis said suddenly,
icily. 'You knew my identity before I had even entered
your room. And a woman with your sources would be
aware of me and my activities. But no matter, no matter,'
he continued on, 'now that we've met again, I'm sure
everything will be fine. Tell me about the man who was
killed.' he said suddenly.

The sudden change in subject caught her off balance,
and while she floundered for a suitable answer, he

388

continued on in the same monotone. 'You see, I know you know something about the man's death. And I'm going to find out. Now there are many ways of asking the questions, pleasantly or unpleasantly, but of course the choice is yours. You see I have proof . . .'

'If you had proof you wouldn't be holding me here!' she snapped.

And suddenly all the pretence was gone. Major Lewis surged to his feet and crossed the room in two quick strides, his right hand lashing out, catching her once across the face and then again as it swung back. The mask was gone and in its place was the old Major Lewis, the same Major Lewis who had beaten and terrified her in the Imperial Hotel, the same Major Lewis who had, according to Katherine, killed an eighteen-year-old pregnant girl.

'You'll tell me,' he hissed, 'you'll tell me what you know. And then you'll tell me the names of your sources in Monto, and then you'll tell me the names of your customers . . . you'll tell me everything I want to know.'

But Tilly shook her head defiantly, blood trickling down her chin to drip on to her breasts. 'I'll tell you nothing!'

He wrapped a hand into her hair and twisted her head upwards. 'I think you will. I think you'll beg to answer my questions. By the time I'm finished with you, you'll be working for me.'

'You can take your questions to Hell – I won't be answering them,' she warned.

'Oh, there are many ways of asking a question,' Major Lewis said, unbuckling his belt, pulling out the leather strap . . .

The night was chill, with a stiffening east wind whipping down the length of Clonliffe Road, bringing with it the promise of rain. Katherine stood in the shadows opposite the major's house and felt the intervening years dissipate in a flash, and suddenly she was a servant

389

again, returning home. Everything she had learned over the years, everything she had experienced, seemed little more than a dream. Then Mickey touched her on the arm, bringing her abruptly back to the present.

'As far as we can make out there's only the major in the house, although up to a few days ago there was supposed to be a woman living there, but no-one seems to know who she is. Some slattern off the streets more'n likely.'

'Could it have been his wife – she is supposed to be ill?'

'She hasn't been seen in years – it's extremely doubtful that she has actually been in the house for the past few years.'

'Well, if the major is the only one living there, then why are there two lights on?' Katherine asked. 'One in the main bedroom, and one in the attic.'

She felt Mickey shrug in the darkness. 'Perhaps he's keeping someone up there,' he suggested.

'My thoughts exactly.'

Katherine looked down Clonliffe Road to where it intersected with Drumcondra Road. She could just about make out the dim shapes of four cabs standing in a line under the trees. Each of the cabs held three men, but they were only there to be used as a back-up if everything else failed.

'I still think you're being foolish,' Mickey said. 'I don't think there's any need for you to go in. Let me do it.'

But Katherine shook her head resolutely. 'No; I know what I'm doing. If I manage to get inside, give me thirty minutes, and if I'm not out by then, you can come in and get me. But whatever you do, don't kill the man.'

Mickey nodded. 'I'll be careful,' he said, but he had already made up his mind that the major had over-stretched himself on this occasion and unfortunately might have to be killed in the struggle.

Katherine crossed the quiet road quickly, her heels clicking and scraping slightly on the cobbles. As she

390

opened the gate and walked up the path, she had to resist the urge to continue on around by the side of the house to the back door, and it was only when she tugged on the brass bellpull set into the stonework by the side of the door that she realized that this was the first time she had ever come to the front door. Somewhere deep in the house the bell jangled, and she ran her fingertips down the verdigris-stained brass roses, remembering the countless times she had shined them to a mirror-bright polish. There was no movement in the house and she pulled on the bell again. She heard a stair creaking – the third from the end she knew – and then a shadow-shape moved behind the decorated stained-glass panels. A chain rattled and a bolt clicked back and then the hall door creaked open.

Katherine stepped back so the light could fall on her face, and tilted back her head. 'Hello, John,' she said simply.

The major stared blankly at her, trying to place the vaguely familiar face. When he failed to do so, he shook his head. 'I'm sorry, I don't think I've had the pleasure . . .'

Katherine smiled. 'Oh, you've had your pleasure from me on more than one occasion – although it was a long time ago,' she added, almost absently. 'Why, it must be seven or eight years ago since we last knew each other intimately.'

Major Lewis frowned, and tried breathing in deep lungfuls of the damp night air to try and clear his head. He had been drinking on and off throughout the day and that, coupled with 'questioning' Tilly, had left him feeling drained and slightly fogged. 'You know me . . .'

'Very well indeed, Major Lewis – although you were still a captain when we knew one another.'

'How many years did you say?' he asked sharply, suddenly seeing the face before him shift, the hard lines vanish and the tired, cold, world-weary eyes give way to a look of expectant innocence. It was a face from his past, a face which had sometimes haunted his nightmares.

Katherine saw the expression in his eyes and smiled savagely. 'I see you remember, John,' she said. 'Can I come in?'

He tried speaking but no sound came out, and he had to swallow hard. 'Yes, yes, of course,' he whispered. He stepped back and allowed the woman to walk past him into the darkened hallway. Before he closed the door he peered up and down the street, more out of habit than anything else but saw nothing.

Across the road, standing stock-still in the shadows, Mickey watched the door shut and pulled out his half-hunter, looking down at the face. He would give Katherine half an hour – no more. If she – and Tilly – weren't out of there, then he was taking his men in, and God help the major then. Mickey half hoped that Katherine wouldn't be out in time.

'But this is extraordinary,' Major Lewis was saying as he ushered Katherine into the familiar sitting room. She looked around quickly, and, as far as she could see, nothing had been moved or altered; the only difference was the general air of shabbiness and disuse that hung over the room, coupled with the more obvious signs of neglect, the dust that covered everything and the cob-webs that hung in the darkened corners.

'What do you mean?' she asked, fully aware she was playing a very dangerous game. She had Major Lewis off balance now, which left her with the advantage; if she was to continue to hold on to that advantage, then she must be very careful.

He indicated a chair and then sat down in his old chair by the unlit fire. He didn't offer to take her coat and Katherine made no attempt to take it off; the room was cold and damp. 'Why, it just seems like my past is catching up with me. I seem to be meeting with a lot of my old . . . well, acquaintances, shall we say, recently.' He leaned forward, resting his elbows on his knees. 'But

392

tell me, what brings you back here? I scoured Dublin for you, do you know that?' He shook his head slightly and sat back into the chair. 'You know my marriage failed – and your departure was one of the main reasons . . .'

'Your whoring and drinking had nothing to do with it?' Katherine interrupted.

It took a few moments for her words to sink into his fatigue- and alcohol-numbed brain. 'What do you want?' he asked, his voice cracking, 'what brings you back here?'

'I've come for something that's here,' she said quietly, watching him carefully, fingering the whistle she had in her fur muff. If Major Lewis were to become violent or difficult, all she had to do was to blow the whistle and Mickey and his men would come rushing to her rescue.

'There's nothing of yours here,' he said quickly. 'Anything you left behind the old cook took away.'

Katherine shook her head. 'No, I have come for something that is here now; something I know is here. And I want it back now.'

'You've a damned cheek to come into my house and begin making demands!' he snapped. 'What have you come for anyway?' he asked, his curiosity aroused.

'I've come for Tilly Cusack!'

His face immediately betrayed him, and when he opened his mouth to deny it, Katherine shook her own head first. 'I know she's here. And I know why you've taken her.'

'I don't think . . .'

'No, you don't think,' she said. 'But I imagine you thought she was Madam Kitten.' She nodded. 'Yes, I can see that you did. But you were wrong, you see, wrong. And now I want you to release her.'

'Get out!' He surged to his feet, swaying slightly, his broad face crimson.

'Not without Tilly,' she said, remaining where she was. 'And there are two ways we can do this. You can release her to me, and we'll walk out of here. Or I can

393

take her. And if I have to take her, then you'll be a very sorry man.'

'Your idle threats don't frighten me.'

'You were always something of a fool, John Lewis.' She stood up, and smoothed the folds of her dress before turning to him again. 'Of course, I wonder what the brigadier would say if he knew one of his officers was keeping a woman prisoner in his house? I wonder what the newspapers would say?'

'I presume you have men outside?' he asked coldly, ignoring her remarks.

'You presume correctly.'

'You realize of course, that I could kill you before they could get to you?'

'I don't think you'll do that.'

'And why not?'

'My friends would take great pleasure in killing you very slowly if you so much as lay a finger on me. Now, give me the girl and we'll be gone.'

The major crossed to the window and peered out, looking up and down the street. But he could see nothing. It could be a bluff of course, but somehow he doubted it; the woman was too confident, too assured. 'What will you do if I don't release the girl?' he wondered.

Katherine smiled as if she were humouring a child. 'Why, we'll take her in any case.'

'Then I don't really have much choice do I?' he asked.

'There does seem to be only one choice open to you,' she admitted. 'Well, one sensible choice,' she amended.

He crossed to the door and then stopped with his hand on the handle. 'You know I'll find you, now I know you're back in Dublin.'

'I never left Dublin,' she said with a smile. 'But tell me, major, just why were you looking for me?'

'I wanted my child,' he said simply.

'Your child!'

He nodded. 'I would have brought it up as my own. But I suppose you got rid of it,' he added bitterly.

394

Katherine was too shocked to reply; for all the reasons she had thought Major Lewis might be looking for her, that was one which had never crossed her mind, and suddenly she found the very idea terrifying. 'But what about my predecessor here? She was also pregnant. Why did you kill her?' She knew she had made a mistake as soon as she had said it. His face hardened and his eyes turned cold and chill.

'Who told you that? Who told you? No-one knows about that girl.'

'Some of us do, Major. Dublin is too small for secrets,' she said quickly, partly surprised that he didn't attempt to deny it.

'She was blackmailing me – or at least attempting to blackmail me. And, in any case, I wasn't entirely sure the child was mine.'

'And so you killed her?' Katherine asked.

The major regarded her coldly for a few moments and then turned and left the room. Katherine reached into The watch pocket sewn into her dress and took out the small fob watch. She had a few minutes left before Mickey came sledgehammering in through the front door. She crossed to the window and looked out, and waved across to where she knew Mickey was hiding – although she could see nothing. Behind her, the door opened and she turned.

Tilly pulled herself from the major's grip and ran into Katherine's arms. She was naked and her body was bruised and cut, especially around her nipples and on her breasts, and there were weals across her buttocks and back.

Katherine looked at the major in disgust. 'You are an animal,' she said softly, 'I should have my people come in and break your legs. I think they'd like that. I think I would.' She pulled off her coat and wrapped it around the shivering girl, and then half carried her from the room, brushing roughly past the major. The man stood and watched her and then walked down the hall and opened the door. He saw movement outside and then two men leaped over the wall and ran up the steps to take the girl from Katherine's arms.

'Just what is she to you?' he asked, 'just how did a servant girl get involved with a whore?' he jeered.

'Tilly is one of my girls, Major Lewis,' Katherine said icily, 'I am Madam Kitten!'

CHAPTER THIRTY-THREE

Anne Lewis stood up as the man and woman entered the room, followed by William Sherlock. The woman was tall and thin, with a sharp, pointed nose which served to accentuate her high cheekbones and deep-sunk eyes, giving her face a slightly skeletal appearance. She carried herself with the poise and dignity of one reared to command, although she surprised Anne by walking up to her and offering her hand.

'I'm Constance Markievicz,' she said with a smile, 'William has told me about you.' Her accent was a surprise also; she spoke with a sharp, English accent. The woman turned and introduced the man, 'And this is Padraic Pearse.'

He was a rather stocky man of medium height, with a fine, sensitive – almost feminine – face, with rather full lips and a high forehead. But it was his eyes which caught Anne's attention; although one had a slight cast to it, they were dark and piercing, and stared at her with an almost frightening intensity. He took her hand diffidently, almost shyly, and almost immediately released it again.

'It is a pleasure to meet you, ma'am. William has told us about some of your troubles, and we offer our deepest sympathies.' Behind him Constance Markievicz nodded in agreement.

'Thank you . . .' Anne said slowly, unsure just what was expected of her.

'William tells us that you have expressed a desire to join us,' Constance Markievicz said slowly, sitting in Sherlock's customary chair by the fire. There's something rather frightening about her, Anne decided, although she was one of the loveliest women she had

397

ever seen, and the sincere warmth in her eyes added to her rather spectral beauty.

'I think it's a worthy cause,' Anne said softly, taking one of the straight-backed chairs across from her.

Pearse, who was standing in front of the fire with his hands behind his back, nodded quickly. 'It's a cause worthy enough to die for.'

Anne, unsure whether he was joking or not, looked from Constance Markievicz and then over to William. 'Surely it won't come to that?'

'That's what the guns upstairs are for,' William said softly.

'When I was ten or so,' Pearse said slowly, his glittering eyes boring right through her, 'I prayed to God to grant me the strength and willpower to make the effort to free my country. I intend to keep that promise – even if it costs me my life.'

'What Padraic means,' Constance Markievicz said with a smile, 'is that what we are talking about is revolution; peaceful if possible, but I would be a fool if I thought we could achieve our ends through peaceful means alone.' She leaned forward and touched Anne lightly on the knee. 'Are you with us?'

Anne looked at William in confusion. This was all so sudden. She wasn't sure if she wanted to become involved in a revolution, she wasn't sure if she cared enough to become involved. But then she thought of Major Lewis, and all that he had done to her, both directly and indirectly, and decided that it might be worth the risk – even if for no other reason than to avenge herself on him.

'Yes, I think I am,' she said slowly.

'But are you sure?' Pearse asked suddenly.

'Well . . . I don't know . . .'

Constance Markievicz looked at Pearse and shook her head. 'Leave it for the moment, Padraic, not all of us burn with your enthusiasm.' She turned back to Anne and smiled, 'You must forgive him, his desire for a free Ireland sometimes clouds his better judgement.'

'Constance!' he protested good-humouredly.

'Can you deny it?' she demanded, and Pearse shook his head with a shy smile.

The door opened and Sherlock's maid, a tiny frail woman of indeterminate age, carried in a laden tray. Pearse crossed the room in three quick strides and lifted the tray from the startled woman's grasp. 'Allow me,' he said quietly. She watched in astonishment while he laid out a small side table, and then turned to go, shaking her head in astonishment, still staring at the neat young man in the slightly oversized charcoal-grey suit. Pearse poured the tea and handed cups to Constance Markievicz and Anne Lewis, and then offered them milk and sugar. The countess refused the sugar but took some milk, while Anne took both.

'Tell me,' Constance Markievicz said suddenly, looking directly at Anne, 'if you do take up our cause, would you be prepared to lend us your support in any way you can?'

'I'm not sure I know what you mean,' Anne said.

'Would you be prepared to do things which you might normally find distasteful?'

She nodded. 'I think I would.'

'You're still only "thinking",' Pearse said from the chair he had taken by the window on the far side of the room.

Constance Markievicz smiled and shook her head, almost despairingly. 'Ignore him.' She sipped from her cup, her eyes never leaving Anne's face. 'Well, would you?'

'If William has told you what I've endured over the past few years, then you'll know that there is nothing you can suggest to me that I haven't already experienced. What did you have in mind?'

The countess stared at Anne for a few moments, almost as if she were trying to work out what she was referring to, and then she nodded seriously. 'Oh yes, quite, I see what you mean.'

'What do you want me to do?' Anne asked.

Constance Markievicz looked over at Pearse and he took up the conversation. 'Tell us what you know of your husband's present occupation,' he said.

'I know very little,' Anne replied, turning in her chair to look at him. 'He initially told me that he had something to do with the recruitment of staff to the post office. But I later learned that he seemed to be involved in watching different people and places, "watching the pot bubble" was how I once heard him describe it.'

'Well, we have our own sources, of course,' Pearse said almost proudly, 'and I can confirm that Major John Lewis is one of the Crown's most important intelligence officers in Ireland. Unfortunately we've never been able to get anyone close to him, so there is still much about him that remains a mystery.' He paused and took a deep breath. 'Would you go back to him?' he asked suddenly.

Anne almost dropped the cup with shock. 'You can't be serious!'

Pearse nodded and opened his mouth, but it was the countess who spoke first. 'We know how he's treated you over the past few years, and it is abominable, but this is a way for you to be revenged on him.'

'How? I'm not sure what you mean.'

'We would like you to spy on the spy,' Pearse said with an almost boyish grin.

Anne shook her head vigorously. 'I won't go back, I can't – and besides, I don't think he'd have me.'

'Oh, he will take you back,' Constance Markievicz said quietly, 'a man in his position cannot afford to be without a wife, and if it ever got out that his wife had run away on him his career would be ruined.'

'And what happens if he locks me up again?' Anne demanded, suddenly angry at these two strangers with their cause, attempting to involve her in it, trying to send her back to the monster who had kept her imprisoned in her own house, who had made sure that she had enough alcohol for her to drink herself into an early grave. And they wanted her to go back! Yes, she had wanted to join their cause to take some small revenge on the man, but she never thought that it would mean returning to live with him.

'If you're not out within two days, we'll go in and get you. We'll put a watch on the house,' Pearse said, 'you'll be safe. I give you my personal word on that.'

'You would be doing the cause a great service,' the countess added persuasively.

Anne Lewis sat back into the chair, looking from the tall regal countess to the rather ordinary-looking young man, and then she looked over at William, and she noticed that they all shared one singular trait. Their eyes were all fanatical, almost mad. She looked down at her cup, and saw her face reflected back in the brightly-polished silver spoon on the saucer. Her own eyes glittered just as madly.

'We're not asking you to make this decision now,' the countess added softly.

'But if you are going to help us in this way, it is a decision you'll have to come to fairly shortly,' Pearse added.

But Anne shook her head. 'There's no decision to make. I'll do it,' she said, almost surprising herself with the ease with which she said it.

'You don't have to,' William Sherlock said, speaking for the first time.

'I do,' Anne said, looking at him. 'I'm not doing this for you. I'm doing this for myself; for too long I took the blows, abuse and humiliation with no way of striking back – until now. I'm doing this in the hope that when the old order falls, Major John Lewis will be one of the first to go.' She looked from Constance Markievicz to Pearse. 'And just how do you see it ending?'

The countess looked back over her shoulder at Pearse, who smiled, almost absently. When he spoke, his voice was soft, slightly dreamy. 'Oh, it will end in blood. Mark my words, in blood.'

* * *

The hall was packed and Mickey, who was standing in the shadows close to the door, was surprised to find that there was an almost equal number of men and women present, and many of these were young couples. A few children ran around, enjoying the last of the summer heat, playing through the open doors at the end of the hall, but no-one paid them any heed – all eyes were on the platform.

Two of the three speakers had already said their piece – a fresh-faced young priest, who was far too plump and well-fed to be lecturing to Dublin's poor, and a short red-faced trade-unionist, who had mouthed platitudes and made vague and empty promises.

Mickey watched with interest as the crowd, who had been growing restless through the lengthy speeches, fell silent while the third speaker stood up and came to the front of the platform. This was whom they had come to see – the famous journalist, Dermot Corcoran, the man who had championed their cause for many years.

'My friends,' he began – and whatever sound there had been in the hall died completely, even the children falling silent to listen – 'my friends, I am going to keep this short. I am not going to make you any promises, I'm not going to tell you how prayer or joining a union is going to sort everything out, put food on your tables and clothes on your backs. I wish I could . . .'

Mickey folded his arms, his fingers touching the butt of the pistol beneath his coat. Because of the recent episode with Tilly, Katherine had sent Mickey along to this meeting to keep an eye on Dermot and to ensure that the major didn't try to abduct him also. The old man watched the crowd, but they all seemed to be hanging on to Dermot's every word, and occasionally a head would nod in agreement. This was the first time Mickey had heard Dermot speak, and he had to admit he was quite impressed. The young man's delivery was crisp and concise, he made no promises, passed no patronizing remarks and, moreover, seemed to believe completely in what he preached.

'You all know that no-one gives you something for nothing in this world. If you want something, you've got to get it yourself. If there is going to be a change in the system, then you are the only people who can bring that about. And I'm not talking about simply changing the system which leaves you to starve and die here, but of smashing it. If we change the system, we'll be doing nothing but replacing English politicians with Irish politicians – the laws will remain. No, we need to write our own laws, create own constitution, an Irish constitution for an Irish people, written by Irish people . . .'

Mickey found himself listening; the boy had the makings of a great speaker.

'It won't come today and maybe not tomorrow either, but some day – some day soon I hope – you will be called upon to make a decision. You will have to decide whether to remain as slaves or to break free and become your own masters. There'll be a price of course – everything has its price – and you'll pay for this one in blood. But that's the one thing they can't take from us . . . it's ours to shed for whatever cause we truly believe in.

'And our cause is freedom!'

The hall erupted into cheers, and Mickey was surprised to find himself joining in.

CHAPTER THIRTY-FOUR

'How do you feel?' Katherine asked softly, touching Tilly's split lip with a hot damp cloth.

'Sore.' Tilly attempted a smile, wincing as the bruise beneath her eye stung. 'But not as bad as I felt two days ago when you hauled me out of that house.'

Katherine nodded. 'I'm sorry,' she said suddenly.

'For what?' Tilly asked, surprised.

'It's my fault this happened . . .'

Tilly reached out and squeezed her friend's hand. 'It's not your fault – there's only one person to blame for what happened.' She paused and then added, 'Mickey told me how you got me out – that was very brave of you.'

Katherine smiled. 'Not really; it's easy to be brave with Mickey and a dozen strong lads waiting in the background.'

'That's what you should have done, Katherine, you should have sent the boys in. Now, Lewis knows who you are and where you are. He'll want revenge. You've cheated him, Katherine, you've cheated him out of Dermot, and now you've taken me away from him, and he's not going to forgive you for that. He's going to come after you, you know that – it's personal now.'

Katherine nodded. 'I know Tilly. And I agree, Lewis is a problem that will need attending to sooner or later. But let's leave it for the moment, eh, I have you back safely and Mickey or one of the other lads is keeping an eye on Dermot for me. The next move is the major's . . .'

Three days later, the brothel, Number Eighty-Two, had a most unexpected visitor. It was evening, and the bells of the surrounding churches and the pro-cathedral were calling the Catholic faithful to evening mass. As the last peal was dying away across the chimneyed rooftops, the doorbell jangled. When Mickey ambled out to open the door, prepared to turn any early callers away since most of the girls were still in their beds, he found he was facing Major Lewis.

The two men stared at each other for a few long moments, neither speaking. Mickey looked up and down the street, expecting to find police wagons clattering up the cobbles, or columns of men marching down the street.

'I'm alone,' the major said quietly.

'You're not welcome here,' Mickey said coldly, 'in fact I'm surprised you dare to come down here at all.'

'I want to see Madam Kitten ... Katherine,' the major said quickly.

'I don't think she wants to see you.' Mickey went to close the door, but the major placed a hand against it, pushing backwards with surprising strength.

'Just tell her I'm here,' he said calmly. 'If she doesn't want to see me, I'll go and there will be no trouble, I promise you.'

Mickey looked at him, and found that there was something like desperation in the man's eyes. 'What do you want to see her about?' he demanded.

'It's about my child.'

Mickey closed the door in his face.

Major Lewis stood on the doorstep, desperately attempting to hold his temper in check. He mentally tried to visualize the old man hurrying up the two flights of stairs, knocking on the Madam's door, telling her what had occurred and then making his way back down to the hall again with her answer. But, by the time he had run through this scenario twice, and the door still hadn't opened, he decided to return home. He would come back tomorrow and the day after that and the day after that again ... until she finally saw him, and he saw his child. He had just turned and begun to walk down the step when the door opened, and Katherine stood

405

outlined against the warm yellow light from behind. The first thing he noticed was that she was wearing a coat and hat, and there was a parasol in her hand. He remained standing on the bottom step while she came down and joined him. 'Let's walk,' she said calmly, striding past him.

Completely stunned, Major Lewis followed her down the street towards Marlborough Street, while behind them Mickey shook his head in frustration.

'I'm more than a little surprised that you agreed to see me,' Major Lewis said quietly, catching up with her.

'And why is that?' Katherine asked, not even looking at the man.

'Well, after that little trouble a few days ago . . .' he stumbled.

'That has been forgotten about,' Katherine lied. She would never be able to forgive what Tilly had suffered in her place and it would be a long time before she could forget the young woman's injuries. The major had raped her repeatedly, and even though Tilly might once have slept with two or three men in one night, that was through choice and a long time ago. This was brutal and savage violation. He had beaten her with his belt across the breasts, belly and legs, raising ugly weals, and splitting the skin in places, and there were cigarette burns across her breasts. The doctors said that her physical injuries would heal in some weeks, but the mental scars would take much longer. No, Katherine wouldn't forgive, nor would she forget.

'I must admit I was half expecting reprisals . . .' the major said with a grin.

'For what?' Katherine asked, sounding surprised.

'Well . . .' he shrugged and had the grace to look embarrassed, 'well, perhaps I did become a little too enthusiastic in my questioning,' he said diffidently.

'Perhaps you did,' Katherine said, 'but Tilly will not be bringing any charges against you – after all, she is nothing but an old whore.'

Major Lewis managed to look surprised that any

charges should even be considered; the reprisals he had been thinking about were of a much more basic nature. 'Is she still on the streets?' he asked, glancing at the woman.

Katherine shook her head. 'Tilly hasn't slept with a man in several years,' she said tightly. 'She manages my house and, as such, has no need to sell herself.'

At the bottom of the slight hill Katherine turned right and then, a little further on, turned left into Findlater's Place. They walked past the spot where the major's man had been killed. She didn't remark on the killing and Major Lewis seemed too preoccupied to notice. Once into O'Connell Street, they turned left and walked down the street, passing the GPO heading for O'Connell Bridge.

'Mickey said you wanted to see me.' Katherine said conversationally, looking around at all the other couples out promenading in the mild evening air. 'What about?'

'You said you had a child,' the major said slowly.

'I didn't,' Katherine shook her head. 'You said I had a child; I didn't deny it.'

'Well, have you?'

She nodded once, briefly.

'Boy or a girl?' Major Lewis asked eagerly.

'Why do you ask?'

'Well . . . well, I think the child is mine . . .'

Katherine turned to look at him. 'And what makes you think that?'

'Well, you conceived it because . . . because . . .'

'Because we slept together?' she finished for him. 'Yes, that's correct, I conceived it because of that, but I still don't see how that makes the child yours,' she added.

The major shook his head in astonishment at her reasoning. 'But . . . but surely you can see that it is my child?' he demanded, raising his voice, making a few heads turn in his direction.

But Katherine shook her head, schooling her face into a mask of impassivity. 'The child is mine and mine alone, Major Lewis. I brought him into this world, I reared him, I taught him everything he knows. There is nothing of you in him now.'

'So it's a boy,' Lewis said smugly.

They crossed O'Connell Bridge and headed up Westmoreland Street, walking past Trinity College on the left hand and the old Parliament Building on the right, and then began the familiar walk up Grafton Street.

'What's his name?' Lewis asked when they had walked in silence for a while.

'Don't ask me Major Lewis, because I won't tell you.'

He nodded, content to wait. And then another question struck him. 'Tell me; what made you come out here with me tonight? You could have seen me in your rooms with your guards to protect you.'

'Oh, I know you won't harm me,' Katherine said slowly, 'and I suppose I was curious in a strange way about the man who took my virginity.' She smiled slightly, 'It's almost as if you have a special place in my heart because of that.'

'You have a very special place in mine,' the major said, sounding almost sincere.

They had reached the top of Grafton Street and were facing the main gate to St Stephen's Green. But the huge gates were just being closed; the park shut at sunset. Katherine slipped her arm through his, and hurried him across the road to the gate. 'That's a pity; I thought it would have been a nice place for a walk and a chat.'

The major grinned boyishly. 'I know a place where we can hop over the railings,' he said.

'I'm hardly dressed for hopping over a spiked rail,' Katherine smiled.

'I'll lift you.'

They walked down the west side of St Stephen's Green, past the shuttered and darkened shops and down towards the Royal College of Surgeons. This side of the Green was quiet and in shadow, and already the evening traffic was dying off. There were few strollers and they had the path very much to themselves. The major stopped a little way down from the College, where a line of young trees shielded them from the road. 'There's a stone here,' he said, bending down and touching her foot with his hand, guiding it to an upraised rounded stone. She moved up on to it, and then the major was behind her and his large strong hands encircled her waist and he lifted her up and right over the spiked top of the iron fence. The ground on the other side of the rail was actually higher than the street, so the drop down was less difficult than she had expected. The major simply gripped the top of the rail in both hands and smoothly pulled himself up and over, landing easily on his feet beside her. 'This way.'

In the daylight St Stephen's Green was a quiet, sometimes magical place, a place of peace and tranquillity away from the bustle of the city, but now, at twilight and completely deserted, it took on an almost mystical quality, an almost otherworldly air. Although she knew it was closed and that there would be no-one about, Katherine almost expected the bushes to part and a vision step out on to the path, or some ghostly figure to emerge from behind a tree.

Major Lewis led her to the wooden seat in a little nook in the greenery beside the artificial lake. They sat without words for a long time, both apparently content with the silence. Finally Major Lewis spoke.

'You must have had a reason.'

'For what?' she asked, turning to look at him, her face softened by the gentle evening light.

'For coming here with me to this quiet, deserted place. Tell me,' he asked, his voice dropping lower, 'tell me why.'

'Because I wanted to talk to you – I wanted to talk to you away from the guards and other listening ears, away from the strains imposed by our different occupations.'

Lewis frowned. 'What do you have to say to me that you couldn't have said in your house?'

Katherine stared across the lake, her face expressionless, her eyes hooded. 'I've survived in my business because I am a very careful person,' she said slowly. 'I do all my business through a third party, I ensure that my word is my bond, and I never make a threat unless I intend to carry it through.'

'I don't see . . .' Lewis began.

'Leave me and my people alone, Lewis!' Katherine snapped. 'I'm warning you.'

Speechless, Lewis turned to look at her, his mouth open in shock.

'Interfere with my business, my personal life, or any of my friends, and I will ensure that you have a fatal accident.' She turned to look at him. 'Do I make myself clear, Major Lewis?'

'You know who I am . . .' Lewis whispered, 'you know the position I hold, and yet you attempt to threaten me? *Me?*' He breathed deeply, holding in check his rising temper. He rounded on her, his eyes blazing. 'Now, let me get some things straight. You are nothing more than a madam in a brothel, and a dealer in stolen goods. Your boyfriend is a hack scribbler with dangerous friends. You are surrounded by whores, thieves and murderers. And yet you threaten me! I could crush you . . . you and all your organization.'

Katherine smiled, infuriating him further. 'Are you so pure yourself, Major Lewis? Would you bear investigation . . .'

Lewis hit her then – a quick back-handed slap that sent her reeling off the seat on to the ground, her head spinning. She could taste blood in her mouth.

And then he was on the ground beside her, his fist at her throat, bunching the cloth of her coat, hauling her head off the ground. 'You're way out of your league, Madam,' he spat. His eyes were large and round in his head, and his expression was terrifying. 'What's to stop me killing you now, eh?' he hissed. 'What's to stop me throwing you into the lake? Just another body in the water.' His eyes glinted malevolently at the thought. 'And then in the morning, a raid on your brothel, in which several of your people could be hurt or even

killed resisting arrest, your boyfriend run over by a tram
... Yes, yes ... I could tie up a lot of loose ends ...
And, of course, your son would have to be taken into
care ...'

Katherine smiled tightly – and stabbed Major Lewis
low in the stomach with an eight-inch stiletto blade.

It took a moment for the pain to register, and then it
burst into a ball of agony that completely consumed
him.

Katherine pushed the major off her, and then she
squatted beside him, listening to his breath whistling
rapidly through his lips, while his blood pooled around
him. A single trickle, coal-black in the dusky light,
curled and twisted down to the lake.

'Consider that as payment for all you've done to me
and those close to me, Major Lewis,' she whispered
venomously, pressing the knife to his throat, the razor-
sharp blade parting the skin. 'That's for taking a young
woman's life, for taking my virginity, for Dermot, and
for Tilly.'

She stood up and arranged her clothes, and then
walked away from him without a backwards glance.
There were tears on her face as she hurried down the
darkening path, tears of rage and frustration and annoyance at her own stupidity and weakness. She wished she
had possessed the courage to kill him.

Two weeks later Katherine Lundy's period failed to
arrive, and two weeks after that she knew for certain she
was pregnant. It looked as if her single night of passion
in Galway with Dermot was not to be without
consequences.

Eight months later, Katherine gave birth to an eight-
pound baby girl. She called the child Senga, after her
grandmother. A few days later – on the 1st of May –
Katherine Lundy finally married Dermot Corcoran.

PART THREE

. . . A Time of War . . .
Ecclesiastes 3:8

CHAPTER THIRTY-FIVE
New Year's Day, 1916

The last chimes of the bells tolled out across the city, heralding the birth of the New Year. In houses, both grand and small, in drawing rooms and dingy hovels, in bars and hotels, glasses were raised and toasts were drunk, wishing health and happiness, wealth and prosperity in the coming year.

But there was little cheer to be found in many Dublin homes on that bitterly cold morning of 1916. The Great War had already claimed thousands of Irish lives; young men who had joined up with the Irish regiments in the British army and had been uselessly squandered on the bloody battlefields of France and Belgium. A series of crippling industrial disputes up and down the country had left many families destitute and, under the employers' system of blacking all those who had taken part in any strike, no chance of securing other employment.

But people still made plans for the coming year, and resolutions which they hoped or intended to keep. It was New Year, it was a time of promise, a time of change.

Katherine Lundy Corcoran raised her glass and spoke into the silence that followed the bells, 'Good Health and much happiness to everyone here in the coming year.'

Glasses were raised all around her and voices murmured 'Good health'.

'To absent friends,' Dermot Corcoran said, slipping his arm around his wife's shoulders and raising his glass. They all knew someone who had lost a member of the family or a friend in the terrible European War.

415

Katherine, sensing the sombre mood that was slipping over her New Year's party, forced a smile, and kissed her husband, 'Happy New Year, Dermot.'

Kisses and handshakes were exchanged around the room, and Dermot stooped down and swept up Senga, his daughter, and kissed her on the cheek, while Katherine hugged them both close. 'Happy New Year, sweetheart,' they chorussed. Although Senga was not quite eight years old yet, she showed every sign of becoming a great beauty.

Patrick Lundy, awkwardly conscious of his status as a young man, solemnly shook hands with his stepfather, and then kissed his mother quickly on the cheek.

'Hey, what about me?' Tilly called, 'do I not get one?'

The boy reddened and quickly kissed Tilly on the cheek, and then shook hands carefully with Mickey, who had a tendency to crush fingers when he had taken rather too much drink – as he had tonight.

Senga yawned, and her yawn was infectious, and suddenly they were all yawning. 'Time for bed,' Katherine said, blinking hard, her eyes gritty with exhaustion and the cigar and curling pipe smoke in the room. The young girl was so tired that she didn't even argue and went quite docilely to her room, while Patrick – usually the most difficult to get to bed – bade his parents, Tilly and Mickey a good night also and left quietly.

While Dermot filled all their glasses again, Katherine pulled the easy chairs in closer to the fire, which had been allowed to die down a little, and stared into the glowing embers, allowing herself to relax, conscious that there would be no disturbances tonight of all nights. She had closed the house for the night, and given all the girls and servants the time off; New Year's Eve, like Christmas Eve was not a good night for business. They were the two occasions in the course of a year in which her customers usually felt pangs of remorse or guilt and stayed at home. The pangs, however, would have faded by tomorrow, and business was traditionally brisk. So, the huge house was empty – and felt it – with only Tilly

416

and Mickey remaining behind at Katherine's insistence. Old friends, they were content to sit in silence in the cosy room, beyond which they could hear the ships' horns still booming and hooting soulfully down the Liffey.

'Like banshees,' Mickey said suddenly, startling them all. He was more than a little drunk, and it was almost as if the alcohol had loosened all the muscles in his face, for Katherine suddenly noticed how they had begun to sag, giving him a terribly aged look.

'Or lost souls,' Dermot said slowly, 'and let's face it, we've a lot of those in this city of ours.'

'The year will bring many more, you mark my words,' Mickey said, tipping his glass back and swallowing the last of the smooth malt whiskey.

'Surely not,' Tilly said quietly, 'let's hope for the end of the war and the return of peace both at home and abroad.'

Mickey snorted drunkenly. 'If we hadn't had the war to distract attention from things here in Ireland, then the bloody unionists in the north would have probably started one here.'

Dermot began to agree, but Katherine put her hand on his knee and squeezed warningly. Irish freedom and 'the cause' had become one of the Mickey passions over the past few years – as it had for so many Irishmen.

'Well, I don't know about you,' Tilly said suddenly, rising slowly to her feet and stretching, 'but I'm for bed.'

Mickey, not so drunk that he didn't catch the hint, came slowly and shakily to his feet, 'Aye, well, I'd best be off myself.' He elaborately offered Tilly his arm. 'Walk you home, ma'am.'

She took it and bobbed a curtsey. 'I would be honoured, sir.' Their rooms were on the floor below.

Dermot and Katherine walked them to the door, and then watched Tilly lead Mickey carefully down the stairs to the landing below. They returned to the fire and Katherine sank back down on to the floor, while

417

Dermot sat in his chair. Katherine rested her head against his legs and looked into the embers.

'Another year done,' she said softly.

She felt movement as he nodded. 'I wonder what the coming year will bring.' His long fingers brushed gently against her hair, stroking the silk-smooth tresses. 'I always feel sad at this time of year,' he continued, 'I remember all the things I meant to do during the year, all the things I'd forgotten about, all the resolutions I made at this time last year and never kept. It makes me feel as if I've lost something . . .'

'Perhaps it's just age?' Katherine suggested.

'Perhaps it is.'

'Do you know,' she said suddenly, 'I've been in Ireland for nearly eighteen years now, and I've spent New Year's Eve and New Year's Day in this house on every one of them since Tilly first brought me here on Christmas Eve, 1898.' She shook her head in wonder. 'It seems like a lifetime away.'

Dermot laughed briefly. 'It is a lifetime.'

They went out on to the landing and into their bedroom which was next door. Katherine crossed to the window and was about to pull the curtains, but stopped, and leaned on the windowsill, staring down at the frost-glittering cobbles. There was no moon, but the sky was clear, and the stars were sharp and brilliant, shedding more than enough light to see by.

The street had deteriorated over the past few years, and the houses looked ghostly and deserted in the starlight with the frost glittering on them. The street held little more than tenements and brothels now, and most of the respectable families had moved out. Even Number Eighty-Two, despite her every effort to keep it more respectable than the others, was almost as decrepit as the rest on the outside, although within it was still as luxurious as ever.

'Penny for them,' Dermot said, coming up behind her and wrapping his arms around her waist, nuzzling at her shoulder.

418

'I'm thinking we may have to move shortly,' Katherine said.

She felt his head move against her shoulder. 'That's fine by me.' Dermot, still with the *Freeman's Journal* and now a features writer, was still ashamed to give his present address, and invariably gave his mother's. Katherine didn't mind; having a brothel for an address was not an advantage. What did bother her, though, was that Dermot still hadn't told people outside his family that he was married to her, and had been since the 1st of May, 1908.

'You're dreaming again,' he whispered in her ear.

'I'm sorry; I'm just thinking back over a few of the things we've done together . . .'

'Don't look to the past, look to the future. This is the first day of a new year – enjoy it. Look ahead.'

Katherine turned to face him and draped her arms around his shoulders. 'To what Dermot, what am I supposed to look ahead to? Every time the doorbell rings I expect to find the police in here looking for you.'

'I think you've more to look out for than I have in that respect,' Dermot said with a grin, taking the sting from his words.

'Dermot, be serious. You've got to withdraw from the Republican Brotherhood – before it's too late. You know the police are watching you . . .'

'Ah, it's not just me love, they're watching everyone associated with the Brotherhood and the Citizen Army. Why, they even try to get into our meetings, or join up – but we nearly always catch them.'

'Oh, Dermot, it's still a game to you, isn't it? You're playing at soldiers, dressing up in your uniform, playing with your smuggled guns, talking of revolution. But while it's only a game to you, it's not to some of the others. People like Pearse want revolution; you've heard him, he's talked of a blood sacrifice. Well, I don't want you to be one of the sacrifices.'

Dermot kissed her on the mouth. 'I've no intention of being one of the sacrifices,' he said quickly, 'and I don't think we'll have a revolution this year – not until the war is over in any case.'

Katherine nodded. 'Well I don't want a revolution at all, but let's pray the war ends soon.'

'Amen to that!' They both knew far too many young men – friends, customers and employees – who had already given their lives in the struggle.

Katherine reached up and kissed him. 'Take me to bed,' she said with an arch smile.

Dermot shook his head and laughed. 'You're going to end up pregnant one of these days,' he said with a grin.

Katherine laughed with him, but in her heart she knew she would never conceive again. In their eight years of marriage, although she had never taken any precautions against becoming pregnant, she had never conceived.

It had been a long time – nine years or so – since the major had last made love, and that last time was an occasion he would never forget. Major Lewis lay on the bed and watched his wife casually undress. He could still appreciate her body, which the years had been kind to, although now there was a little thickening of her thighs, and her breasts were beginning to sag, but the sight of her body no longer aroused him.

And it wasn't just her body, it was any female body. He had tried on numerous embarrassing occasions with either the whores who walked the streets or the brothel ladies, but to no avail.

When Katherine Lundy had stabbed him, she had ruptured more than his stomach and intestines. The emergency operation that had saved his life had traumatized much of his internal organs, and that in turn had destroyed much of life's pleasure for him. Fine food and alcohol were out of the question; the first few occasions had left him agonized and passing blood for days afterwards. And of course he could no longer have any sexual relations with a woman. The doctors had told him that there was nothing physically wrong with him, but the fact remained – John Lewis was impotent.

And he often thought that it would have been better if she had slit his throat.

Anne Lewis slipped naked into bed beside him, and curled up against his body, her breasts pressing against his arm, one of her legs curled across his groin. Her fingers toyed with the hair on his chest.

'Did you enjoy the party?' she asked, whispering softly, although there was no one else in the big house.

'Not really,' he said after a long silence, 'but it was something which had to be done.' He paused and added gruffly, 'Thank you for coming with me.'

'I couldn't let you down,' Anne said, smiling in the darkness. It was not for her husband's sake that she had gone to the grand New Year's Ball in Dublin Castle. She had been asked to attend by Constance Markievicz to whom she had grown very close over the past few years. The tall, regal countess had specifically asked her to accompany her husband to the ball to listen in case anything of interest was let slip by one of the high-ranking police and army officers who would be attending. Anne Lewis was a spy for the Irish Republican Brotherhood.

Her hand moved down Lewis's body and rested on his lower stomach; she could feel the involuntary tightening of the muscles, but there was no other response. She moved her fingers slightly to the right, and traced the long, broad groove of the scar where he had been knifed.

She remembered the day clearly. It had been the night she had returned to Clonliffe Road from William Sherlock's house, following her agreement with the countess and Pearse that she would spy on her husband and his friends for the 'cause'. Walking up the garden path to College House she had been terrified as to how he would react, and even the fact that Pearse had the house watched did nothing to ease her mind. Her husband could have beaten her to death before they even crossed the street.

However, she had found the place dark and empty, and no-one answered her persistent ringing on the bell. She was just stooping down to pull out the spare key from beneath the loose flagstone on the path, when she heard the sound of horses' hooves clattering wildly down the cobbles. She turned as the carriage rattled to a stop outside her gate, and then felt her heart begin to pound when a man in an army uniform came running up the path. But instead of dragging her away, or clapping handcuffs on her, he had stopped and saluted smartly.

'Mrs Lewis, ma'am?'

She nodded dumbly, unsure what was happening.

'I shall have to ask you to accompany me, ma'am.'

'Why – what's wrong? Has there been an accident?' She found the questions tumbling out, although she realized that there was no feeling behind them. She didn't care if her husband lived or died.

'I'm afraid so, ma'am.'

'And my husband – the major?'

The soldier shook his head. 'I'm not sure, ma'am, but if you will be so good as to accompany me . . .'

'Of course.'

Major Lewis had been taken to Mercer's Hospital – the nearest to St Stephen's Green. When Anne Lewis was ushered in, he was heavily swathed in bandages through which blood was still seeping, and he had been drugged with morphine. She stood looking down at him dispassionately, wondering why he had been attacked, wondering how he had come to be in the Green after closing, but not really caring if she ever found out. The questions were mere idle curiosity; there was no interest behind them.

He had opened his eyes, his pupils shrunk to pin-pricks with the drug, and looked up at her. Almost unconsciously she reached for his hand and his fingers tightened fractionally around hers. 'Anne,' he whispered, and then drifted back into his drugged stupor.

When he returned home, nearly three months later, he didn't speak about her 'escape' from the house, nor did he question her as to where she had been, and in return she didn't speak of her long imprisonment.

Now their relationship, as well as their personalities, had changed. Anne Lewis sensed that her husband was an angry, bitter – and in some vague way – a frightened man. He had never spoken about his attack, and any mention of his wounds only sent him into a towering rage. It had been nearly a year before their tenuous relationship had been patched up enough for them to sleep together, and it was only then that she discovered his disability. And that seemed to give her even more power and control over him – and she sensed that he knew it.

He continued in his shadowy position in the post office and, through her contacts with the IRB, Anne learned that he had become even more ruthless and sadistic than before, his injury obviously driving him on.

Anne Lewis resumed the duties she had been denied while she had been kept prisoner. She made contact with most of her old friends – and all of them were shocked by the change that had come over the once timid and shy woman. Physically, she was drawn and thin, and her skin had an almost ugly yellowish pallor to it. Her personality had also changed; she had become aggressive – almost embarrassingly so – and easily irritated. Her temper was short, and the slightest inconvenience would send her into a rage. However, the pains which had beset her in the early stages of her disease had mercifully receded, and as she had gradually abandoned her former drinking her health had at least superficially improved.

Anne was also spying for the IRB, passing on whatever information she managed to glean from her husband or his papers, and John Lewis, in an effort to win back his wife, was more forthcoming about his work

423

than previously. Indeed, he was pleased and more than a little flattered that she was actually taking an interest in his work.

'Will you be going into the office tomorrow?' Anne Lewis asked suddenly, startling him.

She felt him shake his head in the darkness. 'No, not on New Year's Day, not if I can help it. But I have some paperwork which needs completing, so I'll try and get up early in the morning to do that. Otherwise, we'll have the day to ourselves.'

Anne nodded. She wondered what papers her husband would be working on . . . but it didn't really matter in any case. If he followed his usual routine, he would go for a stroll in the late afternoon, which would give her an opportunity to read them.

In the distance, they both heard the churchbells tolling three. The first day of the new year was well under way.

'I wonder what 1916 will bring?' Anne Lewis wondered.

'I hope an end to the war,' Major Lewis said slowly. When he had heard the reports of so many good men being thrown away in stupid battles on the killing fields of Europe, he had not been displeased to learn he was considered too valuable in his present position to send into action. 'Aye, an end to the war.'

And a free Ireland, Anne Lewis thought fiercely, a Republic.

CHAPTER THIRTY-SIX

The new year was three days old when Katherine and Dermot had their first major argument, and it was caused, as so many of their arguments recently had been, by Dermot's association with the Irish Republican Brotherhood.

'Look, it's just for one night . . .' Dermot said, putting down his knife and fork and looking almost pleadingly down the long table at his wife.

Katherine shook her head firmly. 'No. I've told you before, I will not – I cannot – allow this house to become involved with politics in any shape or form. My answer must be no; you'll have to hold your meeting elsewhere.'

'But the pub we normally use is being watched.'

Katherine smiled triumphantly. 'And how long do you think it would be before they started watching this house? Dermot, you know what a thin line we tread and every year that line gets thinner and thinner. If there were even a hint of a political connection with us at all, we would lose all our custom and we would be closed down, and I don't think even our 'friends' would be able to help us – or want to for that matter.' She watched him for a few moments longer, waiting for him to say something further, but he just shrugged and resumed eating again.

Dermot's involvement with the Irish Republican Brotherhood had been a growing source of worry for Katherine over the past few years. Dermot had always been politically minded, from the time she had first known him, and his early investigations had led him to write the series of articles which had made his name, and made him a champion of the poor. He had highlighted the dreadful social conditions that had prevailed in Dublin and even now, almost eighteen years later, many of those conditions remained unchanged. Dermot Corcoran was outspoken in his condemnation and laid the blame for the misery, the poor conditions, the dreadful housing and non-existent sanitation, and the resultant diseases completely at the feet of the British administration in Ireland. He had joined the Sinn Fein movement, but had become disillusioned by its policy of passive resistance which seemed to him to be achieving nothing. And so he had moved on to the IRB. The Brotherhood's aim was to free Ireland, to make her a Republic and it was prepared to use force to achieve that end. Although Dermot was not by nature a violent man, he felt that this was the only way the British government would listen to their case.

He became involved with the IRB newspaper, *Irish Freedom* and its editor Sean Mac Diarmada, and through it met Padraic Pearse, who was a regular contributor to the paper as well as being one of the leaders of the movement. And Pearse, as he did with so many, cast his hypnotic spell over Dermot, weaving an almost magical vision of a free Ireland.

The IRB had looked on the growing conflict in Europe with a great deal of interest and indeed, with a certain amount of approval. Their own movement was still too small – and because of its extreme views unlikely to grow very much larger in the near future – to tackle the might of the British Empire. But if England's involvement in a European conflict were to reach greater proportions, then the way might be open for them to make their move.

But Katherine had no time for any of the political organizations that were springing up in Dublin at this time; a shrewd businesswoman, she knew that they would only cause trouble and trouble meant lost business. And, Katherine also realized that, if by some miracle any of the organizations – Sinn Fein, the Volunteers, the IRB or the Citizen Army – were to achieve their aims, then the bulk of her own business, which depended largely on the military and their entourage, would suddenly dwindle, and the 'trade in flesh' would cease.

She had tried to talk Dermot out of his association with the group, but he had firmly fallen under Pearse's spell and, on the one occasion Katherine had met the man she had fully understood why . . .

Katherine had gone to one of his classes to learn how to speak Irish – the promise she had made on her holiday with Dermot – but her efforts had been short-lived. She found the language beautiful, haunting and lyrical in its sounds, but the fanaticism of its teachers, and indeed the pupils, was off-putting. She had met Pearse on her third and final visit to the Irish class. He was slightly taller than herself and stocky, with a high, broad forehead, straight nose, deep-set and piercing eyes, but with a rather weak chin, she thought. His hair was short and sleek and he was meticulously clean-shaven. His manners were impeccable, and he treated her with the utmost courtesy, and indeed with a certain amount of shyness.

But with his friends he was a changed man; his conversation slipped easily from Irish to English and he was a brilliant, inventive – almost inspired speaker. His hands and eyes did much of his talking, and his eagerness generated a sympathetic air of enthusiasm in his listeners.

And looking at him, watching him then, watching him almost unconsciously bend and twist others to his will and his way, Katherine knew that he was indeed a very dangerous man. She had left the Irish language class and never gone back.

'Where will you hold this meeting?' Katherine asked, wearily.

Dermot shrugged. 'I don't know – we'll find someplace,' he said quietly. 'We can always post guards, and hope we're not spied upon . . .'

Katherine sighed. 'Will Pearse be attending this

427

meeting of yours?' she asked and Dermot knew then that he had won.

He shook his head. 'No, not tonight. Just Mac Diarmada, old Tom Clarke and Eamonn Ceannt. It'll only take a couple of hours,' he hurried on, 'and I'll bring them in the back way.' He paused and added with just a touch of a smile, 'And at least you'll know where I am all the time.'

'Small consolation that'll be to me,' Katherine said returning his smile, picking at her food.

'There are just a few things to be sorted out,' Dermot said eagerly, 'it shouldn't take too long.'

'Well let's hope we're not raided while you're at it.'

Captain Martin Moore tapped respectfully on the major's door and waited the required length of time before pushing it open and stepping in, the evening's report tucked under his arm.

Major John Lewis was standing by the window, looking down over the vista of O'Connell Street that had become almost as familiar to him as the view from his own dining room window. Every day for the past – must be nearly twenty years now – he had stood in this same spot and stared down at the street. Occasionally he paused to wonder at how little it had changed since he had first looked down on it. He had seen the horse trams disappear to be replaced by the electric tram, he had seen the coming of the velocipede and then the motor car, he had seen fashions change, but the street itself remained unchanged.

He turned from the familiar view as Captain Moore coughed discreetly. 'This is the report of the IRB meeting last night, sir.'

Major Lewis waved a hand negligently in his direction. 'Just give me the main points.'

'I detailed four separate men to follow Tom Clarke, Eamonn Ceannt, John McDermott, or Sean Mac Diarmada as he calls himself, and Dermot Corcoran. They met outside their usual meeting place, which is a public

428

house on the corner of Parnell Square and Great Britain Street, where we had men waiting inside. But instead of going in they continued on down Great Britain Street, heading towards Summerhill.' He paused and looked over at the major. 'I think they may have begun to suspect that they were being followed because they took evasive action and immediately split up . . .'

'Hardly surprising, your four men were probably following them in a group!'

'They lost two of them in the back streets, but managed to stay with Ceannt and Corcoran . . .'

'And their destination?'

'A rather shabby brothel . . . but it is only four doors away from Dermot Corcoran's mistress, Madam Kitten's house, Number Eighty-Two.'

John Lewis sighed. Like one of the country's myths, the banshee, the woman came back to haunt him. Her name appeared again and again on reports, usually just in connection with Corcoran but sometimes with thefts or handling stolen goods, and occasionally with other, more serious crimes. But there was never any hard evidence against her, and her highly-placed 'friends' made her untouchable. She was like a cancer growing deep inside him, destroying him. His fingers automatically went to his scar.

'He is still seeing her?' he asked, trying to keep his voice as casual as possible, 'she's more like a wife than a mistress!'

'Our men watched the house and, shortly afterwards, the two other men, Clarke and Mac Diarmada arrived from opposite directions and entered. Two of my men then went in, posing as clients, and although between them they managed to get a good look at most of the house, they saw no sign of the four men, nor was there any sign of a room that was closed off and being used as a conference or meeting room. I think it is reasonable to suspect that the four men used the brothel as a means of escape or of moving into another house – possibly Madam Kitten's.'

Major Lewis had turned back to the window and was staring across the street at the grand façade of Clery's shop with its beautifully dressed windows, displaying the finest in Irish and continental work, while behind the grand shop lurked some of the meanest streets in the capital. 'Your recommendation?' he asked.

'Something is definitely in the air, and my street spies report that both the IRB and the Citizen Army have been particularly active of late. I would suggest a constant watch on the Kitten house, and a particular watch to be kept on all the known members of the IRB, and also this Citizen Army fellow, James Connolly. I have here another report of one of his speeches in which he states, and I quote, "Should a German Army land in Ireland tomorrow . . . then we should be perfectly justified in joining it . . . there is only one enemy in this country and that is the British government." ' He paused and added, 'If there's going to be trouble, then these will be the people to cause it.'

Major Lewis crossed to his desk and rummaged through the papers that had arrived that morning. He pulled out a buff envelope and handed it across to the captain. 'Here's the latest report on Sir Roger Casement; I fancy he may be the most dangerous of the lot.' He sank into his battered leather chair and closed his eyes, still troubled by the reappearance of Madam Kitten, Katherine Lundy, in his life. 'I concur with your suggestions,' he said wearily, 'you may act upon them.'

For the second time in a week, Katherine let herself be persuaded to allow Dermot and his cronies to hold their meeting in one of her rooms. She reasoned it out by telling herself that at least she knew where he was and that, even if the house were raided, the system of alarms and baffles would give the men time to escape and be half-way across Monto before the police managed to reach even the first landing.

This time the group was larger, and included Mac Diarmada, his stick tapping on the polished wooden

430

floorboards, Clarke, Ceannt, Thomas MacDonagh and Padraic Pearse as well as Dermot Corcoran.

Katherine stood on the landing and watched the men file past her, each of them raising his hat and wishing her a 'good evening', and Pearse, last of all, stopping and bowing slightly, thanking her in Irish and then switching to English. He then went into the small sitting room and closed the door behind him. Katherine waited a moment, unsure what to do, until she heard the key turn in the lock, and that decided her: there would be no secrets in Madam Kitten's house – especially not from Madam Kitten!

The room next door was a small cupboard, used to store the brooms and mops, buckets, washcloths and soaps that would be used by the maids to clean up the house the following morning. On one wall hung a large fly-spotted cracked mirror that had been partially covered over with an old blanket. Katherine pulled off the blanket and tossed it to one side, and then carefully lifted down the mirror, revealing yet another sheet of glass. This glass was set directly into the wall, but, instead of reflecting back Katherine's own image, it showed a slightly dusky view into the crowded sitting room beyond. Beside the mirror was an air vent and Katherine slowly moved the lever, allowing the voices to filter through . . .

Her husband was speaking. 'Glorious news from Germany – they will support us! Casement has sent word that the Germans will send us 20,000 captured Russian rifles, pistols, machine guns and as much ammunition as they can spare . . .'

The news seemed to stun the group – as it did Katherine. Up to then she had always thought they were just playing at soldiers, and that their long-promised revolution was nothing more than a pipe-dream. But 20,000 guns from Germany wasn't a game. And now, when they were at war with Germany . . . the enormity of it was almost unbelievable. It was treason.

'Details will be worked out later on. Sir Roger tells us

431

that he is being closely watched not only by the Germans but by British agents in Berlin and he has to be very careful indeed. However, he hopes to return to Ireland within the next few months with the arms.'

The group raised a low, restrained cheer and then Pearse got up to speak. He paused for a moment, looking at each one in turn. 'Let us not be too presumptuous with our congratulations. We all remember the last arms shipment; we'll try and make this a less public affair.'

Less than a year and a half ago, in July of 1914, Sir Roger Casement had purchased 1,500 rifles and 45,000 rounds of ammunition in Hamburg for the Irish Volunteers. Erskine Childers had carried the arms back on his yacht *Asgard*, and they had been landed in Howth on 10th July and distributed in broad daylight to the waiting Volunteers . . . who promptly marched into Dublin with them. However, in a confrontation between jeering Dubliners and a detachment of the King's Own Scottish Borderers, four civilians had been killed and thirty-eight wounded.

'The time is drawing close for our revolution,' Pearse continued. 'As you are aware the Military Council decided that the rising would take place before the end of the war. Well, I can confidently tell you that the rising will take place before the end of this year!'

This time the cheer was louder and sustained and Dermot Corcoran had to jump to his feet and wave his hands to silence them. 'Gentlemen, gentlemen, please, remember where you are.'

Pearse nodded agreement. 'We must be circumspect.'

Katherine continued to watch from behind the two-way glass which, in more prosperous pre-war times had been used for other, rather more erotic purposes. But the main business seemed to be concluded and they spent the rest of the time choosing members for the IRB, a process which, as far as she could make out, was as difficult and rather more painstaking an affair than planning their revolution. About twenty minutes later,

432

when it became apparent that the meeting was due to break up, she concealed the glass again and left the room. A little later, from her own room upstairs, she heard the door opening and closing at regular intervals as the IRB men slowly slipped out the back door into the night.

Katherine was in bed by the time Dermot closed the door to their bedroom. He was a little surprised; because of her occupation, she was usually late to bed, preferring to remain up until the last 'guest' had departed. He imagined that she was annoyed the meeting had been held in the house tonight. He knew it was a foolish thing to do; if the authorities were watching the men, and some of them almost certainly were under observation, then it might mean trouble for Katherine and the other girls in the house if they were caught. The only thing in their favour was that there were scores of private armies in Dublin at the time and nearly everyone was a member of something or other; the authorities couldn't watch all of them all the time – could they? In fact, that might make a good subject for an article, 'Dublin's Private Armies'. If he phrased it correctly, he could make the various organizations look slightly foolish, which might allay British suspicions a little. Of course, it might also make the members look foolish, and a Dubliner liked nothing less than to be embarrassed, and that might even mean the loss of some – and they couldn't afford to lose even a single member now. He shrugged as he unpinned his collar; he'd talk to Mac Diarmada about it, or perhaps Joseph Plunkett, the poet, and editor of the *Irish Review*, the literary paper, and also a member of the council of the IRB. Like Pearse, he was an educated, literary man, and he would certainly know what would be best.

He stood by the window looking down over the darkened street, gently humming to himself, elated at the prospect of the coming revolution, like a child looking forward to Christmas and wishing it were the following day.

'Your meeting went well then?'

The voice startled him, and he felt his heart miss a beat. 'Katherine! You gave me such a shock – I thought you were asleep.'

'I was waiting for you,' she said, sitting up slightly in the bed and looking over at him, outlined against the window.

'It went well enough – there was only a little minor business to be taken care of,' he said quickly.

'You know I can always tell when you lie to me,' she said with a smile that showed her teeth in the darkness.

'Oh Katherine . . . you know I can't tell you what went on. It's supposed to be a secret society, remember?' he said, sounding so exasperated that she smiled again.

'I remember. So, how is the revolution coming along?'

'It's coming along,' he said, pulling off his shirt. 'But you probably know as much about it as I do, what with your sources of information.' On several occasions, Dermot had been almost frightened to discover just how much Katherine knew. Indeed, she was often aware of IRB movements, Volunteer marches or Citizen Army parades before even he knew.

'So we'll have blood and fire in the streets this summer, do you think?'

He looked over at her, unsure if it was a rhetorical question or not, a shrewd guess or an intimation that she knew something more.

'And how far would you be willing to go to win?' she continued, watching the shape of his face intently, trying to make out his expression in the darkness.

'What do you mean, how far would we go?'

'Well, I mean if you're actually prepared to stage your revolution in the middle of the biggest, most destructive war this world has ever seen, you're obviously capable of going to some extremes. I suppose you would even be prepared to enlist the aid of the Germans in your struggle.'

'Yes,' he said simply, 'I would sup with the Devil

434

himself, if I thought it would give us any help. Look, you don't see it the same way as I do . . .'

'But Dermot, most Dubliners don't see it the way you do. Yes, I suppose many of them want an independent Ireland, but not now, not immediately, and certainly not by bloodshed. Given time, we will have it anyway.'

' "We?" ' he asked with a wry smile.

'I've been here a long time, Dermot, I'm as much a Dubliner as you are.'

'But are you Irish or English?' he asked quietly, as if the question had just struck him. He crossed naked to the bed and pulled on his nightshirt which Katherine had laid out earlier, and then he stood looking down at her, 'Do you think of yourself as Irish or English?'

'I never think of myself in terms of nationality,' she said softly.

'But if you had to?'

Katherine took a long time in answering. 'Well, then, I suppose I should think of myself as English.'

'And if – when! – it comes to war, Katherine, where will you stand, beside your husband or beside your King?'

'He is King of Ireland too,' she reminded him and turned over, pulling the blanket up around her as she did so.

But both Dermot and Katherine lay awake long into the night, both aware that the other wasn't sleeping but each troubled by their own thoughts.

Dermot was aware that his involvement with the IRB and the planning of the coming revolution was slowly and inexorably tearing his family life apart. He was seeing less and less of his wife, and their meetings were now coloured by politics and talk of war and revolution. His adopted son Patrick he felt he barely knew, and he hadn't seen his daughter Senga since their New Year's Eve party. But things would be better after the revolution. He would have more time for his wife and family. They would be living in a free Ireland, an independent

435

Ireland, capable of formulating their own policies, instituting a more humane social policy . . .

Yes, things would be better after the revolution.

Katherine's thoughts were running along much the same lines as her husband's. She knew what was happening to him, could see it clearly, but equally knew that there was little she could do. The drive which had made him join Sinn Fein in the beginning was the same that had made him write about the slums of Dublin, and begin a personal crusade to discover the murderer of a young servant girl. His new crusade was freedom for Ireland – whether Ireland wanted it or not. It was almost inevitable that it would end in revolution, and that revolution would end in death. Even she could see that. And she had heard Pearse speak more than once of the need for a 'blood-sacrifice', and that if even they did die, then, like Christ's death on Calvary, it would have been all to the good. He wasn't mad – that explanation was too simplistic – but he just saw his road and the road he would lead others, the road Ireland must take with a terrible, terrifying clarity. He was looking ahead, years, possibly decades, into the future to a free Ireland. But that wouldn't help her Dermot or the countless hundreds of others like him, husbands, brothers, sons, lovers, who would all die in that mad Light Brigade charge against the British forces.

And now there was the German involvement. It had always been on the cards, of course, but she had never really believed that they would involve the Germans in their struggle. How could they invite in the very enemy against whom so many Irishmen serving in the British army had given their lives? Why, two years ago, when Sir Roger Casement had signed an agreement with the Germans which would have allowed the Irish prisoners in German POW camps to return home to fight the British under an Irish flag, not even one of them had deserted his regiment and signed up with the Irish Brigade he was forming. And it was almost inconceivable now to think of the IRB looking to Germany for arms and support.

Katherine wasn't sure what support the IRB had for their plan, but she did know from her own sources that James Connolly's Citizen Army would side with them, and Connolly too had sided with the Germans before in his speeches and writings.

Dermot had asked her whether she was Irish or English . . . well, she supposed she was bound to answer English, but she felt herself to be Irish in nearly all things. However, her parents and grandparents were English, and her father and grandfather had been in the army, and now her brothers had joined up. What would happen to them if a German-backed uprising in Ireland were successful? Would they then be faced with two enemies, one facing them in Europe and one behind them in Ireland?

And then there were her children, Patrick and Senga. She knew what sort of future lay ahead for them in a British-dominated Ireland, but what would happen in the inevitable chaos of a 'free' Ireland, or worse in a German-dominated Ireland? She had a duty to them . . . and a duty to her husband . . . and a duty to her country, both that of her birth and of her adopted one.

But where did her first duty lie?

Captain Moore made his way slowly down Summerhill towards Parnell Square, having just left two of his spies. They had followed the men to the same house, and this time he was convinced they were meeting in Madam Kitten's brothel a few doors up. One of his men had spotted a light burning in one of the back rooms which was not normally used. He wondered how the major would take the news – and he wondered if he would act upon it.

On the few occasions when he had brought him news concerning Madam Kitten, the major never seemed to act upon it – it was almost as if he were frightened of the woman. The young officer was curious; he had read the file on Madam Kitten, which was unusual in that it was not as complete as those on some of the other madams. However, her activities had never included an association with politics of any denomination, and he wondered what had brought about the change now.

Martin Moore was unsure if his department had the power to close the house, but they could certainly place it under a more strict surveillance. If the Brotherhood were holding meetings there – and meetings which they wished to keep secret – then obviously something big was in the air.

And if Major Lewis didn't act upon his recommendations regarding Madam Kitten's brothel, then perhaps it was time for him to bring it to a higher authority, possibly to the mysterious brigadier.

Katherine reached her decision just as the dawn was beginning to lighten against her window; it wasn't an easy decision, and not one she relished making. But if it worked, then it might save her husband and her family – and possibly Ireland too.

CHAPTER THIRTY-SEVEN

As they were finishing breakfast, Major Lewis looked up from the morning post and said, 'I think I shall be late tonight . . . this wretched war,' he added, by way of explanation.

Anne nodded. 'I may be a little late tonight myself. I have tickets for a performance of one of Mr Yeats' plays. It's a small affair in one of the backstreet theatres, but I suppose I really should go – a lot of the old crowd will be there.'

'I thought you had grown a little tired of Mr Yeats' work,' Lewis said, looking down at his letters again, simply making polite conversation, not really interested.

'I found his interest in the metaphysical and the occult to be a little tiresome, and some of his poetical allusions were a little too obscure even for me to fathom,' she admitted, 'but apparently this is a dramatization of one of his earlier works – I'm not sure which one, but it's probably one of his heroic plays.' She smiled as he saw him nod appropriately, knowing she had lost him. What she didn't tell him was that Constance Markievicz would also be present and, with the rising inevitably drawing closer, she was eager to discover if a date had been set. Also, she had some information which she wanted to pass on to the countess.

To date, nothing she had discovered had been of great consequence; there had been some small matters of troop movments, and she had passed on the itinerary of the royal couple during their visit in 1911, and also numbers and ship complements of the Home Fleet when it sailed into Kingstown Harbour in 1911 and 1913. But the Military Council of the IRB knew – as Anne herself knew – that her greatest value would arise when the revolution was closest or actually in progress.

Major Lewis walked into work that morning. It was crisp and sharp, but the night had been surprisingly mild for January, and there was no ice. He preferred the chill weather; he imagined it helped him to think more clearly. As he hurried down the street, limping slightly because of his wound, sucking in great lungfuls of the sharp air, he quickly ran over the day's work ahead of him.

There was revolution in the air, all the signs were there; the various private armies were meeting with greater and greater frequency, and the hard-core element, the IRB, were beginning to become much more cautious regarding their movements and the location of their meetings. This Casement fellow – a knight of the realm no less! – was agitating in Germany for arms, and he desperately needed to be stopped. While it wouldn't kill the revolution, it would certainly slow it down. He shook his head slightly as he strode along, his cane tapping the slick cobbles – how such a brilliant man could become involved with this rabble was beyond him. He had been H.M. Consul in Lorenzo Marques, 1895, H.M. Consul for the Portuguese possessions in West Africa, south of the Gulf of Guinea, Consul in the Gabon and Consul to the Congo Free State, 1898–1905, Consul General, Rio de Janeiro, 1905–1913, when he retired on pension. Knighted by the King in 1911 for his services whilst in Africa – although Major Lewis had read a report which said that the man had previously refused a knighthood, but that he had been forced to take this knighthood, due to the circumstances of its conferment. Indeed there was evidence that he hadn't even written the letter of acceptance himself. But he had always been a champion of lost causes, and this was certainly a lost cause if ever there was one. That was all there was in the report on the man, but there was a single sheet appended to it, which suggested there was circumstantial evidence that he was actively spying for

Germany. There were also other, rather more disquieting rumours beginning to circulate about the man, but Major Lewis preferred to defer judgement on those.

A shiver of anticipation ran through him – the revolution would be soon, and the only problem was that the Castle was refusing to take his warnings seriously.

It was rather a case of the boy who cried wolf; the authorities in Dublin Castle had been receiving reports of imminent revolution and uprising for too many years now to take this renewed warning with the seriousness it deserved. And an additional factor at this time was that no-one truly believed the rising would come now – not in the middle of the war.

Captain Moore was waiting for him when he strode into his office on the top floor of the GPO a few moments later. The young captain snapped to attention, and held the position until Major Lewis reluctantly returned the salute before taking his seat.

The young man laid a folder on the major's desk. 'That is the report on the movements of the IRB men last night . . .' he began, but the major rudely interrupted him.

'You have been with me for how long now?'

Thrown by the sudden, seemingly irrelevant question, the young man shook his head slightly and then said, 'Six, seven years, something like that, sir.'

'And you are aware that we are running a reasonably clandestine operation here?' Major Lewis asked quietly.

Captain Moore stiffened, schooling his anger, realizing where the questions were leading. Major Lewis had ordered him on more than one occasion to dispense with all military associations, bearing, dress and salute while they were in the GPO. Although many of the workers were aware that the office on the top floor was not directly related to the working of the post office, none of them had any indication of the full extent of the operation. 'I'm sorry, sir. I forgot myself.'

'Well, try not to forget yourself again, please. Now, instead of having me wade through these reports, why

441

don't you summarize them for me, eh?' he asked. 'And for God's sake, sit down man, you're making me nervous!'

'Yes, sir.' He perched on the edge of a straight-backed chair. 'Well, sir, this meeting seemed to follow the pattern of the meeting a couple of nights past. The attendance was . . .' he began, but Major Lewis waved him on. He was looking down at a copy of the attendance list. 'It is my guess that the meeting was held in the brothel known as Madam Kitten's, although we have nothing to substantiate this, except its proximity and its association with Dermot Corcoran.

'However, ' he continued, watching his superior's face closely, 'I would be inclined to think that two top-level meetings held within a week indicate that a decision regarding the rising is due very shortly, if indeed, it hasn't already been made.' He paused, waiting for comment, but when none was forthcoming he continued. 'There is a report in this morning from our Consul in Madrid which indicates that Sir Roger Casement has finalized an agreement with the German government for the purchase and supply of weapons to the insurgents. I would imagine the revolutionaries would want to get hold of those weapons very quickly before the Germans change their mind or the tide of war turns and the Germans find they don't need the distraction that a revolution here would provide.'

'Did the report mention anything about troop movements, either from one of the German ports or one of the neutrals?'

'Nothing, sir.'

Lewis's greatest fear was that the Germans would land a small command or brigade somewhere in Ireland, with trained, battle-hardened soldiers to lead the revolutionaries. Of course, with the progress of the war in Europe at the moment, it seemed unlikely that the Germans would be able to afford the men – but then, would the British be able to afford the men to put down a rebellion?

'I've made several recommendations,' the young captain added diffidently.

'I can see that,' Major Lewis said shortly. 'I'm afraid it would be somewhat hasty to act upon these at the moment,' he dismissed them briefly, and closed the folder with his forefinger. 'Right now we need information, and most particularly numbers; we need to know approximately how many men will march into the streets when the call comes.'

'We know that there is not much support at grassroots level for a rising at this time.'

'Granted. But exactly how much is there? How many men will our boys be facing; one hundred, one thousand, five thousand, ten thousand, twenty thousand men? I want you to try and find out.'

'Me? How sir?'

'By following one of your own recommendations!'

'I'm not sure I follow . . .'

Major Lewis looked up at the younger man, his thin lips parting in a cruel smile. 'I agree that there is an excellent possibility that Madam Kitten is involved and that the brothel is being used as a meeting place. Therefore, I want you to become a regular at Madam Kitten's.' He saw the shocked expression on Martin Moore's face and his smile widened; the captain was a Methodist minister's son and engaged to a very respectable young lady. He continued on slowly. 'I want you to become particularly friendly with one girl – make it seem as if you're really falling in love with her, develop a relationship that goes beyond that of a whore and her client. But do it quickly; I've a feeling that there's not much time left. Now the woman to ask for is called Tilly, Tilly Cusack. She is a close friend of Madam Kitten's, and if anyone is party to her plans, then she surely is. Use your association with her to glean as much information as you can, it will also give you the opportunity to be in the house should another meeting take place. Try to get yourself invited there during the day, when the house is closed and you have access to their private apartments – perhaps you might come across papers that would be of some significance.'

'It sounds to me as if we're clutching at straws,' Captain Moore observed tartly.

Major Lewis sat back in his chair and smiled. 'Aye, it does, doesn't it – but it's all we have at the moment.'

To a distant observer, the two older women looked like sisters, or perhaps cousins, and from the cut and material of their clothes it was obvious they were well off. The third person was a young girl, possibly a daughter of one of the women.

This early in the year there were no other strollers in the Green, besides Katherine, Tilly Cusack and Senga. Their carriage was waiting for them at the main gate, before the recently erected archway that had been raised to those who had fought and died in the Boer War. Around them, the stark leafless trees and withered bare bushes gave the park an almost graveyard appearance. At any moment Katherine expected to round the corner and find a tombstone amongst the leaves, or a funeral wending its way along the twisting paths.

'I think perhaps you should buy this place,' Tilly remarked with a smile.

'Well, if it ever came up for sale,' Katherine said seriously. 'I've very fond memories of the Green; it's where Dermot and I first got to know one another, it was our first regular meeting place, our own secret place ...' her voice faded as she looked around, her mind drifting off into memories of all she had seen and done in the Green. Some of the memories were not quite so pleasant.

They took a side turning which she knew would bring them past the seat where, on that strange, almost dreamlike night back in 1907, she had stabbed Major Lewis. It was only later – much later – that she admitted to herself she had actually gone out with the intention of killing him that night.

'What are you smiling at?' Tilly asked, glancing sidelong at her.

Katherine shook her head. 'Just thinking.'

The two women walked on in silence for a while, watching Senga darting through the bare trees and skipping blithly over the 'Do Not Walk on the Grass' signs.

Finally, Tilly shivered and that seemed to be the signal Katherine had been waiting for. 'I need your advice, old friend . . .'

'What's wrong?' Tilly said quickly. Katherine had grown so much in confidence and experience over the past years that she rarely – if ever – asked for advice.

'What do you think of this coming revolution?' Katherine asked, seemingly changing the subject altogether.

'Oh that . . . well, I don't think it will come off at all. It'll be like so many other Irish things – just puff and blow and the excuse to jaw about it in the pub.'

'And if I told you it wasn't just wind, that it really was going to happen, and if I told you that the weapons for it would be coming from Germany, what would you say then?'

Tilly stopped and looked at her in confusion. 'Really happen? You mean it will go ahead. When? After the war surely?'

Katherine shook her head emphatically. 'No, it'll go ahead soon, within the next few months I should imagine. All they are waiting for now is the weapons to arrive from Germany.'

'It'll mean trouble,' Tilly predicted gloomily, 'police and raids, questionings and confiscations and the like. But I suppose the extra army it'll bring will be good for business . . .'

Katherine shook her head in exasperation. 'You're missing the point. It will be funded by Germany, we are talking about treason on the part of those who take part, and treason during wartime is punishable by shooting, isn't it?'

Tilly nodded dumbly.

'And what about all the Irish who have died in this war; surely this makes a mockery of them all, and all that they died for?'

Tilly shook her head in confusion. 'I don't know . . . I suppose so . . .'

'Well, what do you think we should do about it?' Katherine demanded.

Her question caught Tilly by surprise. 'What do you mean, what should we do about it? There's nothing we can do about it, except hope and pray that it doesn't come off. You know how these things are, they're usually just an excuse for men to dress up and march around with guns. It'll probably fizzle out,' she said confidently, and then added, 'You're worried about Dermot, aren't you?'

'Of course I'm worried about Dermot, but I'm also thinking about the wider implications . . .'

Tilly's knife-sharp eyebrows went up sharply. 'I thought I told you a long time ago that your only duty was to yourself and those you cared for.'

'Remember the girl you found in an alley one Christmas Eve, did you care for her, did you know her? What would have happened to her if you'd just turned your back and walked away?'

'That was different,' Tilly said defensively.

'I don't think so.' Katherine stopped and turned to her friend. 'I've got to try and stop it.'

'How? Do you think anyone will listen to you? Do you think those involved are going to change their minds just because you asked them to?'

'Probably not.'

'Will Dermot?'

Katherine shook her head. 'We've argued it back and forth so many times; it's useless even talking to him about it. We even fought about it last night.'

'What can you do then?'

Katherine shrugged, the movement almost lost beneath the heavy fur of the collar of her coat. 'I want

446

to give it one last chance before making any decision. I want to speak to the most important woman in their councils, Countess Constance Markievicz, and if that fails, well, we'll see . . .'

'See what?' Tilly wondered.

'We'll see,' Katherine repeated enigmatically.

'Why did you ask me to come out here with you?' Tilly wondered, 'it seems to me you had your mind already made up before we got here.'

'I don't know. Perhaps I thought you would have some brilliant idea that would solve everything.'

'Short of shooting the whole lot of them, I don't see that there's anything you can do. However, if you want to see the countess, I happen to know for a fact that she will be attending a play by the dramatist and poet William Butler Yeats tonight in some small theatre . . .' she shook her head. 'I don't remember where, but I have a card at home.'

Katherine laughed. 'How did you get that?'

'I bumped into one of my old clients leaving the house, and he gave it to me. He thought it might be culturally uplifting, I think – or perhaps he was trying to justify spending a night in a whorehouse by making an attempt to educate some of its inmates,' she smiled. She was well used to men's rather curious efforts to justify themselves after a night with another woman, and over the years she had received some very strange gifts as they salved their consciences.

'Well, you have solved one of my problems then; I'll attend the play tonight and speak to the woman.'

'I still think you're wasting your time.'

'I've got to try,' Katherine said softly, and Tilly thought she detected a note of desperation in her voice.

CHAPTER THIRTY-EIGHT

The theatre was small and smelt damp, and was situated in a dingy backstreet behind Christchurch Cathedral. When Katherine arrived it was full to overflowing with people from the surrounding slums, and their general odour – that of stale sweat, grease and urine and the other, more indefinable smell of disease – mingled with the stale and rotting smells of the hall. But Katherine had lived amongst Dublin's poor for so many years now that she barely even registered the odour. The people were sitting on hard wooden benches, chatting quietly together, looking expectantly towards the stage and the curtain, which was nothing more than a length of torn and dirty cloth.

There was a woman standing by the door, distributing thick chunks of bread to the audience as they arrived, and she stopped and stared when Katherine ducked her head and came in through the low arched doorway. Katherine felt awkward and conspicuous, even though she had worn clothes suitable for venturing into the slums: a heavy, black, woollen dress and knitted shawl. It would pass a cursory glance, but she knew that her bearing, manner, even her walk betrayed her.

'Her ladyship's around the back,' the woman said, without giving Katherine a chance to say anything. She nodded and walked down the length of the hall, keeping in close to the wall, and up the two rickety wooden steps that led to the stage and then stepped in behind the curtain.

She spotted Constance Markievicz immediately. The woman towered head and shoulders above the rest of the people milling around, her voice clear and demanding, her accent decidedly English. She was ordering around men and women dressed in strange creations that seemed to pass for the costumes, setting up a tableau on the bare wooden stage behind the curtain. The woman eventually straightened up, putting her hands on her hips and glaring at the performers until they had asumed the stance she had ordered, and then she turned away, shaking her head in what looked like disgust. When she spotted Katherine she stopped, immediately taking in her self-assured bearing.

'Can I help you?' Her manner was brusque, almost rude.

'You are the Countess Constance Markievicz?' Katherine said, more a statement than a question.

'I am Constance Markievicz,' the woman said with a smile. 'You may drop the countess.'

'I'd like to talk to you if I may.'

'Of course,' the woman said, and then she turned and snapped at a small, thin man hurrying past with a long wooden sword. 'You! Take your place, the curtain is about to go up.' She turned back to Katherine and smiled an apology. 'We were going to stage one of Willy's plays, but this crowd were not really in the mood for it, so I changed the programme to a series of heroic tableaux. "The Knights of Fianna", "Oisin's Return from the Land of Youth", "Queen Maeve and her Army" . . .' She shrugged again. 'That sort of thing.'

Katherine nodded vaguely, and looked out on to the stage. About twenty people had taken up position almost in the centre of the floor, each of them with a serious, studied expression, their wooden swords and spears held at extravagant angles, while in the centre of the group a pretty young woman stood holding a spear aloft.

' "Queen Maeve and her Army",' Constance Markievicz said by way of explanation, 'about to lead her men into battle. It's taken from an ancient Irish tale, and is supposed to remind the audience of their great cultural heritage.' There was just enough inflection in her voice

449

for Katherine to realize that she wasn't being entirely serious.

'You sound as if you don't approve,' Katherine said cautiously, unsure how Constance Markievicz would take it.

The tall, bitter-eyed woman shook her head. 'Look at them; they may not actually be starving, but they've had little enough to eat today. I dare say if you shook the lot of them you might get ten shillings out of the whole hall. The only reason the audience are here is for the free bread. They don't give a toss for their cultural heritage, they need food, money, proper houses, jobs . . . freedom . . .' She was about to continue when the 'stage' door, which seemed to lead out into a yard, opened and another woman came through.

Katherine looked up at the sound – and felt her heart begin to pound. She recognized the woman . . . even over the years and experiences, she still recognized her. It was Anne Lewis.

When Katherine had first met her, Mrs Lewis had been in her early thirties, which would make her about fifty – certainly late forties – now. She had filled out slightly, although she certainly wasn't plump – it was only Constance Markievicz's extreme thinness which made it seem that way – and her hair was still its mixture of brown and grey, more grey now than brown. Her eyes, though, betrayed her; they were old, old and wearied, the whites discoloured and yellowed, the pupils slightly dulled, and when she looked in Katherine's direction she squinted slightly.

Constance Markievicz, realizing that she had lost Katherine's attention, stopped speaking, and Katherine registering the silence turned back with an apology. 'I'm sorry, I just thought I knew that lady, but I see I was mistaken.'

The woman came over and stood beside Constance Markievicz. 'Everything is in readiness,' she said, still squinting towards Katherine.

The countess nodded her approval. 'Good. We will

450

begin in a moment.' She looked from Katherine to Anne. 'This is Mrs Anne Lewis, my good friend who helped me organize this . . . this affair,' she said, and then she turned back to Katherine. 'And this is . . . I'm sorry, I didn't catch your name.'

'Oh . . . it's Mrs Corcoran, Katherine Corcoran,' she said extending her hand, first to the countess and then, without hesitation, to Anne Lewis.

'Mrs Corcoran wanted to speak to me about . . .' Constance Markievicz began, talking to Anne Lewis, but then turned back to Katherine, 'What was it you wanted to speak to me about? Oh, for goodness' sake,' she suddenly snapped, turning away and darting across the stage, leaving Katherine and Anne Lewis together.

'She's a marvellous woman,' Anne Lewis said, to fill the silence between them.

'Oh, marvellous,' Katherine agreed, watching Constance Markievicz manoeuvre some people back into position.

'Have we ever met?' Anne Lewis said suddenly, turning to look Katherine full in the face.

'I'm not sure, I don't think so – why do you ask?' she said.

Anne Lewis shook her head. 'I feel as if I should know you. You must remind me of someone – but I'm afraid I can't even remember just who that is,' she laughed.

'We may have met at some function,' Katherine suggested.

'Possibly, but I don't attend many functions.'

Constance Markievicz came hurrying back. 'Look, the curtain's about to go up. Why don't we wait until this is over – you can wait, can't you? – and we can talk then.'

Katherine nodded. 'I can wait.'

'Good. Find yourselves a seat, and I'll start this.'

Major Lewis sat in the bar of the Imperial Hotel with the brigadier, drinking hot whiskey. The bar was almost

451

empty; although the night outside was cold it was not as bitter as it had been over the past few days.

'No money so soon after Christmas,' the barman had remarked as he passed the two drinks across the bar to the major, whom he had come to know in a casual way over the years.

As he slid on to the polished, red-leather seat beside the brigadier, Major Lewis reflected that he still reminded him of Dorian Gray and, in all the years he had known him – more than twenty now – the man had remained unchanged. He still looked, dressed and acted the same way, and still carried the same silver-topped cane.

Both men sipped the hot, clove-scented, amber liquid appreciatively for a few moments, and then Major Lewis spoke. 'You've read my report?'

The brigadier nodded. 'I've read it. Your suggestions were, as usual, lucid and to the point. You speak highly of young Moore.'

'He is an excellent officer; competent and decisive.'

'I'm afraid his opinion of you is not quite so high. I received a letter from him this morning which included a copy of a report he claims he made to you and about which you did nothing.'

'Did you read his report?' Major Lewis asked, lifting his drink again.

'I read it.'

'And how did you find his recommendations?'

'Interesting, but hardly practical at the moment.'

'That is very much what I told him.'

The brigadier nodded. 'Well then, do you want to speak to him – or shall I?'

'I'll speak to him myself. I think it would be all for the better if you were to keep a very low profile. These damned IRB, Citizen Army and Volunteers seem to be everywhere, and they're all getting terribly nervous these days, and I don't want to draw attention to myself by having someone strange coming and going in my office.'

'As you wish. Now, why did you call me down from the castle today?'

'I need more information,' Major Lewis said, watching the other man intently.

The brigadier smiled broadly. 'Why, I thought you brought information to us – not the other way around.'

'I know you have your sources. I need you to help me.' He stared at the man. 'Well, will you?'

'Of course, of course. What do you want?'

'We both know the revolution is close – all we need to know is how close. Now, I believe the whole key to this affair lies with this man Casement. He has bought these people arms before, and I understand he's in the process of doing it again, and this Irish Brigade nonsense with the POWs has convinced me that he's quite prepared to deal with Germany to gain his ends. I want you to use whatever diplomatic sources you possess to get me as much information as you can on the man. Also, if this is possible, I want him watched at all times. If – no, when he drops out of sight – that means he's on his way home here, and the rising is about to begin. As soon as that happens, I'll pick up the leaders and we'll nip this in the bud. A few stiff jail sentences – plotting treason and the like – and that'll take the wind out of their sails.'

The brigadier returned his drink to the damp circle on the table and sat back into the squeaking, high-backed, leather seat. 'I can only agree with you. But I'm not sure if I can help you. I know Casement is being watched in Germany at the moment – although not the whole time of course; I'm afraid our English counterparts just don't think he's as big a threat as we've been making out. Nor am I so sure I can get news to you as quickly as both you and I would like. By the time it filters out of Germany, makes its way along a rather circuitous route to London and is sorted, and then finally passed around to the various offices, a month or more may have passed.'

'God help us – how can we fight this war and hope to

453

win?' Major Lewis wondered, swallowing the last of his drink, grimacing as the hot alcohol seared his throat.

'Well, for urgent news, slightly faster methods are employed.'

'But this is urgent!'

'You and I know that, but I don't think they'll believe us.'

'Don't they know we're trying to stop a revolution in England's back pocket?'

'Ah, but they're trying to stop a war in England's waistcoat pocket.' He sighed. 'I understand your concern. I'll see what I can do in the meantime.'

'And what am I supposed to do while I'm waiting?' Major Lewis demanded.

'You could try praying,' the brigadier suggested.

'Usually after one of these things we have to stack the chairs ourselves,' Constance Markievicz said to Katherine, 'so you can imagine how thankful I am that these are benches.' The two women were standing at the foot of the stage watching the last of the audience file out. Behind them, Anne Lewis was gathering up the remainder of the props into a large cardboard box, which would be collected later.

'Do they serve any real purpose?' Katherine asked quietly, turning to look at the countess, her gaze direct and disconcerting, 'other than to give you an excuse to give them bread?'

'Probably not,' Contance Markievicz admitted.

'Why do you do it then?'

'I do what I can for them – until I can do something better.'

'And do you think rebellion will help them?' Kathering asked, her eyes never leaving the countess's face.

Constance Markievicz smiled slightly, her thin lips curving up at the edges, but the smile never reached her eyes. 'Ah, and here we come to the reason for your visit, I think?' Her eyebrows rose in a question.

Kathering nodded, and then indicated one of the long benches with her gloved hand. 'Can we sit?'

The two women sat down together, their manners and bearing startlingly out of place in the drab surroundings. Constance Markievicz was taller than Katherine, and her rather gaunt features contrasted sharply with Katherine's more pleasant, rounded face and high bones.

'I've come to you,' Katherine began, 'because you're the only woman I know of involved in the revolutionary movement . . .'

Constance Markievicz laughed and shook her head. 'And what about the *Cumann na mBan*, which is entirely composed of women? Just because mine is the only name you hear mooted abroad, do not for one moment think that I am the only woman in the movement.'

'Well, yours is the one I hear my husband using time and again.' She smiled slightly, 'I think he, like most of the others, seems rather in awe of you.'

'You didn't tell me your husband's name?' Constance Markievicz reminded her.

'Dermot Corcoran – he's the reporter with the *Freeman's Journal*.'

The countess nodded, and then frowned and looked suspiciously at Katherine. 'I know Dermot; his articles on the conditions in Dublin are a great help to us in promoting the movement abroad . . . but I don't think I ever heard him speak of a wife.'

Katherine smiled tightly. 'I know. He doesn't like to mention that he's married – just in case people inquire about me.'

'But why would he ever want to do that?' Constance Markievicz wondered.

'He's rather afraid that people will find out what I am.'

'And just what are you, my dear?'

'I am the madam of a brothel!'

Constance Markievicz looked at her as if she were

455

mad, and although usually imperturbable, she seemed for once quite at a loss for words.

'You can see why he doesn't like to talk about me,' Katherine continued pleasantly. 'But I must beg of you never to mention it to him or any of his friends; it would embarrass him terribly.'

Constance Markievicz nodded slightly. 'Of course,' she whispered. She looked at Katherine anew, as if she were some sort of alien creature. She had once said that she had seen all that life had to offer, and that nothing could surprise her now, but whatever she had been expecting from this quiet woman in black it certainly hadn't been this.

'What can I do for you?' she asked at last.

'Well,' Katherine said slowly, 'I suppose, like many other wives and mothers with husbands or sons in the movement, I am concerned for my husband's safety. I think I've come here to ask you – plainly and simply as one woman to another – will the revolution go ahead?'

Constance Markievicz looked at her, wide-eyed with astonishment. 'Good God, woman, of course it will. There was never any doubt that it would. Yes, we will rise and, though we may die for it, we will throw off the British yoke.'

'And will you use German aid to do that?' Katherine wondered, keeping her voice low and steady, making it sound like just another question.

'Connolly says that there is only one common enemy,' Constance Markievicz said, standing up and looking down on Katherine, 'and I will make use of any and all means possible to help us take Ireland from the British.'

Katherine stood and stretched out her hand to the countess. Surprised, Constance Markievicz took it. 'Thank you, you've answered my question.'

'If your husband dies, then he will be dying in a good cause,' Constance Markievicz said, by way of consolation.

'Much good that will do me and my children,' Katherine said a little bitterly. She nodded to the countess and then again to Anne Lewis, who was making her way down the benches now that the conversation between the two women seemed to be at an end. 'I'll bid you both good night.'

Anne Lewis stood beside Constance Markievicz watching the woman winding her way down along the length of the hall towards the door. 'I still think I've met her before.'

Constance Markievicz smiled, thinking of Katherine's occupation. 'I really don't think so. I wonder what she wanted though?' she asked aloud.

'I thought she might want to join *Cumann na mBan*,' Anne Lewis said.

'So did I, initially. She said she was worried about her husband's safety if the rising actually took place.'

'But of course it will take place,' Anne said, sounding almost affronted that anyone should even doubt it.

'You and I know that, my dear, but I dare say there are a lot of Dubliners who look on us all as a great joke.'

'But they will rise up and join us when we finally go into action . . . won't they?'

'I hope so,' Constance Markievicz said, 'but I think you must remember something about the average Dubliner; he doesn't like to be disturbed. And for many of them the rising will be nothing more than a great disturbance.'

The two women walked slowly towards the door, and then Anne Lewis waited while Constance Markievicz turned a large rusted key in the stiff lock. They stood together under the arched door, looking out on the wet cobbles – it had rained while they had been inside – and breathing in the damp foul smell from the nearby River Liffey.

'Has any decision been reached?' Anne asked finally.

Constance Markievicz hesitated a few moments before replying, and then she finally nodded. 'Yes, the day has been set. The rising will take place on Easter Sunday, April 23rd.'

CHAPTER THIRTY-NINE

If Dermot had expected an argument when he asked Katherine for the use of the back room for the following night's meeting, he was pleasantly surprised. She agreed without question or argument, and had simply nodded in his direction as she pored over the books of the household accounts, without even bothering to look up at him. 'This will be my last night on the evening shift,' he said as he kissed her on the top of the head and headed off for work, never even stopping to think about her sudden acquiescence.

It was now nearly a week since her meeting with the Countess Constance Markievicz, and so far she still had not come to a decision – indeed, she wasn't even sure what sort of decision she should be making. What she was considering was . . . well, almost unthinkable. However, she resolved to wait and see what would transpire at tonight's meeting, and then she would make her decision – however difficult that might be.

In the distance she heard the doorbell ring, and glanced up at the clock. The large age-coloured face showed a little after eight. Business was good, but then, wars were always good for brothels.

Mickey stood solidly in the doorway and glared down on the man – a stranger – who looked up at him from the bottom step where he had obviously retreated after ringing. 'I don't think I know you, now do I?' Mickey demanded. 'We've strict rules of admittance here; I think you should be looking in on one of the other houses further down the street.'

'But I was recommended to come here,' Captain Martin Moore said, more nervous now than he had ever

458

been before in his life, more frightened even than when he had fought the Boers in South Africa.

'Aye?' Mickey said suspiciously, 'and who might have been recommending you, eh?'

Captain Moore named several of his fellow officers who had recommended the house highly – amid much ribald jeering. Martin Moore's prudishness was almost legendary in the regiment.

'Aye, well I reckon I know them well enough,' Mickey said, stepping back and allowing the man into the hallway. 'Did your friends tell you the rules?' he demanded, taking in the man's military bearing, the highly polished shoes, the well-kept hands, with the fingertips stained by powder burns. He was indeed what he professed to be – a soldier.

'They mentioned that this was a place of great discretion and complete honesty,' Captain Moore said.

'Well, we do have that reputation,' Mickey said, reaching up to take the gentleman's coat and hat and gloves. 'One of the reasons we have such a select clientèle is because we are discreet; no-one will ever speak of what happens here, nor will you ever be robbed of either money or jewellery.'

The captain looked surprised; in most of the other brothels, thefts were commonplace, and many an officer or gentleman who went in with either money or jewellery and virtue and came out with none.

'Now, have you been recommended to ask for any of our ladies in particular?' Mickey asked, phrasing the question the same way as if he were asking what the gentleman preferred to drink.

'Well,' Martin looked slightly abashed. 'I was told to ask for a Miss Tilly Cusack – if she was available, that is.'

'Miss Tilly no longer participates in the activities of this establishment . . . perhaps I could recommend one of the other girls . . .?'

'But . . . if she is here?' Captain Moore began.

'The madam never participates.'

459

'Ask her,' he urged.

'It will be a waste of time,' Mickey warned.

'Ask her – please.'

Captain Moore had barely settled into one of the overstuffed chairs in the luxurious sitting room and ordered a gin and tonic from the waiter, when the door opened and a . . . well, a rather surprising woman came through. Captain Moore wasn't really sure what he had been expecting, perhaps something whorish and brassy, but certainly not this rather pleasant woman who reminded him in some indefinable way of his mother!

Tilly crossed the floor and sat down beside the surprised-looking young man, wondering what had made him ask for her. He was, she guessed, somewhere in his early thirties, round-faced, with a strong chin and bright intelligent eyes. He was also smooth-shaven, which was curious in an age where most gentlemen wore whiskers of some sort. 'My name is Tilly Cusack,' she said, smiling her professional smile. 'It's been a long time since someone asked for me by name,' she said softly, her barely-discernible English accent surprising him even further.

Well, how did one react with whores – even matronly-looking whores, just what were the codes of conduct, Captain Moore wondered in confusion. He stood up and took her hand formally, and introduced himself, 'Captain Martin Moore, at your service ma'am. I . . . ahem . . . I was advised to ask for you. I was not aware that you had . . . ahem . . . retired.'

Tilly hid a smile; well, at least he had good manners. Her long association with men also told her that he was tremblingly nervous. 'Have you ordered a drink?' she asked, making polite conversation, allowing him to settle down.

'Ah, yes, of course, will you allow me to . . .' he asked, but Tilly shook her head, smiling slightly.

'No, no, that is taken care of,' she said, and, even as she was speaking the waiter reappeared with a tray holding Captain Moore's gin and tonic and Tilly's dry

460

white wine. They toasted one another and then busied themselves with their drinks, Tilly realizing that the man was using the time to get a closer look at her.

Captain Moore saw a woman in her late thirties or early forties, tall and rather slender, and with large breasts that moved freely under her salmon-pink evening dress. Her hair was blond and full, the colour looked natural, and her eyes were bright blue. Her ankles and wrists were somewhat thickened, there were wrinkles around her eyes and at the corners of her mouth, and the skin of her slender neck was stretched and beginning to show signs of age. She didn't seem to be wearing any make-up, other than colour on her lips, and her perfume was a delicate floral fragrance that he found quite pleasant. He was reminded once again of his mother, and found the idea extremely disconcerting.

'Why do I get the impression this is your first time in a place like this?' Tilly asked suddenly, startling him.

'I'm sorry, I was miles away. Well, you are actually correct; this is my first time in a brothel,' he said, lowering his voice, even though the room was empty.

The doorbell rang then, and he sat up, looking almost comically guilty. Tilly stood up and extended her hand. 'Come on, we'll go to my room; that way no-one will see you, we'll spare you that embarrassment.'

The captain nodded his thanks and, swallowing the last of his drink, followed Tilly from the room, just as Mickey was opening the door to a man he addressed as 'Your Grace'. It took an extraordinary effort of will not to turn around and look at the person the doorman was admitting.

Tilly's room was at the front of the house, on the second floor, and the captain found himself straining to hear sounds coming from behind the doors they passed, but they were all silent. It was only when he got inside Tilly's room and closed the door that he realized why; there were thick tapestries hanging on the back of the doors. Tilly saw him looking at them and smiled. 'They

461

help kill the sounds, and discretion is our byword,' she added with a grin.

Captain Moore looked around the room; compared with the elegant clutter of the sitting-room below, it looked almost bare. But it was surprisingly large and the furniture was of the best quality. There was a bed in the centre of the room, set with its head against the wall, and with two armchairs and a small wooden table on one side of it. A large wardrobe with a mirror set into the door stood on the other side of the bed, and there was a small, elegant, French dressing table against the wall. Incongruously, on the wall above the dressing table was a picture of the Holy Family. Tilly saw the captain looking at it and, smiling, crossed to it and moved it slightly so he could look at the wall behind it. There was an area of paler plasterwork, obviously covering a hole that had once been there.

'In the old days, the girls sometimes kept knives or bars behind the holy pictures in case a client became difficult. We don't here,' she added.

'I didn't know the practice had died out,' he said crossing the floor and standing by the window, looking down into the darkened street.

'It hasn't,' Tilly said. She sat down in one of the leather armchairs and placed her drink on the table before her.

'How did you know this was my first time in a brothel?' he asked, sitting in the chair facing her.

'Experience,' Tilly said with a smile.

'Have you . . . have you been doing this sort of thing long?' Martin Moore asked. 'The doorman said you were not available . . . that you no longer participated . . .'

He would be a talker, Tilly decided. Some men were; they wanted and needed nothing more than to have a willing ear to bend. But when she looked into his eyes again, she revised her opinion. He would be a talker the first time, but the next . . . well, that might be different.

'That's hardly the question to ask a respectable

woman . . .' she began, and the captain immediately apologized, colouring deeply, but Tilly waved her hand. 'I wasn't being serious. I did work both the streets and this house for a few years, but now I'm the madam, I run the house, and one of the advantages of being the madam is that she rarely – if ever – takes part.'

'I'm sorry . . . I didn't know. But why did you agree to see me?' he wondered.

'Curiosity, I suppose. And it is flattering to have a handsome gentleman ask for you by name.'

'You're not what I expected,' Martin said shyly.

'And what did you expect – a whore, all paint and flash?'

'Something like that.' He sipped his drink and added. 'You're English, aren't you?'

'Once . . . long ago,' Tilly said with a touch of a smile. 'I came over to Dublin in the late '90s, and I worked for a while in the linen-trade . . .' It was a lie she had built up over the years, her little fiction which she felt left her with a certain amount of self-respect. 'But, of course, the linen trade was never the healthiest to work in, and when I became ill, they fired me. My savings quickly ran out and my landlord threw me out of my lodgings. And so I went on the streets. I had nothing else to do, I had to live.' Her story was all the more plausible because such things happened all too frequently. She watched his face, and was surprised to find that he seemed genuinely interested. She sipped her drink and continued. 'I was luckier than most, however. I ended up in this house. Girls working in the houses generally live longer than those walking the streets – well, in the better-class houses that is . . . and this is the best,' she added.

He continued staring at her long after she had finished speaking, and to cover the embarrassing silence she asked him why he had come to the house, giving him the opportunity to speak.

Captain Moore shrugged slightly. 'I really don't know . . .'

'Why did you ask for me?'

Again the slightly embarrassed shrug. 'I don't know – you were recommended to me.'

'Most of the men look for the younger women,' she said with a smile. 'But then, I don't think you knew what I looked like before you asked for me,' she grinned. 'I can arrange for a younger woman if you wish.'

'No!' he said quickly, 'no, that's all right. I mean, I'd prefer if you stayed, I feel I can talk to you.'

Tilly nodded. 'You can. It's been a long time since a man simply talked to me.'

'You've no husband . . . no boyfriend then?' he asked. Tilly grinned and shook her head. 'Have you ever thought of leaving?' he wondered.

Tilly shook her head. 'Not really; sure, what would I do? I can't go back to London, there's nothing left for me there, and there's not many jobs for a retired whore.'

'But if you met someone . . .?'

She considered for a moment and then nodded. 'Yes, if I met someone. But I gave up that dream a long time ago. Can you think of any respectable man who would marry someone like me? And even if they didn't know what I had been, I'm afraid I'm honest enough with myself to want to tell them.' She shook her head. 'No, I can't see that happening.'

'But you're still a very beautiful woman,' Captain Moore said quickly.

Tilly threw back her head and laughed with genuine good humour. 'And you're a very charming man to say so.' She shook her head in fond remembrance. 'Ah, but you should have seen me in my youth – I was beautiful then, and, if I've any regrets, it's that I didn't use my looks properly. I wouldn't be where I am today, that's for sure.'

'And what about your future?' Captain Moore asked, 'what will become of you?'

The question sobered her, and she took her time before answering. 'I don't really know. Everything is

464

changing now. I think the days of the grand houses are dying, especially here in Dublin. I don't know what I'll do in the future, we'll just have to wait and see. But I think I've a few years left in me yet,' she smiled, glancing mischievously across at him.

'Yes . . . yes . . . of course.' Captain Moore slipped his small-faced fob watch from his waistcoat pocket and flipped back the engraved cover. 'Goodness, is that the time, I really must be going.' He stood up and came around the table and then, taking Tilly's hand in his, stooped over it, not quite kissing the fingers. 'I realize you don't participate . . . that is . . . that you're not . . .' he stumbled. 'Perhaps I could see you again . . . tomorrow night . . .?' he finally managed to ask.

Tilly nodded bemused and watched in astonishment as he crossed to the door and quietly let himself out on to the landing, pulling it shut behind him.

Captain Moore stood on the landing for a moment with his back to the door, and then patted his sweat-sheened face with his handkerchief. He found he was shivering, the muscles in his legs were trembling – and he couldn't account for the feeling. He shakily descended the stairs to find Mickey standing in the hall chatting to two men dressed as waiters. Without a word, Mickey produced his hat, coat and gloves, bade him good night and let him out into the chill January night, where frost was already beginning to sparkle on the cobbles, a change from the mildness of the last few nights.

In the room upstairs, Tilly stood by the window and watched the young man make his way smartly down the street, heading towards O'Connell Street, and wondered what all that had been about. She pulled a shawl tighter around her shoulders and shook her head, vaguely troubled. It had been a long time since she had revealed so much of herself to a man; a long time since she had considered her future; that was something which, because of her nature, she usually managed to forget about.

465

Tilly Cusack had met many men in the course of her career, but none of them had ever been like Martin Moore. She wasn't sure if she was looking forward to his visit the following evening or not.

CHAPTER FORTY

Dermot watched the men file into the small sitting room, and experienced an immense feeling of pride to be associated with these men, who would right Ireland's wrongs and set her on the road to freedom. They came in ones and twos, quiet men all, bundled up against the chill of the night, talking quietly together when they came into the sitting room with its small coal and turf fire burning in the corner, and glasses of mulled wine and hot tea on a small side table beside the door.

Dermot had been surprised to find that Katherine had ordered the fire lit and even more surprised when, a few minutes before the first of the men were due to arrive, Mickey had come in with the tray of drinks. The old man's eyes were sparkling; he knew the revolution was being plotted in this room, and when the time came and the call to arms went out, he would be standing there alongside with the rest of them. He put the tray down and looked at Dermot. 'It'll be soon, eh?'

'It will be soon,' Dermot promised, smiling at the older man's enthusiasm. He wished more people shared Mickey's desire for a free Ireland, but he realized that a lot of the poorer people regarded them as little more than trouble-makers, while the wealthier merchant classes looked upon them as eccentrics, figures of fun rather than any real threat. The weekly and monthly marches and parades by the Volunteers and the Irish Citizen Army were usually laughed and jeered at by the passers-by, and Dermot couldn't help wondering when the time came, just how many of them would march out to fight alongside their fellow countrymen. Like the other leaders, he shared their vision, but he was a realist enough to recognize that, unless the common people rose up also, then the rebellion was doomed from the very start.

Pearse had arrived first, stamping his feet against the cold and rubbing his gloved hands together, followed, a few moments later, by Tom Clarke, the oldest of the group, and his close friend Sean Mac Diarmada, leaning heavily on his stick, complaining of his stiff leg. Joseph Plunkett arrived next. He was a thin, frail-looking young man who walked with a slight stoop, and was continually adjusting the wire-framed spectacles that perched high on his nose close to his eyes. He paused at the door and solemnly shook hands with Dermot, congratulating him on having found such a splendid room for their meeting. Last to arrive was James Connolly, a stout, bluff, hearty man, who had set up the Irish Citizen Army and had laboured long and hard for the rights of the Irish worker. He too shook hands with Dermot, his large hands rough and calloused after years of manual work.

The men arranged themselves in a rough semi-circle around the fire, with Pearse at the far wall. Closest to the fire, facing old Tom Clarke who sat on the opposite side, Joseph Plunkett sat beside Pearse, his long-fingered hands stretched to the heat of the fire, while Sean Mac Diarmada sat in the middle, his legs, which had been crippled by polio, stretched straight out in front of him. James Connolly sat beside Sean, both hands resting on his knees, glaring in at the fire, the light gleaming off his high forehead.

Dermot Corcoran passed around the drinks and then he squeezed in beside Tom Clarke and James Connolly. Drinks in hand, they all looked expectantly at Padraic Pearse. He smiled a little shyly and raised his glass slightly, 'Let's drink . . .' he said, 'to Ireland.'

'To a free Ireland,' Connolly amended with a grin, and Pearse nodded. The small group solemnly and silently drank and then, that small formality dispensed with, the tension seemed to seep from the room and they settled themselves for a long discussion.

468

Dermot watched fascinated as Pearse straightened up to speak. The man was a magical orator and, even these hardened revolutionaries, well-used to his oratory, still couldn't escape his spell. But tonight, there was to be no rhetoric, it was just business.

'You all know James Connolly, and he, I think is familiar with all of us. What Mr Connolly didn't know until recently was of the existence of the secret Military Council within the Irish Republican Brotherhood. However, we became aware a little while ago that his Citizen Army was moving in the same direction as ourselves, that is towards an armed insurrection. So, we have invited him to join with us, to pool his men and resources, and this he has agreed to do.'

'It would be foolish to pull against one another,' Connolly boomed.

'This is another boost for us in our struggle,' Pearse continued, 'and his men and arms and training are very welcome at this point. As you are all no doubt aware, the day for the rising has been set for Easter Sunday, April 23rd. But I think, before I continue, we should perhaps listen to our friend and comrade, Joseph Plunkett, and perhaps, Joe, if you would, details of some of your rather interesting travels over the past year or two, not only for Mr Connolly's benefit, but also to remind us how close we are to victory.'

The thin young man nodded and smiled nervously. His long fingers touched his glasses and he looked into the fire, glancing up every now and again to look at the faces around him.

'As we all know,' he began, his voice soft and cultured, barely above a whisper, 'in September, two years ago, it was decided that the rising would take place sometime before the end of the war, and to this end our people contacted our Irish-American brothers, who in turn contacted the Kaiser's government with the object of securing aid for our cause. The Germans were receptive to our plans and sounded sympathetic. Although Sir Roger Casement was already in Germany, his relationship with the government was a little strained at this stage, and also his health, weakened by his long stays in the hot climates, was beginning to break down. So our people decided to send someone to Germany to work out the details and,' he shrugged a little depreciatively, 'for some reason I was asked to go.'

'Joe was chosen because he had travelled extensively in his youth for his health's sake, and we therefore felt he would be able to pass the British authorities undetected – as he did,' Pearse said, almost proudly, as if the plan had been his, although he had not even been a member of the Supreme Council of the IRB at that time.

Joe smiled his thanks and continued, and Dermot felt himself warm to the frail young man – obviously terribly ill and almost certainly in pain, and yet he too was giving what little he possessed in the way of strength towards the success of the rising.

'I travelled on to Spain and then went to Florence, where I took the precaution of changing my name to James Malcome – the initials from my own Christian names ... Joseph Mary,' he explained shyly, 'and then I went on to Switzerland and thence to Berlin, where I contacted Sir Roger. Unfortunately, he had made little headway with the Germans, and his own plans for the formation of the Irish Brigade amongst the prisoners of war had foundered, and this, I think, made him lose even more face with the Kaiser's ministers.

'However, my own representations were received a little more enthusiastically, and they gave me an undertaking – and this was early last year you must remember – that a shipment of arms would be sent to Ireland in the spring of this year. Now that undertaking has recently been confirmed by Sir Roger, and we have confirmation that the guns will be arriving here shortly.' He looked from face to face, his eyes burning feverishly behind his spectacles. 'Before I returned to Dublin last year, I travelled on to New York to report on my progress with our American brothers in the *Clann na Gael*, and they will support us in any way they can.' He finished a trifle breathlessly, looking very pale, and with two spots of colour burning feverishly on his cheeks.

Pearse squeezed Plunkett's arm in a rare gesture of affection. Everyone there knew what a toll the travelling must have taken on the young man's already frail health. 'I think, gentlemen, we have to decide what must be done now,' Pearse said. He looked from face to face, inviting someone to speak.

'Arms,' old Tom Clarke said truculently, 'we need the arms before we do anything else.'

Dermot Corcoran, who was sitting beside him, nodded. 'May I be so bold as to suggest that we contact John Devoy in *Clann na Gael* in New York advising them of the date of the rising? They could pass it on to the Germans and perhaps even suggest that they might help us with a military manoeuvre on the European fronts on that date. It might give us a few days' grace before men could be diverted from Europe to deal with us.'

'Good sense,' Connolly said, rubbing his balding head, which was gleaming with sweat, 'sound military sense.' James Connolly was the only man present who had actually been in the army, having served in the First Battalion of the King's Liverpool Regiment for some seven years.

'What will the Germans give us?' Dermot asked, gaining confidence from Connolly's support. 'How many guns can they afford?' He looked at Joseph Plunkett.

The young man shook his head slightly. 'I'm not sure. The more we ask for the more we will receive, and the bigger our request, the more confidence they will be inclined to place in the rising.' He paused a moment, considering, and finally said, 'We should ask for 25,000 ... no ... 50,000 rifles, a proportionate number of pistols, the new parabellums if possible. We will need some machine guns – as many as possible – as well as some artillery pieces with which to control the ports and the like. I think,' he added eagerly, now caught up

471

in his planning, 'that we should also ask for some trained German officers, who would be of great use to us.' And then he smiled and shrugged. 'However, I don't think they'll send men, and if we even get half the number of guns we'll be doing very well. Perhaps it might help if we suggested that a successful rising in Ireland would divert some . . . shall we say, 500,000 soldiers from the European battlefields?'

'Are you not being a little optimistic?' Tom Clarke growled.

'Of course I am,' he said with a smile.

'I can only agree with everything Joe has suggested,' Pearse said. 'Has anyone anything else to add?' He looked from face to face. 'No? Well then, we'll get this message off to Devoy in New York and he can pass it on to the Germans for us. Did you get all the details, Dermot?' he asked, looking at Corcoran.

Dermot tapped his reporter's notebook with the tip of his pencil. 'Aye, everything. I'll let you see the message before it goes out.'

Pearse smiled. 'It might be better if you let Joe here see it; he's our military strategist.'

Dermot nodded. 'Of course.'

'Well, gentlemen . . . have we any more business . . .?'

As the minor business of preparations for the rising went on around him, Dermot reflected that he was finally doing something for his beloved Dublin people. For years he had written about them, tried and tried again to better their station, to win better housing, better sanitation and better jobs for them, and all to no avail, but these few men sitting around him now, these and a few more, would do it for him.

And yes, there was a price to pay; the understanding of his wife and the love of his children for a start, but what they didn't realize was that he was doing it for them too, and if he succeeded it would be a small enough price to pay. He looked across at Joseph Plunkett; there was a man who was quite prepared to sacrifice his health for the cause; could he then begrudge his wife's anger and misunderstanding?

From her position behind the two-way glass, Katherine wept silently. She hadn't realized the depth of her husband's involvement in the planning of the rising, nor had she realized how closely they were involved with the Germans, nor how much they were relying on their aid. It made her decision easier to make, but it didn't make it any easier for her to accept.

On the other side of the city Anne Lewis and William Sherlock were also discussing weapons for the coming rising.

Anne sat in the corner of William Sherlock's extraordinary library and watched the tall, gaunt man pulling out the boxes of guns from his hidden cupboard. When the cupboard was empty, he broke open each box and almost reverently took out the rifles, German Mausers which had been smuggled into Ireland a year and a half previously. They were huge single shot rifles, that fired an enormous eleven millimetre slug, that made a hole the size of a penny going in but left a wound the size of a football when it came out on the other side, Sherlock told Anne almost proudly. While he cleaned the guns of their protective grease, Anne methodically tore up the oiled wrapping paper and threw the strips into a bucket. Both the paper and the wooden gun boxes would be burned later.

Sherlock looked up at the squat, thick-bodied clock that acted as a bookend. 'We'd better hurry; they'll be here soon.'

'Is the countess taking the guns to her own house?' Anne asked.

'She wants to give her Fianna boys some practice with real weapons for a change,' Sherlock said with a grin, 'although I fancy they'll find these heavy work indeed.' The Mauser rifles kicked solidly to the shoulder when fired, and detonated with an explosion of noise and

473

smoke. If the guns were not held properly, they could very easily dislocate or even break a shoulder.

'But with the rising so close now, everyone who can bear arms will be needed, and the few who can load and clean a gun will be able to show the others. As soon as the guns arrive from Germany, we'll be sending them around the country to our people with Fianna boys to instruct them.' His eyes were sparkling, and he was chuckling softly to himself as he scrubbed grease and gun oil from the weapons, already seeing his precious rebellion finished and won and Ireland free again.

Anne watched him, almost sadly. She was forcibly reminded of the tall, elegant, literary teacher she had once known, who had taught her sentence construction and creative thinking on those balmy afternoons and warm nights so long ago, or of the man of letters, resplendent in his evening dress and his polished manners, whom she had admired with such fervour. That man – that William Sherlock – would never have stripped down a gun, that Sherlock would never have become involved in revolution. But then, she decided, neither would the old Anne Lewis, the wife of a British army officer who had once thought herself an accomplished poetess on the basis of one collection of verse. She smiled gently to herself and shook her head.

'What's so amusing?' William Sherlock asked.

'I'm trying to remember the collection of verse I had published back in '97 or '98,' she said.

'*A Pot-Pourri of Verse*,' William Sherlock said with a grin, 'four hundred copies published, ninety-eight sold and ten distributed free as review copies. What made you think of that now?' he asked, looking across at her as she methodically shredded the heavy brown paper.

'I was thinking the old Anne Lewis would never have become involved in this, would never have sat here tearing up gun wrapping, and I was thinking the old William Sherlock would never have cleaned rifles and plotted revolution.'

'We all do strange things in the name of freedom,'

474

William Sherlock said seriously. 'We've all changed . . . but I think it will be worth it in the end.'

'Do you think so?' Anne Lewis asked, looking at William, the lamplight catching her pale eyes, turning them to water. 'Do you honestly think so?'

'We can't afford to think otherwise,' he said seriously.

Tilly had been right; the first time he had been a talker, but the second . . .

Martin Moore had made love to her gently, taking enough care and paying enough attention for her to realize that he wasn't accustomed to making love to a woman. She lay back on the bed as his lips and fingers drifted across her body, touching her with a gentleness that she hadn't felt in a long time, and arousing her for the first time in many years. When her passion took her – suddenly, unexpectedly, joyfully – it wasn't assumed, and it left her in tears.

Captain Moore ran his fingers down her face and brushed away the salt tears. 'Why do you cry?'

'Why do you think?' she asked, allowing her hands to drift down his back, tracing the lines of old scars, glad the light was off and that he couldn't see the marks which John Lewis had left on her own body nine years previously.

'Most people cry when they're sad,' he whispered.

'Or when they're happy.'

'And are you happy?' he asked.

'Yes,' she said simply, and was almost surprised herself to find that it was true. 'You've done something to me that no-one has ever done before, and it's a frightening but very wonderful experience.'

'And what is that?'

'You made love to me.'

'But . . . I thought . . .'

She pressed her fingers to his lips and quietened him. 'No, what I used to do with men was not lovemaking; it was a rough mechanical act, with no pleasure in it for me. It was a task to be accomplished as quickly as

475

possible, and with as much false passion, emotion and enthusiasm as I could muster.

'But that didn't happen tonight. Tonight, it was real. It's been a long time since I've slept with a man, and tonight was the first time anyone has ever taken the time to make love to me, to treat me as a woman. Thank you.' She kissed him, not passionately, but simply and gently.

They lay together in the quiet aftermath of their lovemaking, her head in the crook of his arm, whispering softly together, like lovers, she realized, like real lovers.

'If you had the opportunity, would you leave here?' he asked.

'If I had somewhere to go,' she said, after a moment's hesitation.

'And if you had?'

'Well then I'd go.'

'Come with me,' he said suddenly.

'What!' She struggled to sit up, but he pushed her back down on the pillows. 'This is stupid . . .'

'I said come with me, marry me!'

Tilly suddenly found herself becoming angry. 'This is a cruel game you're playing,' she snapped.

'It's not a game,' he said quickly. 'I mean it. I'm offering to marry you and take you away from here.'

'But I don't even know you,' she said, laughing.

'We could get to know one another as time went by.'

'And what if we found we didn't like one another?' she asked, still playing the game – if game it was, and she found herself fervently hoping that it was.

'I don't think we would,' he said.

'But I've only met you once before. I don't know anything about you, and if there's one thing you learn early on in this game it's never to take a man on trust and never to believe the word of a stranger. And I'm not insulting you,' she added quickly.

'No, no of course not.' She felt the movement of his head as he nodded seriously. 'You have a point, of

476

course. Perhaps you should think it over, consider my offer.'

Tilly laughed softly. 'Perhaps I shouldn't. Perhaps I should say yes now, because in the morning you'll have changed your mind.'

'Oh, I don't think so,' he said quickly, but Tilly said nothing. She knew that promises made in the heat of lovemaking had a strange way of looking completely different in the chill light of dawn. And, while she had received many strange offers, she had never yet been asked to marry.

And yet the young captain seemed sane enough; he hadn't been invalided home from the Front; he wasn't shell-shocked. He seemed and looked to be a perfectly respectable, perfectly normal army captain, and yet there must be something wrong with him. Why else would he propose to an old whore on his second visit with her . . .?

Unless, of course, he really was in love with her.

Tilly twisted her head to look up at him. He was sleeping now, and in repose his features had settled into an almost boyish expression. She didn't love him, of course, she barely knew him, but she could learn to love him, she reflected.

Tilly Cusack lay awake long into the night, wondering if his offer were genuine, and wondering if she dared to accept it.

CHAPTER FORTY-ONE

Captain Moore usually arrived at the GPO just as the doors were opening and at least an hour or so before his superior. But Major Lewis was already at his desk going through the latest reports on the war when the captain arrived today.

'There will be more casualties arriving at Kingstown in the next day or two,' Major Lewis said without preamble, glancing over at the young man, passing no comment on his delay. 'Some of the men have been genuinely wounded, while others have self-inflicted injuries which they have used to escape the trench warfare.' He pulled out a separate sheet. 'Some of these men are noted here, and we have been asked to report on their conduct and behaviour while they convalesce.' Major Lewis tapped the sheaf of papers in his hand. 'It says here that men are smoking the iodine in their first-aid kits, and this gives them an extraodinarily high temperature, nausea, vomiting and diarrhoea, chronic coughing and spitting of phlegm and blood. They look, and here I quote, "like the walking dead".' He glanced over at the captain. 'Much as you look this morning.'

'It's all in the course of duty, sir,' Martin Moore said quietly, opening his briefcase and pulling out his own files. No papers of any importance were ever left on the premises.

'You met Tilly Cusack again, then?'

'Last night,' he said softly.

'And?'

Martin Moore looked over at him. 'That was only my second meeting with her.'

'I know that. But have you learned anything yet?'

Captain Moore was almost ashamed to admit that he

478

had barely thought about his mission to discover if the house was being used for illegal meetings. 'I think it's a little early, sir. My task is somewhat complicated because Tilly Cusack is no longer actually working in the house – she is the madam.'

'In name only,' Lewis snorted. 'The house is Kitten's!'

'The top floor seems to be used as living quarters, but beyond that I've found out little. I don't know how many people are actually living there, although, last night, as I was going up the stairs to the first floor, I passed the ... the major-domo I suppose you'd call him, who was carrying a tray with about half a dozen cups and glasses on it. I stopped on the second landing, but he continued on up.'

'What time was that?'

'Close on nine, I suppose.'

Major Lewis propped both elbows on the desk and laced his fingers together and then rested his chin on his hands. 'But surely all the girls would have been entertaining in their rooms, or else be downstairs in the sitting room awaiting a guest at that time?'

Captain Moore disguised his surprise at his superior's knowledge of the layout of the house and nodded. 'I suppose so. I came in and was directed to go straight upstairs; I don't know how many of the girls were still ... unaccompanied.'

'By nine in the evening all of them should have been busy. And I know there's only Kitten, her "husband" and two children living upstairs.' He glared at the younger man. 'Are you sure there were more than four glasses?'

'Positively. There were at least four glasses, spirit glasses I think, and certainly the same number of cups and saucers. The tray was silver, I remember that clearly because it surprised me, and the teapot and the cutlery looked to be of good quality.'

Major Lewis shuffled aside some papers and pulled out a series of single sheets. 'Here are the reports on some of the men we're watching. Last night, Pearse,

479

Clarke, Plunkett, Mac Diarmada, and this union fellow, Connolly, all disappeared in or around the Monto area. They all reappeared individually some hours later in Parnell Square, in the vicinity of Tom Clarke's shop there.' Major Lewis shuffled the sheets together. 'Perhaps you have given us some clue as to where they were last night.'

'You think a meeting took place?'

'In view of your previous suspicions and what you've just told me, I'm sure of it.' He sat back in his chair, looking out the window at the tall section of Nelson's column in the centre of O'Connell Street. 'Christ!' he suddenly exploded, 'we're on the verge of an uprising here, and I'm being asked to check up on bloody shirkers.' He slapped his hand down on the casualty reports. 'They're traitors, and should be shot as such. And so should this lot,' he added, tapping the reports from his spies. 'It's wartime and they're plotting treason. I'd shoot the lot of them.'

Captain Moore turned back to his case and began pulling out more papers. He had heard it all before from his superior: shoot the traitors, without trial, without reason, but shoot them now before they had a chance to cause any real trouble. 'Has there been anything further on Casement?' he asked quickly, to break the tirade.

Major Lewis got up from behind his desk and strode over to the window. The pale winter sunlight streaming in through the window washed away what little colour there was in his face, giving it a ghastly appearance. 'Nothing; he's still in Berlin, and the only report I have is that his health is poor. I've spoken with the brigadier concerning him, but he believes the spymasters in London consider the man to be of only minor importance . . .'

He stopped suddenly, staring down into the street below. A tall woman in black was standing at the base of the pillar, her head tilted up, staring directly up at his window. Her face was veiled, and she wore a broadbrimmed black hat, so he couldn't see her face. But there was no doubt that she was looking at this particular window. There was something arresting and disquieting about her, something which sent cold fingers sliding around his spine. Even as he watched, the woman raised a black gloved hand and lifted the veil off her face. And it was the face from his nightmares, the same square, determined chin, the same wide-set, unwinking eyes, deep brown if he remembered correctly. It was a face he would never forget – could never forget. He could still see it closed in implacable hatred as the white-hot needle pierced his flesh, feel her twist the blade, and then wrench it free.

But as he looked down at the pale oval of a face, with its dark, intense eyes, he found he felt no anger, no rage – that had been burnt from him long ago, and all that was left was something approaching his old fear of the woman. As he watched, she stepped away from the railing that surrounded the pillar and crossed the street heading towards the doors of the post office.

'Downstairs,' he snapped, startling Martin Moore, 'downstairs immediately. A woman has just come in, tall, thin, dressed entirely in black. Follow her, see where she goes, find out what she wants.' As the captain raced from the room, John Lewis remained by the window, craning to see down past the pillars that supported the portico. He wondered what had brought her out; Madame Kitten, he knew, rarely if ever ventured out of doors, and it could hardly be to buy a stamp, now could it? She had people who would do that for her. And why was she standing down there staring up at his window, and how had she known which window was his . . ?

The questions were still tumbling through his head when there was a gentle tap on the door and Captain Moore stepped back in.

'Well, what did she do, what did she want?' he demanded fiercely.

'She . . . she wants to see you, sir,' Captain Moore said slowly. 'She's waiting outside,' he added.

'What!' Major Lewis, who had been turning back to

481

the window to catch sight of the woman leaving the building, whirled around again. 'Outside . . . outside this office?' he asked incredulously.

'Yes, sir,' the officer said uncomfortably. 'She said if I didn't bring her up, she would make a scene and tell everyone that the British Intelligence Service had an office in the building.'

'No-one would believe her,' Major Lewis said automatically.

'That's what I said, but she added that it might set some of the employees to thinking about the mysterious office up on the third floor.' He stopped. 'Who is she, sir? What does she want?'

The major looked over at him and smiled rather sourly. 'That is Madam Kitten,' he said, and then added sourly, 'Tilly Cusack's employer.'

'Oh,' the captain breathed. 'But what is she doing here?'

'I cannot imagine.' Major Lewis shook his head in astonishment at the sheer audacity of the woman. She had courage, there was no doubt about that – but then Katherine Lundy had never lacked for courage. He remembered the night she had come to the house in Clonliffe Road for Tilly Cusack, and he remembered the night she had lured him – he had realized that later! – into the Green to stab him.

'What should I do, sir?' Martin Moore asked, nervously.

'I think you'd better bring her in,' Major Lewis said, sounding equally nervous.

A moment later there was a tap on the door, and then it slowly swung open, and Katherine stepped in. John Lewis had forgotten the sheer presence of the woman; even from across the room, he could feel the tangible aura of authority that clung to her. She stood in the doorway and stared at him, and Major Lewis felt beads of perspiration pop out on his forehead at his hairline, and his knife wound suddenly itched. 'Madam Kitten,' he said, with as much confidence as he could muster.

'Major Lewis,' she acknowledged. She strode across the room. 'Just you and me, Major Lewis, if you please,' she said without turning around to look at Martin Moore.

'I would prefer it if Captain Moore remained.'

She smiled thinly. 'Why, surely you cannot be afraid of me? If he stays I walk out of here, Major Lewis, and you will regret it, that I swear,' she added ominously.

Major Lewis looked over at the captain and nodded briefly. 'Wait outside.'

'But, sir . . .'

'Wait outside, I said.'

'Sir, this woman hasn't been searched.'

'I am not carrying any weapons, I assure you,' Katherine said with a smile in Major Lewis's direction.

'Wait outside, Martin, please,' Major Lewis said wearily, and waited until the door clicked shut. The man and woman stood staring at each other for a few moments, and then he suddenly turned away, crossed to the young man's desk and pulled the chair out from behind it. Katherine nodded her thanks and sat down, arranging the folds of her dress around her. Major Lewis eased himself into his own well-worn chair and stared speculatively at the woman.

'It's been a long time,' he said finally.

'Nine years,' Katherine said without inflection or expression.

'I've thought about you – often,' he said, automatically fingering his old wound.

'Tilly Cusack thinks about you too – every time she dresses,' Katherine said, still maintaining the same neutral voice.

'And my son – how is he?' he asked quietly.

'You have no son, Major Lewis. Your child, perhaps, but my son.' The edge in her voice was warning enough for him to drop the subject; it had been his interest in their child, even more than his brutal treatment of Tilly, that had caused her to attack him.

He decided to leave it for the moment – although

there would come a time, he knew, when she would no longer have control over the boy, and then . . . well, he didn't know what would happen then. He had some vague idea of meeting the boy, perhaps getting to know him, befriending him, and then revealing his identity. But that was for the future. 'How did you know about this place?' he asked.

Katherine smiled and shrugged. 'You've never made any secret that you worked in the post office. And you forget that I buy and sell more than bodies,' she said.

'Your famous sources,' he said, a little bitterly.

Katherine nodded, but said nothing.

'Well, what brings you here?' he demanded finally.

'I've come to make a bargain with you,' she said, watching his face intently.

Major Lewis stared at her, speechless. When he finally got over the shock, he shook his head resolutely. 'I will have no dealings with you, woman.'

'That's a pity, major,' she said, but made no move to rise.

'I want nothing to do with you,' he stated flatly. 'You have nothing to say that would interest me.'

Katherine continued to stare at him, her face masklike.

'Now, I think if we've nothing more to say to one another, I would like you to leave. I don't think it's proper for a whore to be here.'

'I find your attitude offensive and inexcusable, Major Lewis.'

'I make no apology for it.'

'Still, it is a pity – especially when I may be in a position to give you the date of the forthcoming uprising!'

For a full five minutes the man and woman looked at each other in silence, almost as if they were willing or daring the other to speak first. Finally, Major Lewis reached for a small bell that was placed on the underside of his desk and pressed the button. Captain Moore immediately burst into the room, his service revolver in his hand, pointing at the woman.

'Perhaps if you could arrange for some tea to be sent up to us, captain . . .' John Lewis suggested, 'or better still, if you were to make it yourself, I would appreciate it.'

The captain rather sheepishly put away his gun and backed from the room. When the door had closed and they heard his retreating footsteps, Major Lewis turned back to Katherine. 'Just one question,' he said, 'and that is "why?"'

'Why am I doing it?'

'Just so.'

'There are several reason,' Katherine said, looking down at her hands which were folded in her lap. 'The main reason is that my husband Dermot Corcoran is involved with the IRB – but I'm sure you already know that,' she glanced up at Major Lewis and saw him nod briefly. 'In return for your guarantee that he will not be harmed, imprisoned or even implicated in the rising, and that my business will be left alone, I will pass on to you whatever information comes my way.'

Major Lewis sat back in his chair and smiled indulgently, feeling on safer ground now. 'It hardly seems reason enough to betray your friends.'

'They're no friends of mine,' Katherine snapped.

The major nodded. 'Just so. However, I'm unsure of the value of the information you possess or, indeed, may come to possess.' He sat forward and placed both hands palms down on the table. 'Perhaps if you were to give me some inkling of the type of information you are party to? I suppose it would be too much to ask how you came by this information?' he added, and then nodded, 'No, I suppose it would be too much.'

'My information concerns the IRB's association with Germany, the quantities and types of arms they have requested, details of their leaders and planners and, in time, the date of the rising.' The date was her trump card, and caution made her hold back from even admitting that she already knew it.

Captain Moore returned then carrying a tray with

485

two cups, a small, battered teapot and a small jug of milk. There were no spoons and no sugar. He set it down on the major's desk and backed from the room, his eyes never leaving Katherine's face.

Major Lewis poured tea for them both and then apologized because of the rather primitive conditions, but Katherine waved it aside.

'There are many in Dublin who don't even have this.'

Major Lewis nodded and sipped his tea. It was scalding and strong, and he grimaced with distaste. 'How do I know you're telling me the truth?' he asked.

Katherine shrugged and smiled. 'I was going to say you have to trust me, but I'm sure you will be able to check up on enough of my information to give you at least some idea whether I'm telling you the truth or not. Revolution makes strange bedfellows,' she added maliciously.

'I'm sorry, but I still don't see why you should betray the rising.'

'I've told you; in return for my husband's safety.'

'And that's the only reason?'

'Whatever else I am, I am British, and while I have a great love and regard for Ireland I am not prepared to see my husband killed for it, and the business which I have spent years building up destroyed overnight.' She paused and looked Major Lewis in the eye and said evenly, 'Nor am I prepared to be ruled by Germany.'

'You never answered my question as to the . . . shall we say, quality of your information.'

Katherine sipped her tea. She had thought about this before coming here. Major Lewis would have to be played along with over the next few months to ensure he would keep to his bargain to see that Dermot went free. So, it would be necessary for her to give him some information which would already be in his possession but which would not be available to the general public.

'You are aware that Sir Roger Casement is in Berlin at this moment arranging for arms to be sent over here?' she asked.

486

Major Lewis nodded slowly.

'But are you also aware that a firm commitment has already been made for the weapons to be supplied?'

Major Lewis continued to stare at her. He hadn't known, but had suspected it.

'And are you also aware that, as well as requesting rifles, the rebels are also looking for pistols, machine guns and, more importantly, German officers to help direct and organize them?'

Major Lewis said nothing. He hadn't known that – although he had for a while feared that that might be the case. But certainly, Katherine Lundy's information was good. All he had to do now was to make up his mind if she was genuine, or if this was all some elaborate trap. 'What you've given me was already in our files, I'll need something else, something solid,' he insisted.

What he was looking for, she knew, was something which would implicate herself, something which would prove her goodwill, which would in effect betray her, give him a hold of some sort on her . . . and there was only one thing she could tell him which might do that. 'Are you aware that top-secret high-level meetings have been held in my house over the past few weeks, the most recent being last night?'

Major Lewis looked at her for a long time and then finally nodded and sat back. 'I've known about the meetings,' he said, 'well, perhaps "known" is too strong a word. I suspected that they were taking place.' He sipped the strong, bitter tea again, and then came to a decision. 'Right, you have my personal guarantee that, no matter what happens, your husband will be allowed to go free.'

'I'll want it in writing.'

'Don't you trust me?'

'What do you think?' she asked.

Major Lewis nodded. 'If you call tomorrow, I'll have it for you.'

But Katherine shook her head. 'I won't be coming

487

back to this building, it's too public. We'll meet . . . in St Stephen's Green in future.'

'That's a little too public for my tastes,' Major Lewis protested.

'St Stephen's Green,' she insisted, rising smoothly to her feet. 'And bring that letter with you. What I would like you to do,' she added, 'is perhaps to adopt Dermot as a British Agent. In that case, if anything does go wrong, then the document can be produced and used to absolve him.'

'You've obviously thought this out well in advance.'

'I've been thinking about it for a long time,' she said. She put her hand on the door handle and then turned back to Major Lewis. 'I'll see you tomorrow in the Green around noon . . .'

'Where?' he asked.

'Where do you think?' she said and stepped out of his office, closing the door behind her.

Major Lewis stood, fingering his old wound, feeling both elated and curiously frightened at the same time. If Katherine Lundy was telling the truth – and it certainly looked as if she might be – he would be able to produce the evidence the British authorities needed to take this planned rebellion seriously. He pulled open the bottom drawer of his desk and lifted out a half-finished bottle of Scotch whisky and a dusty glass. John Lewis did not usually drink on duty, but this, he felt, was a very special day. If he pulled this off, he was looking at a promotion and possibly even a knighthood.

Captain Moore came back into the room, and looked quizzically at the older man. 'What did she want?' he asked.

'She wanted to help us. Would you believe it? Dublin's most powerful madam, and my bitterest enemy – and she wants to help us.'

'Help us – how?'

'She wants to help us prevent the rising!'

488

CHAPTER FORTY-TWO

'I haven't changed my mind,' Martin Moore said to Tilly. 'I meant what I said last night.'

Tilly nodded, but said nothing. The couple were strolling up along the banks of the River Liffey, and had just passed the impressive bulk of the Four Courts. Tilly stared down into the murky waters of the river, not even registering the foul odour that floated above the surface in an almost visible miasma.

They had met around noon on Bachelor's Walk, on the corner of O'Connell Street and O'Connell Bridge, and had walked aimlessly down the quays, past the Ha'Penny Bridge and up towards the Four Courts. During the warmer summer months it was a popular walk for Dubliners, and for most of them usually ended in the Phoenix Park. This early in the year, though, there were few willing to brave the chill wind whipping up along the river and they had the quays very much to themselves. For a while they had walked in virtual silence, occasionally making small talk about the weather – which was fresh and sunny, although still very cold – and it was only as they had passed by the grime-stained frontage of the Four Courts that Captain Moore had spoken.

'I wish . . . I wish I could believe you,' Tilly said finally. 'And that doesn't mean I'm calling you a liar,' she added quickly, seeing his expression change, 'because I'm not. Maybe you do honestly believe that you love me at this moment, but what about in a few weeks or months, or even a year's time, Martin, what about then?' she asked desperately.

'I don't think my feelings will change,' he said resolutely.

489

'Martin, you're a very lovely person and, although I've only met you twice before, I truly like you. I've always thought myself a good judge of men, and I think you're a very sweet and kind person. But you're doing this on the spur of the moment, perhaps out of some feeling of . . . of pity perhaps.' He opened his mouth to protest, but she hurried on, 'You're not looking into the future.'

He stopped suddenly and roughly turned Tilly towards him, looking down into her eyes. 'Listen to me,' he said slowly, his eyes hard and cold, matching his expression. 'I am engaged to a rather pretty young woman – a lifelong friend, a close friend of my family, whose father, like mine, is a Methodist minister. She is a lovely girl, pretty, sweet, dutiful, and she'll make the perfect wife, passive and obedient. But I don't want a wife like that,' he said fiercely, 'and, more importantly, I don't love her. I don't love her! And I think, in time, I could come to truly despise her, and I don't want that to happen. Now I've only met you twice before, but you're everything I'd want in a wife. You're strong and independent, a woman experienced in the world, cautious, cynical and . . . and loving, I believe.'

'Martin, I'm older than you, and not just in years,' she said softly.

'That means nothing to me.'

Tilly linked her arm through his, and they walked up the quays, heading towards the rather skeletal greenery of the Phoenix Park.

'I'd be a liar if I said I loved you,' she said finally.

'I fell in love with you the moment I met you,' he said.

'Martin, listen to me,' she said quietly, staring straight ahead, afraid to meet his eyes, knowing if she did so, then all her resolution would be swept away and she would give him the answer he wanted. 'Martin, every night for years, I "fell in love" at first sight. Old men, young men, rich and poor, men from all classes, every occupation, every station. I've "loved" them all and each

490

of them, I think, believed that they were the first man I ever loved. Certainly they were fooling themselves to make what they were doing seem just a little less sordid, but I helped them maintain that illusion. You see, Martin, I actually fell in love with them – that's one of the reasons I've survived this trade with my life and sanity intact. I convinced myself that I loved them, each and every one, and that in turn helped convince them that they loved me.' She took a deep sobbing breath. 'So you'll understand if I'm not really convinced when you say you fell in love with me at first sight.'

Captain Moore nodded silently.

'I could lie to you,' she continued slowly, picking each word with care, 'I could lie and accept your offer, but I don't think that would be fair either to you or to me. Your offer . . . well it's like a dream – a magical dream – come true for me. I told you before, every old whore wants a respectable man for a husband, and I know of many who'd jump at the chance, and not think twice about it. And I dare say if any of the girls in the house knew that I was even hesitating over an offer like yours . . . well, I dare say they'd call me for all sorts of a fool. And they'd probably be right.'

'No, no. I respect your decision, and your honesty and integrity. But it only reinforces my case, it only makes me all the more determined to have you for my wife.'

Tilly shook her head in exasperation. 'What about your family – and your fiancée? What will they think when you arrive home and say you've become engaged to an old whore?'

'Stop it!' he said suddenly, 'I won't have you denigrating yourself. I know it's only an act, something you are doing to try and frighten me off. But it won't work.' He took a deep breath and continued in a more sombre tone. 'As to my family, well . . .I don't know what's going to happen there. They'll be upset, naturally, and so will my fiancée, but when they find out that we really are in love, I think they'll come round.'

Tilly shook her head. 'Martin, they will never accept me. For a start, I'm too old, and when they inquire about my background, what do I tell them . . .?'

The young captain shook his head. 'I don't know, but I'm sure we'll think of something.' He took her by the arm and led her across the road, towards one of the gates that led into the huge park. 'And now, let's have no more of these "ifs" and "ands" and "buts"; let's just walk in the park like any other young couple.'

Tilly nodded reluctantly. But she knew that they would never be just like any other young couple.

Katherine was waiting for Major Lewis on the seat that overlooked the lake, warmly wrapped against the January chill. The bells of the surrounding churches were beginning to toll noon, the sounds sharp in the cold air, when the tall man with the military bearing strode in through the main gate and began the circuit around the pool to 'that' seat.

John Lewis hadn't been in the Green since the night in '07, but he remembered where the seat was – some things you never forget. As he marched along the smooth cinder path, he touched the paper in his pocket. It was a letter, written by him and addressed from Dublin Castle, which was the centre of British administration in Ireland, to Dermot Corcoran, giving him carte blanche, as it were, to spy on his fellow Volunteer and IRB friends. It also authorized him to pass freely through any British lines and allowed him access to all the buildings which would have been otherwise off-limits to a member of the public. It would, Major Lewis reflected, cover Katherine Lundy's every requirement.

And the document was a forgery.

It had certainly been written by him, but he had been very careful to mis-shape certain letters, and although the paper was from Dublin Castle and bore the crest, it was old stock which had been discarded because it had yellowed and become brittle and, while it might pass a cursory glance, it certainly would not stand up to a more intensive scrutiny ... which was exactly how Major Lewis planned it.

He owed Madam Kitten too much to forgive and forget so easily.

Major Lewis rounded the corner and saw the woman in black sitting on the bench, a small, brown, paper bag in her lap and the ground before her littered with crumbs. Scores of birds waddled or hopped or stalked round her feet, pecking at the crumbs, and from the distance she looked like any one of the scores of widow women – and many wore the black widow's garb in Dublin that year – who fed the birds in the Green. But Major Lewis knew he would never confuse this woman with anyone else; she sat too tall, her movements were too assured, too arrogant. This was a woman who had grown used to command, a controller, rather than one of the controlled. And yet again he marvelled at the change that had come over the timid servant girl he had once known.

He sat down on the far end of the bench and waited silently, until she had emptied the bag and then slowly and carefully folded it up into a small crumpled square.

'You came,' she said, almost as if she were surprised.

'Did you think I wouldn't?' he asked.

'There was always that possibility.'

'Not after I checked up on a little of what you had told me.'

'And?'

'And it turned out to be true,' he said.

'Whatever else I am, Major Lewis, I am not a liar.'

He nodded, but said nothing.

'Did you bring the paper?' she asked eventually, when it was clear that he wasn't going to speak again.

He took the envelope from his pocket and passed it over. She opened it and read down through the short note ...

'I, Major John Lewis, late of the East Lancashire Regiment, and a representative of His Majesty's Service in Ireland, do hereby certify that Dermot Corcoran, journalist, is empowered to gather and report on the activities of the nationalist organizations, especially the Irish Republican Brotherhood, commonly known as the IRB, and the Volunteers. He does so with my full knowledge and approval and is employed by me for that purpose. He is to be afforded every courtesy by His Majesty's Forces . . .'

Katherine re-read it slowly, nodding slightly, approving the contents. She then opened her small purse and took out a single sheet of paper which she carefully unfolded and compared with the sheet the major had given her. He slid over on the bench and saw it was a sheet of Castle notepaper. She held both up to the light and noted the crown and harp watermark in both and, apparently satisfied, returned both to her purse.

'I think some more trust is needed on both sides,' Major Lewis said, a little sarcastically.

'I think we know each other too well,' Katherine remarked.

'Well, can we finalize our agreement now?' he asked.

'I thought we did that yesterday,' Katherine said, sounding surprised.

'I'd like you to state it formally.'

'I've told you, major, I will pass on to you whatever information comes my way concerning the planned rising, in return for this piece of paper. Satisfied?'

He nodded. 'Satisfied.' He sat back and stared into the murky leaf-covered water. 'Well, have you anything for me today?'

'I know the IRB will be asking the Germans for 50,000 rifles . . .'

'You cannot be serious!'

'I am.'

'But there cannot be that many in the Brotherhood!' he said, half to himself.

'But what about the combined Volunteers, Connolly's Citizen Army, Countess Markievicz's Fianna boys, the Gaelic League . . . and even the general citizens who are

494

not members of any of the groups but who might take up arms on the day. Have you counted all of those?' Katherine took a certain delight in watching the colour drain from Major Lewis's face. He had obviously never even considered a combined revolution by all the various parties and private armies that had proliferated in Ireland over the past few years.

'Have ... have you any idea of the other arms they have requested?' Major Lewis asked.

'I know they were looking for a proportionate number of pistols – parabellums, I think they were – and machine guns, and as I told you, some German officers to help them.'

'And Casement is the man behind the weapons?' Major Lewis asked.

'He was aided last year by a rather sick young man called Plunkett, who travelled to the Continent under an assumed name and then went on to Berlin where he seems to have conducted the negotiations which actually provided the arms. There has also been a communication from Casement which said that they would be arriving soon, sometime within the next few months.'

'I need that date,' Major Lewis said fiercely, 'even more than the date of the rising. I must have that date.'

'You'll have it,' Katherine said, watching him closely. She patted her bag, 'this paper buys you a lot of information.'

'Well, let's hope it's good,' Major Lewis snapped.

'Let's hope this paper is genuine,' Katherine smiled.

Anne Lewis carefully sorted through the pile of papers in her husband's desk, looking for anything that might be of interest to her friends. But as usual there was no classified material, and to date she hadn't found anything of startling importance in the large, rolltop desk which had once been hers but which he had appropriated and moved up to the attic room he now used as a study. If he was working on important papers he seemed to carry them around with him and bring them to and from his

495

office in a small leather briefcase, which was not unlike a doctor's bag.

And there was nothing here today either. A sheaf of slightly yellowed and brittle paper bearing the crest of Dublin Castle was the only addition to the contents of the drawer as far as she could see; that and a lot of sheets which contained nothing but parts of sentences and odd letters, which were written in a hand that was like and yet unlike her husband's.

Finished with the desk, she stepped back and inspected it thoroughly, making sure that everything was as she had found it, and then she moved over to the fireplace. The small fireplace was a recent addition to the room, and one which she considered to be completely unnecessary, until she had discovered that her husband never threw anything away but burnt all letters, papers, envelopes and notes. On two previous occasions she had found tantalizing fragments of letters or memos, but so far there had never been anything which she could use.

The stones and grate were still warm and she cautiously poked through the ashes with a hatpin, being careful not to disturb them too much. There were two completely blackened papers on top, and in both cases she could distinguish the Castle crest which was embossed on to the heavy-wove paper and had defied the burning. Both sheets seemed to be copies of something – a pass, an authorization . . . she could make out that word . . . she could make out the name Dermot . . . and the words 'my full knowledge and approval . . .'

There was a second sheet under the first, and in the hope that it might be slightly more legible than the first she went back to her husband's desk, and removing two recently sharpened pencils, she slid them in under the uppermost page, attempting to lift it in one piece. But both it and the sheet underneath crumbled to fine flaky ashes, and she sat back on her heels, shaking her head in frustration. She felt she had been close to something; it looked as if her husband had been authorizing someone

– someone named Dermot – to spy . . . but on whom, on what? It had to be in connection with the coming rising – the Castle couldn't help but be aware that it would be soon – and every Irish rebellion to date had been betrayed by spies, usually Irish spies. She tried to run through the names of those she knew who were connected with the leaders of the rising; but no-one immediately came to mind.

She stood up and dusted off her hands and then looked around the attic room, ensuring that everything was as she had found it. She would pass on the information for what it was worth to the countess later, perhaps she would be able to make some use of it.

Anne pulled out her small-faced watch and looked at it. It was after two, and she was meeting William at three. They were both cycling around Dublin drawing up a list of what weapons the various groups had available for the coming rising.

But Anne Lewis also intended to discuss their future together.

CHAPTER FORTY-THREE

As the chill but dry January rolled into a cold and wet February, the sense of expectancy in Dublin grew. Everyone knew that something was in the air. The Volunteers and the Citizen Army marched and paraded with ever-increasing frequency, and real weapons replaced the dummy guns and sticks they had so often used. But surprisingly, the authorities didn't move on any of the known leaders of the groups or attempt to take their weapons, and the marches were conducted under the almost benevolent eye of the Dublin Metropolitan Police.

But what neither the police, nor indeed many of the group leaders knew, was that the sudden increase in the marches and parades was primarily so that when they gathered for their assault on the day of the rising, it would initially look like just another march.

However, another reason the authorities didn't react was because they had been assured – by Major John Lewis – that his spies would supply the date of the uprising in good time. He had suggested that a combined police and army force could act on the eve of the uprising and imprison the leaders and capture the arms and ammunition. And so his advice – and it was advice that was taken – was to wait; if they held their hand now, he promised them, they would get them all together and end this nonsense once and for all.

Katherine had passed on various pieces of news which she had overheard, including the fact that the German General Staff had committed themselves to sending 20,000 rifles, 10 machine guns and 5,000,000 rounds of ammunition to Ireland on an agreed date. What Katherine didn't tell Major Lewis was that the agreed date

498

was between Good Friday and Easter Saturday in April, and that the arms were to be landed in Limerick, on the south-west coast of Ireland.

Tilly Cusack had left the brothel and was now living with Martin Moore in a small house on Dorset Street, on the north side of Dublin. She refused to marry him and it was her compromise. Tilly also insisted that she appear as the captain's housemaid to ensure his reputation stayed intact, as well as allowing for the possibility of a reunion with his family and former fiancée. But Martin Moore loved her – or at least thought he did – of that she was certain, and she was beginning to feel more than just affection for him.

Initially Katherine Lundy had been delighted to see Tilly finally make a break from the brothel life. She offered to set Tilly up in a business of her own, but she had been politely refused. 'After all,' Tilly had said, 'I only know one life.'

Katherine knew that it was every street-girl's dream to find someone willing to keep them, if not as a wife, then certainly as mistress. This was a whore's dream come true, and if anyone deserved it, then surely Tilly Cusack did.

At first Katherine had been only too pleased to see her old friend settle down with someone who was apparently so much in love with her. However, Tilly's young man, as he soon came to be called, seemed very reluctant to meet with Madam Kitten and broke three separate dinner engagements at the last moment with feeble excuses. Eventually Tilly, putting it down to shyness and nerves, stopped trying to arrange a meeting between the two most important people in her life; they would meet all in good time, she reasoned.

But Martin Moore's apparent shyness had sparked a hidden intuition deep within Katherine, and she instinctively knew that something was wrong. When she investigated the young man's background and discovered his association with Major Lewis, her instincts flared into concrete suspicion. Her first reaction was

499

that he was obviously a spy, using Tilly as a means to get into the house, but when she carried that train of thought to its logical conclusion, she had to admit that something was awry: Martin Moore had moved Tilly out of the house, thus cutting off any chance he would have had of overhearing chance remarks or accidentally observing something amiss. And so, in deference to her friend's growing happiness – Tilly visited her nearly every day – Katherine had said nothing, and decided to wait before acting.

Katherine saw very little of her husband in those weeks, and even the children began to see him as a stranger. He was travelling the country officially on an assignment from the *Freeman*. Unofficially, he was instructing the various groups on the tactics for the coming rising. On the few occasions he had managed to get home, he had promised Katherine that everything would be well, 'when this is all over'.

Katherine meanwhile made plans that both of her children would be abroad for the coming Easter week, though she had determined that she herself would remain in Dublin, no matter what happened. She had planned that when the time was opportune – that is, when the uprising was doomed – she would use Major Lewis's pass to get Dermot away and then they would join the children in Liverpool, where she was planning to send them to stay with relatives. By the time they all returned to Dublin, the rebellion would be over, the leaders dead or imprisoned, and the movements they had organized and run would be disbanded. Dermot would have nowhere to go, and in time – she knew it would take time – things would return to a semblance of normality.

On the 17th of March that year, the feast of St Patrick, the patron of Ireland, Joseph Plunkett, the frail young man who had so excitedly worked out the details of the revolutionaries' arms requirements, strolled around Dublin with Dermot Corcoran with a large-scale map in his hands. Like any other tourists, they

500

paused every now and again to examine some building or stopped on a street corner to consult their map. The day was a public holiday and the city was crowded, not only with tourists, but also because the Volunteers had organized a huge march through the centre of the city, and in the throng the two went completely unnoticed.

At one stage they stopped and watched the Volunteers march by in ranks of four, some of them uniformed but the majority in their Sunday best, with armbands to distinguish them. 'I should be there,' Dermot said almost wistfully.

Joseph Plunkett had smiled and tapped the folded map against Dermot's hand. 'Do you not think this is more important, eh?'

Dermot nodded and grinned, 'Oh, I suppose it is.' He began pushing his way through the crowd, opening a way for the frailer Plunkett to follow.

When they were away from the crowd, and the marching song of the Volunteers was beginning to fade, Joseph Plunkett had said quietly, 'They're marching now – but we will be giving them some place to march to.'

The two men had been given the task of touring Dublin with an eye to the positioning of their troops and deciding which buildings were of sufficient strategic importance to take and hold. So far they had estimated that they needed somewhere near three thousand men to take control of the city, but with the combined forces of the Volunteers and the Citizen Army, numbers should be no problem.

However, they both knew that there were some protests from within the revolutionary movement from men who didn't see the value of a pitched fight within the city of Dublin. They argued that allowing themselves to be boxed in was madness, and there were some suggestions that a guerilla war conducted both in the cities and in the countryside would ultimately be more successful and less wasteful of lives.

But these voices had been overruled; this was not to

be a guerilla war, this was an uprising, and would be conducted to the highest standards of modern warfare. Their thinking was also influenced by the belief that the British authorities would refuse to shell and fire on some of the city's oldest and most respected buildings.

Pearse's orders to Plunkett and Corcoran had been clear; he needed to control and hold the city from its strategic vantage points, but he also wanted a central point, a headquarters . . . their task was to find it. There were several obvious choices, including Dublin Castle and the Four Courts, but these both suffered from being just a little outside the centre of the city. They needed somewhere important, a building which was used by Dubliners but which was unquestionably a centre of British Imperialism; they needed a building which would gain them the attention that they needed abroad, a place every tourist would be familiar with but – and even more importantly – they needed a building which could be relatively easily defended.

Finally, they decided on the GPO for their headquarters.

On the same day that Joseph Plunkett and Dermot Corcoran were working out the fine details for the taking of Dublin, Katherine was meeting with Major Lewis in their old haunt, St Stephen's Green. Their contacts over the past few months had, if nothing else, at least rendered them slightly more civil to one another, and Major Lewis found he had lost his initial fear of the woman – but not the hatred and desire for revenge that nestled deep within him.

Sometimes the sudden intensity of his emotion would frighten him; these sudden flashes of rage always occurred following a meeting with her, just as he was beginning to realize that he still wanted her, still lusted after her. Only then, when he realized that he could never have her, could never have any woman, would the rage take him.

They met on the small, humped-back, picturesque

bridge over an arm of the lake. Major Lewis was already there when Katherine arrived; he was leaning on the parapet smoking one of his Turkish cigarettes and staring up at the white-fronted elegance of the Shelbourne Hotel across the road. Unlike many other Dubliners celebrating St Patrick's Day, he was not wearing a sprig of shamrock in his lapel.

'That husband of yours is beginning to appear with ever-increasing frequency in my reports,' Major Lewis said without preamble as Katherine joined him on the bridge.

Katherine glanced at him and then turned to stare down into the crystal clear water.

'It seems his involvement with the movement is very deep indeed,' Major Lewis continued. Dermot's name hadn't appeared on any of the major's reports, even though his files on the leaders of the forthcoming rising were growing daily, but he had no intention of letting Madam Kitten know that. The more frightened she was for her husband's safety, the more willing she would be to supply the information he needed – and needed desperately now. If anything went wrong at this stage, his career would be finished; he had promised too much to too many people.

'I know you will get him out of any trouble,' Katherine said softly. 'After all, he is one of your spies, remember?' she added maliciously.

Major Lewis allowed a thin smile to hover over his lips and then he too nodded. 'Yes, he does have my authorization.' He pulled strongly on the cigarette and then tossed the butt into the water. It sputtered and hissed and a drake came paddling out from the reeds to investigate. 'You wanted to see me,' he said, more a statement than a question.

Katherine nodded, and then turned away from the water. She felt they were too exposed just standing there on the small bridge. 'We will walk,' she commanded imperiously, and Major Lewis obediently fell into step

503

beside her. 'I have some details on the arms shipment,' she said quietly, not looking at him.

Major Lewis nodded slightly, careful not to react. This was the information he had been waiting for.

'Apparently the German Foreign Office contacted their man in Washington who in turn contacted John Devoy, who relayed the message on to Dublin. Two or three trawlers will arrive at Fenit Pier in Tralee Bay in County Kerry sometime between the 20th and the 23rd of April. They will be guided in by pilot boats who will be lying in wait off the north end of Inistooskert Island.' She glanced across at the brooding man. 'I think that should be enough for you, Major Lewis, don't you? Capture those weapons and there will be no rising. You'll be a hero, and I would say almost certain to be knighted,' she said, adding somewhat bitterly, 'not that you deserve it.'

'But you'll have your husband, children and business,' Major Lewis snapped. 'There are no winners in this game. If this nonsense goes ahead, it is almost certain that your husband would be killed, and everyone and every place associated with the rising – no matter how indirectly – would be subjected to the most intense investigation and search. Your friends in high places wouldn't be able to help you, and I don't think even you have the money to rebuild your house, Madam Kitten. And what about you, personally? Why, as the owner of the house where the meetings were held, complicity would be assumed and you would be taken into custody and charged, and what would happen to your children then? Well, your boy is what now – sixteen, seventeen? Certainly old enough to have been involved in the rising. Perhaps he was even a member of Countess Markievicz's militant boy scouts, the Fianna, eh? And as for your little girl – well, I think an orphanage for her, don't you? No, no,' he shook his head violently, 'you've far too much to lose if this rebellion goes ahead.'

'We both stand to lose much, Major,' she said coldly.

Patrick, her son, was not a member of the Fianna, although there had been a long and bitter argument with him and Dermot, but Katherine had been adamant, and the boy hadn't been allowed to join. The Fianna were rather like the English boy-scout movement, but instead of teaching them wood craft the countess had instructed them in survival and marksmanship, and had drilled them until they were virtually an army in themselves.

'What about the date of the rising?' Major Lewis asked suddenly. 'Have you any idea when that will take place?'

'No,' she lied, 'but if the arms are arriving in April, then I should imagine the rising will be shortly afterwards, when they have had time to distribute the guns around the country.'

Major Lewis nodded, considering. 'The end of May, or early June, perhaps . . .'

'Of course, when you capture the arms, they may decide to rise up immediately.'

'Not without weapons,' Major Lewis said confidently. 'They would be wiped out. No, if we have the guns, we have the rising.'

'Ireland has risen before,' Katherine reminded him grimly, 'and when the guns weren't available, they used pikes, forks and spades, knives, stones, sticks and their bare hands.'

'No guns, no revolution,' Major Lewis said decisively and walked off, leaving Katherine standing alone on the cinder path that led around the lake.

Katherine continued on down the path and came to her favourite seat, the seat of all memory, she had once jokingly called it. Despite the lack of people in the park at this time of year, she did spot one young couple walking around the lake, just like she and Dermot had done . . . oh, so long ago, a lifetime ago. She wondered what had become of them, how had they drifted apart. Certainly, Dermot's personal crusades and then his involvement with the Volunteers and finally with the IRB hadn't helped, neither had her own concern to make the brothel the most luxurious and profitable in Dublin. They had both gone their separate ways, both seemingly oblivious to the break-up in their relationship, and it was too late now. She was honest enough with herself to know that it would never be the same again, could never be the same. Dermot wasn't going to thank her for what she was doing; he was going to see it as a betrayal. Indeed, it might just be the final straw that would break them up completely. But if it was, then at least her conscience would be clear; she would have saved his life, and perhaps that would repay the countless small kindnesses he had extended to her when she had first come to Ireland all those years ago, and then again in the early years of their marriage.

A nanny walked by holding two small children – twins – by the hand. If Katherine had any regrets, it was that she hadn't had more children. She shook her head slightly. She knew that there were many woman who couldn't have any and would have been envious of her two, boy and girl, both strong and healthy, and intelligent. And whatever her feelings for Lewis were, there always remained a lingering sense of gratitude to him because he had given her Patrick. And Senga, glorious charming Senga. Every time she looked at the child, she was reminded of that brief holiday she had spent with Dermot in the west of Ireland. If Patrick had been conceived in passion, she liked to think that Senga had been conceived in love.

Sometimes, when she was feeling depressed – as she was now – she fell to wondering how the years the children had spent in the brothel, with its strange atmosphere, would affect them in later life. And now, of course, with Dermot away from home so much, she wondered how that would affect them. But at least Patrick, who was almost a man now, seemed to show no ill effects. The only thing which troubled her was that, although he was living in a house full of women, where nudity was common and the opportunities for his sexual education frequent, he seemed to show no interest

506

in women, either young or old. She wasn't entirely sure how he reacted to men, but she didn't think he was a homosexual. In many ways he reminded her of his father, Major Lewis, in that he was slightly distant, cold and impersonal, with very little of what Granny O'Neill – Lord rest her – would have called 'nature' in him.

Senga was educated by an order of teaching nuns. The nuns were unaware of Katherine's occupation, and the child was taken by a circuitous route to and from school every day by one of the male servants. Next term she would continue her studies at a boarding school in the country which was also run by the same religious order. Katherine was determined that Senga would never become involved – no matter how indirectly – with her own occupation, and the less the child knew about it the better.

She shivered as a cold gust whipped across the lake, rippling the water and spattering icy droplets across her lightly made-up face. She stood up and headed for one of the Green's side gates. She decided she would slip into one of the cafés on Grafton Street and have a cup of tea to settle her head which was pounding with a tension headache. It invariably happened after one of her encounters with Major Lewis. She would never allow him to know – or even suspect – but Katherine Lundy was still terrified of the man. She hid her fear behind a mask of contempt and indifference, but deep down the serving maid still lurked, and still harboured a serving girl's awe of the strong, handsome, English army officer.

She didn't like betraying her husband and his friends – but it was necessary, and Madam Kitten always did what was necessary. But she couldn't shake the impression – that strange intuitive feeling that had served her so well in the past – that it would all be in vain. The rising had to take place. For the various organizations to survive they needed an uprising, a violent release of all the pent-up energy and frustration. Too many words over far too many years had created a picture of a

507

magically free Ireland. Indeed had almost promised it. And too many people now believed in the promise. They saw only the destination – they didn't see the long and bloody path that led to it.

Many would die, but Katherine was only too aware that in Ireland dead men's words were listened to and heard more than those of any live speaker.

She turned into one of the cafés at the top of Grafton Street and found herself a window seat, where she could watch the people moving to and fro outside. She was still a great 'person-watcher', it was a trait she had picked up from Dermot, and she still took an almost childish delight in ascribing occupations to the people she saw. Some were easy: clerks, messenger-boys, manual workers, shop girls, factory girls – paler complexions – ladies' maids, butlers and police. But as she looked at them, she wondered how many of them were revolutionaries. This smug city would never be the same if the rebellion came.

She spotted a familiar figure moving through the crowd and was about to stand up and wave to him when she saw whom he was with, and then she deliberately lowered her head and stared into her weak golden-coloured tea.

Dermot Corcoran and Joseph Plunkett walked slowly past the entrance to the café on their way around the Green to look at two possible positions for garrisons, the Shelbourne Hotel and the Royal College of Surgeons. The young man was pale and obviously exhausted and was leaning heavily on Dermot's arm, but his face was set and determined.

And looking at him, Katherine suddenly realized that the rising would take place no matter what; it wasn't arms and ammunition which made a rebellion, it was people.

On April 9th, a single ship, the *Aud*, left the port of Lubeck for Ireland with its consignment of arms, 20,000 Krnka rifles which the Germans had captured from the

508

Russians at Tannenberg and had decided to pass on to the Irish rebels . . . because the weapons weren't good enough for their own troops.

The revolution was underway.

Barely five days later, Joseph Plunkett's niece arrived in New York with instructions for the Germans that under no circumstances were the arms to be landed before the night of Sunday the 23rd. Someone had discovered that there was a full moon on the night of Tuesday. But, unfortunately, the *Aud* had no radio equipment on board and there was no way for the message to be passed along, so the dates remained unchanged.

Three days later, Sir Roger Casement left Germany in the submarine U-20, but the craft had to turn back because of faulty diving gear and Casement transferred to the U-19. What no-one knew – neither the Irish revolutionaries, nor the Germans – was that Casement, bitterly resentful of his treatment by the Germans, and appalled by the notoriously defective and ineffective Russian rifles they had sent, was coming home to try and prevent the uprising.

A message arrived in Dublin, advising the leaders of the departure of the arms, and it was followed, four days later, by another advising of Casement's imminent arrival. The news was relayed to the leaders of the revolution by Joseph Plunkett, speaking in a voice a little above a whisper in Katherine Lundy's back sitting room.

It was destined to be the last meeting in the house.

Katherine's meeting with Major Lewis was brief and hurried. She had been standing outside the GPO for over an hour before he had looked down from his third floor office and spotted her leaning against the rails that surrounded the tall pillar. He had marched through the main doors of the building a few moments later, pausing to buy a small posy from the flower- and fruit-sellers that surrounded the bottom of the tall monument. When she saw him approaching she turned away and then surprised him by ducking into the entrance to the pillar itself. The interior was hollow and it was possible to climb the winding staircase to the top of the one-hundred-and-twenty-foot tower.

When he saw what she was doing, he walked across the street and looked in the window of Tyler's shoe shop and waited until he saw the black hat appear at the rail high above his head. Then he quickly crossed to the entrance and paid his penny to climb the pillar.

April had been unseasonally wet and no-one else seemed inclined to brave the possibility of another shower nor the icy wind that whipped about the top of the pillar, and Major Lewis and Katherine found they had the small railed walkway to themselves.

'Were you waiting long?' Major Lewis asked, noting the sodden hem of her long dress and the discolouration on the tips of her shoes. Her umbrella was soaking.

'An hour or so.'

'Why didn't you come in?' he asked, leaning over the edge of the rail and looking down the broad length of O'Connell Street.

'Because I didn't want your assistant to see me,' she said quietly, standing back against the base of the statue of Nelson, shivering slightly in the breeze.

Major Lewis glanced back over his shoulder in surprise.

'I don't want him reporting it to Tilly,' she explained.

'You don't mean he's still seeing her?' The surprise was evident in his voice.

'So I was right, you did order him to become close to her!'

'Only so we could get someone on the inside of the house. We knew the IRB were meeting there and we thought he might see something . . .' he shrugged. 'But then you came along and suddenly there was no further need for him to continue with the mission.'

'You didn't know that they had set up house together . . .?'

'No, I didn't even know he was still seeing the woman. Well, well,' he shook his head slightly, although Katherine wasn't sure whether it was in surprise or admiration.

'I think this will be the last time we'll meet,' Katherine said quietly.

Major Lewis spun around, something like alarm on his face. 'What do you mean?'

'Oh, you needn't look so worried,' she smiled coldly. 'I'm not about to betray you. The arms are on course to arrive sometime between the 20th and the 23rd, as you know. Casement is also on his way here in a German submarine and should be landing on or around the same date.'

Major Lewis's eyes gleamed. To have the guns and Casement together would be quite a coup!

'You will hold to your original promise?' Katherine asked slowly, watching him closely. 'My husband, children and premises will be safe?'

'You have the authorization,' Major Lewis said carefully, 'and my word.'

Katherine Lundy nodded; she had to be satisfied with that. Then she said slowly, 'The rising is planned for Easter Sunday.' She turned away abruptly, walking slowly and carefully down the smooth damp steps.

Major Lewis turned back to the rail and waited until he saw the woman in black appear and hurry down Henry Street. His grip tightened on the iron rail in a white-knuckled grip and the smile on his face was tight and triumphant. He had it now; the rising was his!

CHAPTER FORTY-FOUR

'I'm afraid I have to go into work today,' Martin Moore said to Tilly. He was sitting on the edge of the bed, having just brought in her morning pot of tea.

She opened her blue eyes and blinked sleepily at him. 'But it's Saturday morning,' she said, struggling to sit up. 'Easter Saturday; I thought we were going shopping today.'

He leaned over and kissed her gently on the lips. 'I'm sorry, truly sorry, but something important happened yesterday. I'm sorry I didn't have a chance to tell you but you were asleep when I came in last night.'

She pushed back her hair and nodded as she reached for the teapot, and poured two cups. 'You were late, and I didn't hear you come in.'

'It was around two, I think,' he said. He sipped his tea. 'I don't think I've ever spent a busier day. We captured a German spy bringing in a shipload of arms for the rebels yesterday.'

'My God – so it's true, they are planning rebellion!'

Martin shook his head, surprised at the disbelief in her voice. 'Well, we always knew they were planning a rising, but I suppose we never thought it would actually come to it. But it seems that they did contact the Germans through a fellow named Roger Casement, and he seems to have made the arrangements for the guns to be sent over. Why, the man even had the nerve to come here himself – in a submarine no less. But we caught him,' he added, just a little smugly.

'And what about the guns?' Tilly asked in an awed whisper.

'The German captain blew up his own ship. They're at the bottom of Tralee Bay.'

'Well, that should put a stop to any thoughts of a rising,' Tilly remarked. Like many Dubliners, she had little time and even less sympathy for the rebels and their aims.

Martin finished his tea quickly and then stood up. 'And I'll tell you something else,' he said, enjoying her expression. 'The rising was due to start tomorrow!'

'Easter Sunday?' she asked, startled.

He grinned at her reaction. 'Well, I don't think it will happen now. With this Casement chap out of the way and the guns lost, they can't very well do anything, can they?'

'I suppose not,' Tilly said, slowly allowing herself to fall back against the heaped pillows. A sudden thought struck her. 'But how did you know that the guns were coming?'

Captain Moore looked vaguely uncomfortable. He shrugged. 'I don't know for sure, perhaps the information was passed on by a spy.' What he didn't add was that he was sure that spy had been Madam Kitten.

'Betrayed,' Dermot almost spat, 'we've been betrayed! Casement captured and the guns lost. It's incredible . . . incredible,' he repeated, pacing around the room.

Katherine, who was sitting in one of the large armchairs by the fire, attempting to read the previous day's newspaper, looked up, trying desperately – but failing – to suppress a smile.

Dermot caught the smirk and glared at her. 'What's so funny?' he demanded

'You,' she said, 'you're running around like a . . . like a . . . well, I don't know what you're like, except that it's funny. Why don't you sit down and tell me, coolly and calmly, what has happened, eh?'

She saw the look of suspicion and mistrust that darted behind his eyes and suddenly grew angry. 'Oh, for Christ's sake, Dermot, I think you can trust me; I know almost as much about the rising as you.'

'Do you know when the rising was due to take place?' he demanded, sitting down in the armchair facing her.

Katherine looked him straight in the eye and lied, 'No, I've no idea, except that it must be soon.'

Dermot sat back and folded his arms. 'Aye, well, even your precious organization couldn't find that out. Well, it was due very soon; it was going to take place this weekend in fact, this Sunday. We were getting guns from Germany – and don't look at me like that – and with 10,000 men in the field, and 20,000 guns we could have taken this country.'

'And now?' she asked, looking away from him, carefully folding the newspaper and placing it on a side table.

'I don't know what will happen now. The Volunteers are already split; their leader Eoin MacNeill will have nothing to do with an armed rebellion, but perhaps Pearse will be able to get around him.'

'And if he doesn't?'

'Well then, I think we might just go ahead without MacNeill.'

'How were you going to organize an armed uprising without the leader of the Volunteers being aware of what was happening?' she asked, the smile on her face belying the seriousness of the question.

'We were going to begin our traditional Easter Sunday manoeuvres this weekend – except that they wouldn't have been just manoeuvres.'

'In other words, you'd trick men into taking part in the rising?' she asked.

'I'd hardly call it a trick; after all, when they joined the Volunteers, they knew that there was every chance that it would eventually lead to an uprising.'

'I still think it's a shabby trick.'

'Well, I don't know what is going to happen now. When MacNeill gets to hear of Casement's capture and the loss of the guns, he'll soon put two and two together and realize that Pearse and the others have been only using him as a front.'

514

There was a gentle knock on the door and they both looked up as the door opened and Nuala, Katherine's maid, wheeled in a small trolley bearing a silver teapot, fine bone-china cups with matching plates and a small plate of pastries. 'Mickey thought you might like some refreshment,' she said, looking from Katherine to Dermot.

'Thank you, Nuala, and thank Mickey for me, that was very thoughtful.' When the maid had left, Katherine used the opportunity while pouring the tea to ask Dermot if it might be a good idea to come away for a holiday now, 'Since the rising has been temporarily abandoned,' she added.

'But I can't leave Ireland now, not with the way things are.'

'But you've just told me that it looks as if the whole event is off,' she protested.

'I'll wait and see what Pearse says.'

Katherine pased his cup over. 'I suppose asking you not to see Pearse nor to participate in any of his plans would be foolish on my part?'

'Katherine, it would only lead to an argument, you know that. You know my reasons for becoming involved, and even if you don't like them the least you could do is to respect them.'

'If the rising is called off – if Pearse cancels it – will you come away with me to join the children?' she demanded.

'I would prefer not to leave Dublin . . .' he began, and then he saw the look in her eye and smiled. 'All right then, I'll go. I know these past few months have been hard on you, but it's nearly over now; one way or another the end is in sight. If it comes to fighting, I'll fight, and when the fighting is done, we can begin again, you and I. In a newer, freer Ireland I should be someone of importance in the government,' he added, somewhat proudly.

'What will you be?' she asked, playing the game.

'Well, I'm not sure yet; only a few posts have been

515

settled, and of course Padraic Pearse is President of the Provisional Government. Perhaps I will become the Minister for Information.'

'What position will I hold?' Katherine asked, with a wicked grin, her meaning clear. 'Something horizontal, perhaps?' Dermot coloured deeply and turned his attention to his tea.

Anne Lewis arrived at William Sherlock's house shortly after two that Saturday afternoon. She brought with her news of the guns' destruction and the capture of a man who called himself Richard Morton, but who was actually Sir Roger Casement. When she arrived she found the Countess Markievicz already present. The countess was sitting by the window of the large sitting room, absently working the cylinder on a revolver that seemed far too large for her frail hands. Six silver-topped brass-jacketed bullets stood in a line on the windowsill in front of her.

'You've heard?' Anne demanded breathlessly.

'This morning,' the countess said slowly.

'What happens now?' Anne asked, looking around for William, but he had disappeared to make some tea.

'Now we wait,' the countess said. 'Pearse or Connolly will be in touch.' She picked up the bullets one by one and looked at them closely, and then began to load them into the revolver. 'But if you are asking my opinion, then I think we should go ahead.'

'But with no arms?' Sherlock asked, coming back into the room, carrying a tray, 'and what about Casement?'

'You're forgetting we have some weapons,' the countess said, closing the cylinder with a click, 'and we can free Casement later.'

That afternoon dragged on into an eternity. After the first hour or so conversation lagged, and Constance Markievicz resumed her position by the window, systematically unloading and reloading the pistol. Anne took up a position by one of the other windows that had a good view of the main road beyond the gate. She

516

cupped her chin in her hands and stared through the glass. It was about twenty minutes later that she realized she hadn't in fact been looking at the road, she had been daydreaming. William Sherlock paced the room, his slippers making no sound on the thick-piled carpet, his head bent and with a pencil in his hand, tapping silently against his leg. Occasionally he would stop at his desk and scribble a cryptic note, and then resume his pacing.

Around six o'clock a figure hurried up the driveway, his feet crunching loudly on the gravel, bringing the three inside fully alert. Constance Markievicz pulled back the hammer of her pistol, the sound loud and sharp in the silence. The figure paused with his foot on the step and looked directly towards the sitting-room window.

'It's Dermot Corcoran,' the countess said, breathing a sigh of relief, easing the hammer down on the gun.

When William led the young man into the room a few moments later, both women were shocked at his appearance. He was shivering and almost frighteningly pale, and his lips were drawn into a thin, almost invisible line. He silently emptied the glass William handed him, and then drank a second, not even tasting the fine brandy. Finally he sat down in a chair by the fire and buried his head in his hands.

'It's all off,' he said eventually, almost sobbing in frustration. 'The rising is cancelled.'

A stunned silence greeted his remark, as they all saw years of work blow away like so much dust.

'What happened, Dermot?' the countess asked eventually.

'Eoin MacNeill's betrayed us!' he suddenly shouted, and then immediately sobered. 'I'm sorry,' he apologized.

'Tell it slowly,' the countess advised. 'William, give him another drink.'

Dermot drained half the glass in one swallow, and then gasped as the fiery liquor burned his throat.

517

'There's little enough to tell,' he said finally. 'When MacNeill heard that Casement had been captured in Kerry, and a cargo of guns had gone down, he knew that Pearse and Clarke, and those who were loyal to them, had been planning something behind his back. He went to Pearse's school where they argued violently. It ended with MacNeill accusing Pearse of usurping his authority as leader of the Volunteers.' Dermot drank again and shrugged. 'I'm not sure what happened then; perhaps Pearse admitted that the Irish Republican Brotherhood was working under the cover of the Volunteers. However, I do know that he told him about the rising which was planned for Sunday. MacNeill flew into a rage at this and swore that he would stop it at all costs . . .' Dermot paused and took a deep breath. 'I've just come from the *Freeman*: MacNeill has inserted an advertisement in tomorrow's – Sunday's – paper ordering the cancellation of all Volunteer manoeuvres, parades and marches.'

'When the Volunteers read the newspaper, no-one will turn up,' Anne Lewis whispered.

'We need all the Volunteers – all 10,000 of them – if this rising is to be a success,' Countess Markievicz said grimly.

'Exactly,' Dermot nodded glumly, 'but he's destroyed any chance of that.'

'How could this be allowed to happen?' Sherlock asked.

Dermot shook his head. 'We were afraid of too many people knowing – too many plans have been lost that way in the past. But I suppose we went overboard in our secrecy, and it was probably a mistake to keep MacNeill in the dark about the activities of the movement he was supposed to head. He has always been opposed to a military action, we've always known that.'

'I never thought he would betray us,' Sherlock said quietly.

The countess shook her head. 'He hasn't betrayed us;

518

he has merely stayed true to his principles.' She looked at Dermot. 'What happens now?'

He shrugged. 'Now we wait and see what happens.'

Major Lewis and Captain Moore stood before the Lord Lieutenant's desk in the lush opulence of the Viceregal Lodge. Ivor Churchill, Baron Wimborne, Lord Lieutenant-General and Governor General of Ireland slowly read through the thick report that the two men had presented to him. The large jovial man kept shaking his head, seemingly in astonishment.

'Sir Matthew Nathan has seen this report?' he asked suddenly, startling both men.

'Yes, sir, we passed on a copy of the report to the Under-Secretary as soon as we had it in our hands.'

The large man looked up at Major Lewis from under his bushy eyebrows. 'And what were his recommendations?'

'He suggested that we await your instructions,' Major Lewis said dryly.

'Have you any suggestions of your own, Major Lewis?'

'I would strongly recommend the arrest and incarceration of the leaders of the various groups involved here, the IRB, the Volunteers, the Citizen Army. I would suggest a raid on Liberty Hall where certainly arms and ammunition are being stored, as well as a raid on the Countess Markievicz's house where she trains her Fianna boys.'

Lord Wimborne tapped the paper. 'But it says here that the guns have sunk and this Casement has been captured. Surely that puts an end to this damp squib of a rising?'

'This consignment of guns has been destroyed, sir, but the revolutionaries have received supplies in the past. No, sir; allow me to arrest them all now, rather than leaving it to chance,' Major Lewis said forcibly.

'And yet, if we take action now, it could have disastrous consequences.'

'In what way, sir?' Major Lewis was desperately attempting to control his temper.

The Viceroy looked startled. 'Why, major, it could be the spark needed to ignite a massive civil disturbance.'

'Surely you are not suggesting that we do nothing about this?' Major Lewis said coldly.

'No, I certainly am not. I will discuss the matter with Nathan, and the Commissioner of Police if necessary, and we will draw up a plan of action . . .'

'For Christ's sake, we're talking about an armed rebellion here,' Major Lewis exploded. 'Now you have the facts, the numbers, the leaders, the dates, even the cursed day it's due to happen. You must do something about it!'

'You forget yourself, Major,' Wimborne said icily. 'Your department has done excellent work, but the decision is now mine.'

'You're not going to do anything – are you?' Major Lewis said in a whisper, 'you're not going to do a bloody thing!'

'I will admit I am not convinced that anything will take place this weekend, in view of the events of the last few days.' A perfectly manicured finger tapped the report.

'Well then, you're a fool, a stupid, bloody fool,' Major Lewis hissed.

He had turned and was already heading for the door when the Viceroy, recovering from the shock, called after him, 'That will be all, Major Lewis.'

On Sunday morning, the church bells rang out over a bright and sunny Dublin city, making a pleasant change after two weeks of almost continuous rain.

In the bedroom of the house in Dorset Street, Tilly Cusack stood naked before the window and looked out across the damp streets shining in the bright sunlight, and hugged herself closely. She looked back at Martin Moore, 'I think it's going to be a marvellous weekend,' she said.

Less than a mile away, Katherine Lundy was sitting up in bed, reading the advertisement in the morning paper advising the Volunteers that there would be no manoeuvres this weeked, and countermanding all previous orders. She folded the paper and lay back on the pillow, closing her eyes with relief. She could feel the heat from Dermot's body as he lay alongside her and she gently, delicately ran her fingers down his arm. So, it was all over. And she thanked God for that.

The seven-man Military Council of the IRB met in Liberty Hall just before noon that Sunday morning. Following a brief discussion, they decided the rising would go ahead at noon on the following day, Monday.

CHAPTER FORTY-FIVE

Katherine came slowly awake, dimly aware of a metallic jingling sound in the room. She rolled over in bed, and her left arm reached out to the place where her husband's warm body should be; but the bed was empty.

A sudden chilling premonition brought her fully awake . . . to find Dermot dressed in his green Volunteer uniform. There was a belt draped across a chair with a holster on one side and long bayonet on the other. A Lee Enfield rifle was propped against the end of the bed, and there were two long bandoliers of ammunition curled on the floor. At the foot of the bed itself there was also a pistol, with two small boxes of what Katherine guessed to be ammunition, a pair of field glasses, and a soft brimmed hat, with one side pinned up.

Katherine sat up in bed, something solid and leaden settling into the pit of her stomach, and in silence watched her husband strap on his belt, wrap the two bandoliers around his shoulders, and then check his pistol before slipping it into its holster and closing the strap. Without looking at her he picked up the rifle and worked the bolt, the sound harsh and metallic in the room. Holding it in his left hand he strung the field glasses around his neck, and stuffed the boxes of ammunition into his pockets. Finally, he picked up his hat and slowly turned to his wife.

'I thought it had been called off,' she said in a whisper.

He shook his head slightly. Katherine noticed that he was unusually pale and his eyes were glittering far too brightly. 'There was a change of plan yesterday . . .' He shrugged and sounded almost embarrassed. 'Well, we had to do something, we couldn't just let all the planning

522

and preparation . . .' His voice trailed off. 'The date was set for today, noon today,' he added.

'Why?' she asked simply.

He placed his hat on his head and spent a few moments adjusting it until he thought it was at the correct angle. 'You know why; we don't have to go into all that again.'

'But the order was given to cancel all manoeuvres – you saw the notice in the paper yourself,' she protested, 'you'll have no support.'

'We made arrangements to contact our men yesterday; they'll be there,' he said, but Katherine detected the lack of confidence in his voice.

Katherine threw back the covers and climbed out of bed. Her fine chiffon nightdress was beginning to stick to her with the icy sweat which had suddenly washed over her. 'You don't expect to win, do you?'

Dermot made a minor adjustment to the tilt of his hat.

'Do you?' she demanded.

'Yesterday . . . well, yesterday, I would have said yes. Today,' he shook his head and made an attempt at a smile. 'Today, I just don't know, Katherine. I just don't know.' He went over to the dressing table and pulled open a drawer, and returned with a large, leather-and-gilt-bound bible and handed it to her.

Surprised, she took it without a word and opened it, half-expecting to find an inscription inside the cover. Dermot smiled at her startled expression. 'It's a derringer,' he explained, lifting a small double-barrelled pistol from the compartment inside the dummy book and handing it to her. 'It's silver-plated and the grips are mother-of-pearl.'

'It's lovely,' she said, bemused, turning the gun around and around in her hands. It was a beautiful weapon, small, but with an almost palpably lethal air about it. She realized it was something to do with the fact that, for it to be really effective, one would have to be very close to the target.

523

Dermot showed her how to break open the gun and load in the two snub-nosed bullets in the separate chambers which were situated one on top of the other.

'Why, what's it for?' she asked at last.

He smiled. 'For no reason, other than your own protection if things go wrong today.'

'Do you expect things to go wrong?' she asked, beginning to shiver now as the sweat dried on her body.

He suddenly reached for her and pressed her into his arms. She felt him shake his head slightly. 'I don't know. I don't know what's going to happen today. I only wish the children were here – I would have liked to have said good-bye to them.'

'Don't go,' she said quickly, 'please don't go.'

'I have to . . .'

'No . . . no you don't. You're going out to get yourself killed for a cause that's already lost.'

'I have to go,' he repeated stubbornly. 'I've championed this cause with words for too many years – and where has it got me? Nowhere. Nothing has changed, Katherine, there are still children dying of malnutrition in this city. Well, now I have a chance to do something about it, something definite, something tangible. I'm doing it in the hope that my children will grow up in a better city.'

'Would it not be better if they had a father to grow up with?' she said, and then she moved him away slightly, because his bandoliers were pressing against her breasts. Holding him at arm's length, she looked deep into his eyes. 'Will you be coming home tonight?'

'I don't think so.'

'If I want to find you . . .?'

'I'll be fighting with Pearse and Connolly in the GPO.' He said it almost proudly. 'I should be in the thick of it.'

Katherine's fingers tightened on his shoulders. 'Tell me honestly now . . . What do you think will happen?' she demanded fiercely.

'There are really only two alternatives. Either the British will capitulate and grant our demands . . .'

Katherine smiled derisively. 'Or?'

'Or they'll bring in more troops and kill the lot of us.'

'And which do you think is the more likely?' she whispered.

Dermot kissed her deeply and then stepped quickly away from her. He stopped with his hand on the door. 'I love you,' he said simply.

But Katherine shook her head, the anger and frustration boiling up inside her. 'No, Dermot, you don't love me – you love your cause!' She turned away from him and went to the window, looking out on to the sun-bright streets. 'Well go then; go and die for your cause,' she said, very softly.

She didn't hear him close the door, nor did she hear him hurry down the stairs and open the front door, but a few moments later she saw Dermot Corcoran and Mickey walk side by side down the street. Mickey was wearing a uniform similar to Dermot's, but had an overcoat thrown over his arm. He was carrying a double-barrelled shotgun. Neither man looked back.

Across the city, the church bells began to toll ten o'clock.

Katherine Lundy turned back to the room and began to dress hurriedly.

If she had any doubts, Katherine didn't show them as she climbed the steps to the house on Clonliffe Road. There were still memories, she was surprised to find, even after all these years, but surprisingly only the good ones remained. The memories and the smells . . . she could remember the smells perfectly. Polish; wood polish, silver polish, tart and sharp . . . the rich odours of Granny O'Neill's cooking that always seeped through the house and set her stomach rumbling . . . the smell of tallow in her darkened room every night . . .

525

the musk of her body on the nights she had made love to Captain Lewis. Only the good memories remained.

A short fat girl answered the door; she was ugly and ungraceful and stared at Katherine with an air of undisguised belligerence. Anne Lewis was choosing the servants again, Katherine realized.

'I have come to see Major Lewis; is he at home?'

The girl continued to stare at her, and Katherine was beginning to wonder if she was a little slow, when she abruptly nodded and stepped to one side, allowing Katherine into the hallway. There was movement on the landing above and then Major Lewis came down the stairs, whistling softly to himself. He stopped in shock when he saw the figure in black standing in the hallway.

'This lady wants to see you, sir,' the maid said, standing with the hall door still open, looking from Katherine to the major.

He nodded, without taking his eyes off Katherine. 'Thank you; that will be all.' The girl went to move away, when the major added, 'The door.'

The servant started and looked at the door, almost as if she was surprised to find it ajar. When she had closed it, she clumped rather noisily down the hall, heading in the direction of the kitchen.

Katherine walked past the major, who had remained standing on the stairs, and straight into the sitting room. It was exactly as she remembered it; the wallpaper, the carpet, the furnishings remained the same. The major followed her into the room, and closed the door behind him.

'Whatever you want, make it quick. My wife is upstairs.'

She stood with her back to the fireplace, looking at him, noting the wary – almost frightened – look in his eyes, and then she said slowly and evenly, 'The rising begins today at noon.'

He looked at her, almost without expression, as if the words had little meaning ... and then he smiled. 'I knew it,' he whispered, almost as if he were talking to

526

himself, 'I knew it!' He looked up at Katherine. 'Where?'

'The only building I know about is the GPO.'

'Oh my God!'

'Is there a problem?'

'I have papers relating to the rising, the leaders, and the German involvement, as well as details of Roger Casement's capture in my office.' He paused and added, 'I also have copies of the government's emergency plan in the event of an uprising.'

'I thought you always took your papers home with you?'

'I forgot,' he lied. Recently he had begun to suspect that someone was going through his papers. Major Lewis had an excellent memory and an almost total recall for details and, although on the surface his papers looked untouched, he had noticed small things had been moved and misplaced. He had deliberately left his recent reports and papers in the GPO. He looked at the clock; it was a little after eleven.

'I'll get dressed and go down there . . .'

'Should you not be warning your troops and the police?' she asked.

'Those papers are much more important,' he snapped. 'No, I'll get them first, and then warn the proper authorities.'

'I'll go down with you,' she said, and sat down on the settee, noticing that it was beginning to sag in the middle. She sighed, remembering the old days when everything had been in perfect order. Those days were gone forever.

He paused by the door. 'Why?'

'Why?'

'Why did you come here?'

She shook her head slightly. 'No reason – except that I always keep my end of a bargain.'

The bright sunny weather had brought the crowds out, and the streets were busy with strollers and window shoppers, although there were few trams to be found around Nelson's pillar, most of them having taken Dubliners either out to the coast or to the races for the day.

Katherine Lundy and Major Lewis arrived at the pillar at ten minutes to twelve. They had waited fifteen minutes for a tram and had eventually decided to walk into town. Actually it was more of a run than a walk, and both were red-faced, gasping and slick with sweat. They had come hurrying down O'Connell Street, both half-expecting to find the street filled with flag-waving, gun-carrying insurgents. But there was nothing amiss; it looked like any other bright Bank Holiday Monday.

Major Lewis checked his watch against the large clock on the GPO façade and then turned to Katherine. 'You stay here; I'm going in.'

Katherine nodded; she had no intention of entering the building. She watched as the man ran across the street, dodging cycles and motor cars, running in between the two centre columns and darting in through the right-hand side door. She strode back and forwards nervously; she didn't really know why she had accompanied Major Lewis to the GPO – perhaps it was just to see if indeed the rebels actually attempted to take the building. She knew that a lot of the revolutionary groups were mainly rhetoric and bluster but notoriously short on action. She prayed to God that that would be the case . . . although somehow she doubted it. Deep in her heart she knew there was only one course of action left open to them now . . .

Martin Moore was walking away from the counter with Tilly on his arm when he saw John Lewis run in through the door. He stopped in surprise and half raised his hand in greeting. But the major didn't see him and continued across the floor, his face set and pale.

'Hang on a second, Tilly,' Martin said and then darted across the marbled floor towards his superior.

Tilly, who had been busy folding some stamps so that

528

the adhesive backs wouldn't stick together in her purse, looked up in surprise. She saw Martin Moore stop at the far end of the counter beside the wooden door that allowed access for staff to the upper floors and she saw him speak to a tall, grey-haired man. She had taken two steps towards them when the man looked past Martin's shoulder to stare at her.

Martin Moore had turned to look at Tilly at the same moment. He saw the look of absolute horror and loathing that crossed her face, followed by the look of betrayal as her eyes caught his. Without a moment's hesitation, she turned and walked quickly from the building without once looking back.

'Tilly?' Martin Moore shouted, attracting stares from across the floor. He took a step forward, but Major Lewis gripped his arm. 'You can sort out your domestic problems later, captain,' he snapped, 'we've got work to do.'

'But why should she walk out like that?'

'You'll have to ask her later!'

Katherine was actually looking down the street when she saw the column of men rounding the corner from Abbey Street. The first thing she noticed were the uniforms – the familiar green of the Volunteers – and she felt her blood run cold. Up to that moment she had continued to hope that, with all the confusion, the rising would not come off.

The column, led by three men, wheeled right and marched down the street much to the amusement of Dubliners, long-used to the sight of the Citizen Army and the Volunteers marching and parading. She could see two trucks, their engines howling and gears crunching as they rounded the corner, and beside them two motor cycles. There was also a green Ford touring car, though she wasn't sure it was actually connected with the body of men until it drew near and she could see the boxes and cases of weapons and foodstuffs piled in the back.

The column drew to a halt almost directly across from her. At its head were Connolly, the pale and shivering Joseph Plunkett and the sternly proud figure of Pearse, but she only noted them briefly. Her eyes were on a figure a little way behind Connolly in the right-hand column – the figure of Dermot Corcoran, looking pale and determined and almost a stranger, very unlike her husband. Mickey was walking beside him, but unlike Dermot who looked aged he looked much younger than his years.

'I never thought they'd do it.'

Katherine turned to find Major Lewis standing by her side, breathing heavily but with a triumphant smile on his lips, a bundle of thick envelopes under his arm.

'You sound almost as if you're pleased they did,' she remarked.

'In a way I am – it gives me the excuse to have them all killed.'

'Not all,' she said quickly, looking up at him.

He was about to reply when a bell tolled noon – the pro-cathedral in Marlborough Street reminding the faithful that it was time for the Angelus. Most Dubliners paused to cross themselves and a hush seemed to fall over O'Connell Street.

'Left wheel . . .' Connolly suddenly bellowed, startling everyone, sending pigeons flapping from the windowsills of buildings all around. He pointed with his ceremonial sword. 'The GPO . . . charge!'

For a moment there seemed to be confusion in the ranks – almost as if some of the men were beginning to realize that this was no exercise, and then Katherine distinctly heard Dermot call out, 'Take the post office!'

And the men charged the building.

There was confusion at the entrance as the rebels milled around the doors and then the men all disappeared inside in a rush. From within there were several dull popping sounds, and then the customers and staff began pouring out, most of them stopping to stand in confusion on the street, wondering what was happening.

530

Glass began to shatter as the rebels broke the windows.

'I have them now,' Captain Lewis laughed, 'and when they are dead, with them dies all chance of an Irish rebellion.'

'But don't forget – Dermot won't be harmed under any circumstances. He's working for you!' Katherine insisted.

'Don't be such a fool, woman!'

A score of weapons went off in the post office, blowing out several of the windows, but Katherine didn't hear the sound. Nor did she hear the screams, the shouts, the children crying. She didn't see the people running for shelter, the trams hurriedly emptying. All she saw was the triumphant look on John Lewis's face, all she heard were his words. She looked at him in horror. 'But the letter from you . . .?'

'Forged on old paper,' he laughed, and then he turned and gripped her jaw in his hard hands. 'It's worthless, woman; the paper is worthless; produce it and you'll be shot on sight.'

Katherine looked into John Lewis's cold, hard pitiless eyes and in that single moment all her plans were shattered, and she realized that he had used her – again. He had won. She had been tricked into betraying them all . . . and for nothing. Dermot would die – they would all die – and she would be responsible . . . as surely as if she had put a gun to his head and pulled the trigger herself.

'We . . . we had a deal,' she hissed.

'I don't deal with criminals,' he said, releasing her and turning away. 'You will excuse me – I must contact the authorities. Say good-bye to your husband, Madam Kitten; you won't be seeing him alive again – that I swear.'

The sound of laughter and triumphant shouts drifted out across the suddenly silent street from within the post office building, and Katherine was sure she heard Dermot's voice amongst it all.

CHAPTER FORTY-SIX

Shortly afterwards the flags appeared on the roof of the GPO. There were two; on the left a gold harp on a green cloth, with some words in Gaelic script which Katherine didn't recognize, although she guessed they would read the 'Irish Republic' or something like that, and on the right-hand side a tricolour of green, white and orange.

Like most Dubliners she was numbed and shocked by the events. Even though she had been prepared for it – and far better prepared than most – it was still shocking to see one of Dublin's loveliest buildings taken over by the insurgents. As she watched, the windows were systematically broken, and rifles began appearing everywhere.

She was about to turn away when she spotted the familiar face of Tilly Cusack directly in front of her. Her friend was pale and grim-faced and was pushing her way roughly through the crowd, attracting angry stares and some shouts.

'Tilly . . . Tilly!'

It took a few moments until Tilly realized that someone was calling her name, and then she stopped and looked around in confusion. A hand waved ahead and a little to her right and she finally spotted Katherine. The two women stared at one another through the crowd, and then Tilly dashed across and flung herself into Katherine's arms, the tears finally erupting.

'What's wrong? For God's sake, tell me what's happened?' Katherine demanded.

But Tilly was inconsolable, and all Katherine could do was to hold her, the two women unnoticed in the excitement.

A hush suddenly descended over the murmuring crowd, and Katherine looked up to find that a man had appeared in the portico of the GPO, immediately followed by half a dozen other armed men, who took up positions around him. Then another individual came out of the building and joined the central figure. As they stepped out between the pillars, Katherine recognized Pearse and Connolly. She saw Connolly take a few steps out into the street and tilt his head up to look at the flags, and when he returned to stand at Pearse's side there was a broad grin on his face.

Padraic Pearse then took two steps forward and unfolded a rolled sheet of paper, and in a loud and steady voice he began to read, the words drifting out over the crowd. The revolution was forty-five minutes old.

'The Provisional Government of the Irish Republic to the People of Ireland . . .' He glanced up, catching eyes, noting expressions and the total lack of reponse. 'Irishmen and Irishwomen: In the name of God and of the dead generations from which she receives her old traditions of nationhood, Ireland, through us, summons her children to her flag and strikes for her freedom . . .'

'Katherine, it's Martin . . .' Tilly sobbed, 'it's Martin . . .'

'Martin?' Katherine asked, only half listening.

'Martin Moore!'

'Oh, your captain,' Katherine smiled.

'Katherine, he knows Major Lewis . . . he knows Major Lewis!'

'Tilly, love,' Katherine said as gently as possible, 'he works with the major!'

'. . . Having organized and trained her manhood through her secret revolutionary organization, the Irish Republican Brotherhood, and through her open military organizations, the Irish Volunteers and the Irish Citizen Army, having patiently perfected her discipline, having waited for the right moment to reveal itself, she now seizes that moment and supported by her exiled children

533

in America and by gallant Allies in Europe, but relying first on her own strength, she strikes in full confidence of victory . . .'

'You never told me!' Tilly accused icily.

'I didn't think it would be something you would want to know,' Katherine said wryly, and then she suddenly pointed to one of the men standing behind Pearse. 'Look, there's Dermot.'

Tilly turned to look, but she was still preoccupied. 'How did you know he was associated with Major Lewis?'

Katherine turned to look at her, prepared to shrug off the question with an easy reply, but then she saw the pain in her friend's eyes and knew she couldn't lie to her. She linked her arm through Tilly's and they walked away – like so many other Dubliners who had become bored with Pearse's speech. Katherine turned right into North Earl Street, where they were passed by scores of people hurrying towards the cause of the disturbance. They heard talk of other military actions throughout the city, but strangely, although there were members of the police around, there were no military men present.

'I looked into Martin Moore's background following his second visit, when he professed that he loved you.' Katherine smiled. 'I thought it was perhaps just a little too sudden.'

'So did I,' Tilly confessed.

'I discovered he was Major Lewis's personal assistant, I suppose you would call him his second-in-command.'

'Why didn't you tell me?' Tilly demanded angrily.

'I suspected that he might have been sent in to spy either on me or the activity in the house. Remember, Dermot was holding meetings with his IRB friends upstairs at the time, and I thought the young captain might have been sent in to watch them. And my suspicions turned out to be correct. He had been sent in with the deliberate intention of becoming involved with you as a means of gaining access to the house at all

534

hours of the day and night, with the intention of catching us off guard one day . . .'

Tilly swallowed hard, and found there was a taste of ashes in her mouth.

'But . . . but then circumstances changed . . . and the captain was told that there was no longer any need for him to continue with his mission. It seems he chose not to.'

'What sort of circumstances?'

'Major Lewis discovered he was in a position to gain access to up-to-date and accurate information from another source, and therefore there was no longer any need for Martin Moore to spend time with you.'

'What other source?'

'From me!'

Katherine had walked on a score of steps before she realized Tilly wasn't beside her. She stopped and looked back; the woman was staring at her in blank astonishment. 'I did have a reason,' she said quietly. She shook her head. 'But that's not important now. What is important is that Major Lewis didn't know that Captain Moore was still seeing you, and more importantly, I do believe he truly loves you.'

Tilly walked up to Katherine, but didn't touch her. 'If he loved me, why didn't he tell me about his association with the major?'

'Well, he was hardly likely to, now was he?'

The two women turned left into Mabbot Lane, a small street overshadowed by brothels and tenements, and filled with the ever-present stench of urine and boiled cabbage. The streets, which would usually have been swarming with half naked urchins, shouting, screaming and tumbling in the gutters, were empty. Everyone had gone off to see the revolution.

'Why did you go to Major Lewis?' Tilly asked finally.

'I needed to deal with him.'

'Deal . . . in what way?'

'I was trying to save Dermot's life. I couldn't persuade him to leave the Volunteers, and I knew that if the

535

revolution went ahead he might be killed or captured. Then I learned that the Germans were supplying arms, and I realized that if he were to be captured then he would surely be shot as a traitor. So I did a deal with Major Lewis for his protection.' There was enough bitterness in her voice for Tilly to notice it.

'What sort of deal?' she whispered.

'I betrayed the revolution to him.' There was no emotion, no inflection in her voice.

'In return for Dermot's life?

'In return for a pass, a letter written by Major Lewis on Dublin Castle paper saying that Dermot was working for him.'

Tilly said nothing and concentrated on avoiding the fetid puddles on the ground.

'I got the letter. In return I told Major Lewis everything I knew. Today, I even went to tell him that the rising would start at noon. I came down to the GPO with him – he had to collect some papers from his office – that was what he was doing inside when Martin met him.'

'And?'

'And?' Katherine asked, looking at Tilly.

'What went wrong; something went wrong, didn't it?'

'Major Lewis betrayed me. The paper is worthless!'

'So he wins,' Tilly said quietly, 'after all these years he finally wins.'

'Not yet,' Katherine said softly.

Reports coming in were mixed and contradictory; the rebels – pitifully few in number – had seized control of certain buildings and locations, and while not in complete control of the city had certainly contained certain sectors.

Michael Mallin, with Constance Markievicz as his second-in-command had occupied St Stephen's Green. The rebels had also taken over Jacob's Biscuit Factory, a large forbidding-looking building in Bishop's Street;

and naturally the Four Courts had been occupied, with the heavy leather-bound books of law and statutes being used in place of sandbags on the windows. Boland's Mill, the South Dublin Union and several other key shops and buildings which controlled the approaches to Dublin had also been taken. If the ten thousand Irish Volunteers had marched out that morning Plunkett's strategy would have worked: with the twelve hundred or so men under arms it was impossible.

As the afternoon wore on and Katherine Lundy gradually acquired a clearer picture of what was happening in Dublin and the provinces, she arrived at an obvious, terrifying conclusion: 'They'll be massacred!'

The interior of the GPO was a shambles. The centre of the floor had been cleared of everything movable and the tables and chairs had been moved over to beneath the large windows and in front of the doors as barricades. Every window had been shattered, and bags of mail, books, files, records and furniture were piled before them.

Dermot Corcoran moved from room to room, itemizing the rebels' weapons and ammunition. Although the Irish Volunteers' Equipment Leaflet, No. A1, had recommended that each man bring a rifle and one hundred rounds of ammunition, many of those present had come without guns but with antique swords and pikes, daggers, spears and axes. Others had come armed with shotguns, single- and double-barrelled and a mixture of bores, and the rifles were a curious mixture of ancient and modern: Sniders, Long and Short Lee Enfields, Lee Metfords, Martini-Henrys, Martini-Enfield carbines, the Model 98 Mauser, the 71/84 Mauser, Anson-Deeley high velocity rifles, Mannlicher sporting rifles, .22 target rifles, and even some air guns. Pistols were few and far between, but the Mauser pistol was the most popular, and there were some Colt army revolvers and Webleys. Dermot had one of the new

Webley-Fosbery .455 automatic revolvers, but had only two dozen rounds of ammunition for it – and that included the six already in the cylinders.

He listed the weapons and noted the lack of ammunition and then reported back to Joseph Plunkett on the ground floor. But by now the pale-faced, red-eyed young man was so exhausted that he could barely stand, and Dermot wandered off in search of The O'Rahilly who was on one of the upper floors and was now apparently in charge of the weapons.

He had to push and shove his way past the men milling around on the stairs. Some were good-humoured, laughing and joking together, but their voices were high and the laughter seemed forced, while others were pale-faced and tight-lipped; indeed, many of them had been unaware that today's march was to be anything other than an exercise. When they had left home that morning they had never expected to find themselves actually going into battle.

He was passing the windows that looked up the length of O'Connell Street when he spotted the sun sparkling on metal. His breath fogged the glass and he rubbed at it, his hands suddenly hot and wet. His mouth went dry. A party of Lancers was advancing slowly and majestically down the street, their lances catching and reflecting the early-afternoon sunlight.

'Lancers ... Lancers are coming ... Lancers.' The soldiers had been spotted by the lookouts and the shouts went up and down the building, and he heard men rushing to the windows and more glass splintering, followed by the clicking of rifle bolts.

There were footsteps on the stairs behind Dermot and he turned as a tall man with a curling handle-bar moustache came running down from the floor above. 'Don't fire; don't fire until I give the word,' The O'Rahilly snapped at him as he rushed by, 'pass it around.'

Dermot nodded and hurried downstairs to the ground floor where he spotted Connolly. 'The O'Rahilly says to hold fire until his word.' The stocky, large-faced man nodded, and then startled Dermot by throwing back his head and bellowing out the order. Dermot then raced back upstairs, shouting out the message to everyone he met. On the top floor he ducked into a small square room that was almost completely empty, save for two desks and chairs and a single, empty filing cabinet. With the butt of his rifle he shattered the glass and then chambered a round into his gun and looked down into the street.

The Lancers had fanned out across the street about a hundred yards away on the north side of the street, sitting stock still on their tall horses, while the officer in the centre looked straight ahead. Then the leader's head tilted as he looked up at the fluttering flags and at the broken, sandbagged windows, and an expression almost of disgust crossed his face.

Dermot brought his rifle around and levelled it in the centre of the officer's chest. He saw the man reach down for his sword and then swing it free of its scabbard and up into the air in one fluid movement. It was a brave defiant gesture. The sword fell – and the Lancers charged.

They thundered down the street, all the power and majesty of the British Empire represented in the sheer audacity of the move. Dermot held the gun steady and waited for the order to fire – and then wondered why it didn't come.

And then from below a single shot rang out – obviously early – but it was followed by a score or so of shots, and then a ragged volley. Dermot saw a man fall from his saddle, and then another. He tried to hold the officer in his sight, but the man was twisting around in the saddle, shocked, perhaps dismayed that his men would actually be fired upon in one of the Empire's capitals. Dermot squeezed the trigger and fired; the rifle thumped back into his shoulder and he distinctly saw stone chippings and sparks fly from the cobbles just behind the officer. More shots rang out and another Lancer fell, and then another. A horse screamed and

539

crashed to the ground, unseating its rider who went tumbling to the ground but managed to land on his feet. Another volley, and one of the riderless horses fell with an almost human scream to the ground.

The Lancers were now milling around in confusion, their orderly ranks and pride shattered. There was another burst of firing and the bullets sang against the cobbles and the sides of buildings, but – almost miraculously – no one else fell. Dermot rammed another round home and sighted down the rifle, but his hands were trembling so much that he couldn't hold the gun steady. He lowered it and squeezed his eyes shut; firing at targets was one thing, but shooting another human being was a different matter entirely. The firing died down and when he looked up again the Lancers had retreated, leaving four men on the ground, three of them obviously dead and another moving feebly in a pool of his own blood. The two dead horses sprawled alongside the men, the once graceful animals ungainly in death.

Dermot wiped his face with his handkerchief and was surprised when it came away stained and black. He was still shaking slightly, and his mouth was dry. On the street below he spotted a young boy run out from the shocked and stunned crowd that lined the street. He was barefoot and ragged, an urchin from the slums. He stopped by one of the dead Lancers and looked at the man curiously, and then stooped and picked up the man's rifle, turning it over and over in his hands as if it were some sort of toy. A woman, equally dirty and ragged, darted across and tried to wrest the gun from him, but the boy hung on grimly, and in the struggle the butt of the rifle struck her on the side of the head. She sat down in the street, unhurt but dazed, and started to scream. The boy darted across the street towards the GPO, waving the weapon like a stick, and Dermot craned his head downwards to see where he was going but the windowsill intervened and he couldn't see. Afterwards he learned that the urchin had handed it to one of the bemused Volunteers before

540

running off again. Cheering drifted up through the floors from below, but the cheers sounded high and harsh and more than a little forced.

He was still standing by the window a little more than an hour later when he heard movement behind him, and turned to find Mickey standing in the doorway.

'Dermot,' he said slowly, suddenly looking old and tired.

'Mickey.' He jerked his head to the window, where now only the dead bodies of the two horses and the stained cobbles remained to mark the brief engagement, 'We've done it now, eh?'

'I think we did it long ago.' The large man smiled and leaned his large, rough hands on the windowsill and looked down into the street.

'Our boys are all right?'

Mickey's face twisted in disgust. 'One dead and two wounded, would you believe?'

Dermot looked at him in astonishment. 'But the Lancers didn't even fire a shot.'

Mickey pointed across the street towards the Imperial Hotel where some of the rebels had taken up position. 'He was shot by one of us. One of the wounded was a sixteen-year-old boy, a Volunteer trying to get into the building when he was hit by a stray shot. Another lad dropped his rifle and it went off, shooting him in the stomach!'

'Oh my God!'

'Connolly is sending out Joe Cripps to find some medical supplies. But what we really need is a doctor.'

'Could we get the two wounded men to Jervis Street Hospital?'

'We could, I suppose . . .' Mickey said slowly, 'well, we could always try.'

'Do you think you could get me four men to act as stretcher bearers?'

'That shouldn't be too difficult. Why don't we ask

541

Pearse or Connolly? We've got to do something for them; they'll die if they're left here.'

A semblance of order had returned to the main floor of the building. The windows had been sandbagged and there were two armed men at each of them. Dispatch riders were arriving with reports from the rebel outposts in other parts of the city, while lorries and cars were coming in with food and blankets. The leaders were surrounded by small groups of men either bringing reports or hurrying off with orders, and the mood of both the leaders and men seemed on the whole excellent.

Dermot and Mickey had to wait a few moments, while Padraic Pearse received the latest report from the Four Courts which had been successfully taken by the rebels, and from St Stephen's Green where they were in the process of digging trenches. Abruptly there was a lull, and Pearse looked around, seemingly almost surprised at having nothing to do, and then he spotted Dermot. His usually dour face broke into a rare smile. He nodded at Mickey.

'Dermot has suggested he bring the two wounded men around to Jervis Street,' Mickey said without preamble.

'I was just about to look for volunteers,' Pearse smiled.

'I'll need four stretcher bearers,' Dermot said.

'Well, I don't think we'll have any problem with that . . .' He was looking around when there was a deafening explosion from one side of the room and a man fell back screaming, both hands clutched to his face. There was a moment's confusion, and then pandemonium broke out. Men rushed to the windows, expecting an attack, while others threw themselves to the floor, fearing another explosion.

Pearse and Dermot with Mickey behind them, rushed over to the fallen man whose head and shoulders were black with smoke and blood. But the man seemed very much alive, and his eyes were bright and fierce in his filthy face.

542

'What happened?' Padraic Pearse demanded.

'I was holding one of them bloody homemade grenades,' the young lieutenant said, spitting blood from his torn lips, 'when the cursed thing went off in my face.'

Pearse lifted one of the cannisters – a tin can packed with gunpowder – which had been made by the Countess Markievicz and her Fianna Boys, aided by the Plunketts. He watched as the smoke and blood was wiped from the young officer's face, but miraculously, except for some superficial burns and scorched hair, he was unmarked. 'It should have blown your head off,' he remarked quietly. He looked at Dermot. 'See if you can check these out while I get your stretcher bearers.' He glanced down at the officer. 'And you can bring this casualty with you.'

'Ah sir . . .!'

'That's an order!'

Dermot gathered up a bag of the cannisters – most of the rebels had a dozen, some of them had more – and carried them out past the guards on the door into the street. He stood for a moment in the bright April sunshine and looked up and down the street wondering what he was going to do with them. Finally, he walked over to the base of Nelson's pillar and emptied the bag out on to the ground. He then arranged the cannisters and tins in a neat pile by the railings that surrounded the pillar and walked quickly back to the main door of the GPO. He nodded to the guard on the door. 'Think you could hit one of those?'

The man grinned and brought his rifle up to his shoulder and fired in one smooth movement. There was a thunderous explosion, thick, choking black smoke wreathed around the pillar and shards of the cans and cannisters went clanging down O'Connell Street. But when the smoke had cleared – there wasn't so much as a scratch on the railings.

'So much for our grenades,' Dermot remarked.

* * *

Major Lewis cabled another message to London later that afternoon. 'The rebels have attempted to blow up the statue of Nelson in Sackville Street.' When the rebels seized the GPO, they had hoped they were going to take the telephone and telegraph lines also and by doing so effectively isolate the British authorities in Ireland, and perhaps even delay for a few days the inevitable arrival of British troops. But the lines had been smartly re-routed to Amiens Street telegraph office by the Post Office Superintending Engineer almost as soon as the first shots were being fired, and lack of manpower prevented the rebels from occupying the telephone exchange in Crown Alley.

A few minutes before he had left the building that morning, Major Lewis had used the telegraph office in the GPO to send off a message in code to the Irish Office in London. What he didn't know was that the decoder wasn't present because it was a Bank Holiday, and the message remained undecoded until later that afternoon when it was already too late, and by that time Lord Wimborne had also sent telegrams to the Irish Office and the Foreign Office informing them of events.

Major Lewis had spent most of the afternoon in his house on Clonliffe Road, telephoning around, trying to collect together a coherent picture of what was happening in Dublin. Rumours abounded and estimates of the number of rebels supposed to be on the streets of the capital ranged from one to ten thousand. Besides the GPO, Dublin Castle had been attacked and a guard shot, but surprisingly the rebels hadn't pressed home their attack and the castle remained in Crown hands. St Stephen's Green had been taken – he shook his head at that, there didn't seem to be any military sense to it; rebels had taken the Four Courts and fired on a troop of Lancers, killing two and pinning down the others. There had been shooting between insurgents at Portobello Bridge and the few troops that hadn't a weekend pass and had remained in Portobello Barracks; there were also contingents in control of the enormous Jacobs'

Biscuit Factory, the Mendicity Institute, the South Dublin Union and, possibly the most worrying of all, the rebels had taken Boland's Mill, which controlled the approach to the city from Kingstown Harbour.

Major Lewis began estimating army figures in the city at the time; most, he knew, were on leave for the Bank Holiday, and were either at the sea or at the Fairyhouse Races. He attempted to get some up-to-date data from the police, but was horrified to discover the Dublin Metropolitan Police Commissioner had withdrawn all his men from the city. He spoke briefly on the telephone to Lord Wimborne who informed him that he had already sent telegraphs to Belfast and the Curragh Army Camp for reinforcements. All they could do now was to engage the rebels with what forces they had, try to estimate their numbers and arms, and wait for the reinforcements to arrive.

But Major Lewis wasn't prepared to wait. He fixed himself a quick lunch – idly wondering where his wife had gone – and then, filling his pockets with ammunition and tucking his service revolver into his belt, decided to head back into town to assess the situation for himself.

He ate quickly and then left the house by the kitchen door. At the rear gate he stopped for a moment, breathing in the clean cold air and relishing the quiet of the suburb. It was difficult to believe that little over a mile away a revolution was taking place.

Anne Lewis, wearing the green uniform of the Volunteers, was up to her elbows in soft, wet earth. Naturally she had chosen to go with William Sherlock and there had never been any question that he would not fight alongside Constance Markievicz, who was stationed in St Stephen's Green under the command of Michael Mallin.

It was terrifying, but exhilarating. Anne's only wish was that she could have seen her husband's face when he learned that the rising had taken place. When their troop had entered the Green, their first task had been to

545

clear it of the numerous Easter Monday strollers, and she had entertained a vague fantasy that she might discover her husband walking there – perhaps with the mysterious woman who had called at the house earlier that morning. Like many of the other women present, she had a knife and a pistol in her belt, and she would have shot him – there was no question of that.

When the Green had been cleared, the Volunteers set about securing it and began to dig their trenches across the entrances and main pathways. At one stage, the countess, Anne and William found themselves digging together in one trench, the largest one which controlled the entrance from the main gate. Constance had rolled up the sleeves of her green uniform and tilted her soft-brimmed hat back on her head and was busily shovelling out the thick, sodden muck.

William Sherlock stopped and wiped his arm across his forehead, smearing dirt across it. 'How many men do we have?' he gasped.

The countess shrugged. 'Around one hundred and forty or so.'

'This is madness,' Sherlock exclaimed. 'We can never hold this position if we're attacked.'

Constance Markievicz nodded and frowned. 'We should be in one of the surrounding buildings.'

'I thought some of our lads were supposed to take the Shelbourne Hotel?' William asked.

The countess shook her head angrily. 'They never turned up; MacNeill's countermanding order saw to that.'

'Do you think we will be attacked?' Anne asked, her eyes glittering fanatically.

'I imagine the authorities will have far more important targets to concentrate on for the moment, but don't worry, they'll be here in time,' William said with a smile. The shy, frightened woman had blossomed into a fiery revolutionary.

'What are you smiling at?' Anne asked, leaning for a moment on her shovel.

'I was wondering what your husband would think if he saw you now,' William grinned.

'I wish he could,' Anne said fervently.

'When you see that man,' Constance said quietly, 'the revolution will be over.'

Anne nodded and continued shovelling. Many people were going to be killed in the next few days; she prayed to God that her husband would be amongst them.

Katherine Lundy's information was much the same as Major Lewis's, except perhaps a little more detailed. Her informants were the street people, the shawlies and urchins, the cabmen and delivery boys, dockers, draymen and tramps. Katherine had already passed around the word that she was paying extra for information on the rising.

As the afternoon wore on and the steady flow of informants streamed into the house, two pieces of news began to give her more and more cause for concern. The first was the lack of British troops – she wasn't entirely sure how to evaluate that – and the second was the withdrawal of the police.

'You know what that means?' she asked Tilly, who had been sitting silently by the window throughout the afternoon.

'Trouble,' Tilly whispered silently, 'looting probably.'

Katherine nodded. 'We'll close the house for tonight . . .' She paused as the doorbell rang down below, and almost automatically dropped her veil over her face. She heard footsteps on the stairs and checked her cashbox, wondering how much money she had left to pay informants. The door opened without even a perfunctory knock, and she turned angrily . . . but it wasn't a ragged Dubliner with a snippet of information to pass on – it was her husband!

Her first reaction was one of relief, mingled with disbelief. He was still in his Volunteer uniform, but his cap was gone and he was wearing a heavy overcoat on top of the distinctive green.

'Thank God,' she gasped.

'Don't thank Him just yet,' Dermot said wearily, propping his rifle by the door and shrugging off his coat.

'What do you mean?'

'I'm going back.'

'You're mad!'

'Possibly – probably – but I'm going back in.'

Tilly stood up and mumbled a vague excuse and discreetly left the room. Neither of them even saw her go.

'Look!' Katherine turned and began hauling out sheets of paper, each one covered in her own neat hand. 'Look; do you know how many men you have?'

He started to shake his head, but Katherine hurried on.

'There are a little over two hundred Citizen Army people and about twelve hundred Volunteers on the streets. That's fourteen, maybe fifteen hundred men – against an Empire! Men died this afternoon, British Lancers, some police. That won't be forgiven. Troops are already on the way from Belfast and the Curragh. How do you think you can hope to hold out against the British army?'

Dermot buried his head in his hands. 'We don't,' he said very softly.

'You don't?' Katherine sat down suddenly.

'That's why I'm here.' He looked up at her, and Katherine noticed for the first time how much he had aged, the soft boyish lines and innocent guileless eyes were gone. She was looking at a man and, in so many ways, a stranger. 'I volunteered to bring some wounded men to Jervis Street, but it was only so that I could come around here . . .'

'Why, for God's sake, why?'

'To say good-bye to you.' He saw the look on her face and hurried on. 'You see, I know how bad the figures are, I know how few men have turned out and I know – and the leaders know – that this is a fight we

548

cannot win. But we knew that before we even started. Even if we die – as we surely must – our deaths will serve as an example for those who follow. We're just the spark to the fire that will one day set Ireland free.'

'And what about me, and the children?' Katherine asked numbly.

'I've told you before, I'm doing it for them. I'm doing it so that they can grow up in a free Ireland.'

'Without a father,' Katherine said flatly.

'If that's necessary.'

'Why did you come back, Dermot?'

He looked into her face, reading the pain and hurt there. 'To say good-bye – and to tell you that I love you.'

'If you loved me, you'd stay here with me.'

Dermot shook his head. 'I don't think I'll ever make you understand. You've different values, different needs from me.'

'I love you,' she said fiercely, 'that's a value, a need we share.'

'But I think you love this – all this,' he spread his hands, 'more than you love me. You love the power and authority, the money and prestige. My country comes first . . . even before you, I'd have to say.'

'I had nothing, Dermot; I grew up with nothing . . .' Katherine said and then stopped. 'I won't deny that this is important to me. It's everything I ever wanted out of life. But you're important to me too. There's no point in having one without the other.'

'If I remained here with you, today, would you give it all up?' he asked with a wry smile.

Katherine hesitated just a few moments too long before replying. 'I don't think you would stay here,' she said eventually.

'You didn't answer my question,' he reminded her. He stood up and bent over her, and then he kissed her gently. She responded coolly at first and then with growing passion. Her arms wrapped around his head and she pulled him down into the chair on top of her . . .

They made love quickly but gently, and almost totally silently, both of them aware that this would be the last time, eager to give a little of themselves to the other before they parted forever. When they were finished, Dermot kissed Katherine and then, gathering up his overcoat and rifle, left the room. A few moments later Katherine heard the front door slam closed, the sound loud and final.

She knew she would never see him again.

CHAPTER FORTY-SEVEN

With no police on duty there was looting in Dublin that night. The slums emptied and the poor, ragged men, women and children poured down into O'Connell Street and the side streets that led off it. They smashed the plate-glass windows and pulled the contents of shops out into the street to be sorted and divided amongst themselves, bartered, traded and swopped again and again. People who had had nothing all their lives now found themselves in the situation where anything they wanted – anything, from shoes to clothes, even confectionary – was theirs for the taking. Liquor shops, wine merchants and bars suffered badly, and soon the night was disturbed by the shouts and screams of drunken men and women, the sounds of bottles shattering and glass breaking.

Within the GPO the rebels were silent, some amazed, most just disgusted by the activities of their fellow citizens. The rules and regulations of the IRB and the Volunteers relating to the uprising were rigid, and forbade even the 'liberation' of so much as a sweet from a premises without a receipt. When the rising had been successful, they were told, all the receipts would be honoured in full. Alcohol had always been expressly forbidden within the organizations, and a man found drunk on duty was simply dismissed.

Dermot leaned over the edge of the windowsill and looked down into the street. 'I didn't come here to fight for this scum,' he said angrily.

'Can you blame them?' Mickey asked reasonably, leaning over his shoulder to stare down into the street. 'It must be like Christmas to them ... Look!' he suddenly pointed as a familiar figure hobbled out from the building and into the street, the tapping of his cane lost against the racket. Sean Mac Diarmada, white-faced with anger, tried to reason with the crowd, but even Dermot and Mickey who were straining to catch his words, couldn't make out what he was saying, even though they were almost directly above him. Shaking his head in disgust he limped back into the building. A moment or two later someone on the roof emptied several buckets of water on to the looters below; there were screams and howls of defiance, and the crowd scattered in panic – only to return a few minutes later, but careful now to keep well away from the GPO building. In a final effort to disperse the looters – whose activities would, of course, taint the rebels and the rising itself – a volley was fired over their heads and, when this looked successful, a second ragged volley was fired into the air. But the people quickly realized that the rebels weren't actually shooting at them, and they returned to attack the biggest prize of all, Clery's department store.

In frustration, Connolly sent out one of his most trusted men, Sean T. O'Kelly with a score of armed men and instructions to clear the building.

From across the street, Dermot could see into the huge department store. He was able to watch the crowd stripping the shop like a plague of locusts, taking things which they didn't want or need or, indeed, would never find a use for.

And then O'Kelly arrived with his men. His method of clearing the building was simple and direct. He demanded that the looters leave and when no-one moved to comply – even to listen – he had his men fire a few rounds over their heads into the ceiling, which at least brought a temporary silence, and then on his command, his troops began batoning those overloaded with spoils. The treatment was brutal but effective, and the looters left Clery's like rats deserting a ship in harbour.

In the GPO, Dermot threw back his head and laughed

552

– only to sober immediately when Mickey touched his arm and pointed. The looters were converging on a shoe shop a few doors down the street. O'Kelly and his men followed them, exercising their own brand of justice – and again the crowd dispersed, only to wander into another shop – followed by O'Kelly. But by that time some of the looters had doubled back and returned to Clery's . . .

Tilly Cusack wandered through the crowds of looters like a lost soul, completely oblivious to the shouts and screams, the raucous laughter, the shattering glass, and the shots. She had returned to the house she shared with her lover in Dorset Street when she left Katherine, half-expecting to find Martin home, but the house was still and empty, and there was no sign that he had been home all that day. She wondered what had happened to him; the last she had seen of him was when he was talking to Major Lewis, and after that, well . . . She shrugged. She was probably worrying over nothing; Martin Moore was probably with Major Lewis even now, working out ways to defeat the rebels.

She only really became worried when he hadn't returned home nor had attempted to contact her by nightfall. Coming to a decision, she pulled on her old walking shoes and headed up into Drumcondra.

Tilly waited outside Major Lewis's house for over an hour, standing well back in the shadows, watching the comings and goings. Her memories of the house were vague, and her recollection of her treatment by the major had faded to vague impressions, although the scars were still livid on her body. The house on Clonliffe Road was busy, with messengers arriving every few minutes, and a long line of cars and carriages was lined up along the kerb. Every light in the house was burning, although most of the activity seemed to be concentrated on the ground floor, where she could see movement behind the curtains in the sitting and dining rooms.

When she had first arrived, Major Lewis had been

553

opening the door himself, but he was later replaced by a fresh-faced young man in a crisp, green, army uniform. Eventually, after spending nearly two hours in the shadows and still with no sign of Martin Moore, she finally walked across the street, went up to the door and rang the bell. Her plan was simple: if John Lewis answered the door, she would turn on her heels and run . . . but if the young private . . .

'I've a message for Captain Moore,' she said crisply, standing just far enough out of the light so that her face remained in shadow.

It must have been a night for the unusual because the young man didn't even seem surprised by the presence of a woman on the step. 'I'm afraid Captain Moore is not here at the moment, ma'am, although he is expected. May I take a message? Major Lewis is here.'

'My . . . my information is for Captain Moore's ears alone. I'll call back. Good night.' She turned away and walked down the steps, all the time feeling the man's eyes on her back. When the door finally closed, she sprinted across the road. She had just reached the shadows when the door opened again and Major Lewis stood on the steps, glancing up and down the street, obviously looking for someone. Someone must have called his name from inside, because he turned away almost reluctantly and closed the door.

But Tilly was worried now; if Martin wasn't at home and wasn't with Major Lewis, then where was he? A sudden thought struck her: perhaps he was looking for her! She turned and headed down into Summerhill and Monto, making for Katherine's house.

As she entered the slums the first thing she noticed was the absence of people. It was a mild night and the tenement steps should have been crowded with women talking and laughing together, while their men-folk sat in the gutter smoking and playing cards. But the streets were empty.

When she arrived at the brothel the house was in darkness and she spent nearly five minutes pounding on the knocker before one of the servants answered. And as she hurried into the darkened, silent hallway, she immediately, instinctively knew that Martin wasn't there.

She found Katherine at the top of the house, sitting in a darkened room, staring out across the rooftops to where the top of Nelson's column was just visible. Tilly stepped into the room and closed the door quietly behind her.

'He went back, Tilly,' Katherine said without turning around, her voice soft and emotionless. 'He came here to say good-bye and then he went back to die.'

'I thought he might stay,' Tilly said, groping her way across the darkened room to a high-backed chair and perching herself on it.

'Oh no,' Katherine said with something like bitterness in her voice, 'he couldn't do that. His cause was waiting for him. And his cause was much more important to him than his wife.'

'He'll come back to you – you'll see.'

'You don't believe that any more than I do. There's not enough of them; they're outnumbered and out-gunned. They'll all be killed.'

'I'm looking for Martin,' Tilly said suddenly. 'He hasn't been here, has he?'

'Who . . . Martin . . . no, he hasn't been here,' Katherine said, distracted. 'He's probably with Major Lewis.'

'He's not, I've already checked.'

'Oh, I wouldn't worry, he's sure to turn up.'

'Yes, but where can he be?' Tilly said desperately. 'Where can he be?'

'Where did you last see him?' Katherine asked.

'In the GPO, just before the rebels attacked . . .'

Katherine slowly turned from the window and looked at her friend's pale face. 'There's an English army captain being held prisoner in the GPO,' she said softly.

Tilly passed the pillar and mingled with a crowd standing round a group of urchins detonating fireworks

555

outside a boot and shoe shop. Even as she looked a rocket smashed through the front window of the shop and immediately began to burn on the cloth in the window display. A caution born of too many years on the streets made her move away.

The fire began sizzling on the cans and tins of boot and shoe polish – one cracked and the fire blazed! With a whump the shattered glass exploded outwards, and within minutes the shop was ablaze, and wood and leather, cloth and paper, polish and cord burned. Tilly hurried away as the crowd gathered around the burning shop, watching it silently, like children around a bonfire.

On a whim she crossed the street, while behind her the crackle of the flames was suddenly rent by screams and, looking back, she could see a large struggling woman being carried out of the burning building. Strangely, the woman seemed more annoyed than hurt and it was only when she was standing on the street remonstrating with one of the men that Tilly realized she was very pregnant indeed.

Tilly stopped outside the GPO and peered in. The main doors were open and, although guarded by sentries, there were people coming and going and she could clearly see the frenetic activity inside. One of the sentries tipped his hat to her and wished her a 'good night'. She smiled briefly and hurried on; getting into the building didn't seem to be any problem – getting out would be.

In the first, thin light of dawn the chatter of a machine-gun woke the sleeping insurgents. The rebels had no machine-guns; the ten being sent by the Germans had gone down with the *Aud*.

'They're moving,' Constance Markievicz said, listening to the sound drift across the city, 'they're closing in.' She was speaking to no-one in particular, but everyone knew she was referring to the British troops.

The machine-guns spoke again, nearer this time – from one of the buildings that looked down into the Green. Bullets whickered through the trees and bushes, scything through leaves and branches and digging up regular lines of pocked turf. A few shots were returned by the rebels crouched in their trenches, but they were firing blind and had no idea where the shots were coming from. Bullets tore into the ornamental bridge across the lake, sparking and chipping the stonework, ricochetting around the masonry in a mist of fine dust.

When the firing finally died away, William Sherlock straightened slowly, his joints creaking audibly, for the night had been cold and damp and there was the promise of rain in the air. 'We can't defend this position,' he stated flatly, 'they can pick us off at their leisure.'

Anne Lewis, who was crouched beside him, shivering despite the heavy greatcoat, nodded in agreement.

The countess nodded also. 'I know.' She stood up cautiously, pressing both hands into the small of her back. 'I'll see what I can do.'

As the woman moved away through the low mist which clung to the damp ground, Anne Lewis snuggled closer to William. 'This is foolishness,' she whispered. 'We're going to be killed.'

Sherlock smiled and hugged Anne to him. 'But we'll die together.'

Anne Lewis nodded, but said nothing.

The countess arrived back a little while later. 'We're moving out.' The relief was plain in her voice.

'Where to?' William asked, beginning to gather up his rifle and kit.

'We'll take the College of Surgeons; it's more easily defended.'

About an hour later, the contingent of Volunteers from St Stephen's Green raced across the road and raided the College of Surgeons, successfully occupying it with the minimum of fuss.

The rattling of a machine-gun brought Katherine fully awake. She had been sitting in a rocking-chair by the window, which overlooked the street. In the early hours of the morning she had watched the slum dwellers who

557

lived in and around Monto stream back to their tenements, with nearly all of them carrying bundles of clothing or bags of shoes, and most of them very drunk. She fervently prayed that Dermot would see them, hoping that he might realize now just what sort of people he was fighting for. Several people had called at the house attempting to sell the goods they had stolen earlier that night in the shops along O'Connell, Henry and North Earl Streets. She had refused them all, but she guessed that there would be many more callers before the rising was finally over.

Around dawn she had fallen into a light, troubled sleep. Her dream had been brief but vivid, and in it she had been chased by a laughing Major Lewis, who was waving a large sheet of paper and shouting, *'useless, useless, useless'*.

As she breakfasted she read all the reports that had come in overnight and which were continuing to flood in. A little after ten o'clock, a message arrived from Dermot. It said simply, 'I love you.' He had sent it to her by passing it to someone he had recognized in the crowd, knowing that because of Madam Kitten's reputation it would almost certainly be passed on.

Her information on British troop movements was still incomplete, but she knew that the army still hadn't fully mobilized, although there had been several confrontations between the troops and the rebels. Artillery had been moved into the grounds of Trinity College which, for some unknown reason, the rebels hadn't even attempted to take. There had been widespread sniping and the army had attacked the rebels' posts in the *Daily Express* offices and City Hall.

She drank her tea, which was cold, but she was so preoccupied she didn't notice, and wondered what she was going to do. She considered the facts she had to hand and wondered if there was any possible way for her to get Dermot out of the GPO. But even if there was, she knew he wouldn't come of his own free will. She reviewed what she knew of the rebels' strength and then tried to guess at the figures the British authorities would bring in . . .

Katherine shook her head. The rebels would be crushed and those that didn't die in the fighting would be put up against a wall and shot. It was only a matter of time.

People had been arriving at the GPO all day; some were Volunteers who had only now answered the call. Confused by O'Neill's countermanding order, they had waited to see what was happening, and when it became clear that the rising was actually taking place they had joined up with their comrades.

The guards on the door were surprisingly lax. At one stage a score of men had ambled in, armed with nothing more than long knives, announcing that they wanted to join the rising, and Dermot had remarked to Mickey that, if the British army wanted to attack, then all they had to do was to infiltrate men in civilian clothing.

There were even a few women, not members of *Cumann na mBan*, who came to offer their services to the rising. Some were slum girls, others the wives of the men fighting there, and a few came from wealthier backgrounds, fighting with the Irish insurgents for reasons all their own.

One of the women was Tilly Cusack . . .

At around noon that day there had been a disturbance which had caught the attention of the rebels in the GPO as well as every other person in O'Connell Street. A young woman with flame-red hair and a bundle of clothes in her arms had sat down in the middle of O'Connell Street in the shade of Nelson's pillar and began to strip off her clothing. She seemed completely oblivious of everyone else, and any passer-by noticing her would probably have assumed that she was more than a little drunk. It was only when she pulled off her dress and then undid her bodice and cast it aside, revealing her large breasts, that she had begun to attract her audience. By the time she slipped out of her underskirt and pulled off her drawers to stand completely naked, every eye in the street was on her. And then she began to sort through the bundle of stolen clothing she had brought with her, trying them on and then tossing them aside one by one . . .

Meanwhile no-one noticed the woman in a green skirt that was almost the colour of the uniform of the *Cumann na mBan* walk into the building past the dazed guards.

In the street a light rain began to fall, and the naked woman began to dress more hurriedly; her strip and exhibition had been three pounds easily earned, but she didn't fancy catching her death for it.

Tilly wandered unquestioned through the chaos that was the GPO. She had long ago perfected the expression and stride of someone on an important task – it had taken her past many a policeman and hotel doorman. She tried to remember what the building had looked like only two days ago, but found she couldn't. She also found it difficult to reconcile the noise, the shouts, the occasional laughter and the equally intermittent moaning with the silence and peace that usually pervaded the building.

Her wandering led her to the Commissary where a group of women in the uniform of the *Cumann na mBan* were drinking tea and eating biscuits. She moved around the kitchen trying to look as if she knew what she was doing, while all the time listening to them; from their conversation she learned that they had just arrived and were new to the post office – and that suited her plans. She left the Commissary and walked up to the first man she saw.

'I've been told to bring the prisoners something to eat, but I've just arrived and I don't know where they are,' she said, smiling innocently.

'They're in one of the back rooms upstairs, love; I'm not long here myself so I can't tell you which one,' he smiled apologetically.

'Thanks anyway.' Tilly headed for the stairs, pausing

only when a number of men lumbered over to the door with a settee, which they obviously intended to use for a barricade. She was watching them so intently that she didn't see the man come hurrying down the stairs, walk past her and then stop, before turning back in amazement to stare at her.

'Tilly!'

Hearing her name, she turned, and then realized her mistake. It was Dermot Corcoran.

They stared at each other for a few seconds, and then both began to speak together.

'What are you doing here . . .?'

'What are you doing . . .?'

Dermot stopped, as did Tilly. 'Is everything all right?' he asked quickly. 'Has anything happened to Katherine? What are you doing here? Did Katherine send you?' The questions tumbled out.

Tilly shook her head. 'No, Katherine doesn't know I'm here; she didn't send me.'

'Why are you here then?' His expression began to harden.

'Can we speak together somewhere privately?'

Dermot looked around the room, half minded to call on Pearse, Connolly or Plunkett and ask their advice. Tilly Cusack had no right to be here, he knew; she had never shown any interest in the rising, and her presence here was . . . curious.

'Upstairs,' he finally nodded. He led her to the room he had chosen as his look-out point, the room which had once held two desks but which was now bare of all furnishing. He closed the door behind him and then stood with his back to it, while Tilly wandered over to the window and looked out. The young woman she had paid to undress had gone, and the street was damp from a slight drizzle.

'What are you doing here?' Dermot asked again, 'and don't give me any nonsense about wanting to join the rising,' he added firmly. 'My wife sent you, didn't she; she wants you to try and get me to leave, doesn't she?'

561

'No, Dermot, she doesn't.' Tilly said, turning away from the window, leaning back against the wall and folding her arms. 'Katherine doesn't know I'm here, I've already told you that. I'm here of my own accord . . .'

'Why?'

'To try and free one of your prisoners!'

The sheer audacity of her answer left him speechless.

'Martin and I were in the post office just before your people took it over,' she continued into the icy silence. 'I got out but he was delayed and must have been captured here.'

'This is the man you left Katherine to live with . . .?' Dermot said finally.

Tilly nodded. 'We were going to be married.'

'He's an English army officer,' Dermot said firmly, 'and a prisoner of the Provisional Government.'

'I love him, Dermot,' Tilly said simply. She looked straight at him. 'You must know how much he means to me.'

Dermot slowly nodded. 'Katherine spoke about how happy you were together and how pleased she was for you.'

'But I'm afraid he might be killed – accidentally, of course,' she added hastily.

He nodded again. Originally they had kept the prisoners on the ground floor, but one of them had very nearly been struck by a sniper's stray bullet, which was why they had been moved upstairs for greater safety.

'Dermot, I know you feel nothing for me, I know you regard me with nothing but contempt, but remember I saved Katherine's life once, and if you have any love left in you for your wife, then do this for me. Release him. Please.'

The silence which followed was long and heavy and Tilly turned away from the look on Dermot's face to stare down into the street again. It was drizzling, and although the snipers' bullets were more frequent now – she could hear one whining off the brickwork somewhere below her – the looters were still out in force.

562

'I'll do it,' Dermot said suddenly, startling Tilly. She turned around and looked at him in astonishment. 'I'll do it – because you saved Katherine's life once . . . and because I love her.' He looked past the woman out into the street. 'And I want you to tell her that,' he added in a whisper.

Getting Martin Moore out of the building proved to be surprisingly easy.

As the afternoon rolled on the looters came out again in force. Their chief target was Lawrence's, the photographer's in O'Connell Street. They were looking for cameras and field-glasses, telescopes, microscopes – anything which might be sold later for a few shillings. But then some of the tenement urchins discovered the fireworks. They made a huge pile in the centre of the street and, after several attempts to set it alight, eventually succeeded and immediately turned the whole street into a blaze of terrifying sound and colour. Rebels in the outskirts of the city and the snipers thought a major attack was underway, and the British troops received the impression that the Irish rebels had many more armaments than they had been led to believe. Soon the photographic shop, with all its inflammable chemicals and liquids, was ablaze. The first detonation shook every building in the street, including the GPO, and shattered windows in every direction. When the floors began crashing down one by one, sending sparks spiralling up to the heavens, the crowds cheered and howled. The fire brigade finally arrived but made little headway against the huge conflagration, until finally a score of Volunteers from the GPO went out to assist in fighting the blaze.

But while everyone was absorbed with this new spectacle, Dermot let Tilly Cusack and a bemused Martin Moore out through the building's side entrance in Henry Street.

'Remember,' Dermot said, gripping Tilly's arm and squeezing it slightly, 'tell Katherine I did this for her.'

563

'I'll tell her.'

The door closed, and Tilly and Martin were alone in the shattered street. Tilly was grateful for the rain which had begun to fall; the tears wouldn't show. 'Let's go,' she whispered, her lips brushing his face. The pair drifted into one of the side streets and disappeared.

CHAPTER FORTY-EIGHT

It was a little after three o'clock in the morning when Katherine finally fell asleep. Her spies had been coming in all night, carrying whatever information they could glean and encouraged no doubt by the prices she was paying for reliable news. But for every item of genuine information there were a score of rumours to be discounted. Around midnight she had received a report that British troops had reached Parnell Square, just beyond the Rotunda Lying-In Hospital north of the GPO. At first she had been inclined to disbelieve it, but the report had been repeated again and again, until finally she had no choice. She had paid a dozen men to make their way to the GPO and inform the rebels, without revealing where they had heard this information, and ordering them to say they had seen the men themselves.

The news had raised the insurgents, who had been attempting to doze, into a frenzy of activity . . . and it had proved to be a false alarm. But it was only to be the first of many, and sleep eluded them all that night.

Katherine was awakened from her light sleep by a sound. It was a sound she couldn't identify, something deep and reverberating, rumbling up through the old stones of the building, rattling the windows, setting the chandelier tinkling. She scrambled to her feet, pressing her hands to her tired gritty eyes, wondering what the sound was – it sounded a little like thunder, but bright April sunshine was streaming in through her window . . .

The sound rolled over the city again and then again, and it was identifiable this time as the booming of a big gun. It was followed by more explosions, and then the rattling of the machine guns began in earnest.

Katherine raced from her bedroom on to the landing and then into the next room, which had been her daughter's bedroom. The window there overlooked the back of the house and down over the rows of tenements in the direction of the river. Katherine pulled aside the curtains and peered out through the grimy glass. A tall plume of curling smoke was rising up across the city, coming, Katherine guessed, from somewhere in the direction of Butt Bridge or the Customs House. And the only rebel outpost in that direction was Liberty Hall, the headquarters of James Connolly's Citizen Army.

A little less than an hour later, a ragged urchin reported to Katherine that a British gunboat, the *Helga*, was shelling Liberty Hall, and that British troops were slowly encircling the rebel headquarters in the GPO.

'Hundreds an' thousands of them, all in green, an' with rifles an' swords an' cannons . . . it's grand. Sure, an' it'll be all over soon.' The boy sounded almost sorry that the excitement would finish. He self-consciously rolled up his sleeve and examined a brand-new square-faced wristwatch he was wearing. 'Well, I must be goin',' he said, his bright eyes looking nervously at the veiled Madam Kitten.

Katherine nodded and, reaching into her bag, produced two half crowns and handed them to the boy. They disappeared almost magically into his pocket. His head bobbed in thanks and he began to edge towards the door.

'If you hear anything else . . .?' Katherine suggested.

'Sure, you'll be the first to know,' he said quickly. He looked at the stolen watch again. 'I have to go . . .'

'Of course.' She pulled the bell rope and Nuala her maid appeared immediately. 'Will you show the young gentleman out, please. Oh, and by the way,' she added, smiling at the urchin, 'you've got the watch on the wrong way up!'

The boy grinned a gap-tooothed smile at her, and pulled up his sleeve. He was wearing a dozen wristwatches up along his arm.

A volley of bullets ripped the plaster from the wall of the room directly across from the ruined window, sending Anne Lewis and William Sherlock diving to the ground. When the firing ceased, Sherlock took a deep breath and inched his way up the wall, and then in one quick movement poked his gun through the window and fired off a shot.

With Anne Lewis and a score of others, he was positioned in one of the upper rooms of the College of Surgeons, which overlooked the Green. When the insurgent forces had been compelled to quit St Stephen's Green, the park had been overrun by the army, who had kept up an almost continuous fire on the building they now sheltered in. So far no-one had been wounded, except for a few minor cuts from flying glass and stone chips. The rebels' spirits were high, though. They had discovered a store of rifles and ammunition in the basement, arms which belonged to the College of Surgeons training corps, and, although food was short, they had enough to hold out for a few weeks yet.

Another machine gun opened up, this time from the roof of the Shelbourne Hotel, and shots pattered along the exterior of the building in a line, driving those inside down beneath the windows. In the lull that usually followed the sporadic firing, a dozen rifles opened up, firing blindly into the Green, with little or no hope of actually hitting anything, merely reminding the army forces that they were still there.

The door on the far side of the room slowly swung open – and was immediately chewed up by machine-gun fire, the force of the bullets ripping it from its hinges. When the firing eventually ceased, Constance Markievicz's head, barely six inches above the ground, peered around the jamb.

Sherlock shook his head in astonishment. 'They'll get

567

you yet; they're not going to have any regard for the fact that you're a woman. Indeed,' he added with a smile, 'I doubt if they could even tell that from a distance.'

The countess crept into the room on hands and knees; she was wearing the uniform of an officer of the Citizen Army and had adopted the male attire. Her only concession to individuality was the soft hat with the feather in it which she now had tucked into her belt. She sat back against the wall, sighing gratefully, tilting her head back and closing her eyes. Like most of the leaders of the rising, she hadn't slept since Sunday night – indeed few of them had – and she had made do with snatched minutes here and there, but was beginning to feel it now.

'We're going to try and get some of the wounded out,' she said, looking around the small group in the room. 'We need to stop the gunner on the Shelbourne roof, and draw the fire of the snipers in the Green.' She rubbed her eyes and continued tiredly. 'I would like you to split up into groups of two and take positions in the rooms overlooking the Green. In five minutes exactly, I want you all to open fire into the Green.' She looked at William Sherlock. 'You've got the Mauser – will you try for the machine-gunner?'

'I'll try – I won't make any promises though.'

Constance nodded. 'That's good enough.' She looked at the small, round-faced watch on her wrist. 'In five minutes – exactly.' She crept from the room, followed by the other rebels, leaving Anne and William alone in the room.

William sat with his back to the wall beneath the shattered window. 'Anne . . .?' he whispered.

She was crouched in a corner, nestling a .22 calibre target rifle across her lap. 'Don't ask,' she said wearily.

'Please . . . you could leave now. No-one would think the worse of you if you did.'

'No, William,' she said fiercely, 'no. You're prepared

568

to die here, aren't you – aren't you?' she demanded loudly.

William shrugged and looked uncomfortable. 'There's little enough I'm prepared to die for, but yes, I suppose I am. I'd rather not,' he added with a wry grin.

'I am as prepared to die as you are!'

Her vehemence surprised him. 'Yes, I think you are,' William said, looking at her, as if he were seeing her anew. 'Why?' he asked simply.

'You're doing this for your cause – I'm doing it for myself . . . and for you too in a way.' She smiled at his surprise. 'William, if I die, who will mourn me – you, and only you. And you're here. If I die here, at least I'll be dying beside you . . .'

William Sherlock shook his head. 'No more; such talk is . . .' He shook his head again and looked at his gold hunter. 'It's time,' he said.

The guns opened up from the seven large windows that looked out over the Green. William immediately pulled himself up to the window-ledge and rested his rifle against the sill. 'Take your time,' he said evenly, and then added with a smile. 'I love you.'

Anne smiled tightly, suddenly terrified. Her heart was pounding in her breast and her fingers were trembling so much that she could barely steady the gun. She took a deep breath to calm her excitement, but the adrenalin was surging through her, setting her muscles twitching, her nerves jangling. Her eyes throbbed, and everything seemed brighter, sharper, clearer.

She looked down into St Stephen's Green and watched the grey-black balls of smoke that marked the positions of the snipers, and raised her own rifle. She nestled the cool, flesh-smooth wood of the stock against her cheek and sighted down the barrel, aligning the sight a little above the centre of one of the balls of smoke, and then she slowly, gently, almost like a lover's caress, squeezed the trigger. The rifle bucked against her shoulder, but there was neither as much smoke nor sound as she had expected. She was too far away to see what had happened below, but there was no further firing from that position.

William was firing one of the huge old Mausers that had been part of a shipment of arms that had come in through the port of Howth two years previously. It was an unwieldy weapon, slow and difficult to fire, each round having to be chambered separately, and it gave off a thunderous report. But it could be deadly accurate, and it fired a lead-jacketed hollow-nosed bullet that penetrated flesh with a neat, circular wound but exited leaving a hole the size of a dinner plate.

William's first shot was for range, and it tore a chunk of stone from the roof of the Shelbourne Hotel. His second struck home, killing a lieutenant, and thereafter he laid down a slow but steady fire, effectively silencing the machine gun for over an hour.

Anne, meanwhile, was picking her targets carefully, firing three-round bursts wherever she saw smoke or movement, pinning down the troops in the Green.

But the British troops knew which rooms the snipers were in now, and fire was being increasingly directed towards them – especially the room on the right-hand side where the Mauser was firing.

Anne and William crouched below the shattered windows while the stonework chipped and the bullets sang off the wall opposite. Another machine-gun began its deadly rattling song, pinning them down long enough for the gun on the roof of the Shelbourne to be manned again, and then it joined in. The once-beautiful room was systematically torn apart by the lead, and even the walls began to disintegrate beneath the onslaught of bullets. There was an acrid smell of burning stone, and the whining, high-piched screaming of ricochetting metal was like the sound of children crying.

Eventually the firing stopped, only to begin again, but now it was directed elsewhere, as there was no longer any returning fire from the room.

In the room the dust and grit slowly settled, coating two supine figures in a powdery grey-white shroud. The

570

victorious troops would later find that the man had attempted to shield the woman with his body.

'I thought I said I wasn't to be disturbed . . .' Katherine began, but then stopped when she saw who was standing at the door. 'Tilly!' she gasped.

The two women embraced, clinging to each other with more relief than they could ever express. Tilly stood aside and waved a hand at the man standing back in the doorway, who looked distinctly embarrassed. 'I think you know Martin Moore.'

Katherine nodded. 'We've met.'

Captain Moore smiled vaguely, the events of the past few hours having left him dazed and bewildered.

'I've a message from Dermot.'

Katherine looked up quickly. 'He's all right?'

'He was yesterday – when he let us out of the Post Office,' Tilly said, enjoying the look that passed over Katherine's haggard face. Quickly, she explained what had happened, finishing with Dermot's message. 'He said he was doing it for you . . . because he loved you.'

'I got a message from him yesterday – and one on Monday also – saying much the same thing,' Katherine said quietly, her voice cracking, 'and another arrived today.' She touched the three scraps of crumpled paper on her desk. 'He's giving them to the locals who wander too close to the building; they know if they bring them here, Madam Kitten will pay well for them.' She looked at Martin Moore. 'Answer me honestly now, do they have a chance?' The desperation was clear in her voice.

'No chance,' he said, resisting the temptation to lie to this grieving woman.

'And what will happen to him . . . to them all?' she asked, already knowing the answer.

'If they're not killed in the fighting, then I would imagine they'll be tried, found guilty and shot as traitors. It is an act of aggression within the sovereign realm during wartime – it's treason.'

Katherine nodded wearily. 'I know . . . I know.' She

was silent for a long time, until, almost as if only then remembering they were still in the room, she looked up. 'And both of you, what will you do?'

'We talked about this last night,' Tilly said, looking at Martin and then back to Katherine. 'We think that when Martin isn't found it will be assumed he died in the fighting, and that means he's free of the army and all it represents. We can start afresh, and so we've decided to go to England, north, or maybe to Edinburgh or Glasgow. I've some money saved . . .'

'Tilly,' Katherine said suddenly, 'how much do I mean to you?'

The question took her by surprise. 'You . . . you're like a sister to me. I love you.'

'And Patrick and Senga?'

Tilly was both Patrick and Senga's godmother. 'I think of them as my own children, you know that.'

'Would you love them as your own children if anything happened to me?'

'Of course I would, you know I would. But nothing is going to happen to you.' There was a question implicit in the last statement, but Katherine chose to ignore it.

She opened one of the drawers in her bureau and took out a sheet of heavy writing paper. In her neat, precise hand she wrote a dozen lines, signed and dated the note and then folded it into an envelope. 'Take this.'

'What is it?'

'This makes you my agent, my representative. It will allow you access to the monies and bonds with British banks, my holdings in lands and stocks, the house in Cornwall and the cottage in the Lake District. But swear to me you'll bring up my children as your own.'

Tilly nodded dumbly. 'Katherine?' she whispered.

'I have a final task to do here,' she said, still holding on to the envelope, knowing it contained the sum total of her life's work; her past and her future. 'I'll be happier knowing that, if anything happens to me, Patrick and Senga will be properly looked after.'

'What are you going to do?' Martin asked cautiously.

'If I do eventually get to England, I'll contact you when the time is right,' Katherine continued, ignoring his question. 'Now, there is a boat with the first tide in the morning; I suggest you book passage on it.'

'Katherine . . .?' Tilly whispered.

'Go now,' Katherine said wearily. 'I'll rest for a little while.'

Tilly took her into her arms, and kissed her. There were tears on her face, but she wasn't sure if they were her own or Katherine's.

CHAPTER FORTY-NINE

There were fires in the streets just off O'Connell Street that night and Dermot watched the flames flicker and dance long into the night.

Mickey, who was standing by his side, nodded to the glow that burned redly across the buildings. They both knew it was only a matter of time before the rest of the city would be in flames. 'I think it's nearly over now.'

'A day, two at the most,' Dermot agreed.

'Do you regret it?' Mickey asked.

'No – yes,' he corrected himself. 'A part of it. It's easy to see now what we should have done; perhaps it was foolish to go ahead with the rising on Monday when the orders had been countermanded only the day before, and there was still confusion. Perhaps we should have fought a guerilla war ... I don't know. What sickens me is the fact that we'll more than likely die for what we believed in, and for little or no reason!' He jabbed a finger in the direction of a score of looters going through the remains of a shop like a pack of scavenging rats. 'Do you think they care? Do you think they'll even remember our names? And if they did, all they'd probably do is spit on them.'

'They're the people whose cause you've championed for years,' Mickey reminded him. 'You're just seeing them as they really are. And all they're really doing is what they've always done – take advantage of every situation. You can hardly blame them.'

'But I do blame them; if they were behind us, they'd know that looting isn't going to help our cause.'

Mickey grunted and shifted the heavy shotgun in his lap. 'Maybe the causes are different,' he remarked. 'Dermot, do you honestly think that, if the government changed tomorrow, their lot would also change? And think before you answer me, and if you answer yes, then you're a fool. You've done more good and achieved more with your articles than any number of guns and bombs will ever achieve. They know that when this is over, the police and army will descend on the tenements and no-one will be able to sleep easy in their beds at night. In a rising like this, only the poor will be certain to suffer, both at the hands of the police and at the hands of the rebels.'

Dermot looked up at him curiously; it was the first time he had ever heard the old man speak so vehemently about anything. Indeed, it was the longest speech he had ever heard him make.

'Those people out there haven't had any food all week,' Mickey continued fiercely, 'we've occupied the bakeries, closed the roads, sealed off the centre of the city, including the markets, and brought troops out into the streets. The shops, the post offices, the banks have all been closed, and even the gas has been cut off. Some of them are looting – yes – but others are looking for food just to survive.'

Dermot watched the dim figures across the street for a few moments, and then nodded. 'You're right of course, Mickey. Forgive me.'

'There's nothing to forgive.'

'What made you join us, Mickey? If you felt that this was how it was going to end, why did you join us?'

The old man shrugged. 'I remember standing at the back of a mouldy hall watching a young man speak. What he said made sense ... but, like most of the young, he was impatient for his dream to come true. So were his listeners. So was I.'

Dermot looked down at the flames. 'Will the dream come true?' he asked softly.

'It's coming true now,' Mickey smiled.

'But this is a nightmare!'

The old man gripped his shoulder and squeezed. 'It'll get worse.'

575

'Connolly says they'll never fire on the centre of the city, and destroy the buildings.'

Mickey snorted rudely. 'They'll fire,' he promised.

His prophecy came true the following morning. The rebels were now almost completely surrounded, with the outlying garrisons either captured or cut off. Field guns had been brought into position and with the coming of dawn the army began shelling the insurgent positions in the centre of the city.

From her daughter's bedroom Katherine could hear the shells falling on Dublin and watch the plumes of smoke rising from different positions. She was still standing there at noon, when a massive detonation shook the city and blood-orange flames leapt into the sky. She watched all through the sunny afternoon as the flames roared higher and higher, and soon a dark pall of smoke covered the city down to the river.

Lower Abbey Street, across the road and to the right of the GPO, was ablaze. A shell had ignited the liquids and newsprint in the *Irish Times* reserve printing office and soon turned the building into an inferno – an inferno which rapidly consumed the buildings on either side of it. The flames leapt with almost terrifying speed up to O'Connell Street, and began to swallow up the buildings there. Soon Clery's, the shop directly across from the GPO, was burning fiercely.

Machine guns opened up from all sides and began raking the GPO. Sandbags exploded beneath the onslaught of lead, and the men inside dived for cover as the bullets tore into the walls, tumbling great chunks of plaster on to the floor.

At around noon Pearse tapped on the door of the room Mickey and Dermot were holding, startling them both. The leader of the uprising stepped in and was followed a moment later by a priest! Both men looked at one another in astonishment – there had been no priest in the building up to that morning.

'The father will hear your confessions,' Pearse said with a tight smile and left the room without another word.

Both men stood until Pearse had clumped down the corridor, his booted feet thudding solidly on the wooden floors, and then they remained standing in deference to the priest.

'It's very good of you to come, Father . . .' Dermot began.

'I didn't come, I was tricked into coming here!' the priest said indignantly, 'but sure, we'll let it go. I was told to come and minister to a dying man, and when I arrived here I was presented with nearly two hundred "dying" men.' He shrugged philosophically, looking from Dermot to Mickey. 'If you wish, I can hear your confessions, my sons . . .'

Mickey stepped away, and looked at the younger man. 'You first; I'll wait outside.'

Dermot nodded and then knelt at the priest's feet, and crossed himself. 'Bless me, Father . . .'

A shell, followed almost immediately by a second, struck the Metropole Hotel, not fifty feet away.

'Bless me, Father . . .' Dermot began again.

Mickey wandered down the corridor, absently stuffing his favourite pipe – the one he had carved himself – with fine Virginian tobacco. He hadn't smoked in over ten years, having broken the habit following a chest infection, but on Tuesday morning he had started again.

He leaned against the wall beside a shattered window, careful to stay well back out of sight, and peered down into the street. Even from this distance he could feel the heat of the fires which were raging out of control across the street. With no fire brigade, he knew the destruction of the entire length of O'Connell Street was inevitable.

He was knocked off his feet when the shells hit the hotel beside the GPO, and he remained sitting on the ground; it wasn't worth the effort to stand, and besides he was getting old. At sixty-three or four – he wasn't sure which himself – he was too old for revolutions, but the rising was something he fervently believed in, heart and soul. He had been a follower of Jim Larkin, the trade unionist, and the step into the Citizen Army had been a short and almost natural one. And, while he did believe in the dream, he was practical enough to realize that he would never live to see it. Maybe this wasn't the way to achieve it – but whatever happened, Ireland would never be the same again after this week.

Unlike Dermot, he had no-one to worry about; there was no wife waiting at home for him, no children or grandchildren. Maybe some of the whores he had known in his long career in Monto would miss him, but somehow he doubted it . . .

Mickey never even heard the shell which exploded against the portico of the GPO. The wall he was leaning against erupted inwards, crushing the sitting man beneath a pile of stone. When Dermot reached the cairn of stones a moment later, all that remained of his old friend was a hand sticking up from the pile of rubble clutching a pipe . . .

Behind him, the priest knelt on the floor and began to pray.

Dermot was reaching for the pipe when the first bullet ripped in through the gaping hole in the wall and struck him high in the chest, spinning him around, a look of absolute final surprise on his face . . .

The priest reached out instinctively to him . . .

But the second shot spun the younger man around again, and a third knocked him down. He was dead before he hit the ground.

Katherine was unsurprised when no message arrived from Dermot that day – the GPO was coming under heavy fire and she knew the chances of his getting a message out were very slim. She savagely suppressed the insidious thought that he might not be alive to send any message.

As the evening wore on into night, the sky burned red and, even up in Monto, Katherine could clearly see the flames leaping from the buildings down on O'Connell Street, and Nelson's column was darkly outlined against the fires. The entire street was ablaze and sparks spiralled high into the evening sky. Billowing clouds of acrid, filthy smoke drifted across the city, coating everything beneath its grimy pall. Detonations and explosions were almost continuous now, and the chain rattle of gunfire continued unabated. Katherine didn't know what it was like in the GPO, but she imagined it would be something similar to a scene from Hell.

There was a sudden rippling roar which brought Katherine back to the window, and she watched in astonishment as long streamers of colours soared into the sky. The fire took on a new lease of life with this sudden explosion, and Katherine realized that the chemical and oil store across from the GPO had just gone up. Even from this distance she imagined she could feel the increase in temperature, and tiny beads of sweat popped on to her brow. Through the partially open window, a rank breeze wafted in the sickening odours of smoke and fire, burning wood, leather, cloth and the stench of oils and chemicals.

She realized abruptly she didn't want to know what was happening in O'Connell Street. If . . . if Dermot was dead, then she no longer had any interest in the GPO. She was sure that acts of extraordinary heroism were taking place; she had already learned of some of the acts of bravery and foolishness of those in the outlying garrisons – but she didn't care. All she cared about was her husband. At first light she would send someone out to see what was happening; if there was no news of Dermot, either from or about him – then she would act.

Katherine wandered back into her bedroom and sat down at her bureau. She touched a part of the scrollwork design and a small wooden drawer popped out. Inside there was a bundle of letters tied up in a faded blue ribbon. They were the letters Dermot had written to her when they had first come to know one another, and then later when they had met again. The last one was dated the 28th September, 1907, a few months after their marriage. He hadn't written to her since – not that they had ever been separated from each other for any great length of time. She undid the ribbon and turned up the first letter and, with the distant roar of the huge fire, the falling shells and explosions and the stuttering of the guns, she began to read of love . . .

The sound of the hall door slamming brought Katherine fully awake, heart pounding. She had slipped into a light doze sitting up in the high-backed chair, and as she stood up the letters she had been reading and re-reading through the long hours of night fell to the floor. She looked at them, white and pale cream against the blood-red carpet.

Footsteps pounded on the stairs and she turned expectantly towards the door. There was a hesitant knock, and then the door was opened slowly and a young woman peered around the edge, almost as if she expected to find the older woman asleep.

'What is it, Nuala? I thought you'd be here earlier.'

The young woman stepped into the room and quietly shut the door behind her. She was wearing a man's overcoat, but her heavily made-up face and dead, knowing eyes betrayed her profession. 'The curfew's been extended from six in the evening to nine in the morning, and I'd some problems in getting through.' She paused. 'I've some news, ma'am.'

'Well?' Katherine snapped. 'Come on girl, don't make me drag it out of you.'

'A British general has taken over, ma'am, a Sir John Maxwell, an' he says if there's no surrender, he goin' to destroy all the buildings occupied by the rebels.' She hesitated, and then added softly, 'I think it's over, ma'am; I think the rebellion's over.'

'Did you get any word of Dermot or Mickey?'

The young woman hesitated, before shaking her head quickly. 'I've no word of either, ma'am. The Post

Office's in a bad way; the roof's gone, and there's been burning inside. There's a lot of dead ... they say Connolly's wounded and near dead, and that many others have been killed, but I've no word of Dermot or Mickey.'

'Did you hear anything about Major Lewis?'

'Nothing – I had to be discreet, of course, but the few army officers I spoke to had never heard of him. Or if they had, they weren't saying.' She shrugged. 'I'm sorry, I couldn't find out where he is or what he's doing.'

Katherine nodded. She didn't need to know what he was doing – since he was undoubtedly advising Maxwell. She stepped over the scattered letters and crossed to the shuttered windows. Outside, she could hear the staccato of gunfire, coupled with the heavier booming of the cannons. She rested her head against the polished wooden frame for a moment, and then turned back to the younger woman. 'Thank you, Nuala, that will be all.'

'If you'll be needing anything ...'

'I won't be. The house will remain closed for tonight; we will be accepting no guests. Oh, and thank you, I appreciate what you've done.'

Nuala remained a few moments longer, waiting for further instructions, but when it became obvious that Katherine had nothing more to say, she backed silently from the darkened room. The door clicked shut.

There was a dull thump as an artillery shell exploded close by, rattling the shutters and setting the crystal chandelier swinging, tinkling softly.

No word of Dermot and no message ... and he would have got a message out if he was alive. She bowed her head and accepted his death.

She felt the ice settle into the pit of her stomach, and the raw burning begin in her throat. She had finally admitted it. She shook her head savagely – she wouldn't give in to it. Dermot wouldn't want tears, and she wasn't even sure if she had any left for him. Another explosion rocked the house, and she heard one of the

581

tall windows snap and crack behind its heavy wooden shutter. She couldn't help Dermot, but there was something she could do, something she had to do . . .

Katherine went to the bookshelves that lined one end of the large salon. She ran her fingers down the polished leather spines, the titles familiar even in the semi-darkness, finding what she was looking for in the middle of the top shelf. It was a tall, black-and-gilt bound copy of the bible. She smiled as she read the title and then opened the book. It was a dummy; inside was a red velvet box, and within the box was the tiny double-barrelled silver derringer Dermot had given to her on Monday morning.

She carefully broke the gun and loaded the two bullets, one above the other, and then snapped the gun shut. It looked and felt as light as a child's toy, but she knew if she were close enough it would kill. She slid the tiny weapon down inside the front of her dress, nestling it between her breasts. The metal felt cold, but the mother-of-pearl handle was smooth and almost flesh-warm.

Just two shots, but one should be enough.

Even this far out of town she could still see the red glow on the sky vying with the first hints of dawn paling the sky to the east. The thud and boom of the explosions tearing out the heart of the city were like distant thunder, but aside from that, here on Clonliffe Road, there were no other indications anything was amiss.

Katherine stood in the shadows and watched the house which was in darkness. She realized that she was feeling nothing, no fear, no loss at the thought of Dermot's death. She was numb, numb and cold – except for the gun, the gun was like a coal, burning hot against her breasts.

She crossed the street quickly and mounted the steps. Through the hall-door glass she saw that there was a light low on the floor at the back, coming from the kitchen. She paused with her hand on the knocker and then, on impulse, went back down the steps and around the side of the house. Light from the uncurtained kitchen windows lanced out into the garden, momentarily blinding her. She remained standing back in the shadows and lifted the tiny pistol from her dress. It sat neatly in her hand, like a coiled snake, and just as deadly.

She took a deep breath and looked in through the kitchen window – at exactly the same time as the person inside chose to walk across to the sink. They stared at each other in shock for a single pounding heartbeat . . . and then John Lewis smiled and walked across to the back door and pulled it open. Katherine stepped inside.

'I'm surprised,' he said slowly, looking at her warily.

'I thought I should see you,' Katherine said softly.

'How's the revolution going?' he asked with a tight smile. He looked as if he hadn't slept for days; he was frighteningly pale, and his eyes had sunk deep into his face, giving him a gaunt, haggard appearance. He was wearing a soiled shirt, with the sleeves rolled up and the collar undone.

'Surely you should know?'

John Lewis nodded distractedly. 'I just made some tea. Would you like some?'

It took a moment for Katherine to register what he had said, and surprised, she nodded. She sat down at the familiar wooden kitchen table, the tiny gun still concealed in her hand. The table was covered with reports, most of them on official paper, but others little more than scraps torn from copybooks.

'I'm surprised they're still fighting,' Lewis said slowly, his back to her, busy at the stove.

'They're still fighting,' Katherine said, 'but I think it's nearly done now. Dublin is burning.'

Major Lewis nodded. He returned to the table, brushed a pile of reports on to the floor and set down two cups and saucers on the table, placed the teapot and a jug of milk between them, and then sat down facing Katherine.

'What brings you here?' he asked, pouring the tea, his eyes on Katherine's face.

'I believe my husband died in the GPO,' Katherine said very carefully. 'You had promised me you would protect him. You betrayed him, betrayed me – again. You killed my husband.'

'He went out to die – they all went out to die.'

'You gave me your word! I betrayed the revolution for your promise of his safety.'

Surprisingly, he smiled, but it was a cold, brittle thing. 'Do you know, when I brought the news of the rising – the times and dates, the numbers – to my superiors, they wouldn't believe it, they laughed at me. But no matter . . . no matter . . .' He rubbed his hands down the front of his stained shirt and then searched through the papers on the table. He finally pulled out a slip of pink paper that seemed to be covered with names.

'Did you know my wife?' he asked suddenly.

'The woman who put a pregnant eighteen-year-old girl on to the streets on Christmas Eve? I remember her.'

Lewis didn't react. 'She was killed fighting with the rebels in the College of Surgeons.'

'I don't have the forgiveness in me to say I'm sorry,' Katherine said coldly.

Lewis shrugged and tossed the paper back on to the pile. 'I don't think I'm particularly sorry myself. Just surprised – I didn't even know she was involved with the rebels.'

Surprised by the depth of his callousness, Katherine said quietly, 'But she was your wife . . . you loved her . . . surely you feel something for her?'

He shook his head, his eyes becoming hard and distant. 'No, I didn't love her. Once perhaps, but that was a long time ago . . .' he stood up suddenly, sending the chair crashing backwards, making Katherine drop her cup in fright. 'There was a time . . . when things might have been different, when we had the chance to make a new start. But then you gave me this.' He lifted his shirt, revealing the livid scar which marked the

584

wound she had gifted him with nine years ago. She looked into his eyes again and saw that they were glittering madly. 'You took away my manhood – what chance had I of keeping her, then?' He turned and leaned against the sink, staring out into the lightening dawn sky. 'I have a lot to thank you for,' he whispered bitterly. And then he began to laugh, a harsh humourless sound. 'A lot to thank you for,' he said quickly, nodding his head. 'When this trouble is over, it will be remembered that I was the one who supplied the information – even though it wasn't acted upon. I have to thank you for that. I managed to dispose of that meddling journalist. I have you to thank for that, too.' He was nodding his head quickly now. 'Yes, I have a lot to thank you for. You've humiliated me, made me look a fool to my superiors . . .' He stopped and said very slowly. 'And you took my child, my son . . .'

When he turned around, there was an eight-inch kitchen knife in his hand. 'Let me thank you,' he said, and the look in his eyes was terrifying.

Katherine had sat benumbed as Lewis raged, but that numbness was gone now. It had melted away before a deep, terrifying roar that Katherine dimly recognized as anger. As Lewis advanced around the table, she lifted the tiny pistol and squeezed the trigger!

Lewis staggered back a step . . . and then a deep glistening stain appeared on the front of his shirt.

'I've a lot to thank you for, too, Major Lewis,' she said tightly. 'You took my virginity and my honour. And now you have taken my husband. Given time, you would have left me with nothing.'

Lewis lunged across the table for her, right hand extended, blade upthrust to slash her throat. Katherine's second shot lifted him clean off the table; the bullet had taken him through the eye – killing him instantly.

She walked away without looking back. She had only one regret – that she hadn't had the courage to do it sooner.

EPILOGUE

The woman stood on the cliff top watching the two youngsters explore the rocky beach below, envying them their innocence, their easy acceptance of everything that had happened.

But for Katherine Lundy there was no easy acceptance of all that had happened. It had cost her too much. With hindsight, she realized now how she could have taken different – possibly better – decisions. She should have foreseen Lewis's betrayal, should have realized he would never agree to save Dermot . . . not after all that had happened. She had betrayed Dermot – and had cost him his life.

Katherine turned away from the cliff edge and began to walk slowly down the sandy path, the wind now behind her, blowing her long hair past her face. She knew that what she was feeling now – this ragged maelstrom of emotions – would eventually pass, leaving her in some sort of peace, but until then she didn't want to make any decisions. For the moment, she was content to rest. Later, when she got lonely or if Patrick and Senga grew restless, she would head up to Glasgow to Mr and Mrs Martin Moore.

She had made one decision, though: she wouldn't be returning to Ireland for a while – perhaps she would never return. The country held too many bitter memories, and they overshadowed the good.

And the Ireland she had known was already changing – a little more than a thousand men and women had decided that. It was a change that would have come inevitably, but they, and the fifteen rebel leaders who were executed by firing squad, had succeeded in hastening that change.

Pearse had surrendered on Saturday, 29th April. Less than a week later, he had been shot, along with Thomas Clarke and Thomas MacDonagh. Joseph Plunkett had been allowed to marry his fiancée an hour before he too was shot, alongside Willy Pearse, Padraic's brother. James Connolly, who had been wounded in the GPO, was carried out on a stretcher to be executed. Constance Markievicz was sentenced to death, along with nearly one hundred others, but her sentence was commuted to life imprisonment.

But although Katherine had read the papers very carefully, she found no mention of a body being found in the kitchen of the house on Clonliffe Road.